Un-American Activities

Books by Richard Kluger

WHEN THE BOUGH BREAKS (1964)
NATIONAL ANTHEM (1969)
SIMPLE JUSTICE (1976)
MEMBERS OF THE TRIBE (1977)
STAR WITNESS (1979)
UN-AMERICAN ACTIVITIES (1982)

Un-American Activities

A Novel by Richard Kluger

DOUBLEDAY & COMPANY, INC.
GARDEN CITY, NEW YORK
1982

ISBN: 0-385-13506-8
Library of Congress Catalog Card Number: 81–43440
Copyright © 1982 by Richard Kluger
ALL RIGHTS RESERVED
PRINTED IN THE UNITED STATES OF AMERICA
FIRST EDITION

For Richard Alan Eisner
and James Coleman Freund,
old friends and true

PART ONE

Crimson in Triumph Flashing

"You are young, my son, and, as the years go by, time will change and even reverse many of your present opinions. Refrain therefore awhile from setting yourself up as a judge of the highest matters."

—PLATO, *The Laws*

PROLOGUE

WHEN I WAS A BOY, everybody but the Wobblies knew that America and God had gone into business together. The commercial and the holy spirit were one, and prosperity was the surest sign of indwelling grace among the go-getters. Only the ungodly ran in the red.

When the bottom fell out on Wall Street the year I turned seventeen, some tall explaining was in order. Latecomers among the moralizers said that so much striving in the Lord's name was more than a little blasphemous. Hard bargainers, weaned on the divinity of the profit system, charged that it was God who had shown bad faith. Either way, the partnership was dissolved, along with the delusion that America was paradise.

In my own case, the shock was minimal. The very idea that our family might be among the elect seemed preposterous on its face. Even in my prayers, I knew not to insult the Heavenly Father by pressing Him for special attention. Why should He have cared very much for me in a world full of boys, and Ubangis and moo-cows and grasshoppers and every manner of creature fully as worthy as I of divine favor?

To be honest, I should probably add there was a not altogether attractive element of calculation in that youthful modesty. My reasoning ran that if God or any of the heavenly host accepted requests to comfort innocents below, the divine monitoring system must just as certainly have operated to deliver discomfort to the sinful. And since the exact properties of sin were a source of large confusion in my mind, I knew only that I could not rely on the Lord for protection without the attendant risk of offending Him at every turn. It looked like a bad bargain. The smarter course was to avoid the oversight of Providence—and stir up as few others as I could manage.

My ensuing career in its entirety, then, may be described as a search for a route that neither dared too much nor risked too little; a voyage bound for serenity that was not torpor, steered with prudence that did not paralyze. Having lately reached the stage when my prospects for glory, infamy, or anguish worry me far less than how long I have left to remain upright, I am ready to concede failure in this hopeless pursuit. Aristotle makes a tiresome deity.

For a time there, I thought of belatedly soliciting God for guidance. Even now, though, the possible consequences deter me. Given such long delinquency in the bent-knee department, any heavenward plea of mine would surely receive either no answer at all or one terrifying in its remonstrance. So I am reconciled to dying dumb, which is no more ignoble than having lived that way. Knowing what we do not know can at least be passed off as a species of wisdom.

All endings are melancholy, even those assuring cessation of pain. How much more pleasing to deal, as I fully intend here, with beginnings and discoveries. If my own do not instruct posterity at length, may they serve at least to suggest some measure of the diversion available on the outward trek. All the answers I encountered then, when I was listening more closely than I have been since, were equally ardent in their claim to truth and pledge of justice. Less was said of mercy, as if communion among the doomed were not the only saving lesson in the lot.

ONE

IF HIS FIRST-PERIOD LECTURER had been anyone but Travis, he would have gone straight to the station and sat alone with his thoughts for the hour until the next train left.

His father's telegram had reached Toby just as he was heading out of Hollis for breakfast on that stinging December morning. The news was not unexpected. His mother's decline had been apparent during the Thanksgiving break. In his mind, he had already rehearsed the grief he imagined would assail him when the word came. Its actual arrival left him oddly unable to summon any authentic feeling beyond a perverse relief.

He packed, dropped off a note at the dean's office explaining the necessity for him to miss classes for the next several days, had coffee by himself in a corner of the Union, and decided, on consulting the train schedule, that Travis's lecture would be a constructive way to fend off bereavement a while longer. Practically speaking, it also made sense. A Travis lecture on Shakespeare was so compelling and compact that it was hard to conceive how any absentee could pick up more than a fraction of its substance—or any of its feeling—from borrowed notes. Better to submerge himself in the tribulations of Lear, due for examination that morning, and dash for the train the instant the dismissal bell went off.

A trim, smallish man of around forty, always natty in dark worsted, wispy hair combed back from an imposing forehead, Jeremiah Sterling Travis, Grosvenor Professor of Letters and Rhetoric, consumed quantities of himself as well as his students' notebooks in the course of a single lecture. Laboring under the enormous shadow of Kittredge, still teaching in his seventies, Travis was wise enough not to compete with the nonpareil. His approach was more analytical than romantic, but not dry—a fusion of fire and ice. His eyes would skim over the thronged hall like tremulous vectors as his nasal, slightly metallic voice packed into each immaculately phrased sentence what others took five to say.

In the three months he had been at Cambridge, Toby had come to view Travis as the embodiment of the life of the mind. A man possessed by his calling, he sang of literature as a thing sublime. Writing of the sort that deserved contemplation did not approximate life, was no mere cultural artifact, but living metaphor, the designed effects of artists who were the supreme interpreters of their age. The texture and construction of their language, when intensely analyzed, revealed the social, ethical, and metaphysical values their world lived by. Grasp them, Travis said, and all barriers between art and life would fall away. The study of literature, therefore, was no effete pastime, no idle pleasure reading, but as stern and demanding a discipline as any of the natural sciences—and at least as exact as any of the social ones.

Not everybody loved Travis. He was said to be dour in private and snide toward slow-witted students. He graded stringently, ran his class sections like a star chamber, and expected nothing short of a transfixed audience in the lecture hall. It was this last demand that proved most trying to Toby that unhappy December morning.

He had been listening as closely as he could manage under the circumstances but somewhere lost the thread in Travis's discussion of the duplicities of the princesses Goneril and Regan. The inconstancy of their filial devotion came close to releasing the tears that he was by then only narrowly withholding. All Toby could think about as the hour crept interminably on was reaching the train on time.

When the bell finally sounded, he leapt to his feet and sprang for the door, oblivious to Travis's effort to complete the last point in his pregnant lesson. The impudence of Toby's urgent motion broke the professor's concentration and shattered his civility. "You!" he burst in a voice uncharacteristically shrill. "You—!"

Toby froze as several hundred heads swiveled toward him in unison.

"Might you have the decency, young man," Travis demanded in his most withering tone, "to grant me sixty seconds more of your precious schedule?"

He felt the ceiling rushing down upon him.

Travis continued erupting. "I have been exerting myself strenuously in your behalf for the last fifty minutes, trying to propose an insight or two into one of the immortal works of man. I trust this ordeal has not proven too great an inconvenience for you?"

The obligatory apology refused to form in Toby's knotted throat.

Travis's fury was billowing by now. "My question was not rhetorical, young man!" he shouted. "Have you any conception of what the word 'courtesy' means? Have you—have you?"

The man was quite beside himself. The boy broiled in agony. There was no way to say across a full lecture hall that he was sorry but his mother's death mattered more to him just then than all the immortal works of man. Frenzy seized both of them as Toby stood there pinioned and speechless until asked his name. He managed to get out the syllables in a hoarse whisper. Travis claimed not to hear and asked him to repeat it, compounding the humiliation.

Finally, the professor composed himself and pronounced sentence. "All right, Mr. Ronan—I do not propose to see you in this room again until after the Christmas holidays. Perhaps you'll develop some manners by then."

II

The farther from Boston the train bore him, the more he yielded to melancholy. The world within him took on the emotional coloration of the one outside his window, which for more than a year now had been turning bleaker by the month.

When the bill for the 'Twenties' long binge fell due at decade's end, those then arriving in the adult world were peculiarly stricken by the economic upheaval. The universe of their childhood was stood on its head, and their places in it, cushioned against calamity only a moment before, were suddenly no more accommodating than a rock ledge not yet brushed by the avalanche. Appalled by the distintegrating present, terrified of a future beside the abyss, those whose parents could still afford it were glad to be packed off to a refuge in the collected wisdom of the past.

At Harvard, matriarch of American higher learning, the muted mood was less a departure from the norm than on campuses where banners, booze, and Friday night bonfires best evidenced the gravity of resident scholarship. In good times or bad, the authentic élan of the great university along the Charles was manifested in the unannounced conviction of those who attended it that, by virtue of pedigree, wealth, intelligence, or any combination thereof, they composed the closest thing on the American continent to a native aristocracy. By the time Alonso Tobias Ronan, Jr., arrived there in the fall of 1930, almost three centuries of achievement by his predecessors had lent intimidating substance to that terrible presumption.

In contrast to all happy families, however, not all Harvard men are alike. Indeed if there had been a trophy for the least haughty boy in the Class of 1934 at the moment of its matriculation, Toby Ronan would have been an immensely strong contender for it.

On his mother's side, the only forebear of known distinction was a one-armed horse thief whose noose was said to have been fixed in place by the sheriff of Dorset himself. His father, of comparably low Anglican origins, rose from a modest education at a trade school to become, by pluck, perseverance, and the usual quota of bootlicking, manager of a very large manufacturing plant owned by a very large company. His son and namesake was not taken inside that throbbing monolith more than half a dozen times during his entire boyhood, but he was made unforgettably aware at an early age of the difference between a can factory, which was what his father superintended, and a canning factory. The latter, his mother explained, held a far more humble place in the industrial hierarchy and was invariably unhygienic. Cannery managers, moreover, were not elected to the board of directors of even provincial savings banks, as his excellent father had been.

Class consciousness, then, was a family preoccupation. And when the Ronans and their sole offspring moved into the snug Victorian halfway up the hill on the north side of town near the Grandview line, their exalted standing among the salaried families of Piermont was confirmed.

But there was never enough money for stylish living, even if the inclination had been there. Toby went to school with the rough-mannered children of the local proletariat and, while careful not to wear airs in their company, probably escaped having his nose disfigured only because it was somehow understood, even among dirty-eared urchins, that you did not bloody a boy whose father held the power to deny you your daily bread and sausage.

His report cards suggested that Toby was only a competent pupil, even at a small high school in a Hudson River laboring town. His mother's expectation that he would nevertheless attend a leading university, the cost for which she and her husband had carefully calculated and saved, and thereafter enjoy a respectable professional career was encouraged only by an eleventh-grade aptitude test that indicated the boy was achieving well short of his potential.

Without rank, riches, or record of distinction, however, Toby's credentials to attend Harvard were so suspect that even his mother began to waver in her resolve that only the best was good enough for her cherished chick. Then one golden October afternoon on his way home from Tappan Zee High School, Toby saw a dead cat. Everything changed as a result.

Turning a corner perhaps ten blocks from his home, he had spotted a man lifting the squashed and decidedly dead animal from the middle of the street and was transfixed by the spectacle. The man was not at all squeamish about it. He held the carcass only slightly away from him as he proceeded purposefully down the sidewalk across from Toby, passed the last house on the block, turned the corner, and, without looking back, disappeared from view—presumably to dispose of the animal down the nearest sewer.

The event consumed just a few seconds. And yet the unceremonious bearing away of so despicable a thing filled him at once with an uncontainable sadness. All life's mysteries seemed somehow bound up in its demise, probably because he had had so little direct dealing with death and denial. His mind raced with speculations the rest of the way home. Who had killed the cat and when? How long had it lain there unmourned in the middle of the street? To whom, if anyone, had it belonged? Had it been a good cat or an evil one? Of what did virtuous cathood consist? How old was it? Which of its nine lives had this one been? Would it be reincarnated as a caliph next Ramadan or as a six-day bike racer from Duluth?

Brain seething with such imponderables, he committed both the questions and his fancied answers to paper, one embellishment leading to the next in increasingly exotic sequence. His mother found the composition, which Toby titled "Catalogue," odd but appealing, not unlike the author. Toby submitted it a few weeks later for the senior-class essay contest. Too unorthodox for the teacher's committee judging the entries to take first prize, which went to a demure sketch of the life of Clara Barton, "Catalogue" was designated first runner-up. When both were offered, as was the custom, for publication on the editorial page of the Nyack *Journal*, only Toby's was chosen. The paper ran it under the by-line "A. Tobias Ronan, Jr." and the appalling title "The Passing of a Pussycat."

To provide Harvard with its required sample of his writing, Toby enclosed the clipping from the paper with his application for admission, carefully noting the original title in the margin. There was little else in his folder to recommend the boy to the Harvard selectors.

While his mother saw Toby's departure for Cambridge as the real beginning of his self-awakening, his father took it as a mark of high fulfillment—his own. How many men who worked with their hands most of their lives sired sons who went to Harvard? His only ground for concern, the senior Ronan allowed, was the university's reputation for attracting pantywaists. Mrs. Ronan branded the charge absurd, a slur by the envious and the uncouth. Nevertheless, to counter the possibility of his boy's pansification—and, Toby and his mother suspected, to exorcise his unmanning guilt for having been too old to serve in the Great War—Mr. Ronan stipulated that Toby would have to join the Harvard unit of the Reserve Officers' Training Corps if he wished to attend the university.

Insisting that military service was every citizen's duty as a Christian patriot, he drove Toby one Sunday to the Revolutionary War battlefield at Stony Point above the shoreline at the northern end of the county and retraced the heroic exploits of "Mad" Anthony Wayne and his men. His mother stayed home, saying that killing was neither Christian nor heroic and certainly nothing to be encouraged on the Lord's Day. Toby, on learning that the Harvard R.O.T.C. marched with brooms on their shoulders—a practice he thought more prudent than pantywaist—yielded to his father's condition.

III

On the night before Toby left for Harvard, his father disclosed the orders he had just received to reduce the plant payroll by fully one third. The news dampened but did not spoil Toby's exhilaration. He was sorry that misery was being visited upon so many people everywhere, including families with whose children he had grown up. But he could do no more good pining over it, he told himself, than his father could have by disregarding the directive of his corporate superiors.

From the start, Harvard proved an almost unimaginable release.

There was, first of all, the physical setting itself, so vast and varied, enclaves within enclaves, starting with the simple, mellow perfection of ivied Hollis Hall, where he was assigned a room with a boy from Virginia, and spilling over into the tumult of the historic Yard. Its arterial crisscross of walkways bore all-day traffic to the monumental masonry of Thayer Hall, the warmer curvilinears of Sever, the block-long granite steps ascending like a processional up the front of Widener, that pillared leviathan of learning. Beyond the Yard the ferment spread, and he followed, sampling the treasures of the Fogg, mingling momentarily with Langdell's lawyers *in utero*, genuflecting at all the other shrines and way stations to wisdom whose names he could not keep straight. On every side and as far as his feet could carry was the corpus of human knowledge, no more than a fraction of it encompassable in a single lifetime, let alone one paltry undergraduate career.

Outside the college gates, he carefully negotiated Harvard Square, a whizzing nexus of sedans, streetcars, taxis, cyclists, and pedestrians with flailing elbow patches, and found another world. He toured the galaxy of bookshops, grazed the soft banks of the Charles, and hopped the "el" for the city's museums and bazaars and antiquities, its parks and squares and graveyards and hundred little places to stop for coffee and a sweet roll. But for all the books and buildings, the inspiring sights and quickening sounds, the bright young faces and stirring new ideas that swirled around him in such profusion, a boy lately arrived could feel very lonely indeed in that perfectly thrilling landscape—especially if he bore all the marks of the outlander.

Toby did not know even how to pretend to be otherwise. The evidence was overwhelming. His suits were too short, his neckties too patterned, his hair too long and too red, his laughter (when he managed any) too rasping. By every Harvard standard and tradition, he was nobody. A nothing. He did not stem from Brahmin stock or lesser Yankee breeds. Or, next best, from New York or Philadelphia mercantile people. Or, still quite acceptable, from reverend clergy of the decorous denominations. Or, just qualifying, from the home of a doctor, lawyer, educator, or some other respectable but tedious sort of professional. Anyone of humbler origin was as much a social pariah as those swarthy semimendicants who doggedly rode the streetcar to college each morning from decidedly unfashionable Boston addresses and ate lunch out of brown-paper bags in the ground-floor pen set aside for them in Dudley Hall.

Nor had he personal gifts that might have redeemed low parentage. Genetics had equipped him with small but indelicate features, ears that cantilevered from a narrow head, too little jaw, too much neck, and shoulders precipitously sloping toward unmuscular arms. A stunning specimen he was not. Neither was he an athlete, though he managed a recognizable version of tennis and swam with a firm if unstylish stroke. Nor a musician, though his mother had taught him rudimentary piano. Nor a debater nor thespian nor chess prodigy nor yawler. He did not dance, drink, kiss—or pray, supposing his sinlessness left him with little need of expiation. The truth, of course, was that a hyperactive adolescent fear of rejection had stunted his development as a social being, so instead he bathed a great deal with Lifebuoy, savoring its octagonal tactility and his own raw aroma.

All things considered, then, he was more distressed than fascinated by his new surroundings. What good was it, Toby wondered, desperately mixing metaphor and cliché, to be rated the cream of the crop if you wound up at the bottom of the barrel?

What made it all doubly dispiriting was that the *crème de la crème*, Cambridge division, had hardly gone into hiding in deference to hard times. The depression was other people's beeswax. Nearly all the young gentry spurned the tacky Yard dormitories for the posher apartments along the Mount Auburn "Gold Coast," but they rarely stayed in the hive for long. Their world was bounded by Topsfield and Newburyport on the north and Marshfield Hills on the south and centered in between on brunches at the Ritz, teas with the Terwilligers on upper Beacon, suppers with Uncle Theo and Cousin Eddie at the Somserset, weekends sailing and wassailing off and on the North Shore, and brisk midwinter marches up Charles Street in snow swirling pastel from the shop lights to a musicale featuring the Misses Bosworth of Louisburg Square. The scions of privilege were forever leaving their J. Press overcoats (chesterfield collar *de rigueur*) in the back of someone's coupe. And if the studs so urgently needed for that night's bash had disappeared at the last minute, one could always borrow that wretched extra set in mother-of-pearl that Roger's Aunt Julia had given him for graduating Andover.

Inadmissible to this lot of lochinvars, Toby was consigned to the rank and file who came to Harvard singly or in pairs from the common boarding, country-day, and public schools across America because they (or, more likely, their families) wanted the best education money could buy and the manners—or mannerisms—to match.

Their segregation was impossible to ignore. Every time he looked up from his studies, Toby saw the silver-spoon set pursuing gaiety he was too poor and hard-pressed (and, at any rate, not invited) to share. Besides, he thought it grossly out of keeping with the times. They mocked and sang and brayed, drinking illicitly into the night or locked in nonstop bouts of blackjack for five dollars a pot or whooping away on the rear of a streetcar headed out of the Square at dusk Saturday for the old Howard burlesque hall and afterward a hot dog across the street at Joe & Nemo's and then to watch while one of them risked blood poisoning getting tattooed at Mr. Liberty in Scollay Square. His roommate went with them. Everyone else at Harvard had pals, Toby concluded, neglecting to notice his fellow outcasts who hugged the edges of the slate walks, head down, hoping to dematerialize amid all that brick and stone.

His mother's funeral found him in spirits that oscillated wildly, and almost from moment to moment, between euphoria and despondency. It was raw and overcast when they put her in hallowed ground. He could not have stood the poignancy of graveside sunshine. The box looked too small to hold her, Toby thought and then battled his welling anger because she had deserved a longer life. What good was a Maker who ignored merit in parceling out lifetimes? He had only scorn for the myth of resurrection; death was final and, he saw, never fair. For the first time, he wondered how long an earthly stay he could expect before joining the dear woman who had given him life and sustained it.

To his astonished pleasure, a handwritten apology from Travis awaited him on his return to Cambridge the following week. No doubt the deanery had conveyed the cause of Toby's overhasty departure from the professor's lecture. He offered graceful condolences, chastened the lad gently for having attended class while so distraught, promised to absolve him publicly when his course next convened, and invited him to his Back Bay home for tea the Sunday following. More apprehensive than grateful, Toby knew attendance in this case was not optional.

IV

A maid admitted him to the three-story brownstone. The professor awaited in an upstairs drawing room, hovering in reverie before the large bay windows that looked out over the river, ash gray in the dwindling light. The water eddied madly in spots as the wind whipped across it and rattled the windowpanes along the lower ramparts of Beacon Street. It was a wonderful view, Toby said after Travis had offered his soft, white hand and they stood silently for a time studying the flow of the Charles.

"Yes, thank you," he said, "I cherish it. It compensates for the bother of living away from Cambridge." Distance lent both enchantment and perspective, he noted, the latter being of special value to him since Harvard suffered so from myopia that caused constant confusion between *veritas* and *virtus*. The professor was being wickedly aphoristic, Toby sensed, but his precise meaning eluded him so he offered no responsive grace note and kept smiling for longer than he felt like.

They sat on the cushioned seats built in below the windows. Scissoring one knife-edged trouser leg over the other in a posture Toby's father would have found suspiciously fussy, Travis asked how he was getting on. Well enough, Toby said with thanks, though the work was very challenging indeed.

"I should hope so," Travis said heartily. "And socially, how is it? The place can be downright brutal, I gather, to boys who don't grow up or prep around here. Where is it they tell me you're from— Peekskill?"

"Piermont, sir—on the other side of the river—just below Nyack."

"Well, that sounds practically metropolitan."

"Not exactly, sir."

"But you must have a river view, too, then?"

"Oh, yes, sir. It's the chief attraction. The only one, actually."

"And do you miss it?"

"The view, sir—or the town?"

"Either will do."

"Somewhat—but there's so much more going on here—"

"No doubt. I don't suppose Piermont armed you for getting along famously with our junior Back Bay Borgias. They must seem *teddibly* stand-offish to you—?"

"Well—we travel in different circles, so to speak, sir."

Travis's brows arched. "And your roommate—is he a decent enough sort? That can make a difference, I should think."

"Decent enough—yes, sir."

"Someone you knew from before, perhaps?"

"Oh, no—not at all. He's from Richmond."

"An F.F.V., I suppose?"

"Excuse me, sir?"

"From an old family there—?"

"I—wouldn't know, sir. I thought they all were, though."

The professor brightened a bit at that. "I can assume, then, you're not thick pals?"

"Not really, sir."

"Yes—well, why should you be? It would be dumb luck to be thrown in with someone who turned out to be a kindred soul. You'll find your friends soon enough."

The tea tray arrived in the momentary lull that followed. Travis invited him toward the mahogany sideboard, an elegant piece with delicately bowed legs that looked too fragile to bear so much weight. The furnishings all had soft lines and muted colors that even a novice inspector recognized as the epitome of tastefulness. Toby's eye roamed from the greenish gray damask curtains with their ferny weave to the scallop-backed sofa in rosy velvet, flanked by a pair of Turkish brass lamps that bathed the inlaid tables holding them in gentle radiance from under bell-shaped shades, beige on the outside and pink within, like a conch. Persian rugs of varying sizes and stages of wear seemed to litter the floor rather than cover it. Potted plants stood, sat, and hung everywhere, tall and short, palmy and bushy, succulents and citrus, in tropical profusion. A scene, all in all, of such charm and serenity that the boy almost missed Travis's asking if he wished milk or lemon with his tea.

Sugar, actually, was what he wanted, but the question seemed to preclude it as a civilized additive. Besides, the silver tray held a plateful of small cakes with glazed white icing, which were promptly presented with a dish, fork, and fingertip napkin. Travis, taking only tea, ushered his uneasy guest toward the flameless fireplace, sat himself on a large chair, and motioned Toby into a smaller, straight-backed one nearby.

The visitor chewed and drank more moistly than he wished while his host sipped noiselessly from a Dresden cup. Was there, Toby wondered, a Mrs. Travis who would whisk in wearing a sort of sherbety dress and perhaps brighten up the lagging interview? He caught no stirring in the wings, only an impatience with the company on Travis's part. Toby could think of nothing to say—was uncertain, even, whether etiquette permitted him to speak unless spoken to by so august a presence. Unquestionably, the man was trying to compensate for the unknowing cruelty he had dealt an innocent; how many other imperious Harvard dons would have had the decency to recant an error in public and the courtesy to try to make up for it in private? The arrangement was too contrived, though, and their stations too far apart for an easy exchange. The kindness tendered, Toby wanted only to be gone from there. Yet he did not relish leaving behind the impression that he was an inarticulate lout—not with that consummate communicator.

His anxiety was not lost on Travis, who took a final petite swallow of his tea, cleared his throat gently, and turned sideways to Toby. "Abbott Lawrence Lowell is in some ways a quite impossible man," he began, selecting his words with precision practiced on a platform, "but our esteemed president is also remarkably astute about a number of things, not the least being the internal workings of the student psyche."

He placed his cup and saucer on the pudgy arm of the chair and locked his eyes onto the company. To blink, Toby was sure, would be disrespectful. He did his best to look alert and expend the least possible energy on actual breathing.

"Addressing the freshmen a few years back," Travis resumed, "the president remarked that shyness is not a becoming trait in a college man. He went so far as to suggest, in fact, that it was an impediment to the pursuit of an education."

Toby could draw no other inference but that the sentiment was directed *ad hominen*. He tried not to squirm. Or disclose his peripheral awareness that Travis's teacup had begun to teeter.

"To clinch his point, he urged each of the newcomers to visit that rather baroque painting of Galahad at the Fine Arts—do you know the one, by any chance, Mr. Ronan? I cannot think who the artist is— some acolyte to Delacroix, I should say."

Toby remembered having seen the work and nodded eagerly.

"Ah, splendid—then you'll catch his drift at once. Mr. Lowell was suggesting that even the purest of knights can miss the Grail if he is too modest to come forth and ask what the parade is all about."

Toby nodded again, more slowly now and wiser by the quantity of one leaden apothegm. His preceptor uncrossed his legs and leaned confidingly toward him while his teacup continued to edge more millimeters the other way. "You must not be afraid to ask at Harvard,

Mr. Ronan—anything or anybody, or under any circumstances. You come this way just once—make the trip worthwhile. And having decided upon your route, stick to it. Harvard may not appear to be overly hospitable to nonconforming boys, but it lets them be and that is no mean virtue. I have the sense they are the ones who contribute the most afterward."

He sat back now and drew his head up, oblivious to cup and saucer at the precipice. "As to the boys with the superior airs, Mr. Ronan, they want you to think they own the university as their fathers did before them, and that tomorrow they will own the world. But the world is changing, and you, young man, are not here to polish the boots of bluebloods—or to allow them to be planted in your back."

So saying and without a lateral glance, he rescued the cup and saucer from imminent oblivion by a swoop of his hand and rose to terminate the meeting. Whether it was Travis's counsel or knowing adroitness with the china that struck Toby the more forcefully that afternoon was hard to say, but from then on he never doubted he belonged at Harvard. When the dean's list appeared at the end of January, his name was on it.

V

Other than Jeremiah Travis, there were three people at Cambridge who summoned Toby from within himself. One was his tutor. One was a girl. And the least likely of them was a large, muscular boy from Pittsburgh named Rupert Perry Donovan, among the most raucous members of the Class of '34.

By the time they met in mid-spring of freshman year, Toby's financial circumstances had become a worry. His father, anticipating a lower salary as business steadily worsened, cut his already austere allowance in half and urged him to seek odd jobs to compensate. Given his academic responsibilities and the unemployment plague, the only work that made any sense was typing student papers. While quite young he had learned to run the big, old Underwood that his father brought home from the plant for composing production reports every weekend. Facility with the machine had stunted Toby's schoolboy cursive even as it enriched the content of his prose. Now he exploited the skill, investing in a second-hand Remington and posting a notice of his peerless service on every bulletin board in the Yard and its environs. He was fast, neat, accurate, and cheap—and sometimes threw in a bit of editorial counseling gratis. Soon he had to turn customers away.

Rupe Donovan barged in on him one night when Toby had the

Remington clacking on all cylinders. The son of a Westinghouse engineer and a doyenne of Allegheny Valley society, he was well-bred enough but suffered from sluggish coordination, which, despite his record as a serviceable tackle at Mercersburg Academy, soon parted him from the Harvard freshman football squad. He turned instead for self-validation to the unwholesome trinity of cards, billiards, and bootleg hooch. Equally graceless in victory or defeat, he wielded his cue stick like a lance and drove off other habitués at the Mass. Ave. pool parlor of Messrs. Leavitt & Pierce. Indeed, in every pastime Rupe Donovan undertook—buying out two whole rows at Fenway Park and then trying to dredge up enough recruits to fill them, for instance, or decorating the Tri-Delt living room with the residue of his liquid lunch at Dartmouth Winter Carnival—there was an immoderate quality that bespoke inner turmoil. Least appealing of all were his sniggering intimations of worldliness with women. No one was readier at any hour to lead a brigade to Minsky's Park Burlesk, where if you paid your quarter before noon, you could catch the strippers in the altogether. And when he solicited the boys at deluxe Claverly for a date with their sisters by reassuring them with a leer that his sex had been shot off in the war at Wipers, they dubbed him "good old Rupe Donovan from Bunghole, Pennsylvania." Soon they called him just plain Bung.

Toby saw why the night Rupe invaded his room. Looking as if he had been baying at the moon for a spell, he announced that he needed a paper typed for his British history course—by morning. It was only seven or eight pages, he said and offered to dictate it if that would make it easier. Not a chance, Toby told him, and the intruder immediately turned truculent. "What'sa matter—isn't my money any good?"

"Unless you printed it yourself."

"Hey, that's rich." He began croaking to transparent excess, then stopped short and said, "Look, it's really important."

"Sorry—I've got a five-day backlog."

"Yeah—but they can't all be emergencies."

"They would be if they'd all waited till the last minute."

"And the world'd be flat if it wasn't round. An emergency's an emergency."

Toby's mute response was to turn back to his work. At eleven o'clock at night, Rupe Donovan was in a seller's market.

"Shit!" he spat and sank back into the corner, sulking. "Look," he said after a moment of subtle analysis, "I'll pay extra."

"I don't do that."

"Why not—isn't it a free country anymore? Or are you union labor?"

"It's strictly first come, first served."

"You make the rules—couldn't you make an exception?" He was close to saying please but his abrasive lips could not form the word.

"It wouldn't be fair to everyone else. They all have deadlines."

"Not tomorrow morning—"

"Not if they've got any brains."

Rupe's bleary eyes narrowed. "Are you calling me stupid?"

"I'm trying to earn a little money."

He slumped onto Toby's bed, his gifts in the art of persuasion nearly exhausted. "Look, I'll throw in a free bottle of gin," he tried, "the best stuff. It'll make your balls play 'Yankee Doodle.' "

The ultimate in percussion. "I don't drink."

"Some pussy, then—how 'bout that? I know a very hot number off Brattle a little ways out—available around the clock. Be my guest." Then he added with a baiting sneer, "Or don't you do that, either?"

Toby looked over at him coldly. "Donovan, has anyone ever told you that you have a very ingratiating manner?"

His haze deflected the irony. "Me?"

"Sure. I'll bet you could charm the pants off a lamb chop even with the lights on."

The persiflage penetrated. "Don't shit with me, Ronan, or I'll take you apart."

"Then don't bust into my room and start insulting me because I don't jump when you snap your fingers."

He was used to scorn, not direct reprimand. "How was I insulting?"

"Everything you said, practically."

He seemed puzzled at being held accountable for his words. "I don't get it. I have a need—and so do you—so I just thought—"

"I know your need—what's mine?"

He squinted at Toby to see if he was serious. "Moola," Rupe said. "You don't do this crap for your health, do you?"

"You mean I'm poor so it's okay to push me around all you want?"

The ruddy, piefaced goon actually looked slightly contrite. "Hey, no—I never meant it that way."

"Well," Toby said, "you need a little work on your personality."

"Look, I'm sorry—forgive me—okay?"

"Yeah, sure." Toby turned back to his typing. "But the answer is still no. Why don't you just write it out nice and neat in longhand?"

"Because my handwriting's worse than a field nigger's."

"Practice makes perfect," Toby said, dismissing him and starting up in earnest on his machine.

Donovan sat there hunched silently for a time like an eviscerated hulk, then threw a cavernous sigh, said "Shit!" again, and began to cry. Not very loud and not very wetly but weeping beyond a doubt. "Shit, shit, shit!" he blurted and buried his face in his hands.

Toby stopped typing out of respect for the pathetic. This overgrown infant had been reduced to abject defeat—and not just by him, it was clear. Blandly, as if not noticing his collapse, Toby asked what the big emergency was.

Eyes bolted to the floor, throat phlegmy, Rupe said the paper was already a week late and he would get no credit if it wasn't in by nine, thereby flunking the course. And since he was in trouble in all his others as well, the odds were strongly in favor of his being booted out. Toby asked why he had waited so long to do the paper, and he mumbled that he was temperamentally incapable of functioning on hard things till the last minute. The authenticity of his grief at the prospect of dismissal needed no clinical analysis. Stripped of bluster, the boy was scared silly.

Toby plucked the rumpled wad of pages from Rupe's shirt pocket and, unmindful of the ink and sweat stains that were its principal punctuation, made his way through the paper. A gloss on Charles I and the justifications of regicide, it was not entirely incoherent, however derelict-looking—a C minus or so, Toby guessed. "It's not terrible," he offered.

Rupe looked up like a whipped dog suddenly presented a soup bone. "Really?"

"What it needs most—if you ask me—is more meat on the moral weakness of Parliament's position. Once they started negotiating with the King on how much treason he had to acknowledge, it sounds to me as if they compromised their own claim to hang him on the principle of the thing." Toby urged him to go take a shower, rework part of the paper with that thought in mind, and come back at twelve-thirty. Mute with gratitude, Rupe lifted his blotchy face and nearly granulated Toby's hand.

The paper received a B, the highest grade Rupe had earned all year. To celebrate, he insisted on taking Toby to Jacob Wirth's for a *gemütlich* supper of pea soup, dark bread, and brisket, and afterward donned a hairshirt. His Harvard career had been a disaster so far, he confided with surprising introspection, because he had so much wanted it to go off like a cherry bomb that he didn't know how to settle for a less spectacular launching. "Gross expectations," Toby said and told him to stop worrying about his social status and concentrate on not flunking out.

Rupe shadowed him the rest of the term. It was not a compan-

ionship Toby encouraged. But there was something touching about
this mooselike boy whom the college had reviled as a boor and a
dunce and who turned to Toby almost worshipfully as his last hope
for survival. Rupe's reclamation became the sole extracurricular project of Toby's freshman year. Beneath that gruff exterior was a genuinely neurotic strain—Rupe Donovan had a compulsion to prove the
world disliked him by provoking it to the point where it was certain
to do so. Toby helped him organize his study for spring finals, weaned
him off gin and on to fruit juices, and taught him to knock instead of
barging through the door.

His reward for this private counseling and confessional service was
an invitation from Rupe to room with him sophomore year. The prospect of playing resident nursemaid to so large and loud a foundling
was dismaying. Whether he was just too polite to say no or was reluctantly acknowledging that, for all their differences, they were outcast
birds of a feather under the Harvard social firmament—Rupe's offer
was, in fact, the only one made to him—Toby agreed.

Luckily, two unforeseeable developments blessed the arrangement.
For one thing, Rupe returned to college in the fall radically reformed.
Calmer, quieter, and twenty pounds lighter, he revealed a pleasant
humor and native canniness to go with his sudden academic purposefulness. He was full of talk about a career in law and had the *Evening
Transcript* delivered to their door to keep up with the sobering news
of the day. Occasionally he spoke of perhaps still making Hasty Pudding and then one of the final clubs, but the way everyone except
Toby persisted in calling him Bung soon told him how forlorn a hope
that was.

His disappointment was softened by the other radical turn in their
lives that fall—President Lowell's program to disestablish aristocracy
at Harvard. What an enigma that willowy old man was! He had as
long a pedigree as any of them and was hardly partial to the lower orders. Only a few years earlier, he had made no secret of wanting the
number of Jews admitted to the university to be fixed firmly by quota
—they were not the manly, active sort, by and large, he said; too
many of the Talmudic tribe would induce permanent curvature of
Harvard's spine. And Lowell's role in finally dooming Sacco and Vanzetti had been no less notorious—and equally the product, it was
widely surmised, of his own Nordic predilections. And yet, as the cul-
minating act of his regime in Massachusetts Hall, he had mandated and
found the funding for a convulsive reform of fair Harvard's living
and learning experience.

No longer were the rich boys to be permitted to dwell in gilded privacy along Mount Auburn; henceforth, Fauntleroys and commoners, the sanitized and the scruffy, would be tossed together. Everyone had to room in the Yard freshman year and after that in one of the neo-Georgian "Houses," the gleaming new residential colleges rising beside or near the river. Porcellian, Fly, and the other off-campus strongholds of elitism remained in haughty operation but overnight became redundant. The Houses were where you slept, ate, studied, got tutored, played squash, and—all but clubmen—socialized. The democratizing process, set in motion with a mighty wrench, was irreversible. In the hazy, rarely seen, but ubiquitously felt presence of A. Lawrence Lowell, Toby came to understand the essence of Yankee grace: a capacity to transcend one's caste, however mean or exalted, without in any way disowning it.

Any of Lowell's new brick Houses along the Charles, ashimmer with the showy splendor of their freshly gilded cupolas, would have suited them, but the luck of the draw landed Toby and Rupe in third-floor digs at Adams House. Converted from the old Westmorly apartments that had operated as the lower terminus of the Gold Coast, Adams was old but hardly a tenement. Like all the other Houses, depression or no depression, it catered to its privileged clientele with white tablecloths and linen napkins, gentlemanly place settings, and prompt table service. Instead of the poetic riverside vistas available from Eliot House or Leverett or Dunster, though, its windows gave out on the thoroughly unpastoral prospect of now declassé Mount Auburn Street. They were installed on the avenue of the swells a year too late.

This orgy of fraternity infected Rupe to the point of proposing that his more than ample allowance be used to defray their shared recreational costs like movies and meals out, which he knew Toby couldn't afford without his typing income. He said Toby had better uses for his time, such as staying on the dean's list, trying to write for the *Advocate* or *Lampoon,* or taking out a girl now and then. Toby thanked him for his generosity but thought that even so benign a form of dependency might unbalance their friendship. Rupe swore he would never think the less of him for it. It was more a matter of his own self-respect, Toby explained, than his roommate's estimate. "But friends share things," Rupe persisted. "You've done a lot for me, and I want to reciprocate—what's wrong with that?" His impulse was commendable, Toby told him, but he had to look at it from both sides. "Suit yourself," Rupe gave in, only mildly offended, "but just remember—pride goeth before a fall." And without it, said Toby, you might as well stay on all fours.

It was not their last exchange on the topic of Toby's being prin-cipled to a fault. On the day he learned that his father had salvaged the Ronan family nestegg by what struck Toby as an act of blatant dishonor, Rupe strongly disputed that judgment. "You're being a swinish little turd about this, you know," was how he put it.

His father's letter grieved Toby most because it came so unforgiv-ingly close to self-congratulation. Never a believer in the stock market, he preferred to maintain his modest financial liquidity in the form of savings deposits. Upon his election to the board of the Pier-mont Savings and Trust, where in theory he gained oversight of the soundness of operations, he could conceive of no safer haven for the accumulated morsels he had long set aside from every pay envelope. The crash on Wall Street confirmed his caution for a time—till out of the blue, as he wrote Toby,

> one of my fellow members on the bank board, who must remain nameless, was kind enough to advise me that every last cent in our account would be lost within forty-eight hours. You can imagine my shock and chagrin, and the course I felt obliged to follow. I am sorry to report the bank has, in actuality, closed its doors. While such failures are occurring in many places around the country these days, I never supposed it could happen in Pier-mont, or to an institution with which I was associated.

There was no hint of shame or compunction over having rescued his own skin at the expense of others toward whom he presumably bore a high fiduciary responsibility. Instead, the lesson he chose to draw from the harrowing episode was the necessity in a dog-eat-dog world of maintaining friends in high places. This instruction did not go down at all well. In Toby's mind, his father's failure to concede an ounce of turpitude made him nothing less than a white-collar bank robber. Not that he had ever imagined him a candidate for sainthood but had always arrayed him, beyond a doubt, with the forces of goodness, for which his mother was perhaps the more earnest recruiter of the pair. Yet here his father was revealing an aspect of himself truly ignoble, and it disillusioned the boy to a point very near heartbreak. Nor was the calculating guidance he offered at the close of this letter at all welcome:

> . . . You have gone to Harvard to make the acquaintance of the right sort, and I trust this sobering experience I have apprised you of may be a reminder of how precious an acquisition is friend-ship. Be well and good.
>
> As always,
> Your loving father

It was not something he would normally have shared with Rupe despite their thickening bond. Blood was still thicker. But even as he absorbed his father's shameless revelation, Toby could not help thinking how little he had really known him before his mother's death and how there was even less linking them since. He had not been indifferent to Toby ever, certainly, so much as eternally preoccupied with his dreadful, clanking factory and how the family's whole fate had been bound up with the size and dependability of its output. Parental tenderness he simply ceded to the boy's mother, whom he counted on to administer it sensibly. Yet Toby knew he cared. At the dinner table, he listened, and not glumly, to every account of his son's deportment, upright and naughty alike, and responded in a manner that left Toby in no doubt he retained the man's love if not always his approval. It was plain, though, from the news he volunteered by letter as a cautionary tale, that the moral precepts they each honored now differed sharply. In his distress, Toby blurted all to his roommate. "It isn't a question of honesty," Rupe said, taking Toby's father's side at once. "It's a matter of survival."

"Thank you, Charles Darwin."

"Yes, exactly. All your old man's saying is that you can take your principles and jam them up your rosy red if you're insolvent."

"So every man for himself, and too bad for the poor and the powerless and the guy who didn't get the word."

"No one's saying it's pretty, but that's how it is—yes."

"That's not civilization—that's the jungle."

"Which is what it happens to be out there right now, sport."

"And all my father did was to make it worse."

"And what would he have proven by leaving his money in the bank?"

"That decency still matters."

"How would it have done that? First off, no one would have known what he was doing unless he announced it, which would only have sped up the stampede. Second of all, don't you think he would have done something to change the bank's policies if he'd found out in time? And third, sticking his thumb in the dike at the end wouldn't have stopped it from collapsing—he'd be out all the savings he's worked his entire life to collect, and you, you high-minded babe in the woods, would have had to come crawling to Harvard to make you a charity case. And let me tell you—you're lousy at crawling."

Toby was not so ready to concede the futility of honor, although he recognized the practical force of Rupe's argument. Principle that did not waver under adversity, he was sure, might yet win battles that expediency never would. Suppose, instead of deserting the ship, his father had held fast, as captains are charged to, and urged others to do likewise—might not the outcome have been different? Not every bank in America was closing. And at the imperiled ones, didn't men like his father have a special duty to serve as models of propriety and not to exploit their privileged position? Rupe shrugged that off, saying Toby was holding his father to a standard of saintliness that only dogs and small children detect in their keepers. "Anyway," he wound up, "you may win a battle with dead heroes but not the war."

"But if you surrender your principles to win it, a war isn't worth fighting in the first place."

Rupe snorted. "You think wars are fought over principles? How'd you pull an 'A' from Firsky Merriman? The only principle that counts on the battlefield is 'Might makes right.'"

"The Revolutionary War was fought over principles. So was the Civil War—"

"They were both fought over money—the principles were fancy rationalizations, lyrics courtesy of T. Jefferson. Wise up, Toby."

"I don't happen to agree. America has been more principled than any country in history, practically."

Rupe gave a groan of exasperation. "Look, there's no more sterling character in the United States than Herbert Hoover—but his ship's going down, principles and all, and we're going with him. You've got to know when to cut your losses. My old man's a Smoot-Hawley Republican, and even he thinks the President's being a hopeless jackass. He says if we don't start spreading the wealth around a little, the Bolsheviks'll beat our bloody brains in. He says no one's told Hoover that the greatest American principle of all is compromise."

The Donovan clan may have found expediency to be the highest form of ethics, but Rupe's fast talk brought Toby no balm. The bank incident left him feeling confused and orphaned. His father need not be a shining knight, but no parent of his could knowingly do an indecent thing and then wrap himself in righteousness. He wanted to blame it on the times. But men's souls, he knew by then, were always on trial. Better to get through Harvard by cleaning toilet bowls than on his father's tarnished shekels. That was bravado, though. His impotence drove Toby to rebel less drastically.

Probably because he had been forced to join the R.O.T.C., Toby hated it from the start. He was forever out of step and messing up march orders. The mindlessness of it all galled him. If he had wanted to perfect his muscular coordination, he would have joined the Ringling Brothers, not gone to Harvard. He resigned from the unit and advised his father of it the next day in a brief, brassy letter that made no mention of his old man's scandalous bank job or its part in prompting the step.

"I am sorry you have chosen to desert your country in her hour of need," his father wrote back. "I had hoped they were teaching you the meaning of honor up there."

TWO

MOST OF THE YOUNG MEN at Harvard in the early 'Thirties looked with the same disfavor as their parents on a rash response to the economic emergency. The sky may have been falling, but rushing around beneath it would not make you a smaller target. A common belief was that as the Lord giveth, so He taketh away, and there was nothing for it but to forbear till things turned up.

A remnant at Cambridge, however, thought it sorry folly to blame God Almighty for the breakdown of an economic system conceived by the genius of Man and done in by his nastier impulses. Toby counted himself among these thin ranks, of whom there were never fewer than ten or more than twenty on hand for the biweekly meetings of the Harvard Liberal Club during that autumn and winter of deepening distress across the land.

The only reason for turnouts even that size was that the Liberals were taken more for a lay religious sect than a partisan political movement. Harvard was allergic to politics—a condition probably traceable to the belief among her enrollees that, being the finest flower of the nation, they debased their individuality by embracing parties, causes, or ideologies beyond themselves. One did not attend Cambridge to be submerged; one went to learn how to captain the ship.

Beyond that, of course, was the sordidness of the thing. Politics was a vice that men of taste and breeding rose above. It was perhaps dabbled in for diversion now and then but only at a distance. Or manipulated for sound economic motives but then only with a velvet glove or, still better, hired hands. Cambridge, moreover, was not the best terrain to nurture illusions about the wholesomeness of the body politic, being only a whiff away from Boston, that historic sink of grafters, wardheelers, and solons of the saloon.

If Harvard did not encourage political activism, good citizenship then being embodied primarily in private virtue, neither did it quash deviant social thought. Misfits of any genus were by and large ignored. And that was no small thing. Founded by religious dissenters, led afterward by those who dissented from the first dissenters, Harvard became Harvard, beacon of enlightenment in the New World, as much for her toleration of unorthodoxy as for any other single quality. It may have been a freedom inspired by indifference instead of burning conviction, but it was freedom nonetheless.

Yet for all her openness, Harvard was hardly a place to attract radicals. And it did little to convert anyone tilting in that direction. The sons of the wealthy, even the occasional conscience-stricken ones, relished their station too much to turn any weapon more lethal than cynicism on the shortcomings of society. The poor boys, having come to Cambridge with the unabashed ambition of improving on their parents' lot, were still less inclined to antagonize. And the offspring of the enterprising middle classes, craving respectability above all, were the least likely to harbor incendiaries.

Thus, even against a backdrop of worldwide destitution, these negative factors conspired to trivialize the activities of student political groups and social movements at Harvard. The Liberal Club was perhaps a shade less laughable than, say, the vegetarians, the World Federalists, or the antivivisectionists, but only because no one who did not belong knew what it stood for.

Toby had been drawn at first to this self-conscious band of meliorists because theirs was the sole acceptable forum around for the venting of bootless outrage. He himself felt more emptiness than fury, and less directed than compelled to find a direction. Once he came within earshot of them, the Liberals all sounded maddeningly as if they knew what to believe in—which dragons needed slaying in what order—and that it mattered greatly what they said and felt. Toby hoped some of that radiant certitude would rub off.

Their imperatives were breathtaking in their sweep and simplicity. Oppressive power—of every sort, in every place—had to be lifted from the whip hand of despoilers and dispersed fairly, forever. A balance had to be struck between the appetites of capital and the grievances of labor. Militarism had to be certified as humanity's ultimate lunacy. The universal demands of mankind—liberty, dignity, and the equal chance to flourish—had to be recognized, and all forms of political organization that did not strive for their fulfillment had to yield their claim to legitimacy.

"That's paradise they're talking about," Rupe said with a laugh when Toby reported to him on his first meeting, "your classic one-party theocracy. I'll take a little *laissez-faire* turmoil any day."

For a time, those apocalyptical gatherings excited him more than all his classwork combined. They stirred his head and heart together. The topics aired may have varied—how long would the now unmasked barracudas of Wall Street be allowed to prey without restraint on the gullible public, or the farmers be expected to till the land at a loss, or the workingman be denied decent pay and hours and conditions?—but the intensity of concern each generated was constant. And they were so indefatigably articulate in their righteousness that Toby was reduced to envy because he had no golden tongue and dreaded the prospect of rising amid such glib company to offer some fumbling rejoinder. Yet for not speaking up, for having nothing constructive to add, he was soon stricken with guilt—he was taking sustenance without giving any—and feared he might be asked at any time to justify the heady air he was consuming.

But no one ever called on him, and the meetings would wear down long before they could resolve much of anything. Then out would come the cakes and lemonade and gone was the delusion that they were some magically invested privy council called to rid the realm of its woes.

The earnest but masturbatory nature of these exercises eventually eroded Toby's ardor. He was on the verge of quitting, in fact, when a girl showed up and sat next to him, and he suddenly donned a mask of grave contemplation.

Not many Radcliffe women turned out for the meetings of Harvard political groups, though they had a standing invitation. And nobody remotely resembling this one had appeared among the Liberals during Toby's tenure. She looked a little as if she had been sent by the Wobblies or Anarcho-Syndicalists to monitor the proceedings.

All eyes converged upon her as she undid a tan, billowy poncho with a dramatic swirl and then flicked aside her brown, checked newsboy cap revealing a long fall of straight jet hair, so contrary to the short, ringleted vogue of the day. High cheekbones made her face almost heart-shaped, and beneath a pair of wire-framed glasses, dark, almond eyes swam about absorbing the scenery even when she held her head perfectly still. Her nose was straight but mannishly indelicate, and her mouth, nibbling on the end of a stubby pencil she soon produced along with a small, spiral notebook, was too mobile to fix on but larger and detectably moister than the standard model for maidens of New England. By the criteria of the Yard, she was a high exotic.

For the first half hour or so, her attention never roved from the subject of the evening—a proposal that the government guarantee to unions the right to try to organize industries historically hostile to them. Toby's attention dwelled on matters uplifting only in the prurient sense. Stripped of her outerwear, she was a conventionally enough clad young woman in a white blouse and tobacco tweed skirt.

High, chocolate-brown wool stockings offered the voyeur not an inch of bare gam but a tantalizing anatomy lesson in flowing musculature. She was easily the most desirable creature he had ever sat next to.

His head danced with fantasies of conquest as the meeting dragged on and the girl began to shift about. Then somebody was on his feet saying that once government began meddling with the delicate machinery of the bargaining process, the whole economic system would disintegrate. That galvanized the girl. She began scribbling down notes in heat. Someone else stood and said that the other fellow must have been asleep for the past two years, that the system had already disintegrated, and besides, everyone knew owners never gave workers a damned thing they didn't have to—that was human nature—so government intervention was the only answer. Nodding at that, the girl scribbled harder now and then looked up, shrewd eyes flying about the room to gauge the prevailing sentiment. When they reached Toby, he pursed his lips in bemusement and stared inscrutably ahead.

As that flurry subsided, so did her patience, and after the talk turned to the Sherman and Clayton antitrust laws and their applicability to the labor movement, small sighs escaped from her, and those now anesthetized eyes rolled up into her temples. No word issued from her the whole time, though, and at the end she hurried off before anyone could engage her over refreshments.

To Toby's agitated delight, she came again to the next meeting. Again she failed to utter a word, and her note-taking tailed off to just a few acute slashes of her nubby pencil. But her looks and shifts and now audibly impatient sighs broadcast advancing exasperation with the discussion, this one on the need to restrict naval armaments, poison gas, and other lethal tools of national policy. Her restlessness finally grew so pronounced that the club president turned to her and asked if she wished to be heard.

An expectant stillness encased the room. Toby's throat tightened in empathy. Slowly those excoriating eyes lifted from her notepad and, in a voice a shade husky but by no means coarse, she said, "I beg your pardon?" The chair repeated the question. The girl glanced back down at her notes, then unhooked her glasses from behind her ears with both hands, placed them on her lap, tossed her hair back, and said, without rising, "My only thought was that as the next war is going to be decided mainly by aeroplanes and U-boats, worrying about them in particular might conceivably have made for a more useful exchange." So saying, she shut her notepad with a withering little flip that served to dismiss the entire program as pointless.

Two days later, Toby found himself seated obliquely across from her in the main reading room at Widener. It was unnerving to watch her speed through a thick text, underlining and inscribing tight marginal notes with legendary Radcliffean obsessiveness. Everything about her bespoke assurance and intensity. Oblivious to her surroundings, she never once glanced up to catch the smitten eyes fastened upon her.

He was not retarded, exactly, in developing a fondness for womankind, but being armed with neither looks nor money to speak of nor evident genius nor savoir faire left Toby dubious that he would ever send the ladies into raptures. He viewed the whole business of hunting up a mate as irksome. Romance happened in the movies; love made melodies only in Tin Pan Alley. Growing up, he had witnessed slight demonstration of either. There was more kindliness than acrimony in the Ronan home, surely, but rarely did it swell to affection and never, in his view or hearing, to ardor. His mother could be tender with him at rare intervals, but his father never was, and what feelings they reserved for each other he refused to contemplate.

As a social animal, then, he was a study in wariness. A few party kissing games provided the sum of his carnal knowledge till well into high school when curiosity overcame diffidence long enough for him to disappear into the catacombs of a Nyack movie palace one night and ceaselessly knead the upper torso of a friend of his cousin's. Happily, the young woman was both receptive and in bloom. But she lived in Suffern, which might as well have been on the other side of the world, not just the county, and she was thick in both senses, so he wound up sorrier for her than passionate. Girls with real allure, he was sure, were inaccessible to him.

Harvard hardly transformed him into Casanova, but it undeniably allowed him to walk taller through the precincts of his boyhood when he arrived home after freshman year. His father let him have the car some evenings, supplying Toby's emergent libido with privacy and mobility. But a little summer smooching with musky salesgirls was a far cry from stalking some bright, sleek, deodorized thing who had actually read *Ulysses*.

This one moved now, summoned back to earth by an inner alarm after nearly an hour of transfixed study. Anyone who could compartmentalize herself so completely, he decided, was either a prodigy or a witch. She slipped her head through the slit in her poncho, gathered up her things in some disorder, and, coming around Toby's side of the table, spotted him tracking her.

Her wide mouth formed a soundless hello as she slowed for an instant. Could she have remembered him from the meetings? He had said nothing memorable at them—nothing at all, in fact. Probably she was good at collecting faces, except that his could not have etched its way into her dreams. All he knew was that she was brushing past him now with a directed sweep of energy and, if he let her pass, there would be no other moment. "Is that thing," he asked, lurching to his feet with the grace of a penguin, "as warm as it looks?"

She stopped, wondering what he meant, then quickly realized and threw off a polite smile. "Roasting," she said. "But I'd die without it. I can't think how the Pilgrims made it till spring."

Oh, good God in heaven! She was so—so—he could not think—so alive! So saucy! He wanted to prostrate himself in her path to hold her there a minute more. "I—I—thought you were right the other night," he managed to utter.

She looked blank, rummaged through her mind briefly to place him, then shook her head in failure.

"About planes and U-boats—at the Liberal Club?"

"Oh, of course," she said, leaving in doubt if she connected him with it. "It wasn't my idea, exactly. General Mitchell, you know, has—"

"No one else there bothered saying it, though."

"Maybe no one else there reads the papers."

He shrugged with a grin meant to exclude himself from her charge. Then somehow, more prayerful than bold, he asked her if she had time for coffee.

"Thank you, no—I've got class." But with a darting smile that looked too much like a ray of sun to be perfunctory, she added, "Some other time, though, if you'd like." Slipping from him now.

"Yes—I'd like. When?"

"Call me—we'll decide." Her poncho fluttered.

He took two strides in pursuit. "How?"

"How what?" she called back over her shoulder. Heads were turning toward them.

"How do I call you?"

She would not stop. "At Cabot—just leave a message."

"For who?"

She froze in midstride and tapped her forehead. "Sorry," she said. "I'm Francesca da Silva." A cascade of musical sibilants. A name to suit her charms. "Just ask for Cheska." She tugged at the peak of her cap, and her long, blue-stockinged legs carried her out of range.

He had neither offered nor been asked his name. That did not bode well; indiscriminate invitations, issued in haste, were intended to deflect, not ensnare. That suspicion, added to his hatred of the telephone as a social instrument because it turned your whole being into a disembodied chirp, gave him what slight excuse he needed to wait until the next Liberal meeting to renew the invitation. Meanwhile, her name flowed through his brain with pulsing current. He would say it over and over as it leapt and sparkled like a freshet dancing out of a Keatsian idyll. But all along he knew she would not be there at the next meeting, which turned into an interminable ordeal without her for him to dwell on.

Rupe, noting his Werther-like mopishness, pried the source out of him and would not tolerate such wallowing. Only when he threatened to call her in Toby's behalf, though, did he gird himself and finally drop a note by her dormitory proposing she join him for coffee at four a few days hence at the Hayes-Bickford. It was signed "Liberally yours." There was no provision for her to decline, implying he was a habitué of the Bick at that hour and her showing up or not was more or less a matter of indifference to him.

She arrived at 4:15, just as he was going under for the third time. Up close, her chambered energy, disclosed in short, sharp movements as she talked and smoked and conjured, made her into a still more vibrant grace than he had remembered. She was so warm and charged and busy that the heat steaming her glasses seemed to rise up not from the coffee so much as her own internal combustion. A resident of San Francisco, where her family had a wholesale hardware business, she had come East to prep at Rosemary Hall and then taken a year off to travel abroad with her mother, who rediscovered Catholicism at an audience they had together with the Pope.

"The Vatican, you know," she said with delicious irreverence, "is obscenely gaudy." After three months at Radcliffe, she found the place both stimulating and confining—"like a kennel for high-strung bitches. But some of them are smarter than any boys in the place, and even the drudges have their moments."

Compared to her cosmopolitan background, his own sounded so airless and stultifying that he felt the need to embroider a bit, turning Piermont into Marseilles-on-the-Hudson and hinting that his father was closer to a baron of industry than a dogged superintendent of hellish works. "And doesn't he mind having a rabid revolutionary for a son?" she asked.

Her sarcasm, while confirming what little use she had for the Liberals, struck him as misplaced. "That's not exactly how I see them," he said.

"Oh, I know—I've been. They're wonderfully decorous—"

He tried to parry. "Yes—your enthusiasm was evident."

"I did my best to stay attentive."

"Yes. Well, maybe they ought to have a juggler in for when the going gets slow."

Her dark, emphatic eyebrows wavered, wondering if he had issued a lumpish joke or a crude reprimand. "That's not quite it, you know," she said, having decided whatever he had intended was a dud on arrival. "Your meetings are just fine as far as they go—very informed and very serious—oh, so serious. But they're rather antiseptic, don't you think—or will you take that unkindly?"

By assuming his strong allegiance to the Liberals, she had put him on the defensive. To deny a firm partisanship was to risk looking craven at the first sign of attack. He tried for neutrality. "You mean they're too—what—intellectual? Too abstract?"

She drew on her cigarette with practiced technique—no doubt she had acquired the habit at boarding school, where feigning worldliness was a preoccupation—and ran a hand over a few wisps that had wandered from her waist-long hood of raven hair. "I mean the world is caving in and you're all sitting around there like good little cerebral peas in your ivy pod. Look, starving men are picking through garbage cans in New York. Women are sleeping on park benches in Chicago. Wheat is rotting on the prairies—and cotton in the South—and apples in Oregon." Smoky eyelids raised and lowered, punctuating her words. "Did you know they're throwing live sheep by the thousands down canyons in Montana or Idaho or somewhere because the railroads charge the ranchers more to ship the animals than anyone will buy them for? Next time you see your father, ask him why they've repealed the law of supply and demand."

"Actually, he doesn't own his company—he's just sort of a top official."

"Would it make any difference if he did own it? What do you think railroads are but people who work for them? It's the system. I don't mean to sound contemptuous, Toby, but I just don't understand why anyone would keep going to the Liberal meetings after the first couple of times. I mean it's very fine for a group of bright, public-spirited college students to get together and try to understand what's going on out there—I applaud that. Only you have to be a terrible dodo not to have figured out by now there's something dreadfully wrong with a country that's so big and rich and fertile and everything else but millions of its people still wind up hungry and homeless—and hopeless. The time for brooding about it has passed. It's time to get out and start changing things."

Her face was fiery with conviction that made him uneasy. "You sound as if you're ready to put up the barricades."

"Not really," she said, muting her tone a trifle, "not yet." There were any number of small things a caring person could do to improve the devastated lives around him. Sundays, for instance, she helped cook and serve dinner for destitute families at a settlement house in

Dorchester—"and I don't deserve a medal for it. I read to shut-ins a couple of hours a week, too, and that's even less of a much. But your Liberals are too spoiled, probably, or too lazy or too frightened to get out into the real world. Social service or protest action is *infra dig*, so you all talk-talk-talk for useless hours. You're straight out of *The Hollow Men*—'shape without form . . . gesture without motion.'" She drew deeply on her cigarette a final time before jabbing it out. "And the most discouraging thing is that you dumb simps are the decentest guys in the whole university."

He had never been so sweetly damned with faint praise.

II

It took him about a week to figure out how to turn the bewitching Cheska da Silva's mockery to admiration.

When the Liberal Club was not wrestling valiantly with cosmic questions, it was fond of taking highly principled stands on subjects closer to home, like the slave wages paid to Harvard's cleaning women, free speech for campus communists and socialists (of whom there was said to be at least one or two each), and more help for students from families victimized by the depression. But none of these causes moved the Liberal stalwarts nearly as much as the dubious legitimacy of the Reserve Officers' Training Corps at a seat of higher learning.

In the years since Versailles settled the war to end all wars and America proceeded to turn her fatted backside to the world, "Rotcy" had come to occupy strategic ground on almost every major college campus in the country. Entrenched and truculent at the public universities, "military science"—a euphemism for a little reading on Athenian hoplites, medieval siege weaponry, and the tactics at Gettysburg, and a lot of sweaty marching in formation—was now a compulsory part of the curriculum. At Harvard and most private institutions that prided their independence, it remained an anomalous option, appealing only to a kind of caveman virility and defying nearly all the venerated values of the liberal tradition. The *R.O.T.C. Manual*, a compendium of chauvinism, intolerance, and brutishness, provided campus warriors such spiritual guidance as, "[The] inherent desire to fight and kill must be carefully watched for and encouraged in the student. . . ."

By far the most militant of the Liberal Club's activities was its ongoing campaign to have the Harvard Rotcy unit demobilized—permanently. The club wrote letters, put up leaflets, and circulated petitions against converting the college into a bulwark for mindless militarists. Even kid-glove efforts like these, though, earned the wrath of Mars. When a sheet called *Scabbard & Blade*, proclaiming itself the official publication of the R.O.T.C. "honor society," denounced campus liberals as "peace agitators" and declared all who opposed universal military training as traitors to true Americanism, Toby headed for his typewriter.

To that moment, his Harvard *oeuvre* consisted of two rejected stories for *The Advocate* and five satiric poems (one published—a limerick) for *The Lampoon*. Whether he was inspired now more by Cheska's needle or by the memory of his own abbreviated military career, featuring hateful weekly drills under a fanatic platoon leader, was of no concern to his muse. The piece, which he wrote in half an hour, the "Lampy" ran without a comma changed under the title "Red, White & Blueblood":

[Reprinted without permission from *Leopardskin & Cudgel*, the magazine of the R.O.T.C. cadres.]

It has been the better part of a century since an American army has done a sustained amount of killing. The war with Spain was more like shooting ducks in a barrel than a contest in earnest. And the Great War in Europe, while an invigorating exercise, really ended too soon for the Doughboys to get more than half-baked. The real gainers in that conflict, militarily speaking, were the Old World powers who succeeded in slaughtering millions and obtaining priceless experience in the martial arts.

Thus, America is likely to be caught woefully underprepared in the killing craft when the next international quarrel arises unless the lessons espoused by the R.O.T.C. are taken to heart. While mandatory military training at the land-grant colleges has had a stimulating effect on blood lust, too many other institutions remain aloof from this wholesome and essential form of character development. Alleged biblical injunctions against mayhem and other such false and unmanly distortions of history's great moral precepts have become the refuge of spineless collegians across the land.

Among the foremost gathering places of these pantywaists, who hold Old Glory in no higher honor than a few furls of mildewed cheesecloth, is Harvard University. Harvard men have a reputation on five continents and seven seas, plus the fey principalities of the mind, for being squeamish about killing. Often they ask questions about the purpose behind public policies that are palpably the sole business of those in command of society. Whenever possible, Harvard chaps buy the services of others to perform their patriotic duty. Remember that it was to Harvard that President Lincoln dispatched his son while the Union was embroiled in its most stirring butchery ever.

To rid Harvard of its lily-livered tendencies, the editors of
L & C are pleased to recommend to President Lowell and the
Board of Overseers the following curriculum of required killings
for all matriculated students:

*

FRESHMAN YEAR. Strangle one dormitory rat, preferably
plague-bearing; hides are to be tanned and worn as athletic supporters, the meat (after curing) going to the Adams House
kitchen, where it is a speciality of the chef.

SOPHOMORE YEAR. Blind one deer, selecting the more
soulful eye. While it is bashing into trees, slit its throat and drink
two liters of blood (hot). If a buck, rip antlers from head and
use as hat rack or ornament for auto hood.

JUNIOR YEAR. Kill one worthless underclassman. Method,
optional. Viscera go to Harvard Union mess, where they are a
specialty, etc.; genitals to the Radcliffe Priapic Taxidermy Society, and the husk to Med. School clumsies. Five points for an
M.I.T. man, three for an Eli, one for a B.U.'er. Then write on
a slate one thousand times: "Raskolnikov is alive and well in
Cambridge."

SENIOR YEAR. Bludgeon to death one excellent soul; the
more screaming and agony, the better. The eight receiving most
points for gore, ingenuity, and eminence of victims meet in Soldiers Field tourney; survivor graduates *summa cum loony*.

***Caution:* Killings limited to one per year; more would stain
R.O.T.C.'s reputation. God bless America. And if He doesn't,
He's next.

Since indifference to displays of virtuosity by his peers, particularly
the japery of sophomores, has always been a hallmark of the Harvard
undergraduate, Toby expected little in the way of a response. All together there were three that reached him: the first, almost surely
apocryphal; the second, mephitic, and the third—the third was bliss.

"The Master is gravely offended in behalf of all Adams House,"
Rupe reported, returning from commons the evening after the *Lampoon* appeared just before Christmas vacation. "And word has it that
your little burlesque infuriated the chef, who is thinking seriously
about making you his next *specialité*."

The next night, on his way back to his room after supper, he heard
shouts and scuffles all the way up the stairs and down the hall. Two
disheveled figures fleeing the scene nearly bowled him over. Inside the
room, a bloodied but unbowed Rupert Donovan sat panting beside the
contents of Toby's dresser, which had been strewn across the floor
and garnished with dogshit from every curb in Cambridge. Inverted
on top of the pile was his trusty typewriter, liberally stuffed with

chicken guts. "I almost nailed the dirty bastards," Rupe said, still heaving from the effort. Then he looked up and, a gob of blood aready beginning to congeal under one nostril, added, "Welcome to the brotherhood of the dearly beloved."

He would have left for home the next morning in a sour mood if not for a note Toby found in his mailbox. In big, swoopy handwriting on Radcliffe stationery it read, "Tom Paine, move over! The pen is mightier than the horde. Have a semi-happy holiday & call afterward. Your comrade-not-in-arms, C."

III

There is nothing to buoy the confidence of an uncertain young man like the admiration of a certain young woman. If, moreover, she is manipulative and he is pliable—and has not yet learned moderation in weighing her charms against all the rest of life—the resulting pain will do much to advance his education.

Cheska da Silva parceled her time to him stingily those first months of 1932, and he, accordingly, tried to be at least as economical about asking for it. It did not suit him to compete for her favor with what he took to be multitudes. He saw her once a week, sometimes for a movie and soda (Dutch or not at all, she insisted) or a free concert on campus, sometimes just for a blustery walk along the river and coffee afterward. But it was enough to hurt him whenever a prior commitment forced her to decline his next invitation. Never sure it was so, he would grow sullen and back away until she volunteered an alternate time or day and thus massaged his tender ego.

She was direct enough to say this fragility of his was not altogether endearing and that he had really better learn to be a little tougher with women, some of whom actually preferred swagger in their males. Yet she would as readily slip her arm through his when they walked at night or even, as she did one time after an all-Vivaldi recital had moved her, reach up on the sidewalk a block before the entrance to the Radcliffe Yard, and kiss him firmly on the mouth. Times and places to embrace, even if she had been more inclined, were scarce those icy weeks, and his dread of rebuff served to stymie ardor between them still further.

He was nevertheless determined that they should not be platonic pals. There was too much passion afloat in her, and need accumulating within him. While he waited for the thermometer, and her fondness, and his own boldness, to heat up, politics served as sublimation.

She had drifted into the Harvard-Radcliffe outpost of the Student

League for Industrial Democracy, an unofficial ward of the Socialist Party, and tried to proselytize him with assurances that there was nothing doctrinaire-Left about the group—just an abiding concern for the condition of the common man. When Toby scoffed, she would accuse him alternately of cowardice and callousness and then add darkly that, either way, inhumanity did not become him. It was not a coy overture. When he told her extremism frankly dismayed him, she said the problem was less that he had misjudged the Student League than that he felt threatened by any egalitarian movement. In self-defense, he finally went to a meeting of her group that she had helped arrange at the Radcliffe Institute.

The star attraction that night was a trimly bearded, honey-voiced fellow named Anton Sota, a graduate student at Tufts who was winning a name among concerned college youth in the Boston area as the John Brown of their generation. Cheska had so raved to Toby about Sota's magnetic appeal that he suspected at once that she dated him, perhaps often. While Sota was waiting to be introduced, Toby saw only ambition in those bleary, pinpoint eyes that hinted their owner had lurked too long in shadowy places, training for perfidy.

At the lectern, he wasted no time in identifying himself as the son of a lifelong laborer, lately crippled on the job and dismissed without pension as worthless. This experience left Sota in no doubt as to the source of America's anguish—"a greed so gargantuan it finally consumes itself!" The tycoons had gathered up profits with glee in the golden 'Twenties, he said, and filled their bellies and their pockets and their parlors and their larders, but hardly a dime extra did they allot to those who had created the wealth by the sweat of their brows. It was better business to improve the factories than the men, he said; machines never turned ungrateful. Besides, the more efficient the equipment, the fewer workers needed. And so even in flush times, he said, wages stayed low, hours long, and conditions mean, and the masses of men continued mute in their desperation.

He had avoided the catchwords of Marxism, but there was no mistaking the standard deterministic interpretation of the class struggle, even when prettied up for Radcliffe. The whiff of proletarian fervor was in the air, lending a forbidden quality to the meeting that had no doubt helped quadruple normal attendance.

Sota seized the occasion to announce plans for a student relief mission over Easter vacation to Harlan and Bell counties in eastern Kentucky, where fifteen thousand coal miners and their families were living in virtual serfdom. He held up pictures: Filth, disease, ignorance, hunger, and the threat of live burial were the constant companions of these scratchers in the earth who got fired without warning and pitched out of their hovels—or, if they were very lucky, only had their wages slashed in two whenever the owners decreed.

"To see this nightmare with our own eyes," Sota said in a whisper that coiled through the breathless auditorium, "to bear witness to friends and neighbors how some men can treat others like insensate beasts—and, not incidentally, to bring food and clothes and medicine to these destitute folk," students with enough courage, dedication, and money for the trip would be dispatched from New York by bus. Those who could not afford the pilgrimage were as badly needed at home to raise the relief money.

"Oh, please come!" a radiant Cheska pressed him after it was over and they were walking through snow-clad Radcliffe Yard, bluish white under a full moon. "It's the chance to open up the minds of a lot of people around here."

"Like mine?"

"I didn't mean you, exactly. You never would have come tonight if you weren't open-minded."

"I came because you asked me to."

"Then come to Kentucky with us because I'm asking."

"That's awfully far to go to find suffering," he said, shoving freezing hands deep into his jacket pockets as they came out on Cambridge Common. "There's plenty all over Boston."

"Not like this, Toby."

"Maybe not, but it's a matter of degree, not kind. To me, it smacks of exhibitionism—'College Kids Lend Succor to Beleaguered Miners' —like a field trip for Sociology 102."

"Of course it's exhibitionism! The whole point of it is to dramatize their dreadful condition. What's wrong with that?" He would not answer. Baffled, she launched one of her deadly sighs at him, and they crunched on toward the Square for a while in silence. "Is it the money?" she asked finally. "I think maybe it's the money and you're too damned proud to say so."

"That doesn't have anything to do with it."

"You're lying, Toby. You don't even have a winter coat—"

"They get me overheated—I told you before. Look, I've got a lot of work to catch up on—and two papers to write—and a dozen to type."

"Kentucky is more important."

"Because *you* say so?"

"Because it is." She took his hand. Beneath the poncho she was a regular furnace. "Hey, I'll make you a deal. I pay your way to Kentucky and if it turns out to mean something special to you, you pay me back as soon as you can. And if not, then we both forget it."

"No soap—I don't take loans."

She flung his hand out into the cold. "God, what a dumb, stubborn ass you are sometimes! And you think you're being so very principled. Someone who really cared about his fellow man wouldn't stand on stiff-necked pride like you. There's no shame in taking a little temporary help if it's to a good purpose. Think of it as a social debt—you'll repay it a thousand times over unless I'm terribly wrong about you." She reclaimed his icy hand, nestled it for a moment inside the poncho against her blazing breast, and pleaded, "Oh, come, Toby—I want you to."

"Personally or politically?"

She thought for a second. "Why do I have to separate them?"

"You'll have plenty of political company. You don't need me."

"Most of them'll be strangers. You're—a friend."

She was breaching his outer wall. "Tell me the truth—why does this trip mean so damned much to you? You don't have to go smell the stench if you know a thing is rotten."

She pondered as they moved briskly down Mass. Ave. toward the lights and noise. "Guilt, I guess. I feel guilty as hell."

"For what—for being here?"

"For being young and smart and rich—well, rich enough—and I'm not what you'd call deformed, exactly, except for my astigmatism—"

"And you'd rather not be any of those."

"I'd feel less of a hypocrite if I were poor, at least."

"And be a lot hungrier. And you'd lose your license for moral superiority. Your Anton back there, why, he's an avenger for the downtrodden. But you, an aristocrat—you're a guardian angel, performing selfless deeds of mercy—"

She wheeled on him. "You think I'm just slumming, don't you? What a shit you are!"

He had heard vehemence from her before but never real profanity. Its shock value passed in an instant, but the nastiness hung on heavily between them in the dark crystal air. "You do a lot better dishing out the medicine than taking it," Toby said softly.

All at once she was on his shoulder, half weepy with remorse. "The awful thing," she said, hot face against his ear as the moon danced across her glasses, "is what you said is right."

"I didn't say what you said I said—exactly."

"Oh, come on! It's true—I don't do anything that matters. I run around pretending to be Jane Addams, Emma Goldman, and Krupskaya all rolled into one when down deep all I am is a goddamned stupid little sentimental 'Cliffie."

She hung on to him, throbbing cathartically. There was a softness in her she had hidden from him before. "You're as sentimental," he said, "as Madame Defarge." She sniffed and laughed a little and sniffed some more. "Anyway," he asked as she disentwined herself from him and took off her glasses to dry her eyes, "who's Krupskaya?"

"Lenin's wife."

"Never heard of her."

"That figures. She's only one of history's great women. The Russian Revolution would probably never have gone off without her. She held everything together all through Vladimir Ilyitch's exile—including him."

"And you identify with her?"

"Sure—she's a model of fortitude."

"How do you know so much about her?"

"I read."

"About Lenin?"

"Among others—sure."

"And Marx—of course?"

"Of course. Also Thomas Aquinas, John Stuart Mill, Nietzsche, and a few dozen other guys—that's why I'm here. Why?"

"I was just wondering where your allegiances lay at the moment."

"You mean am I a communist—because I've read Marx and Lenin?"

"That—and the company you keep."

"Who—the Student League?"

"And Sota's not exactly a monarchist."

She gave a splutter of disbelief. "First of all, I don't, as you coyly put it, keep company with Anton—though I wouldn't mind, if you want to know the truth. He's just a guy I know. I happen to know a number of guys, some better than others—and I can't help it if you don't like that. Anton and I belong to the same organization, if you can call it that. Everyone in it has a different slant on things. It's all very undisciplined."

"What's your slant?"

"You mean what label do I wear? I don't know—I'm a radical Jewish utopian or something."

"You're—*Jewish?*" It was as if she had said Martian or leper or werewolf. His tone was not so much disapproving as stunned that she had never mentioned it.

"What did you think I was—a Hapsburg?"

"Catholic, I guess—from what you said about your mother and the Pope. And your name, of course—"

"Oh, my mother's Catholic, all right—well, more or less. She got to name the firstborn—that was the deal she and Daddy made. My brother's name is Joshua da Silva."

"I thought you were Portuguese or something—like Vasco da Gama."

"Yeah, sure—four hundred and fifty years ago. Then they told us to convert or be killed—and you know how clever Jews are. But they threw us out, anyway. We're San Francisco Sephardic, by way of Amsterdam, Curaçao, Newport, and a few other places."

His knowledge of Judaism was drawn almost exclusively from four literary sources—the Old Testament, *The Merchant of Venice*, *Ivanhoe*, and the Baseball Joe boys' adventure series, which included an unforgettable charmer named Moe Russnick, "an oily Jew" whose principal occupation was trying to bribe the hero. Toby also knew that Freud, Einstein, Proust, Louis Brandeis, and Leon Trotsky were all Jews and all titans of the century—and none of them dealt in shekels. Marx and Disraeli, of course, were the nineteenth century's best-known apostates, but he had no sense of any of them as people, only geniuses, and it was inconceivable to him that Jews were any more prone to genius at birth than to the love of lucre. There was clearly something, though, that set them apart, only he had never taken the trouble to think what it could be. Jews were beyond his frame of reference, even the ones at Harvard who, at any rate, seemed a skittish, clannish bunch. He asked Cheska why.

"Survival," she said as they slid into a booth at the back of a coffeehouse on Brattle. "Or so they think—which compounds it all."

"You're not like that, though."

"My family's been in this country awhile—and out of the ghetto a lot longer. The novelty—and terror—wore off about two centuries ago. It's just not the most important thing in my life. But for an Epstein from Brookline, it probably is."

A hundred dumb questions flew out of him, each a new disclosure of incomprehension. Amused at first, she ran out of patience finally as he kept probing for the distinctive element in the Jewish tribal character. "The distinction lies in your thinking it," she said sternly.

When Toby protested that he was only asking, she looked doubtful and took out a cigarette. "All right, I'll confess—if you promise to keep it a secret."

He promised eagerly.

"Have you noticed how a great many Jews seem to have very progressive or radical social views—and some are even openly communist?"

Toby said he was vaguely aware of it. "Well," Cheska said, "some say it's because they've been kicked around so much all through history that they naturally have an affinity for underdogs." She put the cigarette in her mouth and poised the unlit match beside it. "But the actual secret reason is that, next to usury and leeching blood from Gentile babies for the seder, the real passion deep in every Jew's heart is"—she lit the cigarette, drew in deeply, and exhaled in his face— "sturgeon. We're after the Tsar's old caviar concession—the cossacks can keep all the vodka." She stirred her coffee wickedly. "Now will you come to Kentucky?"

IV

There are things in life you must do when you are young or not at all because later on you will know they are pointless or hazardous or exhausting, perhaps all three, and do them warily, missing the pleasure. Not every adventure needs a reason when you are young—not a good one, anyway—especially if it is spring and you are in the right and your destination is far enough away to seem magical.

So Cheska da Silva—Cheska of the expansive heart—went off to Kentucky with a busload of Leftist students to call down the wrath of heaven on monstrous iniquity; Toby did not go. He was either old before his time or wise beyond his years. The truth is, he was much tempted to go. Money was one preventive, though—she had been right about that. It was not a paupers' crusade. And he really did have his work, but then there was always that. Mostly, he did not want to do her bidding, particularly in what he took to be a fool's errand, even if performed on angel's wings.

There were stories in the paper about what had happened to them. At the Kentucky state line, their bus was rudely met by sheriff's deputies who hauled the travelers to a remote county courthouse in the middle of the night, reviled them as Yankee-Red-Jew agitators, and promised to jail them for disturbing the peace unless they hightailed it home. When the students spoke up for their rights, a red-eyed, rope-twirling mob outside was offered as the alternative. Valor yielded to mountaineer justice.

One of the deputies escorting the bus back through the Cumberland Gap got riled at Cheska, who, outraged at the oppression, had refused to doff her cap on command. Reaching for it, the bully caught her a glancing blow on the side of her face. Anton Sota leapt to her defense and earned a gun butt in the back of the skull. She nursed him till they got to Washington, where stitches were taken and a manifesto issued to the press about the denial of liberty in the land of the free and the solidarity of students and workers in the home of the depraved.

Although the relief-bearing part of the trip aborted, its larger purpose had been served. Newspaper coverage no doubt inspired sympathy for the terrorized students and the tale they wished to tell. Back on their campuses, the bus riders were celebrities for a time, and in and around Boston, Anton Sota was a minor martyr. When he came at the Student League's behest to speak at Harvard on the sanctioned venality they had met on their travels, Toby felt obliged to attend lest Cheska accuse him of harboring sour grapes. He brought along Rupe, who had expressed curiosity to see the *provocateur*.

On their way, they stopped for hamburgers at the hole-in-the-wall known as The Greek's at the bottom of the Square and became involved, by chance, in a discussion with a group of law students. At issue was the prudence of the Supreme Court's great dissenter, Justice Brandeis, Harvard '86, speaking against the majority in a case just decided that struck down an Oklahoma law to license anyone who wanted to enter the ice business. It all sounded terribly parochial to Toby, but Rupe had been alert enough to the implications of the case to have read his roommate the *Times* headline a few days earlier when the decision was reported—"Brandeis, Viewing Crisis 'Worse Than War,' Urges Control of Competition by the State"—and a couple of paragraphs to get the gist of it: If enough people disapproved of a system that permitted so much misery in the midst of so much abundance, then the Justice saw no reason why a state should be constrained from writing experimental statutes that tried to head off ruin. As headlines often do, this one had missed the point; the Justice had approved the right to act, not the rightness of the act.

Anton Sota did not see it that way. Addressing a crowd of several hundred, by far the largest the Student League had ever drawn to any of its Harvard functions, the newly celebrated young spellbinder settled on the latest Brandeis dissent to illustrate his sermon for the evening: Bad law, even well-intended, was no better than good law that went unenforced. Even Mr. Justice Brandeis, perhaps the most enlightened jurist in America, he said, did not appreciate fully the rapaciousness of unbridled capitalism. Why, the whole licensing scheme was just doubletalk by owners and operators already doing business to perpetuate their franchise for profit-gouging. "That's not reform—that's bourgeois bliss! And that is the pleasure of Louis Dembitz Brandeis, the finest flower of the system!"

The hall smoldered with discontent. Sota glowered over his congregation, as if to say they were all beyond salvation unless they heeded the words of their redeemer. At that instant of maximum theatricality, Rupert Donovan stood up and declared, so no one present could miss it, "That is *not* what Justice Brandeis said!"

Sota's velvety resonance had so drugged the audience that the intrusion was met at first by numbed silence. Toby felt like vanishing down the nearest crack in the floorboards. Sota, though, seemed unfazed by the heckler. "I have it right here in black and white," he snapped, waving a news clipping. "You can read it after. Now I'd like to—"

"You've distorted the entire point of Brandeis's opinion!" Rupe persisted, folding his arms across his chest.

"You can speak when I'm through if you'd like, but—"

"I'm speaking now! You can't get up there like that and twist the words of a Supreme Court Justice completely out of whack!"

Rupe's determined upbraiding unnerved Sota for the instant. "That's your opinion!" he yelled back. "And I'm entitled to mine if it's still a free country!"

"You're not entitled to fob off something as fact when it's not! You're slandering the man!" Rupe stepped out into the aisle and, arms akimbo now in open defiance, bellowed at the speaker, "Brandeis never said he thought the licensing law was a good or bad idea—only that the state should be free to experiment with social legislation."

"Sure," Sota said, stepping forward from the lectern to meet the challenge, "by granting established profiteers a clear field and keeping out anyone else who tries to make a decent living."

"That isn't what he said!"

"But that's the *effect* of what he said!"

"You're putting *your* sentiments into his mouth! I defy you to read us anything in that article you've got there that supports what you're saying he said."

A powerful undertow began to build around the room. Sota, calculating that he was in alien territory to begin with, squinted hurriedly at the clipping and decided to squelch the intruder before the situation got out of hand. "All right, I will," he said and began to quote Brandeis to the effect that the great social evil of irregular employment could not be overcome until production and consumption were more nearly balanced, and toward that end many people now favored some form of economic control. "And then he goes on to speak approvingly of the licensing law—which is just what I said he said." He closed up the clipping with a flourish as if to clinch the point and turned from Rupe.

"No!" Rupe shouted. "He did *not* go on to speak in favor of the law. What you read was just his statement of the problem and of what some people think the solution should be. Read further on—the part where he says if the licensing law will solve the problem—"

"I'm not giving a public reading here, mister."

"Then I'll read it for you." And Rupe started down the aisle.

Sota turned panicky. "Look, this isn't your meeting—"

"Then read us the part I'm talking about!"

Sota had trapped himself. He re-examined the clipping, then morosely acquiesced. The Justice had said of the licensing law:

> . . . The objections to the proposal are obvious and grave. The remedy might bring evils worse than the present disease. The obstacles to success seem insuperable. Economic and social areas are largely uncharted seas. . . .

"And he goes on from there," Rupe cut him off, "not to endorse the law, as you've been telling us, but to speak of the value of trial and error in social legislation. That's a very different thing."

The room rocked. Voices erupted on all sides. Rupe was pummeled with handshakes and backslaps. Sota had lost command of the gathering. Mass exodus ensued. Harvard turned its back on the Student League for Industrial Democracy.

Toby had a chilling note the next day from Cheska. It said Rupe had fired up an intellectual lynch mob no less brutal than the one they had faced in Kentucky, and that he ought to be ashamed and should have restrained his gorilla of a roommate, well known on campus as a buffoon. "In fact," she went on, "it almost sounded to me as if he'd been coached to pounce on Anton by someone who deeply resents him and his fortitude." Her friendship with Toby, she was sorry to say, was over.

His anger and envy flamed. The outcome of the meeting was unfortunate, he wrote back at once, and Rupe may have gone overboard, but whatever his past reputation, he was nobody's fool and well within his rights to speak up for the truth. "Anton's distortion was the real intellectual thuggery of the evening," he charged. "Since your enchantment with bravado appears to have blinded you in your choice of friends, you need have no worry about my calling."

In fact, Toby was drawn down a whirlpool of bitterness and yearning. He cared for the girl immensely but could offer no dash nor doctrine to dazzle her interest. Fuming renunciation was his only course. Then he hit upon taking revenge by soiling himself.

For months Rupe had been after him to go downtown to Scollay Square and find themselves some floozies. Toby had resisted, claiming the sexual act to be a sacred ritual, not practiced promiscuously by people of quality. Rupe saw it more as a sort of hydraulic function and said that emotion and devotion, while agreeable accompaniments, were biologically irrelevant. "A lay is a lay, old chum—and if you don't turn on your pump soon, it's going to fall off."

Having massaged it solipsistically for years, Toby saw no real danger of that. If anything, it was overprimed for its ultimate purpose. What drove him finally to accept Rupe's standing proposal was the overwhelming conviction that the object of his heart and her bearded Bolshevik were splashing around somewhere in their own bodily juices, probably with great regularity and all the while discussing the fate of the new Five-Year Plan.

Only two things still bothered him about whoring. One was the notion of paying for anything so intimate; some things ought to be beyond purchase. Rupe was understanding. But going to a professional, he said, saved a lot of horsing around. "They know the ropes—they'll turn you into a stud in no time." As to Toby's other concern, the possibility of having to spill his first seed upon the vulva of a slattern, he said it was a buyer's market and there was no need to go with anyone who repelled him; historically, the profession required a certain hardy comeliness of its recruits. "No one pays," he put it artfully, "for putrid pussy."

Rupe arranged the renting of the bodies. Toby's turned out to be hardly older than he was. That equally distressed and pleased him. A veteran of the streets would have been more likely to forgive his ineptness—but also been so much more *used*. This girl was on the scrawny side with not a bad face, short dun hair nearly matted to her scalp, and a pouty little mouth. She never looked at him until they reached her cell of a room, rank with mildew and brightened only by its curling floral wallpaper.

She had a cigarette first, checking him over through the veil of smoke while Toby stood awkwardly in the middle of the room, uncertain how to proceed. "Harvard, huh?" the girl guessed. He conceded as much. She had nothing against Harvard boys, she said in a flat, nasal voice; they were usually gentlemen and almost always clean.

Every conceivable subject of conversation seemed to him a travesty of courtliness under the circumstances. Finally he thought to ask her how long she had been at her trade. Long enough, she said, and had no intention of making it her life. But other work was scarce and she did this sort well and did not mind it all that much. Then she ditched her cigarette and, switching off the blurry overhead light, said she supposed they weren't there to socialize.

He watched her undress by the corner lamp. Even paying for the spectacle, he felt like a voyeur. Had she had a more voluptuous body, he would surely have been immersed in a puddle of sweat. As it was, he observed her almost clinically. She sensed his close attention but hid none of herself; plainly, it was part of the service. She had large, pale nipples that seemed to be misplaced on her small, splayed breasts, and there were splotchy pimples on her upper back just below the nape.

At the point of undoing her stockings, she looked over at him ogling her and stopped until he began to undress himself. No doubt she had had her share of perversions practiced on her temporarily deranged clients. Or perhaps she had been merely expressing a legitimate anatomical interest in him in the event he turned out to be equipped like Man o' War. His loins were full of life, it was evident even before he got his shirt off, but hardly anything equine was lurking under there, he showed her while depantsing. All shyness had left him now as he unsheathed, eager finally to rut his congested pelvis out.

"Oh," she said, timing her revelation to the second, "I can't do it the regular way."

Toby's brow contracted, then his member. He did not understand. How many ways were there?

"I just became unwell," said the girl, gliding over to him. She would be glad, though, to do anything else he liked to make it up to him.

Toby was no clearer about his options. Young but practiced at her craft, the girl undid his underpants while he stood there, fully gorged again, and, with many accompanying sounds of admiration, sat him on the edge of the bed and straddled his legs as if riding a horse and placed his hands upon her breasts and caressed herself with them until he managed to operate without her. Then she brought them to his face and mouth, and he drew on them gently, experimentally, and then more and harder, thinking with boiling brain that he would consume them whole in another moment. Weightlessly, she slid off and knelt before him on the dingy carpet, her hands slowly and surely encircling him, exciting the length and girth and root of him, routing all awareness of what it was he had been denied. The sudden heat and moistness of her mouth made him shudder in pleasure, and he looked down and saw the narrow, uneven part in her hair bobbing away and wondered how she could do that with a mouth so small and didn't her jaw hurt and how could anything so degrading possibly feel so good.

In a rush it was over. She drew away gently while he fell back on the sheets, still quivering. She went to have a cigarette in order, he supposed, to burn away the aftertaste. They dressed in silence and he paid her at the door, three dollars for her time, two for the room. She was still naked on top when he left, not knowing whether to say thank you or that he'd see her again or nothing at all. He settled for goodbye.

With Rupe after, in the toilet of the Park Street el station, he vomited from shame. Whether more for himself or the girl was hard to tell.

V

The rages of youth can be as brief as they are ardent. By May, Toby asked Cheska to the Adams House spring dance. In figuring the risks, he never got beyond her saying no. That he danced with the approximate aplomb of Long John Silver seemed beside the point; it was a nice, neutral, almost impersonal occasion for an armistice that he badly wanted.

She not only accepted happily, but came in a silk dress of blue pastel, left her glasses off the whole time, and, after a few lumpish reels with Toby, danced with half the House under his baleful gaze. Among her partners was that erstwhile gorilla, Rupert Donovan.

As they meshed to "Yes, Sir, That's My Baby," switching from a frisky fox trot for the verse to a frantic Charleston for the chorus, they looked to Toby like Irene and Vernon Castle apprenticing. Most astonishingly of all, she conceded Rupe had been at least half right in the Brandeis imbroglio and that Sota should have done his homework better before shooting off his mouth at a place like Harvard. When last heard from, she said, Anton had quit pursuing his doctorate and gone off to organize textile workers around New England. Rupe jeered that the fellow was addicted to lost causes. "They're better than none," she countered.

It was not a satisfying reconciliation for Toby. Perhaps he had been expecting more from Cheska da Silva all along than she ever gave him reason for. Still, her volatility kept him hopeful. His heart bounded a week after the dance when she asked him to the Bick for coffee and a talk. But then she added curdlingly that maybe Rupe could come, too, because an idea had dawned on her that was either inspired or nitwit and she needed both of them to tell her which.

Her brainstorm was to launch a nonpartisan student activist group on a scale never before seen at Harvard. At first she had thought it might be built up out of the ashes of the tiny League for Industrial Democracy unit, but the fiasco with Sota had shown Harvard to be pitiless toward any movement that advertised itself as labor-related or saw all history as class war. Even the Socialist Club model, which had attracted a wide range of Harvard idealists in its heyday under Walter Lippmann twenty years earlier, would be too divisive now; the Soviet Socialists had seen to that. It was so much easier to embrace Menckenism and, like the *Crimson* editorials, sneer urbanely at all would-be do-gooders. But that was what made it such a challenge to her. Harvard was the nation's intellectual pacesetter: If they could organize a student movement here, of all places, to unfurl a new social vision for America, bringing genuine liberty and justice for all—if a cleansing wind could stir in Cambridge—then it could blow all across the land. . . .

At another time, perhaps *any* other time, such an ambition would have been brushed aside as misdirected, delusionary, and foredoomed. But the depression had deepened that year, a presidential election was only six months off, and change was already in the ocean wind that swirled in off Massachusetts Bay and swept up the Charles. Dubious but noncommittal, Rupe and Toby waved her on.

Well, she had done a lot of exploring around, she said, and concluded the best vehicle would be a Harvard chapter of the National Students League. Independent and militantly anti-fascist, the N.S.L. had drawn socialists and communists to its standard at other colleges, she granted, but also reformist Republicans, Democrats, Liberals, liberals, Progressives, progressives, populists, pacifists—anyone who felt decency and humanity ultimately mattered at least as much as the almighty buck. To succeed at Harvard, the N.S.L. would from the very beginning have to win members of diverse political faiths, and some who had none at all. Would Rupe and Toby join the cause as charter members and help shape the effort?

Rupe was interested but leery. He had announced himself a Roosevelt Democrat and wondered if she wouldn't frankly prefer a more radically minded colleague. Cheska shrugged him off. Her problem with the Democrats, she said, was that ever since Wilson they had been neither principled nor smart—and obviously not much good at national politics. "At least Norman Thomas and William Foster stand for something."

"Sure," said Rupe, "for confiscating anything the little guy has left and handing it over to the state. And Hoover—he wants to hand it over to the banks. But Roosevelt wants to give him a chance to earn more—that's the real difference."

"Excuse me," she said, "but that's soapbox baloney." There could be no social justice in the industrial age, she insisted, until the owning classes were persuaded—or required—to part with a substantial portion of their power. The alternative was certain revolution. "No matter how you slice it, the rich are going to have to be hurt—and I just can't believe Roosevelt is willing to turn on his own kind."

Rupe was offended. "Hell, he doubled the New York state sales tax to feed the hungry—didn't he?"

Cheska folded her hands chastely on her lap. "A sales tax is a regressive social measure," she said, as if reading to him from a primer. "It hits the poor much harder proportionately than the rich."

"It was probably all he could get through the legislature."

"That doesn't make it any better, does it?" She lifted her palms beseechingly. "Look, these are desperate times—we've got to have a coherent plan for national relief—something sweeping. Time and luck—and maybe even God, if you're so inclined—are running out on us. I don't have anything against Roosevelt, but he's just an able politician with a Harvard pedigree who couldn't even make it through law school. And he sways in every breeze. Hearst pressured him to turn on the League of Nations—so he turned. He'll take his support anywhere he can get it."

"That's politics," Rupe said. "He just wants to win. Once he's in power, he'll be his own man."

"That's what they said about Hoover—and he's been a pawn of the financiers ever since."

Rupe looked to Toby for help against an adversary who showed him no mercy. "My ticket," Toby said, "is Abe Lincoln and Will Rogers."

Cheska wangled the Dunster House commons for her organization meeting, at which sixty or so showed up, including half a dozen besides Toby from the effete Liberal Club and maybe twice that many commuting Jews. Starting in the fall, it was proposed, the Harvard N.S.L. would pamphleteer, petition, picket, strike, or take whatever other social action was required to protest social injustice on and off the campus but within student purview. The proposal carried by acclamation. Then Cheska nominated Rupe for president.

It was a master stroke. Rupe was a moderate, he was articulate, he was semi-informed, he came from good solid Republican stock, his father worked for a renowned industrial giant—who better to divert suspicions that the N.S.L. was nothing but a bunch of ethnic meatballs, out to reconstruct the class system, the American government, and the Harvard Board of Overseers?

Rupe was flattered. Rupe was dazzled. Rupe was famished for recognition. He would have given anything to be taken seriously, and here the chance was being handed him gratis. He accepted the nomination and promptly got elected. Cheska, a regular little Krupskaya by now at rigging things, was made executive secretary, and Toby was placed in charge of publicity. In that festive air, all his caution crumbled. He sent the *Crimson* a three-page article in roseate prose heralding the N.S.L.'s coming to Harvard. The paper ran one paragraph, defrilled.

THREE

NOT EVEN HARVARD could escape the leftward tilt that was threatening
to turn the American political landscape perpendicular in the fall
of 1932. The lure of collectivism may not have mesmerized the
university, but there was surprising sentiment around for the gentleman Socialist, Norman Thomas, for President—nearly as much as for
the renegade patrician and son of Harvard the Democrats had put up.
Which of them to favor, or maybe even the Communist candidate,
William Z. Foster, Toby could not settle on; all he knew was Herbert
Hoover was not for him.

His father felt otherwise. Hoover was his bastion in the storm—the
earnest and upright technician, not unlike himself, being cast as the
scapegoat for times he had not created. "You don't throw out the
baby with the bathwater," he wrote Toby, even while advising him
the company had inflicted a second salary cut of 20 percent on him.
Though these blows greatly distressed him, he noted that at least they
were not as severe as the full 50 percent drop in output that had been
ordered at the plant since the depression first hit. This small discrep-
ancy in his favor he chose to dwell on as a measure of his worth to
management. And maybe it was. Toby asked Cheska, who found the
conceit moving but pitiful.

"He's a body to them," she said, "just slightly less dispensable than
the rest."

Yet he could never have mocked the man for this self-deception. He
had worked too hard for his dignity. Besides, his fondest hope was
that his son's life should be an improvement on his own.

If his father chose to believe the bosses could work it all out so long
as everyone bore his sacrifices manfully, Toby himself was becoming
persuaded that bosses were no wiser, only more willful, than the common run of men and therefore not to be subsidized by the immolation
of multitudes. There was nothing subversive to him about dethroning
moguls and ministering to the ailments of the masses. Just how this

could be accomplished without resort to confiscation, and probably a lot of busted heads, he waited eagerly to learn.

This growing tolerance for radical reform would almost certainly have landed him well within the gravitational pull of socialist ideology if he had not fallen just then under the hectoring tutelage of Mr. Graham Halyard, the closest approximation of Byronic temperament among the Harvard junior faculty. For Toby's final two undergraduate years, this keen drillmaster held claim to at least half his soul—enough to check its recurring slippage toward incurable egalitarianism.

Fitted out with a wicked jawbone, owlish eyes in Prussian blue, a splurge of tassel-fine sandy hair, and chalky skin pitted slightly at the cheeks, Graham Halyard had been handpicked for his job by Professor Travis, whom President Lowell had designated chairman of the Board of Tutors in History and Literature when the House Plan was inaugurated. In no time, Graham was more of a fixture in Adams than the Master. His Oxbridge grandiloquence was perhaps pardonable in a fifth-generation Harvard man who had taken a first in literature at King's College a few years back and, thanks to parental indulgence, was now pursuing his dissertation on Miltonic demonology at a pace befitting a gentleman academic. Unapologetic about his origins, secure in his learning, yet hardly insensitive to the crosscurrents at work all around him, he defended proper Boston by missing no opportunity to chide it. Once, after a heavy weekend of socializing, he recited:

> "I kissed her once, I kissed her twice,
> She was a charming creatchaw.
> But every time I brushed her face
> I froze anothah featchaw."

Toby thought that the cleverest thing he had ever heard and spread it all over the House as a patented Halyardism, only to discover soon after, in browsing through a twenty-year-old volume of the *Lampoon*, that the lines were in fact written by that incorrigible revolutionary John Reed, the only Harvard man known to be buried in the Kremlin Wall.

Confronted with a charge of plagiarism, Graham was nonplussed: "I never said it was mine, dear boy—I merely recited it to make a point." He drew pleasurably on his meerschaum and then added, "At any rate, no worthy raconteur reveals his sources unnecessarily."

There was no mistaking the invocation of Reed for a pro-Soviet bias in the fellow, any more than his shameless anglophilia was to be taken for anti-Americanism. Indeed, partisanship of any sort he saw as a defilement of the temple of the mind. Any allegiance other than to the habit of independent thinking was a betrayal of Harvard's whole purpose, he told his charges. "Given a choice between absolutists of any stripe, be they monarchists or *bolsheviki,* and our own crabby, clamorous, thoroughly disorderly *demos,* I'll take the farting rabble every time."

Toby's counselor in matters spiritual (he said anything but agnosticism was pagan), secular (he said all that glittered and was not gold was probably silver and would do as well), and glandular (he said the secret to success with the female anatomy was familiarizing oneself with the cliterature), Graham Halyard was, above all, his instructor in the riches and uses of the King's English. He taught him that "Attila" and "lamentable" were accented on the first syllable and "allies," "vagaries," and "incognito" on the second; never to say "the reason is because" or "different than," and not to commit to paper what Toby had always taken to be the perfectly serviceable Anglo-Saxon word "thing." He had concluded one of his first weekly papers for the tutor —a few reflections on Keats—with the unexceptionable comment that "the total impression of the pregnant instant—blending his own subjective feelings with the sensations of the material world—is the ultimate thing for him." Graham tossed the essay back in his lap and roared, "No!" Toby asked why not. "A *thing,*" he cried, "can not be ultimate! 'Thing' is not even a word—it is an excuse for one! 'Thing' is the dropping of a retarded vocabulary or an unspeakably sluggish mind. There is always a more precise, more vivid, and more pleasing word than 'thing,' dear boy, if you will just take the bloody trouble to locate it."

Nothing gave him greater pleasure than manipulating minds less supple than his own. One week early in the term, he assigned Toby as his weekly essay topic "Friendship, like art, is the technique of selective affinities; spontaneity is the enemy of both. Discuss."

Toby did not know for certain what that meant, but it sounded depressingly like his father's standing advice to use Harvard mainly as an instrument of social advancement. So he heatedly rejected the premise and argued in his paper that Harvard had finer insights into human nature to impart than success through opportunism.

Graham asked if that meant he thought chums didn't count for much in life. "Not if you've actively solicited them," Toby said. "Those aren't real friends."

"And what, pray tell, is a *real* friend?"

"One you don't need—they say."

"They? Who's 'they'?"

"It's a saying."

"I don't give a fig for sayings. It's *your* head on the block. At any rate, I should have thought mutual need, like mutual gratification, was a splendid basis for friendship."

"Mutual need is different from unilateral. Friendship means genuine feelings—they have to come naturally or they're contrived."

"Like art, one might say—feelings being the essence of art—"

"Yes—that's exactly it!"

Graham threw up his hands. "Ah, dear boy! The answer is no—exactly no. Surely you don't suppose *Ode on Melancholy* was a piece of spontaneous combustion? Art is a mesh of the natural and the contrived—an imposition of the will on the disparate materials fortune flings at us. That is the essence of what our beloved Travis instructs us."

"But the creative impulse itself," Toby flailed on, losing ground with every step in the discourse, "has to be natural, that's what I mean."

"Impulses, dear boy, are not what make art happen. The ingredients are well known—a flash of vision, a touch of feeling, and a great deal of sustained energy known as craft."

"That's not art you're talking about—that's artifice—ingenuity—cleverness. That's different."

"How is that?"

"The more authentic and inspired the talent, the less forcing it needs."

"You don't think talent needs cultivation?"

"I didn't say that. Everything needs cultivating to prosper."

"All forms of human endeavor, one might say."

"Sure."

"Including friendship."

"No!"

It was unthinkable that Graham Halyard could be bettered by a single callow adversary during a tutorial hour. A contest developed only those evenings when he opened the door of his apartment to anyone in the House who wished to wander by for a smoke, whatever diluted liquid he was serving, and the headiest talk in Cambridge. The flow was so free, so brightly informed, and so uncharitably caustic that there were moments when even Graham could not neatly contain it.

Toby saw him bested only once, though, and then by the sole intellect at the college he held in higher awe.

To celebrate the four-hundred-fortieth anniversary of Columbus's voyage, Graham had asked half the intelligentsia in Boston down to his dowager aunt's summer place at the Scituate shore—his Adams House flock, a *mélange* of graduate students, faculty friends of various ranks and disciplines, local literati, *artistes* both performing and *manqué*, and half an acre of genteel freeloaders about evenly divided between famished teetotalers and bottomless drunks. With the election only a few weeks off, much of the talk was politics, not a little of it dwelling on the prospects for salvation through a managed economy if the Democrats got in. Harvard's thinking on that score had been conditioned by the fiscal envoy from Bloomsbury, the seminal socialist J. M. Keynes. The British connection appealed to Graham, but it lacked a literary context; he thought all economists unreadable, except Veblen, whose prolixity did him in after a dozen or so pages. So he haunted his own party in search of cultivators of the arts whom he might tutor to shreds.

Toby watched him hover for a time at the edge of a group surrounding the *Evening Transcript*'s second-string music critic, who with painfully provincial pride was complaining because Koussevitzky had been patronized for his "control and cultivation" while recently guest-conducting the Vienna Philharmonic. The Germanic critics, he said, still thought of Boston as the Wild West.

"It's a question of race with them, not geography," Graham put in. "You can't tell a Viennese anyone named Koussevitzky is an authentic Bostonian. A Slav by any other name is still a Cossack to them."

When a graduate student from Munich started taking exception in a husky vibrato, Graham slipped off through the hubbub. Toby trailed him to a claque presided over by the proprietress of Back Bay's least daring art gallery, who was scoffing at the proposition that Walt Disney was rapidly earning a place in American *kultur*. Graham waded in at once by venturing that Mickey Mouse was surely the most notable feral creation in American arts since Br'er Rabbit and vastly more personable than Moby Dick. That drew a laugh as hyperbole but suddenly lifted the subject from the frivolous.

"My only problem with Mickey," said the gallery owner, sensing she had hit on something both trendy and respectable, "is that he *talks* so much." The forgivable excesses of an infant art form, Graham suggested. But why did the thing have to sound like a Kewpie doll, the woman wondered, and look like a little man in a mouse suit?

"Would you prefer him *au naturel?*" Graham asked. "He's not meant to be your *echt* rodent."

He hit full stride on the back porch, where the literary circle was savaging a newly published posthumous work by the dark prodigy of recent English letters. The consensus held that D. H. Lawrence's *Apocalypse* was a crackpot book by a demonic sensualist whose reputation had plunged deservedly and as precipitously as the stock market in the two years since his death. Among the less enlightening features of this new work, a youngish editor with Little, Brown had been saying as Graham joined, was the author's claim that for a time he had been communing with the sun "in a blazing interchange." "That's what happens," sniped the editor, "when you move a Yorkshireman out of the mines and let him broil his brains in the New Mexico desert."

"First of all," a tutor from Kirkland House jumped in, "it wasn't the sun he was having the interchange with—it was a gila monster. Second of all, it wasn't an interchange he was having—it was intercourse. And third—"

"As I understand it," said an instructor-poetaster from the Wellesley English department, "it was a giant cactus he tried it with and put himself out of commission forevermore."

It was all cheap and modishly risqué, and everybody was laughing but Graham. "I grant you it's very jolly to treat the chap as a dirty joke," he said when the smirks subsided, "so long as we acknowledge, finally, he was a creator of catalytic force."

He gloried in delivering such verdicts, and the more apparently aberrant, the better he liked it. Toby sometimes thought Graham would say anything, however deviant, to cause a storm.

"He was not catalytic, old boy," Graham's counterpart from Kirkland picked up the challenge. "He was some brand or other of Protestant by birth—and very surly on the subject. Most of us are familiar, I think, with his doctrine that God is an insatiable libido. Profound and appealing as that is, some of us who've survived the obsessions of puberty prefer not to worship with you at the Laurentian shrine."

Graham twitched his nostrils. "It's beginning to smell awfully as if bluenosed Boston is tossing a new witch on the pyre. The man abhorred the Church because it denies and degrades the human body—"

"Your view of it as well, presumably?"

"Immaterial. It is an arguable position."

"Well, whatever his reasons, there's no denying he was mightily anti-Christian. And against the state and the social contract as ineffectual busybodying. And against democracy as the opiate of the weak. And against any institution or effort dedicated to material progress. With all respect, Halyard, this delightful thunderer of yours was irreligious, illiberal, irrational, and otherwise intolerant of every ethical and scientific premise of modern life."

Graham's tongue flicked over his thin lips as he considered for a moment. "It's not what a man is against that makes him interesting," he said, glancing about him as if on the hustings. "The real problem Lawrence presents is what he was for—it frightens us to death. How much tidier to swallow our wafers and wine in ceremonial obedience than to come to terms with our bodies and blood. All those secret yearnings and mysterious possibilities bouncing around our insides are what he cared about. He wasn't trying to forge a new society—just a whole new kind of private consciousness so mortal souls can fulfill their humanity in the little while they're given. And then the blackguard had the temerity to pull down our pants and show us what it was he was talking about. Oh, yes—burn the infidel!"

They were chastened but not routed. The talk turned to why Lawrence and so many other leading literary lights—Yeats, Eliot, Pound, and Conrad among them—had become political reactionaries or even crypto-fascists. Dread of the Red menace was too facile an explanation, Graham argued, since the literary Right was hardly less condemnatory of bourgeois society than the Marxians. Whatever the cause, he said, it was plain why the collectivist Left had produced no comparable literary harvest: Doctrinal Marxism insisted that art serve ideology, and so no state-approved creative act could be permitted to escape from literalness; all metaphor was suspect of deviationism.

"Except," came a voice from the outer edge of the circle, "that not everyone who thinks as a revolutionist feels as a Philistine—if one may be so bold as to paraphrase comrade-in-exile Trotsky."

A reverential hush fell. That a guest of Jeremiah Travis's eminence had graced a gathering of mostly Young Turks and dilettantes was tribute to Graham Halyard's standing with the scholar. "One may, Professor," he said heartily, "but at risk of bearing in mind what his anti-philistinism earned Comrade Outcast. Do come join us."

A path was cleared. Travis slid smilingly through the pack and took Graham's proffered handclasp. "No lecture," he promised, noting the expectations of revealed wisdom that had enveloped them, "but I was merely wondering if you aren't taking the Soviets too literally. Dwelling on the virtues of one's own time and place is not necessarily fatal to the resilient artist. The art, after all, resides in the form of the creation, not the nominal subject matter."

"But our dear Soviet comrades dismiss form as morally irrelevant," Graham took him up. "Their critics tell us with fanatic cheerfulness that style is mere guile—decadent trinketry and crude gossamer draped by capitalist lackeys over all the social turbulence."

Travis's small smile retracted a bit. "I would characterize that as Marxism at its most vulgar."

"Is there some other sort?"

It came out a touch too scornful to pass as idle jest. "Why, Mr. Halyard," Travis recoiled with mock sternness, "do I detect a note of rancor?"

"A party line, sir, is a party line."

"I'm told there is a bourgeois line as well. If I'm not mistaken, it holds that art exists essentially to organize the chaos of reality."

Graham considered that a moment. "I don't find that so very objectionable."

"More's the pity. It is a doctrine precisely as brutish in its restrictiveness as the crudest Marxism—"

"Not at all—"

"—by condemning art to the level of propaganda and the function of therapy, to say nothing of the moral implications of perceiving reality as chaos—"

"You mean it's not?"

"I mean to grant it is to play the Marxist game—the hungrier one is, the more chaotic one's reality. All hope for serenity, you see, then hinges on one's place in the class structure." As if sensing the exchange was about to turn fractious, the professor stopped it. "I daresay there are civilized refinements to their side of it that you might conceivably find mitigating. I've been looking into Lukacs, who is hardly a vulgarian—"

"I've not tried him."

"Do screw up your courage, then." He administered an avuncular pat or two to Graham's shoulder. "I doubt he'll persuade you, but at least your biases will be better informed."

Toby was dizzied by the rapidity and archness of the exchange— the professor almost epicene in his refinement, the tutor tending to rowdiness in his iconoclasm—but he sensed that Graham had been outpointed at his own game. He took no pleasure in that outcome; between these two finicky exemplars of his, he had no preference nor did he see the need for one. Yet his instincts told him for the first time that evening that a choice might eventually be required. For beyond their mutual respect, beneath the urbanity of their jousts, a loathing lurked and ran far deeper than a simple divergence in their manner.

II

Had he been a less generous or more combative spirit, Toby might have felt betrayed by his roommate for stealing the object of his affections without even bothering to ask if he minded. Instead, he blamed himself for not mounting a more forceful pursuit of his quarry.

Rupe and Cheska were off all the time that fall planning how to build the Harvard cell of the National Students League into a children's crusade that would set New England ablaze with righteous wrath. Toby's natural suspicion that so much purposeful effort had to be accompanied by a certain amount of surreptitious clenching in the balcony at the Uni or the Widener stacks was muted by their including him in many of their activities. They were hardly a *ménage à trois* —their only shared carnality was a darting goodnight kiss she would sometimes give them both when they walked her back to the Radcliffe Yard after an N.S.L. session. But a sweet comradery grew up among them that was at times notably free of concupiscence even on Toby's side of the triangle. Still, Toby did not deceive himself; it was not an equilateral arrangement. He rarely spent time alone with Cheska now except en route to or from class or a meeting or her new job at Sara Blue's bookstore off the Square. She was always friendly and effervescing, but the distance between them never diminished.

Pride lashed him toward tenderer relationships. Graham's fiancée, a lapsed debutante, arranged for him to escort a high-minded if unpropertied cousin of hers at Wheaton to a concert, even lending him a car on that occasion and several others to encourage the acquaintance. Less stimulating mentally but more rewarding otherwise were episodes with the sister of an Adams House sophomore who had him home to Nashua several weekends and a waitress from St. Clair's on Brattle who laughed bawdily in all the wrong places during Laurel & Hardy. These were company of a sort, yet he aspired still to the turbulent charms of the one girl who seemed to have twice the spunk and fifty times the character of any other in view.

When she and Rupe showed unmistakable signs of courtship, taking long rides now and then in Sara Blue's borrowed Studebaker, Toby could hardly complain to his friend for denying him what he never owned. And surely, she was not going off with him under duress. The only seemly tactic open to him was to pretend not to mind or even notice, counting on the incompatability of their politics and personalities eventually to dissolve the uneasy union.

Toby was confirmed in this wisdom late in the fall when Cheska popped up without warning near the end of one N.S.L. gathering and proposed that the group petition the Harvard powers to grant Leon Trotsky academic asylum for one year. Rupe saw red.

If Trotsky's name was then on the lips of many in the Left-liberal camp as the martyred hero of Mother Russia's peasantry, he had become a living god to Cheska. In the fourth year of his enforced seclusion on an island in the Bosporus, he retained for her—as his pitiless captor in the Kremlin decidedly did not—the full moral authority of the great Soviet uprising. It was Trotsky who had led the insurrection, generaled the Red Army to victory, inspired the International, championed the planned economy—Trotsky who was the authentic surviving legatee of Marx and Lenin. Alas, he was no politician; he was a man not of the party but of the people, of the state, of the world, a figure too large to be ruled by expediency, bureaucracy, or dogma, so the party hounded him and surrounded him and finally, in everything but spirit, did away with him. Even in the living death to which Stalin had sentenced him, he towered over his tormentors, unyielding in the call for international socialist revolution and proletarian democracy. Who, Cheska asked, had ever struggled more nobly to defeat the forces of darkness?

That she admired Trotsky because he was, along with everything else, a Jew, she admitted, ranking him with the foremost Hebrew warriors of the past three thousand years, the most notable being David, slayer of Philistines; Judah Maccabee, scourge of the Syrians, "and my father when an account is more than sixty days in arrears." What appealed to her most about him, though, she insisted, was that Trotsky was a man of thought as well as action. He wrote with great verve, and she read everything of his she could get hold of—the autobiography, the sketches of Lenin, the warnings on Germany and national socialism, and the newly issued first volume of his history of the Revolution, featured in the window of Sara Doyle Blue's New Era Book Shop. It was in Sara that she found a preceptor no less stimulating to her than Graham was to Toby, and even more of a confidante.

Everything about Sara was outsized without quite being gross—her brontosaurian bones, her grainy voice, her fried-egg eyes forever runny from cigarette smoke, and her meaty bosom gloriously perceptible even beneath the smock she wore to keep the dust from burying her. For all the apparent disorder of the shop and her own habitual dishabille, Sara Blue knew not only her entire inventory by heart but what was happening on the streets and in every *arrondissement* of current socialist ideology.

"It's all Pope Leo XIII's fault," she explained to Cheska. *Rerum Novarum,* the 1891 papal encyclical that called on Catholics to renounce acquisitive impulses and devote themselves to the weak and impoverished, had moved her late, sainted father, Johnny Doyle, in his young manhood and set the course of his life. He gave his heart and fists to Gene Debs as an organizer and political operative, roaming the land for months at a time while his wife brought up Sara and her two brothers in the front flat of a kelly-green boardinghouse she ran on the edge of Jamaica Plain. The roomers provided the family with its only dependable income, little as it was, but Sara never once heard her mother lay into the old man, especially after he had shown the grit, as few other men did in '11, to march arm in arm with the women's suffrage brigade across the Common. Sara stayed up with him through the night they grilled Sacco and Vanzetti, praying all the prayers he had not recited since childhood for God to spare the cobbler and the fishmonger, but Johnny Doyle had long given up believing in miracles. His daughter's legacy was scorn for the efficacy of candles.

After excelling at Roxbury Latin, graduating with honors from Boston College, and teaching third grade for a time in Dorchester, Sara Doyle married Peter Blue, who shortly began drinking away his civics teacher's salary. She took to the diaphragm without telling him and so bore no baby Blues. When she finally told him, he beat her for the deception and drank more than ever, and she left. With a sockful of savings and a piece of her father's life insurance, she took a six-month lease on the small shop at the corner of Brattle and Hilliard, three short blocks west of Harvard Square.

From the start, Sara specialized in secondhand trade, taking in whatever stock she could get hold of on barter and consignment and claiming the lowest used-textbook prices in Cambridge. When hard times came, her clientele swelled. Her known social views were reflected in the stock—the Marxist-Leninist canon in all the languages of Europe, a whole wall of proletarian novels and the literature of protest, crammed racks of Leftist periodicals ranging in respectability from the grace of *The New Republic* to the groan of *The New Masses*. Soon the New Era Book Shop was mecca for the intellectually aroused and socially discontented.

Drawn by the notorious air of the place, Cheska quickly fell in love with its clutter, its strident wares, and doughty owner. Sara Blue, amid a flotilla of chipped coffee cups with Camel butts sopping up the dregs, broken-pointed pencils mounted above either ear, pocketfuls of illegible reminder notes, and a prized Atwater Kent blaring dance tunes in the back room, was the most thoroughly undomestic woman Cheska had ever known. Just the sight of her navigating in that musty bedlam was enough to rout the dispiriting prospect of a lifetime at homemaking. She began working at the shop a couple of hours a day after classes and all day Saturday, taking out her pay in trade.

Indoctrination in Trotskyism followed in short order. The moral and intellectual exhaustion of capitalism had lent allure to the certitudes of Marxism, said Sara, narrating her own leftward hegira, but it was important not to be inveigled by gospel, whether of the churchly, bourgeois, or materialist variety. She drew no sustenance from terrorist dictatorship masquerading as benign expediency; Stalinism was just as despotic as tsarism. She had examined the domestic strain of communism, supposing that a universal truth could, by adapting, flourish anywhere. But who could serve a party with the primary function of parroting the latest mindless edict of the Comintern? As to the Socialists of the Norman Thomas stripe, she told Cheska, their hearts were in the right place, but the movement, like its leader, was out of touch with the working masses; what a pale, almost dispassionate successor to the lionhearted band for which her father marched and died. Trotsky, though—Trotsky sang to her! Above all, he was a humanitarian, another Lincoln, the hope of the world.

When the London publisher of Trotsky's account of the Revolution solicited her order, Sara took fifty copies and gave them a rousing window display, surmounted by a picture of the author clad as the dashing commander of the Red Army. Noting the brisk activity she was generating for the book, the publisher's salesman drew Sara into the back room of her shop and whispered that half a dozen copies of the *Bulletin Oppozitsii* were to be made available to Trotskyists in the United States. The *Bulletin*, printed in Russian in Berlin, was the exiled prophet's only remaining platform for discussion of inner party matters and reflections on worldwide political developments. There were said to be only a thousand copies run off of each monthly number, the bulk of them smuggled into Russia at dire peril through the network of Trotsky sympathizers. Was Sara interested in becoming his conduit to the greater Boston Leftist community? All that was necessary was to have the *Bulletin* translated and passed to as many hands as could be counted on to treat it respectfully and discreetly.

Sara jumped at the chance. At a moment when America was sinking ever more deeply into depression and there were no saviors on the horizon—only ranters like Huey Long and Father Coughlin—here was a way for her to connect with a legitimate, and radiant, revolutionary movement, however forlorn its immediate prospects. Sara's new disciple naturally became a camp-follower. Toby was not entirely surprised, then, when Cheska got up at the N.S.L. and sprang her proposal to invite Trotsky to Harvard.

"This is not the outlandish notion some of you may think!" she bravely sang out after Rupe, himself in obvious consternation over the idea, gaveled down the initial outcry against it. Trotsky, she reminded them, had just made his first appearance on the world stage in four years, thanks to student Socialist Democrats in Denmark who had invited him to speak on the fifteenth anniversary of the Revolution. And what had that pilloried figure said to the press before being hustled back to his island keep? "Is it a utopian dream," he had asked, "to think I should be able to work at one of the great American libraries for two or three months?" To the tyrannized, she said in a voice quiveringly plaintive, freedom meant only America. And what more

striking way for America to show the world that even in a dark hour
she still stood for liberty of thought and utterance than to invite the
communist exile to her shore to pursue his writings in peace? And
what better haven in all America than Harvard, with her proud tradition of academic freedom? It would be A. Lawrence Lowell's parting
gift to American learning, for however inimical Trotsky's collectivist
social philosophy might be to many Americans, he was beyond dispute a powerful thinker and passionate democrat.

Rupe praised her breathless eloquence. Then, coldly and mechanically, he said that, as far as he was concerned, a communist was a
communist, however exalted, and America was in quite enough turmoil at the moment without inviting in a firebrand pledged to international revolution. Furthermore, in Lowell's final year as Harvard president, the last thing he would welcome was another controversy over
radicalism. And then, annoyance honing the edge to his words, he
asked, "Is this how we want to be known at the college—as the raving
insurrectionists who support one of the arch fiends of world communism? I thought we were trying to build a nonpartisan movement
here, not get ourselves sneered out of Cambridge for pulling offensive
stunts."

Shredded and minced for easy disposal, Cheska stood her ground.
The quiver almost shrill now, she said there was no such thing as non-
partisanship where freedom was concerned. And besides, Rupe had no
business as chairman trying to cut down her proposal before the membership had spoken on it; he was there to lead the discussion, not stifle
it. Rupe, hot himself now, brusquely conceded the point and asked for
the views of others. None was forthcoming. The president at once
said he would entertain a motion for a vote; it was so moved. Cheska
asked that it be secret; the chair ruled her out of order and asked for
hands in favor. Of the two dozen or so in the room, Cheska carried
three votes—her own, a Radcliffe friend's, and Toby's.

Cold calculation told him, of course, that she was being idealistic to
the point of absurdity. But the principle she had invoked seemed to
Toby to go well beyond the merits or evils of Trotskyism. And why
was he bothering with this whole doubtful N.S.L. business if not to
raise the standard of conscience when the rare chance for it arrived?

Afterward, she gave his arm a tight squeeze of gratitude before
turning to face Rupe. He took her into a corner and stormed that she
was trying to incite dissension in the ranks; the correct procedure
would have been to broach her birdbrained schemes to the leadership
council beforehand. "I don't stand for name-calling," she said evenly,
"and, anyway, I knew you'd be against it."

"Then you should have figured out I'd probably have some damned good reasons," he fumed. "Now trot on home to Sara and tell her you tried your best but the bourgeois bums gave you the rush."

Her eyes still jumpy with hurt, she ambushed Toby the next morning after his first class. Would he write a letter with her to the *Crimson* for Trotsky? He asked her why she couldn't write it herself. "I did," she said, "last night. This morning it reads like Hearst bombast. Help me—please."

"Look, this is your thing, kiddo."

"You voted for it, too. Why did you—if you didn't believe in it?"

Her fierce look cauterized him. Had his motive been base? Was he just trying to alienate her from Rupe by siding with her in a doomed cause. No—but it was one thing to be for implausible virtue within a private setting; it was quite another to stand up practically alone in front of the whole university and risk being thought a total ass. "I don't have to write a letter," he told her, "in behalf of everything in the world I think is right."

"But this is very important."

"Anything that happens to excite you is very important."

She pressed her lips in frustration, and her eyes rolled heavenward. "Pretty please," she said, "with sugar on it."

But he did not appreciate her coyness in the wake of so much indifference. Everything in him wanted to catch her by the shoulders and shake her and cry out that he was not her toy, not some accessory just for random use and convenient disposal, not a pet to stroke or ignore as whim moved her. What he said was he had no time for her just then.

She gave a knowing bob or two of her head and said she supposed he was afraid because of what had happened to his room the year before when his piece on the R.O.T.C. ran in the *Lampoon*. Toby denied it, but the charge put him so on the defensive that he could not refuse her plea to come along for moral support when she delivered her letter to the *Crimson* that afternoon.

Naturally, she insisted on taking it straight to the president of the paper; no underling would do. After making them wait an hour, his *Crimson* highness indicated by the vertical tilt of his nostrils that he was granting the campus equivalent of a papal audience. Scion of an old Marblehead family, he had prepped at St. Mark's, spurned Porcellian to join Iroquois, and held forth as precocious eminence in a paneled office five times the size of the one Toby's father had to direct the largest factory along the entire length of the Hudson River.

With a small, silent bow, this junior grandee plucked Cheska's letter from her, motioned them into a black leather sofa against the wall, and, not bothering to look behind him, fell into his carved wooden throne to study the heralded missive. "But surely," he said when he was done, fingering the edge of the sheet as if it were flypaper, "you jest."

Arms crossed, Cheska said softly, "I'm afraid not."

"Oh," said the *Crimson*, "but it's highly amusing."

"Then it should cheer your readers no end," she said.

"Actually, Miss da Silva, I think it might see print sooner if you submitted it to our self-styled humor magazine, the name of which escapes me for the moment—they're generally desperate for material."

"To be honest," Cheska, said, ignoring his snideness, "I hoped you might do more than just print it."

"Something like a two-column box on the front page, perhaps?"

"I thought you might consider endorsing the idea editorially."

The *Crimson* mouth gaped soundlessly.

"I'm sure it sounds odd," she jumped in before she could be slain by sarcasm, "but I think it would be the most courageous and enlightened thing the *Crimson* has done in ages. The whole world would notice."

"Oh, no doubt." He turned to Toby. "Has she escaped from some—?"

"I wouldn't know. I'm just madam's gardener."

"You're a big help," she hissed at him.

The *Crimson* president bounced to his feet and hooked a majestic thumb under each lapel of his herringbone jacket. "Tell me, Miss da Silva, is it that you're genuinely for Trotsky's position or do you simply think he'd be an adornment to the university?"

"My personal views of his philosophy are beside the point entirely."

"Satisfy my curiosity."

"My views are a matter of private conscience. All I'm saying is that granting him refuge here awhile would be a civilized thing to do."

"Harvard being the prime repository of civilization?"

"Well—something like that."

"And what is it specifically that Harvard is to learn from Trotsky— that point keeps eluding me somehow."

"Regardless of what you or I happen to think of his politics, he's one of the towering figures of our times."

The *Crimson* emerged from behind his desk. "I see," he said. "And what shall we appoint him, Miss da Silva—Genghis Khan Professor of Rapine and Butchery? You know, there's a growing body of evidence that communists are not terribly nice guys."

"You can't generalize about them like that—any more than you can about capitalists or monarchists or—or—or Hottentots—"

"Are we talking about the same Leon Trotsky—the one who led a bloody revolution for a cause that preaches merciless salvation? Until they threw him to the wolves, if I'm not mistaken, he was a leading party to all that terror and tyranny. People like him think people like you, who talk about freedom and truth and being courageously civilized, are ruled by foolish, squishy scruples. They're positive they have the answer to what ails the world, and you damned well better agree or you'll get it good when they come to power."

"You're distorting the whole—"

"And to top it all off, they promise us a dictatorship of the proletariat. Well, I for one am not a bit more eager to be dictated to by the proletariat than by Mrs. Astor's horse." He came around to the side of the desk and picked up her letter by a corner. "Or by Harvard females who, unwittingly or otherwise, do the bidding of barbarians." He floated the letter toward them through the air. "Good day, Miss Francesca da Silva '35—and agrarian attendant."

She cut classes the next day and showed up at Sara's shop just long enough to say she needed a little time by herself. Rupe thought she was overreacting and showed no inclination to seek her out. "Let her be," he said. It was his way of winning a lovers' quarrel.

Toby found her on the riverbank below Eliot, a little way from the boathouse. Legs jackknifed in front of her, she was hugging her knees and staring out blankly at the water.

He sprawled beside her without saying a word. In unintentional empathy, his breathing began to mesh with her pronounced rhythm. Trying to will away her agitation, she seemed both oblivious to his hovering concern yet glad for the mute company. In a while, the wind came up strong from the river and tore at the cardigan sweater she had thrown over her shoulders. He had not thought of her till then as someone who could suffer chill—only inflict it. In love, in lust, in longing to speak his anguished mind, he reached out a hand and firmly encased the beautifully rounded ridge lines of her calf.

"Harvard," she said after a moment, placing her hand on top of his, "is a shithole."

To salvage something from her Trotsky infatuation, she had asked her European history professor to intercede with the manuscripts and archives people at Widener so that Sara's set of the *Bulletin Oppozitsii* could be preserved for historical purposes and the noble outcast be assured a home of sorts at hallowed Harvard. The professor, instead, dealt her the final blow.

"He stood there with his bare face hanging out," she reported, voice thickening, "and said he didn't have much use for Stalin but there was probably no other way for him to pull his people out of the dark ages except by imposing monolithic rule. And his opponents are dwarfs and curios not worthy of taking up any of Widener's precious shelf space." She threw one of her mountainous sighs. "The bastard!" she said, gathering herself up off the wind-blown slope. "Anyway, I'll bet Trotsky isn't even circumcised."

III

Ten months shy of being eligible to vote for President, Toby was nonetheless ardent about finding a deliverer upon whom he might pin his hopes. However misguided or misspent her fervor, Cheska had found her Moses in the wilderness. That he could do little to settle America's chaos was beside the point as far as she was concerned; the affiliation brought a kind of order and dimension to her inchoate identity. Toby, as needy for his own candidate, scoured the field for a worthy prophet.

Chief Justice Hughes, all bushy-faced and biblical, Toby rather admired, but the man was too old now, in all likelihood, to make a second run for the White House. And Lindbergh, daring and visionary, was too young. Babe Ruth, surely a forceful personality, offered gravity but no dignity. Doug Fairbanks was too handsome for the part; Will Rogers, too honest. Santayana was in Rome and John Dewey in his dotage, which took care of philosopher-kings, and Henry Ford loathed labor unions and the Jews. Even a benevolent soldier might have suited, but Pershing was superannuated and MacArthur excelled chiefly at mowing down penniless veterans of his own army. Toby was stuck with the current crop of politicians.

Nothing Herbert Hoover had said during the campaign altered the perception Toby's little bunch had of him as a diehard defender of mammonism. Their ranks split badly, though, over the trustworthiness of Franklin Roosevelt, who was at least mouthing the proper sentiments about the plight of the long-forgotten common man. The persistent vagueness that passed in some quarters for smart politics left many on the Harvard Left suspicious of his exemplary rhetoric. Cheska said Rupe was for Roosevelt only because the man sounded the way God would have if He had graduated from Harvard and not merely created it.

N.S.L. sentiment, by and large, was farther Left, where Toby grew uncomfortable. Communism did not excite in him the same xenophobia it did in Rupe, but he had never overcome the sense that it was something sinister and alien, not a fit thing for a people who cherished their private liberties. Only when all else had failed and social paralysis loomed would he entertain the collectivist prospect. But America had not yet begun to redesign her economic system, or even retool it.

The Socialist Party, in the person of Norman Thomas, offered some promising thoughts along those lines—federal regulation of the banks, public spending for housing as well as guns, a minimum wage for the workingman and a modicum of security against sickness, forced idleness, and old age. But they seemed to him a futile crowd, without the remotest chance of electing anyone, unbefitting the allegiance of an educated Christian gentleman.

Toby sought outside guidance. His father's view had not altered. Graham Halyard said Roosevelt was a Throttlebottom but thought it symbolically apt for the nation to turn itself over now to a cripple; at any rate, he saw no practical alternative. Toby's other instructor in heightened sensibility proved a more positive guide.

The N.S.L. chapter had taken up a collection in behalf of the Scottsboro Boys' defense at about that time, and each member was asked to solicit half a dozen professors of his or her choice for a contribution and the use of their names in the cause. Jeremiah Travis was first on Toby's list.

He arrived unannounced late in the afternoon at the professor's cramped office on the second floor of Grays. His look said he was not entirely delighted with the intrusion. Books, periodicals, papers, and index cards covered every available surface—all pieces of an intricate design known only to the resident wizard. He had been working in shirtsleeves, but a vest preserved the sense of high-buttoned dignity Toby supposed he retained even in the bathtub. For a fatigued moment, Travis appeared not to recognize him, although he had taken several courses with the man. Toby hurriedly identified himself and offered to come back another time. While he plainly would have preferred that, Travis said he could spare a few minutes.

Toby's errand interested him less than the health of its sponsor. He wondered how the N.S.L. was prospering and noted that, in his student days in the Yard, only the Lippmann Socialists had stirred up political fire. "A very respectable bunch, by the way—some of them club men and athletes and even boys in the religious societies, as I recall." To be a socialist, then, he said, was to make an almost abstract declaration of concern about human inequities everywhere. His glance wandered over toward the window and the gathering darkness beyond. "I'm afraid the stakes of the game have risen rather dramatically since then."

Without calculation, Toby seized that instant of retrospective mellowness to ask him what politics he thought he might favor if he were a student at the moment. Travis's gaze lingered out the window awhile, then floated warily toward his young visitor's, passed by, and finally fixed on the wide, not quite worshipful eyes addressing his.

"An odd question, Mr. Ronan," he said. "It presupposes one is wedded to virtue only in one's youth."

Smiling, Toby said he had not meant that.

"You just didn't want to pry directly into my present allegiances, is that it?" Toby nodded and confessed the need for guidance in dovetailing immortal art and infernal politics.

Travis offered one of his own wan little smiles and agreed it was a continuous dilemma for every age but harder at that moment than any he could recall. "Some things are clear, though," he ventured and then abruptly checked himself. "So long as you understand that I'm not professing, Mr. Ronan—merely reflecting a bit—?"

"If you'd rather not say, sir—"

"Not at all. You put an honest question to me. It's just not one I'm normally called upon by students to answer." He swiveled around ninety degrees and seemed to address the collected volumes on his groaning shelves. Whatever historic services capitalism may have rendered, he said—"and they were legion, of that there is not doubt"—its heyday was just as surely ended. The glorification of rugged individualism had tamed a continent, but that same profiteering passion tended to debase everything it touched, be it business or pleasure, or faith, or art, or friendship, or any genuineness of feeling. "It has proven a moral disaster—and utterly un-Christian. And if that were not enough, Mr. Ronan, it has now failed the pragmatic test as well." By all available evidence, the free enterprise system was incapable of maintaining production and employment with any semblance of stability. "In its present form, the *laissez-faire* economy is not only cruel and inhuman—it is also inefficient and hopelessly volatile. That leaves it, in my not very nuanced judgment, with no redeeming virtue."

Toby had the sense that, for the first time, he was hearing not petty partisan words but heaven's high verdict of the ungodly works of man. Jeremiah Travis may have lacked a nimbus and the rich drapery of something fluttery out of Tintoretto, but he looked—dour, compact, immaculate—and sounded—civil, certain, resonant—the way a modern angel should have. Toby inquired respectfully of this divine emissary where one might turn, if anywhere, for secular sustenance.

"You mean how shall we fix it all up," he asked, "in three well-chosen sentences?"

Toby's look was sheepish; his hunger for instruction, wolfish.

"To be frank, Mr. Ronan, I don't think programmatically." Science and technology were shaping a new age, he said, that plainly required fundamental changes in human temperament if the race was to survive. Enmity would have to yield to tolerance; preconceptions, to demonstrable truths. Trust in providence could no longer obstruct prudent social planning. "And in place of ruinous competition, we must be clever enough to devise a new form of economy in which mutuality of interest supplants avarice as the ruling incentive. Without material security for the masses, I'm afraid, all our grand folderol about liberty and democracy is just so much tinhorn sloganeering."

As to Toby's request for a contribution to the Scottsboro defense, Travis agreed that the entire spectacle in Alabama was a travesty on justice and promptly wrote out a check for five dollars. As to the use of his name as a sponsor, he thought not. Those who advertised their philanthropy, he said, showed ill grace.

They met again the next day, not quite by chance, at Sara's shop.

Travis was autographing copies of his new book while sipping tea with a slightly less scruffy order of customer than usually attended the place. Titled *The Somber Muse,* the book was described on the flyleaf as a series of probing essays on the Puritan heritage as reflected in the works of a number of New England authors of the nineteenth century. Toby invested two dollars in a copy, the author's swirling signature and the date still drying on the endpaper, and went straight to Widener to hunt through it for epiphanies.

Limpid it was not. But the prose was as rewarding as it was dense, even if its tidings were unrelievedly grim:

> . . . This perceived tendency to sacrifice everything to the grasping individual will reaches its culmination in Melville's Ahab. In him, Emerson's conceit of the new democratic man as a potential sharer in the divine is penetrated and perverted until all that survives that majestic aspiration is an overweening drive for mastery. Thus, the exemplary American was—and has since remained —isolated in the midst of a violently expanding society. . . .

Toby wondered how, in hard times, any publisher could afford to bring out such a book. Sara explained the next day when he came by the shop full of praises and curiosity. The trick was to find reputable authors willing to subsidize their own output. Travis, whose doctoral dissertation on naturalism in Defoe and later compendious study on Shakespearean metaphor had earned him the good opinion of scholarly circles, was perhaps not required to underwrite his own publication to the same extent as others, but whatever the particulars of his arrangement, Sara saw no shame in it. The fault lay, she said, not with scholars reduced to vanity publishing to promote their labors but in the national philistinism that consigned almost all works of cultural substance to commercial oblivion.

However limited its sales prospects, the book was already a *success d'estime.* Sara paraded the clips with almost proprietary pride. It had been enthusiastically if not ecstatically received by newspaper and magazine reviewers from all sectors of the cultural and political spectrum. Only the *Evening Transcript*, Boston's reigning arbiter in matters literary, had not been heard from.

Such acclaim was more than enough for a celebratory soirée to be scheduled under Sara's direction at Travis's place two nights before the election. It sounded uncharacteristically immodest of the professor until Toby grasped that, as a *quid pro quo* for featuring his book in the store, Sara had induced Travis to throw open his drawing room to the Socialist Party for a last-minute pitch to every intellectual in the vicinity whose heart was not irreparably hardened to the politics of conscience. "You kids all come," Sara urged Toby. "It's the literary-political event of the season."

Graham, who gave him a lift to the affair, was at his most vitriolic throughout. His attendance, he grumbled, was an obligatory show of fealty to Travis. They stopped en route to pick up his fiancée, the very social and not entirely useless Miss Valerie Dobson, at her place on Pinckney. Employed as a reader with higher editorial aspirations at Houghton Mifflin, she professed both literary and social interest in the evening, which she thought might be dimmed somewhat by the review of *The Somber Muse* that had finally run in the *Transcript* that afternoon. Toby scanned the clip which she had brought along in case Graham had missed it. The savaging ended:

. . . Professor Travis's new work, while demonstrating his notable intelligence, is regrettably weakened by a prolixity of style, a tendentious reading of the materials he purports to examine afresh, and lugubrious attitudinizing toward the past and future American prospect.

"Mmmm," Graham purred, "that must have given the old boy a bit of a jolt." The tincture of malice in him was unmistakable.

Travis's fusty salon was threatening to disappear in a haze of blue smoke by the time they arrived. The milling went on forever, wilting plant and animal life alike, before the professor finally appeared in front of the fireplace and, with that singular grace of gesture and expression, introduced the guest of honor.

A ranking member of the national executive committee of the Socialist Party, the fellow held forth in a commanding variant of waterfront English that broke across all class and professional lines. "Let America act!" he cried. Let a nation that spent billions on killing to keep the world safe for democracy now spend constructively to end the suffering of so many of her own people. Yes, the wealthy would be hurt by the requirement to share—but they would not be maimed.

And the damage would surely be lighter than if the nation continued to sanction the unscrupulous code of acquisitive capitalism that drove men apart instead of bringing them together as brothers in Christ. "Marxism is godless by preference," he declared, "but socialism, my friends, says that true Christianity has never yet been tried."

It was a message whose largest appeal to Toby lay in its simplicity. When questioners began to pick the Socialist program to pieces, he fled out the arched entranceway and across the hall to the library, where Beaujolais was being poured. At the far end, Graham was paired with a fellow in a hound's-tooth suit whom he introduced as "the professor's great good friend, Julian Fairchild." About twice Graham's age and half again as thick, he had a curly, steel-gray mane, somewhat sunken cheeks, and a filigree of eye lines that gave his face a weathered look just the near side of dissipation. A composer of some fame who was said to have been laboring for years on a major oper-atic work, Fairchild had been lamenting the assault on Travis in the *Transcript* when Toby joined them.

"—and we still have no clue as to who the assassin is," he foamed about the reviewer, who had been identified at the end of the piece, in the paper's usual manner, only by the initials M.V.D. "I'd heard he was some pup on the B.U. faculty, but a few guarded inquiries have led me precisely nowhere."

"Why not just ask the bounders at the paper outright?" Graham wondered.

"We have—through intermediaries, actually. They say it's their business—and then offered polite assurances it's someone qualified."

"Whoever he is has a nice little feel for the vicious."

Fairchild was not taking it with detachment. "I say he's a venal rot-ter—and that someone hateful in the literary department over there has it in for poor Jerry. A man of his gifts and position and attractiveness inevitably invites envy." Graham suggested there was perhaps more to it. "Yes, of course," Fairchild said, gulping at his wine with anger-twisted lips. "The piece reeks of intolerance for—what shall we say—unorthodoxy? They're the ones doing the attitudinizing. Cheap and cowardly I call it."

Graham clucked commiserations and then, to drown his own te-dium-born disgruntlement with the evening, helped himself to no fewer than four glasses of wine in the ensuing hour. By the time Valerie drew up beside his elbow, glad to be done with hearing the Socialist gospel, his tongue had turned sloppily caustic. She told him to pipe down just as the host and guest of honor loomed up behind his shoulder, intent on a few swallows of refreshment.

"Oh, my dear professor," Graham said, wheeling on the pair suddenly, "a quick question that's put to me all the time by the senior boys who are casting their first vote—?"

Travis, dabbing at his high forehead with a kerchief, was immune to the airs of mannered tutors, particularly ones in their cups. "By all means, Halyard. Come fill up, meanwhile."

"Splendid," said Graham, getting jostled in the crush but insensate to it. "These lads, Professor—few of them impecunious, by the way— say to me, 'Why should we vote for Thomas, who hasn't a Chinaman's chance, and thereby boost Hoover, who's hopeless?' Not a thoroughly reprehensible question, you'll admit, even though—"

"Tell them to vote their hopes," Travis said above the din, "not their fears. That's how the candidate puts it." His colleague nodded.

"Goddamn twinkle-toed paragon!" Graham snarled when the three of them were safely back in his car and aimed toward Valerie's. "The man's so bloody virtuous he makes a bootlegger out of Jesus—with all that water-into-wine business, don'cha know? Well, I say a parlor pink is not a rose by another name."

"Shush!" Valerie said to him. "Toby'll think you're serious."

"I will not shush! And I am never anything but entirely serious, as yon Ronan knows full well—and that is more than Travis can say. All this beatific consorting with the Left is perfect therapy for the manchild—it exorcises his guilt for turning out a lot richer than a hod carrier and it rationalizes his grievance at not being born a Lowell. So he professes solidarity forever with the great unwashed, whose existence he has only lately uncovered. But good God, can't he see? There *is* no American proletariat!" He was flying around the corners now on two wheels while whipping himself into a frothy gyre. "Not a working stiff breathes in forty-eight sovereign states who does not want to lay down his pickax and shed his filthy overalls for good and sail into his Model A and putt-putt out to his snug hermitage in the sticks and sniff his mangy greensward and settle in with the evening funnies while his elephantine little woman is out fixing the roast. And why not —there *is* no dignity to manual labor in the U.S. of A. The lowliest gandy dancer cannot wait to hightail it into the middle classes—that is the sole genius of this society. That is what is new about the New World—our drones are not forever shackled to destitution if they will only persevere—and our unslackening entrepreneurs buy their way daily into the peerage. But how could Marx, the furry-faced Hebe, have foreseen all this? He had eyes only for the hoary Hegel—and Hegel's demented eyes were only for the state, next to which the individual life was but a briefly steaming ant turd. So what could his disciples know of liberty in that Teutonic element? Had the Hun a parliament? Could he speak out freely? Was he tried by jury? Not a bit of it! How, then, could the surly Marx have conceived of anything nobler than the dissolution of all that despotism besetting the workers of his world? He knew nothing of America and pugnacious egalitarianism. Travis, though—he does, or should. Perhaps that's it—he leads so hermetic a life in his inviolate tower—"

"Harold Laski's book last year," Valerie broke in at last on his ranting, "disagrees with you, angel. He says the American economic crisis is no different essentially from the European one—that the controlling classes here are no more accommodating to the legitimate demands of labor than they are over there and—"

"Laski? Who is Laski—God? If not for Lowell, they would have slit Laski's throat when he was here and sautéed him for supper. If there's anyone more insufferable than an Englishman trying to dazzle Harvard, it is a British Jew. Jews and fairies—they are the trial of my life—except for you, my dear."

"Graham, you're being hateful—"

"I have no hate in me—only brilliance and impatience."

"We are not alone, Graham. Toby's getting the wrong—"

"Oh, fuck Toby—he's not as fragile as all that. And fuck Travis, and fuck the Socialists, and fuck Harvard, and fuck John Milton—oh, God, Milton is the worst cross a man can bear—"

As the car stopped for a traffic light, Toby got out, said goodnight to Valerie, and walked off. Affectation in witty men was forgivable; defamation and intolerance, never.

He toed his way slowly down the cobblestone binding of Beacon Hill, catching glints through partly drawn curtains from the soft lights and polished woods and fluted crystal. Privilege, he thought, was no more a preventive for the corrosion of character in the salon world than desperation was a builder of it in the tenements. But then, he decided on the streetcar back to Cambridge, there must have been nights when even Byron got upstaged and turned into a dreadful shit.

In the student poll the *Crimson* took the next day, Toby voted Socialist. Norman Thomas received an astounding 17 percent of the total, just four points behind Roosevelt. Hoover, of course, swept the student body, but then no one has ever mistaken Harvard for the real world.

IV

Graham Halyard never let up that winter in decrying the malevolent strain in the German character. Even its most admired champions had been feverish with racial and martial toxins for more than a century, he said, citing chapter and verse from Hegel, Fichte, Nietzsche, and von Treitschke, the last of whom had told his history students at the University of Berlin, "It does not matter what you think as long as you obey."

It came as small surprise to Toby, then, when the Reichstag was put to the torch—the work of communist revolutionaries, according to the new Hitler government. Few at Harvard doubted the incident had been contrived to vilify the Red candidates in the pending election and provide the authorities with a pretext for suspending all civil liberties. What had really expired in the flames, of course, was the residue of German democracy.

In America, democracy still lived. But in the four months between the election and inauguration of Franklin Delano Roosevelt, Harvard '04, as its thirty-second President, the nation had sunk to such a state of fear and paralysis that it, too, seemed nearly ready to forsake popular government. Thirteen million were looking for jobs that were not there, the wheat crop and bread lines both set records, and banks everywhere were closing down to wait and see if the new leader had the will to govern and the power to rally the people.

Remote as they were from the staging grounds of this historic moment, the Harvard members of the National Students League hungered for a mission that would cast them as participants in the rush of coming events. It did not matter that the N.S.L.'s entire active membership nationwide could probably have fit comfortably within the chalk lines of a single tennis court. Directed energy, not numbers, was what counted, Rupert Donovan was fond of saying. As that fateful spring began to stir, Rupe thought he had found the perfect cause.

In February, after a fierce debate in the halls of the celebrated Oxford Union, an undergraduate assemblage of England's finest flower resolved that "this House will not fight for King and country in any war." An uproar engulfed the sceptr'd isle; the imminent demise of the Britons was prophesied. All over the land, collegiate youth endorsed the "Oxford Pledge." And now, Rupe enthused, that spirit was crossing the Atlantic on the wings of the dove. The Harvard N.S.L. could lead its generation to a lifetime of peace and save civilization from a bloodbath that would make the Great War look like a mere scrimmage for Armageddon.

The Harvard version of the Oxford Pledge that Rupe proposed to them read simply: "We refuse to support any war conducted by the United States government." To the swift objection that such a vow was un-American, Rupe responded defiantly. War was a ruthless social policy, he said, adopted by those in power and imposed on those without the power to resist it. "Which means when the older generation fails to solve its problems, the younger one gets sent out to be killed in the name of patriotism." This arrangement was highly beneficial to both industry and labor. War vastly increased demand for goods of all kinds, thereby filling the pockets of every military supplier in the land. And conscription rid the job market of its least skilled element, whose presence chronically depressed wages. "In other words," Rupe roared, "the young are our most expendable natural resource."

He asked the chapter to reflect on the pledge for a week and come to the next meeting prepared to vote on it; meanwhile, he lobbied the membership as if propagating the gospel among the heathens. Meeting arguments that the pledge was essentially a negative act, he contended just the opposite—it was a way of trying to preserve the good things the country had built and the fine ideals it stood for. Everyone knew that liberty and social justice dried up quickly in the fear, frenzy, and irresistible regimentation of wartime. Besides, it was time to bury jingoism as an acceptable policy of state; the government had become too practiced at converting minor international disputes into hysterical pretexts for saving American liberty by going to war on other people's soil. "We're talking about something more than civil disobedience here," he would end his private pitch. His goal was a mass movement to breach the barrier between college students and other young people who would share a common fate as cannon fodder if war came again.

By the next N.S.L. meeting, he had turned into a pure flame of righteousness. Pacifism had never had a more militant champion. He asked every N.S.L. member to take the antiwar pledge that night—in unison would be best—and then circulate petitions bearing it throughout the university. They would set up signing tables in the Yard and every House and maybe even canvass door to door until they had at least a thousand signatures, which would be sent to the new Harvard man in the White House. And then they might hold a peace convention for all the Boston area colleges and then perhaps a larger one for all New England. The thing would sweep westward after that.

The glow of Rupe's conviction was overpowering. He was staking his whole young being on the radiant premise that sweet reason could eventually accomplish what violence never would. Part of Toby was proud to have a roommate who had become such a humanitarian. The rest of him feared Rupe had gone a little haywire. Only one other member, a senior from New York named Melvin Kantor, seemed to agree. "My objection is that the pledge says we won't fight 'any war,'" he said in the discussion before the vote. "There's such a thing, unfortunately, as a just war. I think the Civil War was probably one."

"But it could have been talked out if there was no one willing to fight it," Rupe answered. "Don't you see—once you start making exceptions, the trigger-happy boys can drive a division of tanks through the opening faster than you can say Robert E. Lee."

"Suppose we get attacked or invaded?" Melvin persisted.

"Now seriously, who's going to attack us?" Rupe asked. "The Canadians with harpoons? The Mexicans with jumping beans? The Boche across three thousand miles of ocean? The Japs across six thousand?"

Melvin told him not to dismiss the Germans so lightly and asked if any of them had actually bothered to read *Mein Kampf*. If Hitler was to be even half-believed, he said, they ought to put him away at once instead of sitting back and watching him perform this Wagnerian opera he was planning called *Lebensraum*.

"Oh, I've read him," said Rupe, "or as much as I could take. It's Poland he wants and some of Russia, as far as I can figure out—not Wyoming."

"One thing leads to another—like last time."

"Things are different now—especially in Russia. The point is that it's not our continent."

"It wasn't last time, either. That didn't stop their U-boats from blowing our ships out of the water."

"We were supplying the Allies!" Cheska called out. "That made us a belligerent."

Melvin turned his thick, dark-framed glasses on her. "What were we supposed to do—stand by and watch Britain and France go down?"

"But that's exactly what I'm talking about!" Rupe cried. "Aggression answers aggression in a vicious cycle."

But what about the vicious creature, Melvin asked, who had risen to power in Germany on the frustrations and hatreds of his countrymen and boasted of it? Rupe said Hitler was a direct result of the vindictive peace imposed at Versailles which had done nothing more than stoke the European tinderbox. And instead of combatting militarism by helping build the League of Nations, America had gone off on an orgy of nationalism every bit as narcissistic and xenophobic as anything ever indulged in by the demonic soothsayers of the Reich. Punitive war settlements and isolationism were not responsible substitutes for moral rearmament in a world full of sorrows. Melvin Kantor, looking as warlike as a nearsighted owl, subsided; Rupe had all the answers.

Toby, though, remained unconvinced. He rose slowly and uneasily. Public speaking frightened him. His tongue never quite recaptured the thoughts that would fly through his mind beforehand. It was so much easier and safer to express himself on paper. There was time to rethink and rephrase—and no need to risk stunted delivery, poor memory, or the sudden horror of hearing your own voice honking nonsensically.

"I've been thinking very hard about—all this business," he said, groping to order his brain, "and I definitely agree—war is brutal and immoral and—and I'm against it—what decent, civilized person isn't? But could someone here please explain to me how war is so much worse than all other immoral conduct of the government that we should renounce it alone but still sanction the rest? What I mean is, are guns aimed across borders any more immoral than hatred and neglect and degradation directed within them? If we're absolutely against war, why aren't we also absolutely against a government that allows inhuman conditions in the mills and coal mines—and hardworking people to lose their homes and farms and savings—and children to grow up hungry and cold and sick and ignorant? And—and Negroes to be separated like animals on account of their skin—and denied their rights—and openly terrorized? And the rich to write the laws to suit themselves—and evade them whenever they want? I don't understand why it takes war for us to pledge our nonallegiance to a callous society." He gulped for air and confronted Rupe directly. "I appreciate the sentiment," he said, "but I think this whole approach is pretty juvenile."

Toby stood there, waiting for the Howitzer to unload on him. Instead, there was only the terrible silence of no-man's-land. The vote was taken in a mood of eerie, almost sullen dutifulness. Seventeen signed the pledge; five of them did not. Rupe moved out on Toby that same night without a word.

"Some pal you are." Cheska was wedged in a corner of the Widener steps when Toby passed by the next day after lunch. She slung her bookbag over her shoulder and fell in step with him. "He really feels betrayed, you know?"

"Why—because I said what I thought?"

"Because you never told him how you felt—and then went after him like that in front of everybody."

"He had his mind made up from the first about this thing. It wouldn't have mattered what anyone said to him—except you, maybe."

"But you didn't try. If you had, he might have cleared up your confusion. You didn't seem to—"

"*My* confusion? Oh, I get it now. When I'm on your side—like with the Trotsky business—then I'm very principled, but when I'm against you, then I'm just confused."

She shrugged away the charge. "Look, nothing you said—and you said it quite well—but none of it negated the point of the pledge. The idea is to seize on some aspect of the whole mess that peculiarly affects young people and make it our rallying point. All you were saying, really, was why this issue—and he could have explained beforehand."

"He explained it endlessly. I wasn't convinced, okay?"

"Toby, the N.S.L. is a social protest group, not a debating society. We've got to pull together. Rupe thinks you're pulling the other way."

"Because I didn't knuckle under to him? That sounds like Stalin."

"Your confusion's showing again. It's only repression when the cheese in charge shuts you up—and Rupe didn't. He was too shaken, even, to answer you. I'm talking about self-discipline. Trotsky says you don't become a real revolutionary until you fully subordinate personal ambition to the service of a great idea."

"And what's my personal ambition?"

"I've given up trying to figure that out. But Rupe thinks it's me—and that you're sore because you think he took me away from you—and this is your way of getting back."

"That's—totally—crazy."

"Sure, that's what I told him." She took him by the arm and steered them past Sever. "Toby," she said, voice softening, "I let Rupe kiss me sometimes on Sundays because—well, because I need a little kissing—everyone does. That doesn't make us sweethearts, though."

The sun flared off the round panes of her glasses as they reached Quincy. "Oh, right," he said. "Kissing's kid stuff."

"I told him you and I had this out last year—about my choice of friends—"

"Sure. You're you, and he's he, and I'm me, and that's how it is."

She tugged him to a halt at the curb and reached her fingers up to his lips, dry and taut with sarcasm, and touched them gently. "Look," she said, "you're just as dear to me as he is—you really are."

The sweet directness in her voice and look and touch swelled him with sudden rage. How could anyone who seemed so open be so duplicitous? "Sure," he said, "I just don't happen to be the one you're kissing—or whatever the hell it is you do with him."

She did her patented eye roll, imploring the heavens for help. "This one time only I'm ignoring your slanderous insinuation. I just said everything I have to say on the subject of Rupe and me—but I think maybe he was right about you."

"You tell him that. And give him a kiss for me while you're at it."

"Stop being an ass!"

"Oh, I have—finally. I'm just sorry it took me so long. Who needs enemies when he's got friends like you two?"

"Now stop that—"

"No, I won't stop! The nerve of that sanctimonious son of a bitch telling you I betrayed him when he's been loving you up the whole year!"

"He's done no such thing!"

"Horseshit! That's what that is, Cheska—and so are you, and so is he—pure, unadulterated, Grade A horseshit! And so's Trotsky, if you want to know what I really think—"

"I'm not going to listen to any more of—"

"If Trotsky's so all-fired brilliant and you're such a goddamned self-disciplined revolutionary, why the hell don't you disown your stupid bourgeois family and renounce your inheritance—or were you planning on handing it over to the fucking Comintern and hope they'll—"

"Just shut your ignorant face!" She whacked her bookbag across his arm to end the assault.

He stood there, steaming face bowed, hands convulsively clawing at his pocket bottoms, as six months of frustration seeped away. She could easily have bolted, just left him there that way, having exorcised his fury with nothing to show for the indulgence but two lost friends. Instead, she perched on the running board of a car parked by the curb and waited till he was as calm as he was going to get.

"I'm sorry I called your family stupid," was all he said finally. "They're probably very nice."

"The thing is," she began without looking up, "I think all the time about what you said—the money part, too. I decided once to give it all to Father Flanagan—and then I said to myself if he's only got boys out there, to hell with him." She sighed as if a great, forgiving tranquility had come over her, then plucked at his trouser cuff to make him sit beside her. "Families are like an anchor," she said in quiet explanation. "You don't throw the anchor away when you go for a sail." It was perfectly possible, she thought, to disagree with your parents about a lot of things and even actively dislike them at times without ever stopping loving them. It was kind of primal gratitude, she supposed, for having been created. "My father says children never give their parents back even half the feeling that's been invested in them. He claims not to mind, though, on the ground I'll get repaid with the same show of ingratitude by my kids—it's just a condition of the species." She took his hand and gave it a squeeze and then replaced it, saying, "But you don't make babies from a little Sunday kissing."

He spent the spring in solitary thought. The salutary result was an eight-stanza poem titled *On Contemplating the Enormity of Antares,* after the bright star in Scorpio's tail that he learned in astronomy had recently been calculated by the Mount Wilson Observatory to be three hundred million miles wide. If it only knew, he thought.

The poem came out in the May *Advocate*, where T. S. Eliot, Edward Arlington Robinson, and other artists-as-young-Cantabrigians had first published, and earned him half an accolade from Graham Halyard.

That summer he read the nineteenth-century Russians and wrote obituaries for the Nyack *Journal* at space rates. The two went well together. In between, he wrote Cheska—long, funny letters alive with caring but withholding his soul. She wrote back, in her own sweet time, the answers growing shorter and shorter. Summers, she said after his third letter, were for feeling, not thinking or any mental discipline. He stopped writing her after that.

FOUR

IN THE POSTDILUVIAN AUTUMN of 1933, Toby gathered the distinct impression that half of Harvard was going around trying to sound like Franklin D. Roosevelt.

His own form of identification with the President—who had, after all, lived in Adams House when it was the old Westmorly apartments (Room 27 in the B entry, one over from Toby's)—was to slide his swivel chair over to the window and, remaining confined in it, pretend he was commander of all he surveyed. That was easier than trying to imitate the man's speech, given his own unshakeable rasp. He took heart from reports that even Roosevelt hadn't sounded like Roosevelt when he came to Harvard. The university's legendary elocutionists, George Pierce Baker and Irvah Winter, worked over that larval lordliness in the young aristocrat, training him to project with a voice so artlessly authoritative that no one ever after would take him for anything less than—even when seated—toweringly formidable.

In office, every radiant syllable he uttered shot electrically across the beleaguered land like a telegram from providence. "It may well be," Graham Halyard said, noting that the President carried it all off with easier grandeur than any blueblood who ever pandered to the American rabble, "they'd actually prefer a king."

It was apparent, though, that Roosevelt was appealing less to a latent royalist strain in the body politic than to its stomach. One after another, his emergency measures had been speedily carpentered into place. In a single season, the magisterial man in the wheelchair had begun to restore to the people their land, their shelter, the fruits of their labor, and, most of all, their hope.

His inaugural address had, of course, been the talisman. By naming the dreaded wraith that pursued them all and declaring it insubstantial, the President began at once to dispel it. In the act, he earned a niche in the pantheon of rhetoricians. It was that following fall when Toby discovered that, though the delivery of that justly famous speech may have been pure Roosevelt, the phrasing had first been used by another Harvard man, a quarrelsome eccentric with a large nose who had entered the Yard as a student precisely one hundred years earlier. Seeking a subject for his senior honors thesis, Toby came across Emerson's eulogy to this queer bird, from whose unpublished manuscripts he had chosen to quote in fitting memorial: "Nothing is so much to be feared," Henry David Thoreau had written, "as fear."

The more Toby looked into him after that, the surer he became that this peculiar pantheist was the savant he had been seeking. Without a doubt, he appealed vastly more to Toby than did Karl Marx, just one year Thoreau's junior but light-years away in conviction. While the German shared the Concord man's lament that most of humanity passed helplessly through "lives of quiet desperation," the former called upon the individual to yield up his soul to the common good; Thoreau urged a different course, even more foreign to the American temperament—a turning away from material goods, away from the social contrivances of men, toward an inner song tuned to the simple pleasures in which the earth abounded. He worshiped freedom by loving nature. To Marx, both were luxuries; to the New Englander, they were life itself.

What convinced him Thoreau was, when analyzed, far less ethereal than communism's thunderous progenitor, was a single line by the transcendentalist: *In what concerns you much, do not think you have companions; know that you are alone in the world.* They were at once the most terrifying and most bracing words Toby had ever read, and suited his mood entirely. In a flash, the title for his thesis came to him —"Thoreau: Society and Solitude"—and he knew he had a model closer to his sort of Harvard man than F.D.R. They both, Thoreau and he, lacked means to speak of, tended toward homeliness, and suffered so from inwardness as to be suspected of misanthropy. In some perverse fashion, too, he felt strengthened because Thoreau had been such a total failure in his own time—mocked, reviled, and, more than either, ignored. That fact seemed to give Toby breathing room. He went off to tell the light of his life that there was now another.

To his surprise, she was not indifferent. While she alphabetized a fresh shipment of titles for the new term at Sara Blue's bookshop, he tried to persuade her that they had each arrived at some of the same social positions by different routes. Indeed, the very first chapter of *Walden* took the view identical to Marx's that labor was the only true creator of value, yet instead of rewarding the worker accordingly, capitalism reduced him to an inanimate object, hardly distinguishable from—or nobler than—the machine he tended.

Cheska's left eyebrow, the higher one, curled at this intelligence and remained in that intrigued but wary arrangement until she was done sorting. Then she said, since he seemed so worked up, why didn't they bike out to Thoreau's pond the next morning and venerate him on the spot.

It was at least twenty hilly miles to Concord, Toby pointed out, but she said that was nothing in weather so gorgeous. What he meant was the next day was Sunday, and before the summer her Sundays had been for Rupe.

What had happened between them, she did not volunteer. Rupe, though, asking Toby by mail in August for a reconciliation, hinted strongly at what Cheska had maintained—that their romance had not gone beyond the smooching stage, which Rupe found unbearable and very possibly debilitating to the gonads—and advised that they had reverted to friendship regrettably free from sin. "Well, no one ever woos a 'Cliffie for the whoopee in it," he wrote. "Besides, with her, chastity is a political statement—that is, in case you still harbor ambitions. Or, possibly, she's afraid coitus with Gentiles will dry up her womb."

Toby guessed that her abstinence where Rupe was concerned was more a question of water and oil than Old Testament *vs.* New. But Lord, he was pleased.

It showed all over him that Sunday when they wheeled in tandem down to the end of Mount Auburn, spokes singing in the morning stillness, swung right on to Route 3, followed its long curve to the edge of town, where it joined with 2, and struck out due west on the Paul Revere route, past Belmont and Arlington, skimming up, down, and between the rises of Waltham and Lexington, west past Lincoln, west ahead of the sun, watching it slowly shrink their shadows as it overtook them with festive warmth in that mellowest time of year. Those exquisite calves of hers churned away in a fluid blur uphill and turned to sleek tan steel as she stood on the pedals defying the wind on the downhill runs. The relish she took in the sport revealed itself in dark, damp circles radiating from her underarms. All that brain and the canny look her glasses gave her could not diminish the bursting physical luster of the girl.

They stopped about midway and each took a swallow from the canteen of apple juice he had brought in his knapsack, along with a couple of cheese sandwiches and Hershey bars from The Bick and a towel for after swimming if the water wasn't ice. Without delicacy, Cheska announced she had to pee—and confessed to be stricken, at such moments only, with penis envy. A suitably secretive clump of bushes was located, and she went off to perform, muttering about the perils of poison ivy. Before Toby could disappear for his turn, she asked whether he'd mind if she watched.

From the perfect dispassion with which the request was made, it was plain she was serious. He laughed, uneasily, and asked her why. "Just to see how far it goes," she said. He laughed again, trying not to blush but failing lavishly. "How far does it?" she asked with clinical interest. Roseate by now, he said he supposed that depended on a number of factors but, being housebroken, he had never been at liberty to test all the variables. "Well, what do you think—a foot—or a yard—or a block?" Almost certainly not a block, he said, though probably more than a yard, under full-bladder conditions of the sort he was painfully experiencing at the moment. Her eyes widened. His narrowed; he felt fifteen years past his prime for the carefree exhibition of that sort of virtuosity. "In case you're worried, I've seen them before," she said, unable to ignore his florid condition, and then hurriedly added, to fend off suspicion of promiscuity, that there were two men in her immediate family. He asked why she hadn't had them demonstrate. She said her brother and she were too far apart in years and her father would have thought the idea corrupting. "Of course, if you'd rather not—"

Till that moment, he had not considered the discharge of his wastes either a shameful act or a spectator sport. Distasteful as the forced performance was, he could detect no real prurience in a mere display of bodily hydraulics. Unbuttoning not without pride, he guided a golden parabola far into the sky. She whistled softly at the feat, then laughed and clapped and said she would do it in the open all the time if she were a man and always try for a distance record. By the time they remounted their bikes, his manhood was rampant from such unwonted admiration. Sensing that the moment of innocence had passed, Cheska chose not to notice.

The rest of the way out, he tried to impress upon her the reverence with which they ought to approach the shrine of his sainted ascetic. In tireless profusion, he quoted suitable aphorisms from the Thoreauvian canon: . . . *A man is rich in proportion to the number of things he can afford to let alone. . . . Superfluous wealth can buy superfluities only. Money is not required to buy one necessary of the soul. . . . However mean your life is, meet it and live it; do not shun it and call it hard names. . . .*

Whether transfixed by such pearls or numbed by his salesmanship, she made no response, and they journeyed on in warm silence until the first signposts of Concord flashed by. He felt his insides quicken as they made the required turn south and flew past cordial hedgerows

separating tall meadows from ripe beanfields, none of them changed
much, probably, since Thoreau had taken his last daily trek over those
same roads.

The sign at its eastern end, atop the slope where the water was not
visible through the trees, said Walden Pond belonged to the people of
Middlesex County, whose commissioners solemnly warned that
swimmers proceeded at their own risk. *A man sits as many risks as he
runs*, wrote Thoreau—"or swims," Toby added as they locked their
bikes and skipped down the log steps cut into the hillside. It opened
up suddenly before them, a great gleaming mirror that snatched down
the firmament and spread it at their feet in blazing blue and liquid
gold. *Nothing so fair, so pure, and at the same time so large, as a lake,
perchance, lies on the surface of the earth. Sky water. It needs no
fence.* Or explaining.

Half a dozen sunbathers basted in their juices on the crescent of
beach, and another few porpoised in the water. Aside from them, an
anchored wooden raft about thirty yards offshore, and a tin toolshed
at the rear of the beach, there were no signs of human intrusion. The
land banked abruptly from the shoreline but did not climb far.
Enough conifers still grew to keep it a shady if not dense woodland,
but there were threadbare spots along the rim and only some small
coves and hilly outcroppings off to the west to scallop the regularity
of the vista. A modest setting—the better to show off the gem it
cupped.

He took her hand and set off counterclockwise along the shore toward where the cabin had been. The path did not yield easily to
strangers. Beneath a mat of pine needles, it was jagged with half-
buried stones in many spots and varicose with tendrils of tree root exposed by the steady erosion of the hillside. In places where the path
was washed out altogether, they forded the little inlets barefoot. Well
down the north shore they came at last upon the clearing Thoreau had
picked to construct his tiny house for that famously itemized twenty-
eight dollars and change. Was even a splinter of it left?

The path to the site had long since grown over, and that "young
forest" he wrote of had withered to a paltry stand of mostly scrub
pine. Farther inland, on the soil embankment he had made as a pedestal
for his one-room home of boards, sumach still grew, but no dwelling
stood there now nor any trace thereof. On the lower lip of the earthen
mound, though, a pile of stones, irregular in size and shape, rose as
high as their chests. From the initials and dates, some quite recent, that
were painted or etched on them, it was plain they had been placed
there in primitive homage.

They flopped wearily on the ground a few feet below the impromptu stone monument. He wondered if Thoreau had set eyes on any of these very same arrowy pines when he arrived at the pond—eighty-eight years, two months, and fifteen days earlier, Toby calculated—in order *to learn what it had to teach, and not, when I came to die, discover that I had not lived.* More to the point, how much of it would he himself have perceived, even with senses alerted, had he been Thoreau. Even looking, would he have *seen* the fish hawk dimple the glassy surface of the water, or the grass grow greener after spring rain? Would he have known to listen for the owls, *those wise midnight hags . . . like mourning women,* or heard the hare in its extremity, crying like a child? And felt the cold—*A man has not seen a thing who has not felt it*—by plunging fingertips into it till they tingled, or embraced the darkness of a moonless night by groping blindly through the thicket? Or did it take a rarefied sensibility, all that transforming of raw sensation into sublime spirit? Perhaps nature, being everywhere and everything, was too grand and ubiquitous for his local soul to compass. The facility to shuttle between the elemental and the infinite, he decided, was mostly a matter of mental conditioning; you had to treat existence itself as a rare pastime. *This curious world which we inhabit is more wonderful than it is convenient, more beautiful than it is useful; it is more to be admired and enjoyed than used.* If only men could content themselves with its contemplation instead of possession.

"If only," Cheska said when he offered the sentiment aloud. "And if only Henry had had a family to feed instead of flitting through the woods all his life." Toby recoiled, and she put up a tempering hand and said she was only teasing, that city girls knew nothing of birdsong and it was not arbutus that trailed off the fire hydrants of San Francisco. He told her she had no poetry in her soul.

She rocked her head in the crook of her arm for a moment, eyeglasses flickering with diffused woodland light. "I'm not sure there's anything in my soul," she said. "I'm not sure I *have* a soul—in fact, I rather doubt it."

Even unlimbered and becalmed in that hallowed bower, she would not lapse into wishfulness or summon seraphs. He envied that hardness in her as much as he held it her severest limitation.

"But I do have a stomach," she said, springing to her feet, "and I know *that's* empty. Now don't let me stop you from gathering nuts and berries and other natural treats, but I'm ready for a sandwich and a Hershey."

They lolled at the pond's edge, toes in the water, knowing you got cramps if you swam too soon after eating, and spoke of their separate summers. Hers was uneventful, aside from the usual intrafamily squabbling, but she was genuinely impressed that he had wangled a job on a real newspaper. He said writing mostly about dead people of small distinction and getting paid by the columnar inch were not exactly evidence he had hit the big time.

"Why must you always put yourself down?" she asked. "It's as if you're terrified at being taken seriously. Getting any work right now, especially the creative sort, is an achievement. They must think you're very talented." He shrugged and said obituaries did not have to rhyme. She gave him a scornful shake of her head, then ran a finger down his arm and said, "Excessive humility is your least charming quality—did you know?"

He did not. But neither was he so stricken by the news that he neglected to ask for her roster of his better features. She thought awhile and cautiously ventured that he was tallish, and that she was quite partial to tallish people, and he was quite smart and quite funny, both in an understated way she also favored, and quite talented and quite tender and not a fake the way half of Harvard was, although his overweening modesty almost canceled that out. "Also, you pee farther than anyone I've ever seen."

For that he shoved her partway into the water. She yelped it was really cold but very nice on so warm a day, and she was going in. She scanned the shoreline to make sure there was nobody watching or coming, then stripped off her clothes right there, tucked her glasses well inside one of her sneakers, and raced bare and bold and altogether beautiful into the clear water. Nike at her bath. "It's incredible!" she shouted, limbs thrashing like a rubber hose. "But where'd they move the Gulf Stream? Get in here and warm this thing up!"

His profoundest secret having already been more or less exposed, Toby could not falter. Besides, swimming was one of his stronger sports. With more vigor than form, his bony body churned through the water at a smart clip, as Cheska found on challenging him to a sprint. It just proved, he yelled to her, that not everyone from California was born amphibious.

"All it proves," she shouted between gasps of air, "is that Jews do better on land than in water. Why do you think God parted the Red Sea?"

She went in to shore first. He was discreet enough to hang back a while, giving her time to dry off and dress. But she was lying on the shore still wrapped only in the towel and sunning herself deliciously as he started in, more than a little self-conscious. The icy drink had reduced his maleness to a strawberry nubbin *cum* walnut. Her eyes looked closed as she drank in sunlight; he weighed the odds of slipping past her undetected and into his underpants. Just as he rose from the water at the last possible moment, she squinted up with an assessing smile and said, "My, how we've changed. I trust it's not permanent."

Laughter in paradise. His condition was rectified the instant she peeled the towel off to let him dry with it. They stood there motionless a moment, Adam and Eve on the brink of the primordial ooze, she all ripely round and tawny, he milky white and raw red, until, as if on signal, neither taking the lead, they entwined. And pressed themselves slowly into a tight coil, her smoky heat banishing the cold wet film that still clung to him from the pond and inspiring a different dampness. Before, he had touched her only gingerly and won a few polite kisses. Now, eyes shut, he clung indivisibly to her, caressed her full-length, swayed with her ecstatically, asking himself whether it was virtue or perseverance that had at last been rewarded.

They moved back into the woods, spread the towel over the pine needles, and fell into horizontal, and mutually ardent, exploration. That they were profaning Thoreau's temple crossed his mind briefly. The great naturalist's own interest in bodies was apparently limited to the furry, finny, and feathery sort, toward which he indicated no unnatural passion. Human sexuality he abjured with monkish vows. How any process of nature could qualify as ecstasy and depravity at the same time was beyond Toby. So he delved, to Pan's pipe, rejoicing in every curved surface of Francesca da Silva, who rotated pliantly to his touch.

As he intensified his probing, however, she slackened hers and announced they could not do that, not that way—it was dead against her principles. But there were other ways—"gratification without penetration," she called it huskily and drew his hand to her pelvis for instruction. Her response was so swift and loud and moist and the flexing of her loins so fevered that he marveled at his power to stir that fierce a joy in her, and at her pleasure in displaying it. And when she returned the favor with hands so knowing in their effects, he supposed either she had had Levantine training in the techniques of perversion or that all Trotskyists were natural voluptuaries. The energy of his release drew still keener admiration from her than his morning discharge by the roadside. In one trip, she had exhausted his repertoire.

The spell of the place and the day and their sudden intimacy wore thin on the ride home, and at the risk of disenchanting him, she said she was not so sure about a lot of Thoreau. Suggesting he was something of a glorified sugarcoater, she noted there was at least as much malignity, terror, and killing in nature as in the dungheap society had made of itself. Pantheism, moreover, struck her as much a pagan cult as any other religion, and what was there transcendent about the morning dew if its very molecules reconstituted themselves every so often and deluged the earth murderously?

Feebly he argued back that she was trying to impose morality on mere organic matter, but siphoned of all his tensions, he was too bushed to sustain a debate. He dropped her at the bookshop to do some unpacking for Sara, who eagerly waved them in. Perched on the workbench stool in the back room, beardless now but more gaunt and flinty-eyed than Toby remembered, was Anton Sota.

He was just passing through town, he said, between assignments for the textile workers' union. Cheska gave him a kiss and a hug that, on this day above all, could only embitter Toby's memories. What intimacies had she practiced with *him?* Was she perhaps a nymphomaniacal virgin? Yet for all her evident delight over Sota's appearance, she was full of talk about their trip to Walden Pond and its reasons and looked indignant in Toby's behalf when Anton scoffed at the idea that anyone would seriously bother, in 1933, to write an honors thesis on Henry Thoreau. "Marx could have learned a thing or two about writing from him," she said gamely.

"But not about thinking," Anton said with a smirk. "You redeem the proletariat from enslavement by granting workers their fair share of production, not by telling them to learn how to do without. Revolutionaries destroy a corrupt system. Thoreau just whined about it."

The sight of him poised like a bronze copy of a sinewy agitator fresh off a *New Masses* cover was suddenly unbearable to Toby. It was no longer enough to detest him mutely. Better to aim answering blows, however unequal the contest, than yield to that sulfurous fanaticism of his by default. "The real change has to come from within us —with how we think and feel—"

"Toby, Toby, Toby!" Anton said, tossing up his palms. "That could take till doomsday! Justice can't wait for every man to see the light—any more than law enforcement should vary with the moral standing of every citizen. Both have to be imposed—don't you see?— by an enlightened state. There's no other plausible mechanism."

"But a state has no conscience—only people do. That's the part of the revolution Thoreau was working on."

It was not a debate Anton Sota thought worthy of him. "Thoreau was a romantic imbecile," he announced. "Anarchy would have suited him fine, so long as the flowers bloomed on time." He smiled at his own vitriol, drew a short laugh from Sara, and then glanced up at the wall clock. "I've got a meeting downtown—any chance of my catching some of your legendary java?"

Outside the door, Cheska kissed him firmly on the mouth. Toby pedaled back to Adams more in triumph than rancor.

At their room, Rupe tried to reason with him when he narrated the insufferable return of Anton Sota. "If you want to be coldly analytical about it," he said, "Thoreau *was* practically a nihilist."

Cold analysis was Rupe's game that fall. He had announced the moment the roommates were reunited that he intended to enter Harvard Law School a year hence. There may have been more shoals than depths to his intellect, but Rupert Donovan was a quick study. Everything that came up between them was grist for his litigious bent that season. When Toby hinted Thoreau might be his thesis topic, Rupe had immediately gone off and reread *Walden* and *Civil Disobedience*. His verdict was not markedly different from Sota's: The man was fatuous as a rhetorician and hopeless as a logician. "Look, he said in plain English the state has to recognize the individual as a higher and independent power. 'Any man more right than his neighbors constitutes a majority of one already'—isn't that the whole point of *Civil Disobedience?*"

"And wasn't that the whole point of your pacifist oath?"

"But we were trying to get the government to mend its asshole ways—not deny its legitimacy. Thoreau just begs the whole question of who's to decide what's right. He says it's each man for himself. That may be great poetry, but it's lousy politics. Even in utopia, you've got to be civil."

Nor did Toby win an ovation from higher counselors when he registered his choice of thesis topic. "Saints pray-sahrve us!" Graham chirruped in his execrable mock-Hibernian, a sign of high playfulness. "Holy Henry David himself, is it to be, now? The biographer of the bluebird—inspector of snowstorms—supervisor of sensibilities—celebrator of celibacy—"

Toby argued back that Thoreau was no maunderer in Xanadu but a highly practical reformer. Instead of wanting to kill off private enterprise, like Marx, he preached lower consumption—*That man is richest whose pleasures are cheapest*—so his countrymen would not have to grind away their days in order that a few among them might grow rich.

"So," Graham replied, expelling a sweet cloud of pipe smoke, "instead of an economy of abundance on which our fair land has ripened, you and the pond-watcher would substitute the glories of scarcity—an economy of economy, so to speak—thereby destroying demand. Do I have it right?"

"An economy of *need*—producing enough to satisfy the basic necessities. Beyond that, work is just legitimized enslavement. 'Getting and spending we lay waste our lives,' he said."

"Ah, dear boy, would that you could run a modern society by steering multitudes into the berry patch—or repeal the industrial revolution by punting down the Merrimack." He slid his slat legs off the desktop. "Try to content Americans with a cupboard of necessities and the whole genius of the system is defeated. Why else did God in His infinite wisdom load us up with such natural treasures if not to condition us to the joys of gluttony? No, I'm afraid the late H. D. Thoreau, Esquire, is thrillingly irrelevant to the current well-being of the republic."

Travis was his last hope. His departmental approval, moreover, was required. When Toby told him what his tutor thought of Thoreau, he tidied a wrinkle at the knee fold of his professorial trousers and remarked drily, "Someday I should like to hear the brilliant Mr. Halyard hold forth on the fine line between the passé and the classic."

Despite this cheering start, it was evident as their talk wore on that Travis regarded Thoreau as rather a dog in the manger. Toby pressed the case for his spirituality, contending that Christian democracy would not prevail over godless despotism unless greed were eliminated as an economic necessity.

"His theology and economics are beyond my field of competence, I'm afraid," said Travis. "But I'll confess the man troubles me when he writes, 'The only obligation which I have a right to assume is to do at any time what I think right.' Now I don't require that Thoreau, or anyone, love his neighbor to excess, but I do rather resent his stony indifference to him. May I suggest, Mr. Ronan, that solipsism is as prone to abuse by meditative naturalists as rugged individualism was by the robber barons?"

His enthusiasm blasted, Toby muttered something wan about the handwriting on the wall and the evident need for him to find a new thesis topic that would please somebody or other.

Travis's captious mind turned impatient. "See here," he said, "it's not a question of pleasing—it's a matter of rigor. Doing a thing excellently is what counts, not whether I or Halyard or the Dalai Lama takes a shine to it *a priori.*" He settled back in his chair. "This learning business is not like buying a tin of biscuits at the market, Mr. Ronan, and getting stuck with the lot. To write usefully on Thoreau, you need not defend him at every point—why should you? We all have our strong points and our weak ones. Take what suits you from him, so long as you don't misrepresent him to us—and the same with any other genius, or lesser mortal, for that matter, you happen upon along the way. I should much rather have you hold on to a patchwork of beliefs of your own assemblage than take someone else's readymade. Apostles, may I suggest, are not whole men."

Those instructions alone were worth all of Harvard to Toby Ronan.

II

They both needed money that year, Toby more than ever, Cheska for the first time. His father, having superintended the cutback at his factory as humanely as possible, was rewarded by being demoted to assistant manager and replaced by Pharaoh's No. 1 Lash. Down to half-salary, he considered himself lucky at that. Toby was bitter for him and felt closer to him than any time since his mother died. The latest financial blow forced the elder Ronan to choose between closing down the house or discontinuing his son's modest Harvard allowance. Toby made the choice for him.

A lightened course load, traditional for seniors writing a thesis, gave him time to earn more. But the typing business was glutted by then—a lot of people were working for under the standard ten-cent-a-page price—and he could not make enough at it while still excelling at his studies. Rupe again offered to help out, but more than ever Toby needed to be independent of him. Thanks to his academic standing and character references from his tutor, House Master, and the Grosvenor Professor of Letters and Rhetoric, he was granted twenty paid hours a week behind the circulation desk at Widener. The work was easy and in slack spells let him do his own reading. It was unthinkable —for his first week on the job, anyway—that he would betray such a privilege.

Cheska's position had changed even more than his own. Tired of playing campus radical and then going home to a household of hardly reduced opulence, she had disclosed her unsettled but decidedly anti-bourgeois views to her family over the summer. They were neither amused nor very tolerant, beyond suggesting it was a sympathetic phase she was going through while the country recovered. Given her growing inclination to bite the hand that had been feeding her, her father said perhaps they ought not to corrupt her high principles with filthy spending money; capitalists were well known as hopeless promoters of profligacy in their young. Cheska took the bait defiantly. She would do without her allowance if that was how they felt— would even repay them her tuition as soon as she was able. Temporarily, anyway, the poor little rich girl had liberated herself from the lap of luxury.

Sara Blue was admiring of this courageous act but not to the point of paying cash for her services. With an old, sick mother to care for and a dozen needy nephews and nieces, Sara said the only help the shop could afford was the sort satisfied with pay in trade. And if she were to offer cash wages, it would not be to Cheska, however warm she felt toward her, but to someone in dire need.

When Toby hinted Sara was taking advantage of her, Cheska jumped to her defense. "You wouldn't understand," she said and then tried to make him. Sara fed her several times a week, let her use her small apartment above the shop as an off-campus retreat, lent her her car for part of Sunday, and offered large helpings of street savvy, to say nothing of a comforting shoulder. "Some things don't have a price," she said. Toby agreed but was tactless enough to ask if it occurred to her that maybe she was also providing Sara with highly supportive companionship, to say nothing of a ready receptacle for her pronounced but not always edifying views. "Oh," she said, "that stinks. It really does."

"How come," he asked, "nobody can ever tell you anything?"

Yoked to her deepening entanglement with Sara was a heightening animosity toward Harvard—serving, he guessed, *in loco parentis*. In fact, her displeasure with the place was approaching the pathological.

A prime reason was the university's nominee for the new president. After twenty-six years of Abbott Lawrence Lowell, who, whatever his virtues, was to her an incorrigible Bourbon and certified antisemite, the Overseers selected a man she found unworthier still. James Bryant Conant, another in the mold of lean, large-domed, astringent Yankees Harvard seemed to dote on for its leaders, was a Mayflower descendant who passed the World War as a chemistry professor in the university laboratories turning out poison gas for the army. He had helped save democracy, in her pacifist estimate, by committing atrocities in its name. She considered his wide mouth effeminate and his metal-framed glasses the telltale accessory to a steel heart. The only thing in his favor, she said, was that he was not a Cabot.

To make matters worse, she canvassed catalogues and reading lists and discovered that not a single undergraduate course at either Harvard or Radcliffe dealt with Marxist-Leninist theory, a major social force in world thought for nearly a century. It was an unspeakably benighted and cowardly omission in the curriculum of the nation's foremost university. In sum, she faulted the Harvard administration for intolerance and insensitivity that rivaled the student body's reactionary snottiness. In that combustible frame of mind, she hatched her plot and enlisted Toby in it.

They had gone for a drive in Sara's disintegrating sedan the Sunday after their idyll by the pond. She was a girl just then of such volatile feelings that he could not predict with any accuracy where he stood with her from one moment to the next, or whether, even provided with a place and time for intimacy, they would ever renew their embraces of the previous week. For all he knew, that had been a singular event, brought on by a primeval setting and serene mood; the car, by contrast, was a denatured capsule and Cheska herself now seemed wrapped in a dozen brooding veils.

And yet when he braved her wrath by turning up an untrafficked seaside lane halfway down the shore road to Plymouth, she told him to park and, under cover of dusk, left him in no doubt of his standing with her for the moment. The congested compartment somewhat inhibited their responses, but if the earth did not move under them—only the front seat—all was not lost. Petting to climax was the perfect prophylactic for youth's raging lust.

Recovering from this marginal sin, he listened through a blissful haze as she proposed they sabotage "the system" by stealing books from Widener for sale at the shop.

She had thought it all through. They would take only duplicate copies, nothing rare, and therefore not really be vandalizing a treasurehouse of civilization. She and a couple of accomplices would bring the books from the stacks to Toby at the circulation desk, where instead of filling out the check-out cards, he would simply stash them in his pocket and no one would be the wiser. All signs of its provenance removed, the contraband would be sold through the shop—to spare her involvement, Sara would be told Cheska and the others had solicited the books from neighborhood attics as donations to the N.S.L. indigent students' fund—and the income split among him, the raiding party, and the N.S.L. treasury. It was a way to wage guerrilla war against "them" at minimal risk. Harvard would never miss the titles if the heist was limited to twenty or thirty a week. "Anyway, we can all use the money," she said, lighting up one of Sara's Camels. "But you're the key to the whole thing."

Nothing she could have said to justify it would have made the plot more than malicious mischief. But juxtaposed the way it was with her sexual favors, it seemed to assign him an implicit obligation to make a go of the scheme. Perhaps it was meant more as a dare, as if this were just another form of thrill for them to share: Their libidinal bond depended on her complicity; this one of rebellion would depend on his.

She switched on the car radio while he sorted it out. Connie Boswell was singing, and then Lanny Ross, and then still more incongruously,

Aunt Jemima doing "Stand Up and Cheer," which had the opposite effect on him. He snapped off the sound and said the idea was dumb and dishonorable. She said not to talk to her about Harvard and dishonor. He said she was making a conspiracy out of simple antiquarian policies. She said if that was how he felt about it—and about her—that was okay and she would find someone else, or some other way, to strike a blow for justice.

In short, he let himself be manipulated in more ways than one. For a time, he considered it a fair bargain. The orgasmic rewards continued. And the risk of his crimes being detected was small, though still real enough for him to turn clammy whenever Cheska or her agents slithered up to the circulation desk with the daily haul. Ducking the cards, as it turned out, took a bit of chicanery; other book borrowers and check-out clerks in the vicinity would likely have spotted any blatant sleight-of-hand that wound up with the cards in his nearest pocket. Instead, he stowed the incriminating slips together in the tray —at the end of, say, all the G's—and as soon as he was alone at his station, yanked them. To fend off guilt pangs, he rationalized two ways. First, Cheska was worth it. Second, it was all right to commit the perfect crime if you were otherwise pure in heart and injured no one else in the process. Neither really comforted him—but the money did come in handy, especially when squiring the moll.

She unfailingly kept her side of their unspoken pact. Even the Sundays she was unwell, she tended him, taking pains to disperse his qualms of selfishness. And when the weather turned freezing and the car would no longer do for their private transactions, she got them a few hours by themselves in the apartment above the shop while Sara was off visiting family. Still, he grew to feel there was something unlovely about the ritual; it was too mechanical and too constricted to produce any feeling beyond release. He longed for the real thing, and told her so.

She was understanding but not encouraging. He argued that her purity was largely a technical matter by that point. She objected, insisting she had drawn the line—it ran unmistakably, if invisibly, like the U.S.-Canadian boundary, on a latitude between her clitoris and hymen —and no one would violate it before the man she chose to share her body for life. He could not keep from asking how many others had shared it to the extent he had. She wondered why he asked, noting it was hardly gallant of him. He said it fell under the same general heading of idle curiosity as wanting to see how far a fellow could piss.

Her eyes slid past his to the endtable where Sara kept half a dozen depleted cigarette packs. "Not many," she said, rummaging hungrily through them for a smoke. She must have sensed that such ambiguous candor served more to discredit her than reassure him, because she added, as soon as her match was struck, "And nobody you know."

That helped. But he never could outgrow the feeling that he was an interlude for her, carnally speaking. As a result, he would not believe it was enough that she got as good as she gave in their sexual exchanges; his only hope for protracting the pleasure was to remain her accomplice in the looting of Widener. He had become a prisoner of his own insecurity.

Events after the holidays forced his conflicts into the open. On New Year's Day, Toby told his father he wanted to stay at Harvard for an advanced degree in literature, leaving till afterward whether he would teach or write for a living, or both. Teaching his father thought a thankless sort of life and certainly unremunerative. And writing, to him, was more a pastime than a profession. The choice was Toby's, unarguably, but the family's reduced circumstances left him without means to finance his son's ascent to the higher reaches of academe; it had been all he could manage to get the boy this far. On returning to Cambridge, Toby applied at once for one of the few graduate fellowships available for the following fall.

"Have you the mistiest notion of what you'd be in for?" Graham asked, testing his resolve. Unless he intended to make a career of ministering to runny noses or the masturbatory excesses of boarding-school boys, the tutor assumed Toby had a university career in mind. When he said perhaps, Graham hastened to disabuse him of any Olympian illusions he might have been harboring about the professoriate. It was populated, his counselor said, largely by three sorts: The rich, because they could manage on the pittance attached to most college positions; the sycophants, because academic authority invariably flowed to the most ardent appeasers of the established order; and the effete, not a few of them practicing pansies, because it was possible to survive forever on a university campus doing next to nothing, so long as one was personable and unabrasive. "And you, dear boy, are far too scruffy, too principled, and too gifted to apply for this unworthy team." If Toby wanted to write, then he should go off somewhere else and do it. The muses were not domiciled in college halls.

Graham's own residence there, Toby pointed out, somewhat discredited his counsel. "Not a bit," the tutor said. "I am the exception that proves the rule." And Travis? "Between you and me—and I shall deny it to the grave and haunt you evermore if you tattle—Travis *is* the rule. Aside from being burdened with a reforming conscience, or the semblance of one, he plays the game smashingly. And his output epitomizes scholarship at its most jejune—lucid in spots yet largely impenetrable—slightly original yet safely derivative—spiritual and cosmic yet fibrous and petty—a sort of profound meringue, so to speak, and just as forgettable."

Forewarned, Toby nevertheless proceeded with his application for the graduate grant. But he was incapable of compounding his felony by soliciting Harvard for financial aid while continuing to rob from it. Indeed, if there had been a way, he would have made restitution. Cheska claimed not to see the contradiction. Her turbulence had led her into byzantine moralizing.

The very week he retired from her racket, she reported that Sara would be in her apartment all day Sunday, so their recreation would have to be suspended for the time being. On the chance the two things were unrelated, he proposed they take a room at the Brattle Inn—it was two dollars a day.

"That's repulsive," she said. "I don't need to pay for it."

"But it's all right for me to," he said.

She looked puzzled. Then he said what he meant.

"And you think I wouldn't have been with you all these weeks if you hadn't—cooperated?" she asked. Before he could soften her rephrasing of his charge, she planted her hand against his ear with a stinging force he had always supposed her capable of. "Thank you for thinking me into a prostitute," she snarled and marched off.

III

Cheska's belief that Harvard was a hotbed of anti-semitism and political reaction did not square with what facts and impressions Toby had collected. Such traces of these tendencies as may have existed, he suggested to her, stemmed not from any malevolent growth in the subsoil of the Yard but a kind of generalized, sneering superiority toward the humbler assortment of humanity; the pain of others was a matter of conditioned indifference to certain Harvard gentlemen. These diehard vestiges of traditional Brahminism were best ignored as phobic laments for a tidy world that was gone forever.

She drew some comfort from this reading of Harvard's supercilious syndrome—until the news broke that a ranking official of Nazi Germany had been invited, as an honored participant, to the university's commencement in June.

The courtesy was extended, it had to be said in mitigation, not because Ernst Franz Sedgwick Hanfstaengl was the German foreign press secretary and one of Chancellor Hitler's earliest and closest financial backers but because he was a proud member of Harvard's class of 1909, due to celebrate its twenty-fifth reunion at the commencement. By tradition, selected members of that reunion class served in top hat and morning coat as marshals at the annual university exercises. The chief marshal for this occasion, who happened to be an eminent brain specialist at Harvard Medical School, had asked good old "Putzi," as Hanfstaengl was affectionately known to his classmates, to join the honor guard. Not only did Putzi accept with alacrity; he said he would bring along, for exhibition to the class, a film he had made that "can show better than any words of mine what we Nazis stand for."

"And I suppose you'll be attending?" asked Cheska, furious at the news.

"Which," Toby said, "the movie or commencement?"

"Oh, God—I knew it."

She seemed almost to relish his innocent confirmation of her dread. "Meaning what—I'm like all the rest?"

"More than not."

"Hey, it's my own graduation—not just some two-bit Nazi's big reunion. Why should I let him piss on my parade?"

Up shot those Lord-beseeching eyes of hers. "You know," she said, "you have a disgustingly convenient way of applying and discarding principles. Some people would find it an excuse for low character."

To prove his constancy, she wanted him to circulate a letter to the *Crimson* to be signed by as many members of the senior class as he could get to say they would not accept their diplomas at any ceremony in which a book-burning Nazi played an official part. He told her you didn't fight tyranny by abridging the freedom of people repugnant to you. Rupe agreed. That only made Cheska twice as furious and more determined to stir up a boycott.

She found few Gentile sympathizers. Although the metropolitan papers reported that a number of Jewish alumni had protested in private to Harvard officials, the only public complaint was a letter to the *Crimson* from Melvin Kantor, her N.S.L. confrere, who was by then a graduate student in philosophy. Precisely because Harvard had always stood staunchly for toleration of all beliefs, he wrote, it should not be opening its arms to "the representative of a government which considers intellectuals to be the dirt of the earth and free speech a rank poison." With its usual tastefulness, the *Crimson* headed Kantor's letter "Heil Hitler" and declared in an editorial that "to object to the presence of a Harvard man among other Harvard men in any capacity, on purely political grounds, is an extremely childish thing to do."

Still, the Kantor letter was widely quoted in the press, and a week later word came from Berlin that Putzi would not be coming to commencement, after all. There was no explanation beyond his alleged surprise at the controversy over the invitation "as Harvard, since time immemorial, has stood for freedom of opinion." Then it turned out that Hanfstaengl was only one of fifty men in his class who had been chosen as marshals—and instead of being the brutish sort of Nazi, Putzi was reportedly an oversized clown who belonged to a cultivated Munich family long in the international art business and had endeared himself to Hitler by pounding out Wagner and other favorites of the fatherland on the piano for him whenever *der Führer* summoned. Yet Cheska would not concede that the incident may have been blown out of proportion. "A straw in the wind," she said.

And the wind, after a year of Rooseveltism, was howling afresh. The new President had managed to stop things from getting worse, but anxiety persisted, even among his more avid Harvard supporters, like Rupe and the core of the N.S.L., that the New Deal reforms were mere patchwork and it was only a matter of time before another blowout. Even the N.R.A. looked like little more than a placebo; you did not cure the abuses of a rotten industrial system with good-conduct codes.

Economic recovery, meanwhile, was proving stubbornly slow. Every college graduating class in the country that spring was being advised that one third of its members could not expect to find work soon, and many of those who did would have to take jobs for which they were extravagantly overqualified. As the end of college neared, the panicky reality finally arrived for many of them that theirs might prove a generation all dressed up with no place to go.

Even so, few got hot under the collar. Their insecurity nourished conformism, not rebellion, and radicalism remained an incubator baby —an illegitimate one, at that—on most university campuses. Habitual reactionary fulminators like the American Legion, the Hearst press, and the deadly dowagers of the D.A.R. stood ever vigilant against all critical inquiry and tagged every proposed social reform as communistic. Thus, when the escapist fantasies of the troubled young surfaced, they wafted not toward the Soviet-model Left as much as its arch rival in extremism. The ultra-nationalists overseas were mobilized and already on the march, even as the democracies floundered. Militarism was deemed better than chaos, at least, and fascism's fluttering banners were more diverting than an endless depression.

Mars, then, remained a guest lecturer in good standing on most college faculties. The domestic version of the pacifist Oxford Pledge that Rupe and his supporters had hoped to administer to their whole generation proved unpalatable. And when the Supreme Court ruled that land-grant colleges were within their rights to require R.O.T.C. drilling of every male student, the junior peace lobby was sent reeling.

But it did not expire. And as Imperial Nipponese armies stalked Manchuria and Shanghai, and the new tinhorn Caesar in Rome preyed on tropical victims, and the *Wehrmacht* came bristlingly to life despite the sanctions of Versailles, and even Washington found more money for guns, idealistic American college youth decided to usher in that troubled springtime by striking for peace. Every chapter of the National Students League was charged with organizing a classroom walkout on its campus at eleven o'clock on Friday morning, the thirteenth of April.

It was to have been Rupe's finest hour. He had come far since his boisterous freshman days as "Bunghole" Donovan. Under him, the N.S.L. had given social protest at Harvard viability, if not stature. Its membership did not exceed one hundred, and hardly a quarter that many showed up at the regular working sessions, but the league was always busy with something—picketing or petitioning or sponsoring talks by the morally outraged or drumming up support for the flagrantly victimized. It had never mustered a real crowd, though— never touched the Harvard community as a whole; in the peace strike, Rupe saw that opportunity.

To Toby, it was one big straw man. No one in his right mind would stand up and claim to favor war over peace as a sensible social policy—and expect to stay out of the loony bin. If the N.S.L. wanted something real to strike against, he told Rupe, it should have been nationalism, mankind's worst pestilence. Still, striking for peace was more sensible, he supposed, than trying to sweet-talk young America into forswearing all and any war. He said he would help with the publicity. Cheska, supportive from the start, was gloomy that a peace demonstration would be allowed as long as the university was run by a former purveyor of poison gas. "Once a killer," she said, "always a killer."

Rupe, sanguine to the point of delusion, mapped out a mammoth rally, using the steps of Widener as his stage and the heart of the Yard as his theater. He enlisted the other progressive groups in an *ad hoc* coalition, and a provisional program of speakers was readily negotiated. Everything awaited the university's approval for use of its buildings and grounds; in that era, you did not strike Harvard without asking permission first and still expect her to spare the rod afterward.

Barely twenty-four hours in advance, the official word came: yes. This once, at least, blasé Harvard would formally defer to her romantics. Exhilarated, the N.S.L. chapter flew into motion, nailing preprinted placards to every square of wood and cork in sight, plying passersby with leaflets, getting the word out to every dining hall and residential entry in the college. Rupe, awash in adrenaline, was off consolidating the program, arranging for the p.a. system, finding a friendly clergyman for a proper benediction, and polishing his own delivery to a Ciceronian sheen. As the day lengthened, reports filtered in: The student body, while by and large treating the exercise as so much Leftist flatulence, would condescend to honor the strike but try to stay upwind of it.

Later in the evening, Mel Kantor came panting into Toby's room looking for Rupe. He had heard that a bunch of wiseguys would try to disrupt the rally the next morning. Details were lacking, but he gathered the *Crimson* was behind the horseplay, or certainly encouraging it, as the morning edition would disclose. They collected Rupe, who was rehearsing to himself in the dark on the top steps of Widener, and headed for the "Crime" office. No one was there, though, and it was not till after midnight, when the press run was done, that they got hold of a copy. The story was on the top of the first page in the middle column, headed:

MICHAEL MULLINS CHOWDER CLUB TO PROTEST NSL ACT

Old Organization Wants War Of All Descriptions and Virile Types

---

NSL TO HAVE SPEAKERS

Donovan Chairman of Mass Meeting to Be Held at Widener at 11 Today

The story began:

> Incensed by the actions of the National Students League in protesting against all future war, a second organization in the college will today stage a second demonstration at the same time and place to agitate against future peace. . . .

They stayed up till four trying to figure out if it was all just a hoax or a real threat. Mel inclined to the latter view, theorizing it was the dirty doing of the Friends of the New Germany, a shadowy bunch of Harvard and M.I.T. bruisers who were said to meet regularly at the Riverbank Court in sudsy praise of fascism. Since the *Crimson* seemed to be playing the thing for its maximum sneer value, the rest of the N.S.L. brain trust leaned prayerfully to the former view. If a counter-demonstration actually materialized, however, everyone agreed that Rupe and the other program participants were to let it run its course, however disruptive, and at all costs avoid encouraging a scuffle. Peace-lovers did not start swinging when the bully baited them. Anyway, the Harvard cops would be there to clear out any troublemakers.

The Yard elms had barely budded, the grassless sod was still rock-hard, and the sunlight bore a watery cast as if it could not decide whether the somber New England winter had decamped for good, but spring was undeniably on the wing as the Mem. Church bells tolled eleven, and what better way for young hearts to hail the promise of the season than a convocation in the name of goodness?

They streamed into the Yard from every side, by the hundreds, forming a great, fan-shaped throng at the foot of monolithic Widener. Toby had not seen its like in four years at Harvard. Stationed above them, like a lone watchman in the storm, was Rupert Donovan, all dignity in his best oxford-gray flannel, a nimbus of pride oscillating about his slicked-down head. Toby monitored his trembling, imperceptible to anyone else more than a yard from him. They had weathered their differences; Rupe was the brother Toby never had. Seeing him up there, poised like God's arrow, a former ruffian turned impresario of peace, he never thought Rupe more preposterous—or loved him better.

The crowd was festive and expectant, giddy almost, and when Rupe switched on the microphone and it shrieked and whined, they booed merrily till he shut it off. There was no time to waste on repairs, for fear the whole sea of them would evaporate in an instant, so he stepped to one side and began addressing them at the top of his lungs. That earned him a cheer. Hands clasped behind his back not unlike a gradeschooler reciting *Hiawatha* in assembly, he solemnly thanked them all for coming, said he knew the classes they were missing were invaluable but hoped the future of mankind was worth some small sacrifice, and introduced the first speaker.

A second-year law student who as a University of Minnesota under-graduate had led a successful fight to end compulsory R.O.T.C. train-ing there, the fellow got right to cases. Why was America spending half a billion dollars for national "defense," he demanded, unless her political leaders had swallowed the "inevitability of war" theory propounded by the generals and the admirals? And why was the War Department laying out tens of millions for battleships and cruisers when coastal guns, aeroplanes, and submarines were all that was needed for genuinely defensive operations? "The answer lies," he rumbled, as heads already began to revolve restlessly, "in our unacknowledged policy of aggressive imperialism, requiring a constant show of the flag to affirm our commanding place on the high seas with the big boys of the world."

He got only a few fire-breathing words further when the first discordant strains broke around the corner of Weld Hall. In another moment, a collision of blares, honks, rasps, and whines was assaulting six thousand huddled ears. The speaker bowed briefly to the racket, then tried to reclaim his audience with the help of the microphone, which still balked, and finally plowed ahead gamely as the source of the charivari came into view at the fringe of the crowd.

A roar of approval greeted the sight and spread in waves. The sea parted and the antic band made its way forward in roistering disarray. There were a couple of dozen of them, all in outlandish getups, tootling on bugles, bagpipes, tubas, and kazoos as they came; the non-musicians brandished bells, tambourines, and every manner of noise-maker. Laughter rippled sideways in their cacophonous wake. The speaker saw he was overmatched and let the perverse pageant unfold.

In the vanguard paraded a comedian wearing a sandwich sign that proclaimed "DOWN WITH PEACE!" on the front and "DOWN WITH WAR!" on the back; on his head he had one of the Kaiser's helmets from the World War, its spike skewering a *papier-mâché* likeness of either a duck or a dove—whatever it was, was white with feathers. Next came a trio in Nazi outfits, each with a little Hitlerian mustache, *heil*ing and goose-stepping all over one another. Then there was Karl Marx, enmeshed in a jungle of beard and a necklace of tire chain, juggling a bowling ball with a thick rope fuse; John Bull, in a topper and jodhpurs, waving a Union Jack in one hand and a dueling pistol in the other; Joan of Arc, bearing the tricolor and a pitchfork; half a dozen stumbling Doughboys, armed with hockey sticks and blunderbusses, and the rest, in short pants and high socks, making music and hoisting signs with slogans on the order of "BIGGER AND BETTER IMPERIALIST WARS!" and "JINGOISM FOREVER!" An extravaganza of know-nothingism; Toby's heart fell at the slickness of the burlesque.

They came straight up to the foot of Widener's steps. There was no

movement of the Yard cops to head them off. Soapboxes and mega-
phones with swastikas painted on them appeared from nowhere as the
revelers formed a beachhead on the bottom few steps. One of the
masquerading Nazis climbed right up and bellowed through his
megaphone, "Ladies and gentle peoples, I am being Herr Captain
Schnapps!" The crowd cheered. "I comenzie here before you to
shtand up behind you to shpeak of things dat I meinzelf know notzing
about!" The crowd roared. A second mock Nazi jumped up on the
neighboring soapbox, saluted the four points of the compass, and
screamed, "Piss! Piss—or vore—dat's der kvestshun! Vetter it's better
to suffer der shlings und der arrows fromen zie Versailles Treaty—or
buildin' der U-boaten und der Zeppelins mit der bang-bangs und
makin' dem kaput." Hilarity rampant.

Rupe just stood there at first, biting his lower lip while volley upon
volley of laughter pursued this low slapstick. But then he turned from
it and instructed a couple of aides to get the microphone working.
When the high jinks below him started to wear a little thin and the
first boos began to be directed at the rowdy troupe, Rupe was ready.
"We hope you've enjoyed this little madness we've arranged for your
entertainment," his baritone boomed over the Yard, quelling the tumult, "and now we'd like to offer you a little sanity."

As if on cue, knowing they had ridden the crest as long as it would
hold, the company of grotesques dispersed through the crowd, each to
become a heckling irritant in his sector. The program lumbered forward. The law student spoke on war as legalized murder; an historian,
on the unnecessity of the last war; an engineer, on the hardware in the
next one; a psychologist, on the chauvinist mentality; a medical intern,
on the effects of shrapnel on human tissue; a ministerial candidate, on
why God let men slaughter one another. Throughout, the razzing
went on like small-arms fire—hoots, catcalls, bugle blasts, sez-you's,
and *Sieg Heil*'s—much of it distracting, some of it wounding, but
none of it fatal. They saved the real cannonading for the last speaker,
the only undergraduate one.

Rupe had got no more than a sentence or so into his studied remarks
on what his listeners could do for peace when the first missile, an
overripe grapefruit, landed at his feet with a startling splat. He kicked
it aside in rapid recovery and proceeded. But the pelting, intermittent
at first, grew in volume, variety, and velocity. The rain of gushy fruits
and fetid eggs scattered the other speakers and rally organizers, but
Rupe refused his tormentors the satisfaction of cowering. His dark
suit lit up tomato-red and yolk-yellow, yet on he plodded. "Close up,
Bunghole!" someone yelled; echoing jeers followed and multiplied

across the thinning audience. It was as if the remainder, like so many picadors, was readying him for the kill.

Toby's instinct was to move in and drag him off, but he knew he would be repulsed. And where were the damned Yard cops? Why was this assault being permitted? Something brushed Rupe's face, and he flinched, but kept on. Pennies were being flung now, too, and several stung him, and he lowered his head for fear of being blinded, but he kept on.

In the end, he outlasted the barrage—and more than half the crowd. The applause, at the close, was louder than all the mockery had been. After the benediction, he just stood there in what looked like shell-shocked immobility for a long moment, his suit runny with pulp and albumen, until Toby and Cheska separated him from the microphone and led him to safety.

He sat in their room in his putrefying suit all afternoon while Toby played the radio to get his mind off what he had endured. By any fair estimate, it had been a great triumph. The strike attracted a total of 25,000 students across America, according to later reports; Harvard alone drew three thousand, and the substance of the rally was a model of thoughtful advocacy. Rupe, though, wallowed in his suit as if it were a hair shirt, wagging his head reproachfully—at whom, it was not clear—every fifteen minutes or so. Toby opened the windows wide to air out the place while he stewed.

By suppertime, the crisis had passed. With marked deliberateness, Rupe changed clothes to go down to eat and hung the rank suit in their closet. Toby's dubious look registered.

"Don't worry," Rupe said, "I'll keep the door closed."

"Spanish omelette can get pretty aromatic. I'd think seriously about the dry cleaners in the morning."

"I don't know. Not just yet—unless you mind?"

Who could deprive him of that organic souvenir of his valor, even if he judged it a humiliation? "I suppose if it gets too bad," Toby said, "we can always requisition gas masks from Conant."

Rupe nodded thanks without a smile. He smiled little the rest of that spring.

IV

Competition being the lifeblood of America and the *Crimson* being a self-indulgent journal edited from a narrow social perspective, the *Herald*—said the front-page announcement in its first issue—was a long-overdue addition to the Harvard community. The paper would be issued daily through the end of the term; its future thereafter would depend on what the response to it was. The *Lampoon* lost no time in dubbing it the Harvard *Red*.

The money for it was raised by loans, mostly from parents. Rupe's folks came through with three hundred; Mel Kantor's, the same. An N.S.L. commuter from Dorchester named Alpern whose father was a jeweler got them some from a bank using gems as collateral. And Cheska, too proud to ask her own people after going the whole year without their help, hit up Sara Blue for $150, a fortune for her. Within days, the kitty held just under $2,000, enough to see the effort through until they could convince advertisers the *Herald* was legitimate. A printer starved for business was found at the far end of Mass. Ave. for a rock-bottom price. For an office they rented a two-room, second-floor suite above a bakery on Church, just across the Square from the Yard, and hauled in beat-up desks, typewriters with almost all their keys, more phones than they could afford, and a large coffeepot.

The staff, materializing almost overnight, came for both refuge and adventure. Two editors and three writers who could no longer stomach its smug, clubby attitude defected from the *Crimson* (and were banned for life from returning to it). They were joined by a star cartoonist from the *Lampoon;* a batch of public school graduates who had heeled for the "Crime" and not made it for what seemed to them social failings, day students with Italian and Jewish names who had never had or made the time before for any extracurricular activity, and too many recruits who were longer on Leftist political ideology than journalistic technique.

Cheska took a leave from Sara's shop to run the office, keep the books, ferry copy to the printer, and hover watchfully over the daily editorial conference. Rupe, with his thesis still to finish, was given the honorary title of assistant general manager; in return, he donned Cheska's old newsboy cap and his gray suit jacket, still caked with debris but no longer redolent of the peace rally, and hawked copies of the *Herald* every noontime from a table in front of Widener. Donovan's revenge. And Toby, with his professional newspaper experience as a hard-bitten writer of obituaries, became one of the three associate editors who directed operations co-equally and with little or no acrimony. His specialty was editing out dangling participles and dreaming up story ideas that linked the college world to the real one. It was the perfect lark to wind up his undergraduate career.

In marked contrast to the *Crimson*, which filled its front page with such cerebral items as the freshman ball team's stunning annihilation of the yearling Providence nine, every issue of the *Herald* carried grist for the thoughtful. When the debating club argued Dartmouth on the topic "Resolved, that a national police force shall be created," they sent a stenographer along with a reporter, ran meaty chunks of what both sides said, and commented editorially—strongly against ("Jackboots Don't Fit Uncle Sam," Toby headlined his piece). They investigated the early effects of Prohibition repeal on the college's drinking and studying habits ("Liquor, Liquor Everywhere—But Do You Stop to Think?"). And they even managed to wangle an interview with that most elusive character, the president of Harvard University.

President Lowell had rarely admitted the gentlemen of the press, student variety included, to his ivied sanctum, so few probing policy questions were ever put, let alone answered, except on the university's terms and timetable. Wispy James Conant was more accessible his first year in office, but the sluggish *Crimson* failed to pursue him. The *Herald* applied for an interview its first week of publication, but likely due to reports that it was staffed by irresponsible radicals, he held them off. But not for long.

President and Mrs. Conant served tea Sundays from four to six to any Harvard people who cared to come by their home on Quincy Street. Toby spruced up a bit and, in the company of two younger *Herald* staffers, decided to beard the lion in his den. If he was ever to meet a president of Harvard, this was the moment: Before, he had lacked the social confidence; afterward, he would lack the motivation.

In the flesh, this particular lion bore little resemblance to the arch fiend Cheska had painted. Instead, Toby found a singularly calm, quite genial man with very straight, very silky, very blond hair and a manner attentive even to undergraduates. He expressed polite, if cautious interest in the venture Toby and his colleagues had launched and said it was a healthy thing for the college.

"In that case, sir, would you welcome an open exchange of views between the administration and the student body?" Toby asked, all innocence.

It came out sounding rhetorical, and Dr. Conant, evidently taking it as such, made agreeable sounds. He did not mean then and there, it was evident, but etiquette never being the hallmark of journalistic enterprise, Toby steeled himself for a short game of entrapment.

"Some of us have been wondering, sir," he probed, teacup tremulous, "now that the House Plan has been such a great democratizing step forward for Harvard, if the university is truly fulfilling its destiny as long as it is closed, practically speaking, to the children of the poor."

Dr. Conant examined the question for booby traps, then proceeded to answer it without haste. Harvard had no means test for admission, of course, so the premise of the inquiry was not correct. A number of men and women had always worked their way through Harvard.

"Are you suggesting, sir," Toby countered respectfully, "that hardship is good for the character?"

The broad presidential brow flexed and the pale eyes narrowed. "What did you say your name was again, young man?"

"Ronan, sir—Tobias Ronan '34—sir."

His Serene Harvardness nodded, filing the name permanently in an inviolable recess of that high cranium, and proceeded to deal with the question substantively. "No, Mr. Ronan—in fact, it seems to me a social waste to make a young man of intellectual promise spend long, weary hours performing nonintellectual tasks. It taxes his physical strength and may even break his morale." His goal, Dr. Conant went on, was that 10 to 15 percent of each class at Harvard should receive a completely free education. Already, in fact, he had instructed the admissions office to search out promising scholarship material rather than merely winnow the best from those who applied. He particularly wanted more people from the Midwest and farther away so that Harvard might achieve better balance and keep from growing hidebound.

Toby nodded eager agreement. Then, as offhandedly as he could manage but with throat catching in giveaway anxiety, he said, "I trust you have no objection to our quoting you to that effect?"

Dr. Conant blinked twice and then assumed a suddenly steely look. "I conduct my interviews in the office, Mr. Ronan. If you apply to my secretary, I'm sure we can—"

"We've already applied, sir."

"Well, then I'm sure you'll be hearing soon. My schedule is quite—"

"Excuse me, sir, but I thought you told us a few moments ago that you favored an open exchange between students and the administration?"

"Yes, young man, but I don't necessarily expect it to take place in my own living room—when I'm not prepared—in a social setting. I don't consider that a gentlemanly way to proceed. My remarks to you were informal and not intended for publication."

Toby's courage was all but exhausted. In the nick of time, one of his *Herald* sidekicks put in, "But you knew we were student reporters, sir—we said so right off."

"I also took you for Harvard gentlemen—and they do not bushwhack the president of the university."

"The policies you expressed, sir," Toby rallied, "do honor to the university. Our only purpose is to strengthen it—the same as yours."

There was a long, silent pause. "All right," said the president of

Harvard, "but in the future, anything between us will be on the up and up." And he turned from them in undisguised annoyance.

They pooled their notes back at the office and bannered the story:

FEARFUL OF GROWING STUFFY, HARVARD TO ADD HOI POLLOI

It was their first scoop—and last interview with James B. Conant.

But the paper's impact was unmistakable. It even got under the skin of the *Crimson*, which told advertisers that its upstart rivals were communists, their printer that they were deadbeats, and everybody else that they were the ignorant sons of ill-mannered immigrants. But at Harvard that spring, nearly everybody read the *Herald*.

Their vendetta with the *Crimson*, which conceived of fascism as a distended Mardi Gras, turned uglier in May when the Nazi warship *Karlsruhe* made Boston the last stop on its 'round-the-world maiden voyage. The six-thousand-ton light cruiser was given far more than the courtesy of the port; all Beantown positively fawned over the blue-eyed baron who captained the ship and his heel-clicking crew of six hundred. Governor Ely and Mayor Curley received the officers at the statehouse and city hall, M.I.T. students welcomed the cadets with open arms, and the vessel itself was berthed at the Charlestown Naval Yard directly next to the U.S.S. *Constitution*—"Old Ironsides"—as if in tacit declaration that here were two different but equally legitimate models of the ship of state.

If the Hanfstaengl episode had upset Cheska, the arrival of the *Karlsruhe* drove her close to frenzy. Perhaps the virulence of Naziism had been overdrawn, Toby said; perhaps it would stop pandering to the frustrations of the *Volk*, now that its hold on power was secure. "And perhaps the Pope is a pederast," she said. "Delude yourself all you'd like—that's their whole game."

But he made her come with him to see firsthand if the Hun wore horns.

They toured the ship on a fine Sunday afternoon along with thousands eager to gawk at the floating showcase of *Deutschland* reborn. You could have eaten *knockwurst* off those decks. The crew was as immaculate as the conveyance. Even the turrets, with their thorny cluster of eight-inch cannon, looked as if they were polished and perfumed after every round. Only the antiaircraft guns, with their whiff of burned powder, hinted of any death-dealing mission. In the spotless wardroom, under a wall ikon of the bemedaled *Führer*, the aryan captain suavely lighted cigarettes for the spellbound ladies and politely told the men that his ship made thirty-two knots without straining the boilers.

"God, he's beautiful—the filthy swine," Cheska whispered, holding Toby's hand tight the whole while. "But why do they all look like wire-haired terriers on the top?"

"For sanitary reasons, no doubt."

She shook her head. "I'll bet they take enemas every night."

There was nothing grudging, though, about the notices the vessel won in the next day's *Transcript*. "One was reluctant to leave the ship," the reporter exulted, "so clean it was, so perfectly controlled, so abounding in efficient, proud, capable people." Nearby was a related story headlined "HITLER WARS ON GRUMBLERS, CHIEFLY JEWS," who were blamed for Germany's dwindling foreign trade. So artful was Nazi propaganda that in neither the article nor the heading did the *Transcript* bother to put "grumblers" within quotation marks; allegation had become orthodoxy—and that was what ran in the most civilized newspaper in the most civilized city in America.

Appeasement of the Valkyrie was not quite unanimous. A demonstration was called by maritime workers for the end of the ship's week-long stay. The event grew rapidly into something more than a gesture of sympathy for the hostage status of organized labor under Hitler. The Women's International League for Peace, in which Sara Doyle Blue was a stalwart, denounced the Nazis for "many acts of violence" and promised to turn out in force at the gates of the shipyard. Radical, liberal, and pacifist factions at every college in the Boston area found common cause in the protest. And when word arrived via Sara that Anton Sota was trucking in idled textile workers to swell the ranks of protesters, a confrontation of runaway potential threatened.

Having already proven themselves boot-licking hosts, city officials let it be known they would not tolerate demonstrations against the representatives of a friendly nation. Legions of cops were to be deployed around the navy yard; anyone marching or picketing without a permit would be arrested for disturbing the peace—and, it went without saying, no permit would be issued if applied for.

"Your standard tsarist repression," said Cheska. "Let's all go cover it."

The demonstration was set for late afternoon—after school and after work for most people. The *Herald* bunch went in by the el and was caught up almost at once in the confluence of streaming marchers on north Washington Street on the Boston side of the Charlestown Bridge. A red flag with anti-Nazi slogans that someone had stuck on top of the water tower on the Hoosac Wharf beckoned like a beacon across the river. No one sang the "Internationale" or "Solidarity

Forever"—and Toby was glad of it, for they were not his anthems and he belonged to nobody's party. But he could feel the unison in the vibrating tread as unregimented multitudes trooped across the bridge in a surge of indignation. He was consumed by the fusing power of it.

For weeks he had been doodling swastikas on the margins of books and the backs of envelopes, studying the ancient symbol, so lately disinterred, for the secret of both its allure and menace. Upright, it was a pleasing pattern of parallels and perpendiculars; tilted forty-five degrees, it became a wicked whirligig, each corner a honed blade, each poised arm a blunt instrument of torture—geometry turned lethally jagged. Elbows linked with Cheska and Rupe, he walked into its mad, pummeling path.

The protest was to be staged outside the Wapping Street gate to the navy yard, within theoretical earshot of the Nazi sailors, so the authorities took no chances. The crowd was funneled off the bridge straight up to Charlestown City Square, where the cops were waiting to pen them in. The steady shove of new arrivals put unbearable pressure on the blocked passageway till, at the flash point, the congestion turned into a melee.

In front, the lines swayed and buckled before the cops' rearing horses and flailing sticks. Soon the shouting and shoving spread through the ranks as wedges of police broke the throng apart and everywhere kicks and punches were being delivered indiscriminately. Cheska had been right: It was the Winter Palace guard shattering the St. Petersburg workers in '05; all that was missing were the bullets. But the horses' flying hoofs were savage enough at close quarters, and blood flowed, and the clubbed and bruised went down, and in the confusion and fear and impotence that the sudden terror had injected, the main mass was turned sideways to the fray and driven back, helpless and outraged. Two dozen of the more intrepid combatants were hauled away in paddy wagons, and ambulances were already arriving for the fallen when Toby and the others reached the bridge in retreat. It was all over in a few minutes—a famous victory for the constabulary. The shock of being brutalized, and unable to do anything more heroic about it than duck, left them numb and bewildered.

At the *Herald* office later, Toby was still trying to reassemble the slivers for the next morning's lead story when Cheska telephoned from the bookshop. Sara, having tried to part the scalp of a cop with her anti-Nazi poster, was among the demonstrators jailed. They were to be arraigned first thing in the morning when bail money would be needed. "They're talking about two thousand dollars," Cheska said, her voice at the edge of panic.

"Each—or for the lot?"

"Toby—stop being an idiot!"

Crisis did not add greatly to her charms. He said that was a lot of bail for a charge like that and asked if she could have got it wrong in the excitement. The German ambassador was due in town the next day for the *Karlsruhe*'s send-off, she explained impatiently, and the police wanted high bail to discourage a repeat performance at dock-side. "It sounds illegal as hell," he said.

"I'll tell the judge you said so. Look, we could raid our bank account for a part of what we need—"

"Who's 'we'?"

"The *Herald*. I mean she's not going to jump bail—we'll get it all back as soon as they hold the hearing."

"Meanwhile, we could go bust."

"Or the world could blow up. Now listen, she helped us out when we needed it—and the least we can do is help her when she needs us."

"Not at the risk of losing everything. She wouldn't want that."

There was a pause, then a mighty sigh of concession. "Who do we know with two thousand dollars to spare to help out a real nice lady?"

"A real nice communist lady."

"She's not a real communist, for God sakes. She's just a little bit on the radical side."

"That's enough." The only name he could think of proposing was Travis's.

"Oh, yes! Of course! He's perfect! Will you call him—please—right away—and explain—?"

"You call him. You've got all the dope—and you're Sara's pal."

"But he doesn't know me—and he knows you well—"

"I'd rather not."

"Why on earth not? It's an emergency—and he and Sara are friends—"

"It's a little delicate."

"Why? All he can do is say no."

"It's more than that."

"What are you talking about? Sara's in *jail*—"

"He's reading my thesis—right now—and grading it. Everything depends on it—the fellowship—my whole future—"

"And you think he's going to grade you off just because you—"

"Harvard doesn't exactly throw scholarship money at radicals."

"You—a radical? Travis is twice as far left."

"He doesn't know that. What's he supposed to think if I—"

"Christ in heaven!" she exploded. "Why can't you do something for once in your life without being such a goddamned worrywart?"

"Because I'm too poor," he said, "and too smart." And hung up.

She called back in two minutes, apologized, and renewed her plea. "Do this one last thing—pretty please—and I'll never ask you for another favor as long as I live—I swear to God, Toby—please—"

Travis's friend Julian Fairchild answered. The professor would not be back till quite late. Toby explained the problem. "How dreadful," Fairchild said. "On the other hand, I think we ought perhaps to spare the professor involvement in any of this. It's a sensitive area." Toby started to suggest that the decision might best be left to the professor when Fairchild cut in. "Suppose I simply make the arrangements myself?"

Besides Sara, others in the greater Harvard community—including a couple of undergraduates, an assistant professor's wife, and a law student of Zechariah Chafee, the university's ranking civil libertarian—had fallen victim to the Boston police. The *Herald*'s account of the carnage was accompanied by a front-page editorial proposing that a campus-wide committee be formed at once to protest the intolerable act of police repression.

The call was promptly heeded by nearly every political group as well as the debating club, the *Law Review*, and many of the service organizations. But if the effort was also to attract the endorsement of the faculty and administration so that Harvard might speak out against such barbarism with a single thunderous nay, it was essential to enlist the weightiest voice in the college—the *Crimson*. Since the original proposal had been the *Herald*'s—and the *Crimson* declined officially to recognize its existence—high diplomacy was required.

The Liberal Club acted as intermediary. Its president, a mild fellow of impeccable pedigree whom Toby had known slightly from his days as a member, came by his room to relay the *Crimson*'s terms. They would give full support and generous coverage to the protest if (a) the *Herald* dropped out of the cause entirely or (b) no Jews served on the steering committee.

"Not very decent of them," he apologized. The terms, apparently, stemmed from the *Crimson*'s conviction that the *Herald* was essentially funded and run by Jews of subversive and unattractive character. As for the steering committee, the two Jews tentatively designated were quite objectionable—Francesca da Silva, secretary of the Harvard N.S.L., a notorious Leftist and reportedly a woman of easy virtue, and a fellow named Levin from Chicago, who was the articles editor of the *Law Review* and personified the heavy Jewish infiltration at the Law School.

Toby polled the Christian members of the *Herald*, who made up two thirds of the staff. They were divided about equally, one fraction preferring the *Herald* to quit in order to save the protest movement, the other for telling the *Crimson* to go directly to hell. The division of opinion forced him and the other two editors to choose. Sometimes, he argued to them with irony worthy of Graham Halyard, expediency was the highest principle. They pulled the *Herald* out of it without advising the Jewish staff members till it was a *fait accompli*.

Toby told Cheska over breakfast. All his earlier excuses for Harvard's genteel bigotry tasted ashen to him now. "I can understand how lowlife need somebody to lord it over," he said, "but these people have everything. I just thought Harvard was a lot better about this sort of business than any place else."

"It is," she said. "That's the problem." She stirred her coffee slowly. He had not seen her so composed before at a moment of turmoil. "Do you understand now?" she asked, eyes fastened on the tiny whirlpool she was sustaining in the cup. He said yes, that everyone on the paper did and many others, besides. "Then it's worth it," she said and looked up clear-eyed, which was more than he could manage. "Jesus, you're crying—"

"Hay fever," Toby said.

She put her hand over his. "A common semitic condition—very catching, they say."

The *Herald* stopped publishing on the last day of May, a week before the term ended. The Jewish clothiers, who were its biggest advertisers, said they could afford space in only one Harvard newspaper —and the *Crimson* did far better for them. In the end, the staff managed to return fifty cents on the dollar to their blessed lenders. The whole effort, hastily arranged and devotedly executed, had shamed the *Crimson*, they told themselves, and raised the level of compassion at the university one small notch. At the least—and most—it was a moral victory.

Their satisfaction was short-lived. A week before commencement, the papers reported that Ernst Hanfstaengl had reversed his earlier decision reversing his still earlier decision and was even then on the high seas bound for America and the year-end festivities at Harvard. The *Crimson* compounded its past sins with an editorial recommending that Putzi be awarded an honorary degree at the commencement. A doctorate of fine arts for Hitler's piano player. As a joke, it was callous; as policy, unforgivable.

When he arrived in New York, the press fell all over Putzi, running long, friendly interviews that brushed lightly over his dismissal of the Jewish question as one not fruitfully discussed in American newspapers. In Boston, he was assigned a flying wedge of state troopers and city detectives to fend off any ill-wishers. In Cambridge, both the president and president emeritus of Harvard received the Nazi official in their homes as an alumnus in good standing, and his classmates in the area vied for his attentions. All honor to the vandal.

What had been a bittersweet interlude for Toby at the close of his undergraduate career now turned into active melancholy. To rout it, he drove Cheska down to the Cape for an afternoon. They roamed the dunes above Barnstable, playing back the three years they had known each other and embracing with an intensity they had not reached before. He took it as a spasm of fond farewell; something tender had prevailed over all their irritable ups and downs. Her "easy" virtue, though, remained as obdurate as ever.

On the drive back, he told her he wished there were a way to vent his sorrow over everything that had happened that spring.

"Don't be sorry," she said, "be proud."

"Of what?"

"Of being you—of caring—and understanding—and not giving in." And if he still wanted to tell Harvard off, he could picket the commencement. "I'll help," she said. "We could do it by the Yard gate—" She cut herself short. "But you'll never do that now, not with your nice, fat fellowship for next year." She glanced out the window on her side. "I guess I can't blame you—much."

More than self-preservation restrained him. His father was coming up to see him graduate—a rare fulfillment in a life that had been steadily emptying—and he was bringing along Toby's mother's sister from Poughkeepsie. Aunt Ida was not exactly Krupskaya, he explained, and the sight of him picketing, even in cap and gown, would be enough to shatter his capitalist-lackey father's last pretensions to managerial status. "I couldn't do that to him."

"Sure," she said.

"I'll try to think of something else."

"Sure," she said. "Me, too."

V

Rupe slew his own consuming demons on commencement eve.

Their families had spent Class Day together—the House luncheon, the alumni parade to Soldiers' Field, the confetti fight in the stands, a lobster dinner at Locke's, the glee club concert afterward—and hit it off fine. Their anti-New Deal fathers vied for belly-laugh honors when the Class of '19 marched into the stadium in costumes mocking the N.R.A. and waving signs like "We Have a Code in the Head," "The Blue Eagle Is a Yale Bird," and "NRA = Never Refuses Alcohol." Rupe and Toby were less enthusiastic about the Class of '24 tribute to Hanfstaengl. A couple of hundred strong, they goose-stepped past him and gave the Nazi salute while Putzi, a gangling figure who had spurned his reunion costume for a blue jacket, brown shirt and trousers, class tie, red carnation, and soft dark hat, beamed benignly back. Were they cheering or jeering him? Ah, the ineffable subtlety of Harvard humor! Would that age improved it.

After dinner, en route to the concert, Toby's aunt confided to him that Rupe seemed a refined and well-spoken young man but she wondered a bit about his taste in clothing.

"His jacket, you mean?"

"Yes," she said. "Isn't it rather—?"

"Unsightly?"

"Well, to be truthful—"

"You should have seen it last month."

The thing had turned tastefully dingy and interestingly scaly by then and its former foulness had worn off altogether, but it would still never make the front window at Langrock's. He explained to Aunt Ida that it had become a point of honor with Rupe not to have the jacket cleaned. "How odd," she said—which was the point, of course. The college had hurt and wronged him, and displaying this sartorial disaster it had inflicted was his way of trying to move it to contrition.

Toward the end of the concert, the glee club struck up a medley of college tunes—"On, Wisconsin," the Maine "Stein Song," "Boola, Boola," and finally, the rousing "Harvardiana." Just before the second run-through of the last, Rupe rose in his place in the middle of Memorial Hall. Every head turned toward him in bewilderment. Toby shriveled. Murmurs rode to the rafters; those who knew about his jacket had to explain to those who didn't. And then he was singing, as lustily as he could and louder than the lot of them on stage:

> *With crim-son in tri-umph fla-shing*
> *'Mid the strains of vic-to-ry,*
> *Poor Eli's hopes we are da-shing*
> *Into blue ob-scur-i-ty . . .*

Toby understood. Rupe was forgiving them. He was saying they had never honored him, never even taken him seriously, only rejected him from the first and mocked him to the last, but he loved the university for what it had let him find out about himself—and he was honoring it now, thanking them all for everything, the bad with the good, because adversity had made him a man. Joyfully, pridefully, fraternally, Toby stood up beside him and joined in:

> *Re-sist-less our team sweeps goal-ward*
> *With the fu-ry of the blast,*
> *We'll fight for the name of Har-vard*
> *Till the last white line is passed. . . .*

One by one, then in pairs, then en masse all over the hall, those who would graduate in the morning rose for the imperative chorus:

> *Har-vard!* [like a thunderclap, pause two beats]
> *Har-vard!* [echoing, half a note lower]
> *Har-vard!* [higher and more urgent]
> *Har-vard!* [same note, yet more passion]
> *Har-vard-HAR-VARD-HAAAAAR-VARD!!!* [deliriously].

When the whole place was standing, Rupe, in ecstasy, climbed up on his seat, stripped off his robe of martyrdom, and waved it over his head like a banner as he conducted a third and final rendition in double time. At the end he ripped the putrid jacket straight up the tail vent and heaved the two halves far into the air. A great cheer followed them. Rupert Donovan and Harvard '34 had made their peace.

Toby's own inner turbulence defied such spectacular resolution.

All during the commencement ceremonies in Sever Quad the next morning, he sat unhearing in that ancient, leafy Yard and tried to take an accounting. Rupe, for all his appearance as an adversary, had come to Harvard as a supplicant and was swept up by his yearning for her validation—a need to be told he mattered; Toby was different. He had come as a nonbelligerent and never dreamed of conquest, or even recognition. His adventure with the place was private; his Harvard, not a "she" or a "they" but an "it," there for him to savor and be nourished by. He was not altogether characterless on arrival—even empty vessels have a shape—but cognition turned him protean, and he refused to harden. Harvard yielded not truths so much as infinite paradoxes:

His freshman year, he had learned life is so immense that ambition is probably as pointless as torpor.

His sophomore year, he had learned that neither woman nor justice is bestowed on man by nature—and their high cost in anguish is the world's best bargain.

His junior year, he had learned the length of eternity and the brevity of earnestness; only ice-cream sodas lacked futility.

And his senior year—what had he learned exactly? That each man is an island? He had known that; it just needed pitiless corroboration. Why, then, had he finished that spring feeling so violenced and hollow—so sure that whoever he was becoming and whatever it was he would do were of not the least interest to the wind and the night? The problem was that he had all but abandoned faith in the very conception of moral transcendence. It was impossible to ignore the evidence. Evil was damned well prospering. Good was abjectly failing. And calamity appeared to be no respecter at all of innocence. What if injustice ultimately ruled the world as indifference did the cosmos—and resurrection followed crucifixion just that Once? Of what, then, did the virtuous life consist? Off the events of his senior year, he was unprepared to believe there was such a thing. More plausibly, life's "meaning" was process, not purpose—and ideology was clamorous delusion.

The awarding of the honorary degrees recalled him from his bosky wayside. Was it even remotely possible Harvard herself would help usher in the *Götterdämmerung* by placing laurels on Ernst Franz Sedgwick Hanfstaengl—the apothesis of brutishness? Toby scanned the pavilion that held the dignitaries. No one remotely resembling the Nazi oaf was visible. Why, then, was he holding his breath all through the calling forth of recipients? Because unthinkable things had been happening throughout that year, and everywhere he saw decency invalided or dying.

The honoraries went to President Dodds of Princeton and eight other worthies of whom Toby had never heard. A modicum of sanity still resided in Cambridge.

The luncheon break was a blur of pomp and color. Gowned thousands milling among billowy tents. Hoods shot scarlet and crimson and puce. The band played "Carioca" and other unstuffy tunes while over there prim President Conant chatted with ruddy J. Pierpont Morgan '89 *sans* midget but with stogie at full fume. Dozens of marshals in silk hats and cutaways from the Class of "Naughty 'Nine" circulated but nowhere in that throng, under any tree or tent, behind any bush or Brahmin, was Putzi.

Still, Toby was uneasy. Before dawn that morning, the college had been littered with signs denouncing Hanfstaengl and Hitler, but the Yard police had assiduously removed every trace. No doubt Cheska had had a hand in that bit of diehard defiance. She was unquenchable. All spring, as the outrages piled up, she seemed to him to become more resolute, as if none of it really surprised her. His own response, beyond the almost recreational tour on the *Herald*, remained muted. To the end, no adequate way to express his gathering disaffection had come to mind, short of making a spectacle of himself at the commencement as she had proposed. He had tried more than once to write a poem brimming with acidic disdain but all that kept coming out was molten *Weltschmerz*.

As he sat in drowsy reverie distancing himself from the afternoon ceremonies, an apparition formed to his extreme right. There, twenty yards away, taking seats just inside the railing that closed off the makeshift arena, were Cheska and her friend Bonnie, a townie whose father had been trying for years to organize a union of his fellow high school teachers.

The sight of them alerted his sluggish mind. Why had they come—and how? Casual spectators were not invited to this intramural event. In the morning, every entrance to the Yard had been carefully guarded to screen outsiders. But by midafternoon, apparently, security had turned lax, and the two young women, in proper pastel dresses and smart straw hats, must have slipped by unsuspected. Why, though, on a soft bright June day, were they wearing shawls? His curiosity did not go long unsatisfied.

As President Conant entered the ninth sphere of rapture in his gratitude to the Class of '09 for coughing up a gift of $100,000 to alma mater on this twenty-fifth anniversary of its commencement, Toby noticed Cheska and her accomplice stir in their places. They slipped off their shawls, revealing a most indelicate set of chains bunched about their swanlike necks and handcuffed to their milky wrists. Almost casually, and without so much as a clink, they wound the chains around their chairs and through the railing behind them. Then they locked the chains with a second set of handcuffs, inserted the keys daintily into their cleavages, stood up, and began to shout for all they were worth, "Down with Hitler! Down with Hanfstaengl! No honors for Nazi butchers! Give Hanfstaengl a degree—Master of Torture! Free Thaelman, Michaelson, and all imprisoned antifascists!" Then again, in singsong litany.

Harvard, regally celebrating her two-hundred-ninety-eighth year of existence, stopped.

The tableau lasted a single exquisite instant—a triumph of coarse courage over preening gentility. That the shrill indictment shamed anyone who needed to be was doubtful. Any hope the two perpetrators might have harbored of cueing a sympathetic chorus among the crowd was forlorn. For when their clear, sharp voices penetrated the august gathering from one side of the Yard to the other a third time, the surprise that had momentarily immobilized it gave way to shouts of "Radicals!" and a hubbub of clucking disapproval over so untimely, unworthy, and unladylike a disturbance. Cops converged from the treetops. When it was discovered the still-shouting protesters had anchored themselves to the spot, they were ordered silent on pain of dismemberment. They howled on.

He went to her. Without calculation, without thought of any sort, certain only that he had to stand by her as the cops grew more frenzied in their efforts to disengage these unrelenting harpies.

He bumped and shoved his way through the audience, which had been drawn to its feet in unintended tribute to the disgraceful performance. He kept catching and losing sight of her in the crush. The cops were working frantically now to remove the portion of railing to which the pair was chained. The gap between him and her had become a gauntlet of throbbing enmity. At last he crashed through the circle of hissing spectators around them and groped for her flailing arm as the cops tried to shake and pry her loose. Her hair was swinging long and shiny and wild and her face was on fire with her mission. Then she saw him and shut her eyes with relief and grabbed at his shoulder and hung on for her life. It was like a profane wedding ceremony, lovers locked in desperate embrace while officials and guests readied a funeral pyre instead of a feast to mark the nuptials.

"I wanted to deliver your graduation present in person!" she shouted into his ear and managed a glancing kiss before they began to tug her from his grasp. He yelled whether there was bail money and she burst into a mixture of laughter and tears. "You're incredible!" she yelled back and said not to worry and that Sara was standing by and that she loved him for coming to her like this. And then the clutch of them were being dragged off until something very blunt caught his head behind the ear, sparing him both the hoosegow and the closing rituals of his collegiate career.

"I take it one of those young women was a friend of yours?" Aunt Ida asked afterward, nursing Toby's bump with her hankie.

"Is," he said. "She's been upset—"

"Evidently." She looked a little cross with him. "You certainly seem to favor friends who are rather—rather—"

"Demonstrative?"

"To say the least." And she hugged him—thankful, probably, that his own exhibitionist tendencies were under better check.

The incident hit the front page of *The New York Times* the next morning: "ANTI-NAZIS BREAK INTO HARVARD YARD." Most of the details were right, yet somehow the story made it into an isolated and rather childish prank. It failed to mention, by way of offering context or motivation, that Cheska was a Jew. Or, by way of noting distinction, that she was one of five Radcliffe juniors who earlier that week had been elected to membership in Phi Beta Kappa. Or, by way of telling the world he existed, that A. Tobias Ronan, A.B., *magna cum laude*, Harvard '34 (but two tenths of a point shy of a Phi Bete key) had been orbiting her flame from the first moment he saw her.

FIVE

HE HAD NOT ATTENDED America's finest university in the expectation that, on being graduated with high honors, his survival would depend more on his hands than wits. But manual labor is better than none if you are needy and the world at the moment is undazzled by all you know of Euripides, Diderot, and the metaphysical poets.

The graduate fellowship that Harvard in her wisdom had awarded him carried no stipend beyond a year's free tuition. And no more help was forthcoming from his father. Aunt Ida had presented him with a handsome check for fifty dollars at commencement, along with advice that he study bookkeeping and related aspects of applied mathematics while leaving literature to his leisure. If, therefore, he was to eat at all and lodge somewhere other than Cambridge Common when September came, he would have to provide for himself. And so, even as many of his classmates recovered from their academic rigors by touring the Continent deluxe or plying languorously between Hyannisport and Nantucket, Toby passed that summer in the seamy bosom of the proletariat—and counted himself lucky at that.

His old summer newspaper job as the necrologist of Nyack was no longer available, even at per-corpse rates, which would not have met his needs, anyway. In fact, summer work of any sort was not to be found around his home or the nearby Hudson River towns. He decided not to say he was looking for work that would last only through the summer, thinking that would substantially improve his chances to find something, but the deception made little difference. In New York, where he wandered for a week, his Harvard degree and a nickel got him a subway ride to the end of a lot of very long lines of desperate men applying for salvation.

His life to that point had not been entirely a picnic, but he had surely been shielded from fate's unkinder vicissitudes. Out in the open now for the first time, he found reality bleaker than anything he had imagined. It was plain he could not hold out for a job essentially mental in character; any sort of work would do—for without it, his future could not begin.

Louis Tulipani, if no one else, was properly respectful of his Harvard imprimatur. During the weeks his little job shop at the upper end of Mass. Ave. was printing the *Herald* Louis was forever reading over Toby's shoulder when he came by to check page proofs. A gabby sort shaped like a bowling pin, he missed no opportunity to advertise himself as no "guinea slob" but a high school graduate and the son of a native-born postal worker. Their parity thus established, Louis noted approvingly from the *Herald*'s editorial content that they shared compassion for the downtrodden—of whom, he steadfastly insisted, he was not one; it was just that he had to work a ninety-hour week to feed his family.

To keep his costs down, Louis used part-time labor as the flow of business necessitated. "Besides, it's hard to find good people," he explained to Toby. "You get a lot of boozers in this business, and drifters lookin' for a pot o' gold when all we got in here is lead." But it was an honest trade requiring a wide variety of high skills, he expanded in a transparent bid for esteem. Louis took a half hour one night to induct Toby into the mysteries of the Mergenthaler linotype, which Toby had always supposed was just a kind of enlarged typewriter—the same way he had thought "etaoin shrdlu" was some sort of Albanian cheese pie when in fact it was the two left-most lines of the lino keyboard. "Come work for me if they don't make you a professor," he concluded heartily, "and you'll get a real education."

In mid-June, without anything else in the offing, Toby called and asked to take him up on it. Louis was by no means displeased. "Sure," he said, "we need a little class around here."

At forty-five cents an hour, he was overpaid for a beginner. And hung on to every cent he could. Sara had gone off to Provincetown to operate a bookstall for the season, taking Cheska with her, and he was offered free rooming in exchange for safeguarding the shop at night. He walked the two miles to work to save carfare and feasted on nothing finer than the small but tasty nickel-apiece hamburgers at The Greek's stand on the Square. For recreation, there was the radio, an occasional movie, and any title he wanted from Sara's vast stock. Mostly, he slaved.

He began with every menial chore on the premises—sweeping the floor, reading proof, taking orders, counting letterheads, fetching lunch—and in no time was advanced to more physical scutwork: breaking down forms, sorting handset type back into trays, scrubbing the dead lead with flux for return to the pot. All performed speedily and unerringly as befit a printer's devil with a Harvard A.B. "Six more months," Louis said, "and you'll be earning half your salary."

His apprenticeship in fact lasted hardly two weeks, at the end of which he was moved to the makeup stone and, at Louis's elbow, instructed in the high art of composing in lead. It was not a process that could be profitably rushed. Every slug had to be scraped free of filings and certified type-high before being set in the chase, or it would not print. A momentary lapse of attention all but assured inverted lines, misplaced paragraphs, or a trayful of pied type. Odd-sized rules and boxes had to be trimmed endlessly to fit flush. Typos had to be tweezered out gingerly, proofs taken by mallet with enough force to get a clear impression but not mash the type, and chases locked tight enough with quoin keys and every line inside snug or the form would disintegrate en route to the press. Toby's soft pink palms were blistered by the second day.

Only after they developed genuine calluses was he tutored in the intimidating complexities—and molten furies—of the linotype. It strained his meager mechanical aptitude to the limit. The damned thing took constant tending. The pot had to be kept at just the right temperature, for if too cold, the lead came out in pieces instead of lines; if too hot, it could take your fingers down to the bone. The width of the pot-to-mold channel had to be precisely right or too much metal would be fed down the monster's unforgiving craw and produce dreadful indigestion. The tiny toes on the matrix of each character often bent on the way down from the magazine housing it, and if a misshapen one landed askew to the plunger, hot lead flew. Each night before retiring, the intricate chutes and arteries within the gulping, spitting, extruding beast had to be lovingly lubricated with graphite so the characters and space bands—the lifeblood of the amazing apparatus—would flow freely on the morrow. All of which care and feeding reduced him to quarter-hourly hemorrhages. Louis counseled patience and taught him to perform prodigies of repair with a surgical scout knife.

By comparison, typesetting itself was a breeze, as long as he remembered the Mergenthaler bore the same approximate relationship to his Remington as the Sahara did to a sandbox. Slow and steady was the only way to operate it. Louis said he had never had a typesetter before who not only corrected spelling and grammar in the copy as he went but even knew where to hyphenate words of more than two syllables.

Minor mishaps were frequent at first—he jammed every machine, including the pencil sharpener; selected horsy typefaces for wedding invitations; dumped just-set galleys back into the pot; added a zero to a job ticket and got a brochure overrun by a factor of ten. Once, he failed to detect a soft spot in a chase he had artfully composed and, while hauling it to the flatbed, scattered the Cambridge V.F.W. newsletter all over the shop floor. Not to mention nicking his knuckles four or five times on the carbide saw in the trimming cage and a couple of near-misses on his thumb. Four-fingered compositors, Louis cautioned, were a decided liability, Harvard or no Harvard. In time, though, he got the hang of it all and was kept gainfully, if perilously, occupied nearly fifty hours a week throughout the summer. By the end, he had put enough aside to be assured of lodgings for the school year ahead.

Something more than money sustained him in that hot, hard, messy work. It was not so much the satisfaction of learning a craft as the sheer flow of physical sensation his bookish nature had not been exposed to before. He wallowed in the constant assault on his senses by Louis Tulipani's print shop: the rhythmic thrum and surge of the presses, clank and clatter of the lino, rasp of the steel saw, oily smell and gleaming viscosity of the jet oil, ominous whiff of boiling metal, and grime everywhere in stark chiaroscuro with the spotless, razor-edged stacks of forest-fresh paper.

Most palpable of all was the insidious metal. It made him into an anti-Midas; everything he touched turned to lead. The shavings got under his nails, into his hair, down his neck, beneath his skin. Its very baseness gave it both a menace and beauty. Like bullets, the castings that came out of the linotype were called slugs. They were hard and bright and jagged and turned cold fast. And like bullets, they could burn you and bloody you and blind you. But they had messages stamped on them instead of death. And there was something wonderfully substantial about their heft, their density, their infinite grooves and ridges and facets. He trafficked all day in those shiny, linear bulletins, trying to decode their meaning with his fingertips, relishing them as if they were so many pieces of eight. Four times out of five he could tell how many points and ems a slug was just by the feel.

Lugging lead all over the shop and shifting around seventy-pound brass magazines every time he changed type sizes on the lino made the threat of rupture a reality. He no longer distastefully bypassed the truss advertisements. But his sinews strengthened soon enough, and he came away from work each day with a feeling of earned exhaustion. It made whatever he read while steaming in the tub that night seem facile and cosmetic. For the first time since coming to Cambridge he began to suspect that life revealed its deeper truths in ways more tactile than cerebral. At that depressing thought he would be overcome with drugged sleep.

Some nights that summer of sensory stimulation, he kept company that miraculously banished all traces of fatigue.

Bonnie Quigley was no Helen of Troy, but she had a womanly body, directness of manner, and good, throaty laugh. Cheska's friend from town and accomplice in the commencement outburst, Bonnie had lost her job over the incident and just taken a new one as a cashier at the Woolworth's on Mass. Ave. seven or eight blocks below the print shop. He ran into her one night in the lobby of the Fine Arts, where she was coming out of the show on the arm of Anton Sota, that prince of the proletariat. She had large bones and big violet eyes that were curiously lusterless but sparked with recognition at the sight of him. Sota, without a rampart to mount just then, asked Toby to join them for a beer.

They greeted the news of his enlistment in the working class— indelibly grimy rims on his fingernails were proof positive—with more amusement than sympathy. Harvard was not often humbled. "But surely a genuine gentleman," said Anton, "must know someone who knows someone who could have spared him the shame. Didn't they teach you anything up at the manor house?"

"A genuine gentleman doesn't ask for help," Toby said. "He rises above his advantages and gracefully accepts grubbing like everyone else—for a while, at least."

Anton smiled but said he still had Toby down as *petit bourgeois*— concerned for the destitute so long as his own condition remained trying but at heart a beliver in *laissez-faire* and the class system.

Only because everything else seemed as bad or worse, Toby answered.

"That's your Harvard syndrome again. The trouble is that secretly you still think you're someone pretty special."

"Actually, I hadn't planned on its being all that much of a secret."

Bonnie laughed and gave him a there-there pat on the wrist. But Anton thought he saw the beginnings of a convert. "Well," he said, "your enlightened boss will probably recognize your virtues before twenty years are out and sell you a small piece of the business for twice what it's worth."

"There's your capitalism for you."

He could not be headed by levity. "But suppose you'd been born with only half your brains? And suppose there wasn't an operator like Tulipani around, trying to puff himself up by working a poor Harvard boy to the bone—"

"Tulipani's not the system—he's a victim of it."

"Everyone who tolerates it shares the blame. He just happens to be one of the system's less successful predators—the woods are full of them these days—and he's helping you survive, so you're partial to him. But suppose his business was booming—do you suppose for a minute that he'd cut you in on the profits?"

"Why should he—they're his machines—it's his risk—"

"Because he exploits his labor to get the money to buy the machines so he'll have something to risk. He's just doing what comes naturally in a system run by greed. Which is why workers have to act collectively or accept their permanent enslavement."

"I don't feel particularly enslaved."

"No, four weeks won't quite do it. It's a novelty still. But imagine if you'd never made it to Harvard—and were just another poor, helpless drudge—with nothing to look forward to but interminable days on a mindless job for the rest of your life—and not even knowing when or if the boss might take it into his head to boot you the hell out on your dumb ass. How high and mighty do you think you'd be then about submerging your precious ego in a common cause with the teeming masses?"

"Precious little, probably. And that's what people like that should do."

"But not the better sort?"

"There you go," Toby said. "The Harvard curse."

Bonnie Quigley was less voluble about her social thinking but not short of discontent. Her family was of several minds on the state of man and the reign of divinity. She had a brother in the seminary and a mother who rarely missed morning mass; she had an older sister who worked for the city home relief agency and a father who taught mathematics at Ringe Technical High School—both of them strongly socialist in their views and after-hours activities. Bonnie herself, not having carried her studies beyond high school, was not much given to disquisitions. Her feelings, though, were pronounced and mostly negative. She thought the rich were cruel in their indifference and deserved to be taken down. And she could not love God for making a world like this one. When Toby suggested, as any liberally educated fellow would, that God had given man not only life but freedom of moral choice as well, she said merely, "Freedom to hate more than love." That, he contended, was man's fault. "No," she insisted, "it was whoever made him that way."

He dropped by her five-and-ten on his lunch hour the week after bumping into her and Sota. Business was slow so they talked long enough for him to establish that she and Anton were not fast sweethearts. "I think he likes my father better than me," she said. "When he's signed up every mill in Massachusetts and Pop's got all the teachers organized, I swear to God they're going to join up and try to unionize the Holy Church." She saw him fairly often and admired his intelligence, dedication, and courage. "But between you and I," she said, "he isn't much fun. I mean he's trying to save mankind all week long, y' know? That's hard. When I'm out with him, I keep thinking it's like I'm dating Jesus."

That Sunday they took the streetcar to Fenway and watched the Sox destroy the Indians. She knew a lot more about baseball than he did, including how to stick two fingers in her teeth and expel an earsplitting whistle in appreciation of Max Bishop's home run. Between innings, they fed each other peanuts and compared lives. Her passions were not complicated. She hated her job, her Church, and being a girl. She loved the Sox, the movies, her family, and, most of all, Cheska, whom she thought the swellest person she had ever known but did not pretend to understand. Bonnie's mother and Sara had been friends since childhood, and between them they had become almost a surrogate mother to Cheska since her estrangement from home. Bonnie's affection for her was therefore almost sisterly.

"She's high on you, I know," Bonnie said, "almost like family, too. She never lets on what's inside her, though—past a certain point—if you know what I mean. Sometimes I'm not sure she knows, herself."

"Uh-huh." He kept shelling the peanuts with dedication.

She looked at him sideways. "You're still stuck on her, huh?"

"Leave the skins on," he said, presenting her a palmful of nuts, "they're good for you."

"That bad, huh?"

"I didn't say that."

"You don't have to—it's all over your face." She shrugged. "I can understand—she's a very—very—fine person." So much so, in fact, that her last act before leaving for the Cape, Bonnie disclosed, was to offer to repay her the twenty-five dollars each of them had been fined by the court for their show-stopping performance at the commencement. "She said it was the least she could do for getting me into it. I let her pay part, only I still feel funny."

"You shouldn't—she can afford it."

"That's beside the point. I'm just trying to tell you why I—"

"I know what you're trying to tell me, and I'd just as soon skip it if it's all the same to you." He was done investing in emotions that fed only inward on themselves. And anyway here was Bonnie Quigley, alive and at hand, and if semi-educated and no more than half as buoyant as Cheska da Silva, she appealed to him powerfully with her unnuanced character and wide-hipped design. They stopped by the bookshop on the way back and kissed. She asked if there was anything hard to drink in the place, and when he said no, she said to please have some for next time unless he had religious scruples or some other kind against it. Only financial, he said, and she offered to split the cost of a bottle as long as it was nothing too extravagant.

So agreeable was that artless quality after all the mystery and moodiness of their mutual friend that he did not wait for the next weekend to see Bonnie again. He scrubbed up extra hard after work on Wednesday, and they went to a Jack Holt movie at the Uni, holding hands and talking the whole time till an usher shut them up and they left, giddily indignant. She suggested they take sandwiches back to the shop, and he got out the Four Roses he had bought and they made a feast of it on the worktable. She drank twice what he did and refrained from more only with obvious effort. Afterward he turned the lights off and the radio on and they swayed to somebody's orchestra doing "Avalon," which she said was one of her very favorites, and kept swaying till their lips fused and mouths explored and he drew her tight against him to feel the warm mass of her breasts and she felt his hardness and did not shy from it.

"You don't like to drink much, do you?" she asked, lips brushing his ear.

"How could you tell?"

"The way you almost puked after each sip."

"That's a little party trick I learned. It always wows 'em."

She laughed. "I used to get nauseous from it, too."

"So why bother?"

"It's wonderful for making me forget everything—for a while."

"What's 'everything'?"

"Who I am—what I'm doing—"

"They don't seem so terrible to me. Or am I missing something?"

She sighed and held on to him, deciding how much of her heart to spill. Finally she said, "Look, I'm trapped." He said he didn't understand. She said he was being dense, then. Times were bad and she wasn't rich or beautiful or brilliant or a boy, and there was nothing to do about any of it but to take a couple or three belts every night and hope some guy on a white horse would ride up in the morning and carry her off to the North Shore. "And fat chance of that," she said.

"Is that what you really want?"

"I want to be happy," she said. "How doesn't matter."

"Don't let the commissar hear you say that."

"Who?"

"Anton. It's a little joke."

"Oh," she said. "He's too busy listening to himself to hear what I've got to say. You're different."

Next time, he drank right along with her until they both got giddy and she said they would probably be more comfortable upstairs. Desire mastered nausea as he guided them uncertainly to the apartment sofa. By degrees his sultry siren revealed a body of lavish curvature that she shared unstintingly. He relished each offering and primed it with industry till her moans turned steamy and she stayed his hand. "I think," she said huskily, "you'd better—get—ready—"

"I—I'm not—what do you—"

"A rubber—now!"

"I—don't—"

"Whaa-a-t?"

"I didn't—uh—think—"

She gave a groan. "Think what?"

"That—you—"

"That I'm 'that kind of a girl'?" She sat up, suddenly sober, and gave her hair an angry shake. "Jesus Christ, Toby, I'm a grown woman. You know what my life is like—do I have to write it on the ceiling for you?"

"I—"

"Look, if you think wanting a little pleasure from my body now and then makes me a hussy or something, I can't help it."

"It's not that. It's just—"

"Just what?" She looked at him hard to decipher the message. Suddenly she buried her head against his chest. "Oh, you poor bunny—you're cherry, aren't you?"

"Well—only technically."

She thought that was hilarious for a man. Then she ran a hand through his hair and said she was sorry for seeming to mock him and would take care of herself right afterward if he wanted to do it then. Gorged with unexpended wanting, he drowned happily in her pelvic undulations and rode out her immense and terrifying spasms till, recharged and nearly raw from her accomplished encouragement, he released again within that musky cavern. "I think," she said, "you're getting the hang of it."

When she was done with her elaborate ablutions, they lay unspeaking in the dark for a while, hands entwined. Then she said, as if having to absolve them both from the censure of their absent friend, "You know what I told you about Cheska and my court fine?"

"I'm not thinking about her right now—"

"It wasn't the only thing of mine she offered to pay for."

A backroom abortion sprang to his mind. "What do you mean?"

"Last year she said she could probably get her parents to loan me the money for college if I really wanted to go."

"Very nice," he said. "She can be very nice."

"She meant it."

"I'm sure. And you said you wouldn't dream of taking charity from a friend, even though she said you could pay it all back."

"How do you know? She wouldn't have told you—"

"I've got a rich friend, too," he said, "and that's how I kept him."

On that note of mutual self-respect, they kissed and he started to get dressed to take her home. She watched him slip on his underpants and, with her usual guile, she said, "You've got a very nice thing, Toby. Go get it something to wear."

It took six mortifying turns around the block the next day for him to work up the nerve to enter the pharmacy. Waiting till there was no other customer, he cleared his throat and forthrightly asked if the store sold prophylactics. The pharmacist, disapproval collecting behind his wire-framed glasses, asked what brand. Toby mentioned the only one he knew. They were out of those, the man said. Then any kind, Toby said. The pharmacist asked how many. Oh, the ignominy. No one should have access to such intimate data. Six, he blurted—it seemed a potent number: hardly virginal, not quite lecherous. They came six in a box—did he want six boxes or one? There was no end to it. Next he would be told they also came small, medium, large, and pachyderm and which did he take—or would he need to step into the fitting room in back?

After that, Bonnie and he dispensed with the movies on their twice-weekly nights together. It was such easy pleasure he began to feel sinful about it. There was no hint of real courting. Even on their Sunday walks or picnics by the river, bed was the true destination. How was he different from any other young Harvard lord dandling a wayward wench—except that he was as poor as she was? Wasn't he leading on this simple, earthy girl when carnal companionship was all he sought or contemplated?

The simpleton set him straight. Lovemaking without real love, she said, was perfectly fine as long as (a) there was honest affection between the parties and (b) the rewards were mutual. If marriage had been heavy on her mind, she would not have bargained for him with her body. "Easy lays," she said knowingly, "wind up with shit. Fun is all I want with you—and if that's a sin, why should I love God even a little?"

Whatever it was, was free and painless and left him strutting around all summer with his manhood perpetually distended. But paradise, unlike purgatory, rarely outlives its season. He had a card from Sara saying they would be back from the Cape the evening of September 1. The night before, Bonnie and he had a marathon go of it, not knowing when or where they would resume, or even if. That veil upon the future added a piquant touch to their protracted grinding and thrusting. They dozed off in an embracing nap—only to be awakened by Cheska's clattering through the front door close to midnight. Bonnie and he parted as if cleaved by a lightning bolt.

"Toby!" she yelled through the bedroom door. "We're back— we're dirty—we're hungry—we're dead." End of announcement. "You okay?"

In semi-shock, he managed to croak sure before she could barge in on them. "Why so late?"

"Oh, Sara had it wrong," she said, opening the door a crack and addressing the darkness. "They make you get out the last day of the month. She thought we had till noon tomorrow, like in a hotel." He grunted as engagingly as possible. It did not do. She stood framed in the door for a minute, then asked irritably, "Aren't you going to get up and say hello, at least?"

"I'm bushed," he murmured. "I'll see you in the morning, okay?"

"It's not okay, as a matter of fact. You don't greet someone you've missed by yawning in her face. Besides, Sara needs some help with the heavy stuff—if it's not too much trouble for you to haul yourself down to the car. You've got all those big muscles now, right?"

Oh, yes. Very big. His mind reeled. "I'll be there in a minute."

She receded from the doorway and scuffled around with the bags she had brought in. Then: "Hey—what the hell! Who's in there with you?"

"In where?"

"In there!" She was back at the door. "There's a girl's shoes out here!" Much agitation of voice and windmilling of arms.

"They're the maid's," he tried, doom imminent.

"With high heels? Big joke!" She kicked the bottom of the door. "What's going on here?"

"Hey, it's not against the law," he said, sitting up, "so take it easy."

"It is the hell so—you're not married! There's a name for that. Sara's going to blow a gasket!"

"It sounds like you're the one doing the blowing."

She was silhouetted in the doorway now, arms at her sides and fists clenched. "That's a real nice way to repay Sara's kindness—turning her apartment into a whorehouse!"

"Don't you go calling anybody names!" Bonnie spoke up out of the dark.

"Who the hell is that?"

"It's me—and you try acting your age!"

"Oh, sweet Jesus on a stick!" A summer with Sara had ripened her iconography. She snapped the light on to see if it was true, gasped, and snapped it back off. Nothing came out of her for the longest moment. Then she said softly, "And to think I kept meaning to write and tell you to look each other up."

II

Labor strife erupted all over the country that year in a way it had not earlier in the depression. Roosevelt's encouragement of the legitimate hopes of the common man lent heart to the union movement at a time men everywhere would do any kind of work under any set of conditions. Militancy among workers, like the muse among poets, does not usually flourish in the face of famine. Yet that was precisely the moment organized labor decided it could not gracefully settle for crumbs off of industry's table.

Amid much parading and fanfare, the new National Recovery Administration codes had been adopted, promising the American worker minimally tolerable pay, hours, and safety conditions. Compliance, however, was largely voluntary. Industry hailed the blithe spirit of the Blue Eagle—and then argued it could not both improve the conditions of labor and add jobs to its payroll so long as the economy remained seriously depressed. Labor answered that the economy would never revive if workers were not put back on the job and consumer demand thus restored. Each side was gored by the horns of the paradox. When the unions tried to organize intransigent industries, owners responded by calling on their political hirelings to send in the militia. Immoderation reigned.

Thus, when a nationwide general strike was set in the textile industry at the beginning of September, the prospect was for sustained strife, even in beleaguered New England, where employment in the mills had steadily eroded since the turn of the century. Only the woolen business remained an important textile employer in the region. Anton Sota, as an operative for the United Textile Workers, the major force behind the ordered national shutdown, was charged with winning compliance from every milltown in New England.

Sota must have made a dozen speeches that Labor Day—Cheska, Sara, Bonnie, her father, and Toby went to hear him on Cambridge Common—and he never said a kind thing about communists. The route to salvation for the American workingman, he preached, was to gain economic and political parity with the owner class. The only way for labor to escape peonage and achieve independence was to organize itself by whole industries, not through the old exclusionary craft unions that the owners could play off against one another forever. A united front had to be established with enough numerical and moral strength to require amendment of the laws of supply and demand. The marketplace had to serve humanity, not the other way around.

They all gathered for a bite at the bookshop toward the end of that afternoon while Anton and a couple of his less articulate but more muscular cronies unwound. Reports came over the radio of the speech by Norman Thomas calling the projected textile strike potentially the greatest assertion of labor solidarity in all of American history. The likely industry response could be predicted, Anton said, from an editorial he read to them out of *Fibre & Fabric,* a New England trade journal that declared "a few hundred funerals will have a quieting influence" on the strikers. Gunpowder was in the air.

As it turned out, the response, at least throughout southeastern New England, was highly encouraging during the first week. Jobless hordes on the streets were readily marshaled in intimidating numbers outside of mills that, ever since the big strike of '22, had used the threat of shutting down and moving south as a club to maintain virtual sweatshop conditions. Only scattered plants under intransigent management stayed open with the help of workers whose vision did not extend beyond their next pay envelope. One such exception was a rayon mill in Woonsocket, just across the Massachusetts line in northern Rhode Island, less than an hour's drive from Boston.

Anton's chief henchman in the organizing business—a burly fellow named Jack Reynaud—was a native of Woonsocket who monitored the situation there closely. A city of ninety mills and fifty thousand joyless souls, Woonsocket had two distinctions besides its name (Indian for "at the very steep hill," Jack reported with residual pride): Abraham Lincoln had spoken there during his 1860 presidential campaign, and something like three quarters of the current population were of French-Canadian ancestry, including Jack, born Jacques. The rather inbred and suspicious nature of the Canucks, who had been imported in the nineteenth century to man the then burgeoning mills, had caused them to reject the intense organizing efforts of the United Textile Workers. Their subservience to the owners, though, was not limitless. In 1932, they had formed a town-wide independent union that claimed seven thousand members. And almost all of them were out now in sympathy with the industry-wide strike.

"It's only the fuckin' rayon outfit what's holdin' out," said Jack. "We gonna hafta go in an' bust some fuckin' skulls together."

The Woonsocket Rayon Company had claimed exemption from the general strike on two grounds—that it was not a textile company but a manufacturer of synthetic fibers, and that as a large-scale user of chemicals, it was all but impossible to shut down operations without heavy losses of materials and equipment.

"Well, shit on that!" said Jack Reynaud. "If it looks like a duck and walks like a duck and swims like a duck and flies like a duck—and goddamn well *tastes* like a duck—then that's a fuckin' duck no matter what its feathers are made of!" As to losses from a forced shutdown, Jack offered an equally elemental analysis: "Fuckin' du Pont made twenty-six million last year—and nobody fought harder than them to keep us out. So it don't matter nohow whether you got lotsa chemicals or a little—nobody gives an inch they don't gotta."

On the strength of those singleminded convictions, Jack was sent off to Woonsocket the next week to recruit a squadron of demonstrators and bring the rayon mill to its knees. One holdout might give other companies ideas, the union chiefs feared. Jack, knowing the territory, was charged with whipping up local malcontents—the overworked and underpaid, the jobless and the hopeless, the drinkers and the drifters, the bullies and the brawlers—and leading them into the valley of death if it came to that. Toby was asked to help supply their ammunition.

"Look at it from the historical perspective," Anton appealed to him, coming by the print shop the last week he was scheduled there as a fulltimer. "Rhode Island was the cradle of the American factory system—if old Slater hadn't stolen the spinning jenny out of England and set it up in Pawtucket, we'd all still be out raising corn and killing Indians. And if we don't win this strike—and really get labor organized in every industry—we might as well hand the country back to Pocahontas." All he wanted Toby to do, he said, was drive down one of the trucks the union was sending full of rocks and brickbats for Jack's goon squad the following night when Governor Green was threatening to call in the National Guard.

Toby was doubtful at first. Anton may have been right in predicting that each passing week in the print shop would make it easier for him to conceive of a life at repetitive labor as a prison without bars. But if ten weeks in a benign sweat shop had left him incomparably more sympathetic to the goals of the union movement, they had not turned Toby into a radical. "I promised him I'd work tomorrow night," he said, indicating Tulipani, who was fiddling with the air vacuum on the Miehle vertical and cursing in tempo with the automatic feed.

"Ask him to switch things around—or get someone else."

"I don't know. I'll have to think about it."

"Sure," he said, "you do that. Just call and leave word with my secretary."

"You've got a secretary?"

"And a Rolls and chauffeur—and a little duplex on Beacon—nothing fancy, though." He eyed Toby darkly. "You've got to make a choice one of these days, friend. Either you're with us or against us. Neutrals get shot down in the crossfire."

"Who's 'us'?"

" 'Us'? 'Us' is everyone who has to like it or lump it—who's too dumb to know he's being shat on—or too scared to do anything about it. Some of 'us' don't want to wait any longer to inherit the earth because we think it's rightfully ours already." Anton put a sharp, damp hand on his shoulder. "We need help, Toby—not nods of understanding."

As a precocious orator, he had moved Toby mostly to scorn. He always had the sense Anton was too well rehearsed and the lines were somebody else's. He could not remain indifferent, let alone hostile, to him now, though. Anton had sought him out and stroked his conscience; it was no longer a question of Anton's personality but of his own character.

Still, Toby had trouble subscribing to Anton's world, one composed solely of oppressors and the oppressed. It was a vision of ceaseless strife, one wave of force overwhelming its predecessor with Darwinian inevitability, the winners claiming that one's lot in life was essentially what one deserved. To reduce all humanity to such a never-ending play of power was to feed the pathology of the race. Every act of selflessness, by that standard, was suicidal. Where were reason and compassion in such a world? Where were conciliation and justice?

Anton saw him wavering. Just the moment to throw a curveball. To be honest, he said, asking Toby's help was not his idea—it was the girls'. They would be driving down to Woonsocket as well, Cheska in a truck with him and Bonnie in another with her father. But if Toby didn't want to risk his neck a little in the aid of the downtrodden, he would understand fully. Subtle, Anton was not.

Louis Tulipani might conceivably have been more accommodating if he had not been struggling to repair the crankiest press in his shop. "Hell, no, I need you then," he said with little room for debate. "I'll vouch for you with the lady if it's any help." Toby thanked him but said it was not love calling. Louis asked what then, and he explained. Louis never looked up. "That's communist shit."

"Oh, come on," Toby said. "It's—it's industrial democracy."

"In a pig's ass. Unionism is communism, sonny boy. What do you think the 'U' stands for in the 'U.S.S.R.'?"

Toby thought at first he might be fooling. But he kept wrestling with the grippers on the feed board and offered no further hint of mirth. Quite the opposite. "The first union snot puts his head in the door here, I blow it off or I'm out of business. All they are is trouble-makers and clockwatchers. None of 'em got incentive like you. They don't want work—just your money. It's a holdup." He slid the feed board back in place. "You know why they fried Sacco and Vanzetti? Not because they were poor—and not because they were guinea—and not because they did it—it was because they were Reds. Reds don't belong in America." He spit on the floor in contempt and then finally looked up. "You want to go down there and help out the Red sons of bitches tomorrow, you go, Toby—it's a free country. But don't bother comin' back here."

The perfect end to an instructive summer. "You'd better get me detailed directions," he told Anton. "I've never been to Rhode Island."

The union man squinted across the shop curiously. "You worked it out?"

"I told you," Toby said, "he is one of nature's noblemen."

The back of the pickup truck had a canvas cover over its jagged cargo. The plan was for him to park it right on the street a couple of hundred yards from the mill long before the police showed up to oversee the eight o'clock change of shifts. If anyone stopped him, he was to say it was a delivery to the mill. If they looked under the canvas, the worst they could get him for was lying. And since they were stopping only local people driving vehicles they ordinarily didn't, the risk was minimal.

All the way down, he felt chased. Drums beaten by unforgiving avatars were summoning him to trial by combat. Unless he met and felled his adversary lurking in the bush, he would remain a perpetual eunuch, tending the fires and bearing away the bodies of heroes till shame consigned him to his own unmarked grave. To pass a manly life, in the bright clearing, with head held high, required a display of valor—an overt, physical act. The convictions he had registered throughout college were all nuanced gestures—group acts, cerebral acts, acts of complicity, at one remove or more from the imminence of severe pain. His choice now was either lionhearted defiance of peril or psychic castration. He cursed the former as savage and against his every instinct, but unable to evade it, he jounced across a small bridge over the Blackstone River and drove into Woonsocket, Rhode Island, half prepared to die.

It was an unlovely settlement of sooty brick and sallow paint that drew no mellowness from the crepuscular light. Its low, somber silhouette was punctured only by an occasional chimney or belfry and the saw-tooth roofs of the factories. A Gallic flavor was detectable at once in the names. The stateliest church along his route—a gabled brick Victorian Gothic with great twin towers—was called *Precieux Sang*: Precious Blood. He took it for a sign. The stores, every third one empty and the rest revealing the slackness of trade through dusty windows with limp tinsel, were mostly Canuck-run: J. Roberge's Market . . . Cadoret Jewelers . . . Simoneau Furniture . . . Pirault & DeNevers Hardware. There was a French movie house, too, and even a newsie peddling a local French paper. That *soupçon* of the exotic, though, was not enough to transform slouching tenements and gray-faced *habitants* into something picturesque. Woonsocket, in its extremity, was a *pissoir*.

He came through at suppertime, and no one intercepted him. The others were waiting for him when he rumbled to a stop in the shadows, as instructed, midway between two lampposts. Cheska, in knickers, a baggy wool pullover, and peaked cap that hid her coiled hair, led his surprised welcoming party. "So this is our mysterious accessory to the crime," she said, half to him, half to Anton. "Hamlet joins the Jacobins."

"Slings and arrows promptly delivered," Toby said, bursting with bravado. "Who were you expecting—Andrew Mellon?"

Her look gave him the distinct sense he was stealing her scene. "No," she said, "you've got more to atone for."

"I thought my invitation was your idea—a double-dare by the Trotsky Twins."

"Who said that?"

They all turned to Anton, who was gravely surveying the street for police patrols. "Well," he said, "desperate times require desperate measures." He reached a hand toward Toby for the truck keys. "Anyway, stick with us now, friend, and you'll be richly rewarded for your fortitude."

Jack Reynaud was operating up the block out of the back of a soup kitchen and flophouse called Father Laliberte's Canteen, a mission that had been practically overrun by the hungry since the start of the textile strike. In his three days back in town, Jack had earned the status of folk-hero thanks to his fresh supply of bilingual bawdy jokes, vegetables for the nightly soup pot, and french bread for every comer. "Mmmm," Bonnie said, tasting the crust, "where'd you get this?"

"Same place I get the vegetables," said Jack, blotting mouth on cuff. "Steal 'em outa the backs of trucks when they're makin' their morning deliveries. Everyone's too fuckin' groggy then to see straight."

Money he used for more important things, like greasing the palms of local union leaders to make sure they turned out bodies for the evening demonstrations. Also, he had hired a dozen Hessians from out of town to spearhead the assault and bought a couple of cases of whiskey to keep his hulks rabid. A core group of about a hundred would function as catalyst, shaping and directing the crowd. "Should be a cake-walk," Jack reassured Anton. "There's a lotta hate bottled up in this one-horse town—only no one's told them where the fuck to stow it."

He instructed them to wet a rag and keep it handy in case they got hit with tear gas. Remembering the ambush of the *Karlsruhe* demonstrators by the Boston cops not many months before, Toby yearned for a shield instead. Getting his skull crushed by a rearing horse was no way to die. The Woonsocket police lacked cavalry, Jack advised, and would be outnumbered that night about three or four hundred to one. Under the circumstances, the cops' only mission was to prevent the rayon mill from being overrun. Reassured by the arithmetic and fanaticism of their wolfish agent provocateur, they melted into the throng, which had already grown to several thousand.

In his ear they were hollering hellishly. Arc lights, caged in mesh to repulse pelting, glared down white-hot and lunar-cold and bathed the streets in ghostglow.

Anton had drifted off to agitate and left behind Bonnie, whose father seized her hand and drew her close for safety. Toby did the same with Cheska, who yielded him the lead as they cut through the shifting, seething crowd. Hairy-eared old men stood shoulder to shoulder with gap-toothed young ones. Shrill wives and sisters in bandannas stoutly reinforced husbands and brothers. Boys and girls, in bits of bright ribbon and jerseyed motley, tumbled unattended, ragamuffin harlequins delighting in the disorder.

Ahead of them, in front of the mill, its windows boarded tight with raw wood looking newer still against the sooty stone, police clustered by the fence gate—a tiny crew to brave a raging sea. Their only arms, leather-thonged billy clubs and yard-long sledgehammers, bespoke a certain resolution. A hundred feet of no-man's-land separated them from the barricades.

A mighty swell of sound boiled up and over as cop cars arrived to shield shuttling workers during the shift change. In Toby's ear they bellowed their hate and celebrated the fellowship of misery: "Close it down, you chickenshit bastards—close-it *down!* close-it *down!* close-it *down!*" Wrath fused in their righteous fury, they sounded invincible.

Through the roiling air stones curled aimlessly in an almost playful spattering. The cops ducked and bunted away the floating missiles like so many lobbed baseballs. But slowly, as the cars pulled out, the tempo and trajectories changed with the caliber of ordnance. Stones turned to rocks, slung lower and swifter, and brickbats, edges bladed as they whirled, and long-necked beer bottles spilled out of the sky like World War potato mashers. By the gate, policemen teetered and buckled, blood rouging their cheeks, their brows, their scalps. The scent of it drew yet more missilery as howls of pleasure ventilated the compacting crowd. The fingers of Toby's free hand closed about the single blunt rock Anton had jammed into his pocket. Amid that forest of flailing arms, his right one lifted and locked its grip and aimed and yet would not release. The enemy was beyond his range and loathing.

Fearless, hulking, lip-smacking masses breached the barricades as the hurt police fell back behind the mill gate. The siege army closed to within half a dozen feet of the fence. Rubble soared over it and rained relentlessly against the stout facing of the bulwark. A storm door splintered, globe lights shattered, but most of the outrage spent itself in vain against the seamless bastion. Within, chemical compounds thickened, shuttles flew, and the work went heedlessly, despicably, on.

Up in front, a sortie of strikers, Jack's goons among them, rushed the gate, catapulting great boulders to cave it in and scattering firecrackers to rattle its guardians. Victory was within grasp. Any instant an avalanche of bodies would burst through the gate, cast aside the feeble keepers, and lay waste whatever stood in its path.

At the brink, tear gas stanched the onrush. Three small bluish puffs of smoke rose where the grenades fell in an arc around the gate, and a billow of fumes assaulted the front ranks. The crowd recoiled with an ooohh and aaahhh and fell back to receive the gasping, staggering victims. Mingled fear and resentment rippled back over the vast herd. Toby, too far away to catch the fumes, reached for his damp piece of cloth just in case, but it had already dried. For the first time now, he felt more claustrophobic than heroic: feet tangled, breathing cramped, compass gyrating. He doubled his grip on Cheska, whose darting looks betrayed her fright. Bonnie and her father were nowhere in sight.

Their thrust momentarily foiled, the demonstrators slowly shrank from the fore. Instead of disbanding, they turned hatred outward. Streetlamps, not covered elsewhere as they were around the mill, went dark from attack. Down came a stout wooden fence in front of the big American Wringer factory. Borne off in the mandibles of the milling swarm, its boards were formed into a pyre in the middle of the street and torched against the lowering night. Pushcarts, warehouse barrels, parking signs torn from their moorings, and anything else portable in sight were fed to the blaze. Windows danced with reflected hellfire, then shivered in a cascade of fragments and turned to hollow holes in offended walls. In the distance, the wail and clang of coming fire engines sent cheers of triumph funneling up with the smoke. From its sound, the street population was tripling every few minutes. Toby skittered along its edges, dazed from the foment, consumed with his own complicity, clinging fiercely still to the girl he loved but certain that if the undertow drew them beneath it now, the two of them would not resurface in this life.

In ponderous trucks two streets over, babyfaced militiamen with rifles and helmets ran a gauntlet of jeers and hisses. Brick and stone attended the crouched warriors' wake. The mob's own progeny, outfitted in the service of the system, were not to be spared. Rock-riddled, the convoy went through. Even as it secured the rayon mill and rendered it impregnable, martial law ceded the surrounding streets to unimpeded rampage. Vandals darkened every light in view, plate glass imploded up and down the avenue, and store windows were emptied of every last shoelace. Pillage in the moonlight became indiscriminate. Bars and grills were commanded closed, cars overturned, buses stoned to a halt, unanswerable fire alarms set at every corner. Civilization, adieu.

Trapped in a downspout with ten thousand strangers, Toby fought to stay sane. His limbs splayed, his temples distended to kettledrums, his brain spiraled through vertical geography. Packed amid stampeding swine, red-eyed and howling hellishly in his ear, he had only Cheska's warm, quick breath for sustenance.

Drunk with destruction, the marauders wheeled and retraced their route through the strewn debris for a second assault on the mill. On the far side of the restored barricades, a hundred soldiers patrolled, rifles shouldered. Behind and in front of Toby, twenty thousand feet tramped toward a kill. He could neither flee them nor march to their tempo. There was simply no choice but to flow forward in the savage tide. Cheska's hat was gone, and her long hair hung loose and wild. He tried to calm her trembling with a circling arm, as if remembering finally who was whose protector.

The young faces of the guardsmen, already pallid in the ghastly illumination, grew taut before the oncoming mass. Jack Reynaud, shirt pasted to his body by the exertions of the night, led the first wave to the fringe of no-man's-land. New sorts of missiles flew—whiskey bottles thoroughly drained, potatoes and pulpy fruit plundered from the A & P, chunks of gravestones kicked down in a swerve through a churchyard. The soldiers groaned in pain and dropped. Why was the crowd so sure their guns were toy? It closed to within fifty feet and heaved still more rock, glass, clubs, metal. The round cut, bruised, smashed more brutally than any before it.

"*Allons!*" cried Jacques Reynaud, a rag wrapped around his scalp in case more gas was put down. Toby tried spitting into his cloth, but no juice was left in him. Neither did he heed Jacques' command. What was the objective—to brain the soldiers and blow up the mill? Was havoc justice? They moved forward past him, pressing in on the militia, taunting, daring. Suddenly their commander barked, there was a terrible timpani, and a wall of cloud was rolling toward the surging crush.

Toby bunched the cloth over his eyes and nose and turned from the gas, but the stuff was already on his lips and burning his throat, and when he coughed, it crept up his nostrils and scorched his eyeballs until a single flame tortured every aperture in his body. Blind, breathless, staggering, lost in a crazing miasma, he felt he could not endure another moment: The short, sweet life of A. Tobias Ronan, Jr., snuffed out on a faraway plain in a cause they told him was just.

Swept back a block from the barricades, he revived enough to retch. Puke-stained but clearer-headed, he reached out for Cheska, who was not there. Gone, wrenched away in the panicky retreat. She would perish, he was certain, if he did not find her. Eurydice racing barefoot over the burning coils of hell. But there was no way to search, for they were going in once more. Leaders passed the word that the gas had been used up. The guardsmen could be rushed now and their rifles wrenched from them. "*Allons!*"

Toy soldiers on one knee took dead aim at the clamorous citizenry. Their commander hoisted his riding crop as the air filled once more with detritus and raw throats bellowed bloody oaths in a massive lunge to glory. The commander's signal flicked earthward. Rifles crashed. Motion halted. Lips kissed macadam. A shattering silence. The front ranks were all down. A coil of hovering gunsmoke was the only motion in that terrible tableau.

A head stirred. Then another. Then many. Someone gave a mordant laugh. Nobody had been hurt by the bulletless warning volley. They rose up, sorry at their craven response and furious now that sham tactics should have quelled their righteous host. Ecstatic, the resurrected legion coiled for its final rush. A howling sheet of flesh sailed forward ahead of him. So fierce was the din he could barely hear the shooting. But the shrieks just afterward peeled back the layers of the soul.

Toby was nearly ground under by the backward-galloping horde. Near him three bodies writhed where they had fallen. One not five yards from him tried to keep the glittering insides of his abdomen from spilling out onto the street. No one went to them. In the trampling, they were being left to die. Toby shrank away with the rest, not looking back now, dreading the blast that the next instant would blow his spine apart. Beside him as they ran, a boy was screaming—his leg. Blood erupted from a hole in his thigh. His pants, many sizes too big, darkened from the flow as he dwindled to the ground. He was

small, and Toby reached down for him. They yelled to him to leave
the boy to the soldiers. What could that mean but death? He was light
to lift. Before the summer, he could not have toted such a weight a
dozen yards. He waddled down the street trailing blood. In his ear the
boy was screaming out his life ungratefully.

At the truck, Cheska and the others were waiting, and Anton stood
guard with a baseball bat as Toby staggered up, the weight of the
wounded boy now all but unbearable. "What the Christ are you
doing?" Anton yelled.

"Hospital!" Toby gasped.

"I don't know where it is—and you can't get through! We'd be
arrested, anyway. Put him *down*, you stupid bastard—they'll take care
of him!"

The boy's leg was red-black pulp. Toby placed him gently down on
the sidewalk and blurted "Key!" at Anton. Anton backed away and
told him to climb into the passenger side. "Key!" Toby repeated, maniacal now for his mission, and moved after him. Anton retreated
warily to the driver's door. Toby yanked out the rock he had not
hurled all night and flexed his hand over it with maximum menace.
Anton's burning eyes widened. Toby shouted at him a final time for
the key, and when he stood there motionless and unblinking, Toby
drove the rock through the windshield with his last parcel of energy.
As Anton turned in disbelief toward the violent spray of glass, Toby
launched himself at him to tear away his bat. The sluggish lateral motion failed. Reflexively, Anton swung. The blow sliced down, nicking
Toby's temple but bringing its full force against his right arm just
below the elbow. The pain shredded him as the horrid night went out
at last.

They fixed him up a little medal and pinned it to his cast at Mass.
General. "It was your own damned fault, of course," Anton said at
the presentation ceremony.

In the narrow sense, he conceded as much. But why had all the
pointless violence been necessary and all those innocents hurt?

"It's not a matter of individuals," Anton said. "You've got to get
over that. And anyway, it wasn't pointless at all—they've shut the
mill."

Toby's arm was six weeks mending.

III

His fling with Bonnie Quigley ended as abruptly as it had begun.

For one thing, there was no place for them to be together. She still
lived at home, and Toby took a tiny attic apartment in the home of an

astronomy professor whose churchly wife made it plain he was to do no "entertaining" under their roof. And no other spot beckoned that was private, convenient, and cheap.

More to the point, Bonnie could not cope with the emotional overload once Cheska was back in town, knowing all. Partly she felt she had betrayed her best friend; partly she felt Toby was employing her as a surrogate lover. On the latter score, he felt guiltless. Bonnie, after all, had defined the nature and extent of their sexual activity with admirable candor, and when she took up in earnest with Anton in the fall, he wished her well.

As to whether either or both of them had acted dishonorably toward Cheska, Toby conceded even less culpability. To characterize his simple, sweaty rutting with Bonnie as violating the purity of his true but unrequited love might have worked as a medieval morality play but rang hollow a third of the way into the twentieth century. He was merely a normal young man with his juices running. The ethical efficacy of chastity eluded him; he was not even clear how abstinence advanced the compassion of the priesthood.

Cheska did not view the matter quite so casually. "The mere fact a man can achieve an erection," she said to him as he was packing up to leave Sara's apartment, "is not a license to install it indiscriminately."

"Who said I wasn't discriminating?"

"You know perfectly well what I mean. Premarital relations are no different for a man of refinement than for a woman."

"I couldn't agree more—both should be allowed to participate. Certified virginity is a demeaning state. But you kept refusing me."

"Very funny."

"I'm not trying to be funny. It's a perfectly normal human activity —and I'm only human. What gives you the right to tell anyone else how and when to practice it, I'd like to know?"

Her eyes rolled upward. "For God sakes, Toby—why did you have to do it with *her*—of all people?"

"Why not—isn't she a nice person?"

"That isn't the point, and you damned well know it!"

"Then what is the point?"

"The point is—the point is—it's like thumbing your nose at me."

"No one exactly sent you an orchestra seat to the performance."

"So it was okay as long as it was behind my back? Boy, you've got some sterling character!"

Her presumption reduced him to inarticulate fury. But in a way, it pleased him that she was disturbed, for what else could it mean but that she cared enough for him to feel wounded by his assigned infidelity? Her own inconstancy toward him, the tacit demand that he remain on the string, to be tugged at her convenience, she would never concede.

Whether from unvarnished jealousy or admiration stirred by the momentary valor he had displayed in Woonsocket—or both, or neither—Cheska chose to relent while his arm was recuperating and displayed a tenderness toward him that he had nearly surrendered hope of ever inspiring. She came to his room with coffee and sugar buns two Sunday mornings after Woonsocket. Surprised and in his pajamas, he let her in quickly, then checked the driveway to be sure his landlords were off at church as usual.

"It's your room," she said. "Can't you have any visitors you want? After all, you're convalescing."

"She's a demon on immorality—at which I am a past master, as I'm sure you can testify to her *ad nauseam*. It's the only reason I didn't list you as a character reference."

"Very amusing."

"I'm glad you think so." He saw that her habitual combativeness was missing and softened his defensive irony. "I'm glad you came, too."

"I thought you could stand a little visit. Doesn't the arm bother you? Isn't it hard to manage with that sling?"

Such solicitousness baffled him; could she be fevered? Or was it pity, a sentiment she had never evidenced toward him in the slightest before? "Just getting dressed and undressed, really."

She dropped their continental breakfast on his dresser and turned to him with a playful smile. "Would you like any help in that department?"

Her sudden, unsubtle affection stirred him at once. Her reasons, always a mystery, he chose not to pursue. "I didn't know you were a registered nurse."

"More the practical sort," she said, coming closer. "Speaking of which, you seem to be straining your pajamas very badly. You'd better get into something more substantial. Here, I'll get them for you—"

On the bed, his immobilized arm required somewhat delicate logistics. He remained on his back, and she directed operations from above him. The enforced passivity of his posture lent an antic note to the seriousness of the proceedings. It was plain within a short while that, without further ceremony or pledges of mutual ardor, she was about to bestow her virginity upon him. Or, more precisely, to impale it on his overcompensatingly rampant maleness.

"Isn't this rape?" he asked, smiling up.

"Shut up and put your thing on."

"My thing's already on—it's between your legs."

"Not that thing—the thing that goes on your thing."

"They're in my drawer—the second one—behind the socks."

She dismounted nimbly and drew out the little box. "They're ugly," she said, examining one closely. "They smell so—industrial."

"I think they're supposed to be more functional than decorative."

She handed him the folded white device. "Okay, so function."

He fumbled with it, trying to break the seal.

"Good Christ, here, give it to me." She slid off the paper impatiently, handed it back, watched him fumble with it again and look up at her appealingly. "I get it—you want service with a smile."

The act of sheathing him heightened her excitement still more, and she fed his coated firmness into herself gently, a little at a time, eyes fastened fiercely, mouth slowly contorting while he reached his good hand out and dug his fingertips into the fleshiest part of her taut thigh. Fully encased, he could not long endure her powerful, hungry churning. She shrieked with gladness at his swift expenditure, then quickened her lunges above him in hunger for gratification that steadily more eluded her with each almost desperate movement. In the end, she slipped off him and pressed her body over the length of his in careful, ungrudging embrace. When he reached his hand down to attend to her pleasure, she stayed it and said it did not matter.

The onesidedness of it troubled him. And he wondered about her pain and why there had been no blood.

"All my bicycle riding," she explained just above a whisper. "I think I lost it when I was nine."

He pressed her to him with a joy muted by their awkward, unfulfilling arrangement, more a sacrificial immolation on her part than shared bliss. She felt weightless upon him as he stroked the supple curvature of her back with his wide-open palm. This was, without doubt, the most extraordinary, unpredictable, merciless and merciful creature on the face of the earth at that moment. How could he love what he did not understand? Or was that precisely why?

Her face was hot and motionless beside his, their skin meshing in momentary contentment. His tongue wandered to her cheek and the tip probed along its lateral axis, dimpling her face in playful adoration. She emitted a tiny laugh and drew her own cheek away. "You're so funny," she said. "Did you know?"

"Mmmm."

"No, I mean it." She lifted one drowsy eyelid of his with her fingers and compelled his attention. "You're so gentle and—and unaggressive most of the time—and then you can suddenly turn into this—flaming pillar of rectitude." She tensed her pelvis against his. "And I don't mean that one."

"Mmmm."

"Don't 'mmmm' me—I'm being serious. You're a very strange person, Toby. One minute I think I understand you perfectly and decide you're an unmanly weasel—and the next you're a holy terror I don't understand at all but want to love with all my might."

He ran his hand through her long, smooth hair. "You have a terrible problem, miss—almost as bad as mine."

She molded her hands against his temples and looked down on him with the full force of her being. "Toby," she whispered, "what are we going to do with each other?"

His words were as hushed as hers: "I thought what we were doing before was pretty good for starters."

"Oh, you're horrid," she said, grasping a clump of his hair with a short, punishing tug.

She came the following two Sundays, too, and while he succeeded in protracting his own tumescence and pleasure, he could not sustain it enough for her fulfillment as well. Their unnatural deployment, he told her, and not any physiological lack, was responsible. The male was meant to assume the superior position. "Where is that written?" she asked, irritable now that she had not been able to accommodate herself to his supine position and still rejecting his offer of manual relief.

By the fourth Sunday, his arm was better. The sling was gone, he showed her with delight as he let her in—"a whole week ahead of schedule," he said and posed for her like Popeye. She smiled briefly and caressed the repaired area with delicacy to test it for pain. He evidenced none. In fact, he looped both arms around her shoulders and tried to gather her to him. But she tightened and held back, and her eyes refused to meet his. "What's the matter, Chessie—you prefer me crippled?"

"No—not at all." She busied herself with the coffee and buns.

"Then what is it?"

"Nothing—it's nothing. Hey, I'm really glad."

He let her be, and they had coffee together, but she was sullen and avoided going anywhere near his bed. "What is it—your period? Just say so and don't grump."

"I told you—it's not anything."

"Then why don't you want to go to bed and do it the real way? I mean what we've been doing is no good for either of—"

"I can't anymore, Toby."

"Why not? Because I'm better?" He gave a laugh of disbelief at the perversity of the notion, then all at once understood he had hit the mark. "What was all that, then—a mission of mercy or something?"

She turned her head from him.

"Or a goddamned reward for trying to save that kid in Woonsocket? Shit, I don't want any reward, Chessie—I want you."

"I'm—very—sorry. I just—can't now—okay?"

"No, it's not okay. One minute you're tending me like a passionate earth goddess and the next you don't want to have anything—"

"I'm not the same person every week—or every day, even."

"Oh, I can see that."

"Hey, don't get shitty with me, Toby—I don't owe you a blessed thing."

"Sure—right. Nobody owes anybody anything—except a little decency, maybe."

"A little indecency, isn't that what you mean? The second you're better, you can't wait to jump me. I think that's pretty crude, if you want to know what I think."

He sat on the edge of the bed, shaking his head. "You just have to be in charge with me, don't you? That's what it's all about, isn't it?"

"Spare me the Freud."

"Maybe you'd go for boots and a whip."

"Thank you," she said and headed for the door. "Don't overdo the arm—okay?"

He reached for the bun beside him on the dresser top and hurled it at her back. "Thanks for breakfast."

After that, half-addled with confusion and anger, he told himself it was done finally. How could he share a future with anybody so mercurial? And their backgrounds and temperaments were so hopelessly different. Perhaps the fault was his. What did he have to offer her, really, besides intelligence, devotion, and cloud-high dreams? He had no material resources or calculable prospects—and was nobody's idea of Don Juan. How could he think she would ever have him in marriage? It was so remote a likelihood as to seem preposterous. But to lapse back into a platonic friendship now after having come so close to an intensely erotic one was equally unthinkable. Grace dictated a clean break between them.

Yet he would not relent altogether. Or take her unsmitten state for a judgment of his merits. He viewed his hopes as untimely rather than forlorn; she would come around yet. Meanwhile, the two of them had their separate preoccupations that final season in Cambridge.

SIX

THE FORMAL PURSUIT of knowledge beyond the baccalaureate is not much fun as chases go. The magic of discovery is gone and all but impossible to recapture. The scholar's purpose is no longer innocent. Free-roaming curiosity, that priceless resource of the unformed undergraduate mind, is rarely an asset at the graduate level.

The lasting lessons of his final year in Cambridge, not surprisingly, were all learned outside of class. A common enough experience, certainly, but more ironic in Toby's case because he spent so much of his time in matriculated study. There was his erstwhile tutor to thank for that. The corrosive Graham Halyard, having discouraged his entry upon an academic career, nevertheless urged him to be practical about it. And so by day, Toby delved into Middle English syntax, Spenserian imagery, and similar arcane delights under the guidance of Travis and other Harvard illuminators of literature. By night, he wallowed in the still less scintillating study of educational methods at Boston University so he might be certified to teach at the pre-college level if and when the need arose. With extraordinary kindness, Graham even helped line him up as a B.U. teaching assistant, grading papers and taking over class sections in emergencies in return for free tuition.

The dual regimen forced several choices on him. The first was starving or swallowing his pride long enough to ask Aunt Ida for a loan. Indebtedness to family may be just as mortifying as to outsiders, but it is at least easier to rationalize and somewhat less likely to wind up in court. As between devoting himself to social movements or bowel movements in the precious little time available to him for either, nature similarly dictated. Yet if that wearisome curriculum cut down severely on acts of conscience and friendship, it did not spare him altogether from exposure to shortcomings of character that suddenly surfaced in those to whom he had been closest.

Rupert Donovan was the most egregious case in point.

Having tasted the bitter fruits of martyrdom, Rupe decided he was done with losing battles. Being right was fine, but without power it was nothing. And in America no one was more skilled at getting and using power than lawyers. They ran the country, and that was what Rupe wanted to do. Once he was in charge, there would be plenty of time for reforms.

Harvard Law School was—and to a considerable extent remains—a factory. Very eminent of its sort, of course, but still a factory: large, impersonal, mechanical. Those who geared themselves to it prevailed. Its highest form of reward was membership on the board of the *Law Review*, a distinction then based solely on the class rank of students at the end of the first year. There was a good deal more justice to this than, say, election to Porcellian, but the selection criterion turned the fateful first year into a terrible grind for all who chose to compete.

Rupe warmed up for the game by taking on the protective coloration of his new milieu. He wrote Toby over the summer that he thought it best if he roomed with another law student and hoped his decision would not impair their friendship, which he valued so highly. Already he sounded like a corporation lawyer. Even so, Toby was not prepared to hear him announce over supper at the end of September, when the general textile strike was broken by goons the mill owners hired with the connivance of law officers, that the unions got what they deserved. The N.R.A. textile code had just been negotiated in June and the mills appeared to be honoring it, he said. Child labor had been abolished and, according to the papers, hourly rates were up 70 percent and the work week shorter by one third. "What more do they want?"

"If you earn twenty dollars a week instead of twelve," Cheska said, joining them for the occasion, "it's still practically slavery."

"Nobody's making them work," Rupe said, "so don't call it that, okay? And there still happens to be a severe depression on, so you can hardly expect the owners to be overly generous with wages—they're probably doing the best they can commensurate with economic survival. Just because the unions don't think so is no reason to organize assaults on people who want to exercise their right to work. Either you have law and order or you have chaos."

His pacifism, at least, was consistent with his undergraduate values; only his sense of justice had changed. "But laws don't mean anything," Toby said, "unless they're enforced against the powerful as well as the weak. Anton says the N.R.A. code enforcement is a joke—umpteen hundred grievances against management have been turned over to the National Labor Relations Board and they haven't decided one yet in favor of the textile workers."

"Maybe so—it takes time."

"It's criminal neglect!" Cheska snapped at him.

"What's criminal," Rupe said, "is trying to improve the system by intimidation and violence. The N.R.A. is a creature of the Congress, and you don't thumb your nose at it with flying squadrons of hooliganism."

His rightward shift grew with his vocational attachment, particularly after Roscoe Pound, in his twentieth year as dean of the law school, went off to Germany to accept an honorary degree from the University of Berlin. To compound matters, he called the Nazi regime a strong, stabilizing counterthrust to "agitating movements." Cheska, by then vice president of the N.S.L. chapter and a campus celebrity over the Putzi affair, organized an immediate protest. When she asked Rupe to take charge of circulating an anti-Pound petition within the law school itself, he waved her off with a jaunty, "Hey, the guy's just cashing in his chips."

"'The guy,'" she said, "is dean of Harvard Law School. Fascism is a travesty on the law. How can you stand by and crack wise?"

The unspoken answer was that Roscoe Pound, for all his lofty standing as a sage of jurisprudence, was known to become very testy with his detractors. And they were legion at the moment. The school has been sharply criticized by leaders of the "legal realist" movement for being far more expedient than principled in its approach to the law and for serving primarily as a blind conduit of talent to the big mills on Wall Street and other centers of corporate practice. There was some naïveté and more than a touch of jealousy in the attack, Rupe reassured them. The law, after all, had evolved mainly as an instrument for the protection of property—a cudgel for the haves to restrain the have-nots—and was thus largely responsible for moving mankind out of the caves into the lush groves of permissible greed. Harvard, therefore, performed its highest professional service by training lawyers accordingly. It was all very well for Yale and Columbia to try lately to accommodate law to pressing social issues, but it fell to Harvard, the fount of American legal education, to maintain its rigor and not tinker with the verities. "And nobody," Rupe contended, "knows more about Roman imperial law than Roscoe."

"Which no doubt explains his partiality to tyrants," said Cheska.

It went farther than that. Pound was very much an autocrat in his own right. He ran the law school, as one of his faculty was said to have remarked, "as if he owned fifteen percent of the stock." Such hauteur had hastened the flight of some of the school's best legal minds to join the New Deal in Washington. The trend embittered Pound, as much for the experimental nature of the laws they were helping promulgate as for the act of desertion itself. And no one was said to have aroused the old boy's ire more than Felix Frankfurter, who remained on the faculty but jumped back and forth like a shuttlecock between Cambridge and Washington, siphoning off academic talent to man the national recovery drive. You could get a nice argument whether Pound's displeasure with Frankfurter, the only Jew on the law faculty, was due to the professor's alleged disloyalty or the dean's alleged anti-semitism. Pound's attitude on the latter score was ambiguous at best. He had openly backed Brandeis for the Supreme Court—by no means a universally favored position at Harvard (President Lowell, for one, being dead against him)—and sided with Frankfurter in several of his run-ins with Lowell over civil liberties. But Pound had failed to confront Lowell's bias against Jews as it affected the law school admissions policy and faculty appointments, and his acceptance now of academic honors from the Nazis was strong circumstantial evidence of the dean's latent sentiments.

"That's crazy," Rupe said. "The law school is full of Jews. And the *Law Review* is at least one-third Jewish. What more do you want?"

"I want you not to count," Cheska told him and turned away.

Rupe's conversion to orthodoxy intensified, if anything, at the end of the first term. His grades tied him for ninth in the class and made him a shoo-in for *Law Review* if he held on academically. In the political positions he took, the places he frequented, and friends he saw, he did as little as possible to awaken controversy or ridicule. He had become, in Toby's view, purposeful to a fault. When the state legislature, convening after the turn of the year in a mood of exceptional benightedness, proposed that membership in the Communist Party be made a felony, Rupe had to be dragooned onto the university-wide protest committee the N.S.L. helped enlist. So widely was the proposed state law perceived as a rape of First Amendment freedoms that almost all of liberty-loving Massachusetts joined to defeat the bill, but Rupe's participation was never more than perfunctory.

Worse, he avoided entirely the protest effort, led by President Conant himself, which greeted the legislature's successful drive to impose a loyalty oath on every member of the teaching profession, public or private, in the state. Thanks to the inspirational leadership of Governor Ely and Mayor Curley, those twin pillars of Boston-brand reaction, any kindergarten teacher or Harvard philosopher who did not swear eternal fealty to the federal constitution was in violation of the laws of the commonwealth and subject to dismissal. Rupe trivialized the step as an act of mindless but harmless obeisance to the right-wing —a bone for gnawing away its frustration. "The thing is more stupid than dangerous," he said. "I mean, no dedicated Communist would hesitate to lie under oath, so what practical good can it possibly do?"

"Even so," Toby argued, "why single out teachers and make them into a suspect class? Why not make butchers take an oath, too?"

"Because poisoning meat isn't as bad as poisoning minds. Teachers are supposed to be moral exemplars. Would you want a murderer or a pederast teaching your kids? I say Communists are no better. They're dogmatists—they've hocked their intellectual integrity—they believe in doctrines completely alien to the American way—it's a movement that thrives on conspiracy and calculated deceit. Why should we let people who've declared war on our society and everything it stands for teach the next generation of Americans?"

"But this law doesn't penalize them for *teaching* communism—or for doing anything. It makes it a crime just to *believe* in it—or even to *think* some other political system besides ours might be better. That's the beginning of the end of intellectual freedom. That's Nazi repression."

"Christ, everything even vaguely patriotic now is Nazi." He looked away from Toby impatiently. "Well, I won't buy that. I think your bunch is going a little overboard."

"I don't have a bunch," Toby said. "I never have had—except you."

When Cheska invited him to serve on the steering committee for the second N.S.L.-led peace strike, planned for the anniversary of the one he had run the previous spring from the steps of Widener, Rupe declined the honor. "You're a hero now," she persisted, "a legend in your own time. Your being there could make all the difference."

"The issue isn't whether I'm there," he said. "It's whether there should be *anyone* there. Flops don't rate encores."

"Last year was *not* a flop—half the university turned out."

"Sure—to laugh its ass off. The point's been made—leave it."

"The gutless bastard," Cheska said to Toby after. "He makes me sick."

The chameleon did not revolt him quite so much until late in May when the Supreme Court, with Rupe's blessing, dealt a massive blow to the reforms of the New Deal. The Justices had been chipping away at Roosevelt's recovery program for a year or more, but now they used a meat cleaver to dismember the blue eagle, the very symbol of the renewal effort. The N.R.A. codes, governing more than five hundred industries from automobiles to pants pressing, had been conceived to revitalize the economy by alleviating the worst effects of murderous competition—vicious price-cutting, unfair trade practices, oppressive labor conditions. The only way the complex codes could be thrashed out in time to be useful in the emergency, Congress had decreed, was to leave their specific provisions and enforcement in the hands of the President and his administration. No, the Supreme Court ruled now—that was a legislative function of enormous magnitude and could not be constitutionally delegated by Congress.

"Absolutely not," Rupe concurred. "Once you start hollering emergency and changing the rules, you've got a whole new game."

"There's a difference between changing them and bending them a little," Toby suggested. "Isn't the real genius of the American political system supposed to be its flexibility? The Court doesn't seem to have any give."

"Because principles aren't elastic. You just don't understand the rule of law. It's like legitimacy—either you have it or you don't. And I'll tell you something else—with all this talk about fascism, you should be damned glad that there's still a Supreme Court sticking up for democracy. You can't impose strict regulations on all of American industry without the consent of the governed and still pretend you've got a free country. You can't hand over that much power to one man and not wind up with a Caesar. Franklin Roosevelt is becoming one dangerous critter."

"But you helped elect him."

"The impetuosity of my youth," he said mirthlessly. "The man's got to be stopped. That's what the Court is there for."

"Maybe the Court's wrong."

"Toby, the Court was unanimous—including Brandeis. No one's against humanitarianism, but don't you see—tyranny can come in a wheelchair as well as jack boots."

He had answers for everything now. But when he nearly flunked Williston's contracts course and wound up the year ranked twenty-third in the class—out of the money—his only response was a three-day bender during which he repeatedly vilified the Jews who had usurped his rightful place on the *Law Review*.

Rupe's metamorphosis had run full circle. Toby never did say good-bye to him.

II

Besides helping run the bookshop that year, Cheska also became Sara's housekeeper, nurse, and bedtime storyteller after she began to reveal the excruciating effects of a duodenal cancer.

Cheska moved out of the Radcliffe dorms and into the spare bedroom in the apartment above the shop—"Toby's seraglio," she called it with only mild distaste and made him help her flip over the mattress he had performed on all summer. She kept the shop operating, cooked when Sara felt like eating, stopped her from dosing herself with morphine, and read to her through the long nights of pain. For diversion they labored together over a letter to Trotsky, expressing their immoderate admiration, likening him in ways to Jackson and Lincoln and Whitman, and hoping his days as a wanderer might yet end in America. Cheska got it translated and mailed it off to Paris, though his publishers advised that the hounded outcast was living clandestinely in the South of France and a response was unlikely. Just sending it was fulfillment for Sara.

"She hasn't had a whole lot of laughs from life," Cheska remarked more to herself than to Toby when he came by the shop one afternoon to help out for an hour. "The woman doesn't deserve this ending."

A softer soul would have taken her affliction as divine disapproval of waywardness from the faith and wrapped herself in piety in hopes of eternal forgiveness. Sara, on the contrary, found the arrival of the disease corroborative only of her rage over life's unmeaning. As it started to waste her body and haunt her eyes, she grew surer the church would eventually reward her for having lived the gospel of compassion. "Saint Sara—it has a beatific sound," she would say whenever the stigmata did not draw too badly.

"The hardest part," Cheska confided once when Toby came for a visit, "is making sure she doesn't see me cry. At least I'm down to once a day now." Then she got out her old poncho and went to drape it lovingly over the defiant, dwindling patient.

The net effects on the nurse, who through all this kept her studies at honors level, was a heightened impatience with nonsense and perpetual fatigue that nearly eliminated her social life. The sole link she kept with her activist past was to serve as second-in-command of the Harvard-Radcliffe chapter of the National Students League. With Rupe gone (as well as skittish fellow-travelers like Toby), the chapter tilted leftward, in some ways too far even for Cheska's comfort. A new crop of more vocal, more radical recruits pushed the N.S.L. into provocative activities like sponsoring Marxist study groups to fill that continuing void in the college curriculum, inviting C.P. officials and prominent foreign socialists to address all who would listen, and picketing the statehouse noisily almost all spring while the legislature was busy trying to outlaw political heresy.

"They practically make me into a tsarist," Cheska said, fearful the new breed's militancy, though swelling N.S.L. ranks for the moment, was getting them all branded as extremists. At Harvard that could lead only to derision and, before long, oblivion.

Thus, when the national leadership of the N.S.L. scheduled the second annual peace strike for April, Cheska welcomed it as a chance to reaffiliate the chapter with Harvard's other political reform groups—as *primus inter pares*, to be sure, but decidedly away from the frenetic fringe. Since pacifism had begun to turn into something of a milquetoast cause even in the Left-liberal camp, no one begrudged her the job of organizing the rally. She was determined that it avoid the mockery it had become the previous year. This would be her swan song as an undergraduate rabble-rouser, and she meant to exit in style.

The preliminary signs were encouraging. In the interest of political ecumenism, she enlisted the president of the Harvard Liberal Club to be master of ceremonies. The speakers' roster was to include a prominent Quaker from the American Friends Committee, the dean of Tufts Divinity, a Harvard chemistry lecturer partial to orating from inside a capitalist coonskin coat, and a national officer from the Socialist Party—no communists. Then she stormed the deanery in Massachusetts Hall and extracted a promise that the campus cops would not stand idly by this time while hecklers dismantled the proceedings. What she did not get in the end, however, was the university's permission to stage the rally on the steps of Widener and thereby commandeer the entire Yard. The peace rally would be held on the lawn of Mem. Hall, a far more confining site but one accessible to the Cambridge cops if the heckling turned brutal.

Spurned by Rupe in her bid for moral support, Cheska turned to Toby. "All I need you to do is play counselor," she said the day before the rally. "We've got a group going around to the high schools with handbills, urging the kids to hold their own miniature rallies. I didn't bother with a permit—there's too much rigamarole, and we'd probably get turned down, anyway—so technically it's illegal. If you could just more or less sort of keep an eye on things—" The wily Krupskaya, Jr., den mother to conspirators-in-training.

He went more out of love than conviction, getting his priorities wrong still one more time.

Toby's brigade got no farther than the second high school stop, Ringe Tech, where Barney Quigley, Bonnie's father, taught. His presence was a decidedly mixed blessing. It kept the Ringe officials, who considered him a sincere but misguided troublemaker, from chasing the Harvard agitators out of the schoolyard. Instead, they got the police to do it.

They came on in a flash, paddy wagons at the ready, announcing that the pamphleteers were in violation of city ordinance #47, demanding that the crew cease and desist, and ordering the lot of them to step lively into their mobile custody. All done with a Germanic efficiency that would have had Herr Himmler salivating buckets. Unfortunately, two of the N.S.L. desperadoes, shaggy sophomores, kept distributing their handbills until a galoot of a cop with a horsetail mustache jabbed them hard in the ribs with his nightstick and tried to drag off one by his hair. The boy resisted, the cop swung his stick at the boy, Quigley swung his fist at the cop, another cop shoved Quigley to the ground and began to kick him—and Toby felt Woonsocket ignite in him again. Every synapse shot blue pain—they were kicking the shit out of the father of his friend, like a large sack of guts pudding. What was peace worth if they beat you in its name? Some jungle cat detonated out of his skin and clawed the kicking cop's leg. It was so swift and sure and insane that it wrenched the villain over and down. Six steel muzzles were aimed instantly at Toby's head. They were trooped off to jail in handcuffs.

In short, he had helped accomplish precisely the sort of incident Cheska had sent him to prevent.

The terror he might otherwise have felt on being arrested for the first time fled in the heat of resentment. Their crime was victimless; the police were the thugs. It was a chance to boot some Harvard pansies around—little communist bastards, at that. The hectoring continued in the stationhouse. And in the district court after the booking. The judge himself evidenced a vigilante lust for the hide of anyone radical enough to declare war immoral. He asked the boys who had not been involved in the actual scuffle what their political persuasion was. "None," said the bravest. "We're concerned for the well-being of the whole human race." The others nodded.

The judge was less cosmopolitan. "Then I suggest you start," he said, "by obeying the laws of this city and stop trying to peddle your anarchist filth to the poor, honest boys and girls of Boston. You wiseacres aren't good enough to polish their boots. I think maybe it would be a useful thing if you were all taken out and shot."

He settled, though, for a ten-dollar fine that he said they could work off in jail at fifty cents a day—"just in case any of you angels happens not to have been brought up with a silver spoon." They pooled their cash and made a few phone calls, and within hours all were free.

As to the three of them charged additionally with striking an officer while resisting arrest, His Honor was retributive justice personified. The student pleaded guilty and was fined fifty dollars. Being under age, he was released in the custody of a probation officer and went to raise the money. Quigley pleaded guilty with an explanation—that he had every right to be on the premises and was simply observing the Harvard incursion to make sure it did not turn disorderly; it was the police, in his view, who instigated violence. For his temerity in staying the long arm of the law, he was fined a hundred dollars, an unconscionable sum for a non-Harvard man. They kept him in the lockup past nine that night till Bonnie arrived with the cash scraped together all over town. And Toby—Toby pleaded not guilty, actually believing it. Defiance earned him bail of three hundred dollars.

The Quigleys, Toby gathered, had been too shaken to worry much about him. Bonnie barely nodded over at him in his nearby cell. And on the eve of the big peace rally, he chose not to distract Cheska or to trouble the ailing Sara, neither of whom, in any event, had that sort of money under the pillow. Graham Halyard, who may well have, did not answer his phone—partying in Marshfield Hills, no doubt—and Rupe, the study worm, did not return to his room till nearly midnight. "I think I've got your first client for you," Toby said, chipper as he could manage when Rupe finally lifted the receiver.

He listened to Toby's story and at the end, sounding very far away, said, "I think you're getting a little old for this sort of horsing around." He did it for a friend, Toby said, swallowing his annoyance. "Her, too," Rupe said. "There's nothing more pathetic than an aging *enfant terrible*." Or more judgmental than a first-year law student. Toby was in no position, however, to debate the issue. Rupe agreed, grumbling all the while, to wire home for the money and come rescue his ex-roommate as soon as it arrived the next day. "But you have to promise you won't jump bail," he added.

"Why would I do that?"

"Because it sounds like an open and shut case—you're guilty."

"I was only trying to stop a barbaric act."

"That's your story. Six cops will deny it—and the people on your side have all pleaded guilty already. I'd try Clarence Darrow if I were you—or maybe Our Lady of Fatima."

All that night in a cold, dark cell, rank from feces in a bowl that wouldn't flush and a cellmate reeking of booze and bad memories, he fought a bellyload of methane induced by the chef's blue-plate special —moldy bread and crusty beans—and told himself he was Henry David Thoreau in irons, a wronged majority of one.

Dreams transported him intermittently. It was always the same one: of a terrier tearing the flesh from a kicking cop's leg. Between delicious, if conscience-stricken, bites, he listened to his scrofulous roomie reciting tales of survival through hard times and pissing in the corner of the cell nearest Toby's head. Both were intended as fraternal acts. After his bladder drained, the vagrant's memory refilled and Toby would hear how he had picked peas for a penny a pound in Ohio, and almost had a leg ripped off at the knee jumping a MoPac freight out-

side St. Jo, and staved off frozen feet plodding the winter streets of
Chicago in two layers of socks, bunched wax paper, and a pair of old
sneakers he patched with adhesive tape every time they sprang a leak.
"Speaking of leaks," he said and revisited the corner, passing wind as
well as urine and returning to advise that Boston beans were better
than the cinderized potatoes, coffee full of sand, and occasional shred
of sour chicken on which he had learned to live. Now he was working
the docks two days a week—all his leg would allow. In between, he
panhandled and tanked up, winning arrest whenever he got too aggressive about either. "And you, boy," he asked, blearily focusing on
his company, "what'd you do—kiss a nun?"

Rupe showed up at two-thirty the next afternoon, unfazed about
the possible ill effects of Toby's languishing in durance vile. The
money had come late and, besides, he had been sufficiently overcome
by nostalgia to attend the peace rally. "The crowd was very small,"
Rupe reported with unseemly satisfaction—"I'd say less than a third of
what we had." That the chilly, rainy day Toby discovered when they
left the jail may have affected the turnout, Rupe would not concede.
Piecemeal, though, he testified that the program had gone off well.
Except for a contingent from Hasty Pudding that arrived in helmets
and trenchcoats and was swiftly escorted from the scene by the Yard
police, nothing more unruly occurred than a few stink bombs and occasional hooting. Nationwide, the peace strike drew 200,000, an eight-
fold increase over the year before.

They were buoyant at the bookshop later that afternoon, partying
on bologna and cheese sandwiches and paper cups of chianti. On
every side the talk was of a popular front forming out of the Left-
liberal-labor elements—a great consensual upsurge of social consciousness. Everything seemed suddenly possible if good men could
ever get together, doctrine be damned! Toby edged past the jam into
the back room, where the heroine of the hour was accepting plaudits.

"Toby!" she shouted and broke through a ring of well-wishers.
"What on *earth* happened to *you?* You missed *every*thing!" A touch
of the grape had turned her theatrical.

"I was unfortunately detained."

"God, you are such a damned drudge! I mean, how could you miss
it en*tirely?* Even Rupe showed his face—or should I say his two
faces?" She touched her temple and swayed toward him. "That was a
joke—did you notice?"

"I did."

"I think I'm a little—"

"I noticed that, too."

She latched on to both his hands and pulled herself slowly upright.

"God, I heard about your adventure at Ringe. Did you really tackle a cop? What a dumb, wonderful thing to do! But how are we going to pay your fine?"

"There isn't any fine—yet."

"What do you mean? They fined everyone else but let you off?"

"Everyone else pleaded guilty."

"And you didn't?" Her head shot back and her glasses flashed. "Oh, God—you mean you've been in *jail* the whole time?"

"Or a place very like it."

"But why didn't you plead guilty?"

"Because the cop was kicking the crap out of Bonnie's father."

"So?"

"So that's not right—so I tried to stop him. Mr. Quigley will explain what was going on—"

"Who told you that?"

"I was trying to help him—that's why I did it—he knows—"

"Toby, they'll fire him if he testifies in court against the cops to help out a Harvard radical."

"That's—absurd. It's not fair!"

"Why do you think he's been working so long for a teachers' union? There's a lot they put up with that's not fair. That's why Bonnie didn't come over to your cell to talk to you—so no one would catch on you were in cahoots with him. She figured you understood—"

"And where did she think I was going to get the money to get out with?"

"Borrow it, I guess—the way she had to. It's what I figured when you didn't call."

"You had a hundred things on your mind—I didn't want to bother you. And, anyway, I was supposed to be helping out, not adding to your problems."

"Oh, God!" She clung to him publicly for a long moment, ignoring the swirl around them. "My poor, dear, demented hero! You just didn't want me to think you were a clod—is that it?"

"Well—"

"Jesus, you are a jerk for someone so smart! I love you, Toby—you are a person I genuinely to God love—don't you *know* that? I care what happens to people I love—there aren't very many of them. Would I have ever let you rot in jail? Did I let Sara?"

"I can't keep track of who you love—or how much—or when—or why. I gave up trying a while back."

"Don't blame it on me!" she hissed.

"Who, then?"

"Look, buster, you're still trying to figure out who in the hell you are—and what you believe—and feel—"

"What's the crime in that?"

"Oh, none—none at all—it's very damned collegiate. But why aren't I entitled to do the same? Haven't you noticed—I am not the adorable sweetheart of Sigma Chi! I don't love 'em and leave 'em—love's too precious to spread around like—like goddamned mayonnaise. Your trouble is you want someone to love you like your mother did. Well, I can't do that, Toby—I'm not that kind of woman—nobody can be for you—and you better get used to the idea."

They were interrupted by the sound of Sara in the bathroom, vomiting up her bologna and a frightening quantity of blood. The shop emptied almost at once.

So, too, did something vital in Cheska. From then until the day she left Cambridge two months later, her spunk began to drain off daily in brackish despair. Part of it, surely, was the emotional letdown. Within that chambered place, she had invested all her being in the most passionate of learning processes and emerged, by any standard but her own, resplendent. Harvard, though, she had always recognized, was only a playing field, a laboratory, a stillness in the storm, a prism to squint at the world through—and when it came out looking all skewed, she could rail away at it with impunity. Now that luxury was over, but the world remained intemperate and unreasonable, and very large, and altogether impervious to the will of one feeble-fisted 'Cliffie about to enter it. Sara's malignancy became for her the private harbinger of a universal doom, and whether rot overtook goodness sooner than later hardly mattered to her anymore.

When they took Sara in to Mass. General for surgery and postoperative treatment, Cheska's normally acute awareness of events around her turned ethereal. Politics was all a folly now; by it the lowest forms of humanity held the highest ones in thrall. The Supreme Court's ruling against the legality of the N.R.A. blew out her pilot light. A little afterward, she assaulted Toby with a copy of *The New Republic*, the only thing current she continued to read. "I knew it would come to this!" she wailed and read to him from the magazine's editorial. The *Schechter* decision, it said, proved the nation either had to learn to put up with the confusions and miseries of an essentially unregulated capitalism or be prepared to replace it with socialism—"there is no middle way."

"I'm not sure I agree with that," he said.

"You're never sure of anything," she said.

She was not herself; he would not be baited. "I love the magazine— I agree with it ninety-eight percent of the time—but it's overreacting

—and so are you. Social change takes time. It's happening but not overnight. It's two steps ahead, one back. The court will change—Roosevelt hasn't named anyone to it at all yet. There'll be different decisions someday—"

"Why are you always so goddamned sweetly reasonable?"

"Why are you getting abusive?"

"Why don't you—ever? Why are you so impossibly civilized? Why do you—keep hanging around—all the time—hoping? All your hoping makes me sick—did you know that, Toby? Sick! Literally makes me—"

He grabbed her by the shoulders. "Shut your mouth, Chessie!"

"Oh, do! Do that!" She yanked off her glasses. "Yes, shake me!" She began to undo her chignon. "Lock the shop door and put out the 'Closed' sign and come upstairs—we're going to fuck like bunnies for three days!"

He dug his fingertips into her arms until she was still. "What is it, Chessie—what's this all about?"

"Isn't that what you want—isn't that why you keep hanging around? Isn't it?"

"Is that all you think of me?"

"I don't know what to think—about you or anything." She gave her hair a violent shake and let it fall. It reached halfway down her back. "I'm leaving," she said with sudden softness. "I'm going home Friday. Bonnie's taking over the shop for the time being—" Her eyes, refusing to settle on his, swam past and floated away.

He groped for any straw. "What about—commencement?"

"I've been to one—that's enough. They can send me my diploma."

"But I thought you were on the outs at home?"

"I was. We've worked something out. I'll see how it goes—"

"And—what'll you do?"

"Look at the Bay a lot."

Then she was crying, openly in surrender, and he held her. She may have had the strength of ten, but it was not bottomless. Indignation, however just, consumes its habitual sufferers. "I think it's a good idea," he said after the tears slowed.

"You would," she said, laughing and sniffling together.

"You need a rest—badly."

"What I need badly," she said, taking his hand, "is upstairs in bed."

It was not a joyful consummation. Even as he relished that cleaving act of love, there was no triumph in it, only desperate spasm before the certain dying of warmth. What did any of it matter if she was going to the other end of the earth?

The bargain she had struck at home became clearer the week after she left.

There were three letters from her. The first went to President Conant, who disclosed it to the *Crimson* as an object lesson for all undergraduates but took pains to refer to the sender only as "a member of the Class of 1935." She could not accept her degree from Harvard in good conscience, she wrote, until making restitution for books that circumstances and weak character had driven her to steal from Widener Library. The enclosed money order was for five hundred dollars.

The second letter went to Bonnie. It had two money orders, each for five hundred. One was for Sara's hospital costs. "If more is needed, please let me know," she wrote. "I am here mostly because I cannot bear being there with her now. I will write her every day, though, as long as I can." The other money was for Bonnie—two years' worth of college tuition. "It is a gift, not a loan, and the only way to repay it is to go. You *must*, dearest friend, or I shall never forgive you."

The third letter was to Toby. It insisted that he change his plea to guilty at the impending trial over the incident with the cops and enclosed a hundred dollars for the fine. "It would never have happened," she wrote, "if I had applied for a permit in the first place. I will not have you on my conscience—only in my heart. From the far side of Saturn, I send you: Much love, C."

The day of her commencement, another letter arrived at the shop— this one addressed to both Sara and Cheska and postmarked Grenoble. Toby translated the French at Bonnie's request. The sender apologized for the delay but said his situation made the mails impossible. He thanked his correspondents for their warm greetings, declared his admiration for the proud spirit and great energy of America, and shared their hope he would live long enough to see it—and them. It was signed "Trotsky."

When he reached the New World the next year, Sara was no longer in it.

III

From the outset of the year, Toby could see the ugly end approaching to the brush war between Graham Halyard, arch overseer of his intellect, and Jeremiah Travis, high-buttoned shepherd of his soul. He was powerless to heal the breach between these severe superintendents of his and equally incapable of choosing sides; each mattered to him too much.

All junior faculty tended to orbit about one or another luminary in their department. That Graham was nominally a Travis man was well understood despite their undisguised political disagreement. On that score, Graham had plenty of company. Most of the literature people were Tory and took the bemused view that Travis's leftward flirtation was so much patrician slumming. When the revolution came, few of them doubted he would be in—not pushing—the tumbrel. Everything about him bespoke aristocratic affinities, except what he said and wrote. Graham, sharing much of his background, manner, and sensibility, could never quite accept that Travis had come out on the opposite side of the political arena. The only explanation, to Graham's way of thinking, was that Travis had to be a fraud.

This uncharitable view became fixed in him following the departmental response to Graham's doctoral dissertation, which he had delivered in Toby's senior year. Titled *The Demonology of John Milton, as Extracted from His Works 'Paradise Lost' and 'Paradise Regained,'* it was a prodigious piece of exegesis, shrewd, stylistically elegant, and rather more partial to Satan's plucky band than the heavenly host. "Sin has the virtue of arousing us," he wrote in the preface, "as virtue suffers the sin of fatiguing us." Travis was said to be unamused. While there was no question of depriving Graham of his doctorate, he was graded off for what the dissertation committee called "alluring technique that cannot quite conceal the candidate's inability to order his materials and unwillingness to grant morality a fair hearing."

"And he's put the old kibosh on my chances of being published," Graham complained. Toby said that sounded unlike Travis. "Because, dear fellow, you don't know him at all well," Graham insisted. "He's plum refused to write me up a letter of endorsement to circulate to the presses." Toby didn't see how that amounted to the same thing. "Because," Graham said, "you don't understand how the game works. Lavish encomia from one's doctoral advisors are a *sine qua non* for publication. Their absence is tantamount to a thunderous veto." Toby asked if there weren't others in the department to whom he might turn. "None half so well regarded," Graham said. "And, at any rate, they all defer up the ladder."

"Then why don't you sit down with him and talk it through?"

"I have, dear fellow. We're irreconcilable. Travis believes man is perfectable; I don't even think he's improvable."

"You might try bending a little."

"A little is not what he'd like," Graham said with a leer. "Shall I tell you what he actually said to me? 'Mr. Halyard,' he said, 'you are gravely infected with the nineteenth century's notion that each man is his own messiah.' When I conceded the charge and took up the party line on free will, with a dash of Bergsonism for diversion, he began to speak of 'aberrations of hyperindividualism' as the source of all modernity's woes. Which got us back to Milton, Satan, and overweening pride. 'But you seem to savor it, Mr. Halyard,' he said, 'and I, sir, find no other hope for salvation but humility through a love of God.' The hypocritical bah-stid."

"Maybe he means it."

"Then he's a pious fool masquerading as a *boulevardier*."

Because he now conceived of Travis as less mentor than tormentor, Graham sensed that his own position at the college was growing untenable. He made no secret of his concern the first time Toby returned to Adams House as an alumnus that fall to play squash at his invitation. The games became a weekly ritual and Toby's sole physical recreation. Graham covered the fee for him; his payment, aside from getting soundly whipped, was to hear out Graham's grievances while keeping his own as brief as possible.

"I may not be long for these hallowed halls," Graham told him, climbing spiderlike up the back wall to retrieve Toby's meanest corner shot.

The ball dove in a diagonal blur for the front wall, hit two inches above the metal base strip, and caromed unreachably to the floor. Game, 15–4. Graham had hardly raised a sweat. His rangy, tubular limbs were ideally suited to the sport. Still, Toby was competitive enough to insist that he not be distracted like that while play was on. At once Graham offered to play the clinching point over, as if a tournament had been at stake. "Proper decorum in the future will do," said Toby. "Now what's all this about imminent doom?"

He gave his racquet a couple of playful twirls. "It's quite true—I'm an ideal candidate for Conant's chopping block, so don't be surprised if you ring me up one day and hear I've shipped off for Patagonia."

There was more to the speculation than his incubating paranoia. On fund-raising jaunts around the country, Harvard's new leader had been assuring the alumni he was no fuddy-duddy administrator and would prune the faculty as an economy measure if the need arose— the deadwood among the younger teachers, mostly. When word got back to Cambridge, Conant was obliged to assure the college that no wholesale purge was contemplated; on the other hand, junior faculty stood warned that only those demonstrating "a high standard of intellectual ability" would be advanced or retained. And what, precisely, did that mean? The president hemmed and hawed and then allowed that "unless a university teacher is carrying on research of some sort— some sort of scholarship, some sort of writing—he will not be a fit instructor for mature students." Which translated to: publish or perish.

"That's absurd," Toby said. "You're held in the highest esteem as a teacher. Who doubts your intellectual ability?"

"Thank you, dear fellow. I may call on you as a character witness. The fact remains, nevertheless, that I haven't published a thing—and the immediate prospect is not bright. I had the most preposterously admiring rejection from the Columbia Press only this morning. That makes an even dozen." There were plenty of other places still to try, he granted when Toby told him to have heart, but the process of circulating a scholarly manuscript was interminable. "Most of these genteel establishments appear to be staffed exclusively by hundreds of blind mice, all of whom evidently inspect each and every submission, tiny pink noses atwitch from beginning to end. I'll be dead and buried before a word of mine ever sees type."

He proceeded to win the second and third games handily, though Toby made each a little closer. At the end, Graham flopped on the floor in the corner and balanced the racquet across his prominent kneecaps. His only hope, he said, was to find "a heavyweight sponsor. Or, of course, I might take the Jeremiah Travis route and simply pay off the publisher."

"That never seemed quite cricket to me," Toby said. "Or that he's the sort. What's the distinction in that?"

"The distinction is in having the funds to arrange it—and keep the details hush-hush." If that was so, Toby wondered, how did he know Travis indulged in the practice? "One hears," he said delphically, "one knows." Then how did Travis get away with it professionally? "Why, because he's in considerable company—and his work is well above the usual donnish drivel—which is not to say distinguished." Then why didn't Graham follow suit? "Because, dear fellow, I have principle."

Strapped financially, Toby was not above accepting a monthly dinner invitation to Graham's fashionably cluttered apartment on Charles. His wife of one year, the radiant and very social former Miss Valerie Dobson, had resigned as an apprentice litterateur and taken up teaching at a girls' private school in Concord, so the meals were catch-as-catch-can. The talk, ranging from merely bright to pointedly savage, compensated. An inordinate amount of it was directed at the defenseless Travis. The more of it Toby heard, the less amusing it became.

Cheska had joined him once at their place for cheese casserole and claret, after which Graham proposed they go to see a Soviet film called *Petersburg Nights*—"Bakunin's been urging it on me every day this week," he said, using his code name for Travis. "He assures me the protagonist is neither a truck nor a reaper."

In fact, the film had proved infinitely more artistic than Hollywood's usual fare. It featured superb scenery, remarkable attention to

detail, and powerful close-ups of, among others, a bevy of Mother
Russia's haunting beauties, long lashes flecked with snow. Cheska and
Valerie were captivated. Graham and Toby groaned at the painful
blatancy of the story, centered on the pre-Revolution rivalry between
two violinists, no less. By the end, it was clear that the original and
unaffected compositions of the young purist would find an appreciative audience after the revolt of the workingman whereas his ham-
handed, money-grubbing antagonist would be swept away with the
aristocracy and all its decadent culture.

"Aside from the total falsity of the premise—" Graham began on
the drive home.

"Namely?" Cheska jumped in.

"Namely, that the artist is better appreciated by one form of tyranny than another," he said, "I thought it wasn't half-bad. Midway
through, I even began to see why Travis was so taken with it—in fact,
I think I finally understand what's behind his whole rosy political
complexion."

"Do share with us, duckie," said Valerie, resigned to his target practice.

"He romanticizes the common man, you see, because he himself is
so uncommon. He relishes the natural, you see, because he is so—unnatural. He identifies himself with Igor back there because, you see,
they are both outcasts—alienated but deserving—"

"Wait," said Cheska, "I don't understand. How is Travis an
outcast?"

"Discretion, sweetie," Valerie warned him as she had been doing for
several years now whenever Graham went foaming off excessively.

"I believe his proclivities are well known," he said.

"Not to me," said Cheska.

"You say you're a Radcliffe senior?"

"In my spare time."

"That would explain it, then. The professor, my dear girl, is a
flaming faggot—a homosexual—a queen—a queer—a consummate
fairy—"

"Oh, please!" Valerie moaned in despair.

"Oh, God!" Cheska whispered, more at Graham's vehemence than
his revelation. "The poor man."

"He's not poor at all, of course—which contributes to his uncom-
monness, don't you see?"

"What's the crime in what he is," Toby asked, "so long as he's discreet about it?"

"It is a perversion, my dear fellow, so recognized by the estimable
Hebrews of yore and unsanctioned in the Commonwealth of Massa-

chusetts even to this day. As to his discretion, I'll grant you he's not
been caught laying so much as a cuticle on a Harvard boy, but he car-
ries on notoriously with that pathetic Fairchild, as devoted a buggerer
as fawned over any oily-loined discobolus in all Attica." He jammed
on the brakes for a red light. "And there are stories I need not relate
of his climbing into exotic getups and prowling the waterfront saloons
for a tender young sailor—"

"Graham!" Valerie almost screamed. "Leave off!"

"They asked."

"No," she said, "you provoked."

"I'm merely trying to explain him. Don't you see—the man is strad-
dling two worlds, but he's at home in neither. He loathes himself for
what he is, no doubt—and the rest of us for loathing him on account
of it."

However much Graham's invective stemmed from understandable
frustration, it succeeded in diminishing not the object of his ire but
only its author. After the turn of the year, the attacks intensified as
Travis took several political positions in public that stirred enmity in
many besides Graham Halyard.

When exploratory meetings were arranged throughout the academic community to debate the merits of a Greater Boston federation
of university teachers, few tenured faculty lent their names to the
effort—it was mostly younger people, after job security and decent
pay. Harvard teachers in general saw no advantage professionally, or
any other way, in consorting with the riffraff. Travis, to his credit,
was not so squeamish. He not only attended a gathering devoted to
the subject; he served as its cutting edge. Graham was on hand as well,
ever the moth to the flame—and, to his credit, was not squeamish
about challenging his departmental superior. Barney Quigley, an old
hand at trying to organize teachers of less exalted rank, smuggled
Toby into the proceedings.

In his unexceptionable keynote remarks, Travis argued that now
was the time for enlightened men, whatever their faith or calling, to
step forward as brothers and restore balance to the social system. And
if ever there was a group equipped to help identify the larger needs of
society and frame their solutions, it was the professoriate. "In union,
our single voices grow exponentially. I commend this endeavor to you
most heartily."

Seconding sentiments flowed harmlessly for a time until Graham
stood and said, "With all due respect, I would like to propose that our
profession ought properly to remain above the battles of our age."
That was precisely the proper place and perspective for the university
community. "We may act forthrightly as individuals, of course, join-

ing in the political process if, as, and when we are so disposed. But we vitiate our special contribution to society, I submit, to the very extent we throw in together as just another partisan crowd. The very essence of our function lies in its dispassion."

Most who shared that view had had the courtesy to stay home. Yet it was not a point to be dismissed lightly by a company of thoughtful men. It fell to Travis to blunt the lance of his junior colleague. "Mr. Halyard prescribes for us a life of contemplation, which I endorse, and of inaction, which I deplore." His tone never varied; the edge was in its constancy. "I had not realized ours was so effete an occupation. If we are professors, may we not profess? And as we are workingmen, may we not band together to ask to be fed and clothed and housed as befits our station?"

Graham was on his feet before the chair recognized him. "We surrender our station, sir, when we negotiate like dock workers. Collective bargaining is a demeaning practice when linked to the cultivation of the mind. Wisdom should not be reduced to the lowest common denominator."

Almost elfin compared to Graham, Travis seemed to expend minimal effort in cutting him down to size. "I do not take so lofty a view of our calling," he said, addressing the room generally, almost as if his antagonist were beneath direct notice. "And I am doubtful that any profession can properly claim to fulfill its highest responsibility by exempting itself from the commonality. We are entitled, furthermore, to be as practical about our needs as normal men. Either we are allied with the propertied interests, or we work for wages. Power resides overwhelmingly with the former unless the latter act in concert. And that is all we are proposing here tonight—to join the vast coalition of workers to seek the social and economic improvement of our society."

"Is the professor proposing an American labor party?" Graham blurted. "If so, he misconceives the character of our countrymen. We have largely left the rigidifying evil of class stratification on the shores of the Old World. The spirit of individuality is the principal distinction of our people. Every workingman in the United States prefers his independence to the dubious rewards of collectivization."

Travis wore the look of a man heroically patient while being lectured to by a grape. He turned directly to Graham now. "No one, Mr. Halyard, has said a word here about collectivization. There is a sizable difference between mutual interest and mutual possession. The members of a harem share a mutual interest with the sultan, but they cannot be said to achieve status because he is their mutual possession; it is rather the other way around." There were smiles on all faces but Graham's. His objections were shunted aside thereafter.

He simply could not bear being put down like that. And yet unaccountably—perhaps deluded by animus—he invited a public reprise later that spring. It was at a full-dress departmental meeting, summoned to hear President Conant explain why Harvard, having fought against passage of the state's teacher loyalty oath, would not tolerate disobedience to the iniquitous law. Accounts of the session were all over the college next morning.

This time, the two of them had started out on the same side. Toby had run into Graham in February right after the departmental party for Kittredge's seventy-fifth birthday, and all the talk there, he said, had been against the loyalty oath and for Conant's vigorous testimony before the state legislative committee, calling the requirement a blow to free thought. Graham himself was as much opposed to the oath as to a labor union for professors, and for some of the same reasons. The state was justified, perhaps, in demanding an oath from its own employees, "but it's none of their damned business who thinks what at a private institution."

Once the law was on the books, though, a great row arose over Harvard's proper response. Sentiment was strong with some of the faculty to resist the oath and challenge it under the First Amendment in the courts. Others, however, of whom Conant was foremost, viewed such blatant defiance of government as anarchic. Harvard's obligation, her president insisted, was to set an example of responsible citizenship. The university had made its position forcefully known during the legislative process and, having lost, could and should work now for repeal; meanwhile, however, it was "unthinkable" that Harvard, repository of civilization and beacon of democracy, would tolerate unlawfulness among her faculty.

Opinion at the English departmental meeting was closely divided. Most of the men in the room had spoken by the time Graham got up. His opinion, as possessor of one of the keenest minds and slyest tongues among the junior faculty, was awaited with interest disproportionate to his rank.

He had given the matter much serious thought, he said—"as is my wont"—and whereas he yielded to none in his allegiance to personal liberty, he held Harvard to be a unique institution which, at critical moments, depleted her moral force if she spoke to the community at large with disparate voices. For himself, he would as soon defy the oath and take his chances in the courts. But the wiser course, he thought, was for each of them to abide by the consensus of the faculty as a whole, whatever it proved to be. "This is no time for hyperindividualism," he said—all reports agreed he used that word, which could not have escaped Jeremiah Travis. "We owe Harvard a display not of our overweening pride but of our devotion. Not the mindless sort—we would be disloyal to ourselves in that—but once we have thrashed it over, let us vote, close ranks, and stand as one before the world in this matter. The alternative is ineffectual bickering—and this proud place deserves better from us."

Amid a swell of approving murmurs, Travis took the floor.

"I had planned to keep my own counsel," he said, "until hearing Mr. Halyard's seductive line of thought. I do not derogate it as unworthy. I say merely it misconceives the nature of a university—certainly this one. If, as our esteemed president decrees, Harvard must not set herself above the law, then I say neither must she set herself above the consciences of her sons. Yes, she may indeed expect devotion from us, but she may not impose orthodoxy on us. Long ago, Reverend Mather demanded an oath of religious purity of this faculty, even as the state is now demanding one of political purity—and Harvard, according to the annals, gave the Reverend Mr. Mather the heave-ho. In that abiding spirit, may I commend to you not only tolerance of unorthodoxy within this venerable college but also the right of each scholar, as of any man, to meet his oppressors as he alone sees fit?"

It was a contest Graham could not win. As his distaste for Travis turned to bitterness, he found in the professor's inconsistencies of view only fatal flaws of character. He could not conceive—or would not grant—that the man's intellect thrived on its very effort to reconcile life's contradictions. Anyone might champion causes that were thrillingly unambiguous; to forge truth out of dark polarities was high art. Jeremiah Travis loathed materialism as only the rich can. He saw beauty amid vulgarity as only the aesthetic can. He suffered the benefits of injustice as only the privileged can. He fled madness through faith as only the sanest can. He distilled rectitude from his own impurities as only the self-lacerating can. Were all these the feats of a sublime honesty—or the ruses of a supreme hypocrisy?

Graham's not implausible proposal on the oath issue was quietly forgotten in the wake of Travis's memorable rejoinder, and throughout the rest of the year most of the faculty, Graham among them, limply complied with the Conant directive. Travis, however, did not. He neither signed nor refused to sign the oath. And he issued no flaming manifesto. But everyone knew; his silence resonated. How long he would hold out—how long Conant would wait—nobody could say. Heresy, while not unknown before at Harvard, was not habitual.

By mid-spring, the fastidious little professor of literature had added cubits to his stature. No one in that part of the woods had been more civilly disobedient since Henry David Thoreau. Toby kept dreaming

Travis would hold fast till the whole faculty recanted its surrender and fell in with him—and the state, unable to humble fair Harvard and not quite peeved enough to close her down, would relent. In the midst of this reverie, he had a note from the departmental secretary that Travis wished to see him. Before an appointment could be scheduled, word circulated that Graham had been let go.

On the face of it, he was just one of several dozen victims of Conant's springcleaning. Unproductive scholars had been duly warned the deadwood was in peril. But it was impossible to think of Graham Halyard in those terms. He was embarked on a career luminous with promise—everyone agreed. The only explanation was the one on all lips in the department: Travis had done him in. Or, more accurately, he had done himself in by being indiscreet once too often.

As Toby heard it, Graham had been putting it about that Travis's failure to sign the loyalty oath was not an act of principle at all but of simple prudence: to sign would be to perjure himself because he was in fact a communist sympathizer, if not an actual enrollee in the party. Indeed, it was well known that he had aided and abetted radical Leftist causes for some years now, giving his time, money, and even living room to avowed critics of the American system. On top of which, Graham took open note of the man's alleged turpitude—what he called, in swinish euphemism, "tiptoeing through the tulips." And, most cutting of all professionally, he charged the professor with being "at best a mediocre scholar, subsidized by a first-class bank account."

Aside from its unutterableness, all of that was arguable. But none of it would have been spoken if Travis had not been so illiberal toward Graham's dissertation, confusing moral preference with intellectual rigor. One ungenerous act begat others in response, and it was no longer easy to say what validity, if any, there was to their judgments of each other or which of them, in the end, had proven the more vindictive. Graham's gravest sin might well have been a simple want of deference.

Toby suggested as much after Graham failed to show up for their weekly squash match and he found the grieving tutor hunched in his office with the shade half-drawn. "Perhaps so," he said softly from the depths of his spring-popping leather chair. "I have reverenced no living thing since a sulky Labrador retriever named Hollingshead—it died of distemper on Christmas Eve the year we were both six. Poor devil."

That was the extent of his acknowledging culpability in his own downfall. He seemed more removed than distraught, thinking ahead rather than back. "The thing is, dear fellow, every other place is such a drop-off from here." Toby suggested six or eight schools that might

suit him. "The job market is tight," Graham said, "unless one is thinking Washburn or, say, Upsala." Toby tried to cheer him, saying it
hardly mattered where he went since Harvard would soon be begging
to have him back. "Harvard rewards," said Graham, "and Harvard
punishes—Harvard does not beg. Ever."

Toby was edgy as he went for his appointment with Travis. It
deeply troubled him that these two who had orchestrated so much of
his education had come to a sorry parting. Neither meant the world to
him, exactly—both were such remote men, in their ways, though
given to sudden saving flashes of warmth—yet their falling-out left
him feeling reduced by a factor of two. It all seemed so unnecessary.
He wanted to indicate as much to Travis.

"If you'll forgive an impertinence, sir," he began, "may I say how
greatly I admire the position you've taken with regard to the oath?"

Travis was reading the last few lines of a term paper on the pile in
front of him. "You know about that, do you?" he said without looking up.

"Everyone does, sir."

"More's the pity."

"Why, sir? There's a good deal of support for your position."

"That's odd," he said, red-penciling a grade on the top page of the
paper and looking up now with that wafery smile he wore when
straining to be pleasant. "I didn't think I'd taken any position at all as
yet."

"But isn't that tantamount to resistance—sir?"

"Thou sayest so, Mr. Ronan."

His reserve softened a bit. He did not mind a little worship.
"Would it be entirely out of line, sir, to ask your intention?"

"Entirely." He swiveled sideways in his chair and glanced toward
the window. "If I knew myself, actually, I'd say. Somewhere between
petulance and running Niagara Falls in a barrel there is a proper response to this sort of repression. I've just yet to locate it." He paused
and then added, "Perhaps events will obviate the need."

"I've been hoping others might join you as time goes on."

"Perhaps," he said and then almost at once seemed to regret it. "I'm
afraid you have rather a more romantic interpretation of all this than
may be justified. Mine is a private act, Mr. Ronan—I'm not leading
any crusade, you understand—"

"Not actively."

"Not in any fashion. It is essentially a disagreement between me and
Dr. Conant, whom I find an otherwise exemplary gentleman. My preference is that such intramural matters remain nobody's business but
the parties' involved."

"Yes, sir. I didn't mean to pry—"

"Nor I to rebuke. Look here, Ronan—I'm flattered by your concern —and very glad for your spiritual support. Life has its decidedly lonely moments. This is one of mine—and properly so."

"Yes, sir." That rare flash of warmth, one of those temporary rents in his defensive armor when he seemed entirely accessible and detectably human. Toby dove for the opening. "In that same vein, sir—I wonder if I might be candid with you for a moment—"

"By all means." He sat back, though, inserting space between them.

"I was wondering about Mr. Halyard, sir. I've studied with him for some years, as you may know—"

"Oh, indeed."

"And I found him to be an excellent teacher—"

"So I've heard."

"Well, that's why I was wondering, sir—if it's not overstepping the bounds of propriety—"

"It is, rather, if I may say so." He made a Gothic arch of his fingertips. "You're positively brimming with impertinences this morning, Mr. Ronan—"

"I'm sorry, sir." He bent his head in supplication. Then, more or less letting the words dribble down his chest, he ventured, "It's just that you once told me shyness is a liability in a college man."

"Did I? Well—you appear to have put it to thorough rout."

"I withdraw the question, sir. Forgive me, please. It was just that he's been such a part of Harvard for me—"

"Yes," he said, "of course. I quite understand." He met Toby's eyes with his own jittery pair. "This is never a pleasant business, you must understand, from our side of it as well. A fellow like Halyard is a hard case. I'm sure it doesn't seem so to him but the university is acting in his own best interests by separating him now—while he's still a young man and an attractive candidate to other institutions." He began to twiddle his red pencil. "The alternative, you see, is to leave a man basking in the sunshine for fifteen years or so and then suddenly tell him he'll have to move on. That is a blasting sort of experience. The new policy is to make a decision on tenure at the earliest possible moment—surely you see how that's more merciful all around?" He tapped the pencil against his palm. "Not all these decisions, alas, can be favorable—rather few, in fact. In Halyard's case, it was thought best for him to get away from here just now. Inbreeding is a perennial problem with us, I'm afraid. No doubt it comes with being perceived as the pre-eminent university—"

"But *why* was he let go, sir?"

The ice age returned. "Because the tenured faculty so voted." He glanced at the wall clock. "Now if you'll forgive me, Mr. Ronan, I asked you to come by because I'm obliged to share some unpleasant news with you." Toby had barely time for an insulating intake of breath. "The university will not be underwriting you after June." The graduate fellowships were one-year grants only, as he was sure Toby had understood, and the departmental consensus was that they ought to be handed around to as many people as possible. Only two or three students were having their fellowships extended. He was terribly sorry but Toby would have to finance the balance of his master's study on his own.

"I see."

"It's strictly a matter of dollars and cents, I'm afraid."

"Yes, sir."

Travis bent toward him slightly. "Will you be able to manage it, Toby?" He had never called him that before. Diminutives fell heavily from his lips.

"I don't know, sir. It's been something of a struggle as it is."

"I understand." He flipped the pencil onto his desk. "And something tells me you're not much of one for passing the hat."

"Not much, sir."

"They say knowing when to compromise one's principles is sometimes no small virtue in itself."

"So I've heard, sir."

"No doubt," he said, tossing off a short sigh. "I'm not much at Polonius, you can see."

"It's a hard role, sir—easier to mock than play."

"Ah, yes—you've heard me on it." He smiled almost sweetly. "It's where we were introduced, as I recall. Or was it something else that day?"

"*Lear*, sir."

"Yes—of course. You hardly needed reminding of filial devotion."

"No, sir."

"Look here," he said, tilting backward and folding his arms over his chest, "why don't I ask around a bit—about the money—"

"You're very kind, sir—"

"Not that I'd be terribly sanguine if I were you—"

"—but that won't be necessary."

"Oh?"

"I may want to try teaching for a little—to get a sense of it. I'll have my certificate in June—"

"A good idea! A year off from the grind here might be beneficial. And by then, the budgetary pressures may have let up a bit, and perhaps we can—"

"Yes, sir." Toby reached for his hand. "You've been more than helpful."

Travis looked glum in returning the clasp. "Not at all," he said. "Not at all."

He was a man easy to admire but impossible to venerate. For all his marvelous articulation, there was something chronically evasive in his manner, as if the fine web of words he spun was so much upholstering for a terrible turbulence within him. Or perhaps that was just Graham's rancor coloring Toby's perception. At any rate, it was clearer to him as he left Travis's office that final time how Graham's connection with the man had taken a pathological twist somewhere along the line. Too many recessive impulses colliding in the undertow. Toby resolved to see Valerie Halyard at the first opportunity and inquire what his prospects might be to teach at the secondary level.

His timing was unfortunate.

They had gone to see *The Gay Divorcee* to lift their spirits. Graham bore more than a slight resemblance to Fred Astaire, and Valerie saw in herself a touch of Ginger Rogers. Whatever their associations with it, the film proved a dubious cathartic for Graham's despondency. He woke in the middle of the night—if he had ever been asleep—and drove out to the middle of Anderson Bridge. There must have been a moon to guide him or some other mighty pull on his circling demons. He never shared with anyone but them the ferocity of his disorder.

In the morning, his long, pale body was found washed up on the Cambridge bank, a few hundred yards down the Charles. The note in his car read:

> *Bitter constraint, and sad occasion dear,*
> *Compels me to disturb your season due. . . .*

He postured to the end, taking no chance posterity would undervalue him as Harvard had. Every graduate student of English knew the lines that came next:

> *For Lycidas is dead, dead ere his prime,*
> *Young Lycidas, and hath not left his peer. . . .*
> *He must not float upon his wat'ry bier*
> *Unwept, and welter to the parching wind,*
> *Without the meed of some melodious tear.*

Toby looked it up. Milton wrote the poem the year after Harvard opened. Indeed, the elegy might have been as aptly addressed to the college's namesake as the poet's friend, Edward King. He and John Harvard died hardly a year apart. The three young men had been to

Cambridge; this fourth one now, too. He was back with them in their century and their country, more than his own.

Unforgiving as Valerie was toward him for quitting her and life at his first defeat, as if between them they had not enough blessings to survive, she flayed herself still more for tolerating his mania toward Travis. "It was that damned review," she said, taking Toby aside in a roomful of mourners. "I never should have consented."

He sensed all along that Graham had written it. It had his high style. It crackled with antipathy. And it ran in the one journal a proper Bostonian would employ to savage another. Just how he had obtained access to the pages of the *Transcript*, Toby was uncertain; people with money and family had connections—in this case, his yet better-connected fiancée. A Wellesley graduate fresh off a year of study at St. Hilda's, Oxford, and hopeful of a literary career as a bright young thing in the editorial department at Houghton Mifflin, she had the credentials to do some pieces for the *Transcript* book page and entrée to it through a cousin who served as its assistant editor. Like most of the reviews, hers were signed only with initials—M.V.D. for Merrill Valerie Dobson. Merrill being her mother's family and, to her own thinking, not a fit first name, she dropped it except on formal occasions or, as in this instance, when wishing to cloak her identity. Publishing-house employees who wrote book reviews of other firms' titles were about as dubious a commodity as young academicians covertly using them to assault their superiors in cold print. The mischievous combination produced by far the nastiest review anywhere accorded *The Somber Muse* by Jeremiah S. Travis. "It was not a clever thing," Toby conceded to the widow Halyard.

"I'm sure he's known all along—I always felt it but never told Graham—what would have been the point? When the dissertation came in, Travis took his revenge—naturally. Everything fell apart after that." Her clouded face turned from him. "I thought I would make it different for him."

Those who mean to do themselves in usually find a way; collaborators are only incidental to the process. But what comfort would there have been for her in that unpleasantry? Instead, he offered the epitaph she duly ordered for the headstone in Marshfield Hills—

Tomorrow to fresh Woods, and Pastures new.

—the last line of *Lycidas*.

At the graveside, Toby was full up with his unrepayable debt. Travis had taught him to love the language. Graham Halyard had taught him to use it—to build with it and tear down, to soar upon it and plumb, to compact and elide, vivify and solemnize. But more to mask feeling than reveal it; the tragedy was that, for all his adoration of language, he could not bend it to a more prosaic usage—as a tool to relieve the emotional congestion that was choking his vitality. Surely he was capable of such expression, but that prickly irony in which he so gloried was the sole outlet he ever chose to employ in public. This stoppered anguish, Toby had no doubt, and perverse reluctance to unburden himself in little words of telling weight, killed him.

Travis showed up at the burial. Whether from sorrow or shame, or some of both, there was no telling. Toby was too far away to read his face, and there was no chance to catch up as the strung-out procession of mourners retreated down the hillside.

He found himself falling into stride with a second-year graduate student, one of Graham's glossier products. "Hard luck on the fellowship," he said to Toby with proper modulation. "Seems as if himself down there has been working overtime." He tossed his head toward Travis's fleeing figure. Toby looked befuddled. "Everyone's certain he did you in, too," the fellow went on, "but opinion's divided as to whether it was by being for you or against."

"That's—absurd. I get along with him."

"So did Caesar with Brutus."

"No, but I mean we get along quite well."

He glanced at Toby sideways. "Not *that* well—I hope."

It was a cheap and offensive gibe. "Well enough," Toby said and turned away.

"Yes—well, that would tend to favor the opposite school of thought."

"If you'll excuse my—"

"They say the department thought you were too political—and that Travis held out for you as long as—"

"What total rot!"

"I'm sure. Nevertheless, you're down as an agent of the proletariat —and haven't been keeping cool with Coolidge, exactly."

"I see. And—and how does it go—Travis tried to save my hide?"

"You two being kindred spirits—politically speaking—until they called him on it—for favoritism, I suppose—and he backed off."

None of it made sense. Travis would not have lied to him about the fellowship—or turned on him because of Graham—or failed to support him on the political issue. "Assuming your spies are not misinformed—which I don't," Toby offered back, "I'd suppose he could fight only one battle at a time. This business with the oath has put him in a hole with the department, don't you think—making the rest all look awfully weak-kneed? He's got to have a care for himself—"

His glance stopped Toby from rattling on. "Haven't you heard?"

"About what?"

"He's caved in—complete capitulation."

"Since when?"

"There's a small item in the *Transcript*—he signed up yesterday. Even issued a short statement urging the other holdouts to go along."

"I see," Toby said, not seeing at all. The ground blurred to match the slate sky. A spring storm threatened. "Well—he made his point, I suppose—"

"Rubbish. The man's a titmouse."

"Because he compromised? He's still twice the man anyone else is around here."

The fellow looked at Toby hard. "I believe I just heard Halyard revolving in his box."

IV

To cap off that inglorious springtime, his father closed up their house. It was too large for a man living alone and too costly to maintain, and he could not bear to see it turn ramshackle before his eyes. He tried to sell, but there were no offers except at distress prices, so he carefully boarded it over for the time being and rented a small apartment on the third floor of a once grand house in South Nyack. A tiny bedroom was allocated for his son's use, but the arrangement, which Toby recognized as eminently sensible, meant that, practically speaking, he was homeless.

Accordingly, he looked for work where he was.

The only two pre-college teachers he knew in the world bestirred themselves in his behalf. Barney Quigley, though preoccupied with plans for Bonnie's midsummer marriage to Anton, managed to look into the hiring situation in the Boston school system. Totally hopeless, he reported. There had been substantial layoffs two years before, and the dismissed teachers had fanned out over the state, filling every available job and leaving a backlog of five applicants for every opening that developed. Besides, Toby had neither experience nor an advanced degree—indeed, nothing to recommend him beyond a Harvard sheepskin. That, at least, meant something in private school circles, according to Valerie Halyard, who welcomed the opportunity to concern herself for a moment with something other than her own aimless rage. While Toby came highly recommended, none of the dozen places she called had anything for him or knew of anything elsewhere.

Pedagogy could wait; his stomach, not. He began to apply at every print shop within reach of public transportation. But no one needed help; hadn't he heard—times were still rotten? He scoured what want ads there were and tramped the streets in search of help-wanted signs in any window, ready to accept temporary status as Boston's most literate dishwasher. Every opening, though, had its waiting line, or else he had always arrived fifteen minutes too late.

As his resources and stamina dwindled by the day, the early stages of panic overtook him. Despair was yet a ways off—he did not expect to be left in the gutter to die untended—but increasingly he saw himself as misfortune's foundling, lifted up from obscurity, exposed to grand ambition, and then, still bursting with promise, indifferently discarded as useless for combat with the world's infinite catalogue of ills. Should he admit defeat and beg mercy? Or search elsewhere, colliding with a million other drifters? What was to become of him in such a heedless universe?

It was at this moment of failing courage and accelerating self-sorrow that Barney Quigley left a message with his very correct landlady. Toby was to waste no time getting down to see the assistant state supervisor in the Boston field headquarters for the U. S. Office of Education. Formerly vice principal of Barney's school, he had indicated there just might be something.

It was a three-hour wait. And when Toby finally got inside the door, the official drew a blank on his name, though he had no trouble with Barney's. "He's always sending me people—and I have to be careful. The army isn't keen on radicals."

The connection was not immediately clear to him, but Toby sensed the less he said, the better. "I'm the fellow from Harvard."

"Oh, right," the official remembered. "We have a special situation—"

"You need someone a little stuffy?" Toby said it with a smile.

The man's look announced he recognized the levity but had no patience for it just then. "A little crazy would be closer," he said. "It's out in Pittsfield—do you know the Berkshires?" He pointed out the spot on the map behind him.

"Only by reputation."

"Yes, they're very beautiful. It's the camp commander who isn't."

It was all too cryptic for Toby. "What kind of camp are we talking about?"

"I thought you said Barney Quigley sent you?"

"Yes, but he left a message—no details. I'm afraid I'm in—"

"We recruit C.E.A.'s for the C.C.C.," he said with practiced bureaucratese. "If you're not interested, I've got twenty other people waiting who are."

All Toby knew about the Civilian Conservation Corps was the

hearty stuff he read in the papers and saw in the newsreels. A device to keep jobless young men between seventeen and twenty-five out of trouble and off the labor market, it was by wide assent the most popular and immediately successful of the New Deal relief programs. America's land had been as deeply scarred as her spirit, and these largely uneducated lads were put to work repairing it. Every week yielded a flood of pictures of these plucky throwbacks to frontier days as they swarmed over the eroding soil with their picks and shovels and tractors, contouring parched fields, damming wayward streams, replanting denuded forests, turning inaccessible wilderness into parks and recreation areas. It was all so wholesome and patriotic that the public, without a great deal else to cheer about, acclaimed the readily visible accomplishments. When the President sent his $5 billion public works program to Congress earlier in the year, the only part to win bipartisan support was expansion of the C.C.C. By September, Toby had read, it was expected there would be 2,500 camps in operation around the country, enrolling half a million young men.

"What," he asked, "is a C.E.A.?"

"Camp educational advisor. It means you run the whole teaching program—subject to army supervision, of course."

"And what gets taught?"

"Whatever can be—which is not a lot of Aristotle. There isn't any hard and fast program. And there isn't any budget for books—or equipment—or other teachers. You've got to beg, borrow, or steal what you need, including people. It's not your typical classroom situation, is what I'm saying, and these are not exactly model pupils. If these boys had been any good at school, they wouldn't be in the C.C.C. in the first place."

"You mean they're delinquents?"

"I didn't say that. They're just not long on brains, most of them—and the few who are haven't had much chance to show it. Unfortunately, the army people are not very eager to give it to them—or to the rest. The boys are supposedly there to perform an honest day's work—and if they do, the army figures they're too tired to learn much of anything at night, so why bother? The situation varies from camp to camp, but by and large, I would not call the military attitude terribly supportive of the teachers."

"What would you call it?"

"Hostile."

"And you've got plenty of applicants, you say?"

"Overrun with 'em. The pay's one sixty-five a month as long as you last. But of course there's no job security whatever. If you don't get along with the C.O., you're out on your ear—which is exactly what's

happened at the camp in Pittsfield. The captain has run through three
C.E.A.'s in a year—and they were veteran high school teachers—really
experienced, capable men."

"Then why take someone like me?"

"Basically, we think the captain's problem is he doesn't want anyone
around undermining his authority. We thought a younger man might
prove more—"

"Compliant?"

"I was going to say cooperative. The man, you see, is evidently
quite capable—the liaison officer at Fort Devens assures us his camp is
one of the best in the whole First Corps area—that's all New England
and New York—which means we can't send him just anyone. If it's to
be someone young, he should be special somehow—"

"Like having a degree from Harvard?"

"Very good." He reached for a stack of forms. "Lodging is free if
you live in the staff barracks. The food cost is minimal—which is
about what it's worth. The camp area is buggy as hell in summer, they
tell me, and a glacier in winter, and for culture there's usually someone around playing the harmonica." He shoved an application across
the desk. "Do you want it or not?"

Toby filled out the form in triplicate and was told to come back in
forty-eight hours. That night, Anton added his authoritative view on
the charms of the C.C.C. "It's an army chain gang," he said. "The first
true wave of American fascism."

The subject was of no small concern to the labor movement, as it
happened. The C.C.C., Anton charged, was nothing less than a massive
program to militarize the American working class. The enrollees, desperate and therefore highly manipulable, were separated from their
homes and communities, put to work under often barbaric conditions
for coolie wages of a dollar a day, and subjected to strictly regimented
living arrangements—all so that the government would have a vast
strike force ready to beat back any radically inspired uprising against
the capitalist system. And this was not only a partisan perception; the
Assistant Secretary of the Army had written right in *Liberty* magazine that the C.C.C. would be an integral part of "a system of storm
troops that could support the government's efforts to smash the
depression." William Green, head of the A.F. of L., had opposed the
C.C.C. from the start because it served to make near-starvation
wages on relief projects a fundamental policy of the New Deal. And
Norman Thomas denounced the scheme as anathema to everyone who
endorsed the dignity of labor.

"Now if you want to go work for an outfit like that," Anton concluded, "then you go right ahead. Send us a snapshot while you're at it

—but make sure first your boots are polished and your armband is on straight."

Barney Quigley was a good deal less troubled by the C.C.C. strictures than his future son-in-law. "He gets hot under the collar now and then," Barney said. "Fortunately, I'm not the one marrying him."

For one thing, the conservation corps was run by a well-respected union man who had been a vice president of the International Association of Machinists. That he would not tolerate brutal conditions in the camps was testified to by the fact that he used to lecture on labor relations at Harvard. More to the point, all the relief work actually undertaken by the C.C.C. was directly supervised not by the army but by civilian overseers picked by and answerable to the U. S. Department of Labor—and Miss Frances Perkins, in Quigley's view, was no fascist. "Anton's all wet on this one," he said. "These kids are the lowest of the low, and F.D.R.'s giving them a chance. He's pulled them in off the streets, fed them and clothed them and housed them, and made 'em do something useful for their country in exchange so maybe they'll learn skills and habits that earn them a fresh start in life. Is that bad? Anyway, who else besides the army could keep a lot of tough, restless punks in line while they're shaping up—the Ladies' Petticoat and Pussycat Society?"

There was a story Toby had heard about Le Baron Briggs, who served at Harvard as a popular dean of the college. One day while he was a teacher, a student of his came to him and said he had not completed the assignment because he was not feeling very well. "Young man," said Briggs, "please bear in mind that by far the greater part of the world's work is carried on by people who are not feeling very well."

Tonic words, for Toby was low on leaving school for the world's work. He felt more saturated than fortified and, all in all, overwhelmingly tentative: not quite poor, not quite orphaned, not quite friendless—not quite anything, frankly, except uncertain about the world and everything in it. He had sampled abundantly and sensed salvation nowhere—not in the love of God, or the mercy of men, or the justice of the state, or the clamor of the market, or poetry's diaphanous beauty.

Still, he was disinclined to become a sour solitary, like Thoreau, waging passive resistance against society's grosser habits by trying to remove himself from them altogether. Like the naturalist, Toby Ronan chose now to go into the woods for company and instruction. His hinterland was to prove no asylum.

PART TWO

The New Dealer

"A very few, as heroes, patriots, martyrs, reformers in the great sense, and *men*, serve the state with their consciences also, and so necessarily resist it for the most part; and they are commonly treated as enemies by it."

—HENRY DAVID THOREAU, *Civil Disobedience*

SEVEN

WEST STREET runs directly out of Pittsfield without a swerve in
its rippling climb to the edge of the dark Taconics. After two placid
miles to nowhere, the road ends at the corporate limits of the city and
turns into a rocky upland trail. A few hundred yards farther west lies
the New York state line, a fact of such indifference to neighboring nature and man that it goes unannounced by any feature of the landscape or imprinted marker. The border, unoffended, sits peaceably
astride the ridge line of these low, ancient mountains, their majesty
whittled eons ago to soft pleasantries. They are scarcely more than
foothills now, these interlocking Berkshire ranges—the easternmost
branches of the great Appalachian chain. From their brushy hollows
Massachusetts slopes away in a nearly unbroken plain all the way to
the sea. When he met them for the first time, what these mellow senti-
nels lacked in Alpine splendor they purchased with other gifts. Height
is only incidental to the beauty of a mountain.

The man who gave him a lift out from town was not enthusiastic
about the C.C.C. "Nothin' but a dumping ground for delinquents, truants, and parolees—just a lot of punks on the take, if you ask me," he
said. The whole enterprise baffled him, especially its therapeutic purpose. "Well, maybe it'll do the trees some good," he allowed, "but
what happens with this low-life element when you put 'em back in the
cities afterward? They got no trails that need buildin' there—so we've
bought ourselves a generation of good-for-nothings."

His calcified soul softened long enough for him to slow at a small
rise and point out the northward vista. A break in the roadside shrubbery revealed a shimmering slice of pine-rimmed water that stretched
away to terraced tiers of hazy blue hills—a picture postcard too perfect
to believe. "Onota Lake," he said. "Best fishin' water 'round here—
bullheads and perch, mostly, and some trout when you can find 'em."
The graceful hump at the midpoint of the horizon was Greylock,

highest point in the state. "A nice-climbin' mountain," he added. "All these hills are good for that—if not much else."

A short way past the lake he turned off the main road, swung north, and let his passenger off at a street that veered to the left between a meadow and a cornfield. He was late to pick up his wife at the doctor's, he said, or he'd have driven straight to the camp. It was only a short walk, though, around the big curve—"they're bivouacked up there right below Lulu Cascade. Used to be the prettiest spot for miles around—real cool and splashy—only I hear they went and dammed it for their drinking water. That don't sound like progress, exactly. Maybe you can set 'em straight, son."

A navy flannel sport jacket, the only one he owned, slung over one shoulder and his crammed, broken-cornered suitcase in the opposite hand, Toby set off around the bend in that soft road. Only shrill insect drones spiced the hot stillness as his pace dwindled to a sweaty trudge under that high August sun. All the omens continued bleak.

At the two-day training session they had sent him to at Fort Devens, about a dozen miles out beyond Concord, the educational advisor for the First Corps Area took a glance at him and then at his aptitude chart and began twitching his head. "I can't imagine what they had in mind," he said.

"I'm marginally literate," Toby offered, "and very needy."

His name was Corcoran. "We're talking about professional qualifications, Mr. Ronan—not degrees of desperation. You're supposed to be a trainer, not a trainee. You've got absolutely no experience at teaching or camping or in the military—or scouting or the 'Y' or in competitive sports—or psychology or counseling or social work —anything that might be useful."

"Well," Toby said, "that's not entirely true. I did have almost a year with the R.O.T.C."

"And?"

"I hated it."

"Yes," he said, "well, that's very helpful, Mr. Ronan." He closed the folder with a sigh. "What you've got on your hands are a few hard-boiled, sophisticated officers and a whole lot of tough, active, and probably pretty angry boys running around the woods out there. You have no authority whatever except what the commanding officer delegates to you—and he'd as soon you never came. The entire education program, of course, is completely voluntary—which means you've got to persuade fellows who've spent all day swinging a pick or tearing out tree stumps that they'd be a lot better off if they'd devote their evenings to cultivating what brains they've got instead of playing poker or shooting pool or listening to 'The Lone Ranger.'"

He moved off to a closet and took out a batch of instruction manuals, guidance pamphlets, lesson plans, book reference lists, and other paraphernalia of enlightenment. "I'd spend about an hour with the lot," he said, "and then forget all about it—none of this stuff works in the bush. If it did, you never would have been hired."

The only literature worth consulting, he suggested, was the *Handbook for Educational Advisors*, the official manual of the U. S. Office of Education. It would serve as Toby's Bible and Bill of Rights, and while it would not keep the savages from pitching him into the campfire if he riled them, quoting from it at strategic moments might have a certain talismanic value with the captain. "You'd better get it right, though," Corcoran said, shepherding him into a quiet corner, "because he's already memorized every page of it."

The handbook confirmed that the camp educational advisor's powers did not exist without the blessing of the commanding officer, "in whose sole discretion . . ." etc. The C.E.A.'s functions, though, had the official approval of the American government, and his sanctioned goals included developing within each C.C.C. enrollee "his powers of self-expression, self-entertainment [autoerotic?], and self-culture [like the oyster?] . . . an understanding of the prevailing economic and social conditions, to the end that each man may cooperate intelligently in improving these conditions . . . and an appreciation of nature and country life." Socrates himself had no broader mandate. Or better equipment.

Corcoran sent him forth to battle with three instructions: (1) Use whatever methods work, (2) avoid controversy, and (3) call the C.O. "sir" at every opportunity. "Undoubtedly there will be a lot of times you'll be ready to quit in despair," he said, "but before you do, just remember you've got some important people in your corner. There's the President—the Corps is his pet, don't forget. There's Secretary Ickes, who signs the teachers' paychecks. And there's me. Forget about the first two, though, and call me if things get out of hand." He gave Toby his home telephone in case of an after-hours crisis. "Fight fiercely, Harvard," he added with a wink, "but don't overdo it—you're badly outnumbered."

II

No other wayfarer intruded on his steamy hike along Cascade Street, and no car passed. Each stride carried him one more league beyond civilization. He had come about as far from Harvard Square as it was possible to travel and still remain within the Commonwealth of

Massachusetts. But he no longer felt that he was anywhere geographically definable. Under a cloudless dome of sweet blue, his own steps were the harshest sound in a world drenched with light. A downpour of sunbeams washed the enameled meadows going by him, slipped off every upturned surface, and streamed back into space in ceaseless transit.

At its second right-angle turn, the street offered an alternate route— an arbored spur into the woods. The brown wooden sign with incised yellow letters read, "PITTSFIELD STATE FOREST," and under it, "Lulu Cascade/Berry Pond." He went that way, relishing the patches of shade from the leafy overhang. Grazing cows paid him no heed. Birds twittered that he could not see. Smaller winged things buzzed and hummed in steady serenade. Barns, fences, farmhouses, haystacks— all objects more of painterly contemplation than his transformed reality. He was stepping off a dream.

His pastoral reverie was abruptly broken to the left, where something red-brown and dog-sized burst through a hedge and made for the far fence, its plumed tail the tuft of a racing arrow. He paused and blinked to be sure he had not imagined that overland flight: Its feet seemed never to have touched the ground. Within moments of his having been deposited in her bower, nature was offering him intimate glimpses; there was no polite way now for her to rescind the invitation.

He plunged for a time into a thicket of such impenetrable shadow that the clearing was a welcome sight. The compound was hardly more than an opening in a dense ring of dark forest. The painted sign, far less permanent-looking than the one at the head of the road, said, "CAMP 127, AREA 1, U.S. CIVILIAN CONSERVATION CORPS." Suspended beneath it by chain link was an auxiliary sign: "Capt. Gordon T. Sparhawk, Commanding Officer." An odd and forbidding name. In all the various allusions to him, how was it possible nobody had ever said his name? It was unlikely that, having heard it once, Toby could have forgotten.

Beyond a short, pointless run of log fencing stretched a ragged grassy quadrangle about the size of a football field. Clustered on each side were five long, low wooden buildings of identical monotonous design. Perhaps twenty feet by one hundred, they hunkered in parallel formation, short end facing in toward the campus. At either end of the field sat a similar building but with its long side to the field and commanding a clear view of its whole length—plainly the mess and social halls. Hardly more than distended shacks, their tar-paper roofs broken by an occasional stovepipe outcropping, they had all been painted a deep evergreen, as if the camouflage might somehow let them squat there undetected by the woods.

Minimal human stir broke the scene that sultry forenoon. Half a dozen fellows in denim work clothes were hauling, installing, and whitewashing large rocks set at decorative intervals along the gravel path that formed the perimeter of the camp square and around the wooden spar flagpole that stood at its center. Several other boys tended the shrubbery halfheartedly bestowed upon the entrances to the two community buildings at the head and foot of the campus. Somebody else was repairing a screen door to one of the barracks. And through an open window at the far end of the compound but suffusing it a radio played "I'm Gonna Sit Right Down and Write Myself a Letter."

He got halfway to the flagpole when the welcoming committee finally appeared. Eddie Spain had curly black hair and a slight stammer that inhibited him not at all as he came loping up with a taller, skinnier fellow in tow and introduced himself as Toby's assistant. "And this is Bing-uh, Bingo Barnes—a buddy o' mine in Bug-uh, Bughouse C." He motioned across toward the middle barracks. Eddie had a good, foursquare handshake. Bingo's felt more tentative. Toby tried not to focus on his top incisors, which were so severely bucked that they canted out almost like small tusks.

The brass, Eddie explained, was otherwise occupied. The C.O. left every Saturday morning at ten and returned by Sunday supper. The adjutant was in Pittsfield just then, seeing people at the electric works about the camp's inadequate power. And Sergeant Carmichael, the supply officer, was over behind the mess, supervising a food delivery. "He said to say he'll, uh, see you later." As to the enrollees, they were spread out all over since the camp didn't really operate as one on weekends. Some were playing ball by the reservoir, some were in town, a lot were up swimming at the pond—"they'll all be back in for chow"—and maybe a quarter of the company was on weekend leave. "These guys here," Eddie added, grabbing his bag and leading Toby across the field to his quarters, "are on B.S.—that's the beau-uh, beau-uh—the beautification squad. It's like K.P., o-o-only outdoors."

"How do you get elected to it?"

Eddie's bird-quick eyes blinked, trying to decipher the slightly skewed wording of the question. "Oh—just, uh, hor-hor-horsing around—or showing at report with-with-with dirty fingernails—or fucking up in the field—"

"Or looking cross-eyed at Nesbit," Bingo said with a snort.

"The a-a-adjutant," Eddie explained. "He's the big doggie."

"Not the captain?"

"Who—Smilin' Jack? He's the k-king, all right, but Lieutenant Nesbit's the hangman." Eddie tilted his pug nose back up toward the flag. "He's-he's-he's West Point—very big on regulations."

"Shit, he wrote the book," Bingo said and then ducked off.

Toby's bunk was a separate cubicle at the rear of the officers' quarters, the last building in the colony, across the lawn from the barracks and catty-corner to the social hall—"it's just called the Rec," Eddie advised. "Nothin' is fancy around here—except the captain's, uh—the captain's, uh—his boots."

Eddie Spain's expansive pleasure at Toby's arrival was evident. An assistant educational advisor without anyone to assist soon found himself assigned to a work detail under the blazing sun. Eddie had been pushing a wheelbarrow for three weeks now and thought that unsuitable work for a high school graduate, especially one dedicated to becoming a courtroom reporter. The twenty-five dollars a month the government sent directly to his family in Brockton—the other five he earned went, like everyone else's, into his own pocket—was being banked to pay for his continued education, probably at a business school, as soon as he finished one more six-month tour "with the C's."

A whistle blast drew Eddie out the door. He was back in a moment, summoning Toby excitedly. In the ten or so minutes he had been cordially detained, a premeditated extravaganza was unfurled on the lawn. And raised on high. There, he saw, fluttering lackadaisically but legibly enough fifty feet above the campus and just below Old Glory, was a giant pink pennant with a scallopy white fringe. In the middle, painted on in red letters of diminishing height, flew the glorious name of "HARVARD." In case he missed the message, a mass of enrollees—three or four dozen of them had assembled out of nowhere—pulled handkerchiefs out and flapped them in his direction with their best effort at a limp wrist. "Woo-woo-woo!" they hollered till his face registered a satisfactory flush.

Eddie saw his florid response to the tribute and took no chances. "It's-it's-it's a joke," he said.

"I can tell."

"You, you-uh—you don't look it."

He let out a small smile of appreciation and gave a short, sporting wave of acknowledgment toward the jeering horde. They paid him back with a hearty cheer and, pocketing their teasing hankies, came *en masse* to shake his hand. There was a warmth to the rowdy welcome surpassing any formal salute that might have been arranged in its place. Over lunch, Bingo delightedly explained the complicated arrangements that had gone into the prank. Half a dozen discarded women's slips had to be secured from town and sewn together to make the pennant—no easy trick in an all-male subculture—"and a lotta guys chipped in to get the lace shit at the five-and-dime. Could you see the edge was lace?"

He commended both their craft and initiative, then said it was too bad they had gone and ruined it by spelling Harvard wrong. All their animated faces froze while Toby continued chewing his cheesed macaroni deadpan for as long as he could manage—about five seconds. Then he laughed at their discomfort, and they laughed back twice as hard in relief.

On his way out of the mess, the supply sergeant extended a pudgy hand in official greeting. Denis Carmichael, a moon-faced man with jug ears that gave him something of the look of an aboriginal stew pot, jerked a thumb over his shoulder and emitted a trilling laugh. "I just seen the boys' valentine," he said. "Sure is purty."

"It was very thoughtful of them."

"Yeah," he said, "they went to a lotta bother." A confession of complicity. Then a sign of contrition: "They don't mean nothin' by it, ya know?"

"I understand."

"They were tellin' me we'd have to lay in a supply of Modess now —and other dumb-ass jokes like that. It's just that most of 'em never been within ten miles of a Harvard man before."

"Sure."

"They're good kids but a little crude—ya know?"

"Sure."

"I got a cousin went to college."

"That's nice. Where?"

"Vermont somewhere."

"Middlebury, maybe?"

"That could be it. I don't see him ever except Thanksgiving. He's a little high-falutin' with me—ya know, bein' regular army like I am."

"What's wrong with regular army?"

"I never asked the twerp." He gave another high laugh and patted Toby good luck on the shoulder, promising to get him bedding and other supplies by supper. "An' don't let the boys bullshit you too bad."

Eddie toured him up the line of buildings that bordered the east side of the campus—the company headquarters and supply depot, the work superintendent's shed, the foremen's barracks, the infirmary, and the now familiar officers' quarters in which Toby occupied the caboose. The captain lodged at the front end, Eddie said, in allegedly palatial surroundings, though he had never been inside Sparhawk's den and wanted to keep it that way. A genuine brick chimney, the only one in camp, testified to the inhabitant's exalted rank.

"Why do you call him Smilin' Jack?" Toby asked. "Doesn't he ever?"

"Uh, not—not much. And when he does, wa-wa-watch out."

"I take it you're not a great admirer of his."

For once, Eddie measured his words. "He's—a-a-all right."

"But not a big booster of rustic education, I hear."

"Huh?"

"I mean he's not keen for what the C.E.A.'s are sent out here to do."

He gave his curly head a toss as if to deflect the probe. "I think he thinks they been, uh—been, uh—been full o' malarkey."

"And do you?"

"I think they thought they were at, uh—at Har-Har-uh, Harvard. Everybody figures a real Har-uh—real Harvard man'll know better."

III

Coming up the steps to the Rec, he was waylaid into umpiring that afternoon's softball game between B Barracks and D Barracks, a contest popularly billed as the Bedbugs *vs.* the Dogfaces.

His protest that he hardly knew the strike zone from the Canal Zone ceased the moment someone said maybe it really was a dumb idea, "seein' as all they ever play at Hah-vid is jacks and potsy." That drew a pitifully chauvinistic rejoinder about the marvels of the Crimson football team. A rah-rah went up for that, and he found himself being indoctrinated in the mysteries of the infield fly rule while borne on a wave of bare-chested youth to a lush glade a few hundred yards above the camp. In winter, the spot served as the base of Ghost Trail, a ski run they had finished hacking up the mountainside only the February before. Now, laid out with G.I. bases, including an authentically spade-shaped home plate and a backstop made of chicken wire and two-by-fours, it was a slightly overgrown ball pasture, and occasional foul flies wound up in the reservoir below it.

Full of cheer and bluff irreverence, they all promised to bear with his predictable ineptness. Then the game began, and the promises were at once forgotten. Play was distinguished largely by the fury of its invective. Sodomy was the wholesomest act alluded to. After Toby, the prime target of playful abuse was the Bedbugs' catcher, a low-slung boy named Justin Bloomgarden. In his nonathletic role as company clerk, he bore the affectionate tag of "Skeezix." On the diamond, they called him "The Hammerin' Hebe"—a no less admiring reference, it was explained to Toby between innings by the Bedbug pitcher, to Bloomgarden's co-religionist, slugger Hank Greenberg of the Detroit Tigers, who at the moment was tearing up the American League with his batting prowess. In the C.C.C., Toby detected, insult was the sincerest form of flattery.

Whether out of kindness or his own victimization, Skeezix seemed the only one on the field to spare him the hectoring groans, hoots, howls, and oh-shit's that greeted almost every call Toby made from his post behind the pitcher. Sensing its therapeutic value to the tormentors, he withstood their barrage better than the heat, which threatened to dehydrate him into unconsciousness until Skeezix provided him with a Coke and peaked ball cap. The catcher's darker motive surfaced in the bottom of the sixth inning when, with the Bedbugs narrowly ahead and a fleet Dogface on first base, Skeezix approached the mound. "After the next pitch," he disclosed out of the side of his mouth, "we're gonna pull the hidden-ball trick on Wolfbait —he's the animal dancin' off first."

Toby asked him to explain the subterfuge. He said just to be sure to glance toward first base when the pitcher got ready to unload—but under no circumstances was the umpire to stare over at the runner or he would tip the gambit.

They pulled it off with admirable finesse. After Toby called the next pitch a ball—it was feet wide of the plate—the pitcher let out a terrible stream of profanity over the ump's failing eyesight and distracted the enemy from Skeezix's moves. The third baseman met him halfway to the mound and was shuffled the ball as the catcher proceeded to console his battery mate. Meanwhile the ball got smuggled around the infield so that when the tempest quieted in the vicinity of the mound, the Dogfaces had all been snookered. As the pitcher readied for delivery, the empty pocket of his glove carefully shielded from view, the runner took his lead and was emphatically tagged out by the Bedbug first baseman.

"That's against the fuckin' rules!" roared the unfortunate Wolfbait as Toby thumbed him out. Half the Dogface team joined at once in the tumult. Given the umpire's conceded ignorance of the game's finer points, peaceful adjudication yielded to anarchy.

He watched them surge and shout and shove one another half a head below him, these eighteen- and twenty-year-olds rescued from the wrong side of the tracks and off a freight deadheaded for forlorn adulthood, and he wanted to knock their blocks together for such idiotic bickering. But as they barked and bobbed and thoroughly ignored him, he saw the sense in that senseless tumult. They may have been short on chest hair and gray matter, had too many crooked or missing teeth, and taken the language of the gutter for the noblest expression of manhood, yet there was a zest among them you could not miss from the start. Born of shared need, honed in combat, and sustained probably by a common loathing of their elders and keepers—the very ones who had begat the system that failed these progeny so badly —their whole hope resided in that spark. Woe to its would-be quencher.

"Shut your traps!" he finally yelled above the din.

No doubt charmed by such a decorous reprimand, they obeyed.

He took three steps back from the clot of them. "I say he's out, so he's out—that's the rule."

The beautiful simplicity of that solution eluded them. "You don't know dick about da rules!" Wolfbait snarled at him.

"He tagged you when you were off base," Toby said, "so you're out." A rock of rectitude.

"They ain't allowed t' hide the fuckin' ball, mistah. This ain't a chickenshit Easter egg hunt." Nostrils flaring like a cornered beast's, he knotted his arms across his chest in defiance. "I'm stayin' on base till hell freezes over."

His tragic grandeur in the face of disaster restarted the uproar. A Dogface wielding a bat yelled that the pitcher couldn't step on the rubber without the ball. The Bedbug third baseman rejected that claim with equal vehemence. The pitcher shouted he hadn't actually toed the slab yet. Tempers frothed. Temporal authority had to be imposed, or his future stock with that clientele would be worthless.

"I'm counting to three, Wolfbait"—for all Toby knew that was his Christian name—"and if you're not off the field, the game is forfeited."

"Holy Christ! Now where'd you get *that* one from, Mr. Perfessor— the funny papers or sumpin'?"

"*One.*" In an unswayable voice.

"He means it, Wolfbait."

"He can go kiss mine!"

"You're just pissed 'cause you got caught with your head up your asshole."

"That's where *your* head's gonna be in a second—"

"TWO—"

Mayhem imminent, Skeezix stepped forward and held up both his hands for silence. "Look, we all ast Harvard here t' be the ump—an' he done it. That means what he says goes—an' since he jus' got here, he don't know any of us, so you can't say he's playin' favorites, see?" He looked hard at Wolfbait and then said, "Now stop givin' the guy a hard time, Ivan, an' move yer pork butt."

The "Ivan" was what did it. Glowering all the while, he went. No other Dogface reached base.

The frilly pink pennant heralding Toby's arrival was history by the time they reached the compound. The only sign that it had ever flown was a stern notice on the company bulletin board outside the mess hall. The flagpole was nobody's private property, it said, and "definitely inappropriate for the perpetration of pranks and/or other unofficial activities." Enrollee Anthony Barnes was assigned to K.P. for one week for his part in the malfeasance, and others participating were expected "to come forward like men and take their medicine." The edict was signed "Lt. M. C. Nesbit, Adjutant."

"Bingo takes the rap," said Skeezix, turning away from the board in disgust. "The poor bastard."

"Why him?" Toby asked.

"Someone fingered him, probably. The place is crawlin' with stoolies." He slung his drenched body to the ground and took out a cigarette.

"What happens to comradeship?"

He lighted up with practiced dexterity, sucked in hard, and held the smoke deep and long till only a thin film was left when he finally exhaled. "Nothin', mostly. Everyone's tryin' to save their own ass— they're either buckin' to get rated or afraid of gettin' skunked, like Bingo." There were eighteen "rated" enrollees, he said—six leaders and twelve assistant leaders, who got half again as much pay as the rest of the company and basically ran the place under the army's ceaseless scrutiny. "We're their hired guns," said Company Clerk/Assistant Leader Bloomgarden and spat.

Toby told him he would speak to the adjutant in Bingo's behalf. Skeezix said to save his breath. "The lieutenant gets his kicks bein' a prick."

There was no mistaking the aroma of spit and polish about Mitchell Nesbit. They had supper together in a corner of the mess, and Toby could not recall having taken a less easy meal. An attractively proportioned, even-featured fellow his own age, with brush-cut brown hair and dark, hard eyes, Nesbit was guarded and almost entirely impersonal in his conversation. He came from Decatur, Illinois, had graduated from "The Point" in '34, and considered monitoring the C.C.C. a pretty tame assignment for a career soldier. But his pride and devotion were unmistakable. In the two years since it opened, Camp 127 had reforested more than a thousand acres, he said; planted well in excess of 200,000 trees; cleared some twenty-five miles of hiking, bridle, and ski trails; and, with dynamite and grueling hand labor, built a five-mile circuit drive all the way up the mountain to Berry Pond—"the highest body of water in the state," he noted to emphasize the achievement— and rough-graded the return leg.

The staff had had to sacrifice lovability among the boys, he insisted, for the process to work. The main benefit the corps had to confer was regimen. "Unless they develop habits of regularity—eating and sleeping and cleaning their dirty necks—and performing steady, dependable work—in every kind of weather—doing what they're told whether they like it or not, and doing it well and snappy—most of them are never going to amount to anything. We're trying to save their lives, if you want to look at it that way. It can't be done by tucking 'em into bed at night and kissing their pimply butts."

All that was clear enough and admirable. Toby wondered, though, if perhaps the lieutenant wasn't being a bit hard on enrollee Barnes for his part in the Harvard prank. "I really didn't mind at all," he said. "It just seemed like a little good-natured razzing."

Nesbit's narrowed eyes declared before his lips that Toby was defiling hallowed ground. "The problem wasn't with putting up the Harvard flag," he said, "but the fact they had to lower the Stars and Stripes to do it. Nobody treats the American flag like that—not if I've got anything to say about it."

Chastened, Toby retreated to quarters and made up his bunk. Waiting for him was a stack of government-issue supplies: sheets, olive blankets, towels, khaki uniform, boots, socks, underwear, and a bottle of citronella with a typed label that said, "Compliments of the House —For External Use Only."

The uniform gave him pause. The unspoken command to wear it brought home to him as nothing had before then the distasteful nature of his entanglement with an undeniably militaristic enterprise. It was one thing to view himself as a civilian specialist, ministering to the intellectual needs of these soil soldiers; it was another to be forced to masquerade as part of an authoritarian apparatus. No amount of rationalizing could convince him the difference was merely cosmetic. He thumbed through the C.E.A. *Handbook* for liberating word about exemption from dress regulations, but there was none—only the menacing reminder that he was under the C.O.'s orders every waking moment.

He decided to explore the topic gingerly with the adjutant that

very evening while lounging in the Rec. The hall, while not disorderly, benefited from the lieutenant's subliminal patrol. Every inch of
the place was vibrant with sound or motion. Pool balls clicked, ping-
pong balls clacked, the punching bag went *rum*tumtum-*rum*tumtum-
*rum*tumtum. On the radio in one corner, "The Hit Parade" floogled
"Begin the Beguine" and "Lovely to Look At." Across the hall, a
colored boy, all bones and wire, sat crosslegged, massaging his harmonica to the tune of "St. James Infirmary." In between, ranks of
dress green hunched over checkers, tumbled on the wrestling mat,
wrote letters, browsed the glass-cased library (four or five dozen volumes of Zane Grey, Horatio Alger, and other escapist–fantasy adventures), consumed ice cream and candy bars by the canteen window,
and generally shot the breeze with hoarse gusto.

"Nice setup," he complimented Nesbit, who was seated in a her-
niated old sofa near the checker boards scanning the *Berkshire Eagle*,
the local daily.

"Yeah," he said, "we've got a regular little resort here."

Toby asked if anyone else had confessed yet to the great pennant
prank. Nesbit, turning pages, said nobody ever confessed to anything.
"We've got to get the goods on them—which usually takes some
doing."

"And thumbscrews are against regulations."

He looked up to read Toby's meaning, detected nothing hostile in
it, and conceded the handicap with a grim curl of his lip. Speaking of
regulations, Toby dropped in, did it really matter to anyone what he
wore around camp? Nesbit glanced over his plaid shirt and gray trousers. The supply sergeant would soon provide him with officers'
khakis free of charge, he said, although Toby was obliged to pay for
them to be laundered. And were the khakis mandatory? "Unless you
want to run around all day in your underwear," the adjutant said neu-
trally.

"What's wrong with the way I am now?"

"In civvies?"

"Since I'm not actually *in* the army, I think I'd feel a little more—"

"This is an army post—practically speaking."

"I thought it was the *Civilian* Conservation Corps?"

"Sure. But we run it. And you're part of the administration. Your
khakis are how the kids can tell. Otherwise, you're nobody here."

"I just think I might be more effective if I were distinguished somehow from the rest of—"

"Look," he said evenly, "it's bad enough we give over control to the
Lems eight hours a day during the week." Wood nymphs? "L-E-M—

it's for 'Local Experienced Men,' " the civilian woodsmen and their assistants who supervised the corps' work projects. In the field, the Lems were boss; in camp, the army. "That includes you." He folded the paper neatly and set it down beside him. "You'll look fine in khaki. It's amazing—everybody does. Come on, have a chocolate cone on me." A carrot before the stick.

IV

Sunday, August 25, 1935

If I do not force myself to write every single day I am here, I will forget how. There is so much to discover, and feel, and know—and no place to hide even if I were inclined to. (Does the C.C.C. shoot deserters?) My plan is to put down at least a few paragraphs daily as long as I remain. It will serve as both a record and regimen.

Eddie Spain, dutiful apple-polisher that he is, offered me a guided tour of the forest today, but I declined, preferring solitude for becoming acquainted with my surroundings. There are no snakes, Eddie assured me, though he says a brown bear was reported on Potter Mtn at the north end of the forest a few yrs back. Porcupine the most lethal creature in the vicinity, he advises—forgetting to mention flies, bees, gnats & mosquitos, which cluster in maddening profusion. I shall forbear.

Stuck mostly to the trails & ridges, using the little map Eddie made me, and somehow never got lost. A special providence perhaps overlooks newcomers to paradise. And it is that. Pittsfield State Forest blankets nearly four thousand acres (acc. to Nesbit) of such grandeur as I have not known before. A main ridge serpentining northeasterly forms the backbone. Its vertebrae are mountainettes—what is bigger than a hill and smaller than a mountain?—resembling great long green tender loaves of bread. Smaller ridges ramify off of them, scattering valleys & ravines you could get lost in forever with no effort at all.

Fearing bears, I lost myself only figuratively. It is almost impossible not to if you are sentient. My spell, no doubt self-induced, transfigured the elements. The air itself is tonic. The sky, heady elixir. The hills, sweet and tufted. The brooks, molten silver, as in the gaudiest pastoral, and everywhere amid the greenwood shade, a pulsing intimacy. Even the tallest trees, for all their towering sinew & tissue, seem less ferocious than benign hosts. Sunbursts through their tops drew me up from the gullies, picking my way over cliffy ledges, sometimes on all fours trying not to slither off over the slick moss

*patches, until I made the ridge line again. And what vistas there! An
endless circuit of rippling horizontals, all gentle arcs of marvelous
grace rolling away to the misted margin of sight. The landscapist is
anonymous.*

*Berry Pond lies at the dead center of the forest. Cupped in a little
ring of hillocks, it is smaller & less dreamy than Walden. Before the
Corps got here, they tell me, it was almost bare along its shores. Now
it sprouts birch, maple & pine. The C.C.C. boys swim naked in it, and
fish the stocked trout, and have made an art of skipping rocks across
its preternaturally calm surface. Six skips is considered expert. I cannot count them after three. They say it is all in the angle of the wrist.*

A light breeze swept away yesterday's oppressive heat. . . .

"They tell me you were out reconnoitering on your own all day,"
the captain said on ushering him into his pine-paneled quarters.

He had arrived back in camp late and had his supper sent in. Toby
was asked—told, actually—to report to him afterward. Far from
displaying testiness, he was hospitality personified, supplying his guest
at once with brandy from a decanter on the mantel above an outsized
stone fireplace. "Yes," Toby said, thanking him, "I thought I ought to
see where I am. It's very breathtaking—especially if you've been stuck
in a city for five years."

The captain nodded his sleek head. "I was not a spiritual man before
coming out here, Mr. Ronan, but I don't mind telling you I've felt
powerfully close to the divinity since arriving." He hoisted his glass
slightly in Toby's direction. "Glad you're with us." It sounded a
touch mechanical but more cordial than one had a right to expect
from an advertised ogre. Toby returned the gesture, and they each
took a swallow, the captain's deeper. "Well, I'm glad you didn't get
lost in the hollows," he went on, "or eaten alive by the bugs."

"Beginner's luck—plus about half a bottle of citronella."

He gave a chesty chuckle and invited Toby to take a chair across
from his in front of the open fire. It had only a few logs on it, apparently just enough to drive off the evening chill. "I use birch," he
said, indicating the low, even flames. "It burns warmer and longer—
and chopping it keeps our delinquent enrollees gainfully employed."

Gordon Sparhawk's reedy, cultivated voice denied Toby's precon-
ception of him as a swashbuckling ignoramus. A somewhat oval six-
footer with an overbarbered mustache, he bordered on foppishness,
even in the least dressy military wear. Perhaps it was the razored
crease to his khaki gabardine trousers. More likely it was his hair, of
an almost patent-leather luster as it gripped his scalp like an aviator's

cap and ran straight back from his forehead in little wavy rivulets. His eyes added to this curious air of fussiness about him. Doe-brown, they were of no remarkable size or shape or intensity, but they blinked a great deal, like a tic, and made it hard to keep more than momentary contact with them.

He was an army reservist, he said, who had volunteered to serve with the C.C.C. "despite my advanced years." A man in his early forties who possibly never had a prime to be past—the padded heft that lent him a certain authoritative bearing appeared congenital—he was comfortable dispensing flaccid ironies. The depression he had regarded as no less of a national emergency than the World War, in which he was quick to advise he had served in France at Second Army headquarters, and could not shirk his duty when the C.C.C. was whipped through Congress as one of the New Deal's first relief programs. Besides, rehabilitating luckless young men was a lot more satisfying to him than sitting around his office in Springfield, waiting for insurance brokerage to perk up. It had been bad enough getting clients to meet their premium payments, let alone writing any new business. "My wife's minding the store for the time being—she's a very competent gal." Toby scanned the room for a framed photograph, but there was none. The man was not entirely without taste.

After refueling their glasses, the captain reached for a folder of paperwork on Toby and leafed through it silently awhile. "Well," he said, "a gen-u-ine Harvard man—we're honored." There was only teasing affability in the remark, no scorn. And no allusion followed to the flagpole welcome of the previous day, feeding the suspicion he had not been told of it.

"The honor is mutual, sir."

"Excellent," he said without looking up. "You also seem to have some interesting professional experience—newspaper work, print shop, typing."

"Yes, sir. But I'm a little shy on teaching experience at the moment, I'm afraid. In fact, I haven't taught at all—I hope they told you that, sir."

"First thing. Corps Area headquarters seems to think we need wits more than experience out here—and a bright young Harvard fellow might be just the ticket." He closed the folder and looked up, blinking steadily. "It's not my place to argue. Anyway, you can't beat Harvard, can you?"

"Yale does often enough—sir."

"Yes," he said indifferently, "well, you get my drift."

"I think so, sir."

The blinks abated somewhat as he fondled his glass and studied its depths. "I'm a Purdue man, myself."

"Oh—I didn't know."

"Finest engineering program in the country between Rensselaer and California."

"Yes, sir." Precisely where in that expanse Purdue was situated, Toby did not know—Illinois or Ohio, he guessed, or perhaps Iowa.

Civil engineering had been his field, the captain explained. After the war he had stayed in the East and gone to work for the Springfield Water Company. "Pretty tame stuff, I'm afraid." When his prospective father-in-law opened the door to him at the family real estate and insurance firm, he did not hesitate to put engineering aside in the quest for a more lucrative calling. But it had all come back to him, he said, when they assigned him to regenerate the forest. He took special pleasure in superintending the road-building crew, although the codger who directed the work projects disapproved. "It's our only bone of contention—otherwise we get along hand in glove. In fact, we're all pretty congenial out here."

"Yes, sir."

"It's funny," he said after a pause, "Harvard's not very strong in engineering—did you know that?"

"I don't think I've ever thought about it, to be honest, sir. But now that you mention it, I guess that's why M.I.T. got started."

He looked disappointed at such ready agreement. "I wouldn't be at all surprised," he said drily. "To tell you the truth, Mr. Ronan, you'd be better off out here if that's where you'd gone. Practical skills are what we thrive on—there's nothing philosophical about this operation —or these fellows. They're a salt-of-the-earth bunch—men who'll make their living with their hands when they're done here—if they get the chance. Their hands, Mr. Ronan, not their heads—if you get my drift. I'd like to impress that upon you at the beginning of your tour. The point escaped your predecessors."

"I understand, sir."

"These are not Harvard types."

"No, sir."

"They're here to be reborn, in a manner of speaking. We don't want them being frustrated. We teach them good work habits and upright citizenship—not Shakespeare or Thucydides or calculus."

"No, sir."

"Nor do we like to stir them up with any radical ideas that might make them discontented. This is a place to make these boys feel good about themselves—that's a luxury most of them haven't had before—

and about their country, too. We don't want them being fed any utopian schemes or collectivist subversion, either. Enterprise and perseverance are what we're peddling."

It seemed not the moment to point out that the camp itself was testament to the failure of the unbridled enterprise system—and functioned at state expense very much as a rural collective. "Yes, sir."

Having probed and found the new arrival flawlessly pliable, he chatted thereafter with a measured amiability about the pleasures of life, of which music was for him a prominent component. "To soothe the savage breast," he said, "or is it beast?"

"I've heard it both ways, sir."

"But which is right?"

"I'm not sure, sir—breast, I think."

"I thought Harvard men knew things like that?"

"I'd hesitate to generalize—sir."

He forgave Toby his ignorance—appreciated it, even—and invited him to drop by any afternoon before the boys got back from work or after lights-out to listen to his records on the Victrola. Naturally he kept only a limited supply of albums at camp, given the rough-and-tumble of the place, but he was sure Toby would find some selections to his liking. Toby thanked him and was ready to be gone—the brandy was beginning to moisten his temples—but the captain insisted on knowing who were his favorite composers.

"That's hard to say, sir. Bach, I suppose, and Mozart."

"Yes—well, I have a few of them. I'm inclined to Beethoven and Brahms, myself, and some of Tchaikovsky." He offered Toby more to drink, which he declined, then helped himself to another splash and a half. "And how are you on Sousa?"

"Sousa, sir?"

"John Philip Sousa—the march king?"

"Yes—of course. Well, he's—very—rousing."

"Now there's an understatement if I ever heard one." He forced a laugh that turned into an unpleasant gurgle. "The man is an absolute genius—history's greatest composer of martial music. Just because someone is American doesn't mean he can't be a cultural giant."

"Oh, no, sir. In fact, I think some of our writers—"

"I happened to have attended Sousa's final concert, you know."

"Why, no, I—"

"It was in Reading in '32—I grew up in Easton, which isn't far away—and was there at the time visiting my late mother—" And off he wandered for what seemed the better part of eternity, alternating between the laborious details of his precious collection of Sousa recordings and incoherent vignettes of his Pennsylvania boyhood.

At last he glanced at his watch, said they ought to part since reveille was at six, and urged Toby to take a day or two to get his bearings and then come by for a more substantive talk. Meanwhile, had he any questions or problems so far?

"Well, there is one thing, sir," Toby ventured, thinking Sparhawk's guard might be lowered at that late hour and nicely laced with alcohol as he was. "About my clothing—"

"Carmichael's your man for all that. Hasn't he given you what you need yet?"

"It's not that, sir—"

"Well, if it's about the fit, get yourself a tailor in town. The army's not much for style."

"It's the clothes themselves, sir."

"What is it—you'd prefer pinstripes in worsted?"

"I'd prefer my own, sir."

His blinking began in earnest again. "What's wrong with ours?"

"Nothing, sir. I just think I'd communicate better with the men if I weren't seen as an authority figure."

"I see." He set down his glass with excessive precision. "Unfortunately, Mr. Ronan, authority is what makes this place tick. It's exactly what these fellows need most when they get here—and we supply it to them. You dress like a civilian, you'll have as much success with them as their schoolteachers did."

"That's a chance I'd be willing to take."

"But we wouldn't. We can't risk undermining the authority structure that's been built."

"But why does it have to be within an exclusively military context?"

"Because anything else would confuse them. Too many cooks."

"But don't the men already take orders from civilians—in the field?"

His grogginess had fled. His lids were flicking with the ferocity of hummingbird wings. "Because we delegate them authority outside of camp. But you're inside it, with us—and you should look and act the part of a soldier."

"Nobody told me that—sir."

"I can't help that, Mr. Ronan. I'm here to clarify these things for you from this point on."

"And—and am I supposed to salute, too, and be saluted?"

"We don't require that."

"Why is that—sir?"

"Because you're not—actually—in the army."

"Then why do I have to wear a uniform?"

He stood up and, on the brink of demonstrable anger, collected himself. "Because, Mr. Ronan, I said so. Goodnight—and I'd go easy on the citronella if I were you—they tell me it's addictive."

V

Monday, August 26th, 1935

Had breakfast with the boys—stewed prunes, runny eggs, gristly ham, glutinous oatmeal, blazing coffee flavored metallic, and all you want. Eaten doubletime out of mess trays at tables holding a dozen men each. Yum.

Now I know why it is called the mess. It means the eaters, not the eaten. Better manners are practiced in a stable. They clutch utensils in their fists, shovel in the grub as if famine loomed, chew with mouths full and open, spray food particles as they talk, scrape leftovers from their neighbor's trays, and constantly lick their fingers, evidently regarding napkins as effeminate. An exercise in communal bestiality. They scarcely noticed me there.

The fare is fair but filling. Heavy on bread, beans, rice, and macaroni, they say. The beef is purportedly tanned instead of cooked, the hash made of squirrel, and everything drenched with saltpeter (the latter alleged ineffectual at immunizing Bingo Barnes & other randy rascals from fucking Pickles, the camp dog). . . .

Ashbel Cummings owed his disposition to earned bitterness. The depression had cost him his lumberyard business, and he was full of contempt for politicians in general and Franklin Roosevelt in particular. The New Deal he saw as bread and circuses accustoming a formerly proud people to the dole.

But when they asked him to be the superintendent of works at Camp 127 outside of Pittsfield, he had no recourse but to accept. He might have made a legendary hermit in those hills, only he lacked the intestinal misanthropy. So he reported with grim resolve to the site everybody in the C.C.C. beside him called "Lulu," after the waterfall that used to spill out of the cool darkness in the woods just above where the barracks compound now stood. They made him dam it up, though, so there would be drinking and bathing water for the camp, and thereafter the sight of the harsh concrete sluiceway that replaced the cascade, famed for the primeval purity of its silver-white water tumbling fifteen feet over black rocks into a broad, limpid pool, fired scorn in Ash Cummings toward the notion that men could ever improve on nature.

He was indisputably competent at his job, however reluctantly he had undertaken it. Toby's arrival he viewed as merely another of those pestiferous items he was forever jotting down on the clipboard hanging off a wall nail just behind his head. Toby had come by the superintendent's office in the work shed to introduce himself and ask if he might go out with one of the crews without getting in the way. "Probably not," Ash Cummings rasped but turned at once to check the daily budget and see who was assigned where.

"I'll keep to one side," Toby promised.

"That's where the poison ivy grows, son." His forehead and face around the eyes were imprinted with deep cracks, like the parched bed of some forgotten arroyo. He looked not just weathered but beyond further incursions by time and the elements as he spread his bony legs, hooked a long, knobby hand over each knee, and hoisted himself upright for another day of coaxing blood from turnips. "You go on out with Will Bassett's gang—they're doin' tree-stand improvement, and he's a very educational sort. Don't go blamin' me, though, if you get a toe lopped off."

By the time they were done straightening their bunks, policing the grounds, and enduring Adjutant Nesbit's white-gloved inspection of the barracks, the enrollees were sated with domesticity and eager to hit the road. With purposeful bustle around the tail of each truck, they loaded on picks and saws and shovels and axes and mattocks and long brush-pruning hooks that reminded Toby of poles that clerks in food markets used for plucking packages off of top shelves. Yet the tools were not thrown clattering into corners but carefully laid in storage racks, and the men themselves, for all their buoyant hooting and the taunts that flew thick and fast between the boarding crews, took their places on the wooden benches without any fraternal pummeling or other rowdiness.

At a quarter to eight, Ash Cummings gave a pair of clean, shrill toots on his brass whistle, and the trucks geared sluggishly into motion. The others were driven by Lems, Toby's by enrollee Joe Calabrese, the only officially designated chauffeur in the twenty-man camp detail. He recited the manpower inventory as the truck leapfrogged over the forest trail, jouncing Toby around the cab and shaking loose the remnants of his indigestibly hearty breakfast. The work force was divided into two main platoons of ninety men each, subdivided into three sections of thirty each, broken further into three squads of ten each. The rest of the men were assigned to the camp as clerks, orderlies, medics, janitors, and kitchen help. Plus one chauffeur. To Toby it sounded like the antebellum plantations, divided between bent-back field hands and a relatively pampered elite servicing the manor house.

"What the fuck," Joe said, "a slave's a slave."

A narrow-chested boy with a massive head and thick, dark brows that gave him a top-heavy look, Joe Calabrese came from Swampscott, where there were too many mouths to feed at home and no work. He knew a lot more about motors than how to turn them on and off. When he was not ferrying the work crews or delivering lunch to the project sites or picking up supplies in Pittsfield, he serviced the camp fleet of five trucks with a diligence bordering on fanaticism. No one messed with his machines—or aboard them. When Toby asked how he kept the boys in the open back of the truck from horsing around, he said, "'Cause I'd go for the first bump in the road and flip 'em the fuck out on their heads."

The forest was still damp and sleepy, and the shouts of purposeful intruders carried in defilement of that unwalled cathedral. They peeled off from the truck in twos and threes, bearing tools in accordance with the barked instructions of the foreman. Toby waited till he had dispatched them all before approaching chubby, open-faced Will Bassett, who looked as contented in those surroundings as a well-fed woodchuck.

He was at once generous in extending his friendship and downright lavish in volunteering instruction. Without reference to Toby's Harvard tie—with which, presumably, the whole forest was by now familiar—Will advised he was a college man, too, and no mindless backwoodsman. "I did a couple o' years at Connecticut Aggie down in Storrs," he said, making the stint sound penitential. From there he had gone to work for the leading Berkshire nursery until getting axed when economic conditions turned bad. Adversity, though, had not soured his innate delight in the seasonal miracles of the life process. He knocked around trimming topiaries and taking any other odd jobs he could find until a spot opened up for him in the C.C.C. He claimed to like his new job better than the old one—and seemed the rare sort who probably always would.

His mission, he explained, was to save and rebuild the forest. Most of what was visible around them was third growth. The first had been thinned nearly to extinction to provide lumber for early settlers. The second had gone mostly for charcoal used by local smelters. The C.C.C. was sent to help redress the plundering.

"First thing is you got to stop 'em from dying," said Will, marching Toby off with him on his supervisory rounds. The boys in the corps were applying a two-pronged preventive—one against disease, the other against fire. The former was the worse enemy. For thirty years, an unwelcome refugee from Europe called blister rust had been ravaging the eastern white pine. Its disease spores propagated in gooseberry bushes in and around the trees and got wind-borne onto the pine needles, where they burrowed into the cellular structure of the tree, threw a ring around it, and choked it to death. The blister rust took two years to show itself, by which point the disease was terminal.

"Nasty little bugger," Toby said.

"The shame is your *pinus strobus* is a real gem. Grows fast—adapts to a wide variety of soil and weather conditions—excellent for construction—it's soft and light but she warps and checks less than most timbers. And there's no prettier pine if you're just talkin' ornament." As far as Will Bassett was concerned, the white pine was a damsel in distress.

The only cure was to go after every gooseberry bush in sight. Poisoning was the less laborious way, but since a lot of poison cost a lot of money and the C.C.C. was rich in nothing but labor, the more direct strong-arm method was employed. Will's charges stripped to the waist and grubbed the bushes with mattocks, flinging up soil and roots all around them in frenzied assault on the stubborn foe. Their lean torsos were streaming with sweat after each encounter—and there was never an end to the fray.

The forest's other main scourge was fought by trying to deny it nourishment. Fire breaks, from ten to fifteen feet wide and picked clean of every piece of flammable material, were laid out in a giant checkerboard across the hills, some of the cuts doubling as truck and ski trails and all serving to contain or at least slow any blaze that might take hold. Hacking these swathes through the mountains was also grubby, endless work, sustainable only by supple, young limbs, and the finished clearings required regular tending. To further the conservation effort, the corps scooped out twenty-foot-wide water holes at random spots in the forest, taking pains to tilt one side up toward the lip so any wildlife that fell into the deep end had a way out.

"Very thoughtful," Toby said.

"Balance of nature," Will said.

After two years, their primary effort at fire prevention now was to keep the forest floor clean. The very notion amused Toby. How, and why, would you clean dirt? It wasn't the soil he was talking about, Will said, any more than the trees themselves were a problem, especially the hardwoods, which were probably the least flammable thing out there. It was the ground cover he meant—dead underbrush killed by the density of the forest itself, and the perennial grasses that thrived in the spring rain and turned to long thatch as the waning summer seared them. Living evergreen plants and dried moss were other deadly bearers of flame, hurrying it to downed branch wood, rotting logs, and pitiably vulnerable snags, the woodsman's name for dead, barkless, but still standing trees punky with broken, broomed tops. "Fires shoot the whole height of a snag in a second," Will said, condemning one with a rap of his knuckles as they passed it, "and pop off their rotted tops in brands that spread the thing to hell and back." Half the crews under his command were therefore hard at clearing away nature's combustible refuse.

It went beyond that, though; they compensated nature. The crews fanned out with their mattocks and seedling trays to plant pine in sectors where the dead and crippled trees had been taken down and space was opened in the combed-out stand for new growth. Will checked the site of each one for growing room and light and drainage and monitored the men against careless handling of the baby trees. The more practiced of them worked at a steady pace, rotating the mattock expertly, pick end first to break through the earth, then the cutter end to slash through roots and turf and subsoil debris. The novices excavated too slowly and too much—or too fast and too shallow. Will came on one fellow making a mess of it in a muggy copse. Toby recognized the unlucky Bingo Barnes, cursing as he crawled about trying to reclaim the spilled contents of his seedling tray.

"Okay now," Will steadied him when Bingo returned to the hole he had dug, "fill it in and start over."

"Huh?" Bingo's perplexity showed in his upturned display of buck teeth.

"Keep the topsoil piled separate from the rest—you're not makin' mud pies."

Bingo bent to the task. For a moment he looked tempted to toss the mattock aside and perform the operation with his hands and teeth. "'S that deep enough?"

"A little more maybe—then loosen up the soil nice on the bottom and get rid of any sticks and leaves you feel. Worms you can leave." The debris took too long to break down into soil, he told Toby, thereby threatening the treelets with malnutrition by blocking their roots.

Bingo picked up the seedling with misplaced delicacy.

"Hold it by the stem, dammit!"

Bingo tried to make the change without switching hands and dropped the plant down the hole. In retrieving it, he made matters worse by brushing soil from the frizzy root system, as if it needed to be dusted before reinterment.

"You're killing the thing, Barnes! Those are roots, not a whisk broom. Now you kiss it and make 'em better."

Bingo gave the plant a quick peck and looked up for forgiveness. Will nodded, then told him to spread the roots out carefully in all directions—"Keeps 'em from matting and girdling," he explained, "so they won't choke each other off"—and to make sure they were all placed in the hole below ground level but not as far down as the subsoil. At the end, the flustered enrollee shaped the soil surrounding the plant into a little mound a few inches high so when the exhumed earth settled, rain would not collect in a depression and eventually rot out the roots. Will instructed Bingo to tamp down the soil when he was all done to give the plant support and because roots would not grow through air pockets. "With your heel, Barnes—not your toe! You'll break off the goddamn roots—if by some miracle they still happen to be alive." Will turned away in despair. "That's why he's been on wheelbarrow detail for five months," he said. "Not a bad kid, though."

Toby joined Will for lunch under a clump of maples. Joe Calabrese had trucked out meat-loaf sandwiches, cake, and coffee. Stick-to-your-ribs cuisine was about the limit of the military's gastronomic arts. Half a sandwich of that density left Toby full. "Whatsa' matter," asked Will, "you got something against porcupine?"

"No wonder I didn't recognize the taste."

"You're not supposed to. That's why they douse it with ketchup." Will said it without a glimmer of a smile.

"Tell me you're kidding."

"Why—did you get mustard on yours? Sometimes they—"

"It's *not* porcupine!"

"It's not? Well, then it's some kind of rodent."

"Oh, God."

"I think you're wrong, though. At least they cleaned out all the quills this time. I've had porkie hash in camp where you could actually—"

Toby gave a groan and slid the rest of his sandwich to one side. Will, not one to coddle the squeamish, never slowed his discourse. Rodents got a raw deal, he said, from people who were ignorant about animals. As a subspecies, they were very intelligent and resourceful. It was true, however, that porcupines in particular were one of nature's more useless creatures, and in fact were highly destructive to the forest. They browsed the hell out of the pine bark, laying the trees open to insect infestation and other perils.

Overcoming revulsion, Toby began to listen to what Will was saying. All at once it seemed remarkable that porcupines trundled about not only looking a little like horizontal pine trees but actually thriving on their bark—as if there were some zoöbotanical link between the two. "That couldn't possibly be, could it?" he asked.

"You mean the pine bark makes them grow needles?"

"I guess that's ridiculous."

"Who knows? I used to think it worked the other way around—that the animals thought the trees were their earth-mothers or something."

That sounded to Toby more like Aesop than science. "Just tell me the sandwich isn't porcupine."

"Well," Will said, eyes slitting with speculation, "not much, anyway. But I think I tasted a little whoa-Dobbin in there."

Toby roamed on his own as the tempo of work ebbed perceptibly in the afternoon and their civilian taskmasters began to tonguelash the wilting corpsmen. One who needed no goad was a tall, husky fellow he came upon wielding an ax against a thirty-foot scrub pine in a thin dell being readied for reforestation. Others in the vicinity were pecking at their snags, but this one sized up his prey and went after it with vicious precision. A nice-looking boy except for a lopsided nose—it ridged about midway and the lower half veered to the right, suggesting it had been punched in that direction and never mended properly —he kept his blade moving at an unflagging pace. His look never wandered from the deep divot he was taking in the trunk. Chips spat in all directions at the conclusion of each fluid arc, and in no time his undershirt was pasted to the dark mat of hair beneath it. Toby was surprised how long it took, even with that sustained intensity of attack, to fell a tree—and a sick one at that.

It was an hour before he made an incision on the side opposite and a bit above where he had been chopping. The tree creaked and shivered and then swooned in its muffled extremity. Only then did the slayer pause to acknowledge his company. His name, he said, was Kevin Dundy, he came from South Boston, and he served as leader of C Barracks. It was clear enough why.

While he took a few moments to rest, Toby asked if he could help him get a headstart reducing the felled tree to logs. "Ever use an ax?" Kevin asked.

"Never—but I've been watching you."

"Watchin' is different than doin'. Go nice 'n' easy."

Toby was taken with the hard beauty of the ax. It was almost perfectly balanced between the gleaming head and the in-swept hickory handle. Kevin told him to trim the branches off the side opposite the spot he had chosen so the ax would not glance off a knot and do him in. Then he was to position himself so that what he was chopping al-

ways stayed between him and the ax. Toby gave his palms a few pre-
paratory rubs and started flailing eagerly at the prone deadwood.

"Not such big swings," he was instructed. "It can't hit back."

He rained short, economical blows at the target, marveling at how
little damage each did.

"Slide your top hand up the shaft after each shot and then bring it
back down as you swing—gives you lots more leverage."

Also blisters. In two minutes he had his first; in another two, each
palm was threatening to balloon with lymph.

"Bend your back more," Kevin said. "Half the time you're either
overswinging or underhitting."

He was relieved just before succumbing to fatigue—and as Ash
Cummings appeared on the crest of the rise. A dent no deeper than
one eighth the way through the trunk testified to the feebleness of the
axman.

The superintendent collected Toby with a chuckle and led him off
to tour other provinces. At the crown of the rise, he handed Toby his
ax while he knelt to lace up his boots better. At eye level, he caught
the glint of metal. "Never hold the blade down like that," he said.
"Always out." He unburdened Toby of the lethal tool and shouldered
it, blade parallel to the ground and aimed away from his stringy neck.

"Yes, sir," Toby said, gaze fixed to the bobbing blade. Honed to
guillotine deadliness, it looked mean even in an official safe position.
"Isn't your ax—very—sharp—Mr. Cummings—sir."

"Damned right. And hold the 'sir.' That's for the troopers." He
practically bounded over the pine needles strewn everywhere across
the floor of the forest, soft now with diffused light and shadowed
gold.

Toby lengthened his stride to keep pace. "Excuse me, but isn't it—
dangerous—to carry around that sharp an ax?"

Cummings puffed up his cheeks and filtered the air out in a thin,
antic whistle. "There's two times an ax is dangerous," he said. "When
it's in a fool's hand—and when it's dull." His own he tried to keep
keen enough to shave with, he said. "This man's army even got us a
jim-dandy portable gasoline-powered grinder in the back of the shed
so's no ax comes out here without my men first sharpenin' her up nice
—an' that's each and every morning I'm speakin' of." His own ax,
though, he tended to himself on a whetstone. "Seems more personal-
like an' appropriate, seein' that I made 'er from scratch. Handle took a
week's carvin' and two for sandin'."

They walked on in silence for a time. "You give these boys a nice
workout," Toby offered with as much conviviality as he thought the
superintendent could stand.

"This section's nothin' much," he said. "The ones that got it hard is the road gang. They got to tug out stumps and boulders till they're blue in the face. Sometimes they got tears rollin' down their cheeks from all the creosote in the tar. It burns like piss."

"Is that—strictly—necessary?"

"Which—the tar or the road?"

"The tar, I meant."

"The tar is if the road is."

Joe Calabrese's truck pulled in below them at the edge of the trail. "You mean you don't think the road is?"

"It's a matter of opinion."

"I thought there wasn't any other way the public could get up the mountain into a recreation area?"

"That's what they tell me—so that's what I'm doin'." He shifted the ax to his other shoulder for the final stretch downhill. "Sometimes, though, you get more from it lettin' the mountain set an' goin' the long way 'round." The flint came wrapped in homespun.

Company Clerk Bloomgarden was waiting for him with a message when Toby's truck pulled back into camp a little past four. "His highness the adjutant requests the presence of your carcass at H.Q." Skeezix's eyes spun knowingly. "That's what you get for fraternizin'."

"Who with?"

"You'll find out."

The public-address was bellowing "Semper Fidelis" while the men trooped across the compound to rest, shower, and groom themselves for lineup. The music, presumably, was meant to insufflate their souls with intimations of military transcendence. Soil soldiers on parade, bedraggled or not. He asked Skeezix if these ballads of belligerency were a daily ritual. "Sousa and booza," the clerk said and let it go at that.

The music changed to "The Thunderer" as he pulled open the screen door to headquarters, a three-desk office in the front end of the first building on the staff side of the field, adjacent to the mess. The door was rigged with a new spring that crashed it shut louder than the blaring brass on the p.a. "Hi, Mitch—sorry—"

Whether the raucous door or the bluff greeting rubbed Mitchell Nesbit worse was hard to say, but no kindly glow lighted the adjutant's pert features. His orderly, a boy with a face as pitted as Nesbit's was unblemished, shrank out the door at the sight of Toby.

The lieutenant reached into his top drawer and pulled out a booklet. Turning to a page premarked with a paper clip and not inviting Toby to sit, he read, " 'Supervisory personnel shall under no circumstances eat at the same table with enrollees. Such familiarity inevitably breaks down respect for authority.'" He flipped the booklet shut. "Things are a little loose around here on the weekends, but the rest of the time there's a table by the window in the southeast corner of the mess reserved for officers and any of the foremen who elected to stay for supper. That's where the C.E.A. is assigned to eat." He barely looked up.

"You left out, 'And that's an order.'"

Eyes still averted, Nesbit shoved the rule book back into the drawer and said, "I thought that was apparent."

What was apparent was his uncertainty how to deal with Toby, so he had settled for the moment on a posture of junior martinet. "I used to eat at the same table with my father and mother," Toby said. "They were supervisory personnel—and I didn't lose respect for *their* authority."

"Very funny."

"I'm not being funny—I'm trying to understand."

"This isn't a debating society, Ronan—it's a camp run under military regulations. You want chicken with Mom and Pop, go home for it. But here you can't cozy up to the men one minute and kick ass the next."

Captain Sparhawk delivered him much the same message in a brief interview at his quarters that night. "Your job is here," he said, "not in the forest."

"I thought it would be useful, sir, to see what the men go through so I'd be better able to—"

"That's commendable, Mr. Ronan. But now that you've had a look around, I think it would be best to leave the field work to the Lems. That's what they're here for."

"I didn't have the impression I was interfering—sir."

"You're a distraction out there—just like me—and distracted men foul up. I'd like you to concentrate on your specialty, not everyone else's."

"My thought was to make sure they're properly connected."

"Use your Harvard-licensed brains for that, Ronan—that's why you're here. And that's an order from your commanding officer."

Jailer, too, from the look of it.

EIGHT

Tuesday, Sept. 3, 1935

Have done next to nothing for a week now but eat starch, get con-stipated & learn to play passable poker with Sgt/Carmichael, Skeezix and Eddie Spain (50 lima beans the pot limit). The whole trick is not to bluff unless you know how.

Camp a tomb while men are gone. First the capt. told me no point in organizing ed. program till after Labor Day. Now he says wait till new enlistment period at end of month since a third to a half of men will quit. Leaving me nothing to do while he rides off Sheridanlike, black boots agleam, on a rented steed to inspect the work projects.

Evenings more stimulating. Capt. invites me, Nesbit & Dr Haseltine (when he's in camp) to qtrs for brandy & bull. The talk devoted of late to Mussolini & Ethiopian situation. Sparhawk admires Il Duce's energy & says fascism, while bad for America, is only thing that could have dragged Eyetalians into 20th cent. Muss. started out just like me, he claims—well-ed. intellectual steeped in lit. who taught & wrote till mid-twenties. But he was young socialist & Capt Sp. has no doubt I am unsympathetic to that doctrine.

Feeling restless & useless. There must be something I can do.

WHEN HE ASKED Eddie why the glass doors were always kept locked on the bookcase in the corner of the Rec, his wary face flooded with amazement. "Because," Eddie said, "o-o-otherwise the guys would always be tak-tak-, uh—would be borrowing books all the time."

Toby asked if that wasn't the general purpose of a library, and Eddie agreed. The boys could of course borrow whatever they wanted; all they had to do was ask for it. "But if the case is locked," Toby wondered, "how can they browse to see what they'd like?"

"That's why it's-uh, it's-uh—got glass doors."

Eddie's precocious mastery of the bureaucratic mentality aside, he conceded, when pressed for details, that enrollees were not exactly encouraged to read. The captain liked the men to be active, preferably athletic, and if they were going in for sedentary entertainment, it had best be movies or radio. In fact, *Radio News* and *The Saturday Evening Post* were the only reading matter the camp officially subscribed to.

"What's the captain afraid of?" he asked Eddie.

"Uh-uh-uh—softies." It was Sparhawk's catch-all epithet for anyone inclined to think too much. Heavy thinkers were likely to be brooders, and they were bad for morale. That explained why the few books theoretically accessible to the boys were all escapist pap. Even so, they might have had a better grade of it. Why hadn't the camp appealed to the townspeople of Pittsfield and the surrounding communities for old or duplicate titles? Surely they would have been forthcoming in view of the good works the C.C.C. was performing. The captain was very sensitive on the score, Eddie disclosed, ever since the previous winter when the camp boys were denied permission to use the gymnasium at Pittsfield High School in the evenings. Excessive costs for heating, lighting, and janitorial services were blamed, but the captain suspected it was on social grounds—the enrollees were perceived as lowlife and best kept quarantined from the town, especially its nubile daughters.

The captain's policies seemed so obviously freighted with his own fixations on this score that a frontal assault was out of the question. Instead, Toby pretended there was nothing at all at issue, even while prosecuting his case. Finding him alone in headquarters shortly before evening lineup, he asked Sparhawk if he would please announce that the bookcase was henceforth to be left unlocked and anyone wishing to borrow a title had only to write it on a slip of paper along with his name and put it in its alphabetical place by author in a shoebox on top of the case.

"Do you think that's wise?" the captain asked.

"You mean it ought to be alphabetical by the enrollee's name? I was thinking that too, sir. Whichever way you'd prefer would be—"

"That's not what I had in mind."

"Oh—you mean about putting the boys on their honor? Well, I think that would be a healthy thing, sir—a sign of trust and confidence. As a matter of fact, I'm going to add the six books of my own that I brought to camp—you know, just by way of—"

"That seems excessive, Mr. Ronan."

"Thank you, sir, but really, I think it's the right thing to do. Since the very first of the 'dominant aims' of the educational program as defined in the C.E.A. *Handbook* is to develop within each man his powers of 'self-culture,' I think I ought to set an example by—"

"Exactly what books are they?"

"What books are what, sir?"

"Yours—the ones you—"

"Oh, they're each American classics. Let's see, there's *Typee* and *A Connecticut Yankee*—and *The House of the Seven Gables*—and *Walden*—and a collection of Poe's, *The Fall of the House of Usher*—I think 'The Pit and the Pendulum' is in the same volume—and a book of Emerson's essays—you know, 'Liberty,' 'Character,' 'Self-Reliance' and that sort. All first-rate things."

"Yes, certainly. But I'm not sure I see the point, Ronan. I doubt if any of these men are up to works of that caliber."

"What's the harm, sir? If even one or two of them stumble upon something they like, it might enrich their lives immeasurably."

"I wonder."

"In fact, sir, I was hoping you might—actually consider—at least the possibility—well, no. I'll withdraw that. Excuse me, sir."

"What was it you wanted to say, Ronan?"

"It was impertinent, sir."

"Why don't you leave that for me to judge?"

"Yes, sir. Well—what I had in mind—was if perhaps—"

"Out with it, man!"

"—you might add one or two of your books to the camp collection —on loan, of course. If your name was in them, I'm sure no one would even dream of—"

"*My* books? My own *private* ones?"

He had a nice little shelf of military history prominently displayed in his quarters—Thucydides, Xenophon, Livy on the Punic Wars, *The Iliad*, Caesar's *Gallic Commentaries*, the memoirs of U. S. Grant, biographies of Alexander, Napoleon, and a couple of other all-time, all-star bloodletters. "I thought they might conceivably inspire a few of the boys—you just never know. But of course, as you say, they're your own private property, and it's not my place—"

"That's not the point, Ronan. If I felt there was any chance at all boys like these had the capacity to absorb the great lessons—and the thoughts—"

"You know, sir, you're right—it might help if you explained some of them in your own words. We might arrange—well, I know this is jumping the gun some but the thought's been in my head—suppose we had a course in military history once the education program gets going—that is, if you'd even consider the possibility—sir?"

"Well, I don't know about—"

"I think a surprising number of the men would be interested."

"It seems rather—irregular—" The eyes were flickering.

"Oh, no, it would be part of the larger curriculum—of course."

"—and more up Nesbit's alley than mine, anyway, so I don't—"

"You could both do it, then—alternating lectures, perhaps?"

"Well," he said, not displeased at the inferential sanction of his intellect by Harvard authorities, "it may be worth a thought or two."

"I'm sure of it, sir. And think about your books, at any rate—I mean if you could see your way clear to—"

"Yes." He brushed a microbe from one of his boots. "I'll consider it."

Thus were elided the prospective softening or otherwise debilitating tendencies of literature on the raw young minds in his charge. Captain Sparhawk announced the new open-door policy with some fanfare and much as if he were its originator. The addition of his and the educational advisor's personal books was cited as evidence of an abiding concern with the mental as well as physical development of the enrollees.

That first modest concession by the forces of darkness spurred Toby's efforts. He rode into Pittsfield two mornings later with Joe Calabrese on the daily trip for supplies and, self-conscious in his insignia-less khakis, stopped by the public library. A formidable structure of Victorian Gothic graystone, made all the grander by its name, the Berkshire Athenaeum, it gave the immediate sense of being excellently fusty and thoroughly used.

After stating the nature of his mission twice to noncommissioned harpies, he was shown to the office of a Miss Keyes, identified on the door as the assistant librarian. Miss Keyes, alas, was out at the moment. Indeed, she was often out, he was told, dividing her time as she did between the library and the Berkshire Museum around the corner, which she served as a volunteer curator. This highly versatile creature was said to be overseeing the installation of a diorama just then. Word was being dispatched; if he might be patient for a few moments, Miss Keyes would appear.

The click of a hitched gait preceded her down the hall, causing him to anticipate still another sere old maid, probably arthritic. Miss Keyes proved to be young—approaching her middle twenties—and, except for a slight but unmistakable limp in the right leg, quite brisk. She had on a no-nonsense navy dress with a little white scalloped collar that picked up the bleached purity of her gloves, which she unpeeled smartly before taking his hand. "Temple Keyes," she said. "What can I do for you, Mr. Ronan—or are you Lieutenant Ronan or Leftenant

Ronan or something equally dashing? I'm a bit vague on military matters."

"Just Mister," he said. "The army is fond of imposing its dress code on unarmed civilians."

"Ah, yes," she said, scanning her desktop for mail, messages, or anything that might have accumulated there in her absence. Without beauty and despite her handicap, Miss Keyes was by no means dowdy. Of a slenderness accentuated by the severity of her dress, she had short, bobbed, dark-blond hair; blue-gray eyes of extra width that emitted deft rays of patrolling sensibility; a small, thin mouth rescued from oblivion with a daub or two of lipstick, the only makeup he could detect on her, and a nose that formed a nearly perfect right triangle. This somewhat angular austerity was not modulated by her voice, which had a decidedly regal clarity and command, as if it were performing rather than merely uttering sentences.

"I'm sorry to have interrupted you," he said, hoping to dispel a few of the preoccupations visible on her high brow. She looked to need a bit of jollying. "Is it an Eskimo village or a pack of elephants thundering across the veldt?"

She moved some envelopes about in front of her and glanced up with a slightly pained expression. "I beg your pardon?"

"The diorama."

"Oh," she said, "oh, yes. No, I'm afraid Eskimos and elephants are beyond our means. It's owls, actually. We're quite strong on owls. We've cases of them, in fact. They get dreadfully dusty. I thought we might do something rather more dynamic with them."

"One doesn't think of owls in terms of dynamism."

"No," she said, "one doesn't—which was my point precisely. They happen to be quite fierce and accomplished predators."

"I didn't know. I thought they just sat up there like the Sphinx—all-seeing and all-knowing."

"Well, you've got part of it right. Those big eyes of theirs help them see wondrously well at night—no rodent within miles is safe. They also have remarkably sensitive hearing. That's what we're trying to show—a pair of great horneds on the wing for their supper."

"No fears of inducing nightmares among your smaller visitors?"

"Don't laugh—the point's been raised, and more than once. But I've argued that if Peter Rabbit is capable of learning *realpolitik* in Mr. MacGregor's cabbage patch, then a museum should be permitted to display a few of nature's less benign aspects. We are, after all, a teaching institution."

"Absolutely," he said with studied agreeableness. "Perhaps you might even add a panel showing your owls making off with Mr. MacGregor."

She stiffened at that, taking his playfulness for mockery. There was nothing left, given her apparent tenderness, but to state his errand. Was it possible the Athenaeum had some old, ill-bound, duplicate, or otherwise unsuitable volumes stashed away somewhere that it would be pleased to part with? If so, they would be gratefully received by the C.C.C. camp.

"Really?" asked Miss Keyes. "I wouldn't have thought they were readers—from what little I've heard of those boys."

"They're not, to be honest. I'm hoping to change that."

"How very high-minded of you, Mr. Ronan. And if you have any luck, I'm confident the trustees here would be happy to extend borrowing privileges to your boys—provided they behave better around here than they manage to when they come to town for the movies or whatever recreation it is they find."

"They work hard all day, Miss Keyes. I think they might be permitted to let off a little steam after hours."

"It's my understanding that they're loud and profane a good deal of the time. That is not the way to ingratiate themselves to this community."

"Perhaps if the community were to extend a welcoming hand—"

"It's not easy to welcome an army that's been imposed on you."

"It's *your* forest they're out there restoring—and your merchants they buy supplies from. Doesn't that somewhat mitigate their boorishness?"

"It might—if one knew what it was they were doing out there in the first place. It's all been kept very secretive—save for the vulgarity."

"Without doubt there's a problem here in public relations. But it is a work area, after all. I believe they're to be finished by the middle of next year. Till then, I understand, parts of it will be open to skiers."

"So I've heard," she said and clasped her hands in front of her. "Skiing happens not to be one of my own pursuits, but I'm sure the community will be most grateful to your organization when all's said and done. Meanwhile, as I say, we'd be happy to consider individual applications for a card from the better-behaved boys."

"That's quite impractical, I'm afraid. They're out in the field during most library hours."

"Then perhaps you might want to apply, yourself. I'm sure that—"

"You say you have no expendable titles whatever?"

"I don't remember saying that, Mr. Ronan."

"Oh. I guess it's just the impression I got."

"The fact is, the Berkshire Athenaeum has one of the very highest circulation ratios in the entire country, Mr. Ronan. We take pride in putting all our books to work and not leaving them stuck away somewhere, as you suppose."

"I didn't suppose—I inquired. And I'm sorry your undoubtedly deserved pride doesn't extend to the labors of the earnest young men out there in the woods. Thank you for your time, Miss Keyes."

"Mr. Ronan." She sat there, understandably disinclined to offer her palm in farewell.

He was sure he had overplayed his punishing exit lines until he received a postcard at the camp a few days later asking him kindly to telephone. It was signed "T. Keyes." He dialed her promptly from the pay booth in the corner of the Rec. She sounded, if possible, more chillingly remote when compressed into electromagnetic impulses. "Oh, yes," she said, "Mis-ter Ronan—you've been preying on my conscience."

"You seem oversupplied with predators, Miss Keyes."

There was a crackling pause. "I beg your pardon?"

"Nothing. Don't let me—"

"Oh, the owls!"

"Yes, but forgive me, I didn't mean to—"

"You know, you have a slightly skewed wit, Mr. Ronan."

"I've heard that said."

She actually laughed. The notes were neither a freshet nor a ratchet but as identifiably a laugh as her limp was a limp. "Be that as it may," she said, "I've some news for you." Her assumptions had not been entirely correct: She did some snooping after his visit and came across a cache of nearly a hundred somewhat battered volumes that had outlived their usefulness and been replaced over the years. "Quite a number of them seem to have been very popular with younger readers —*Kidnapped, The Red Badge of Courage*, Kipling, and that sort of thing. I thought perhaps—"

"Perfect! They'd be perfect!"

"Well, I thought they might, so I've had a word with the librarian and he says you're welcome to them. And that, in turn, inspired me to make a few other inquiries. . . ." All she had really done, she said, was to mention his request to her father, who was "associated," as she put it, with the General Electric plant, Pittsfield's largest employer, and her mother, who was active in the local women's club and had been president for a number of years of the Pittsfield home-and-school association. Both of them agreed the book program would provide an excellent means for improving the chilly relationship between the camp and the town, and so they mobilized. The following week—

"pending your approval"—collection bins were to be placed at every entrance gate to the G.E. complex as well as at the Crane and Eaton paper plants, all the public and parochial schools, the post office, and England Brothers department store. "And the women's club plans to canvass door to door in the better neighborhoods." She paused for a breath. "I'm afraid my folks are rather irrepressible once they get their teeth into a thing."

The collection drive was to be announced by a story in the *Berkshire Eagle* as soon as Toby presented himself at the newspaper offices for an interview. The only *quid pro quo* being asked was that he or the commanding officer or anyone else from the camp who was marginally articulate make themselves available over the winter months to address area groups wishing to learn what it was exactly the C.C.C. was doing to their hills.

"You drive a tough bargain, Miss Keyes. I'm afraid I'll have to consult the camp commander about all this."

"Oh, dear," she said. "And I hoped you'd be pleased."

"Only ecstatic, Miss Keyes."

Sparhawk, predictably, was less so. He had been attending the goldfish bowl beside his desk in company headquarters when Toby reported Miss Keyes' offer. "We don't accept charity, Mr. Ronan," he said. "This is an installation of the United States government. And the fact is, the townspeople have been unkind to us in the past, and I'm not the sort to go begging for further favors."

"No one's begging for anything, sir. This is a spontaneous gesture of gratitude for what we're doing out here."

"They haven't the vaguest notion what we're doing, Ronan, so don't hand me any snake oil. Besides, you initiated the thing by soliciting the local library in the camp's name—and without my approval—which happens to be a definite breach of regulations."

"It never occurred to me that you might possibly object—since the C.E.A. is specifically invited to draw upon the resources of surrounding communities for teaching materials—"

"With the C.O.'s approval, Mr. Ronan. Shall I quote you chapter and verse? What you teach and the materials you use require my permission."

"But I was under the impression we agreed the other day that books were basic. So I thought we'd start by building a presentable library."

"I don't recall discussion of anything that grandiose."

"I'm afraid I don't really understand, sir, what your reservations are about books. Reading is an excellent recreation for the men. It occupies their minds and their time constructively. It keeps them out of mischief—and away from Pittsfield. And it's been clinically proven, I believe, that mental stimulation is at least as fatiguing as the physical sort, so strictly as a device of behavioral control, reading is every bit as useful as baseball or swimming."

The collective force of this epistemologically stunning argument occupied him for a moment or two as he bent closer to examine the pair of resident goldfish, which were exhibiting every sign of ingratitude at the captain's introduction of their eighth meal of the day. The white of his eye, ghoulishly distended to Cyclopean proportion by the liquid prism, loomed unblinking over the tiny porcelain castle at the bottom of the bowl and sought to drive the finny denizens from hiding. "I wonder if they're overfed," he murmured.

"I wouldn't know, sir."

"Odd—you seem to know so many things." He pinched one last granule from the little box of fish food and let it flutter to the already filmy surface. "Well," he said, "let's call a spade a spade, Mr. Ronan. Leaving aside the method of accumulation, I'm concerned about what sorts of trash are likely to find their way in here if you were to expand the book collection. These are impressionable young fellows—"

"Oh, sure, sir, but they'll cultivate a taste for the better things once they get into the reading habit. My own opinion is that almost any book is better than none."

"It's not their taste I'm concerned about, Ronan—it's their politics."

"Sir?"

"I don't want the comrades preaching to them. Red literature is the last thing we need around here. Are you aware labor organizers have infiltrated some camps, trying to foment strikes?"

"I hadn't heard that, sir. But I can assure you I wasn't planning to import any foreign social documents."

"They have plenty of domestic allies."

"Yes, sir. And that's why I was hoping you might be able to spare me a little time to sift over whatever came in from the town so between us we could weed out any objectionable titles."

"Hmmmm," he said, "I suppose that's a possibility."

He phoned Temple Keyes back and asked if he might repay her kindness by taking her to lunch when he finished his session at the newspaper the next day.

"That won't be necessary, Mr. Ronan—it's a civic gesture, not a personal one, as I'm sure you understand. Thanks just the same, though." She was expert at imbuing her voice with an institutionally impersonal quality.

"Oh, you're welcome—Miss Keyes."

He wondered why she limped. The subject had not engaged him before then. No doubt the affliction limited her social life and outlook.

It was not much of a limp, actually, and she had no shortage of compensating features. Perhaps she knew. What she definitely did not know was that he was A Harvard Man. That might have changed her tune—and tone. He resolved to drop the fact in passing when he visited the *Eagle*.

The books were gathered in an intensive one-week drive and brought to the camp the following Saturday afternoon in piles of a dozen or so, each well secured with twine—four hundred of them. A convoy of delivery trucks, volunteered by Pittsfield merchants, pulled up in front of the camp gate but was required to disgorge the gift on the edge of the lawn. The adjutant, in charge as usual during the captain's weekend visit home, would not permit the trucks to proceed directly to the steps of the Rec—no outside vehicles were allowed in the compound.

Until well past twilight, a human chain operated, with Toby at the head and Eddie Spain at the delivery end on the Rec porch, handing the books across two hundred yards of turf. At the close of the pointless ordeal, what they had to show were raw hands and, according to a later advisory from Corcoran at corps headquarters, the biggest C.C.C. library in all New England. Nesbit won an oak leaf cluster for obstinacy by refusing to let them stack the books indoors, claiming they would take up too much space. Toby was mercifully permitted, however, to shield the books against the damp with tarpaulins until their ultimate disposition—a bonfire was the adjutant's apparent choice—could be determined.

Toby's plan to avoid mass ruin of the homeless library was to work all day Sunday building shelves against the long back wall of the Rec to surprise Captain Sparhawk with a *fait accompli* on his return. Ash Cummings called a lumberyard owner he knew and arranged for Joe Calabrese to make a special pickup in exchange for a full-grown pine, to be taken out of the forest some time during the week following. "So long as everybody's bein' so goddamned charitable," said Ash, "I'll even take the tree down myself." When Toby expressed his appreciation, the superintendent said it was the least he could do for staying out of his way after the first day.

Will Bassett lined up a couple of other Lems willing to sacrifice a day off to help him put up the shelving on a crash basis, and Toby set Eddie Spain to alphabetizing the books on the tarpaulins they spread out over the campus grass. All was in readiness for the wood when Nesbit caught up with the pell-mell arrangements and squelched them. "I can't authorize a major piece of carpentry," he said. "That's up to the captain."

The captain, Toby argued, had already approved the installation—

"in principle"—when he authorized the book collection. "You don't think he intended for them to be left outside to rot, do you?"

"I don't think he expected the camp to be turned into a branch of the public library, either. You're just going to have to wait for him."

"If we don't get the shelves up and the books indoors today, it'll have to wait till next weekend. A lot of them could be mildewed by then."

"That's not my concern."

"What *is* your concern, Lieutenant—besides making sure everyone around here has his fly buttoned straight?"

The outburst was an indulgence he rued the instant it escaped him. All he had done was to encourage the bean-eyed zealot's dementia for orthodoxy.

Sparhawk returned to camp in a mellow mood, as was his Sunday evening wont. "Good Lord!" he boomed upon inspecting his new, badly jumbled, and unexpectedly enormous library. "I thought they were going to clear out a few attics around Pittsfield—not ship us the entire contents of Harvard's main reading room." The outpouring pleased him even more than had the appearance of his picture beside the newspaper story on the book drive (along with casual mention of his Harvard-educated teaching aide).

"What bothers me," he said after Toby sketched out the carpentry plans for the shelving, "is taking down a healthy pine. I don't think it's an honorable way to use the forest."

"What way, sir?" Toby asked, accepting more of the captain's prime brandy.

"For our personal pleasure."

Toby swirled the brandy about and studied the birch logs crisping in the fireplace. "We do it all the time, sir—out of necessity." He nodded toward the flames.

"Yes, but we try to take out just the scrub."

"The principle's the same, though, sir. I think the relationship between the camp and the forest can truthfully—and morally—be described as symbiotic. Each side has to give as well as get."

"Well," he said, "I suppose there's something to that."

"Balance of nature, sir."

He ordered the Rec closed for the next two nights while Will Bassett and his crew, supplemented by half a dozen enrollees, installed the shelves amid much belching and lowing from the pool-shooters and ping-pong set. As the finishing touches were being applied, Toby proposed (1) to send a letter of thanks, over the captain's signature, to the townspeople via the *Eagle* editorial page; (2) to invite their photographer to camp to snap the finished and filled bookshelves—and while he was at it, a shot or two of the new picnic sites, the firebreaks, and the mountain road with its access to Berry Pond, and (3) to advise Corps Area headquarters of the camp's fresh cultural bent by sending them the news clippings. Only the last caused Sparhawk to hesitate. "I'm not much for tooting our own horn," he said.

"I was thinking of couching it in terms of our gratitude for community recognition."

"Yes," he said, "I think that would be the way." Then, with the glum tenacity of a Watch and Warder, he added, "And you and I can begin reviewing the titles one at a time in the morning."

"I thought Eddie and I might get them in place first, sir—so they don't get knocked around any more than necessary."

"Oh, right—good thought. Let me know, though, when you're ready."

Toby promised. Fast talk was becoming his mother tongue.

II

Monday, Sept. 16, '35

Began counseling interviews with enrollees OK'd as holdovers for new enlistment period. Capt. calls it coddling the boys, says their pasts don't matter—they're here for a fresh start. I claimed process would yield info. on what jobs men can best fill. He says baloney, this isn't vocational guidance institute but place for slackers to learn how to take orders & not bitch. But he agrees that questioning might allow me to plan more useful ed. program.

Rec too noisy so I see men one at a time in corner of mess for maybe 10–15 mins. each. Most are highly suspicious & closemouthed. Sullen, nearly. Probably first time any adult ever sat down & showed any interest in them & their probs. When I ask at end what they'd like to do with their lives, seems most never before thought they had a choice.

Record sheets revealing. Enrollees range from 17 to 23 yrs old, avg. is 18.2, has 9th grade education (15% are h.s. grads), came to camp poor, dumb, hopeless & 12 lbs. underweight (acc. to Dr Haseltine's notes), stays 10 months & gets up to normal weight by end. One third come from home where mother is only parent. . . .

By the time Ivan "Wolfbait" Stubbs slouched in, Toby had nearly exhausted the annals of despair.

Nothing was volunteered to him; it all had to be extracted orally or interpolated from the papers—years of adolescence passed amid sickness, drunkenness, beatings, and desertion; growing up foodless and coatless and loveless; begging at back doors, panhandling at the bus depot, stealing from the fruit and vegetable wagon, moving constantly to stay one jump ahead of the rent collector, hanging out in pool halls and saloons to find cold comfort with equally miserable companions. They almost all said they had joined the corps to help their families by unburdening them of still one more unproductive body around the house. But in a larger sense, their common purpose was to end the chaos of their own lives. "Besides," one of them told Toby on the second night by way of explaining their willingness to be regimented, "anything's better than gettin' nagged the fuck to death."

Wolfbait's woes, even among so many sorry biographies, approached the epitome of blasted innocence.

His father, after several years of irregular work at a bottling factory, deserted when Ivan was twelve. His mother worked part-time to support him, a brother, and two sisters, then married again, probably in desperation. But his stepfather proved a boozer and a bully, beating them all up by turns until Ivan swung back one night and got his jaw fractured. Soon the brute eloped with another woman, and Ivan's mother turned hopeless harridan, shrieking long laments in her anguish until his sisters had to go live with an aunt and his brother went west and was never heard from. Ivan tried to manage the household, but his mother could find no honest steady work and so she turned to the other sort, to the boy's revulsion. Between customers, he took to abusing her, verbally and physically, until their mutual antipathy was out of control. The mother was forcibly institutionalized, and Ivan, at fifteen, ran wild, drinking and stealing and driving around with anyone he could find for who-knew-what favors and sleeping in any half-warm hallway. The aunt who had his younger sisters took him in briefly, but he was unmanageable by then and went off to live with his older sister, who found work for a while until she got pregnant and ran away. At the time he signed up with the C.C.C., he was living in the seediest tenements of Lynn with a woman of sordid renown. Her sole act of virtue may have been to dispatch the boy to country air before he could become incurably alcoholic and syphilitic.

A clawing, untamed animal when he arrived at camp, Wolfbait was promptly restrained by its disciplinary arm. Caught robbing from a nearby orchard his first week, he was put to peeling potatoes and chopping firewood for two weeks straight yet never went over the hill. Somehow he knew, for all his anger and shame, the disciplining was long overdue.

"Does it say in there," he asked as he watched Toby reading through his file folder, "that she used to kick me in the nuts every time she got loaded?"

"Who did?" Toby asked after a moment of further scanning, calculated to encourage the boy to open up a little on the horror story he had lived.

"My old lady. Had fuckin' good aim, too."

"Why did she do that?"

"Couldn' stand the sight o' me, I guess." Or of any man, probably, by that point in her downfall.

"So what did you do?"

"After I stopped rollin' on the floor, ya mean?"

"Yes."

"It's like your whole insides is fallin' out—"

"I believe it. So what'd you do—hide?"

"Shit, no. I punched her tits in. She got nice, big ones—probably coulda been the star slut in any cathouse if she'da set her mind to it. But all she ever did was bring home drunk old farts in dirty long johns who needed a derrick to get it up, ya know? What a waste o' talent."

On the face of it, Wolfbait's post-C.C.C. career prospects seemed limited to pimping. "When's the last time you were in school?" Toby asked.

"I did some ninth grade. I'm no dummy, neither—I coulda got t'rough high school, maybe—if things wasn't like it was." And why had he stopped going? " 'Cause they wasn't givin' away candy apples," he said with a laugh. But Toby stuck with the question, and Wolfbait shrugged. "Lotsa reasons. Teacher was a cunt—didn' put up wit' no shit if you didn' do da lessons. An' we was always movin' around an' I woulda hadda go to differen' schools—which I didn't like nohow. An' I didn' have no money or nuttin'—an' my goddamn shoes was fallin' off—an' my pants was shredded so bad my dick was half hangin' out." He patted the outer thigh of the rumpled but substantial green cotton trousers the government had issued him. "I mean, could you go to school like dat—even if you was in da mood?"

Like almost all of them, he granted that he would have been better off with more schooling. The very subject, though, seemed a closed book to him. When Toby asked if there was anything special he might like to study during the next enlistment period with an eye toward his future well-being, the scrawny boy said sure: how never to lose at blackjack and where to get his hands on a loaded submachine gun.

Putnam Salter, who came before Wolfbait alphabetically but was

still working in the kitchen when his turn was due, had a more positive attitude. His background was no less discouraging, but his dossier
was notable mainly for its brevity. It said he was nearly eighteen,
stood five-three and weighed 110 when he enrolled, came from "Carolina," had lived with unspecified relatives in Roxbury for a year after
leaving the South, and was of the Negroid race. Next to "Education,"
there was a blank. Next to "Skills," it said, "Plays harmonica and
whistles well."

"Where in Carolina?" Toby asked him.

"De bottom," he said.

"South Carolina?"

"Ah guess."

A permanent member of the kitchen crew, where he washed pots
and hauled garbage and did any other scutwork they assigned him, he
was the only colored boy in camp. Nobody reviled him exactly, beyond the nickname "Link" (as in "Missing Link") he had been tagged
with, and he was allowed to sleep in the barracks with everyone else
(albeit at the very back of Bughouse C) and play his harmonica in a
corner of the Rec. It was true he ate alone in the kitchen, but he told
Toby he preferred it that way, being around food as he was all day
and on a different schedule from the rest of the enrollees. Lithe and
smily, he was regarded, when at all, as a mascot—of a higher species
than Pickles, the ever-muddy bitch hound and official camp pet, but
of her devoted and pattable order.

To show their fondness for the darker persuasion, the enrollees got
Link sprung from his kitchen chores long enough each night to listen
on the radio with them to the rambunctious adventures of "Amos 'n'
Andy," the latter of whom was said, not unkindly, to be the only
black man in America dumber than Link. He had also appeared by
popular demand in a camp minstrel show the previous Fourth of July,
winning plaudits for his harmonica version of "I Got Plenty o'
Nothin'" from the new Gershwin musical *Porgy and Bess;* the program assigned him the stage name "Sportin' Link."

"Did you get any schooling down home, Putnam?"

He looked amused by Toby's formality. "Some," he said. But the
schoolhouse was seven miles from where he lived—"an' dey wairn't no
bus." Besides, he was needed in the fields much of the time. Even so,
he had learned how to read the alphabet and make out a few words
and knew numbers up to twenty-five, which corresponded to the total
of his fingers and toes plus the chickens his family had out back. But
he could not write worth a lick, and his only other accomplishment
was the harmonica, which he had been taught by his uncle, an itinerant preacher who presented the little shiny instrument to the boy

when he was twelve. It was his only treasure on earth and never left his keep.

It had been mostly to escape the grinding life of the fields and possibly to get some learning that his family had sent Putnam Salter north to Boston, where relatives of friends had a place. He was too big for grade school and too ignorant for any real job, so he hung around the house trying to be useful—"only dey was near to starvin', so I wairn't doin' nobody no good." Through a janitor who worked at the County Welfare Board office, they got him into the C.C.C. It was a lifesaver—and at least the boy knew something about cultivating the earth. So at the camp they naturally stuck him in the kitchen all day.

When asked if he wanted to do any learning with Toby, Link was leery at first and then plain incredulous. His life at the camp, while mostly hard work, was not the worst he had ever had it. And when they let him come to evening lineup with all the white boys starting the day the man from Washington had come to inspect, his life seemed to be a definite upgrade. But to be tutored now by a graduate of the great university across the river from Boston was beyond his remotest imagining. His eyes wet as Toby sketched the possibilities.

His note to Temple Keyes—somehow Toby had no wish to speak with her directly—explained the special needs of his first pupil. Two days later, there was a reply, saying that several old primers, a copying book, a geography, and a beginner's arithmetic would be waiting in a package for him at the circulation desk whenever he could come by. "I am taking the liberty of adding one other book that you might wish to read from aloud to your student," she wrote in a postscript. "The author grew up in Great Barrington, which is just fifteen or so miles down the highway from here, and attended, unless I am mistaken, your own revered alma mater." It was *The Souls of Black Folk* by Dubois.

"It's all up to you, Putnam," he said, showing the colored boy the collection and supplementing it with a box of needle-sharp pencils. Link nodded doubtfully while fingering through the mysterious texts. No less fascinating to him was the operation of the eraser on the pencil he drew carefully from the box; he had never used either end of one before.

With time on his hands for the moment, Toby drilled him an hour each in the morning and afternoon between his shifts. He tailored the curriculum to the boy's needs and interests, taking him from two-letter sounds to syllables to short words to longer words to phrases to sentences, using as subjects mostly parts of the body, food, and other things he dealt with daily around the camp. Each time he learned to read and spell a word, Toby made him write it as well, and keep writing it, dozens upon dozens of times, day and night, in all his spare time, and drilled him until he could never forget it. What he lacked in quickness he made up for in diligence. Indeed he pursued his writing exercises with such intensity that in the beginning he kept breaking his pencil point every fifteen minutes or so. Sharpening it all the time with a kitchen knife was what first got him into trouble with the cook. Reading from his primer while shelling peas at a less than lightning rate produced a still more rabid outburst of anti-intellectualism. Study on the job was thereafter forbidden. But almost all the rest of his waking hours, save for a short midday serenade to himself on the harmonica in the woods nearest camp, were devoted to the pursuit of literacy. The day he mastered the difference between "ask" and "ax" (as in, "I ax him dat"), arithmetic was added to his studies. In two weeks, he could add a column of five single numbers; in two more weeks, the column was up to twenty. In a month, he was starting the multiplication tables. By then Toby sometimes saw him eying the headlines in the *Eagle* that was usually left on a sofa in the Rec—but he never did it more than furtively for fear his sudden new facility would be noticed and disparaged or, worse, held against him.

Still, his growth in dignity as well as knowledge was unmistakable. For one thing, he began to look people in the eye when he spoke to them, starting with Toby, who insisted on it, instead of fixing abjectly on the ground. And he no longer came willingly—or, in time, at all—to the nightly command performance of "Amos 'n' Andy," the humor of which he began to understand and not appreciate; he suddenly sensed the white boys were laughing at him and not with him as he had supposed before his awakening. Even with Toby, there were flashes of pride. One day, he forgetfully called him Link instead of by his real name. His deep brown brow furrowed and Toby could see the hurt, although he said nothing. "It stands for Lincoln," Toby suddenly proposed to him. "Think of that next time someone calls you it."

He considered the consoling and ennobling virtues of the idea and then shook his head. "Sheee-it," he said, "I cain't tell dem dat."

"Just tell yourself, then."

He thought some more. Then he said, "How you spell Lincoln?"

The effects of wisdom on his barracks life were disheartening. The more he learned, the less he was favored. Only Joe Calabrese, who slept in the bunk beside his, was supportive. During the day, whenever each was not otherwise occupied, and even sometimes at night, when the noise level and antic spirit surrounding them were high, Joe would help, hearing him read, pronouncing new words for him, correcting his spelling, checking over the written exercises Link was to present to Toby the next morning.

The situation took a turn toward open resentment after Nesbit, during inspection one morning, deducted points because Link's books and copying paper had not been arranged on his foot locker to geometric perfection. The penalty cost Barracks C the weekly inspection prize and, with it, the free passes that the Pittsfield movie houses donated to camp on a rotating basis, now that an era of good feelings had been established. Racial slurs without redeeming fondness became habitual soon thereafter, and then mushroom crowns closely resembling dogshit were left in his bed, followed by some of Pickles' genuine leavings. And then a tar-baby doll with a cord around its neck was slung from the rafters over his bunk. When his primer and copying book disappeared, Link came to Toby, softly narrating the whole sad sequence. Toby counseled fortitude, replaced the stolen books from the surplus Temple Keyes had sent him, and suggested Link store the batch of them in his quarters for safekeeping between study sessions. But something vital in the learning process had been stunted.

The matter came to a boil when Link's progress proved so intolerable to several of his barracks mates that they baited the black boy into a furious fist fight that cost him a tooth and Joe Calabrese, his prime protector, a cut lip, bloodied nose, and woefully swollen eye. Only heroic efforts by Kevin Dundy, the barracks leader, prevented a lot of broken bones.

As a result of this overt display of enmity, Toby began to debate with himself whether Putnam Salter's small black person had not perhaps been better off, certainly in terms of social adjustment, in its previous state of blissful ignorance. Maybe the camp-wide attention drawn to his schooling had benefited Toby's needs more than his.

This concern was much on Toby's mind a few days after the infamous hostilities when he came upon Joe Calabrese, still wearing the disfiguring effects. Each day after lunch, Joe went over another of the camp's five trucks, scrutinizing it from cab top to tire tread in a ritual conducted as thoroughly and methodically as a master mechanic might. Toby sat beneath a nearby tree, watching as Joe flushed the engine, cleaned the plugs, filled the batteries and the grease cups, checked the oil, tested the tire pressure, and polished the windows, mirrors and even the gas-tank cap. Near the end, when it was plain Toby was merely a spectator and not about to bring up the subject, Joe asked without lifting his head from the hygienically flawless engine block, "Why do they keep him rottin' away in there on kitchen detail? It's been almost a year now—like all he's good for is nigger work."

Neither of them had had to preface the conversation; just the sight of each other was enough to tug on their linked concern. "Maybe he's in there," Toby said, "for the same reason they've got you doing what you do."

Joe worked a rag around the carburetor a little and then accordioned the hood shut. "Don't horseshit me, Toby," he said. "This here is skilled labor. He's just a galley slave in there." He stuck the rag in his hip pocket and looked up in distress. "Why don't they give the burrhead a chance—the way you did?"

"Maybe they will."

"Oh, sure. Christ, they won't even give me a shot at being rated." He swabbed the sweat from his hairline with a grimy hand. "You think I wanna be a goddamned grease monkey the rest o' my life? I got almost all the way through high school—I'm not just another one of these asshole truants, ya know?" What he wanted most in the world, he said, was to become a real engineer, to design things from the start, new machines and products and systems—if he could ever afford to go to college. Toby told him it was not impossible to work his way through if he was really determined and that he himself had done so partly.

The news surprised Joe, who thought Harvard was for rich boys only. "Sure, but you're a fuckin' brain."

"And how about Link? He's doing it right here. So could you—if you really wanted. Maybe I could work out something with the Pittsfield school officials. You can't go to college till you've finished high school."

Joe looked nearly as overwhelmed as Link had. "Ya think?"

"It's worth a try. All they can do is say no."

"And Sparhawk? He'd shit blue first—"

"Red, white, and blue, probably, and salute when he was done. But I'll go for it if you will."

Joe laughed till his split lip made him wince.

III

Saturday, Sept. 21, '35

Dinner chez *Keyes, a manse of many turrets and thick gingerbread. Spacious veranda o'erlooks a graceful bend of the Housatonic. Half-expected a paddleboat chunking down from Natchez any sec.*

Keyeses a formidable clan. Père a Yalie ('oo) of massive dignity & irrepressible civic pride (saved from Babbittry only by Mme.'s gently deflating barbs). A General Electrician, cum *company pin in lapel, he directs their High Voltage Laboratory (devoted no doubt to building*

*a better electric chair). Also pres. of the Stanley Club, apparent locus
of townie social power, and mem. of Pittsfield City Council—all in all,
large, albeit pear-shaped, pillar of the commun. Mere, who issued my
invitation in lavish cursive, is gifted with more grace than lace. Her
delivery understated but devastating. Among the poobahs of the local
symphony, hospital, library, and probably anything else Mr. K.
doesn't have his finger in. Fils Carl, Temple's younger bro., a sr. at
Union Coll., got mother's manner & the guv'nor's tonsils. Intimations
of rebellion in that tousled, clubby hauteur. Fille: Bejeweled by the
finest china, crystal & silver before her, aglow with candlelight, Temple as unearthly & inaccessible as a storybook princess.*

    *Other guests: young couple named Curtis (he instructs in history at
Williams, she Temple's old roomie at Conn. College now teaching
piano) and the Very Rev. His Holiness Samuel Brandt, rector of St.
Thomas's-in-the-Field and spiritual advisor to the K's. Jellied madri-
lene, rack of lamb, raspberry sherbet, bully banter, rampant
toryism. . . .*

While wiping away a smear of lamb fat from the corner of his
cupid's-bow mouth, too small and sweet for a man of his frame and
flesh, Lawrence Keyes announced for Toby's benefit that Pittsfield,
Massachusetts, was the most beautiful industrial city in the United
States.

He had begun to enumerate the evidence—the broad, tree-lined
streets; the generous parks and playgrounds; the stately homes and
dearth of slums, and outlying but still within the city limits, the lakes,
the hills, the forest—when Carl Keyes gave an impertinent groan. His
father made sniffish pause and asked the boy to name a stronger contender.

"First of all," Carl answered, "and with all due respect, the term 'industrial city' is a redundancy. All cities are industrial, more or less—if
they weren't, they'd starve. So what you're really claiming is that
Pittsfield is the most beautiful city in America—period."

"And you reject the premise?" Mr. Keyes was indignant.

"In the sense that it's an unfounded judgment. How many cities in
America have you actually visited, Father—ten? Twenty?"

"Whatever the number, I've never seen one even remotely close to
this one. I'm allowed to interpolate a little without being put down in
my own dining room for petty boosterism."

"Nothing petty about it," said Mrs. Keyes.

"The problem," Temple put in, "is semantic. Father may be right in
his way, but then he's set up a straw man. It's playing fast and loose
with the dictionary to refer to Pittsfield as a city. Cities thrive on mul-

titudes and everything they generate—infinite variety, filth and
congestion, fashion and wickedness—and any number of other mixed
blessings we pride ourselves for being spared."

"And what would you propose calling a settlement of fifty thousand
souls?" Mr. Keyes indulged her.

"A town," said Carl. "It's a good-sized, very nice town." He gave it
the pejorative edge of one who had glimpsed the larger world and
precociously determined to stake his claim there.

"Absolutely not!" his father declared. "A town is something usually
preceded by the term 'one-horse.' It smacks of hopeless provincialism
and—"

"But of course we're provincial," Carl insisted. "The provinces have
their charms, and we have plenty of ours, but—"

"I utterly reject the charge. Here we are, equidistant from the two
most dynamic and civilized cities in America—not even half a day's
travel from either yet with bucolic pleasures their residents are denied.
What could be a more perfect compromise?"

"You left out," Mrs. Keyes inserted softly, "that we are the county
seat."

Everyone laughed, especially the guests, who had witnessed the
playful family squabble—if Toby's own response was any guide—
with more patience than amusement. Throughout it, he could not help
comparing their well-being, Temple's affliction notwithstanding, with
the fled fortunes of his own family (such as they had ever been) and
wondering if he would someday arrive at such a state of solidity, bordering on smugness.

However excessive Lawrence Keyes's aesthetic claims for his community, there was general assent around the table that Pittsfield was,
by objective criteria, a place of several genuine distinctions. Its landscape drew tourists summer and winter. Its climate sparkled. Its people
were obliging. Its daily newspaper, literate, informative, and attractive, was the match of any outside the great metropolises. Head
G-man Hoover himself had commended the quality of its police protection. Its department store was as well stocked with sensible merchandise as the Berkshire Athenaeum was with worthy reading matter.
Its extensive musical activities included a spirited little symphony orchestra; a chamber music festival of growing renown, presented in an
exquisite mountainside setting south of town; a winter program of internationally eminent artists on tour—"Everyone in our audiences may
not be a connoisseur," Mrs. Keyes remarked, "but the one thing we
cannot abide is being played down to"—and a projected summer
music school, housing the Boston Symphony for the season, down at
the Tanglewood estate on the Lenox-Stockbridge line. Nor was its lit-

erary heritage without notable bench marks. Melville wrote *Moby Dick* in a Pittsfield farmhouse less than a mile from the Keyeses'. Hawthorne used to come over and visit him from his place on the north shore of Stockbridge Bowl. Oliver Wendell Holmes the elder was often in residence—indeed, Wendell Avenue, named for his forebears, was long the town's plushest street. And Longfellow lived for a time at Broad Hall, which had been converted into the main house of the Pittsfield Country Club, to which the Keyeses of course belonged. "Perhaps you might have Mr. Ronan over for a tennis match one of these weekends," Mrs. Keyes proposed to Carl.

No aspect of the town, however, surpassed his employer in excellence, according to Lawrence Keyes's view of things. "I don't say we're philanthropists," he conceded, "but there is no more enlightened management in the nation than General Electric's. Everyone in Pittsfield, from the common laborer on up, regards it as the very model of good industrial citizenship." Work there was steady, safe, and justly paid. The plant complex, including a unit that produced more and bigger generators than any other on earth, was off unobtrusively in the northeast sector, and no unsightly tenements of the sort that blighted most factory towns had sprung up in the vicinity. "The company's relationship with the city government, I might add without fear of contradiction, is exemplary."

"In fact," said Carl, "you *are* the city government." Three other G.E. executives besides his father served on the council, he explained.

"Leaving seven who have no ties whatever to the company—"

"And only two of whom you need to win over for an absolute majority." His father's partisanship earned only scorn from Carl. "We may not be a one-horse town, Mr. Ronan, but we sure are a one-company town."

"Not so!" cried the senior Keyes. "The Crane and Eaton operations are very substantial." He turned to Toby. "It may interest you to know, Mr. Ronan, that every single piece of the thread-impregnated paper on which American currency and federal bonds are printed is manufactured right here in Pittsfield. The Crane plant is even known locally as 'the Government Mill,' and there are guards who—"

Only Mrs. Keyes's intervention saved him from being surfeited with local lore to the point of stupefaction. She managed to engage the minister and the historian in an exchange on the morality of the Italian incursion in the horn of Africa. Reverend Brandt was of the view that policies of state were, alas, rarely framed with considerations of morality. Instructor Curtis made the less-sweeping observation that Ethiopia had been an Italian protectorate for half a century and the League of Nations was therefore unlikely to heed Selassie's plea. Mr. Keyes, suddenly adopting a trans-Berkshire perspective, was inclined to treat the episode as an inconsequential comic-opera war between a cardboard despot and a self-styled "King of Kings." "Why, on top of everything else, that black beggar's a blasphemer," he said, looking to the rector for confirmation.

"What interests me," the clergyman offered instead, "is how all these charismatics invariably overreach themselves and undo whatever good they had to bring their people. It's this incontainable egomania that I rather think is the blasphemy." Mr. Curtis asked, as all good historians must, for examples. "They're almost anywhere you look throughout the ages," the Reverend Mr. Brandt replied, "and I don't restrict my indictment to military conquerors. Mr. Wilson's downfall comes at once to mind, gentleman though he was—and the recently departed Senator from Louisiana, ruffian that he was."

Reference to Huey Long, whose assassination two weeks earlier had nearly escaped Toby's notice at the camp, reactivated Lawrence Keyes's adrenaline. Plainly an unbeliever in *de mortibus nihil nisi bonum,* he bit off the end of a stubby cigar from the fresh box he had passed among the male guests and declared the linkage of Wilson and Long a sacrilege. "Forgive the profanity, Sam, but I think the hillbilly bastard got exactly what he deserved."

"Whether any of us gets what we deserve—assuming we *deserve* anything at all—is debatable," said the rector. "I had his character in mind rather than his politics—in the sense that he seems to have brought on his own end."

"I'm not sure it's possible to distinguish between character and politics," said Curtis, "at least not in his case."

"He didn't have any politics," said Keyes, "just guff. That's what made him such a menace—pandering to the rabble so shamelessly."

"In principle, Father, it isn't guff to spread the wealth," said Carl, "not by the standards of people who haven't any."

"It amounts to Bolshevism, whatever anyone calls it," his father bellowed and then paused to light his smoke.

There was a long moment of respectful silence over that dreaded invocation. Then Mrs. Keyes asked, "Is that what you think as well, Mr. Ronan? Or perhaps Harvard doesn't worry itself with such scruffy adventurers?"

Toby had been all but drugged into inarticulation by the steady flow of talk in front of, behind, over, under, around, and across from him, happy enough as a stranger to remain the proverbial fly on the wall. Invited to participate at a flash point, and to bring with him the authoritative weight of his university, he went blank. "Well," he said, "they've been covering quite a lot of terrain."

"Yes," said Mrs. Keyes, "quite. I meant just about Huey Long."

He fought for time to unscramble his brain. "Well—to be honest, I've never actually thought of Robin Hood and his sort as collectivists."

"What then, Mr. Ronan?"

"I'm not sure. I just think Americans have a tendency to call anything they don't like communistic. If someone steals back from the rich what they allegedly stole from the poor in the first place, I suppose it could be justified as a form of retribution—or at least it's arguable."

"Oh, come-come, Ronan"—Mr. Keyes landed on him at once—"a bandit is a bandit. Let's leave the moralizing to Mr. Brandt and his brothers of the cloth."

"Lawrence," his wife said stiffly, "Mr. Ronan is our guest, and I'm interested in *his* views just at the moment, if you don't mind. Yours I'm perfectly well acquainted with—and very admirable they are."

The floor was Toby's again, though he wanted nothing more than to waltz across it and out the door. "Yes—well—I'm not sure I have any very coherent thoughts on the subject—and I can't say that I recall all of Long's specific proposals—he made so many—or which ones he wanted to be taken seriously—"

"Perhaps Mr. Curtis can refresh our memories."

"—but by and large I think he may have been on to something."

A forbidding hush fell. Mrs. Keyes, nothing daunted, sailed past it. "And what was that, Mr. Ronan?"

"Well—as I understand it—that there ought to be limits to wealth and to poverty in any truly civilized society."

"How fascinating. And what should those limits be, Mr. Ronan?"

Long's proposals, he said, did not seem entirely implausible. "It's hard to believe any family would be deprived if the government were to confiscate its income in excess of a million dollars a year. And at the other extreme, I think perhaps every American family may be entitled to whatever dignity can be purchased with two thousand a year. As a matter of fact, I would also endorse his proposal of free college for every young person of academic ability—"

"You say dignity!" Keyes detonated. "What dignity is there in the dole? Roosevelt and his people have the same problem that Ronan here does. You're all a bunch of Bad Samaritans if you ask me." He appealed to the table. "I do not understand, frankly, by what stretch of Christian charity any living being can be said to have the right to a free ride on this earth."

Toby glanced at Mrs. Keyes in hope of locating a sympathetic eye, but her gaze was fixed on the blue haze that had enveloped the chandelier. He was on his own in the high grass. "I'm not for free rides, sir," Toby said. "That college student who's given an education at public expense is far likelier to become a substantial property holder and taxpayer—and otherwise constructive citizen—than if he had never had the opportunity. Similarly, the family that's relieved from fear of grinding destitution is likely to produce happier, healthier workers—and be more alert and responsible members of society."

"That's better political theory," Curtis put in, "than social psychology, in my opinion. Also, entirely undemonstrable. Give a man something out of compassion, and soon he's convinced he's entitled to it."

"Exactly!" Keyes boomed, delighted at the reinforcement. "And once you let a fellow think he's in a bad way, he starts feeling terribly sorry for himself, and there's no end to it. I say the dignity Ronan here has in mind consists in doing the very best you can in life—whatever your lot or station—and without asking or giving quarter. That's the spirit I've always tried to inculcate in our children—"

"Otherwise known," said Carl, "as the survival of the fittest."

"Not at all," said his father. "It's simply a matter of success flowing to the meritorious."

"But isn't the point," Toby asked, "that many are denied the chance to demonstrate their merit? We don't start out even in life."

"And where is it written that we're supposed to?"

"I think you'll find it prominently stated in the Declaration of Independence."

"That," said Curtis, the voice of strict construction, "refers to equality before the law. It's well understood to mean there should not be one brand of justice for the rich and another for the poor."

"And there is the further interpretation," said Brandt, the voice of strict transcendence, "that the equal creation means in the eyes of the Lord, whatever the outcome of our earthly travail."

Toby dug his trench deeper as the shells fell. "Well, I like to think it has something to do with opportunity—and liberty."

"Ah, now you're talking, Ronan. For me, freedom is the opportunity to work my fool head off for my children to have all the advantages I can provide them." Keyes sounded almost plaintive. "Would you deny me that?"

"No—but I might be inclined to deny your children their unearned benefits."

"They're not unearned at all—I earned them! Why isn't that enough for you?"

"Because, sir," he answered with deliberateness, "I happen not to think anyone should be advanced or degraded in life on account of parentage. To me, equality means everyone starting out even. And liberty means the chance to sink or swim—without interference from anyone—or the deck being stacked against you. And all I really believe beyond that is if you're given a fair chance—which is what this country likes to claim it stands for—and you still sink, you shouldn't just be left to drown."

"It's plain, Lawrence," Mrs. Keyes inserted as moderator, "that Mr. Ronan is a committed New Dealer—whether you think that makes him a Wobbly or any other form of fuzzy-headed anarchist—and I think we must respect his convictions as a professional social worker. If he were not in earnest about his ideals, he'd hardly be giving his time to all those unlucky boys in the forest—would he?"

Thus mercifully patronized, he was permitted to withdraw again to the sidelines. By evening's end, no hint of displeasure with his quaint highmindedness was detectable, and Toby was warmly served with fresh invitations. The Reverend Brandt prayed that he would pray with him some Sunday soon and stop by the rectory afterward for tea and a few introductions if he were so inclined. Curtis asked him up to Williamstown to sit in on classes and be shown around. Carl Keyes proposed tennis at their club, promising the loan of a slightly warped but serviceable racquet. And his host insisted that Toby's social thinking would be immeasurably enriched by a visit to the G.E. factory. This last offer he accepted on the spot, asking if he might bring along a young fellow from the camp who had a talent for motors and future aspirations in the field.

"Delighted," Keyes said, "bring the whole gang of 'em."

When he came into town the following week with Joe Calabrese to run a few errands, he did not call Temple ahead of time, fearing renewed rejection, but went right back to her office and asked her on the spot to join him for lunch. She usually had just a snack at home, she said, but if he wouldn't take it personally that she hadn't much time to spare, a short bite would be all right with her.

"Don't let me inconvenience you," he said. "If you've got things to do, I can make it some other time. Or you needn't at all, really—you've been more than kind to me."

"Oh, my." Her lips pressed together in a mirthless smile. "And I thought I was thin-skinned. I'll get my purse from the locker."

Perhaps it was the prospect of walking beside a stranger that had given her pause, although both the hesitation and self-consciousness may well have been in his mind alone. Her stride was far from spastic —it had just a catch, really, and a slight tilt to starboard. But solicitousness made him slow his own normally long and rapid pace, throwing off the rhythm and turning him into the more awkward walker of the pair. As they moved unsynchronized along South Street, passing

City Hall Park with its traffic-clogged oval, he could not think which
was less discreet—chattering away mindlessly to obscure the unmentionable or lapsing into silence that would only accentuate the physical fact.

"I got polio when I was ten," she said without preface, "since
you're too polite to ask—or even notice, I'm sure."

"I—really didn't—"

"The right leg wound up about an inch shorter than the left and
slightly shriveled—otherwise there were no lingering effects. No, it
doesn't hurt when I walk, I can manage a pretty fair game of tennis if
the whole world's not watching, and I hike like a maniac when I get
the chance. I'm fine on a horse or in water but bike and dance not
quite so well. That's really all there is to say on the subject, and having
said it, I hope you aren't concerned further. Now about the other evening, I thought you coped with Father quite well . . ."

There was hardly a breath between the two topics for him to assay
her clinical recital for traces of incipient martyrdom. She was no more
inclined, on the face of it, to apologize for rugged individualism than
her father was. "He's a gentleman of firm opinion," he said. "I hope he
wasn't offended by my back talk."

"Not in the least. In fact, that was precisely what Mother had in
mind—a little ferment. She adores spirited table conversation, but it's
not easy to come by when Father gets wound up. Mother supposed
that your being a Harvard man and all would cow him a bit."

Over sandwiches in a booth at an ice-cream parlor on North Street,
he suggested to Temple that her mother was apparently suffering from
an idealized notion of Harvard and he did not want her family to be
under any misconceptions about his pedigree. "I'm working at the
camp because I need the job," he confessed, "not out of altruism."

"Thank heavens," she said. "I'm not keen for self-righteous types."
She took off her gloves and began to attack her sandwich with a certain awkward daintiness. "The only thing is," she went on after
disposing of an unladylike mouthful, "your being ordinary will break
poor Father's heart. He's the one, you see, with delusions about Harvard."

Lawrence Keyes had attended Yale, all right, but its Sheffield
Scientific School, not the college. They were quite different things, he
had been made to feel and, as a result, incubated a rancor that sadly
persisted. His hope had been that Carl would attend New Haven and
exorcise the demon, but it had not worked out that way, and so now
their father had converted his antipathy for the university into
unalloyed admiration for its great rival. And Toby, as its latest and

handiest embodiment on the Pittsfield scene, was naturally an object of high curiosity to him.

"You have to understand," Temple explained, "this is very much an industrial community underneath the cosmetics." There were few enough college men of any sort, leave aside Harvard or Yale, and two out of every three workers in the city were employed by G.E.—an affiliation that scarcely recommended any would-be gentleman callers to her parents. Well over half the population, moreover, was Catholic —an impermissible category for a suitor, in the estimate of the highly selective Keyeses. So depleted was the eligibility pool as defined by the family, she said, "I think they're almost ready to settle for a presentable Jew—assuming they don't think that's a contradiction in terms."

"And you—don't?"

"The whole topic couldn't matter to me less. I'm just filling you in on the cultural anthropology of the Berkshire Hills—so neither of us is laboring under a misconception. It's stultifying here, no matter what pretensions to cosmopolitanism Father and Mother like to harbor. Most young women of intellect leave sooner or later—unless they're settled on spinsterhood."

"And you're not, I take it?"

"You mean I'm suspect—because I wear dark things—and no makeup—and limp a bit? That's hardly conclusive. Romance just hasn't happened to be on the top of my list—which turned me into something of a scholastic prodigy, I'm afraid. Mostly I've overcome that. But then it's comfortable for me around here. We know everyone worth knowing—and a great many who aren't. And Father's famous sink-or-swim pronouncements aside, he babies me terribly—and I don't resist nearly enough. No doubt he and Mother pulled strings to have me appointed to my positions—they deny it so furiously that I'm certain of it. Not that I'm all that unqualified, you understand . . ."

He asked if she would go hiking with him in the hills some weekend. She said that would be lovely—and perhaps they might ask the Curtises to join them in the interest of propriety. The rest of the world might have been teetering on cataclysm, but gentility, in both its pleasing and offensive aspects, was still manifest in the Berkshires.

IV

Monday, Sept. 30, '35

Departing enrollees req. to crawl over lawn in underwear thru gauntlet of re-enlistees flailing belts at wriggling arses. Many shouts, groans, threats & curses re allegedly sundered genitals.

Arr. enrollees initiated at once into protocols of hair-shirt heroism. Capt., brassy & booted & slicked to faretheewell, with riding crop smartly skewering underarm, spellbinds lineup thus:

"There was nothing here when this camp opened, gentlemen, but trees & brush & mud. It rained all the time, tents leaked, bugs swarmed, food was vile, clothes misfit by five sizes, shaving & showering with ice water or not at all. But when someone jammed a shovel in their hands & said, 'Fall to,' they did—men just like you. They built this camp & regrew this forest & took pride in every inch. I expect nothing less from you. Think of this as West Pt. and yr C.C.C. greens as a cadet uniform."

Gulping & shuffling, they are commanded to stand to while capt. scales himalayas of testicular oratory: "Give thanks," he hymned, "you have been spared the sordid sinks of city life for this beau. spot closer to God—and chance to build up yr bodies & souls & morals [what happened to minds?]—and privilege of 3 sq. meals a day & good night's sleep on clean sheets & clothes to stay warm & showers & flush toilets & honest work & reg. hrs. & good buddies." Then he flicked out his little wand of power & snarled, "But this is not a resort, gentlemen, and this is no democracy! You're here to learn to take orders—& get on with people even if you hate their guts—& endure drudgery & foul weather & a bursting anus. You're here to pick yrselves up because no one else can do it for you." In voice warm as stained-glass pietà, he adds, "If things get rough, don't pray for an easier life—pray to be a better man. . . ."

After the captain, the adjutant read the regimental act to the newcomers but without any of Sparhawk's smarmy uplift. If they had felt inadequate about themselves before arriving, Nesbit left them humbly grateful at least that the government had consigned their worthless hides to the keeping of the military.

"The captain referred to you as 'gentlemen,'" he went after them, "but where I come from, 'gentleman' is a rank you have to earn. Going by the record, most of you knuckleheads barely qualify as civilized. You've got barnyard manners—don't practice the common rules of sanitation—probably half of you can't even tie your own shoelaces without complaining. And worst of all, you just plain won't do what you're told. Well, that's all over, starting now." The small, even features bristled with fervor. "You're the guests of the United States Army while you're at this camp, and you'll do things the army way or find yourselves on the next train out of here."

He told them to begin with their own mangy bodies. They were required to brush their teeth once a day and bathe once a week—more often if they stank the way they were supposed to after busting their behinds on the job all day. They were to keep their hair and their nails short and clean, and soiled clothes or bedding were a sure ticket for being put on report. Alcohol, gambling, and fornication were strictly forbidden on camp grounds—"and I'd go easy on them in town, too. They're all usually expensive and often infectious." Rookies were likely to undergo a little hazing from the holdover enrollees, and if they didn't like it, they could complain to their barracks leaders. "By and large, though, my advice to you is keep your nose clean and ass wiped, and nobody will give you a hard time. Good luck."

A less scatological but equally pointed message was delivered before supper by the circuit minister, a Lutheran from town who conducted one Sunday service a month at camp and appeared on other random occasions lest the eternal souls of the enrollees be wrested away without a fight by animism, Rooseveltism, or some other form of paganism. The reverend's grace invoked "the Supreme Forester of the Universe," whom he begged to fill the boys' hearts with a love of nature so they might hear her voice of gladness, see her beauteous smile, feel her emanations of love. "Help us, dear Lord," he intoned, "to grasp that genuine happiness consists not in what we possess but in what we share. May we therefore serve as living examples of cheerfulness, gratitude for our blessings, loyalty to one another, and devotion to our mission. . . ."

All of which was unexceptionable. But at the end Toby grieved to hear him pray, "And above all, Holy Father, teach us to accept and obey the orders of those in constituted authority—a lesson that, once learned and practiced, will make us all better citizens, ample providers, faithful husbands—and true Americans. Amen."

The unholy terror of yoked church and state was thus loosed. In case any doubt lingered among the novices in the flock as to the purposefulness of their shepherds, the crook came cracking down on them in the opening days of the new enlistment period with a force Toby had not seen at the camp before.

While he leaned against a table in headquarters, reviewing the files of the new men and resenting the indignity of not having been assigned a place to perch, Lieutenant Nesbit bustled out of the captain's office and instructed Company Clerk Bloomgarden to draw up an order to the barracks leaders to have all bunks shifted around at the end of the day so that no two men from the same hometown were side by side or, if possible, even across the way from each other.

"What's up?" Skeezix asked.

"Captain just thinks mixing helps the new men adjust better."

"Divide and conquer," Toby mused aloud.

Nesbit ignored the comment and the commentator. The two exchanged few words directly anymore. "In fact," he added to Skeezix, signaling that the educational advisor's disapproval could only inspire him to rasher acts, "let's make everyone move around—the older men, too. Keeps 'em from getting into a rut."

"Shake well before using," Toby muttered just before Nesbit slapped on his hat and left, nearly separating the door from its hinges.

Skeezix smiled and shook his head. "I hope you got life insurance."

"What for?"

"The guy's a killer. When he's done fuckin' over the rookies, you're his next meat."

"Nah," Toby said with bravado, "West Point guys always stick by the Geneva Convention." Then he asked what Skeezix could do to keep Link Salter and Joe Calabrese from being separated in Barracks C.

"It's against regulations," Skeezix said. "You just heard."

"The regulation is stupid—can't we get around it?"

"I'll tell Dundy you said so—that'll cut a lotta ice wit' him." He stuck a piece of paper into his typewriter and began to draft the captain's order.

"What would?"

The keys clattered on for a sentence, unheeding. "Basketball," he said. "Kevin's an ace—I seen him play at the 'Y' once back home. You get him a basketball court and he'll spit wooden nickels for ya."

"Tell him I'm working on it—and why."

"You don't want me to do that."

"Why not?"

"'Cause you don't come through, your name's mud."

Skeezix had a better idea. All Dundy had to do to accommodate both the adjutant's order and Toby's request was have Link and Joe swap beds.

"You're a genius."

"So don't make me come to class, okay, teach?"

No such facile remedy was available to the trio of new recruits from A Barracks who showed up at headquarters after supper to protest the order separating them. Buddies from New Bedford, they had signed up together and grabbed bunks next to one another's and didn't see any point in breaking them up.

"The point is, it's an order," Nesbit told them. "This isn't a Boy Scout troop."

But the rookies were not satisfied with that and asked to see the captain. Sparhawk was processing papers as Nesbit marched the complainants into his office. Toby hovered at the door. Eyes flickering faster as he listened to their story, the captain did not lift his head from the documents on his desk until they were all done. Then he said simply, "If you don't move, you're going home."

His wrath was all the more terrible for its economical expression. One of their number braved it. "But *why* do we have to move—could you just tell us that, at least?"

The captain regarded him with a look that seemed to tell the boy he was not quite good enough to lodge in the fishbowl on the table beside his desk. "There happen to be several reasons," he said, "but you're not going to hear any of them." He turned to Nesbit. "If these fellows haven't moved by inspection tomorrow morning, Lieutenant, have Sergeant Carmichael take up their things and the clerk draw up their discharges."

The New Bedford boys made the mistake of staying put for one more night, as permitted, and pretending they had won their point. Word circulated, as a result, that those who objected to the order strenuously enough would be exempted from it. By morning, while the prime felons were preparing to move as directed, seventeen other emboldened new men marched into headquarters to protest. The captain, boiling by now but keeping the steam from view, said only that he would give them all until the end of the workday to decide if they still wanted to appeal his ruling—then he would respond accordingly. But as the trucks prepared to pull out for morning detail, the ringleader of the New Bedford Three, who by then had moved their bunks, was summoned to headquarters and summarily discharged. The testimony of his vacant bunk at day's end proclaimed the efficacy of protest to all newcomers in Camp 127.

Next morning, the second of the New Bedford boys was hauled from his work truck just before it departed. When the platoons returned that afternoon, there was no sign he had ever been in camp.

The third boy, Toby heard, whimpered in his bunk half the night, but dawn brought no surcease in the captain's implacable ways. Fearful of guilt by association, the other enrollees shunned the marked man at breakfast and all during cleanup. Skeezix, head hung low, fetched him just before loading time. There was no mirth in the trucks that morning, nor much in the woods, either, as the winds began to rise and the migratory birds to wing away.

A different sort of ax fell at lineup the next afternoon.

The captain ordered a rookie named Gilchrist to stand forward. The boy stepped out with his adam's apple bobbing frantically. "The supply sergeant reports you failed to return your tool after work today," Sparhawk charged. "Is that true?"

"I—guess so—sir."

"You *guess* so?"

"I—forgot it—sir."

"I see. And what have you got to say for yourself, young man?"

"I should'na done it, sir. I'm real sorry—"

"Anything else?"

"I—don't—oh, I'll look for it first thing tomorra—unless—maybe someone else coulda brought it in—"

"Or unless maybe someone else stepped on it and cut his foot up." The captain raked his eyes over the rest of the ranks. "When the government of your country entrusts a piece of equipment to your care, we expect you to cherish it like your last crust of bread on a desert island. And if you're careless, you'll have to pay the price." In this case, the price—if the ax failed to turn up next morning—was set at $1.25 for a replacement and a like amount so Gilchrist would remember never to misplace another. That amounted to half his monthly allowance. If the ax showed, he would serve two weekends on the Beautification Squad instead.

As the lineup broke and the men headed into supper, Nesbit pulled Skeezix aside for a word. The clerk's dark eyes were hard with resentment as Toby came up to him afterward. "Dirty work, huh?"

Skeezix looked by him as his anger yielded to resignation. "I gotta sick a fuckin' bloodhound on the clown." His mind was already riffling through the list of likeliest candidates for the distasteful assignment. "Bingo," he said. "Maybe it'll get him off the shitlist for a while."

Toby was being obligingly routed at chess by the captain in his quarters later when Sergeant Carmichael, mopping his moist moon-face, came by to report he had taken a later count of the tools and all axes were present and accounted for. One of the Lems had evidently picked up Gilchrist's and returned it to the supply shed.

"Let's not announce it," Sparhawk said. "The boy has to be taught a lesson—they all do."

Gilchrist returned to camp next afternoon and presented the supply sergeant with two axes—one he had been given that morning and the other allegedly lost the day before. At lineup, the captain asked him to stand forward once more. Confident for the instant, the enrollee crisply complied.

"Is it or is it not true, mister," the captain demanded, "that last evening just before lights-out you removed an ax without permission from the supply shed, hid it beneath a bush, then retrieved it on your return to camp this afternoon and handed it in as if you had found the one you lost?"

The boy's whole body seemed to shrivel. He swayed back and forth and almost pitched into the ground. His swallowed voice was confession enough.

"As I calculate it," the captain continued, heedless of the boy's distress, "it's two crimes now—a second to cover the first. Or are you going to tell us you were only *borrowing* the second ax for a few hours?"

So lavish an application of scorn strangled whatever movement may have remained in the boy's vocal chords. But Sparhawk insisted on an answer. A hideous rasp of culpability passed for compliance.

If Gilchrist had denied the charge, the captain revealed, he would have been discharged on the spot. As it was, he would have to pay for both axes now and work K.P. a week in honor of each. Toby looked over at Bingo Barnes while justice was being dispensed. His eyes never left the ground.

Having dramatized the necessity of blind obedience and the sanctity of government property to the new men, the captain completed his indoctrination course with a lesson on the inviolability of the work ethic. It was presented at the regular Tuesday evening meeting of the full company as a theatrical event titled "How to Be a Goldbrick," starring Will Bassett as the Lem narrator and Kevin Dundy as a delinquent enrollee.

Dundy first demonstrated the popular how-to-stand-like-a-statue technique, performed with a long-handled shovel, the only kind experienced goldbrickers used. The top of the handle was gripped by the fingers of both hands, Will explained as Kevin unlimbered one knuckle at a time, and drawn into the breast bone, allowing the arms to hang loose and relaxed. This soothing posture encouraged its perfectly idle practitioner to daydream about the joys of being paid to do absolutely nothing compared with the thankless ordeal of serving as a company leader. Dundy frowned broadly at that to let the onlookers know they were allowed to laugh. They never stopped after that.

Sugar-coated, the pill was nonetheless potent. After the laughing died, the captain privately instructed the work superintendent to have each of the six section foremen winnow the poorest worker from his forewarned ranks and, by the end of the week, present him with a list of lambs fit for slaughter. One, drawn by lot, was discharged just before Friday lineup and his name *in absentia* and the reason announced to the full company. The five dishonorable mentions were assigned to the Beauty Squad for a month of weekends.

Will Bassett looked somber after the sentencing. The discharged boy was the one he had tapped. Relative to the others under Will's watch, he had been a bit of a shirker, but Will suspected the fellow just lacked the muscle power to sustain the required effort—and was too proud to admit it. "The law of the jungle," Toby said to him. "The weakest always get it in the neck."

"Yeah," Will said, "but I don't like it coming from me."

Ash Cummings, to Toby's surprise, felt as bad. So uneasy was the superintendent over the arbitrary act of humiliation that he offered the discharged boy his own handcrafted ax along with advice to practice on the nearest woodpile so he could re-enlist in a few months and show them all. Such generosity should have gladdened both donor and recipient, but Ash looked excessively dour. "Hell, no," he said, "Sonny Boy told me to shove it up my toot blade first."

NINE

Sparhawk devoted 2 hrs in qtrs tonight justifying scourgelike policies to Dr Haseltine & me. Thru history, he says, military discipline has had just one aim: securing absolute obedience in face of mortal terror; singlemindedness is the sole path to victory. Fred. the Great (one of capt's five favorite absolutists) said he wanted his troops to fear their own officers more than enemy. In said spirit of utilitarian despotism, he oppresses peavies every chance he gets.

"Since these little palookas are their own worst enemies," he explains, "we supply the intimidation." His logic impeccably woolly: Because most enrollees have never held a job, at least not for long, they have naturally not learned true meaning of work & responsibility. From which it follows further, sez he, disregarding society's failure to provide them the chance, that "these boys are morally weak & lacking in mental stamina." Main purpose of camp in human terms is to provide discipline of workplace so men can learn to endure in civilian world. . . .

"YOU MAY NOT LIKE IT MUCH," the doctor said as Toby walked him to his car behind the infirmary, "but in his own way, our captain manages to achieve something with these boys."

In his mackinaw and tam-o'-shanter that sat like a large flapjack on a griddle barren except for a little cluster of white fuzz at the edges, Arthur Haseltine did not much resemble the classic American medical man. Before his retirement from private practice a year earlier, Toby was advised, he had affected all the standard accessories of the profession, including invariably gray suits during office hours and a habit of ascetic understatement that patients and admirers took for drollery. These constricting mannerisms vanished, however, when as a widower quickly bored with his solitary existence, he volunteered to be part-time medical officer for four C.C.C. camps within a thirty-minute drive of his home on Onota Lake, a mile or so west of Pittsfield. The task turned him into a bluff and volubly avuncular observer of the human comedy, Berkshire division. His rigorous intellect was so tempered by compassion that Toby's sole mark against him was his propensity to give the devil not only his due but a medal for valor.

"By beating them over the head for their own good, you mean?"

"You're taking him too literally," Dr. Haseltine said. "Look at what he's actually doing, not what he says or thinks is going on with these fellows." The camp routine served to build up the boys' confidence in themselves by a steady series of small triumphs. Every creditable day they logged on the job, no matter how menial the labor, armed them better for meeting the demands of society.

"By turning them into automatons?"

"Ah, there's your liberal education doing you in. Their aptitudes aren't yours." Anything that taxed them beyond their limited native capacities worked against the rehabilitative process. "That's why he's so hesitant to encourage you. Start a program that gets their minds functioning—and pretty soon confused and probably frustrated—and you could undercut everything he's trying to do here."

"He's a Frankenstein in reverse."

"If you want to be uncharitable about it—yes. Which is why he's always at loggerheads with whoever gets sent here to inject a semblance of academic respectability."

An appalling prognosis. With the onset of the new enlistment period, Toby was required to set in motion some sort of teaching program and keep the corps' district educational office apprised of his progress in weekly reports. "You mean anything I try beyond a token effort is doomed?"

The doctor took out a cigarette, another new habit, and tapped one end against the package laconically until the tobacco shreds were firm. "Unless you can figure out how to adjust for the authoritarian mind." As a matter of fact, he thought, the Nazi experience in this area might prove a useful model. The doctor had traveled in Europe the year before and been apprised of the changes in the *Arbeiterdienst*, the work camps for German youth after which the C.C.C. had been loosely patterned. First run by the theoretically retired military in order to get around the Versailles Treaty ban on German rearmament, the voluntary camps were denigrated by Hitler as ineffectual playgrounds where philosophy was discussed around the campfire by useless high domes. But when their potential for indoctrination became apparent, attendance was made mandatory and regimentation stiffened. "It's become their way of eliminating the impractical tendencies of the intellectuals and preparing the youth for a life of manual labor and unquestioning obedience."

"How very Sparhawkian."

"That's my point. Try taking a strictly vocational and patriotic approach that he can see as complementary, not conflicting." He turned on his car engine and pushed in the cigarette lighter. "A clever instructor can work in a lot of perfectly useless information in the bargain and maybe save a few souls." Then, issuing an invitation to join him fishing at his lake on the weekend, the healer drove off puffing contentedly into the starry night.

The key to the co-opting process, Toby told himself, was the adjutant, with whom he had remained at sword's point for five weeks. In every possible instance of conflict, they crossed. The latest had occurred when, on seeing Link Salter duck into Toby's room one morning to pick up his school books, the lieutenant was ready to slap him in irons. "It's against regulations," Mitchell Nesbit snapped. "No enrollees allowed unattended in the officers' quarters."

"But he's got my permission," Toby argued. "What's the point of making him chase all over camp after me every time he wants to get in a little studying."

"The point is it's a rule. No unattended enrollees in the officers' quarters."

"I'm not an officer, though."

"But you're living in the officers' quarters."

"What about your orderly—and the captain's?"

"That's different."

"Why—because they're white boys?"

"Because regulations provide for personal attendants to some officers. They don't say anything about anyone else sneaking around—"

"He wasn't sneaking—that's only in your one-track mind."

"My track's the one the camp runs on. Keep your Sambo out of here."

Their chemistry was combustibly contrary. All Nesbit's energy was as tightly channeled as Toby's was ineffectually dispersed. Nesbit's whole ambition was to command; Toby's to delve, to sample, to collect. It was an uneven match. But then came a stroke of luck, the first of several that blessed his struggles that trying season.

He happened to have been at the supply shed when the Lem foremen returned from work one Friday to check their tool counts with Denis Carmichael and hand in their daily work sheets to Ash Cummings. While Will Bassett was dealing with the supply sergeant, Toby glanced over his tally of accomplished works. Some of it was descriptive in nature—which firebreaks had been cleared and where the underbrush had been swept clean—but a few of the items were quantified: how many seedlings planted, snags felled, gooseberry bushes removed. The first item lodged in his memory: 528 white pine seedlings had been planted that day by the squad in Will's subsection assigned that task. Curious, he asked if that performance was normal, and Will said yes, consulted the clipboard behind the superintendent's desk, and reported total plantings for the week came to just under 2,600.

That evening, when Toby went by the captain's office to hand in his own brief but artfully portentous weekly report for approval, Sparhawk invited him for the first time to inspect the so-called cumulative performance chart assembled by the adjutant—a summary of everything of note that happened in camp that week. Transmitted under the captain's imprimatur, the document served as the official communiqué to corps district headquarters at Fort Devens. Part of the two-page report was devoted to good works: how many camping and picnic sites constructed and landscaped, how many acres of forest restored, and how many seedlings planted. Beside the last item, the number read something better than 3,400.

After telephoning Will to make certain no other subsection but his had reforested that week, Toby joined Nesbit in the washroom the next morning when the adjutant went in to shave. He attended himself frostily in the mirror for a time while Toby lingered, in apparent wait for the basin, and whistled a few bars of "Lullaby of Broadway" with a studied unmelodiousness that could only have added to Nesbit's annoyance. Suddenly he stopped and asked as offhandedly as he could manage, "Lieutenant, how come our official weekly report inflated the number of trees the men planted by more than a third?" After a pause to let the shaft sink in, he added, this time with prosecutorial bite, "Or are all the items padded?"

Nesbit shaved on in silence, weighing his options. Finally, when to wait longer would have been tantamount to a confession, he said, "You must be mistaken."

Toby quoted him the numbers for the week so he could not doubt the basis for the charge. Nesbit shrugged and said he would double-check the figures in case there had been a mistake in his addition. "Math," he noted, rinsing his razor and hastening to finish up, "was never my strong point."

It was the only plausible defense. Toby had to gamble. "I guess not," he said, "because the numbers have been off that much every week. And the funny thing is, they're always on the high side."

"You don't know what you're talking about," Nesbit shot back accurately, though failing to mention that Toby had not been privy to the reported data before that week.

The rapidity and truculence of his response were self-incriminating. "We'll see about that," Toby countered, husky with menace.

Keeping clear of Nesbit the rest of that morning while the captain made his usual Saturday departure, Toby arrived at lunch in anticipatory spirits. But the adjutant was nowhere to be seen. Toby concluded he was consulting either his conscience or the nearest mobster about having the camp educational advisor erased. In midafternoon, though, as Toby plunked away on the spinet in the nearly empty Rec, Nesbit approached crabwise and weaponless, settling an arm on a corner of the piano as if he were planning to break into vocal accompaniment. His snub face was shadowed with concern. When Toby paused after a tinkling rendition of "Lovely to Look At," Nesbit said softly, "The captain doesn't know."

He fought off an impulse to strike up a medley of triumphant Sousa, submerged his animus, and said only, "Do you want to talk about it, Lieutenant?"

"You don't give a guy much choice—Mr. Ronan."

Toby sensed they were nearing parity.

Although Gordon Sparhawk was only a standby soldier, Mitchell Nesbit held him in higher regard than any reservist he had dealt with. "You have to understand—this camp is more than an assignment to him," he confided as they strode past the ball field and began hiking up Ghost Trail. "It's a chance for him to leave his mark on a plot of earth and a thousand men—and to him, that's a lot."

"It's not bad for any man."

"For him more than most, maybe," Nesbit said, pinching out the words with pained precision. "I suppose his life has been something of a disappointment." It was nothing Nesbit could pin down—just a kind of inner desolation about the man that he had tried to repair by turning the camp into a model of ordered efficiency and disciplining its degraded occupants so they might emerge with a chance for a halfway decent life. "And I happen to think those are pretty admirable goals, even if we have to knock some heads together to reach them." So dedicated, in fact, was the captain to his temporary calling that Nesbit had begun to fear Sparhawk might be incapable of separating himself from it—and the domain over which he held, for all practical purposes, omnipotent sway. The lieutenant, for his part, was eager to get on with his military career and more rewarding missions than wet-nursing lazy, pimply, black-toothed lunkheads. For the moment, that meant yoking his fortune to the captain's. But since for Sparhawk the camp was a salvation sure to dissipate the moment it was completed, the lieutenant had found himself having to function in contradictory ways in order to serve both his own ideals of patriotic duty and the somewhat unorthodox needs of his commanding officer.

The clearest instance of this dilemma was the serpentine road the men were building up the mountain to Berry Pond—the so-called circuit drive. When it was finished, so would the life of the camp be. The state forest would then be thrown open to the public that Sparhawk now so avidly repulsed, and his suzerainty would be a memory in the wind. So the snail's-pace roadwork proceeded rather like Penelope's wedding dress: forever in process. To compensate and maintain the camp's ranking among the better outfits in the district—it had stood twelfth out of sixty-one in Massachusetts after the last semi-annual assessment in early July—Nesbit filed somewhat exaggerated reports on all the rest of the work carried on in Sparhawk's paradise. Camp 127, in short, was even more therapeutic an undertaking for its commander than for its needy conscripts.

"You mean he's wacky?" Toby asked Dr. Haseltine later that afternoon while they fished the jittery waters of his moody lake. Nesbit's reluctant disclosure required a seasoned appraisal.

"Mental health is not a field in which I'm clinically competent," the doctor said, "but it's probably a safe guess that our captain is somewhat overinvested emotionally in the camp." The three other C.O.'s whom the doctor dealt with evidenced little of Sparhawk's compulsion as either taskmaster or disciplinarian. "But then none of their camps in half as shipshape—they've got busted pipes and muddy walkways and doors coming off their hinges and kitchens I wouldn't feed a skunk out of, not to mention an unforgivable number of cases of impetigo." No instance of slovenliness or insubordination was beneath Sparhawk's meticulous notice, and no achievement failed to fire his zeal. "Your library, for instance," Haseltine added. "He was like a little boy with butterscotch pudding when the commendation came down from corps area headquarters."

"Then why am I the last to hear about it?"

"Who said anything about *your* morale? It's his we're talking about. In fact, he made a point of asking me not to mention the commendation to you. The last thing he wants is another arrogant C.E.A. around his neck. For his money, the library is all the education program the camp needs." He cranked himself vertical at the edge of the dock and began to reel in his line. "The only reason I've violated his confidence is that I think a purpose is served by your having a fuller understanding of the man. But I'll thank you to show more discretion by keeping the news to yourself." It was hard to say no to a man who sealed your lips with fresh poached trout and two iced bottles of beer.

If the captain's excesses were truly more a matter of pathology than sin, Toby could see no harm in a little coercive use of the knowledge for his own advancement. Nesbit, after all, had extracted tacit benefit from enlisting an accomplice. It was not an easy bargain to seal.

"What I'd like," Toby told him after Sunday breakfast, "is for you to teach the men a course called 'The Art of War'—sort of a light survey of military techniques through the ages. It should be duck soup for a man from The Point. And I think the captain would enjoy introducing you and maybe making a few final remarks each time—he practically said as much to me when I broached the idea. It would take you only a few hours a week for six weeks. And your being involved would matter a lot, believe me."

At first Nesbit said he had no time for that sort of thing. Toby conceded the imposition but noted that there were, after all, eight hours in the middle of the lieutenant's day when the camp was empty and his duties minimal. Nesbit then denigrated the educational value of the proposal. "You think these monkeys are going to listen," he asked, "if I start telling them the Macedonian hoplites were named for their heavy shields, which were three feet wide and carried in their left hands while in their right they wielded a stout spear eight feet long— or maybe it was seven?"

Total recall, it was plain, was what passed for cognition at The Point. "I think they'd be fascinated," Toby said. "And we'll get you the biggest garbage-can cover in captivity to demonstrate with. It'll be a smash."

His surrender was painful to behold. But Mitchell Nesbit all at once seemed as much a realist as his superior officer did a fantast.

II

Sunday, Oct. 5, '35

Slightly singed chicken dinner with Will & Trudy Bassett at their cottage in Richmond, about a mile from the state line. Snug nest is in need of small squaller, but eminently fertile Trudy says they're waiting till times improve some.

Hiked with them after in the hills, now one fierce torch song. New England autumns truly unique, acc. to Will, who says no other place at this latitude boasts comparable variety of trees & brilliance of color. Other colors always there, only masked by chlorophyll, which stops getting delivered as leaf stem clogs like hardening arteries—ergo, red, orange, yellow, gold revealed till chemical breakdown composts everything shitbrown.

Charmed by this tale of pigmento mori & other lore in his store-

house, I beseeched Will to teach elementary course on "Forest &
Wood" to enrollees at my Harv. U. West. A way to combine botany,
chemistry, agronomy, entomology, ecology & woodcraft. "Pay's
lousy," I inveigled, "but satisfaction immense." Bottomlessly affable,
Will said okay if Ash agrees, but I shouldn't count on that.

"It don't pay to bother with the run of 'em," the work superintendent said when solicited the next morning for Lempower to help
smarten up the lambs.

"We're going in mostly for practical things," Toby contended.
"The more they understand how the world works, the better job
they'll do."

"There's a lot of damned fine mules I can think of that that don't
apply to," said Ash Cummings, taking his clipboard down from the
wall and reaching for his ax in the corner.

Toby sat there gloomily for a moment. "Funny," he said as Ash
headed for the door, "somehow I thought you were more sympathetic
than that."

The wrinkles mapping the woodsman's long face veered south by
southwest. "Sympathy never landed no one nowhere but hind tit," he
said. "Give me sweat, son, and then I'll give a man a boost. Or someone like the Dundy boy—we try to help his sort along." As to his
foremen helping out, they were hired to work, not to teach, and
shouldn't be expected to pitch in after a full day in the field, not without additional pay, anyway, even if Lems elsewhere were doing it.
"But if Will Bassett's birdbrained enough to want to, I got no objection."

Recruiting the balance of his faculty took him and Joe Calabrese to
Pittsfield later in the week for a tour of the G.E. factory complex that
Lawrence Keyes had promised. An immense and frightening hive of
coordinated movement with a ubiquitous smell of oiled steel, it was
less noisy than the can plant his father had run but five times the
leviathan, extruding a hundred different products in a thousand throbbing operations. Toby was nearly swallowed up around one turn by a
tangle of heavy copper wires that had snaked off their drums. Joe,
though, practically danced through that grid of thronged aisles and re-
ciprocating hardware. By the time Mr. Keyes began to explain how
successive induction coils on dynamo rotors were wound in alternate
directions to ensure that the generated current always flowed the same
way, it was Joe who seemed the college whiz and Toby the waif who
hadn't made it past algebra.

His flannel jacket earned him a luncheon invitation to the Stanley
Club, exclusive redoubt of the G.E. engineering brass, while Joe in his

C.C.C. dress-green fatigues had to drive back to camp and deliver liverwurst sandwiches to the details in the forest. "Bright boy," Keyes said as soon as Joe had left. "Too bad."

"Let's not bury him yet."

"No, no—I just meant—"

There were a number of them out at the camp like Joe, he said— fellows who had never had a break and were worth trying to reclaim for useful service to society. "That's what I'm supposed to be there for."

This unimaginable news, with the example of Joe Calabrese's native aptitude so fresh at hand, gripped Lawrence Keyes's considerable frame with some force. When Toby told him of Joe's ambition to attend engineering school and enter the profession if he could just manage to complete the last year of high school, his executive plumage flared with indignation, and he took the bait at once. "Why don't we see that he gets it done right here?" he asked. "It seems to me a boy like that—exceptions can surely be made—a phone call or two, I think—"

His prospective good deed left Lawrence Keyes so suffused with benevolence that before the meal was done, he was beaming praise at his guest. "It's just a grand thing, I don't mind telling you, for a fellow of your quality and background to contribute a part of his priceless youth to the betterment of those less fortunate."

"You're too kind, sir," said Toby, the embodiment of *noblesse oblige*.

"Not at all. I only regret there aren't more of your sort around here —modest lads—refined—educated—idealistic. It's very refreshing to run across such a combination of qualities. If there's anything I can do to make your task easier, feel free to call on me at any time. And you're more than welcome at our home whenever you'd like, I can assure you. Please think of it as your home away from home, as it were. And if you won't take my intentions wrong, I'll confide in you a little, son. The ladies at our home share in admiring your activities and character."

With disingenuousness befitting the ungenteel, he took his benefactor up at once on the offer of assistance. Was it even remotely possible, Toby wondered, if the director of one of America's most sophisticated laboratories could spare a few hours a week to instruct the boys of Camp 127 in basic mechanics? Young Joe Calabrese, who was pretty handy with a monkeywrench, would do the dirty work but he just didn't know enough science or engineering to get into the principles of how and why a thing worked—"it'll be a case of the halt leading the blind, if you know what I mean, sir. Now I know it isn't Har-

vard or Yale, exactly, sir, but I thought it might be great fun for
you—and Lord knows, the boys would be thrilled to have a man of
your—"

"Say no more, Tobias!" The pleasure would be all his.

Joe Calabrese was more restrained in his response to Toby's solicitation. "You gotta be outa your fuckin' skull," is what he actually
said.

Joe feared first of all for his status. "I tell 'em all I know an' anybody can do my job, so the second my ass gets an inch outa line, I'm
up shit's creek without a paddle."

"You want to get your high school diploma?"

"Yeah, sure, but I don't—"

"Then consider yourself volunteered."

"Hey, look now—I know a little about how to make car motors go,
but I don't have no real training—I can't explain why the—"

"I've lined up a little help for you in that department. It'll be fine."

"Shit," Joe said, "you're pretty slick," and mopped his brow with a
grease rag. "Now I know what they teach at Harvard."

Sparhawk sniffed cautiously at the package Toby had assembled.
The first two elements in it he supposed were unobjectionable—Nesbit's commendable willingness to instruct the men in history at its
most heroic and Will Bassett teaching woodcraft and forest lore. But
the course in mechanics was another matter. Joe Calabrese was just an
enrollee, and not even rated. Just because he kept the trucks running
in roughly satisfactory order was no cause to glorify him as more than
a common garage hand. As to the offer to admit him to Pittsfield High
School on a part-time basis—even if the scheduling could be made to
dovetail with his job at camp—the captain viewed that as a sop and an
insult to the rest of the men. Access to the gymnasium in that very
school had been denied them the previous winter on dubious grounds,
and Calabrese could not be designated a privileged character. As to the
eminent Mr. Keyes's generous gesture, it would be a waste of the gentleman's time; the boys were incapable of absorbing that level of instruction. "At any rate, you've already got somebody in camp who's
both technically qualified and speaks the boys' language. I take it you
wouldn't object too severely if I brushed up a little and then took on
Calabrese as my classroom assistant?"

"Well, sir—I hadn't—that is, it seems a great deal to—"

To his credit, Lawrence Keyes reacted with exemplary understanding to Toby's allegation of ignorance of C.C.C. regulations: Outsiders, no matter how eminent, could not be enlisted to teach at the
camps unless all staff personnel were already being utilized for that

purpose. "But I was wondering, sir, if I could possibly prevail upon you to exchange one offer of kindness for another." There was a certain feeling at the camp that the city fathers had rejected the captain's request for use of the high school gymnasium the previous winter because a large number of the C.C.C. boys were Catholic. "I realize that's ridiculous, of course, sir, but you can see how it looks from their side—what with the snappers all going to the parochial schools in town, so that an influx of overage, somewhat uncouth R.C.'s, even just to play basketball after school hours, might be perceived to have a corrupting effect on the bloodlines of the community—"

"My God!" Keyes said. "We can't have them thinking that. Pittsfield is a very enlightened city."

Christian charity swiftly prevailed. All it had needed was a bit of deceitful priming. The "Y" would be available to the camp boys for an hour and a half Tuesdays, Thursdays, and Saturdays at hours to be arranged.

Before disclosing the news to the captain, Toby took it to the leader of C Barracks, well known for his athletic prowess. It was an elemental transaction. If Toby could arrange for the enrollees' regular use of a basketball court, would Kevin Dundy make sure his charges turned out in force for the first six-week session of the camp school?

"How many you need?"

"Half the men to show up for at least one of the courses—and you've got to come yourself every time."

"Whew!"

"Take it or leave it."

With a faculty and student body thus assured, he lacked only classroom space. The mess hall was the obvious place, but the matter had to be closely negotiated with the supply sergeant, whose hegemony over those premises had never been countermanded by the C.O. As it was, Denis Carmichael was forever bellyaching about the burden that evening activities imposed on the kitchen crew. They had to work doubly hard, he alleged, to clean up and arrange the hall on Tuesday nights for the company meeting and movies that followed and on Fridays, boxing night. Toby's request to have the place tidied and set up by seven o'clock the remaining three weeknights was greeted as the eighth labor of Hercules.

"I'll be glad to help with the tables and benches," he said, "and so will Eddie Spain."

"Yeah, terrific—but that's the least of it. My boys are only human, ya know? Eight o'clock's possible—just maybe—if we get enough help. But seven, forget it."

He needed two one-hour periods with a fifteen-minute break between. That allowed half an hour for the men to unwind in the Rec afterward and then fifteen minutes in the barracks before lights-out. Tighter than that would never work. "Eight is too late."

"That's a fuckin' shame, pal, but I can't make miracles."

"Look, the captain's approved all this."

"Then you bring the captain down here to clean up—and the adjutant, too, while you're at it. Maybe they got hot-and-cold-runnin' slaveys at dear ol' Harvard, but here there's just us slobs."

A different tack appeared in order.

"Please? It means a lot to me—and it might to the men."

"Please, yourself. Go cry on someone else's shoulder. Mine's busy."

"Thanks—Sergeant."

"Anytime."

"I guess we'll just have to hold classes in the barracks."

"Suit yourself," he said, without visible regret at losing the franchise. But as Toby turned to go, Carmichael called after him. "Hey, the barracks ain't no place to learn nothin' but jerkin' off without missin' a beat." An accompanying phlegmy snuffle signaled a new and more congenial round of bargaining. The supply sergeant had a deal to offer.

He pulled Toby into the farthest corner of the empty mess and itemized the particulars of Carmichael's Catering Service, as it pleased him to call it. For a modest charge—in Toby's case, twenty bucks a month—the sergeant would both ready the mess for classes when needed and see that his creature comforts were attended to just as those of his other distinguished clients were. Under his direction, the labors of the captain's and the adjutant's orderlies, the K.P., unspecified "others" on camp detail, and weekend "volunteers" were pooled to provide "twenty-four-hour personalized service" to the officers, the Lems who stayed in camp overnight during the week, official visitors, unofficial "guests," and even Dr. Haseltine, who required certain domestic attention since his retirement to widowerhood. If he subscribed, Carmichael promised him, his quarters would be cleaned daily, bedding changed weekly, laundry done on request, shoes kept shined, hot water guaranteed when desired, mail delivery expedited, food served him of higher quality than what the enrollees ate—"You been gettin' a free ride on that one so far"—transportation to and from town supplied day and night, and, at no extra charge except the labor and room costs, sexual needs satisfied. "In a nutshell, pal, you got to live like a white man even though you're stuck away in Coolietown." At a bargain, too. "Hell, the lieutenant, he pays almos' twice that an' he only makes forty-five more'n you. 'Course with him, everything's gotta be spic 'n' span, startin' wit' his undies."

His choices were: (1) resist—and not have a schoolhouse when he needed it; (2) blow the whistle on Carmichael as an extortionist—unseemly in view of his own not entirely admirable tactics, and (3) submit. He submitted—like a white man.

Finally, he adopted a few pedagogical techniques he thought likely to enhance the school's chances for success. Instead of conventional classroom seating, he arranged for the benches to be placed on all four sides of the teacher—a kind of theater in the square—so that no student was more than three rows distant from him; sleep, at such close range, would prove difficult. Instead of textbooks, he invested the thirty-five dollars left in the camp educational budget in a beat-up mimeograph and dipped into his own pocket to buy stencils, ink, and paper. At the start of class, a one-page mimeographed "dopesheet" would be handed out to each man with the highlights of the lesson in clear, double-spaced English. Each attending enrollee would be asked to exert himself only to the extent of (a) saving the dopesheets in a plain manilla folder provided for the purpose and (b) reading the previous one over before coming to the next class. And instead of letting his instructors wing it, he reviewed the contents of their lessons with them, the captain included, requiring each presentation to be recorded step by step on filing cards to assure proper organization of the material. Entertainment value was not required.

The enrollee turnout surpassed everyone's expectations but Toby's. Where C Barracks led, the others followed. They not only came, they listened, too, even to Lieutenant Nesbit, whose recitations on Greek and Roman soldiering, by their very remoteness from the boys' lives, took on an almost magical cast. Among the nonattendants was Wolfbait Stubbs, lounging on the mess porch and drawing hard on someone else's discarded butt. "Call me in," he told Toby, "when they wipe Napoleon's ass at Waterloo."

Will Bassett, so much closer to the men than the adjutant was, got hectored by them steadily, but when he would explain things like how trees grew from the outside in and their centers were really deadwood, they followed with interest—in their fashion (*"Ya' crazy, Will—dat's where dere babies come from!"*).

Naturally, they gave Joe Calabrese, as one of their peers, the hardest time of all when he took over from the captain. But between them, they managed to clarify more than they muddied about mechanics, hydraulics, kinetics, thermodynamics, and other friendly forces of the universe—and mostly in words of one syllable. So caught up in these lessons did Sparhawk become that after the first week he returned to camp Sunday night towing a whole engine block from an eviscerated Studebaker. "Should make things a lot clearer for the men," he announced, delivering the thing a paternal thwang on the flank with a professional wrench of recent purchase.

III

Sunday, Oct. 21, '35

Temple Keyes. Strength in the name. And its bearer. What sort, exactly? The quality of quality? Surely that, but it begs the question. Compensation, perhaps, for nature's having dealt her neither fair face nor form? If she had beauty to match her other gifts, she would probably be unbearable—and surely beyond my reach. I like the way she looks: preoccupied.

Keyes & skies. But what rhymes with Temple? Or daunts her? Not mountain climbing, certainly. Granted, they are not exactly craggy, these big old hills, melancholy now that the leaves have mostly dropped and the conifers darkly reign, but she moved up Jiminy Peak today goat-sure as we left Guy & Holly Curtis half an hr behind. And we were the ones wearing the lunch knapsacks.

I am 9 months younger than she though we grad. college the same time because of yr she lost to polio. The ordeal seems to have stolen her childhood. I can detect nothing giddy left over in her. . . .

Two thirds of the way up, and having so far outstripped their escorts as to appear eager to evade their surveillance entirely, they paused for five minutes beside the trail and talked.

On the climb, she had said little, attacking the incline with mannish strides and ducking her head into the wind whenever it swirled in out of the northwest or gusted at them in the clearings. She had dressed for the terrain and weather, not to charm him, in a rough wool shirt, heavy ski sweater, gray slacks, and sturdy oxfords. Only a knitted white cap with a pompon that nicely set off her bobbed, dirty-blond hair lent a saving softness. He asked her what she thought about while climbing so determinedly, then supposed the honest answer was "About not falling" and offered to withdraw the question if it intruded too boldly on her privacy.

"Oh, no," she said. "My concertos—I do them all the time in my head. Mother's convinced I'm so distracted that I'll disappear down a rabbit hole someday and not even notice I'm gone."

She had played the flute more or less seriously for years, applying large doses of desire and patience to supplement the meager gifts her muse bestowed. Years of diligence, though, had turned her into no more than a passingly accomplished flautist; she practiced two or three nights a week with an ensemble that performed occasionally at musicales and weddings. Her ambition at the moment was the third chair in the Pittsfield Symphony Orchestra, for which she had tried out the past several years without success but not without encouragement from the maestro.

"I'd love to hear you sometime."

"I'll let you know if I make the varsity," she said, taking off a pair of knitted white gloves that matched her cap.

"I meant before then."

"Well—if you'd like. But I've a ways to go, I'm warning you—especially my vibrato."

"You're a perfectionist, I can tell."

"There's no other way to be, I'm afraid, if one is serious about it. My trouble is that I'm not quite driven enough—I slack off when I reach a certain threshold of competence instead of forging ahead all the harder."

"But you have other things in your life."

"Yes—well, that might explain the slackness but not excuse it. I think that's the real problem—my life's too comfortable. The entire arrangement of it, I mean—everything's literally *arranged* for me. If my father could have bought me a place in the orchestra, no doubt he would have. He's a wonderful arranger. I guess one has to be to run a laboratory."

Her ambivalence toward the man was manifest in every allusion she made to him. Already it was plain to Toby that when and how to diverge from the guidelines her father had set out for her would prove the shaping conflict of her life—assuming it was to unfold at all. Possibly she would remain a chambered nautilus indefinitely. "I gather that you haven't told him I'm not exactly titled," he said to break her musing.

She looked up wide-eyed. "And how do you gather that?"

"His comments over lunch. He still seems to feel I'm Dr. Livingstone or someone, bringing the one true faith up the Zambesi. I'd have had to lick my plate clean to convince him I'm really just one of the restless natives."

She laughed and said, "I think he may actually have you down for a sort of young Father Flanagan in training—lay variety, of course."

"Why didn't you tell him the truth?"

"What—that you're a street urchin who struggled through Harvard fishing coins out of sewer drains with chewing gum and a piece of string—or was it something still more odious?"

"Not quite."

"I'm glad. Whatever it was, though, is your business—not his."

"Or yours?"

"Or mine—unless you choose to share it sometime."

Her tone conveyed neutrality, not any high curiosity. "Still," he said, "don't you think he should know?"

"If and when there's a point to it." She rubbed her hands together to ward off the chill. "You have a father, too," she went on, "or don't you keep in touch?" Toby said he wrote him now and then. "Well, if you had happened to mention me in one of your letters—" Oh, he had indeed, he said, as well as the great kindness her family had shown him. "All right, then my telling Father about your economic hardship would be precisely as if you had told yours first thing off the bat that I'm a bit disfigured." She took note of his startled look but then mistook the cause of it. "Or perhaps you did."

"Christ," he said with low annoyance, "you can't think that—or that I think of you at all that way."

"But why not? Don't be silly—you've got eyes. I think of you as someone tall and slender and red-haired and so forth—those are physical facts. You can't be oblivious—"

He took one of her chilled hands and clasped it hard, as if to pump warmth into it, and she fell still for the moment, not rejecting the gesture. "It's a lousy analogy," he said after a while.

"It isn't at all—and you're making a much of it." Standing now, she yanked him upright after her and withdrew her hand. "Besides, you brought the whole thing up in the first place."

The rest of the way, she narrated a childhood episode that disclosed something of the journey her emotions had traveled while she grew up. Not long after it became clear that her deformity was permanent, she found herself repelled by the perfect, pink, curly, immutable beauty of her favorite girlhood doll. Retired to a far corner of her closet several years earlier but never discarded, the unblinking, glossy thing in its buttercup crinoline suddenly struck her as not only a mockery of her own newly flawed figure but a cruel denial as well of all human frailty. She conspired to give the doll a real life by creating a mortal cycle for it of exactly one year's duration.

The metamorphosis was worked in a no-longer-used servant's room on the third floor, across the hall from her mother's sewing room, where Temple would duck in to perform a half hour's clandestine stitchery when no one else was around. With cloth and clay and cosmetics and whatever tools it took to perform her perverse miniature surgery, she aged the doll month by month from fair sylph to stooped crone, adding breasts and then drooping them, drawing on facial lines and slowly incising them, turning the braided blond tresses ashen and blowzy and finally bleached white, gnarling joints and twisting limbs, and refashioning her outfit from beribboned pastel to ripe green to withering brown to varicose blue and funereal black. Aspiring to verisimilitude to the very end of her lugubrious game, she glued the eyes closed and packed the decrepit little corpse in a shoebox that she buried behind the garage, never once sharing her secret. Only after a week, when a small bouquet of sweet williams appeared in the doll's old hiding place, did she learn that her mother had known all along of her obsessive hobby and had the understanding not to intervene. "I ran to her then and cried and cried—I must have cried for an hour— for the doll, for my leg, for my dead Nana, for everyone who was lost in the war—for everything, I suppose, that couldn't stay beautiful forever." She stiffened her shoulders as the summit came into view. "I don't think I've cried since."

They had lunch spread out and waiting for the Curtises by the time they reached the lean-to on the south face of the peak. A lively and attractive couple hopelessly overprivileged, they regaled Temple and Toby with talk of their shopping trip to New York the day before and visit to the Hayden Planetarium, which had just opened to the public.

"I mean to say, you know perfectly well you're looking up at a counterfeit sky," Guy Curtis effervesced, "but there must be something they've figured out about the proportions of the place and how the mind perceives them in pitch darkness because you'd swear you're outdoors by your lonesome under an awesomely perfect sky. That's the thing, actually—it's ultrareal—no one's ever seen a sky like that. And I tell you it's totally spellbinding—a classic case, you might say, of that willing suspension of disbelief Shelley speaks of."

Temple expressed a professional interest in how the celestial museum worked. The core of the sky show, Holly Curtis explained, was a kind of huge stereopticon mounted on a platform in the center of the theater. "It's really the wierdest-looking thing," she said. Whirring like some enormous insect as it slowly revolved during the performance, the machine had the miraculous power to portray the heavens past, present, and future.

"It's all very God-like," said Guy. "They show you how the night sky must have looked to Abraham, and then Jesus, and then Mohammed—with all the changes in the horizon and relative positions of all the heavenly bodies. And then they show you how the sky is going to look over New York in 14,000 A.D.—can you imagine? They say Vega will be the pole star then and the Southern Cross will be visible at this latitude."

"How can they know that?" Temple asked.

"Mathematical computations," Guy said blandly. "It's all very predictable, I guess, if you take the trouble to chart it."

"But who says there'll even be a world here then?"

"Oh, have a little faith," Guy laughed and turned to Toby. "Temple can get a bit dour now and then."

"But a giant comet could come along at any time," she persisted, "and bash us into oblivion."

"They're presuming it won't, Temp," said Holly, humoring her. "It's just hypothetical. *My* only complaint is I won't be here to see it."

The vastness of the time warp seemed to have unhinged Temple slightly. "Comets actually worry me a lot less than human idiocy," she soliloquized. "Considering how many millions were butchered in the World War—and all the deadlier weapons we're busy devising—I wouldn't bet on anything animate being around in 14,000 except ants and cockroaches—and possibly a few Rosicrucians."

"On the other hand," Guy said, "all the lunatics may have destroyed one another by then, and paradise could have arrived."

"Father tells me," Temple ran on, not acknowledging Guy's postulate, "that G.E. has come up with some sort of gadget that transmits bullets of light. He says it's just supposed to be for communications—no doubt the same way dynamite's only supposed to be for building tunnels. The fact is, we're going to have armies running around shooting death rays at one another in fifteen or twenty years—fifty, tops."

"But if everybody has it," Guy tried to sooth her, "no one will use it after a while—like poison gas last time."

"Everyone had the machine gun, too, last time," Temple said, "and nobody put *that* away." Having made her point, she dismissed the whole topic as unworthy of such a grand, gingery day.

After packing up, they circled the shrubby mound of a mountaintop and took in the patchy evergreen prospect on all sides. Toby pointed out about where he thought the camp was across a pair of intervening ridges. Hatless as she let the wind strafe her hair, Temple drew several deep breaths of exhilaration and remarked, "Isn't it odd how the mood of the sky thoroughly colors the temper of the day down here? If it's overcast, so do we tend to be—and sunny, then our hearts all leap."

"Don't all living things respond to their environment?" Guy asked.

"That's my point," Temple said. "One doesn't generally think of the sky as environment. It's conceived of as more or less a backdrop when really it's the determining influence—as if all we were down here is a large irregular mirror of heaven." She glanced at Toby sideways. "Or is that so very obvious?"

"The essence of poetry," he said, "is the contemplation of the familiar with fresh eyes."

She pressed her thin lips together in an economical smile and put on her cap for the downhill trip. "And is the essence of Toby Ronan the coining of homilies to avoid straight answers?"

"I didn't think you really wanted an answer—you were delivering yourself of a revelation."

That brought a slightly broader smile, and she took his hand and drew him after her as they started down, having allowed the Curtises a few moments' head start. "How do you like them?" she asked. "And don't quote me Samuel Johnson for an answer."

"They seem amiable enough."

"Very up on things, don't you think?"

"Oh, definitely."

"They're my lifeline to the real world. They go down to the city once a month without fail, shopping or play-going or something or other thrilling and usually quite expensive."

"You disapprove? I thought a little dissipation was the prerogative of the young rich? There wouldn't be any revolutions otherwise."

"It's just that Guy's such an intellectual butterfly—one of your dollar-a-year scholars who's never had a less than respectable thought in his whole academic life."

"His scholarship's not impeccable, either. He mixed up Shelley and Coleridge back there—but I guess that's outside his field."

"Oh, how I wish you'd called him on it. That's so typical—he's more or less familiar with everything and serious about nothing. He plays the field because he doesn't really have one of his own."

Downhill was more dangerous for her, he could see and took the lead, not relinquishing her hand on the steeper stretches. She did not object.

"And you?" he asked. "What are you serious about—if not your music? Is your heart set on becoming directress of the Athenaeum?"

"Hardly." She swerved clear of a ragged clump of rocks and glided away from him. "But I'm not sure what instead. Some form of research, possibly. I'll have to go on with my studies, though—that's clear enough. I'm thinking of Columbia next year—if they'll have me—" So saying, she skidded over an exposed tangle of tree root, turned her left ankle, and went down emitting a shrill "Oh, shit!"

He sat beside her while the initial pain subsided and a duller throbbing set in. She was infuriated with herself. The spill could have happened to anyone, but occurring then and there and to her, it smacked of physical incapacity, a condition she did not acknowledge. To her mind, her problem was aesthetic, not functional.

When she repeated for the third time that such things never happened to her, Toby told her to relax and stop worrying that he took her for a cripple, considering how she had nearly vaulted up the mountain. Becalmed by that, she sat for a time, massaging the tender ankle. Her face was damp and much less pallid than he was used to seeing it. The color gave those gray-blue eyes a kinder setting and a welcome glisten. "Now you," she said, putting the shock of the fall behind her. "What is it Harvard '34 is serious about? I can't tell if it's everything or nothing."

"Me? Oh, you know—money—power—fame—lust—the usual young-man things in a free-enterprise society."

"My God," she said gravely, "don't tell me—you're a communist!"

"Not exactly."

"What, exactly—a socialist?"

"How about an anticommunist? Also, antifascist, antiroyalist, antibourgeois, anticolonialist, antiwar, anti- —"

"Good Christ, an anarchist! That's even worse."

"No, definitely not that."

"Then what? If you're poor and smart and not religious, you've got to be some sort of radical."

"Your father would say if I'm really smart, I won't stay poor."

Temple sighed. "For a moment, I thought you weren't really a Leftist."

"Think what you want, but I don't happen to operate on those terms anymore. Why do I need a label?"

"If you believe in things—"

"I believe in a lot of things—some of them highly contradictory."

"For instance?"

"Does it matter?"

"If you think it does."

"And what would that prove?"

"I'm not sure—until I know what it is. You're quite mysterious, you know."

"Just guarded."

"I suppose you have your reasons—and I'm not one to pry."

"I've noticed. Is that good manners or indifference?"

"Oh, my," she said, tugging her cap off and giving her hair a shake.

"You're not exactly bursting with self-confidence, are you?" Her eyes skidded past his. "I care," she said, "all right? Now tell me some of those contradictory things you believe in."

"I wouldn't know where to begin."

"Begin anywhere."

"Liberty and justice, okay?"

"Oh? What's wrong with them?"

"Nothing—except that given human nature, they're probably mutually incompatible."

"I'm not sure I follow that."

"I'm not surprised."

"Don't sneer at me, Toby—I'm not a fool by a long shot."

"Then you think about it."

"I will—once you enlighten me."

"Free men tend to seek their own advantage—of wealth—or power —or position. Mastery is their life's mission. Justice is what saints and weaklings cry out for."

She said nothing for a moment, then merely, "I see."

"I doubt it."

"Well, that *is* rather pat—and a terribly broad indictment of humanity, wouldn't you admit?"

"Sad but true."

"Aren't you confusing liberty and license? Isn't there a moral element in real freedom that you're omitting—a concern for your neighbor's well-being?"

"I hadn't heard about that—not in America. I think you're confusing it with Christianity. Charity here is conscience money, not a civic obligation. The only thing success breeds is contempt for failure."

"You mean genuine compassion is the exclusive province of the under classes?"

"I wouldn't go quite that far. But it's the tendency, certainly."

"That's horrid," she said.

"Perhaps. But it's not love that makes the world go 'round."

"And what would you substitute for liberty—benevolent despotism?"

"Look, why don't we just drop it? I'd rather not argue politics with you if you don't mind."

"You mean I'm only my father's daughter?"

"I mean there's no point going into it with people who already have their minds made up."

"You're the one who seems all decided about everything."

"It's just the opposite. I've decided not to decide."

"I don't understand you—not at all—unless you're toying with me again, in which case I'm not at all appreciative."

"I'm entirely serious. It's quite simple, really. I'm for all the virtues —just like you. Liberty, equality, fraternity—hoorah! Truth—beauty —justice—three cheers and a puppydog. Faith, hope, charity—strawberry sundaes in every porringer, even—you name it, I'm for it. And who isn't? That's the problem, don't you see? Every party claims a monopoly on virtue, so what point is there in taking sides?"

Her high forehead grew agitated. "What are you saying—because all social philosophies present themselves as revealed wisdom, they're all equally invalid?"

"That's pretty close to it—yes."

"That's beneath your intelligence, Toby."

"I don't think so—not when everything can change overnight— leaders—loyalties—doctrine—slogans—strategy—friends and enemies. It's all a big, lousy game—and games aren't worth dying for."

"But being neutral is nothing. It's—giving up."

"I didn't say I was neutral. I'll take a stand when there's a reason to —but not out of blind allegiance."

"But there's *always* a reason to take a stand—always a lesser evil."

"Today's lesser evil is tomorrow's total disaster. That's why I won't make any commitments—except to myself."

"But alone, everyone is powerless—a crank, more or less, really."

"Alone is what you are, though, really. Taking sides or joining a party is just to hide the fact."

She thought about that for a moment. "You sound as if you've been through some things—and suffered some wounds."

"A few. Nothing epic."

She searched his face for a further clue, but he was not ready for wholesale disclosures—not on the downward slope of a mountainside with an injured companion. "Well," she said, reconciled to his reticence, "they seem to be healing nicely in our good Berkshire air, as Father calls it. Now let's just hope my ankle does."

He helped her up slowly. After a wince or two, she decided it was not broken and said she could get down to the car if he didn't mind her leaning on him. There was not a lot of bulk to her, he could feel as she looped an arm around his shoulder and he encircled her waist with one of his. On impulse he took advantage of that linked pose to brush a kiss across her small, shrewd mouth—more of a good-luck wish than a furtive flick of ardor. Her response was not virginal. They hung together a nice, moist moment. She may have lacked density but there was depth there—and the hint of more warmth than he had supposed.

IV

Thursday, Oct. 25, '35

Everyone waiting vulturishly for midnight when David Schumacher is going up to the pond to fetch a sack of grunion, leave them in a washtub at the rear of the mess, and then sneak back into C Barracks. David does not know that (a) the grunion never was, and (b) the captain himself will be among his welcoming party.

For insertion in my Berkshire Bestiary: The Grunion (as described to David) is a suicidal little fish, silver with blue striations on its sides, ranging from five to eight inches in length, and virtually transparent—some would even say invisible. Their unique characteristic is an irresistible urge, when crooned to beguilingly enough after midnight, to jump up out of the water en masse and wriggle around the shore just waiting to be gathered up by the armful. They have a strong but highly palatable flavor, said to be tunalike.

Have been debating for 24 hrs whether to spare David this misadventure or let them keep abusing his spongy hide till it toughens. I'm not sure he can endure the transformation. . . .

There was no way to overlook him when he arrived.

Two or three others in the pack of eighty or so boys who came at the start of the new enlistment period were on the plump side, but he was the only one wearing brown corduroy knickers. They might as well have had "Kick Me" stitched across the buttocks, for if ever anyone was conceived as the perfect mark for barracks bullying, David Schumacher was it.

Link Salter, at least, had a certain litheness of person and attracted some sympathy for having been born into his unfortunate race. Besides, Joe Calabrese was ready to tear off the head of any man who abused the black boy. But David Schumacher possessed neither defenders nor natural qualities likely to enhance his safety. His record said he was seventeen, stood five-feet-six, and weighed 195 pounds. He looked shorter and heavier. His skin was of such a milky whiteness that it resembled a pickled specimen of albino locked away in the cabinet of some mad Mendelian geneticist. He wore his long sandy hair parted in the middle and slicked fiercely down with pomaded sludge that made it nearly brittle. There was only down on his ample cheeks and, except for occasional oscillation between a lingering, roughened soprano and a marginally male alto, no other sign of pubescence.

The staff, sniffing trouble, read his file with uneasiness. The youngest in a Quincy family of five children, he was an authentic victim of poverty and, more arguably, illness. His father, a sailor, had contracted an exotic disease in the Far East and succumbed several years earlier, leaving his widow only a pittance of a pension. The woman hired herself out as a housemaid till turning sickly herself from overwork. Although the other children pitched in with what earnings they could scrape together in the midst of the depression, the family was barely getting by, and there were no relatives who could help. David's roundness, belying this record of deprivation, was attributed to a glandular condition, apparently unrelated to his daily food intake, and a mild case of asthma, which apparently discouraged much physical exertion. The idea was that both conditions would benefit from six months, or longer if the boy could cope, in the bracing forest environment. In short, he was a rare species—a pampered pauper. "Little Lord Fatleroy," remarked Mitchell Nesbit after reviewing David's folder within range of his orderly; minutes later, the searing sobriquet was abroad in the woods.

David's mother, with the best of intentions, did not help. There was a little something for him every day in the mail—a letter, a postal card, or a small packet of candy bars, which he was obliged to share, notwithstanding his protest that sweets were unconnected to his weight problem. Early on, reports circulated that he might be a eunuch—no one could say for sure because he hated disrobing in public view and made a point of using the showers when no one else was there. One night after supper, a group of doubting bunkmates trailed him into the wash-up and had a good look. Even then, given the suspiciously mammalian fleshiness of his chest and the overhang of belly that threw his pelvic region into shadow, David's gender remained debatable. "If he's got one," Bingo Barnes wondered, "how's he find it under all that?"

Toby's dealings with David Schumacher began midway into his second week at the camp. In the half an hour between mail call and evening lineup, Toby usually went off by himself into a little glen above the camp and flipped through the organization cards for that night's classes—just in case problems arose or one of his instructors was suddenly incapacitated. On this particular day, instead of tranquility he encountered David Schumacher scuttling about with a baseball bat in his starfish hands and cooing, "Here, kitty-kitty-kitty!"

Disaffection for cats made Toby hang back a moment in unseen witness. But the only darting fur in view belonged to the band of squirrels who inhabited that corner of the forest and were Toby's nightly company. A few clumsy, halfhearted lunges revealed that the squirrels were in fact David's quarry and he simply did not know what else to call them. With suppressed hilarity, Toby watched the galumphing hunter flail his bat after those bushy targets who seemed to delight in scurrying just out of reach—or between his legs, which amounted to the same thing. He looked every inept inch the model for the proverbial marksman unable to hit the broad side of a barn door.

"What's the problem?" Toby asked, breaking in on the fat boy's frenzied swipes.

"Oh," he said, perspiration ringing his stubby neck, "nothin', sir."

"Looks like a lot of effort for nothing."

He seemed to welcome the respite. "Yes, sir—they're very fast."

"Is there a revenge motive here?"

He put the bat down and caught his breath. "Excuse me, sir?"

"I mean did one of them do something to you?"

"One of who, sir?"

"The squirrels, David, the squirrels. You seem to have it in for them."

He threw a puffy sigh. "Not really, sir."

"Then what's all the action for—or shouldn't I ask?"

The small, watchful eyes floated free in his pudding face. "I'm not 'aspozta say, sir."

"Some sort of initiation ritual, is it?"

The eyelids drooped. "Sorta."

"And what are you supposed to do with your victim—wear him for a winter cap or something?"

"No, sir—eat it."

"Where—here?"

"No, sir. I gotta bring it to the cook an' skin it. Then he fixes it up for my supper. After that, I'm an official forester."

"How come I haven't seen any of the other new fellows eating squirrel for supper?"

"Oh, they do. The cook fixes it nice an' brown so you can't tell what it is wit' the gravy an' stuff on it."

"If you can't tell, how can they?"

"Who, sir?"

"Whoever's making you do this."

"I gotta show 'em the tail first."

"Show who?"

"I—I'm not 'aspozta say."

"Or what happens?"

His lips bunched up. "I'll get it—for tellin'."

"You haven't told anything, David. I found you out here trying to clobber some poor squirrel."

He nodded a few times, considering that version, and then took on as resolved a look as a bowl of mashed potatoes can. "I gotta do it," he said, "or they won't leave me alone."

Toby tried to relieve him of the bat, but he clenched it closer to him, repeated that he had to get a squirrel, and asked please to be left alone. It was perfectly plain to both of them that the feat was beyond David's powers, but a wave of desperation swept through him, and he spun away from his interrogator. Toby, seeing the boy's anguish, promised to help if David would tell him what sort of travail he was undergoing—without the names of the perpetrators. Given his options at the moment, and then exacting a promise that the whole thing would remain secret, he told.

"They nailed my shoe to the floor the first night—an' the next they did the other. An' then they put dog crap in 'em. An' then they all pissed in 'em. An' now they short-sheet my bed all the time—an' steal my towel—an' knot up all my clothes—an' rub toothpaste in my pillow—an' read my letters all over the barracks—an' take everything my Ma sends me—an' call me names—that I'm fat an' a fairy an' a lily-liver an'—" His face sank lower and lower as he reeled off the atrocities, but when he looked back up, there were no tears of self-pity showing.

Toby put a hand on his shoulder. "They're just testing you, David."

"But when's it gonna stop? I didn't do nothin' to them."

Beyond the ceaseless taunting, he confessed to a feeling of profound bewilderment about the camp. It was all so strange and disorienting—the endless whistles and bells and bugle calls, so many new faces and names to go with them, the rules to remember and places to keep straight, the foul language and the ill-fitting clothes and the food being flung at you, and the crushing lack of privacy, even on the toilet. For all that, he said he wanted badly to stay on and make the grade—if only they would quit picking on him.

"If you kill a squirrel, though, just because they tell you to, they'll think of something else for you to do next as the price for leaving you alone."

"They said they wouldn't! They said this was my test of courage—an' everything would be okay after."

"You'll show more courage if you refuse to do their bidding, David."

His face flushed, and his eyes filled. "You said you'd help!" he cried.

"Killing a squirrel for them is not helping you, David."

"But you said!"

He turned his back and began to whimper. It was hard to say where Toby's sudden anger was directed—at this jelly-belly boy, at the unfathomable cruelty of youth, or at his own self-appointed membership in the Sacred Order of the Bleeding Heart. Who made him righter of the world's wrongs? Claimants to the best intentions sinned as surely as brutes performing vile acts in maniacal causes.

Toby wheeled at the peripheral flash of a squirrel. The turn startled it for a second, and it froze. Muddled fury seized control within him. His foot whipped out and connected with the small, soft body. It sailed ten feet through the air and landed stunned on its side. "Go get it!" he snarled.

David stood there gaping, the bat immobile, as the squirrel began to recover. It twitched and wriggled midway between them. Paralysis overcame the boy while he had the chance to strike. Toby glanced around, scooped up a baseball-sized rock, and advanced on the animal, upright now and moving off in a series of short, skittering turns. Its steering mechanism must have been damaged. At a dozen feet off, Toby hurled his rock. It grazed the thing enough to drop it on its back. The white underbelly beckoned. "Get it, for crissakes!" he screamed.

David took three timid steps toward the distressed animal and looked as if he wanted to pick it up for nursing.

"I said I'd help," Toby yelled. "I didn't say I'd do it for you."

He riveted on the furry casualty for a moment, then looked up and said woefully, "I can't."

"Do it! Do it, goddammit!"

Tears rolled off of him. "I never killed nothin'," David said and stood there, watering the forest floor.

Toby grabbed the bat from him and, uncertain for an instant of the preferable victim, turned it madly, blindly on the squirrel. Half the blows missed wildly. The rest, though, were plenty. The quenching of that small, harmless blob of fur and once-fleet musculature became an urgent duty, a work of wrath that turned his righteous arms into punishing cylinders and his club into an undeniable scimitar. Death to the loathsome creature! Beat it to bestial dust! At the end, his breath was hot and racing.

For a long moment, he could not contemplate his handiwork. Then, intoxicated savagery waning as quickly as it had arisen, he inspected his kill. The eyes were open in the tiny crushed head and the mouth and jaw all bloody. The belly had been split from halfway down to the anus, and raw, glittery jelly erupted.

David, lips parted, could not take his eyes off the thing till Toby handed him back the bat, its head moist red. Then he fixed the killer with a wordlessly accusing look.

"Isn't that what you wanted?" Toby asked, his voice a blade.

His mouth closed, and his lips tried to form an answer, but none came. Toby walked on past him to the edge of the copse. David still was standing motionless, the bat dangling at his side.

"Come on—pick it up."

David stood there.

Toby looked at his watch. It was nearly time for lineup. He told David that, and still he did not budge. Rage returning, Toby shouted, "Pick the fuckin' thing up and bring it back or I'll kick your fat ass in!"

One brutality fed the next. David stirred. Leaning over, knees unbending, he grasped the squirrel by the tail. The animal gave a terminal shudder, its death rattle. David screamed and let it go. Then he began to beat it with the bat. He beat it and beat it until it was a mess of raw pulp and fur by the time he was done. Toby had to take the bat away from him. He fumbled in his pockets for a scout knife he had brought along and with quaking hands severed the tail from the mangled, oozing carcass. Without another word between them, the boy hurried back to camp, tail in fist.

He did not see David Schumacher up close again for another week. His hair had been shorn in the interim at the adjutant's command and by the none too tender scissors of Murray "Boxcar" Malone, the barracks barber. His waddle, too, seemed less pronounced, or perhaps it was just that there was less of him. He had been pushing a wheelbarrow and pulling a rake out on the firebreaks, but his work output was said to be about that of an able-bodied gnat. To shape him up, stigmata were applied.

It was late morning and Toby was conferring with Ash Cummings in his office about some curriculum plans when David dragged in out of the forest. He had walked all the way in from his work detail and was breathless from the effort. "A couple of big trees are teetering," he reported between gulps, "and Mr. Bassett says could you please let me have some sky hooks fast."

Ash squinted at the boy without mercy. "Bassett said that?"

"Yes, sir." Pant-pant.

"Hell, he oughta know better."

"Excuse me"—pant—"sir?"

"We're outa 'em. They're on order. You tell Bassett he'll just have to make do with the air wedges and rat beams and no messin' around. You got that straight, son?"

"Yes, sir—air wedges and the rat beam."

"Good. Now you better giddyup back out there or we're gonna have a disaster." David nodded, heaved a small sigh, and dragged back out the door. Toby watched his squat figure retreat up the trail as fast as his columnar legs could carry him. His glance back at Ash did not hide disapproval of this wasteful form of torment. Ash shrugged. "How else you s'posed to teach the runt of the litter?"

By the end of that work day, David had been reduced to yet crueller humiliation. After lunch, he had had to move his bowels—bad. But Kevin Dundy denied him permission to leave the work crew on the ground that, as he explained later, "Everyone's gotta learn to keep a tight asshole or what good is he out there?" David's immature sphincter, alas, lacked discipline. As soon as his leader turned away, David ran off into a thicket and relieved himself. Kevin, in wait, discovered the violation and reported it to Will Bassett, who reported it to the adjutant. Abandoning his work detail without permission cost a man two weeks on K.P., David learned at the flagpole that night. There was something about the boy that invited collective sadism.

After a few days of enforced scullery, during which Sergeant Carmichael and the cook worked his puffy hands raw, David was receptive to a side-of-the-mouth proposition by the supply officer. If he would bring back a sack of grunion from Berry Pond the next night for the officers' mess, the sergeant would use his good offices to have David's sentence reduced. He would even arrange for a bike belonging to one of the Lems to be put at David's disposal for getting up to the pond and back. As to the grunion-gathering itself, Carmichael said the fish were known to be partial to, among other high-spirited ballads, "She'll Be Comin' Around the Mountain When She Comes." And the best way to scoop them up was to hold your flashlight in your mouth and the sack in one hand while brushing in the fish with the free one.

As word spread that he had taken the bait, the whole camp wagered on whether David would squeal that Carmichael had put him up to it when he got back from the pond and met his horrific fate. If he ratted, another week would be added to his K.P. for breaking curfew; if not, he would be given a stiff reprimand but freed forthwith from the kitchen.

All day Toby considered whether to tip David off on the ruse. Part of him argued that if the degradation arising from revealed gullibility is great enough, its sufferer will gain heavily in character—and henceforth be cured. Yet what was that train of thinking but a license to flay the objects of our hatefulness for not having the strength or adroitness to avoid our persecution in the first place? Complicating David Schumacher's case beyond the fact that he was a misfit from the start—a round peg in a square hole, so to speak—was the suspicion Toby nursed that the boy had been sent as a trial to his oppressors. There could be no other reason for this orgy of victimization. He said nothing to him.

More than that, he joined the throng that piled into the post-midnight darkness of C Barracks to await the return of the rodless angler. Circumnavigating the enrollee on guard duty at the camp gate (who, at any rate, had been instructed not to challenge the mock-heroic cyclist, however loud he clanked), David could be expected to take the better part of an hour churning up the mountain road to the pond, perhaps half an hour trying to coax the grunion from the brineless deep, and twenty minutes or so coming down empty-sacked. Having set out shortly after the captain's regular eleven o'clock bed check of the barracks, he was due back around one. A couple of pickets were put out to flash word of his approach so all would be silence on the truant's return.

By one-thirty, there was still no sign of him. By quarter to two, apprehension grew that he had fallen in the pond looking for grunion. By two, there was talk of organizing a search party. At two-ten, though, his roundness reappeared at last, weaving none too steadily down the road, across to the back trail, and noisily onto the camp's gravel street. An undercover agent he would never make. Lithe as a baby brontosaurus, he lifted the barracks window nearest his bunk and climbed in painfully over the sill. A hundred breathless spectators huddled in the dark, sides about to split.

David hovered by his bed a moment, sensing peril. In another instant, he saw there was someone lying in the bed. Someone large. Suddenly that prone form flashed a light in his eyes. "Good evening, Mr. Schumacher," said the captain. "Out shopping?"

A sharp expulsion of tailwind was David's first response. His faulty plumbing again. The barracks walls nearly exploded from the muffled glee. David's normally puttylike face was a rigid mask. He stood there embalmed with dread, a circle of accusing light playing upon his gaped mouth.

"Come, come, Mr. Schumacher—where have you been?" the captain asked quietly, still from his horizontal position.

There was no response.

"The toilet, perhaps?"

The obvious alibi. "Uh, uh, uh—yes, sir," came the ragged whisper.

"'Yes, sir,' is it? Quite an extended visit, don't you think? And a most unusual form of re-entry. Have you something against doors?"

"Uh, no—no, sir."

"Better come clean, Schumacher—it's your only hope."

"Yes, sir." His parched throat rattled. "I was—fishing."

"Fishing—at this hour? Without a rod? The truth, Schumacher, the truth!"

"It *is* the truth, sir!" The voice was cracked and desperate.

"Very well, Schumacher. And why, pray tell, were you fishing at this ungodly hour?"

"That's the—only time to catch them—sir."

"Really? I've always thought fish lived in the water 'round the clock. Mine do. Is this some special breed?"

"Uh—yes, sir—very special. The grunion, sir."

"Grunion? Grunion, you say? Never heard of it. I suppose it jumps up out of the water at you if you sing to it."

"Uh, uh—yes, sir! That's just what I heard."

"Heard? Who from?"

A monolithic pause. Then: "I—don't—exactly remember anymore."

"I see. And did you catch any of these—so-called grunion?"

"No, sir."

A spell of frigid silence followed as David tried to squint away the glare. Then, with steel in his delivery, the captain demanded, "Do you expect me to believe a fish story like this, Schumacher? If someone put you up to this flagrant violation of camp rules, I strongly suggest you owe it to yourself to come clean. Otherwise, you'll have to accept the consequences."

The stillness was overwhelming. The boy's lids were fastened, no doubt in prayer. Expectation grew exponentially. Finally, David opened his mouth. The words crept out barely above a whisper, but in that electric hush, carried perfectly: "It was—all my idea, sir."

Three forty-watt bulbs jumped on overhead, and the flimsy wallboard dwelling rocked with cheers. At which point, David's bladder let go entirely.

For a week, he stopped being everybody's favorite butt. In his eagerness to gain full acceptance, though, he laid himself open to renewed abuse as a natural buoyancy flowed through the barracks upon the arrival of payday.

Ivan Stubbs, who had been switched to C Barracks at the beginning of the new enlistment period on the theory that Kevin Dundy was more likely than any other leader to keep Wolfbait in line, ran the hottest card game in camp. He had a reputation for cleaning out every sucker who wandered into his web—and then sticking it to the sharps as well. Wolfbait, spotting a sizable morsel in the eager-to-please David, lured him into a game with other novices, let them each win a few hands, and then polished off the lot one by one. David he let go in the hole with him, agreeing to double-or-nothing hands that Wolfbait insisted eventually had to get his victim off the hook. After five dizzying losses in a row, David was seventy dollars in arrears and consigned to permanent peonage.

Toby learned of his newly reduced station on seeing David shimmy off to the laundry one dusk under a double load. Guarded inquiry of Eddie Spain disclosed that David was paying off the gambling debt by tending to Wolfbait's wash, shoes, bunk, cleanup detail, letter writing, and any other errand it moved him to assign his lackey. Toby thought the arrangement inhumane and wondered why no one else did. "The code of the camp," he was told by no one less than the adjutant.

"But I thought gambling was forbidden in the camp."

"They can gamble if I don't know about it," Lieutenant Nesbit explained.

"But you do know about it."

"I know what I want to know." Card playing, Nesbit confided, had both a recreational and educational value. It allowed the men to blow off steam harmlessly around payday, and it taught the losers they were fools to toss away their hard-earned allowances. "Besides, it's better than their going into town and paying for a case of clap."

Then why, Toby asked, proscribe gambling in the first place?

"So they can think they're getting away with something."

David's plight moved him enough to carry an appeal to the trenches. He asked Kevin Dundy why he had let Wolfbait run up the score so badly. The nostrils in the barracks leader's skewed nose dilated at the challenge to his honor. "That's his lookout," he said of David's sullied innocence, "not mine. All I care is there's no cheatin'—the rest is each man for hisself."

Skeezix Bloomgarden snorted at the reported exchange. "That's a laugh. Everybody knows Wolfbait'd cheat his old lady if it meant winnin' a pot." As the company clerk who ran the canteen every night, Skeezix knew whereof he spoke. He had sold Wolfbait half a dozen identically patterned packs of G.I. playing cards. The hustler kept a batch of extra face cards in his right-hand pocket and aces, deuces, and treys in his left, for use as needed. This underhanded provision made him unbeatable at blackjack and hardly less formidable at poker. And there was no way to prove that his palmed additives were crooked since they were indistinguishable from the rest of the deck.

Then why did Dundy let him get away with it?

"Figure it out," Skeezix said, reluctantly teaching the teacher. "First off, it's no skin off his ass. Second, it's Wolfbait's payoff for not givin' him much trouble. Third, it's Kevin's club over 'im. So who cares if Fatleroy gets taken? Live 'n' learn."

That struck Toby as beyond any tolerable code of the camp. He urged Nesbit to have a word with Dundy. Nesbit urged him to mind his own business. "Open approval of moral corruption falls within the province of the camp educational advisor," Toby announced without citing temporal authority and said he would have no choice but to take the matter to the captain.

To preserve pretenses, it was all handled through Sergeant Carmichael. Word was passed to Wolfbait to lay off the fix, or else. Assuming David to have been the stoolie in hopes of getting his debt excused, Wolfbait dragged him out behind the barracks that night just before lights-out and began to beat him unmercifully. Only the speedy arrival of Link Salter, Joe Calabrese, and Boxcar Malone interrupted the maiming.

At three that morning, Toby heard the officers being awakened and joined them in a dash to C Barracks. David Schumacher had his head out the window, gasping for air. His terror-stricken face filled them all with momentary panic. The eyes bulged, the veins stood out in his forehead, perspiration beaded his cheeks, and his whole frame shuddered with irregular paroxysms of whistling breath. Dundy and the adjutant wrapped the suffering body in a blanket and rushed it to the infirmary. The captain rang up Dr. Haseltine, who arrived within fifteen minutes.

"Chest distended—diaphragm immobile—hypertrophy of the bronchial smooth muscle—increased amounts of tenacious sputum producing wheezing," the doctor recited as he examined the panting boy. "He's hyperventilating—it's an asthma attack."

"How serious is it?" Sparhawk asked with a flurry of blinks.

"We'll have to see."

With great difficulty, David told the doctor he had no allergies, the commonest cause of the disease. Further examination indicated no respiratory infection. "It's probably idiopathic," said the doctor, "and psychophysiological—he may just be reacting to some sort of stress he's undergone."

Dundy was summoned and confirmed there had been a short scuffle involving David. "With him," Haseltine noted, "short is long enough."

In an hour the worst was over. David was exhausted from battling the sudden constriction of his air passages but otherwise showed no lingering effects. By morning, he appeared entirely normal. Sparhawk, however, was shaken by the episode and pushed Haseltine to rule the boy unfit for further service at the camp. "He doesn't contribute much as it is," said the captain, "and we're not operating a health spa."

The doctor re-examined David and found everything in order. "In mild asthmatics, pulmonary function tends to be quite normal between attacks," he advised, "and, after all, this one was not exactly self-induced. The boy's no invalid, and all that discharging him will do is feed any fears he has on that score."

Feeling responsible for the chain of events that resulted in the seizure, Toby added his voice to the doctor's. Might not David himself, he suggested, be asked how he felt about staying on?

Sparhawk balked at that. "It's not his choice to make. We just can't have somebody up and die on us. If the boy's fragile, he's got no business in the C.C.C."

"A lot of them are fragile when they join," Toby said.

"Not like this."

Exactly why David Schumacher's condition on this earth should have mattered to him especially, Toby was unsure. The boy was ungainly. He was not very bright. He was pathetically fearful. And he did almost everything badly. But he never betrayed his tormentors, despite all the provocation in the world, and that redeemed a lot. "If you let him stay," he told the captain, "I'll make his health my personal responsibility."

"Only God," said Sparhawk, "can do that."

"And not always well," added the doctor.

On the understanding that further complications would doom him to swift discharge, the runt of the litter became Toby's ward.

TEN

Debuted as teacher tonight. No curtain calls, or rotten tomatoes, either, so far, but the show's just begun. Hoping for minimal att. & crit, while I get hang of it. Capt. & adjutant preoccupied with own courses (though Ackermann, Sparhawk's orderly, is on hand to spy).

Go-ahead granted in view of my calling it a class in "Self-Expression" instead of English (cf. C.E.A. Handbook's first of six "dominant aims" of ed. program: "To develop in each man his powers of self-expression . . ."). The word "grammar" is never to cross my lips. . . .

"EXPRESSING YOURSELF in clean, clear, correct language," he began Lesson One, "is not unmanly. People with brains will respect you for it and listen to what you have to say. People without them will resent it only because they feel inadequate themselves." He paused to let that sink in, then looked over at Skeezix. "What's that mean, Bloomgarden?"

"What?"

"What I just said."

His prize pupil. The other boys respected him as much as they did Dundy but showed it in different ways. He had come because Toby asked him to. "It means if you talk nice, not everyone'll think you're a fag."

"What was wrong with what Bloomgarden just said?"

"He should-uh—should-uh—he was s'posed to say 'talk *nicely*,' " Eddie Spain said.

"Yeah, talk *nicely*, Skeezix!" someone called out.

"Hebes talk backwards—like they write!" someone else yelled.

"Shit on you!" Skeezix shot back.

"And what's wrong with what Bloomgarden said just now?" Toby asked.

" 'Shit' is slang," said Joe Calabrese. "Very crude and low-class."

"Yeah—talk *nicely*, Skeezix!"

Bloomgarden clamped his mouth tight while Toby shushed the heckling and called their immediate attention to the sentence on top of the mimeographed sheet each of them had been given: *Me and him wasn't doin' nothin'.* He asked if it was a good or bad sentence.

"Bad!" they chorused. "Dumb!" "Crude!" "Low-class!" "Not nicely!"

He called on Barnes to say what specifically was wrong with it. Bingo studied the words closely for a moment. "He can't read diddlysquat," a voice behind him said.

Barnes spun around. "Who the fuck says?"

"Crude!" "Lewd!" "Talk *nicely*, Bingo!"

He returned gloweringly to the page. "It should begin 'Him and me,' " Bingo said. There were snickers. Toby asked him why. "It's politer to put the other person first."

"More polite, you mean."

"Yeah."

"Okay, that's something. What else—Salter?"

"Shouldn' it be 'He and me'?" Link ventured. "On accounta 'him' is no proper beginnin' word?"

By the second lesson, he began work on vocabulary, calling it instead their "word supply." They did five new ones every lesson, fondling each long enough to learn how to say it, spell it, and use it. There was always one hard word in the batch, starting that first time with "hypocrite." Kevin Dundy, no ninny, pronounced it as if rhymed with "type-o-write." He was corrected and asked to define the word. "A hypocrite," he said, "is an enrollee who comes to class with a smile."

The aim of the course was to get them to put their new knowledge to work as promptly, practically, and painlessly as possible. That meant letter writing. Most of them wrote home, anyway, or to somebody, at least irregularly, and the chance to show off their freshly acquired gift of expression was irresistible. Toby urged them to try writing about some aspect of their camp experience with vividness and specificity—friends, food, their jobs, the Berkshires as the seasons changed, how they felt. "English is the richest language in the world," he drummed, "and it's yours completely free." There were no folk poets among them, but with encouragement, their pens and pencils flowed. In class, he asked them to describe the trees they worked beneath every day.

"Which trees?" Bingo wondered.

"Any of them," Toby said, "or all of them."

"Big." "Gigantic." "Beautiful." "Peaceful." "Green." "Shady."

He explained the difference between literal and figurative description, told them what metaphor was, and asked them to try again.

"Mighty," said Ackermann, Sparhawk's boy.

"Tow-uh, tow-uh—they're towering," Eddie got out.

"That's better, but let loose now—imagine!"

"They're holy," Joe said.

"Why that?"

"I don't know exactly. They're like a church, sorta—so huge—and hushed, ya know—and—and eternal, like. They make you feel so—so—"

"Puny?"

"Yeah, that's it—puny."

"Is that what you feel in church?"

"Sometimes. But good, too, ya know—and clean. Same in the woods."

"Good. Now spell 'puny.'"

When he proposed that they each write a letter to President Roosevelt, telling how the C.C.C. had affected their lives, they were intimidated enough to advise him, with unanimity, it was a stupid idea. F.D.R. had too much else to worry about besides reading dumb letters from semiliterate mugs in a Massachusetts forest. Maybe, Toby said, but according to current legend, the President himself had conceived of the C.C.C. Besides, he had had to overcome his own handicap, just as they were doing, and would understand their problems and be eager to learn how this pet program of his may have helped them along.

They all wrote something. Despair and hope vied in every fractured sentence. He went over the letters with them word by word, suggesting revisions; after all, they didn't write the President every day—and surely they didn't want him to think they were ignoramuses. Eddie reviewed them with special attention to spelling, punctuation, and neatness. Of the batch, Kevin Dundy's was easily the most affecting. Worked over, it read:

Dear President Roosevelt:

The winter before I joined the C's because my dad (he's a smelter) couldn't earn enough to support us, I was on relief, staying in one of the city welfare shelters. I never want to see that side of life again if I can help it. The food constipated and cramped me. The bedbugs and roaches never let me rest. The men were all crabby and worried, some turning to cheap liquor, some to begging, some to stealing and even worse vices. I could never accept shelter life anymore. I want to advance in life, not lower myself.

Here I have worked for my keep and my country. I think I have done us both some good. The pay isn't much, but I have gained in self-respect and self-discipline as well as a love of outdoors. I just hope when I leave that I can make my way.

Most of all, I want a steady job (not like my dad's) and a nice home (nothing real fancy) and the companionship of a decent woman. I am no shirker and willing to work hard. The world does not owe me anything, but I do not think it's fair to have to fight or steal to get by.

If I cannot live and love and lead a happy, healthy life, then God help me and forgive me if I degrade myself. And God help America to be a better place.

Thank you for everything you are trying to do.

Toby fastened a clasp to the whole bunch and affixed a short note, explaining the origin of the group correspondence and calling special attention to Dundy's letter and his fine record at the camp. Eddie chased down an envelope big enough to hold the lot and painstakingly addressed it to 1600 Pennsylvania Avenue, making sure the return address was printed large and clear in the corner.

Not only did the President of the United States direct a letter three weeks later to one Kevin Dundy, commending him on his character and efforts and asking him to thank his campmates for their devoted labors, but someone at the White House sent a copy of the exchange of letters to *Happy Days*, the national C.C.C. weekly, which printed them in a box at the top of the second page. Letters of congratulation to Sparhawk followed from corps area and district headquarters. This time he shared them with his educational advisor over a stout belt of brandy. All the man craved, Toby thought then, was a nod or two of recognition.

Determined to capitalize on his rising stock with the captain while the market lasted, he asked to start up a camp newspaper. A lot of camps had them. Putting as many of the boys' names in print as possible would bolster morale, he contended. Mailed home, such a paper would cheer parents and give them a better sense of camp life. Sent to corps area and district headquarters, it would serve as testimony to the camp's high spirit, put the best possible face on its activities, and help in the drive for an improved standing. Not entirely incidentally, it would be a logical outgrowth of his class in "Self-Expression" and give the men the thrill of seeing their work published.

The Lulu Bell was not destined to win Pulitzer Prizes. But considering the level of literacy among its staff, it was a creditable, if somewhat heavily varnished rendering of camp life. Boxcar Malone did up a sketch for the masthead, depicting the curvaceous Lulu with her arms entwining a large bell cracked Liberty-style. Toby's English class contributed most of the motley contents—cheery accounts of field work in progress (under the heading "The Forest for the Trees"), barracks gossip ("Someone you might not want to double-date with is Alfie 'Rubberneck' Poteete of E Barracks—he's triple-jointed. On your guard, girls!"), reports on the new intramural basketball league ("C Barracks' Cathouse Five is paced by sharpshooting Kevin Dundy and his antique but still effective two-hand dribble . . ."), an interview with the cook ("Is it true your last job was as a chimney sweep?"), impressionistic pieces on local flora and fauna ("Pickles, the Pride of the Pittsfield Forest"), and even a poem or two, metrically impure but unabashedly felt. The captain added a brief yet turgid message on the need to stay fit and moral; Ash Cummings, a couple of salty paragraphs on the use of tools and the lore of the woods, and Toby, a *pensée*-of-the-week from sages past and present.

It went fine until the third issue when a short humor column edited by Eddie and Bingo, those inimitable masters of jest, was introduced. A part of it labeled "Useful Hints for New Peavies" began:

1. If your clothes are too big, just ask Leader Dundy to have his friend the President send over the White House tailor.
2. Overwork is unpatriotic. Stay in shape by resting two hours for every 15 minutes you log on the job.
3. When you're running late for a date in town, tell the Captain you'd like to borrow his car . . .

This uproarious stuff failed to reach Sparhawk's funnybone. "Unconstructive and unnecessary," he snapped. When Toby tried to dismiss it as innocent clowning, the captain said, "I decide what's innocent around here," and ordered the text of the entire paper to be submitted for his approval before cutting the stencils from then on.

In the hope he would soon weary of surveillance, Toby made sure his quixotic censor had slim pickings in the next issue. But the week after, their first and only real news story broke. While Joe Calabrese was working over one of the trucks in the service garage, static electricity caused a bucket of gasoline to burst into flame beside him. Tearing off his burning shirt, Joe had the presence to shut off the valve on a 900-gallon gas drum, drive the truck out of the shed, and then summon everyone else on the camp detail to help him put out the blaze. If he had not acted rapidly and courageously, the whole camp might have gone up—and the forest with it.

It was a perfect incident for teaching his students how to put together a news story—full of action, color, and heroism. Everyone took a hand in gathering the details, interviewing Joe and the others involved, even doing a sidebar on the camp's fire-fighting preparedness. Toby pulled all the pieces together, trying to incorporate at least a little of the language of every contributor in the finished story, to which the entire front page was devoted. At the end, they all shared in the sense of accomplishment—until Sparhawk killed the whole thing.

"It makes the camp look bad," he said, pinching fishfood into the bowl beside his desk. "The first question to occur to me as I read your story is how come our safety standards were so lax."

Toby pointed out that the story went into that and concluded it was just a freak accident that could have happened anywhere anytime. But the captain found that unpersuasive. And beyond planting the suspicion at district headquarters that Camp 127 had poor fire-hazard surveillance, the story would unduly alarm enrollees' parents. He was also uneasy about turning Calabrese into an unalloyed hero—Joe was already singled out from the rest by privileges extended to him. The possibility existed, furthermore, that he had caused the fire himself by smoking too near the gas bucket or some other careless act. And since Toby's class members had already derived full benefit from the writing exercise, Sparhawk concluded, no good reason remained to run the story.

"Except that it's supposed to be a camp newspaper—and this is the biggest news story we'll probably ever have."

"Well," said the captain, "it's not exactly a newspaper, now, is it? Let's be honest, Ronan—it's more or less of a propaganda vehicle."

"I prefer not to think of it like that."

He poked a pencil down the goldfish bowl to rouse its inhabitants. They remained barricaded in their little porcelain castle. "No," he said, "I suppose not. But the commanding officer is entitled to his opinion."

That was his final word, he made clear by pursuing his fish with such determination that Toby thought he might be trying to spear one for lunch. "With all due respect, sir," he said, "you're putting me in an untenable position with the men."

"Am I?" Sparhawk's arm was in the bowl practically up to the elbow.

"I've lectured them at some length on the meaning of a free press in a democracy. There can't be any further pretense after this that our paper has any integrity—or that my judgment of what's printable means anything at all."

"It seems to me that you're the one who's put yourself in whatever position you think you're in. The newspaper was your idea, Ronan—not mine. We were doing nicely without it."

"Or me," Toby said. "Is that your point—sir?"

The captain drew his face away from the evasive prey in the bowl and looked up at Toby kindly, as if he were by far the lesser irritant. "Where did you get that idea? You're the best C.E.A. we've had here."

"Then I want to run that article, sir."

It was too crude a gambit, too nakedly combative. Sparhawk took out a handkerchief and dried off his hands from the underwater expedition. "I'm afraid you're not going to. Sometimes a subordinate has to accept orders he thoroughly disapproves of—I've had my share. But everyone can't be a chief." He folded his arms across his chest. "I can understand your disappointment, Ronan—it's a tribute to your dedication. But this crisis will pass—these boys have short memories. Now you explain it to them any way you'd like and I'll—"

"I deeply resent this, sir."

"—be glad to play the fall guy."

"I find it personally humiliating and professionally very—"

"I've been thinking, Ronan—considering your responsibilities around here—it's time you had an office for yourself. You need a desk —room for your assistant—space for the mimeograph and supplies. I'll have Sergeant Carmichael fix you up in the front part of the supply shed—and we'll pick up a couple of desks in town. And don't you think it's about time you stopped dipping into your own pocket for the printing supplies?"

II

Thursday, Nov. 8, '35

Five years, practically, since Mother died. Seems infinitely longer. Why do I think of her so rarely? Suppressed pain from the emptiness? Not good enough. My duty to remember—what? Her calm dignity most. It, not Father's position, made us white-collar. That's gone, too. Nothing abides. Not a filament of her, not a vapor even—just a rare brain wave in the head of her only issue. Why was she taken so soon? Does it matter? Does it "matter" how long anyone lives? Or if at all? I view us as a strictly private transaction, a germinal confluence, a growth & ebb of tissue, entirely fortuitous & passing strange. Pitiful delusion to imbue cellular processes with spirituality. Marx right about that, at least.

* * *

Withering on my brain: it's the season. Will Bassett explained trees merely shut down operations by shedding leaves to lock in their water supply before frost hits. A big oak—W. sez some have up to 700,000

*leaves—can give off as much as a couple of thou. gallons a day. Oak
leaves last to appear, last to drop. Hanging on now like stubborn old
men huddled in rags.*

*   *   *

*Somebody stole Link Salter's harmonica from under his pillow
while he showered yesterday. . . .*

To make it up to him, Magowan, the rock-ribbed bugler who everyone thought had a heart of stone to match, gave Link a dented old
bugle he had brought to camp from home. To avoid seeming a senti-
mentalist, he told people the horn was good for nothing so why not
let the kid blow away his black sorrows with it. But he gave Link
some lessons, too, on breathing and tonguing and helped him forget
his hurt.

He would wander a couple of miles over the lower hills till reaching
a properly muffled hollow, where instead of studying in his time off as
he always used to, he trained his lungs and lips to coax something
fluent out of that dimpled bugle. Now and then a blare from it would
reach camp on a freak eddy of the wind. At first it sounded like a
wounded moose, then a rehearsal for a cut-rate fox hunt. But before
long, a less ragged sound bolted from the hollow, and soon it became
smooth and clean. All of which did nothing at all for his spelling and
diction but put light back in those dark, downcast eyes.

When Magowan was discharged a few Fridays later to take a job in
a bakery in Framingham, the adjutant scurried around all weekend trying to find a replacement among the enrollees. Link was the obvious,
and only, candidate—toward the end of his enlistment Magowan had
even practiced the regular camp calls with him in the woods—but
there were obstacles to his selection. It was a position of some prestige,
as camp jobs went, carrying with it an assistant leader's pay. And it
would not do to have a bugler redolent of sweat from scrubbing pots
and peeling spuds all day. Or of Link Salter's color. He was no *café-
au-lait* leftover from a white greatgrandpappy's summer dalliance; he
was a chocolate darky from deepest Dixie, the melanin of equatorial
Africa shading his every molecule—the unsightly sort the military
hardly cared to display when the right colors were being paraded.

By Sunday night, however, Lieutenant Nesbit concluded that he
had no choice for the moment and recommended to the captain that
the black boy be given the assignment, at least temporarily, when the
company reassembled the next day. Probably both officers expected
Link would be so bad that they would have to resort to blasts on the
adjutant's brass whistle until a real white bugler could be obtained.

But Link's reveille was ear-splittingly abrasive. The mess calls sounded right. The flag-raising, at which the small colored boy appeared in fatigues ironed wrinkle-free, was marred by a clinker or two but otherwise recognizable and rousing. After initial nervousness, and with benefit of a full day's authorized rehearsal in the empty Rec, he was practically rhapsodic by nightfall. His flag-lowering had a ceremonial cleanness to it; his tattoo, a mellow lilt, and taps, a reverence of nearly overflowing poignancy. No fledgling first trumpet in any philharmonic ever soloed more feelingly.

Next day, the adjutant was nowhere to be seen. The captain said only that he had gone to Boston on camp business and would return late that night. The purpose of his mission was revealed the following dawn. The camp was summoned from slumber not by Link's spirited horn but by the grating call of a phonograph record played over the p.a. Link, after two prideful days as camp bugler, was remanded to the kitchen fulltime. "More efficient this way," was the only explanation Nesbit gave. But everyone knew better.

Toby took it on himself to tell the captain that the change to a mechanical apparatus had every appearance of a racist action.

"Nonsense," Sparhawk said. "A lot of camps use records. It's more modern and reliable."

"Also unpleasant and dispiriting."

"If it's concerts you want, Ronan, buy a ticket to Carnegie Hall. And if the colored boy isn't happy with the provisions we've made for him, he's welcome to leave. They freed the slaves seventy years ago."

And had been kicking their black asses around ever since. But he did not say that to Gordon Sparhawk. He had enough battles to wage with this blinkered, blinking militant.

Link's friend, Joe Calabrese, was uninhibited by any such need to be politic. He repaid the captain's callousness that evening by stripping all the trucks of their batteries, hiding them deep in the woods, and taking off for the hills at daybreak. The work details had to proceed to their jobs on foot. Sympathetic with the protest and pitying the protester his sure fate, nobody minded much.

By noon, the captain was almost frothing blood. "This is what comes of treating a dago like a gentleman," he brayed. "He's worse than the little nigger." And what, Toby asked, had Link done wrong? Sparhawk glared at him furiously. "He claims he doesn't know where Calabrese is—or anything else about this," he said, turning away. And did the captain think the Negro was lying? "They all do—it's a habit of the race. They lie, cheat, and steal to beat the band."

"The race," said Toby, "is what we made them into."

"Spare me the sentiment, Ronan," he said, staring off through his heavily screened window. "I come from abolitionist Quaker stock on my mother's side—I know the thinking. But goodwill can't alter congenitally low character. Or maybe you think they played harps all day when they were savages in the bush?" He suggested that Toby find Calabrese on the double and bring him back by suppertime, or a dishonorable discharge and possibly a stretch in Leavenworth would follow his certain apprehension.

"Why me?"

"You're his patron. You sponsor all the troublemakers around here."

Toby found him trying to stay warm beside the fireplace at one of the camping sites the enrollees had built a little below Berry Pond. He answered Toby's hallooing readily enough but seemed uncontrite when his options were spelled out. His grudge against the captain, and the system he epitomized for Joe, had been years brewing. "King Shit," he said and spat. "He's the same pricky people my ma's been takin' in scummy sheets from for long as I can remember. 'Marblehead Quality,' she calls 'em. Well, Marblehead can come kiss Swampscott's smelly ass—tell him that for me."

"I think you already told him yourself."

He gave his large head a laughing wag. And that was how he wanted to leave it. He would try to find a job somewhere—grease monkeys could always latch on to something. Toby reminded him about finishing high school. "What's that gonna get me?" he asked, feeding fresh kindling to the fire.

"Farther than a grease monkey."

He thought some. "Maybe I could find work in Pittsfield while I'm finishin'."

"The pricky people won't let you stay in school if you quit the C's."

"How do you know?"

"They wouldn't be pricky otherwise."

He saw the point. "Okay, but I'm not gonna come back in on all fours—tell the bastid that."

The settlement he negotiated stripped Joe of his recently awarded rating as assistant leader, which hurt both his pride and pocket, and his job as Sparhawk's teaching assistant, which did neither. But he was allowed to continue attending school in town and not even assigned to the Beauty Squad on weekends—so lenient a rebuke that Toby suspected the captain's Quaker ancestors must have paid him a chastening visit during his afternoon nap.

The night following, Link Salter found a small package under his pillow as the canned version of taps affronted the tender darkness. Inside was a shiny new five-dollar harmonica, purchased out of the camp canteen's surplus that Skeezix Bloomgarden administered. A little typed note that came with the box said, "From Lulu and all your pals."

Link saved the card and the box. No one ever messed with his new harmonica.

III

Saturday, Nov. 10, '35

Took Will Bassett's sis.-in-law to St. Mary's R.C. autumn dance last night as a favor—and she's not half-bad. Her name is April Janowicz, she just turned 20, works as a telephone operator at G.E. & has excellent set of knockers (they seem to run in the family). Not exactly a mental hvyweight but expect to see more of her (and them).

P. S. We won the door prize, a Schwinn bike, which she insisted I keep since she already has one & I can use it. Got our picture in today's Eagle. . . .

Since arriving at the camp, he found that his libido had lapsed into a curiously distracted condition—garrison gonads, you could have called it. So constantly embattled did he feel that his hormonal output was diverted from stirring sexual impulses.

Not that he was consciously courting celibacy. With Temple Keyes, hardly the promiscuous sort, he had to sublimate his urges. It was harder to reject Denis Carmichael's several offers to set him up with "a sure thing" in town—part of his regular service, he stressed, to valued clients. There was no point, though, in declining Will Bassett's proposition: If Toby took his wife's sister, April, to the big church dance in town, he would lend him his car for the occasion and promise not to ask him a thing about it—or her—afterward. She might not be Miss America, Will said, but she was a fine, nice-looking, "regular" girl—which Toby took to mean neither a prude nor a tart—and the only reason he wanted to fix her up with him was that he and Trudy felt she ought to meet a higher caliber of fellow than the ones she was accustomed to seeing at the G.E. plant. "We're not snobs or anything," Will said, "but everybody wants the best for their family."

It was too high and guileless a compliment to rebuff. Besides, Toby was needy of a little "regular" companionship.

April Janowicz may not have dated many college men, but she was not shy with her first one from Harvard. If anything, she was too eager to demonstrate her indifference to the animal passions aroused on the dance floor and her fondness for what she took, and surely intended, to be cerebral chitchat. After Toby had revealed his classic lumbering footwork for three or four fox trots, she gladly drew him to the sidelines and into a running quiz designed to reveal the contours of her winning personality. Her other contours, crowded into royal-blue velveteen, he found more alluring. But these fairer charms would plainly remain inaccessible if he did not play her gauche game of comparing favorites from the popular culture.

His answers must have struck her as dishearteningly odd. When she said her favorite band was Bix Beiderbecke, Toby said his was McNamara's. Her favorite radio program, she advised, was "The First Nighter"; he went for "The Lone Ranger." In movie stars, she adored Doug Fairbanks and Ronald Colman—and hadn't he loved *A Tale for Two Cities?* He said Ben Turpin and W. C. Fields were more his speed and that he had been bored stiff by Charles Darwin's novels so could hardly be expected to attend their movie versions. Furthermore, his favorite public personality (she had picked Lindbergh) was Gerald L. K. Smith, his favorite flavor (she was for strawberry and vanilla, tied) was licorice, his favorite ball team (she was for the Braves, she said, because everyone else in town was for the Sox) was the Green Bay Packers because they needed some support in the East, and his favorite book (she alleged fondness for all the Brontes) was *Stover at Yale.* "I don't know that one," she said.

What actually interested him about her was how she found it working at General Electric. Her answers were those of an ideally pliant employee. The company was "nice," the people were "kind," and her job as a telephone operator was "quite interesting." "You can get to tell a lot about a person by the sound of his voice," she said. "You know—about his manners and background, the kind of mood he's in, how important he is—or thinks he is."

He asked what her acute ear told her about Mr. Lawrence Keyes.

"How do you know *him?*" Her tone was of obeisance tinged with distaste.

"I get around."

"Oh." The very hint that he somehow had connections to her superiors made her clam right up. "Well, he's nice enough, I suppose."

"And what can you tell about my voice?"

She stared down into her fruit punch, fortified herself with a sip, and said, "That you're bored stiff and wish you hadn't come."

That put him in his place and altered his estimate of her above the neck. She not only had feelings that his cavalier manner had succeeded in hurting but also possessed the courage to call him on the unkindness. The problem, he told her, was that she had him down wrong, that he came from no fancypants family, and she did not need to posture with him. Learning that he worked in the woods for the same reason she ran a switchboard let her relent visibly and begin to have a good time. She loved to dance, she admitted, and wished he did. She hated the news and politics, much preferred the movies—any movie—to reading—any book. And she found her job, while respectable enough, mostly pretty boring. "What you're doing seems a lot more important."

"That's what I tell myself—every time the fellows curse me."

She laughed and saw that he really had left off baiting her. By the time they announced the winning ticket for the door prize—April let out a thoroughly uninhibited shriek of joy—a warmth born of frankness was setting in. Her insistence that he have the bike bespoke a generous nature that only misplaced gallantry could have denied. He thanked her and promised to make it up to her. "You already have," she said and excused herself to go to the powder room before their picture was taken for the paper.

All during the drive to her home, his brain sizzled and fingers twitched at the nearness of April Janowicz's beautiful bursting blue breasts. They strained every fiber of their taut sheathing, not to mention his underpants. There was poetry in their very volume, swelling roundly beyond the margin of her rib cage when viewed frontally and surging in profile as perfectly conical prows. Those warm twin weights had pressed flush against him during their last dance of the evening, producing a reciprocal thrust against her abdomen. A tiny gasp escaped from her as she felt its friction and approved. Thus, his hopes were fired for the homeward trip. Why was it that Catholics had the best tits—except for nuns, which was why, of course, they were nuns—and Protestants had the best legs, even if half the pair was slightly withered? He told himself it was impossible that so pleasing and prominent an arrangement as breasts had evolved in woman solely for the occasional and short-lived purpose of giving suck. Their shape had to have been adapted to satisfy not the gaping mouths of babes— what did they know of symmetry or aesthetics?—but the full span of the adult male palm. Form followed function.

She lived up near Pontoosuc Lake. They parked a few streets away and kissed, and she let him run his famished hands over her scorching promontories a few times before pulling away in obvious regret. "It seems funny," she said, "after a church affair."

"Why—you think all that's a sin?"

"It depends—on whether you care for someone enough—"

"And if you do?"

"Then I think it's beautiful—most of it."

"Which part isn't?"

"Well, you know—it depends—whether you think it's—not just some—you know, animal act. It should be—well, natural—to be really beautiful—you know?"

"You're against birth control, you mean?"

"Well—it just seems so—mechanical—and selfish—"

"Not to mention sinful."

She studied her lap. "I just think all those devices are horrid—not just because the Church says they're wrong."

He started up the car. "Your sister evidently doesn't feel that way."

"She's married to a Congregationalist."

"Is that so bad?"

"I didn't mean that." She smoothed the top of her dress in case his heretical fingers had caused any telltale rustling of the nap. "I mean, weren't there any Catholics at Harvard?"

"Some. I roomed with one, but he wasn't very religious."

"No," she said, "I guess he wouldn't have gone there if he was. I'll bet they don't treat the religious ones very nice."

"Better than they do the Jews."

"Well," she said, "I should hope so."

It was not his only church shindig that week. The Tuesday night following, Sparhawk and he had been invited to address a few remarks about their work to the Pittsfield Symposium, a monthly gathering devoted to civic and intellectual uplift under the joint sponsorship of the very proper Berkshire Women's Club and the interdenominational church council. The site of the meetings rotated among the church parish houses, and when the Reverend Samuel Brandt's St. Thomas's-in-the-Field was the spot, Toby found himself drafted for the cause. Sparhawk declined the dubious honor but designated Nesbit in his place. The lieutenant, having scrubbed every last lichen from his personage, fairly glittered on presenting himself to the ladies. Just looking at him left Toby feeling musty, and that mannequin-trim, olive-and-khaki uniform made his own lumpish jacket, parting at the seams and elbows, seem a loan from the Salvation Army.

The symposium was a kind of endurance marathon. Two speakers shared the first half of the program, followed by an open discussion of a current book of literary repute or social significance. Nesbit and he were bracketed as a single performer; the other half of their half of the twin bill was Temple Keyes's formidable mother, who also happened to be co-chairing the event with the minister. They were kind enough to send Nesbit and him each a copy of the book up for discussion in the second half of the program—*It Can't Happen Here* by Sinclair Lewis. Dutifully, Toby sped through its four-hundred-odd pages and, while in full sympathy with its message against tyranny, found the delivery shrill and obvious. Nesbit had no such problems with it. His copy languished unread on a corner of his desk.

At the head of an assembly room, in a severe black silk suit and matching cloche, Constance Keyes conveyed an even more austerely majestic presence than in paler, kinder costume at the foot of her own dining table. Her astringent style of speech and carriage, no doubt evolved out of self-preservation over the course of her marriage, had put its stamp on her daughter, who sat two rows in front of Toby and listened with unstraying attention. The woman was a model of concise statement and unaffected elocution. By marching straight up to her subject and attacking it forthrightly, she carried her audience, even when championing a cause so apparently prosaic as the need for community support of the struggling Pleasant Valley Bird Sanctuary, of which the Keyeses were prominent benefactors.

"Birds," said she, "help to maintain the balance of nature, and any serious diminution in our bird population results in a serious increase in the ranks of our insect and vegetable foes." No argument there. But she at once struck a dire note by reporting that the birds of Massachusetts were being killed off from unnatural causes at the distressing rate of more than two million a year. The audience stirred at the news. And who was the chief villain in this grim drama? None other, charged Constance Keyes, than the household tabby. "The cat, artificially introduced, bred, and sustained in domestic comfort, does not belong to the natural scheme of things." There followed pithy data on the voracious pesticidal appetite of birds and a plea to help these winged wonders through the winter by putting out sunflower seeds and balls of suet wrapped in mesh.

His own talk was not half so instructive or well received. Nesbit, denied the celebration of war as a topic, rambled on about the variegated benefits of spartan camp life—a source of thrilling reassurance to listeners who had never experienced it and were fully prepared to settle for this vicarious savoring.

"My only quibble with your mother," Toby told Temple over coffee and cake, "is whether you can justifiably claim that birds killed by cats die of 'unnatural' causes."

He had meant it as a pleasantry, but she pounced on it. "You're playing with words. It's plain you weren't following Mother's line of thought too closely."

He had begun to tell her that he yielded to no one in his suspicion of cats when she made it clear she was more interested in meeting Mitchell Nesbit and hearing about the rigors of West Point and the concerns of the modern military mind. He left the two of them tête-à-tête and went off to compliment Mrs. Keyes.

Toward the conclusion of the program, it was natural that, Toby being a former graduate student of literature at Harvard and Nesbit an officer in the U. S. Army, their views should have been solicited on Sinclair Lewis's glum projection of America under despotic rule. Wary of excessive candor before such a crowd, Toby tried to dodge the Reverend Mr. Brandt's inquiry. The country had been on the verge of insurrection only a little while before, in the view of some, he noted. Whether the outcome might have been anarchy or despotism was anybody's guess—although one school of thought, to which he did not happen to subscribe, held that the nation was already presided over by a despot of sorts.

The clergyman brushed aside this tactful commentary. "But in the event of a still more appalling emergency, Mr. Ronan—?"

He was not to be let off with platitudes. "That's likely to depend on whether we value our liberty or our prosperity more."

"Why must it come to a choice between them? I've always harbored the impression our freedom and our faith were the sources of our wealth."

The correlation of religiosity and material plenty he declined to speculate upon, pleading that metaphysics was not his field. With the rest of the rector's equation, he said he agreed—"except that too often freedom turns into a license for greed—at which point there is neither liberty nor justice for all—only for those in a position to enforce their claims to them."

Buzzing greeted this heresy. "Meaning what, Mr. Ronan—that you think our system fatally flawed by low human character?"

"No, sir—but I think it makes greater demands on human character than any other system man has devised—and that temptation is sometimes very great—and the flesh weak. I think our ambitions perhaps need to be moderated by laws that insist on concern for our less aggressive neighbors. Otherwise, I believe the only thing left for the meek to inherit will be heaven—which might produce grave unrest down here meanwhile."

And what, the Reverend Mr. Brandt wondered, had Lieutenant Nesbit to say to all of that?

Nesbit's neat, squarish face hardened. To tell the truth, he said, his duties had not permitted him to get very far in Lewis's book as yet, but at any rate his oath of service limited his efforts to protecting national territory against foreign powers and to safeguarding the social order against domestic subversives. Taking sides in political contests or on policy questions was not the soldier's privilege.

Toby was irked by the applause this sanctimonious sidestepping earned. "But the army invariably takes sides when push comes to shove," he said. "Almost every time labor has tried to organize an industry, soldiers show up with bayonets bared."

Nesbit looked at him with disbelief as the room awoke in surprise at such ungenteel dissension. "Well," he said, "only when the mobs are out of control and the government orders troops in. It's not a personal thing."

"It's personal to the workers who get beat up and shot."

Nesbit struggled to remain soft-spoken. "They only get hurt when they threaten other people's property."

"If you want to look at it that way, the very idea of organizing for better pay is a threat to reduce someone else's property. And the very act of massing brings in the army—always on the side of industry. They don't come to protect the pickets."

Nesbit glanced at the rector in the apparent hope he would intervene. Under the obvious misapprehension that such collisions of viewpoint were what a symposium was for, Dr. Brandt missed the signal. "It seems to me," Nesbit fought back, "that if a group tries to prevent a man from making use of his own property, then they're a lawless mob and should be dispersed."

"And what is it when a company, or a whole industry, conspires to prevent a man from making use of his own body to earn a decent living?" Toby was not quite shouting. "That's inhumane as well as lawless."

"It's not inhumane," Nesbit shot back, "if nobody's making him work against his will. It's still a free country."

"His belly's making him work against his will—and so is the cold—and his children—"

"I think," said Reverend Brandt, "this is getting a little out of hand. But we thank you gentlemen for so much food for thought."

"My only quibble with you," Temple said acidly on the way out, "is that you think all soldiers are proto-fascists." She looked back over the crowd for her mother. "We'd offer you a lift," she added, eyes scanning past him, "but I understand you have a nice new bike for getting around. Do be careful on it at night."

It had not occurred to him that she would learn of his having taken April Janowicz to the St. Mary's dance—or care about it in the least. The girl was obviously not of Temple's social station, and the date had been instigated by a friend. Even if these mitigating factors did not adequately define the casualness of his involvement, the extent of his acquaintance with Temple could hardly have led either of them to claim dictatorial rights over the other's social calendar. He supposed she had other fellows calling on her. And he would surely not have taken great offense on seeing a picture of her with one in the *Eagle*,

especially at a large church function. Only on meeting the full force
of her hostility at the symposium did he understand the nature of his
sin: He had ignored the social structure of the community. Still, he
asked himself, what should he have done—advised her about the dance
ahead of time, and the innocent circumstances of his attending, and
asked her dispensation? That would have been demeaning and im-
proper. And explaining it after the fact and in view of her manifest
disapproval would have smacked of apologizing when he had done
nothing at all, really, for which to be sorry.

The depth of Temple's annoyance with him was confirmed by the
news that Mitchell Nesbit had been invited by the Keyeses to be their
supper guest the following Sunday and afterward to attend a musicale
at St. Thomas's in which Temple's ensemble was to perform. Toby
took it for an act of reprisal on her part, but its calculated nature did
not reduce the hurt, particularly since he had made a point of saying
he hoped to hear her play at the earliest opportunity. What pained
worse was that Nesbit returned from the evening full of praise for the
warmth and highmindedness of his hosts and an offer, promptly
relayed to the captain, to arrange for several dozen families in the
Pittsfield area to have two or three enrollees apiece join them for
Thanksgiving dinner. The captain, touched, was amenable.

All the boys who elected to go for an intimate glimpse of home life
among the refined class—it turned out to be nearly half the company,
necessitating a still wider effort by the Keyeses to line up enough
cooperating families—were ordered to attend a crash course in personal deportment given in place of Toby's regularly scheduled class.
"I certainly think manners qualify under the heading of 'Self-Expression,'" said the captain.

Something in Toby rebelled at playing Henry Higgins and applying
an overnight gloss to a hundred boys' underprivileged upbringing so
the social distance between them and polite society would not be
revealed by slurps of gravy on a linen tablecloth. But he followed orders and rehearsed the men on how to stand up in a living room and
how to sit down on a sofa ("Don't spread your legs like that, Bingo—
it looks like you're auctioning off the family jewels"), how to introduce themselves and hold a conversation free of four-letter words,
how to use which utensils, tip their soup bowls away from them, employ napkins modestly and not park them beside their plates or wear
them like bibs. "And don't ask for second helpings—they'll be offered
—and don't belch to convey your compliments to the chef—that
went out of style a while ago—and if you have to go to the toilet,
take careful aim and be sure to flush when you're done—this isn't the
camp latrine."

Not until Thanksgiving eve were all the logistics arranged. Almost as an afterthought, the camp officials were also invited—the captain to join Reverend Brandt at the home of his sister; Nesbit and his orderly, to the Keyeses', and Toby and any two enrollees of his choosing were to accompany Guy and Holly Curtis to her family's place in West Stockbridge. He took his unofficial wards, Eddie Spain and David Schumacher, and tried to forget that he had been pointedly excluded from the home he would have preferred to attend.

Holly Curtis was a Larrabee by birth, and the Larrabees were basically New York socialites who divided their year between the city and the Berkshires. Their country home was one of those places grand enough to have a name of its own—Nimrod it had been called since being put up as a grandiose hunting lodge toward the close of the nineteenth century. It had twenty-six rooms, each with a fireplace, honeycombing an eclectic jumble of gables, dormers, round towers, and steep roofs that once dignified itself as "the Norman Style." Every inch of the interior appeared to be occupied by the most luxurious of objects, from the Aubusson rug in the entrance hall ("It's a bit *outré*, if you ask me," said Holly) to the massive carved-oak chest in the foyer ("A genuine native artifact—pre-Revolutionary Connecticut Valley, Mother thinks") to the Flemish tapestries on the walls ("Only eighteenth-century, I'm afraid—nothing vintage") to the sixty-piece Lowestoft tea and coffee service on display in the library cabinet. Dinner was served on a Hepplewhite table ringed by authentic Duncan Phyfe chairs—"so long as you've an eye for this sort of thing," Holly threw in to complete Toby's instruction. The effect of such wall-to-wall sumptuousness was to inflict a case of permanently popped eyes on his pair of C.C.C. hardship cases.

Mrs. Larrabee, for all her blessings, was incapable of sustaining a conversation of longer than two minutes without disparaging somebody or other. Toby's presence raised Constance Keyes's name in connection with their talks at the symposium. Sniffing at the very idea of a bird sanctuary as a community necessity, Mrs. Larrabee said she suspected the entire project had less to do with benevolence toward "our feathered friends" than its sponsors' need for a new cause to occupy them. "Poor Connie," she remarked, "can't tell a yellow-throated vireo from an indigo bunting." For good measure, she directed her forked tongue at Mrs. Keyes's wardrobe: "She's got to get rid of that ghastly suit of hers—it makes her look like an aging governess out interviewing for a position—and start shopping somewhere besides *England* Brothers, for heaven's sake!"

After dinner Holly told him she had something private to say and asked that he join her for a short walk through the grounds. She guided him across a flagstone terrace the size of two tennis courts, out past a topiary garden, and down a marble-chip path rimmed in box-wood that curved among small beds of now-dormant flowers till it reached a cloister of ginko trees. On the way, they conversed gaily about the piano, which she taught laconically to some of the more pampered moppets in the county at a walk-up studio on East Street in Pittsfield—"It lets me pretend I've something to do." He told her he had toyed with the instrument since being forced to take it up in boy-hood and wished now that he had more of the knack. "Perhaps a few brush-up lessons would help," she said with a light laugh.

"Is that a solicitation?"

"Well, don't make it sound so tawdry. If we did it for nothing, my professional ethics wouldn't be sullied, would they? The damned trou-ble is I'm booked virtually solid—the price I pay for being so divine at it. You'd have to take what time there is."

The blithe mood vanished as she sat them on a wrought-iron bench and touched him affectionately on the forearm for a moment. It was not her place to tell him how to live his life, she acknowledged, but Temple was her dearest friend and so she was taking the liberty of offering him some advice "if you care for her in the least."

"Of course I care for her. There seems to be some doubt the feel-ing's mutual."

"I can't vouch for the extent of her fondness of you—you've barely met, after all. And then she's a very inward person about many things. But I can assure you she cares. Only you can't have it both ways, not in a place this tight."

"Both what ways?"

"You can't go running around town with a working girl one night and then expect to be welcomed with open arms the next at one of the finest homes in the county."

"Why, is working a crime for a girl? Temple works—you work."

"In a manner of speaking—but out of choice, not necessity. This—girl—is obviously a prole—and Catholic, at that."

"Which is worse?"

"Now don't be an ass, Toby! I know all about your flaming idealism—it's just grand as hell. But I'm talking about social realities."

"The social reality is what I told Temple from the start—I'm not nobility, and I'm not trying to pass myself off that way."

"But you're an elitist, like it or not—an aristocrat of the intellect. It's your passport to society, and who cares if you didn't make a final club at Harvard?"

"I didn't *make* anything at Harvard—except a little trouble for peo-ple who think the 'proles,' as you delightfully call them, are only fit to step on."

"I never said *that!*" She stood, recoiling with angry energy. "All I said was this girl is from a different class—and you can't consort openly with that one and still hope to present yourself in good standing on the doorstep of Temple Keyes's house."

"I see. And have you been formally deputized to deliver this swell edict—or are you translating loosely from the royal tablets?"

Her wickedly lipsticked mouth formed a slim red crescent. "You're cute," she said, "you're really very cute—and smart enough to figure that one out for yourself." Three of her strong, slender fingers strummed a chord on his shoulder. "May I make a somewhat unladylike suggestion to you, Toby?"

"Can I stop you?"

"Not for a moment," she said. "What I really think is that you have sex on your mind in seeing this April person—what else could you conceivably have in common with a girl like that? My suggestion is that if you must satisfy your cravings that way, you handle it as a straight commercial transaction—I understand the commodity is plentiful enough in town. Otherwise, you see, you're going to disqualify yourself from—well—all of us. Is that what you want?"

In the library, Everett Larrabee, Wall Street barrister, was telling Guy Curtis, his scholar son-in-law, how Sinclair Lewis had missed the real point in composing *It Can't Happen Here*, apparently the only book anyone was reading just then in Berkshire County. "It's not complacent capitalism that's going to open the gates to an American Caesar, no sir. It's your clamorous democracy—your multitudinous 'interests'—that'll reduce orderly government to a nullity."

Out of the corner of his eye, Toby spotted Eddie Spain, across the room, longingly finger a small silver matchbox.

I V

Wednesday, Nov. 28, '35

David S. has lost 17 lbs. since coming to camp but still is a butterball. Doc H. gives him a weekly checkup & finds no ill effects of asthma. Only trouble is D. has been very listless on the job of late, acc. to Will—bushed by 11 a.m. & bleary-eyed. Exam. this morn. disclosed nausea & headache as well. Sounds a little as if he's pregnant. . . .

"Or it could also be incipient alcoholism," the doctor said after David dragged out of the infirmary and moped off toward the barracks to finish cleanup.

Dr. Haseltine, Will Bassett, and Toby monitored the sluggish boy's condition closely for the following week, but there was no improvement. Mornings, after a couple of hours in the forest, he could barely lift his shovel. The loss of weight went on, giving his soft face the first lineaments of a definable shape. It began to seem possible there was even a neck somewhere under there. Yet the chronic fatigue, loss of appetite, red eyes, and irritability when questioned about his condition all contributed to the unavoidable diagnosis.

By deduction, it was easy to narrow the time available to him for clandestine drinking. Kevin Dundy, who kept close watch over the goings-on in C Barracks until the work details headed out in the morning and then again after lights-out, reported nothing funny about David's behavior so far as he could see. During work Will had his eye on him and reported the same. Before and right after supper, there was a lot of activity in the barracks, and covert drinking would have been impossible then; anyone's regular absence in the woods for that or any other purpose would have been common knowledge. That left unaccounted for only the evening teaching hours, neither of which David attended. Toby asked him why.

"I don't much care for school, sir—and they said I don't hafta."

"It's not just a question of having to or not, David. It's what you're planning to make out of the rest of your life."

"Yes, sir—only I'm pretty tired at night."

"So is everyone else. The courses are set up so they won't strain your brain too much. I'd like to see you at least try my class. The others seem to think it may be doing them some good."

He was beginning to look edgy. "Yes, sir—only I can read pretty good—pretty well—already. I got a book out now, even—one of those Jerry Todd ones. It's very enjoyable."

"You can do better than Jerry Todd."

His eyes, at half-mast, asked why Toby, too, was tormenting him so. His tongue said only that he would try something harder. But he did not show up for class.

Toby began to check up on him during the first teaching period, when he was free. David was usually around the Rec, listening to the radio or watching ping-pong or reading a book, even. Wolfbait, Boxcar, and most of the other notorious unteachables were also on hand up until the time Toby had to leave for his class. Toward the end of the hour, he sensed David was growing fidgety. During that second period, while Toby was occupied and the three most responsible of the enrollees—Dundy, Bloomgarden, and Calabrese—were off playing basketball at the "Y" a couple of nights a week, was when the drinking had to be going on.

Instead of calling the problem to the attention of the adjutant, who was as likely as not to solve it by having the victim discharged, Toby turned detective himself. Slipping out of the mess directly after class instead of hanging around as usual, he hurried up to the Rec and looked around. Only a handful of the regulars were there. David was nowhere to be seen. Toby strolled back down the company street on the barracks side of the campus, where the staff, by tacit understanding, was not invited to venture at night except on official business. He felt eyes tracing his every step, but the only visible pair belonged to Boxcar Malone, who was slouched smoking a cigarette beside his barracks door. The noise inside could reasonably have been taken for a bacchanalia. He asked what the rumpus was, and Boxcar said, with only second-degree truculence, it was a big card game. Conduct in Bughouse B had reportedly been loose for several days since the barracks leader left for home to help care for an ailing father and while the captain waited to learn if the departure would become permanent. He urged Boxcar to tell the boys to pipe down or the adjutant would be on their tails. The enrollee took a surly puff on his hand-rolled weed before nodding at the advice and then hurried Toby along with those enemy eyes.

Next night, someone else was posted in front of B Barracks having a smoke when he came by, and the noise level within was lower. His warning had at best curbed, but surely not quenched, the festivities. Toby decided to go under cover.

Avoiding the gravel street next time, he cut over behind the washup shed and stationed himself by the window on the latrine side of the structure. After a short wait, he was rewarded by the sight of a panting David Schumacher coming through the brush lugging what appeared, from a short distance, to be a case of empty soda-pop bottles toward the rear windows of B Barracks. He stopped at the sound of Toby's approach, gave a remote hello when he saw who it was, and continued on his painful course as if nothing abnormal were happening. He was overtaken about midway to the barracks. "Are you the refreshment committee?"

He pretended not to understand. When the question was explained, David said he had only been washing out the bottles for Skeezix and was taking them back to the Rec. That Toby had just come from the washup and must have known he had not been in it was lost on him; that was simply the best lie David could make up on the instant. Anyway, by then Toby had caught the cutting smell of rot-gut gin with which the soda bottles were filled. David stopped on command and looked more resigned to his doom than fearful of it. Toby said he could not understand why David was debasing himself this way.

"It's a service," the boy tried. "I'm just helping out."

"I mean drinking the stuff yourself."

"Oh," he said. "Well, I get mine free."

"Is that a good enough reason to ruin your health—or do you think it's making a man of you?"

He stood there, silent and sullen, unwilling to surrender the heavy bottle case to the ground—or to look at his examiner. Toby said it was time for him to stop being a frightened rabbit and Wolfbait Stubbs' private slave. "I'm not his slave or nobody else's!" he answered, pea-small eyes active in their rheumy white gells. "I get paid for this."

All claims to innocent revelry were forfeited by that slip. He would have to tell who was paying him, Toby said, if he expected not to be reported. A stand of hemlocks behind them rippled from the night wind in towering reinforcement of the threat. Toby might as well go ahead and turn him in, then, David said bravely though not loud enough to rile the wind.

It was hard to know whether the boy suffered more from a misconceived notion of honor or a simple death wish. Toby proposed a different bargain: If David retired from the gin-running business after that night and came to class beginning the next, Toby would pretend their encounter had never taken place. David took a deep breath, squared his shoulders against their straining cargo, and said he would think about it.

He did not come to the next class session. Or the next. Almost certainly, he had decided that going straight would mark him as a stoolie, prospectively if not in fact, and invite renewed assault and battery. He could not entirely be blamed. His arch tormentor was another matter. Toby decided to confront him directly.

"Shi-i-it, a little hooch never hurt no one," said Wolfbait, fists balled and rat-quick body ready to dart out of range the instant he had room.

"It's turning Schumacher into a regular alcoholic."

"Nahhh, it's just takin' him a little while to get used to the stuff. The same wit' the smokes—I got Fatleroy workin' on them, too." He gave a lewd snort at the enormity of his aptitude for promoting corruption, as if he resented the least survival of innocence in anyone else when his own had been wrenched away so soon and so savagely.

Toby understood to the full range of his intricately tuned social conscience what had made Ivan Stubbs into such a vile little punk, but all that failed to excuse him. His will seemed to have surrendered unconditionally to adversity. He was the same flailing, miserable package of hatefulness Toby had met his first day in camp—and determined not to accept the smallest caress from life lest he be lulled into turning his back on it a moment and suffering a new boot in the ass. "Lay off David," he said, "for good."

"I ain't makin' him do nothin'—he's a fuckin' liar if he tol' ya that. He's smartenin' up—he's in it f' the dough now. An' he likes the way the booze puts him out nice."

"It also wrecks him for the next day. Now lay off him, Ivan—I mean it!"

"Oh, my ass is tremblin'." He turned his wiry body sideways, looking for a wriggle hole. "Anyway, whattaya leanin' on me for? This here's a big operation—the mob, ya know? I'm just small potatoes."

To authenticate his claim, he said he got only a nickel a bottle on the nightly case of gin the camp was allocated, and he gave a penny of that to David for serving as his delivery boy. That left forty-five cents unaccounted for in the purchase price paid by the enrollees, two or three of whom split each bottle—"just enough," Wolfbait noted, "to souse 'em good by taps." And who supplied the Lulu franchise? If he knew, Wolfbait was not saying. Threatened with disclosure and the likelihood of discharge if he refused to talk, he issued a crooked-tooth laugh. "First off," he said, "I don't give a shit. Second of all, you wouldn't do it. You're not part o' the asshole army. You're a pussycat, Ronan—wit' a big, squishy heart—'cause you went to Hah-vid an' all you wanna do is knock a few brains in some thick noggins—not like Cap'n Craphawk an' his looie asslicker. They get a hard-on from kickin' crotch."

Such a wholesome lad. The gin ring had not only activated his wayward bent but also, he confided, numbed him to "all the rest o' this chickenshit racket." The best deal Toby could strike with him was a twofold promise in return for not being turned in: He would fire David as an assistant bootlegger, and he would attend class for a month —and behave himself in it.

Just who was smuggling the bathtub gin into camp did not long remain a mystery. David was not the only one showing the ill effects of drink. Dr. Haseltine was obliged to so advise the adjutant, who launched his own investigation at once. Owning the keys to every lock in camp, he searched everywhere, high and low. Low was where he found what he was looking for. While Skeezix was in the company office typing out the monthly payroll forms, Nesbit turned his canteen closet upside down. At the bottom of a stack of soda cases, its bottles appearing as empty as the rest, was one filled to the gunwales with gin.

The lieutenant waited till Sparhawk left camp for the weekend before bringing charges against Bloomgarden. Skeezix had no alibi, only an explanation. The gin traffic yielded him very little personally, he said—a cent a bottle; the other four cents that he skimmed from the selling price went straight into the canteen kitty for buying things the

men collectively needed and the government did not provide. There
was nearly enough now for a new washing machine. Anyway, he said
he didn't see how selling guys alcohol was all that different from peddling them ice cream or cigarettes. "Baloney," Toby told him, feeling
Skeezix had betrayed a trust he had invested in no one else, boy or
man, at the camp. "You know the rules."

"Some rules are dumb," he said. "You tol' me that."

Nesbit gave him twenty-four hours to make a clean breast of it,
naming his suppliers and everyone in camp involved. That, in view of
his previous record, might reduce the punishment; anything less would
end his C.C.C. career on a note of dishonor.

For some of those boys, like Eddie Spain, the only code of the camp
was artful dodging; safety was everything. For more of them, it went
well beyond honor among outcasts. They had been thrown together
at a time and place not of their choosing, for reasons beyond their
fathoming, and had only the fellowship of mutual loneliness to sustain
a hope for something better. Skeezix vowed he would implicate
nobody else, whatever it cost him.

Disenchanted with him as Toby had suddenly become, he could not
help admiring that resolve. His effort at selling Nesbit on the comparable benefits of illicit gambling in camp—a practice he chose to
overlook—and those from drinking—which he did not—somehow
lacked conviction. Both, he argued, were victimless crimes, recreational rather than destructive. Why overreact? Just stamp the blight
out here and now and save really stern measures in case it recurred.

"No soap," Nesbit said after hearing him out. "We can't have two
standards of justice here. Bloomgarden's problem is that he thinks he
runs the camp. He's got to be taught a lesson."

"A lesson is different from an execution." And why, furthermore,
was Bloomgarden to be made the fall guy for an arrangement of
which he was almost certainly not the author? Someone had to be
made an example, Nesbit said. "Of what," Toby asked, "summary
judgments? Isn't that the essence of military law?"

The lieutenant threw him a contemptuous look. "Ronan, you
couldn't command a squad of goddamn pixies for two minutes without wanting to tie their little booties for them." But in the end, the adjutant agreed to give him two days to get to the bottom of the bootlegging. If there was no change by then—and if Skeezix still refused
to talk—Nesbit would have to go to the captain with the whole mess.

Toby's chief suspect was Denis Carmichael. All sorts of merchandise was trucked into the camp every day under the supply sergeant's
solitary supervision. It would have been no problem at all for him to

divert a case of bootleg booze to the canteen when no one was looking. As it was, he pocketed an immoral share of every staff member's
pay for marginal services poorly rendered.

"Hey, what kinda horse's ass you think I am?" he growled by way
of answering Toby's pointed inquiry. It was one thing to solicit
among consenting adults, he said, thorny with indignation, and a very
different—and loathsome—thing to corrupt youth systematically. Was
he forgetting, furthermore, that Carmichael was regular army? "One
of them little farts rats on me for pullin' a dumb stunt like that an' I'm
out on the street. It don't make no sense blowin' a pension for a couple extra bucks a week."

But it had to be someone, Toby calculated, with regular access to
town by car. Maybe one of the Lems. He went down the list with
Ash Cummings. Four of them were drys who had staunchly favored
Prohibition; two others were church vestrymen; one was highly active
in scouting; another was a substitute schoolteacher of unassailable integrity—which left only his son-in-law, for whom Ash reluctantly
vouched, and Will Bassett, indisputably the most devoted of the lot to
his work and to the boys.

Who else, then? Obviously not the officers or Dr. Haseltine. It had
to be one of the enrollees. And only three of them had wheels at their
disposal.

Joe Calabrese swore on his mother's life that he knew nothing of
the gin ring. Which brought it down to Ackermann, the captain's orderly, and Bavasi, the adjutant's. Nesbit kept his acned factotum on a
short leash and sent him into town on errands only rarely. The very
idea of his attempting skullduggery under the lieutenant's nose, in imminent danger of being skinned alive if detected, was all but unthinkable. But Ackerman—Ackermann added up. He was twenty-one and
knew his way around the taverns. He took the captain's car to town
every afternoon to get him the newspaper, pipe tobacco, or whatever
other little comforts Sparhawk had his heart set on. How difficult
would it have been for him to make a daily liquor pickup and drop it
at a secret rendezvous somewhere in or near camp on the drive back?
He also had ready access to the captain's ear and derivative power
over anyone who might think of crossing him. And in shrewdly picking the bluff but reliable Bloomgarden as his conduit to the customers
—and the only one in camp who could finger him as the operator—he
would have reduced to a minimum the possibility of being informed
on. Finally, he was bright enough to appreciate the irony of the commanding officer's own orderly also being the camp's leading racketeer.
Yes, Ackermann.

Distasteful as he found stooping to furtiveness, the practice undeniably had its uses in the maze of intrigue. Toby commissioned his assistant to shadow Ackermann's every move. The regrettable strategy yielded swift results. Eddie secreted himself in the toilet of the headquarters shed fifteen or so minutes before Ackermann showed up for his usual Sunday afternoon hour of arranging the captain's paperwork for the next morning. When the orderly telephoned his mysterious outside collaborator to say that the heat was on and the gin was off, Eddie heard every murmured word through the painted beaverboard partition. He piled out of the W.C. window before Ackermann was off the phone and raced to Toby's quarters, where he nearly bit his tongue in two trying to sputter out the grave revelation.

Nesbit and Toby took another of their little walks up the Ghost Trail. The news of Ackermann's turpitude reflected badly on the captain's command. How effective a disciplinarian could he appear in the eyes of district headquarters if he had failed to inspire rectitude even in his personal aide and been forced to discharge him on moral grounds? Any black mark against Gordon Sparhawk, moreover, and the performance of Camp 127 was a setback to Nesbit's own hopes for advancement. Self-interest, loyalty to the captain, and the demands of the rule book all warred in him, leaving the lieutenant receptive to Toby's proposal for creative adjudication.

Ackermann would be put on unofficial probation—a status known only to himself, the adjutant, and the educational advisor; one false move and he was through. The arrangement would have the unspoken added advantage to Nesbit of purchasing Ackermann's allegiance, such as it was, from the captain and any of its useful confidences. And it would have the decidedly unmentionable advantage to Toby of greater privy to the adjutant's practiced deceits in the line of duty.

Such a disposition of the case would also necessitate finding a suitable reward for Eddie Spain and punishment for Skeezix Bloomgarden, the only others in camp aware of Ackermann's malfeasance. "Why not transfer Skeezix to Bughouse B and make him leader," Toby proposed, knowing somebody had to be appointed in there momentarily, "and put Eddie in as company clerk?" Bloomgarden's new assignment, though a promotion on its face, would have the attendant punitive effect of unseating him from his cozy desk job and putting him into the field during the bitterest weather of the year. Eddie, who would no doubt be pleased to begin his professional climb to court clerk, could be counted on to seal his lips in return for this first judicious elevation of his career. And David Schumacher would take Eddie's place as Toby's assistant and be saved from ruination. Four birds with one stone.

"Thanks," Skeezix grumbled on getting the word and suspecting that a fine Harvard hand had shaped the punishment to fit his crime, "thanks a bunch. If I freeze my fuckin' nuts out there, I'm comin' after yours."

ELEVEN

*Two days of soft, sifting snow, followed by a night of sleet &
today fierce sunshine glaring off dunes of crusted hillside. It is all so
bewitchingly pure, and the trees so expertly candied—powdered
pines, maple branches dipped in delicate glaze, birches filigreed with
icicles—till the wind whirls madly down & its dry harping through
the twiggery sings a sinister warning not to contemplate the frostscape
too long.*

*Work goes on despite all. The men have been issued winter gear
(dark blue mackinaws, arctics, heavy gloves, caps with wool-lined ear
flaps) & told to keep moving. The trucks go out with plows always
hooked on front, and nothing halts crews on the mtn. rd, where half
the co. is to be concentrated till spring. The other half seems to be
chopping wood for barracks stoves (3 each) & to keep camp habit-
able. Ash says not to believe if winter comes, spring can't be far
behind. . . .*

IT WAS PROVOCATIVE OF HIM, no doubt, to try to teach the rudiments
of democracy while posted to that authoritarian place. But the camp
education program had prospered to the point where the curriculum
needed expanding, and he had his obligations.

One of the other Lems began a woodcraft course to complement
Will's class in forestry. Will now concentrated more on gardening
and landscaping with a mind toward future work opportunities for
the enrollees. Similarly, the camp cook, a World War veteran, of
whom a limited number had been admitted to the C.C.C. from the
start, gladly took up Toby's invitation to teach the boys some tricks
of his trade. A trained technician with the Pittsfield Buick dealership
was procured through the continuing efforts of Reverend Brandt and
took over the auto mechanics class from the captain. And Sparhawk

himself laid out a course called "Basic Business," glorifying property and its accumulation as every American boy's birthright, if not duty. Was it any wonder, then, that as an antidote to this overdose of *laissez-faire* Toby conceived his second course, "Basic Citizenship," and hoped the captain, busy beatifying the profit motive to boys whose folks had been all but pulverized by it, would not notice?

Civics Lesson ⚹1, sparsely attended as Toby had expected—what, after all, had memorizing the Preamble to the Constitution ever put in anybody's lunch pail?—proposed that the consent of the governed was the linchpin of democracy. "Obedience to law is a requirement of the civilized community," he began, "but it is not the highest virtue of a good citizen." Soldiers had to obey their superiors; citizens had no superiors in a democratic state—only magistrates to whom they delegated authority by choice. Having made that assignment, the citizen who prized his freedom did not forfeit it to his government; he watched his governors, petitioned them, argued with them, censured them if need be. "Eternal vigilance is the price of liberty"—who had said that, he asked them, and what did it mean?

Nobody knew.

"Ivan, who was Thomas Jefferson?"

Wolfbait took his feet down from the bench in front of him and squinted in thought. "Third President of America," he said. "Also he wrote the Declaration of Whosis and was the one that invented kites."

"Kites was Benjamin Franklin, you asshole," yelled the studious Boxcar Malone. "Jefferson bought Louisiana and fucked his slaves."

"He didn' have no slaves—that was Washington. He was so busy screwin' he lost at Valley Forge."

"Valley Forge wasn't no battle, you asshole—it was a retreat an' cold as shit. Colder'n here, even. After that, he won at Bull Run."

"You mean Bull Crap—'cause you got the wrong war, so stop callin' me asshole, you peckerhead!"

"You don't know diddlysquat about—"

"Jefferson believed that unquestioning docility results not in democracy but a dumb mob," Toby outyelled them. "Now you've just seen a demonstration of what a dumb mob is, but who can tell me what 'docility' means?" He spelled the word.

"Something medical!" "Something French!" "Something communist!" "Jefferson wasn't no commie—he was a Democrat!" "They didn't have no Democrats back then, you peckerhead! He was a Tory —wit' a wig." "He didn't have no wig—he had red hair, like Toby!" "Hey, don't go callin' him Toby in here—he's *Mr.* Ronan, the big brain trust—ain't that right, Mr. Ronan?" "Yes, *Mr.* Stubbs."

They made haste slowly.

The second week was devoted to studying how to reconcile two prime impulses of the American character—rugged individualism and the spirit of brotherhood. The former, Toby duly noted, had carved a mighty nation from the wilderness, and in record time. But unchecked ambition often turned into ruthlessness, he added and appended as testimony several passages from Matthew Josephson's new book, *The Robber Barons*.

"And what happens to the *un*rugged individual under such a system?" he asked them. "Freedom is as much an economic as a physical condition." Capitalism, by its nature, was disinclined to regulate its excesses, so the American government in the form of the New Deal had been forced to step in and reduce the victimizing effects of the rampant free-enterprise system—that was the meaning of the political events through which they had all been living lately. In the end, though, he suggested to them, the well-being of the community was not based on abstract principles or more equitable numbers but on its shared humanity. At the bottom of that evening's dopesheet, he added this excerpt:

. . . and herein lies the tragedy of the age. Not that men are poor—all men know something of poverty; not that men are wicked—who is good? Not that men are ignorant—what is truth? Nay, but that men know so little of men.
—WILLIAM E. B. DuBOIS

The horsing around subsided, and they began to listen. By the third week, there were twenty in the class. Toby decided, while the platform remained open to him, to sketch for them the great ideological clash of their own time. The dopesheet he prepared for the lesson took the form of a grid:

	USA	**USSR**
MAIN SOCIAL VALUE	Freedom	Equality
SOURCE OF POWER	The individual	The state
PRIMARY GOAL	Material success & personal advantage (inducing selfishness?)	Classlessness & collective advancement (inducing lethargy?)
NATURE OF RULE	Minimal restraint (mass exploitation?)	Maximum control (totalitarianism?)
STATE OF MIND	Dynamic & insecure	Static & regimented

Q1. Which provides the greatest good for the greatest number?
Q2. Which is the more benevolent?
Q3. How is Q2 different from Q1?

It was rash of him to try to reduce such monumental matters to a stark, simplistic grid, as if the powerful emotional overlay could be omitted from the comparison. Yet it seemed at the time a worthy attempt to inform unnuanced minds in a neutral way.

Sparhawk had no interest in neutrality, of a scholarly or any other kind. Even as the enrollees were piling numbly out of the trucks on their way back from the frozen forest, he yanked Toby into his office and slammed the door. The spinning turntable at the edge of his desk fed a Sousa march into the p.a. system in a forlorn effort to reinvigorate the drained men. "I know all about you now!" the captain blurted, blinking hard and fast, voice just below a shout.

"All what about me—sir?"

"What sort of subversive I've got on my hands—that's what!"

He took up the civics course dopesheets from his desk. No sooner was Toby given a free hand with the men, the charge went, than he started preaching civil disobedience to them as a legitimate form of social action. Not only did that directly defy the very principle of majority rule but it also revealed a grave misunderstanding on his part of the democratic process.

"I wasn't preaching disobedience—I was telling them not to be passive about their government—to speak up and make sure their views and interests were fully considered."

"I know exactly what you're telling them, Ronan, and I don't care for it, not one damned little bit." He flipped the top sheet aside. "And then there's this blatantly antibusiness guff you're feeding them about robber barons—as if every hard-working Joe who's up to all hours running a grocery or a pharmacy or a hardware store is an avaricious son of a bitch!"

"I didn't say anything like—"

"And then you have the gall to tack on this sentimental slop by a coon writer from some colored communist group as if it's got something to do with economic reality. Hell, it's a dog-eat-dog world out there, Ronan—always has been and always will be, and I won't stand for you pretending otherwise to these poor clucks!"

"Dr. DuBois is a scholar and a gentleman," Toby said as unfractiously as he knew how, "as well as a highly skilled champion of his people. And the N.A.A.C.P. is a very respectable organization. The point I was trying to make is that people are better than dogs—even colored people."

"I'm not having a debate with you, Ronan! I'm laying down the law —do you understand?"

Toby bowed his head, mistrusting his tongue in the face of this mean harangue. How much of this crazed, phobic case had to be endured?

"And then—and then there's *this* thing you mean to hand out tonight," he foamed on, waving the sheet with the comparison of the American and Soviet systems. "Is this your bright idea, or does it come straight from the Kremlin?"

Toby let the question hang in the air rhetorically until pressed. When he did no more than ask what the objection was to the sheet, the captain flew off again.

"My God, man—just to ask the question shows how little you respect my intelligence—or your country's honor!" Why, the very act of listing the two systems side by side like that declared that they were equally valid. And the questions at the bottom of the page revealed Toby's bias. When he tried to protest this reading of the sheet, Sparhawk cut him off at once and said, "Don't bother, Ronan—I've checked up on you." That very afternoon he had called the R.O.T.C. commander at Harvard on the chance the man knew something about Toby—and got an earful. A. Tobias Ronan '34 was well remembered, it seemed, as an ardent campus radical and pacifist, a prominent member of the leading Leftist student group, an organizer and editor of a Red-tinged protest newspaper, and a jailed agitator who was reportedly also involved someplace in Rhode Island in a violent labor uprising. " 'You've got a doosie there,' the man said to me—a doosie!"

Toby hardly recognized that tissue of half-truths in which he had been wrapped, sealed, and delivered unto his churlish master. To distill the facts for him from that much rubbish would have taken a month of Sundays and required at least a partially open mind—but Sundays he was never there, and any ventilation of that gnarled medulla would have constituted overexposure. He said only that the report the captain had received was grossly unfair.

"See here, Ronan, I'm tired of your trying to pull the wool over my eyes," Sparhawk snatched up his riding crop from the desk top. Not everyone who hadn't gone to Harvard was a total boob, he insisted and began rapping the leather shaft against his palm in unconscious rhythm to "Semper Fidelis" as it flooded the white-carpeted campus. From the start he had surmised that Toby was something of a radical. There were all those books—did Toby think he didn't know how many un-American ones were among them? Or that some of those magazines besides *Boy's Life* and *Radio News* that he had subscribed to behind the captain's back—*The Nation* and *The New Republic*—were socialistic? Or that Nesbit hadn't informed him of Toby's expressed pro-labor leanings? "And now *this*—this undeniable evidence of party-lining Marxism! It can't go on, Ronan—I tell you it can't go on!"

This endless seesawing of his between dogged combativeness and cheerless sanction where all Toby's activities were concerned was the mark of a man unbalanced in more ways than one. What he yielded one day, he reclaimed half of on the next. The habit had turned Toby into a conniver, not a profession to his liking.

A sudden wave of strength swept over him just then as he sensed that he had less to lose from the collapse of their relationship than the captain did. Whatever the source of the derangement that whipped Sparhawk into these periodic foul humors no longer concerned him; it was enough that they had served to intimidate him, had backed him off from every prior confrontation with this transparently troubled man, leaving Toby to treasure what crumbs he had salvaged from it and already half-dreading their next encounter. It was time to risk a showdown.

"What are you so afraid of, Gordon?"

Sparhawk's blinking stopped. His bewilderment at such effrontery was total. For a moment he looked as if all his springs were about to pop through his tight scalp. The air had been let out of his blimp. Bemedaled Humpty had a great fall. The plumped ruddiness was gone; the pomposity, a wizened husk. The facial lines pulled and cut. It was not pretty.

Very slowly the blinking resumed. "I'm not afraid of anything, *Mr.* Ronan," he said with simulated bite. "And I'm not out in these God-forsaken wilds for my health—all year long, in all kinds of weather, seeing almost nothing of my wife—and my friends—and my home surroundings—not for my health, *Mr.* Ronan, I can tell you—and Lord knows, not for the measly three hundred a month—not by a long shot." The pilot light to his piety had reignited. "I'm here because I want to do something for the country I love in her hour of terrible distress—can you grasp that, *Mr.* Ronan?—and I'm not about to have all my efforts undermined by some young, disloyal know-it-all who wants to kick America when she's down!"

So saying, he larruped his riding crop hard against the edge of the desk. It cracked with a terrifying report, then caromed out of his control against the goldfish bowl on the table alongside and drove glass, water, castle, and fish smashing into the phonograph turntable and cascading to the floor.

Sparhawk stood in stupefied contemplation of his performance. There was no clue in that taut blankness whether he was moved more by anger at Toby, annoyance with himself, or some deeper transfixing power. Analysis was not required for awareness of the puddling mess, the squawking p.a. system deprived of its Sousa finale, and the two wriggling orange blobs in mortal peril on the floor.

Toby called out for Eddie Spain, stationed in the anteroom, his ear almost certainly cupped to the keyhole, to come to the rescue. In he ran with mop and a dustpan, juggling a couple of water-filled Dixies for the fish, which he gave to the still traumatized captain to hold. Using a file folder as a scoop, he retrieved the fish, delivered them undaintily to the cups, wiped up around the p.a. system turntable and microphone, and took the jarred record away to be dried lovingly with a cloth and examined for scratch damage. Behind him, Toby saw, he had left the little red light glowing on the p.a. control panel.

Standing directly over the mike, he addressed the captain, who hulked across the desk from him, a fish in each hand and nowhere to put them. Sparhawk's eyes shuttered spasmodically. "You can accuse me all you'd like, Gordon, of being disloyal," Toby said, "but I'm not the one who's lost faith in his country—you are." America, he said, was great enough and strong enough to face the truth—namely, that it had undergone a grave illness and still needed a good deal of rehabilitation—without having to tar every criticism or suggestion for achieving better health as an act of treason. "It takes as much caring, as much patriotism, as much love, to say the flag is flying upside down and backwards as to stand there saluting it blindly."

He could hear the muzzy resonance of his own words as the p.a. spewed them to the lavender dusk. Sparhawk, though, seemed not to notice, staring at him just below the neck and never quite connecting with what was being said to him.

It was not enough, Toby went on at a quickened tempo, for America to be *against* communism, the way the captain was so passionately against it. A people did not flourish because of what they opposed—it was what they were *for* that mattered. And what America stood for now, after the debacle of economic collapse, had to be more than a chicken in every pot again and two cars in every garage. The country had to restore more than prosperity. It had to reimbue in itself the belief that each man was entitled to his dignity in this life. "We've lost that," he said, "and that's the worst thing—and that's what *I'm* trying to do out here—teach each of these men who you think are such dolts that they matter—not like Einstein or Lindbergh, maybe, in the eyes of the world but to themselves and those dear to them—and that they have the right to exist and to become the best that's in them, whatever that happens to be. And if that doesn't turn out to be enough to sustain a halfway decent existence, then I think the rest of us—out of care and respect for our common humanity—

should help them out. And if I can't say that—and whatever else I feel with my heart—then America and this camp you're running aren't any better than Nazi Germany or Soviet Russia. But they *are* better, a lot better, and I'm going to have my say, Gordon, whether you like it or not—and if you want my resignation for that, then you've got it. And if you don't want it, then from now on I'm going to do my job with all due respect for your views but I'm going to do it as I see fit—without an army uniform on—and eating with whom I like—and joining the men in the field from time to time—and teaching them what and how I think will help them most."

Sparhawk's stillness at the end was terrible. His only response, when it came, was inaudible over the p.a. but unmistakable to Toby: Slowly, expressionlessly, the captain squeezed the water, shape, and life out of the little cups he held and then stood there with the crumpled residue dripping from each hand. Toby left him that way and went to pack.

The giant square, fifty men to a side, that the company formed around the flagpole broke apart to let him through, carrying his suitcase and braving the cold in his tattered sport jacket. He had left his mackinaw and everything else G.I. back in his bunk and stood there now in the middle of the field, alone on the opposite side of the flagpole from the captain and the adjutant, who saluted stiffly as Old Glory made its wind-whipped descent with stately slowness. Bareheaded, Toby held his hand over his heart. It was all probably for the best, he thought, and fought back tears that would have likely congealed before they crept halfway down his cheeks.

At the command "Dismissed!" they mobbed him, just as some of them had after the Harvard banner was unfurled the day he came. The handshakes and shoulder grabs and mumbled regrets over his leaving were more reward than any grandiloquent tribute could have been. He had never sentimentalized his distance from them in quality of intellect or (God help him) refinement of sensibility, for there was no profit for him in that disparity. His own demanding expectations made fulfillment no more promising a prospect for him than for them. He envied most of them their openness and their resilience and their absence of self-pity. He was for them because life had snubbed them; not until the end could they have thanked him for that allegiance.

When the crowd had cleared and headed into mess, only Sparhawk and he were left standing in the center of the field. It was nearly dark, but there was no mistaking the turbulence of the captain's emotions at that instant. They penetrated the encroaching gloom and drew Toby up in them. Immensely saddened, he extended a hand toward the officer, who was as much a victim of his furies as any man. Sparhawk let the hand hang unattended in the freezing air. As Toby sorrowfully withdrew it, the older man turned his eyes up and told him hoarsely, "I never said you weren't a helluva teacher."

"Thank you—sir."

He screwed up a little smile. "I think we know each other well enough now for you to call me Gordon."

In the dark Toby let his eyes fill. They had degraded each other with equal rancor; which of them deserved it more was lost in the fragility of this terse reconciliation. Toby had stated the terms from his end, assuming their unacceptability; Sparhawk's perverse triumph was that Toby should have assumed as much. As adversaries went, this one was at least a benign enough fiend. "Okay—Gordon."

"And when your class is done, come by for a nightcap, Toby—Doc is bringing some Debussy."

Anything but Sousa.

<h1 style="text-align:center">II</h1>

13 Dec 35

Dearest Toby,

Blame it on the imminence of the holidays—they have me dripping with nostalgia like a sentimental slob. The half year since we parted seems a century, but I cannot bear to let the season pass without reaching for you to say I think about Cambridge and us and everything, and that I hope it goes well with you—or at least not awfully.

Bonnie and Anton (who were kind enough to ferret out your remote address from the Boston bureaucrats) report you've gone Thoreau. I didn't know whether to clap or cry at the news. First I thought it was a simple case of escapism, which God knows, would have been understandable. Then, remembering there is not much about you that's simple, I decided the job situation still being what it is, you probably didn't have a lot of choice. No doubt life among the salt of the earth has clarified your convictions wonderfully. But please go easy on the nuts and berries—pantheism is not yet a viable political doctrine!

Bonnie is studying nursing, I'm happy to advise, and Anton is now with something called the Greater New England Labor Council and very respectable since the passage of the Wagner Act. They are not your classic love birds, from the sound of it, each being away from the nest so much, but seem happy enough and send you their best.

As for me, after a summer of California hedonism I concluded that dying for a cause is not necessarily better than living without one,

Monsieur Malraux to the contrary not withstanding. (You would adore the latest cause out here, by the way—has Townsendism penetrated the woods of western Mass.? Everyone over 60, according to Francis Townsend, a Calif. coot, is to get $200 a month from Uncle Sam provided they agree to spend it fast so the economy will gyrate and young people can get work. Alas, the money for this vast boon is to come from a national sales tax—not exactly your most progressive innovation—and the whole operation of the Townsend clubs is strictly autocratic and slickly promoted. I think it's just a national hustle and pray the Social Security kills it quick.)

Anyway, I am settling for now for small pleasures and daily satisfactions, the more innocuous the better, instead of my former messianic delusions and have accordingly entered the law school at Berkeley. It is neither splendid nor terrible, which is something of a relief. I should like to become a government prosecutor, delivering unto the iniquitous their just deserts.

Write if you find time. I'll be home through New Year's. Now I know what they mean about loving someone always if you did once—and even if the form and intensity change as your own life does. So please believe me, Toby, when I wish you all the best for '36 and send you my

Love,
CHESKA

Her letter came from beyond the grave and stirred too much pain and longing for him to answer. He saved it, though, and valued its good thoughts. For warmth, there was April Janowicz in the foreground, and warmth, not the distant glow of an old flame, was what he needed then. April was so warm, in fact, that she heated up the whole camp.

There was nothing the least immoral about it. She was quite the heroine, actually, after the fight broke out at the "Y" between the camp basketball players and a bunch of townies who baited them. The taunting had started over Kevin Dundy's distinctive two-handed dribble and turned nastier over a crack that had appeared not long before in *Collier's*—to the effect that any girl who eloped with a boy from the C.C.C. didn't know enough to come in out of the rain. Soon the court was littered with pummeling bodies, and the townies came off second best, to such an extent that, despite the provocation, the C.C.C. boys' playing privileges were revoked and a "Y"-sponsored Christmas dance, to have been held at the camp with local young ladies imported for the occasion, was summarily canceled.

That was when April came to the rescue. The "Y" affiliates were mostly Protestant; hers were not. She lobbied the presiding cleric at St. Mary's, who was very much a workingman's priest, and won church sponsorship of the dance, provided ample chaperoning could be found. Other strong R.C. participation was enlisted through the local K. of C. and American Legion post until more than enough partners were in prospect to allow the affair to be rescheduled. All that had to be done then was teach most of the fellows how to dance—which is how April became the sweetheart of Camp 127.

Every night after work for two weeks, she and a couple of girl friends drove out to the forest and conducted dancing classes accompanied by whatever was on the radio. April's excellent topography drew an admiring turnout of horny boys who lined up to do the two-step with her. In time she brought some of them as far as the French dip and the Lindy. On none of her partners did April have a more aphrodisiac effect than Wolfbait Stubbs, who pressed himself boldly close to her and solicited her intervention in his behalf with some comparably constructed maiden of the village. "What a set o' jugs on her!" he suavely observed after one evening session. "I hope you're gettin' your share, perfessor."

"That," Toby remonstrated, "is not gentleman talk, Ivan."

"I guess that means you're gettin' it good—you lucky dog!"

Wolfbait's smarmy surmise overstated the case: Toby was getting it fair to middling. But that was a lot, seeing that his collaborator was a faithful daughter of the Mother Church. From the turn of December, she had carnal sin to confess—and did, she claimed, although more intermittently than its commission, which was about once a week, usually on Friday or Saturday nights, on the sun porch at home when her parents were out visiting, or at the Bassetts' when they went to the movies and, intemperate matchmakers that they were, invited the dating couple to curl up in front of the big fireplace that Will himself had put in.

On full disclosure, April Janowicz's breasts had an almost unhealthfully downy softness that defied supple manipulation—they spilled out of his hands like great hot pillows and sort of sloshed from one side of her torso to the other. They were not a disappointment, exactly—more of a superfluity. The only form of The Act that she permitted was *coitus interruptus*, probably a prudent practice, all things considered, although Toby found it an even more unnatural prophylactic than the ones she forbade. Worrying which contraceptive technique would minimize her wickedness in the eyes of the saints seemed to him hardly more than jesuitical diversion. Just precisely where he de-

livered his seed was, he conceded, a minor matter compared to the accompanying neural release. Her way was messy, if technically immaculate, but not painful.

Afterward, they would talk—beforehand, hardly at all—about the
diversions of her life. In most ways she was an uncurious, unadven-
turous girl. Her pleasures, other than horizontal ones, were confined
to dancing, bowling, swimming—it was nothing for her, she said, to
span the entire width of Pontoosuc Lake on midsummer days, dodging
boats all the while—and demure bits of sewing, her specialty being
appliquéd sofa pillows that were always in demand at the annual
church fair. But she never skied—that was for the rich—or climbed
the low mountains that surrounded her or even knew their names.
Nor, despite being Will Bassett's sister-in-law, could she tell a pine
from a spruce or elm from a maple, and the flowers to her were all a
generic miscellany. What she knew flawlessly were the names and
sounds of all the big dance bands on earth which she listened to endlessly on the radio after unplugging from the G.E. switchboard. It did
not occur to her that work could ever amount to more than mere
time-serving.

This obliviousness to almost anything that mattered in the world beyond her own sensory equipment discouraged him, especially because
she appeared so content within her native orbit. She prided herself on
the severely impersonal politeness she had perfected at her work station and for learning hundreds of names and voices and their whereabouts, but there was no craft, no growth, no promise in her purely
repetitive function. Yet that was exactly what she appreciated most—
that it demanded so little of her except endurance.

One night he told April he could never work for a big company
like G.E. so long as it had no union. "I'd feel like a complete slave," he
said.

She thought that odd. The company paid better than the going
wage, she said, and was nice to its workers. It had been especially so to
her father, whom they kept on all through the worst part of the
depression. That he might have been owed that much after more than
twenty years of devoted labor had not occurred to her.

"And what about all the others who got laid off?" he asked.

"Well," she said, "that's business."

"But that's the point—business is inhumane by its nature—which is
why unions are needed to balance things out." And if companies really had any hearts or insight into employee morale, they would extend to their blue-collar workers the same kinds of benefits they did to
their executives—health care, insurance, pensions, and profit-sharing.

"Not to the same degree, maybe, any more than you should get paid the same thing as Lawrence Keyes, but something—something proportional so you'd have a sense of belonging, of working for your own good and not just for a lot of rich, faceless stockholders."

She thought about that for a while, but it proved too much. Succumbing to the warmth of the fireplace at their feet, she remarked only, "Pop says they'll give the boot to anyone who talks union, so what's the point?"

"The point is that's not right."

"There's a lot of things that aren't right."

"But some you can try to do something about."

"Pop has a saying—'Anyone who looks for trouble can find it.'"

His chief reservation about taking up with this sweet, uncomplicated girl was not the poor prospect of remaking her but that he might plant false expectations in her even if there was no fertilizing going on. She was no Bonnie Quigley in that regard, sulky at life and its paltry rewards, using her body to lash back without guilt and disdainful of the Church as a smothering narcotic. April Janowicz had a bovine soul. And while he gladly embraced the body it came in, he was not enraptured by either aspect of her. He did his best, without again being hurtful, to indicate as much. She said she understood he was a transient. But whenever he called, she was availably grazing.

Availability grew as a virtue in his eyes that holiday season, particularly after he tried and failed to patch things with Temple.

He had stopped by her office late one midweek morning and asked if they might have a talk over lunch. "I'm afraid I already have a date," she said, uneasy at his abrupt appearance. "Some other time if you'd like. You might think of calling first."

"I thought of it."

She studied the papers on her desk. "Pity—you might have saved yourself the trouble."

"I'll remember next time—"

"Yes, do."

"—if there is a next time."

"Suit yourself."

"Temple, break your lunch date."

She looked up, disbelief elongating her pensive face. "I beg your pardon?"

"Cancel your date—we need to talk. There are some things that should be straightened out."

For an instant she seemed to soften and consider the brassy proposal. It said he cared enough to confront her at risk of curt rebuff,

But his term in her Coventry was not done. "I'm not the one who needs the straightening," she said firmly and lifted the phone to make a business call.

Without destination, he drifted along the slushy street, distantly appraising the pyramided gifts and gay ornaments in the store windows and demanding who Temple Keyes thought she was, anyway. Before long, he arrived at a small, elegant brick-front with a dress shop on the ground floor and a stone-banistered staircase alongside. The painted directory sign listed, among other upstairs tenants, "Holly Larrabee Curtis/Piano Studio."

Sweet, airy, but slightly ragged sounds, recognizably Mendelssohn, begun, broken, and relaunched, assailed her studio door as he parked himself on the stairway outside and waited for the lesson to run its course. What sort of pupil attended her at the tail end of morning? Her natural clientele was presumably all in school. Whoever it was attacked the piece with unstinting purpose. At the end, though, it was coming out just as imperfectly as it had been at the start.

He was on his feet, pacing the hall impatiently, when the door opened at last to expel the diligent student—a wimpled sister in orders, looking damp around her starched gills. Bidding adieu alongside was her cool, chestnut-curled coach, in a properly high-buttoned white blouse and pleated tartan skirt, without so much as a daub of lipstick on. "Well, well, well," she said, "Mr. Paderewski—what a lovely surprise," and ushered him in. It was not true, she whispered as soon as the door was closed, that they smelled.

"Who?"

"The holy sisters. At least mine doesn't—although she does get a tad steamy toward the end. God, I'd die being wrapped up like that all day."

"That's just her winter habit. You should see her bathing suit around the convent pool—a one-piece shroud."

Holly laughed and gave him a peck on the cheek and said she was glad to see him and sorry but she had to run momentarily. "Was there anything special," she asked, swiftly curling on a maroon film of lipstick in the closet-door mirror, "or were you just planning to audition for me?" He said he happened to be passing and wanted a few minutes of her counsel. "What a shame—I'm booked solid from two on—the kiddies' hours, you know." But she promised to try to cut short her luncheon appointment and hurry back. Meanwhile, he was welcome to stay and play. And out she swept, wrapped in gray persian lamb and a matching pillbox hat.

It was a large, uninviting room, with a mostly bare parquet floor and heavy dark-green drapes, presumably to hold in the sound when drawn. A lumpish sofa flanked by a pair of upholstered armchairs in old chintz sat on a small, weary oriental rug in front of the unused fireplace—the only furnishings in the studio other than the gleaming black Knabe grand, angled out from a corner with its top up. Except for a few knickknacks on the fireplace mantel, the bare-walled chamber was devoid of personal imprint. It gave off a sense of having been used as a piano studio, furnished exactly the same unloved way, since the building went up.

He fiddled at the piano awhile, taking out a book of Mozart sonatas from the bench and trying to struggle through a few pages. The treble he could more or less manage but the base was hopelessly intricate for his unpracticed fingers. After perhaps twenty graceless minutes, he reverted to Cole Porter and *Porgy and Bess* numbers that he had picked up by ear and rendered by hoof. Holly's sneering disapproval rang from the walls. Out of fear she would walk in on this trippingly inept performance, he retired to the fireplace and inspected *objets* bunched on the mantel. Among them were a scrimshaw ashtray bearing half a dozen cigarette butts (who smoked?), a lovely little clock of gilt and malachite that said the time was shortly after one, and a copy of *Man's Fate* with the front flap tucked in about midway through the book.

The novel struck him as curiously out of place. Every politically conscious person in Cambridge—which was to say about a hundred students and perhaps that many faculty—had read the Malraux when it came out in English the year before. Its exalted language and exotic setting brushed a romantic patina over the Frenchman's version of the revolutionary struggle; to Toby, his communists were confections of a utopian intellect—there were no gritty workers manning Malraux's soviets, only heroes and martyrs of doctrinal purity.

He was leafing through the book when Holly's key clicked in the door and she flew in with apple cheeks and frost still clinging to her long, dark lashes.

"I've a bulletin," she said, tossing her heavy coat and hat onto one of the chairs and falling in beside him on the sofa. "Our mutual acquaintance is still what my dear, dead grandmother Larrabee used to call a mite tetched in the lobes—about you and your working girl, I mean. But your bravura performance this morning helped, I'd say— she was beginning to think you didn't care at all."

Somehow, he had sensed they were lunching together, chewing over his fate. He was less sure either of them knew of his continuing friendship with April.

"Oh yes," she said, "your West Point lieutenant sees to that. Evidently your seamy romance is common knowledge in the barracks and no doubt something of a sensation—Harvard's quite a catch on their side of the tracks." He was in luck, though, she added with malicious delight; thanks to her suggestion, he was to be invited to the Keyeses' annual gala costume party on New Year's Eve, provided he came stag.

"Swell—and am I commanded to come as an army officer—since *mademoiselle* seems to prefer the type?"

"Actually, she doesn't. But she'll see only one of you at a time, considering what great pals the two of you are—"

"But we're not pals at all!"

"Yes, Toby—that's the point, Toby. And you will not be milady's chosen so long as you persist in dandling the downtrodden." She poked her index finger into his upper arm. "Too bad you haven't taken my advice. I've checked with Carl Keyes, by the way, and he confirms it: Pardon my French, but there's plenty of pussy for sale around here if you must have it that badly."

The calculated crudity, the savage superiority, the expensive clothes, the coquettish lashes, the touchy hands—she was a monstrously provocative creature without a hint of softness in those elegant bones. "Pardon my English," he said, "but that still happens to be none of your business."

Her smile registered approval of the rebuke, as if she had been testing his tolerance for her abusiveness. "Then why did you come by, sweetie?"

"Not for shopping instructions."

Her smile lingered. "You're quite a charmer, you know—in your disingenuous way. You don't fool me for a moment—Mr. Ronan the *roué*."

"Me?"

"Absolutely. Your walk gives you away—those long, confident strides—the disarming slouch—the roving eyes. Very manly."

It seemed the moment to ask if she had told Temple he'd stopped by.

"That," she said, running a fingertip two or three inches down his sleeve, "is strictly between us—unless I'm reading you wrong." He nodded his appreciation and, to glide from the subject, pointed quizzically to the Malraux lying on the sofa between them. "*Mais oui*," she said, "I am a voracious consumer of the literature of protest. Guy says it's the only way to head off the revolution—know thy enemy. Last summer he had me into *Studs Lonigan* and early Dreiser—pretty grim." *Man's Fate* she was finding more stylish and melodramatic, almost a poet's vision of the class war. "In fact, Guy says you rather remind him of the Russian—what's-his-name—"

"Katov."

"Right. Oh, I do so much better with all those polysyllabic names in Dostoevsky. At any rate, I'm afraid Guy has you down as a bit of a fanatic in your idealism."

"Because he doesn't know me very well."

"You mean you're not an idealist?"

"I mean I'm not a fanatic, like Katov. I don't find the prospect of self-destruction particularly ennobling, whatever the cause."

"But you do admit to not much fondness for the stinking rich—or what's left of them?"

"No, not a great deal."

"I might have thought distance lent enchantment in your case. Isn't that what lures most poor boys to Harvard?"

"Well—"

"Guy says it's just envy, but I don't think intolerance of any group happens to be a very attractive trait in someone with your brains. Don't you think we deserve a chance from you? At least Tolstoy could claim an earned revulsion—the bloody hypocrite—"

"I'm not against anyone who gets rich honestly—honorably—by hard work and decent enterprise—or maybe genius that brings benefits to the masses—like Edison. It's those who get it by blind luck or by ruthlessness I find objectionable—"

"And inheritance, too, I gather, from our evening at the Keyeses'. You must be thrilled to pieces with Roosevelt's new death tax."

"I think it's appropriate social legislation."

"Because you don't stand to inherit anything."

"I doubt if that would change my thinking one bit."

"But it would test the purity of your idealism, wouldn't you agree? It's too easy to oppose privilege in the abstract. Of course, you might still marry into money—if you play your cards right—though, heaven knows, you seem quite determined *not* to. Or are you against that, too? I'd think about it—a rich wife can be wonderfully liberating for a man more interested in mental and moral pursuits than grubbing for a buck—ask Guy. Unfortunately, it also appears to transform the lucky beneficiary into something of a eunuch."

She sprayed her venom indiscriminately. It made her more dangerous and twice as alluring to all would-be tamers. "Marriage isn't much on my mind just yet," he said.

"No," she said, glancing at the clock and rising, "just intercourse, I gather." At the mantel, she examined her appointment book. "Well, if you'd like me to teach you to play, you could come tomorrow at noon—I've an open hour then."

They never did reach the piano bench the next day, or any of the other Wednesdays he came by her studio at noon and left punctually before her one o'clock pupil. That timed, almost frenetic scheduling of their play on the dusty, faded sofa made it all the more passionate. There could be no pretense of sharing anything beyond the physical pleasures of that stolen hour. They could not be seen outside that room together—not even communicate because the risk of exposure was too great. Despite that, because of that, their hour of hermetic intensity diminished the rest of his week to prelude and recessional.

Even unclothed, there was nothing tender about Holly Curtis. Probably its abbreviated nature lent a jaded briskness to her infidelity—how could it have been otherwise? Whatever the conditioning agent, she used her body, all rounded corners and tapered ridges without a subcutaneous handful anywhere besides her dainty breasts and fleshy rear, almost as an offensive weapon. That first time, she wielded her hips and pelvis with such hungry energy that he could not contain himself long enough to satisfy her. "Christ!" she cried at his distressed convulsions and drove herself furiously against his wilting flesh without success. Only his perseverance in the manipulative arts won him a reprise for the following week. After that, he learned to battle her back; she approved vocally and with fingernails that almost but never quite drew blood. With a satisfied little laugh, she said, "*Mon cheri sans-cullotte*" after their first synchronized success and fell back against the pillows with a lighted cigarette. Postcoitally was the only time she said she smoked.

Those secret sessions in that bare studio were easily the most consuming sexual encounters he had yet known—because it was forbidden fruit, because it was so flattering to service and be serviced by an heiress apparent, and most of all because he did not care for her in the slightest. "This has nothing to do with Guy," she explained away her adultery, citing a unique aptitude for compartmentalizing her life. "It isn't as if he's being deprived."

"And Temple?"

"You mean I'm being disloyal?"

"The argument could be made."

"*Au contraire*—this is my supreme act of friendship," she pertly insisted, "keeping your divine dicky bird out of the clutches of the proletariat. Greater sisterly love hath no woman."

Thus, as winter granulated those ancient hills, he was fueled by a lust that twice weekly attained combustion. Well into his twenty-fourth year, a priapic spell seized him that knew no politics or party and asked no reasons. All this free and footloose fornication produced a perpetual tingling in the loins, a perceived pouchiness about the seminal storage area, a suspected swelling of the delivery duct, and fantasies of precocious retirement to Araby as a full-fledged harem master. Yet an element of exuberance was somehow missing from all this loveless, guiltless rutting. He was sowing his oats, all right, even while defying the howl of the arctic gales. But the haughty girl whose body he most wanted to lie beside and share was having none of him.

III

Saturday, Dec. 15, '35

Fancy ceremonies, replete with remarks by aide to U. S. Sen. Walsh (D., Mass.) and incantations by C.C.C. circuit padre Ullman (Luth.), rechristening spiffed up Rec as Roosevelt Hall. Just in time for The Big Dance (also end of Dist. rating period). New (i.e., old) furniture via various contributors: overstuffed morris chairs, victorian davenport, lamps, tables, rugs (including large floral number sent by Mrs. Sparhawk herself). For woodsy effect, there's a big deer's head from overstock at Berk. Museum, thanks to Temple's efforts (at N's instigation—the creep).

Capt. vetoed proposal to invite enrollees' families & went thru roof on learning boys in my Eng. class sent letter to his wife thanking her for Rec rug & asking her to attend ceremonies. "We're not running a ladies' sewing circle!" he ranted & that was that. Mrs. Sp. hasn't written back. Well, what could she say—"I'd love to come, boys, but Mr. Dragon, better known to you as Capt. Dragon, is all in a tizzy at the very thought"? . . .

Sparhawk himself delivered the benediction, invoking divine approval of "these Christian good works." The captain's certitude that it would be forthcoming was more than likely misplaced, Dr. Haseltine remarked the next day when Toby stopped by his house for Sunday supper. He illustrated his distaste for such parochialism by recounting a legend, set in almost the very spot where his house stood, "about a deer and the Indians and another pious Christian soldier of high probity."

It seemed that Onota Lake, with its graceful contours and pleasingly varied backdrop of field and wood and hill, had been a beloved watering place of the Indians long before the white man set foot in the valley of the Housatonic. And the tribes of the region took note of a deer of complete and spotless whiteness that would come to drink each summer and fall from the clear waters of the lake. No Indian ever raised his bow against the perfect animal, for so long as the white doe came to Onota to drink, ran the belief, famine would not blight the Indian harvest nor pestilence visit their lodges nor foemen lay waste their country.

"But it came to pass in the days of the French and Indian wars," the doctor continued, "that a bold young officer in the service of the king at Versailles was dispatched from Canada to try to stir up the Housatonic against the British." A skillful agent, the soldier was welcomed as an ambassador to the lodges of the Indians and given an honored seat at their council fires, where he listened attentively to the marvelous stories that were told, including the legend of the beautiful and sacred white deer.

Impatient at the slow progress of his mission, eager for the fame and favor said to attach to those adventurers who presented to the French Court some exotic trophy from the wilderness of the New World, the Christian soldier thought to obtain the peerless pelt of the Onota deer. His hints of purchase rudely rebuffed by the pagan tribal chieftains, the Frenchman directed his persuasive powers toward a brave by the name of Wondo, whom he knew to have been debased by the use of the white man's firewater. Promising Wondo a perpetual supply, he overcame the native hunter's reluctance to do the fateful deed, and when Wondo was sufficiently besotted, he came upon the unsuspecting animal, so trustful of the friendship of man, and slew it.

As soon as the soldier had stowed the prize in his luggage, he set out for Montreal. According to the legend, however, the white man never reached the Canadian border. Wondo, too, paid the price for his impious slaughter, but from that day forward, the culture of the red man in the valley of the Housatonic began to wither away.

The doctor inhaled slowly on his cigarette after finishing the tale. "The instruction I draw from this bit of regional lore," he said, "apocryphal or otherwise, is that the evils of heathenism are comparable only to the callousness of Christian peoples—or you might say that piety comes down to a matter of whose deer is being gored."

Toby was not slow to apply the lesson to a social context. If truth and virtue were hardly the monopoly of any religion or race or nation, how could more be claimed in the name of any political faith or economic creed? "Only the trouble with moral relativism," he lamented, "is that it leaves you out on a limb, feeling very frail—and fallible—and finite."

"And doesn't all wisdom," the doctor asked, emptying the last of a beer bottle into his glass, "flow from that awareness? It may not be a very heroic thought, I'll admit—"

"Sure, but what bothers me is that good old wisdom doesn't give much of a damn about rectifying the basic human condition. All it seems good for is rationalizing it."

"You're angry there's so much suffering and injustice in life?"

The question had an uncharacteristically puckish edge, coming from a lifelong healer. "Yes," Toby said, "shouldn't I be? Why isn't everyone—that's what I don't understand. Some things aren't relative. Some things are just an egregious sin against humanity. There are certain moral absolutes that override all parochial differences, only they get forgotten as soon as partisanship turns into fanaticism—the way it usually does. That's what gets me angry—all this free-floating self-righteousness that strips the breed of any real compassion."

"You," said the doctor not quite wearily, "are a classic example of why anger is a young man's luxury. Who else would assume the breed wants to improve itself morally when almost all the evidence is to the contrary?"

"I don't care what the breed wants—and I can't answer for it."

"So why take it on yourself to give it moral instruction? I've watched you at the camp, Toby—you're out there on a crag, wrestling with the devil—and holding your own pretty well, I'd say. But he's a mighty slippery fellow, and only one of you is likely to hang on. That's the trouble with moral crusaders—they don't usually lead very long or satisfying lives."

"I believe the expression is 'Virtue is its own reward.'"

"And you don't want to believe that—I can see."

"I'm more worried by reports that the good really do die young."

Dr. Haseltine pressed his fingertips together in contemplation. "Within my limited range of experience, I've never found any clear correlation one way or the other. Of course, I may have lacked your gift for telling the good ones from the rest." He drained his glass and ran a hand over the rear tassels of his silvery aureole.

"I take it you don't hold a very high opinion of idealists."

The doctor looked unhappy at the inference. "I'm not sneering at you, son—far from it. If everyone said what's the use because everything in life is pointless, we'd be in one helluva fix—nothing but debauchers and immoralists. I guess all I'm trying to say is that you can work at virtue privately as well as publicly—and maybe in the end that's the most anyone can hope for."

"Fine with me. Then all we have to do—if you'll pardon the Harvard semantics—is define virtue."

"Ah, yes. Unfortunately, cracker-barrel philosophy isn't exactly up my alley. We've got Gordon to turn to for that—although I guess his is more the gun-barrel variety. But now there—you take soldiering, for example. I suppose virtue for a real fighting man consists of living life as intensively as possible regardless of its duration—and perhaps the same might be said of a poet. For the financier or industrialist, no doubt it's a question of quantity—virtue is how vast a fortune can he gather. And with the politician, the amount of power—and with the performer, of acclaim. But a medical man has a slightly different slant on things. For myself, I'd venture to say that the ideal life is one that neither imposes nor suffers pain. I doubt if you'd rate a negative virtue very high, and I wouldn't blame you in the least. Frankly, if I'd resigned myself to man's fate at your age, I'd have stuck my head in the oven a long time back—instead of sitting around like this, waiting for the end not very serenely."

He had never before emitted a hint of geriatric melancholy. Ministering exclusively to the young seemed somehow to have exempted him from the aging process; good cheer was the principal elixir at his dispensary.

"I hadn't noticed your doing much sitting around."

"Poetic license. Let's face it—I'm a codger, and trying hard to be graceful about it."

Toby looked across at the green-black timber that formed a bulwark on the opposite shore of the lake. "Does anyone die serenely, Doc?"

He drew a deep, draining breath and thought hard a moment. "It's hard to say. Depends what you've been through—and your conception of eternity, I suppose."

"Mine's a void, I'm sorry to say."

"Nothing to be sorry about—that's painless, at least. I've never been sold, myself, on the torments of hellfire."

"Or any everlasting reward, I take it, for earthly virtue?"

"Well, now," he said, "it wouldn't have been very virtuous, then, would it?"

On his way into the kitchen to put something together for supper, Dr. Haseltine banged his shin against an end table and nearly knocked over the lamp it held. Toby thought perhaps the beer had affected his bearings, but he blamed it on a new pair of glasses. "At least I don't have Gordon's problem," he added, rubbing the spot with embarrassed concern.

"Which one?"

The doctor managed a short laugh. "Vanity—the man refuses to wear glasses. Haven't you noticed how he blinks?"

"I thought that was nerves."

"More narcissism, I'd say. He doesn't think officers in glasses cut very commanding figures." He pulled out a handkerchief and daubed a spot of blood from where the skin had broken. "But at least this way he's not much of a threat to the deer."

IV

Tuesday, Dec. 18, '35

Latest Calabrese uproar has produced rebellion in ranks. Group led by members of Citizenship class has drafted petition to capt. protesting Joe's punishment for the truck freeze-up (everyone convinced he's innocent; most sure who culprit is). They want me to endorse and join in presenting resolution as follows:

"The judicial power of Camp 127, Mass. District, Corps Area I, U.S. Civilian Conservation Corps, shall henceforth reside in a Kangaroo Court, consisting of one representative elected from each barracks who shall select a presiding judge from among themselves. Jurisdiction of this court shall be limited to matters affecting the welfare of the enrollees and concerning their conduct in the barracks, throughout the camp, and in the field. Decisions and punishments of said court shall be subject to approval by and appeal to a Judicial Review Board, consisting of the commanding officer, the educational advisor, and the work superintendent. . . ."

An enrollee named Fraser Jones from E. Barracks had got himself chosen authorized representative in camp for purveyors of cheap jewelry all bearing the C.C.C. insignia. Jones, known as "Farmer" because of his big hands and feet and familiar ways with the soil, was among the two or three strongest men in camp—the fact of which he did not hesitate to remind the customers when pushing his merchandise. "Just the right keepsake for the girl who is waiting," he would recite as coached by the company literature, "whether it's Mom, Sis, or that Someone Special. She'll be proud to wear your beautiful, official C.C.C. ring." If that didn't do it, Farmer leaned on the customers a little. And if that didn't work, either, his eyes would narrow and nostrils flare and his hands would start to clench and unclench uncontrollably. That usually did it.

Among those who proved surprisingly resistant to Farmer Jones's mercantile charm was David Schumacher. His appointment as Toby's assistant had earned David virtual immunity from casual bullying, but his still-pudgy appearance and retirement to the comparative comforts of the camp detail must have excited Farmer's intense displeasure when coupled with David's refusal to buy a silver-plated C.C.C. ring to give his mother for Christmas. Farmer wrapped one of his large, callused hands around David's soft, pale throat. David screamed. Wolfbait, of all people, launched himself in gnatlike assault at the hulking Jones, who swatted him aside and then paused in indecision over which of them to kill first.

It was into this brief interlude in the mayhem that Joe Calabrese—he of the boundless fortitude and washboard chest—charged. Calculating the odds against him, Joe submarined the bigger boy with a sudden tackle around the ankles that sent him crashing facedown to the floor and drove his skull hard into the edge of the nearest bunk. Dazed but dauntless, Farmer rose with hatred in his spinning eyes and a profane curse on his bloody lips and came clattering on spavined legs after Joe. A dodge, a feint, a short left jab to the nose, and a well-directed right cross just below the ear, and the contest was over. The supersalesman was out cold for a good thirty seconds—and on recovery did not clamor for a rematch. But when three of the five trucks of which Joe was in charge turned up at dawn a few days later with their antifreeze drained and radiators frozen and cracked, suspicion of Farmer Jones was widespread in the barracks.

The captain, however, professed no interest in rumors and guesses. Joe was in charge of the trucks, the trucks froze up—ergo, Joe was the culpable party. His insistence that he had properly serviced the vehicles with antifreeze and they must have been sabotaged—by whom or why, Joe would not venture—fell on deaf ears. The captain, as everyone knew, had not really forgiven Joe for his spectacular protest of Link's demotion from bugler. "The guy is livin' on borrowed time," Skeezix said after that episode, voicing the camp consensus.

Only Joe's passionate declaration of a frameup saved him a second time from outright dismissal. He was docked twenty dollars, his entire allowance for the remainder of the enlistment period, and reassigned from the trucks to the grueling road detail—so severe a punishment that everyone expected him to quit the corps on the spot. At the least, they thought he would tell the captain about Farmer Jones and his revenge motive. But Joe did neither. Finishing up at Pittsfield High meant too much to him to leave now of his own volition, and he hoped his good behavior would cause the captain to relent. As to Jones, Joe told Toby, "Naww, he didn't do it—he's too fuckin' dumb. Anyway, he swore to me on his mama's left tit it wasn't him, so what'm I gonna do?"

Others in the company resolved to do what Joe was powerless to—organize an *en masse* challenge to the arbitrary judgment, based as it was purely on circumstantial evidence and spurred in all likelihood by the captain's known animus. Exactly what form this complaint should take was vigorously debated after lights-out throughout the barracks. Toby's contribution to the process was a timely discussion of the judicial system during his Citizenship class. The specific proposal for a kangaroo court composed of enrollees came entirely from the men, however, after they read about similar camp tribunals in *Happy Days*, the C.C.C. weekly. Their plan, with Bloomgarden and Dundy in the lead, was for Toby to endorse their petition once they got a hundred signatures on it—half the company—and then, if the captain proved receptive, ask that the judgment against Joe be vacated and the whole case submitted from scratch to the new court of his peers.

"I'm not sure my name on there would help much," Toby told Skeezix. "The opposite, I'd say." His stamp on their action would be all too clear to Sparhawk as it was.

"He's just yella'!" Wolfbait charged.

"Shut up your fuckin' face!" Skeezix told him and then pursued Toby with a touch more diplomacy. "Well, couldja talk to 'em for us, maybe? Hawkhead listens to you." Away from the clerk's job, he had lost his sure sense of intramural politics.

"Sometimes. But this is your grievance, not mine. If I'm in on it, he'll assume I put you all up to it—which won't do any of us any good."

"See? He's just bullshittin' his way out of it!" Wolfbait yelled.

"No, Toby's right, you asshole!" Boxcar Malone weighed in. Dundy concurred, and Skeezix relented. An ounce of complicity, in this case, was worth a ton of solidarity.

They got their hundred signatures and a dozen more for good measure. When Toby was summoned to Sparhawk's quarters to view their handiwork, the captain wore a sweetly reproachful look instead of, as usual when crossed, spouting sparks like the Wabash Cannonball. "I suppose you don't know a thing about any of this?" he asked, handing him the petition for inspection.

It had been neatly done on the company clerk's typewriter, and almost certainly by Eddie Spain himself, although his name was not among the signatories; Eddie was nothing if not politic. "I was consulted," Toby acknowledged.

"And what counsel did you offer?" The captain cast a coy glance at Nesbit, who was pacing about in the corner.

"I told them to make sure their spelling, punctuation, and grammar were right—I'm the education officer, not a political agitator."

"Naturally. And you didn't encourage them beyond that?"

"This is their idea, Gordon."

"Of course. And their susceptibility to the power of suggestion is extremely low, as we all know."

"It's a spontaneous reaction to Calabrese's sentence."

"And they didn't ask you what you thought of the idea?"

"Not in so many words."

"Well, then, suppose you tell us."

He took Sparhawk's subdued tone for a trap and responded with equally subdued enthusiasm. With one modification, he said, the idea was perhaps worth considering on a trial basis. It might teach the men greater responsibility, improve their morale, and even help the camp's standing with district and corps area by introducing democratic procedures in the ranks. "There may be more to gain than to lose by giving them some rope."

"Even though they're trying to pull our pants down in the bargain?" The sweetness was fading fast.

"I don't quite see that."

"Maybe that's because they're not your pants," Nesbit sniped.

Sparhawk nursed the brandy he was cupping without offering Toby one. "Mitchell thinks we'd be abdicating our responsibility if we let the boys be judges of their own conduct."

"Maybe. But you'd retain the right to supervene if they abused the privilege."

"Correction," Sparhawk said. "For me, Ash, and you—and the two of you aren't even officers. And the other one here who is seems to have been left out in the cold entirely."

"Yes—well, that's where the thing needs to be modified. The boys obviously didn't think it through all that far. There's got to be a set procedure for initiating charges of misconduct." Left to their own, the enrollees would probably never stir. The natural party to do the prosecuting was the adjutant—leaving the captain, in his Olympian detachment, to intercede if and when barracks justice failed.

Sparhawk sipped some more of his cognac and then turned to the grimly sober Nesbit. "What do you say to that, Lieutenant?"

"I say it's a smoke screen—and it'll only serve to undermine my authority in the eyes of the men still further by—"

"Just the opposite."

"—giving them the opportunity to dismiss any charges I bring as some sort of nuisance—which they probably won't be able to resist doing."

"It seems to work in other camps."

"They aren't this one."

"But if the idea works for them, I don't see why—"

"Just because Russia's communist, do you think we should go for it, too?"

"What's Russia got to do with this?"

"If you like it so much, why don't you just pack up and go there?"

"I didn't say I liked it! But you can learn from everywhere—"

"Like these men here are learning from you—"

"I should hope so! That's what I'm paid for."

"—all about undermining authority and inciting social revolution!"

"All right, now, simmer down, both of you." Sparhawk extended a conciliating hand toward each of them. It was apparent he was enjoying the contest, even without suspecting the stakes, both inside the camp or beyond it. He drained his glass with satisfaction, seeming to sense his dominion had been bolstered by his underlings' deadlock, then licked his lips and announced, "Well, I'm inclined to try it for a while—with Mitchell prosecuting as Toby proposes. The boys can have their pick of the camp for a defense attorney—Pickles included —and we'll use Calabrese as a dry run. So long as we're stuck with the ornery bastard, let's not turn him into a martyr."

Joe's problem was trying to enlist the right lawyer. Toby was his first choice. "You got more drag with the guys than anyone else— they'll listen to you."

"They're on your side already," Toby told him. "Besides, I can't— I'm on the review board."

And neither Dundy nor Skeezix could argue his case since they had been elected along with the other three barracks leaders to serve on the Kangaroo Court. Link Salter was his closest buddy in camp, but he couldn't put that sort of burden on Link, said Joe. That was when he came up with the notion of enlisting Farmer Jones to represent him.

"I don't think that's such a hot idea," Toby advised.

"Look, he didn't do it, if that's what you're still worryin' about."

"How do you know—because he told you that?"

"And looked me in the eye at the same time. Anyways, I already asked him and he said he'd do it. If he's the one that fucked me, how come he's willin' to be my lawyer, tell me that?"

"Out of guilt."

"He's *not* guilty!"

"But a lot of guys think he is. And if he did it, or even might have, then you couldn't have. Take him out of the picture, and all you've got to offer is your word for it."

He brooded for a moment. "I get it—I should make a heavy outa Farmer to save my own ass. That stinks."

"If I were your lawyer, that's what I'd have to advise."

"Sure—'cause you stink, too. The whole fuckin' system stinks to high heaven, you want my opinion."

Even with Farmer Jones as his lead-tongued Darrow, a court of his peers found Joe Calabrese not guilty as charged by the adjutant and recommended that he be restored to the truck detail. But, mindful of the collective responsibility of the company toward government property, the judges urged that his twenty-dollar fine be paid for out of the canteen kitty, and to hell with a new washing machine. This last consideration, a sop to the captain, weighed heavily enough with him to agree to uphold the decision. Ash and Toby concurred. Justice, of a sort, had arrived in the trenches.

So buoyed was the company by this development that when corps area headquarters staged a surprise inspection of the camp just before the end of the rating period, every last man was on his mettle. The work details functioned through the cold with nary a grumble, completing the new Shadow Trail for skiing even as the visitors watched. The barracks were immaculate; the mess, relatively decorous; classes, packed and with everyone eerily attentive, and the Rec, a tableau of rustic conviviality as the men began hanging it with cheery streamers for the dance that Saturday night before Christmas. On departure, the headquarters team confided to the captain that he might look forward with confidence to the posting of the new camp standings in January.

"And just to think," said an effervescent Sparhawk, toasting Toby after taps that night in his quarters as Doc Haseltine joined them for a smoke and a briefing, "I was accusing Professor Ronan here of conspiring with the boys to pull my pants down. Hell, this kangaroo thing is an inspiration—'sgot all the earmarks of democracy in action, only the reins stay nice 'n' tight right where they belong. Wish I'd thought of it myself. Gentlemen, I respectfully give you—due process of law."

V

Tuesday, January 1, 1936

Joseph Marco Calabrese (1915–1936).
He made 1936 by about an hour and twenty minutes.
More as a favor than out of faith, he drove a small group of men from our camp and the one on West Mountain to town to attend a special midnight mass at St. Mary's—newly instituted as a kind of counter-rite to the usual dissipations of the evening. Truly, the Lord moves in mysterious ways. Joe did not drink a drop beforehand, they tell me, although some of the others did and hoped to pray away the effects so as to start the new year in a blessed state.

After the service he drove back first to West Mtn with everyone in the rear singing to stay warm. On the way down from West Mtn camp, the truck hit a bad patch of ice and flipped. He got pinned under the steering wheel. They said it sliced into him like a can opener. Too much blood was gone by the time the ambulance came.

*A couple of fractures and lots of bruises but no one else was badly
hurt except Bingo. They think he may wind up permanently paralyzed. Only time will tell.*

I was very fond of Joe.

From the beginning, it was not the most joyous night of his life.

First, and inexcusably, he had had to lie to April to get out of
spending New Year's Eve with her.

Then, to make good the lie, he had gone home to pass the weekend
with his father, winding up at an early supper Aunt Ida was kind
enough to give for them in Poughkeepsie on New Year's Eve. The
sight of him for three days running did nothing for Toby's spirits.
The can company had demoted him by then to day timekeeper, a
strictly clerical job that paid accordingly, yet the only thing about it
that made him feel bad, his father said, was that they had fired the
previous incumbent to make room for him. The next step down was
night watchman, but instead of bitterness he continued to profess appreciation for still being kept on at all. There was no percentage, by
that point, in Toby's disabusing him of his gratitude; it would have
only ruined their reunion. As it was, he was not pleased when on the
ride up to Aunt Ida's, Toby handed him an envelope with a hundred
dollars he had put aside from his C.C.C. pay. "What's this?" his father
asked.

"More than I need for now."

The elder Ronan never took his eyes from the road. If he had, they
both would have probably burst into tears. Swallowing, he thanked his
son but said Toby had his whole life ahead of him and would need
whatever it was he was offering. Toby tried to argue, but his father
wouldn't hear of it. Besides, he said, having lately sold their old house
in Piermont, he had enough to keep out of trouble. And if Toby
ever got in a real jam, the old man would always be there to help.

They put him on the train to Albany so Toby could make his alleged curfew—one lie leads inexorably to the next. By the time he got
a hitch east over the mountains, stopped by at camp for his "costume,"
made it into town, and hiked the last half mile to the Keyeses', it was
well after ten. Even so, guests were still arriving. No one else, though,
came on foot. Or approximated the authenticity of his outfit: the
olive-drab fatigues of a C.C.C. peavie. For dramatic effect, he carried
a hoe.

Lawrence Keyes outdid him in cutlery. He presided over the gaiety
as a slightly paunchy Father Time, gotten up in a scraggly white
beard, several pleated bedsheets, beach sandals, and a small egg timer
hung around his neck. On his shoulder he hefted a genuine-looking

scythe. "Well, well, well, we haven't seen you around here in a dog's age, my boy," he boomed. "Eat, drink, and be merry—and let's swap our tools in an hour, what do you say?" Then he was off on a rollicking greeting to the costumed couple who followed Toby in—Hamlet and Mary Pickford in something diaphanous.

To one side of an enormous cut-glass bowl of eggnog that sat in the center of the hall table, Constance Keyes held court, draped like Lillian Russell in miles of mauve taffeta and topped with a wide-brimmed fiesta of ribbons, feathers, and bows. On almost anyone else, it would have been merely *de trop;* on her, with her usual severity of wardrobe, it was straight vaudeville, and all the more saucy for it. Toby praised her stunning appearance and won a lilac-scented kiss, along with the hope that his public-speaking career was flourishing. As an afterthought, she noted his forestwear and made a connection he had not known existed before, expressing regret that Arthur Haseltine could not attend the party. "He took care of all of us, you know, right up until retiring," she said, "and now he seems to have climbed back into harness out there with you and your boys. I only pray his eyes hold out."

"I wasn't aware there's a problem."

"Oh," she said, "oh, my. Perhaps you weren't supposed to know."

"Is it serious?"

"Glaucoma. I can't think it's safe for him to be driving for much longer."

Dampened by this news, he ladled himself some eggnog and drifted into the front parlor. On the far side, hanging over the pianist and joining half a dozen others in song, were Temple, in a depressingly wholesome apple-green Alpine dirndl, and Mitchell Nesbit, in the uniform of the United States Army. Uneager to crash that circle, Toby clung to the fringe of the crowded room, sipping his drink and mentally awarding prizes to the attendees in various categories of ludicrousness. The Slapstick Medal went to Carl Keyes, in a tilted bowler, epauletted John Paul Jones jacket buttoned to his chin in brass, striped baseball pants with ceremonial scabbard dangling at the side, and a pair of patent pumps with buckles that looked just right for whirling off in to a minuet. It was his statement, Toby supposed, on the inanity of the whole occasion, which he nevertheless declined to boycott. "Hey, I'm glad they let you back in," Carl hailed him as Toby stood admiring his outlandish getup.

"Special holiday dispensation—the usual house rule is one free pass per government camp."

"So I gather," he said, eyes traveling across the room to Nesbit. "He's a terrible stick—I've told her."

Toby shrugged. *"De gustibus . . ."*

"And all that other Harvard shit," Carl laughed. "Say, I'm sorry as hell we didn't make it to the club for tennis. Actually, I haven't been home much the fall semester."

"Actually, I'm not much for tennis."

"Actually, I'm not much either. Give me the indoor sports anytime."

"Your reputation precedes you. Rumors abound you're something of an authority on the fleshpots of the region."

"Who's been spreading that filthy slander?" His hand went for his sword. "It happens to be absolutely true," he said, shifting the hand to cover his mouth, "but let's keep it from the guv'nor, shall we? He's death on social diseases—thinks they're the exclusive privilege of immigrant stock."

He was so jocose about it that to suggest wastrelry had gone out of vogue since the world crashed would have been unsporting. "My source is unimpeachable," Toby said, nodding toward Guy and Holly Curtis, who swept into the room with a bow and a curtsy in their direction, "but I can't vouch for her discretion."

"Oh, Lord," said Carl, "the Wit of Williamstown and the Vixen of West Stockbridge. My secret's safer with the gypsies."

She was dressed as a *doña* in black lace, with tiara, mantilla, and a busily fluttering fan. Guy was a matador, his satin gold britches too snug in the fanny for adorableness. "My, my," Holly said on taking Toby in, "how authentically agrarian. Are you coolie or kulak?"

"It's what the boys wear at camp."

"I might have guessed. How tediously apropos." She gave her fan a backhand wave, as if to keep upwind of the very thought of manual labor. "And the hoe—what's that for? I hadn't heard the lads went in much for vegetables."

He glanced past her and saw that Guy was busy bending Carl's ear. "Among its other uses," Toby said, giving it a twirl, "is disemboweling spoiled bitches."

The fanning stopped abruptly, and the mock-Castilian sneer slipped to a wan smile. "There's a W.C. at the head of the stairs on the second floor," she said in a husky whisper. "Be there in ten minutes—and knock four times."

She excused herself with a farewell flutter and a touch on his arm as she slid past Guy, who turned to him then with a hearty, "Well, so it's the return of Comrade Ronan. I admire a fellow who goes in for social realism even at costume parties."

"Agit-prop knows no season."

"Quite so. Still teaching your boys out there that socialism is the moral necessity of our time?"

" 'Still'? As a matter of fact, I've never done that—or expressed that view to you or anyone else."

Guy was unprepared for the sudden switch from japery. "Strange. It's more or less of a cumulative impression I've got—some of it from the lieutenant over there who's seen more of you in action than I have. He's quite a decent fellow, by the way, or don't you think?"

"Oh, quite—if a little careless with the truth," he said and went for an eggnog refill.

What struck him on the way upstairs to his rendezvous was not how royally Guy Curtis deserved to be cuckolded but how little pleasure his debasement yielded its perpetrators. It was not to spite Guy, she swore, that his wife spread her legs or that Toby happily berthed there; the gull was irrelevant to the act. Failure to advise him of it was the only immoral thing, and not the soiling of their sacrament. Unless, of course, she had informed him, laughing in his face without naming her paramour. Was anything beyond her? And how many lovers had she? Happily, his own vested interest in the answer was slender; the mystery was all.

A lissome arm snaked out from behind the bathroom door the instant his fourth rap sounded and drew him inside as if he were a turkish towel. "Is this wise?" he asked, setting his cup of grog on the porcelain washbasin.

"Oh, do get rid of that asinine hoe," she said and reached past him to lock the door. The hoe landed in the bathtub with a clatter. "Well, I knew one of you was asinine." She drew herself up close to him and wrapped her fingers around the back of his neck. Her warmth and musk were overwhelming in that dense cell, so much more confined, even, than their other trysting lair. "So I'm a spoiled bitch, am I?" she asked, tugging herself upward till their faces were flush.

"Incredibly."

"Funny—I never noticed." Her fingers traveled his neck as if examining a woodwind for the perfection of its grain. "But you, on the other hand, are very sweet and very sexy—did you know?" Her frilly costume enmeshed him as her whole weight ground hard into his chest.

"Incredibly," he said and fell to separating her lipstick from her. Her mouth responded by touring his face clockwise, then counterclockwise, as her hands fell and found him where he had risen and clutched him until a moan escaped from her and she slumped into his arms with the whisper, "Happy new year, sweetie."

It took a full minute for her to scrub the lipstick off him, and another for her to replace it, and another for him to subside. Then they raised and matched palms, patty-cake fashion, twined them slowly together, held each other hard for a long moment, and parted.

"You left your dumb hoe!" she hissed as they passed later in the dining room.

On the buffet line, he found himself behind Nesbit. The lieutenant was so caught up in conversation with Carl and his date, a broad-shouldered girl in the powder-blue dress of a Colonial dame, that he never gave a backward glance. But he knew Toby was there all along, for after they had each helped themselves to some meats, Nesbit said over his shoulder, "Your costume is completely out of line—the corps isn't a joke."

Toby kept still for a moment, uncertain whether to answer or ignore him, and then settled on, "I don't address the backs of people's heads."

Nesbit remained ramrod stiff. His voice seemed to come out of the cole slaw as he added, "You've got a nerve, dishonoring the men like that."

They were side by side now, attacking different targets in the salad sector. "It's a tribute," Toby said, "not a joke. Anyway, who gave you jurisdiction around here?"

His snub profile glowered above the lettuces. "It's not a question of jurisdiction," he said, still avoiding Toby's look. "It's just bad taste, pure and simple. You're mocking the C.C.C."

"And what about you—what are you mocking?"

"I'm not in costume—it would obviously be inappropriate."

"Lucky you, having a rule book that tells you when to breathe."

"It isn't a matter of rules—it's responsibility and common decency." He flicked a venomous sidelong look and then swiveled away with a parting "Sarcasm doesn't help, either." The flawlessly bristled back of his cubed head retreated before Toby could lacquer it with blue-cheese dressing.

His insides were still churning by the time Temple and he finally confronted each other. All night he had stayed as far away from her as possible without actually hiding; he suspected the plan was mutual. His emotions were too raw and the scene too public to risk exchanging more than the shallowest amenities with her. But as he seated himself on a wicker loveseat in a corner of the empty conservatory off the library to poke at his food, she came by for her flute, resting on a music stand near him. "Oh, Toby!" she cried, clearly more startled than pleased at the dual discovery. "I'm—so glad you could come."

"Me, too—good eats." He extended his plate. "Have some?"

"Oh, no thanks—I've been nibbling all afternoon, I'm afraid."

"Well, at least sit for a minute."

"Well, I've got to—we're playing after dessert—"

"A minute."

She sat; not to would have been pointedly discourteous. Her high forehead fretted despite the clenched set to the rest of her. "I—I didn't think you'd come, to be honest. It's nice to see you again."

"Nice to see *you* again." Which exhausted their supply of spontaneous civilities. They both fell to studying the contents of his plate in silence while groping for words to cover the rupture in what had been so brief but promising a friendship. "Why didn't you think I'd come?" he tried. "Obviously I'm lacking the decency to know my place."

She shut her eyes and lowered her head annoyedly. "Please—"

"Forgive me—I was just curious."

She tossed off an impatient sigh. "All I meant was—I supposed you'd be otherwise occupied for the evening."

"I unoccupied myself." His eyes found hers. "You didn't, I notice."

"You notice the wrong things—it's not that sort of party. It's more or less of an open house, can't you see? Everyone in the family gets to invite friends. I'd be glad to introduce you around if you're at all uncomfortable—"

"No, thanks. I know all the ones I care to—and some I don't."

She gripped her flute tightly. "You're not terribly subtle, you know."

"Vulgar, almost, you might say—a duck out of water."

"Look here," she said, "if you're not enjoying yourself, don't let us detain you. Evidently you're used to running with a different crowd."

"Common people, you mean?"

"I wouldn't care to characterize them."

"Oh, but you have—and made me do penance for it."

"No one's made you do a blessed thing, Toby!"

"Then why *was* I invited—if not to be shown what I've been missing?"

"You were asked because Mother thinks I've behaved badly to you —and Father still thinks you're the eccentric son of some sort of tycoon." She softened a trifle. "And Holly's a fan of yours, if you must know."

"You left out Carl."

"Carl's in his own world."

"But more for me than against, don't you think?"

"I haven't polled him."

"Well, that leaves just you—who deign to speak to me only through your devoted bearer of pointed messages."

"You shouldn't require any messages. The situation should be perfectly clear to a real gentleman."

"What situation—that your callers must never soil their hands dealing with the fetid masses? Working girls are human, too, Temple."

"Your *hands* aren't the issue," she snapped. "Father's inquired about her at the plant a little—you may as well know. The girl's evidently one level above a trollop—'an easy lay,' I believe the term is. How do you think that makes *me* feel?"

"I think it should make you feel ashamed for having put your father up to it in the first place."

"It was not *my* idea, as it happens."

"Then maybe it's time you expressed some where he's concerned."

"Oh, Toby," she said with more exasperated feeling than he had had any hope of wringing from her.

"And whatever she is, she's no proto-fascist, as you so aptly called our good soldierboy that night at the—"

"I didn't call him that—it's what I said *you* thought he was."

"And was I wrong—or don't you two ever bare your social consciences to each other—so long as we're going into who's exchanging what intimacies."

Her knuckles were nearly white by now from strangling the flute. "You're upsetting me," she said and sprang to her feet. "I can't play when I'm upset." He tried to grasp her free hand, but she pulled it away and hurried off without a backward glance.

By midnight he had discovered there was enough rum, however diluted, in their keg of eggnog to turn him heavyhearted and lightheaded. As through a gossamer curtain, the toasts to the New Year floated mistily but with enough vituperative timbre to summon him from impending blotto. "Ladies and gentlemen—I give you Nineteen Hundred Thirty-six!" heralded Father Time, scythe aloft. "May it signal the return of true prosperity to our sorely tried nation—and good health and gladness to each of our beloved friends gathered here."

Cries of "Hear, hear!" and "God bless!" rang out through the thronged center hall, followed by a brisk chorus of "For He's a Jolly Good Fellow." Whereupon a reciprocal toast to the host and hostess and all their kin was offered by the visiting matador, *El Gran Dilettante* (known in English as "The Not-So-Wise Guy"). After commending the Keyeses for their generosity of spirit, he demonstrated his own deficiency of same by concluding, "To Nineteen and Thirty-six—may it bring the restoration of liberty to our occupied land—and the timely demise of the New Deal!"

Cheers and laughter attended this death wish, and then somebody broke into "My Country, 'Tis of Thee," in which everybody spiritedly joined.

Massive indignation, lubricated beyond restraint, seized him as the anthem died in that packed hall, and he raised his hoe high in the air and called out, "To Nineteen Thirty-six and Franklin D. Roosevelt—the man who brought hope back to America—long may he wave!"

Earth had not witnessed such a stillness since dawn the day after Creation. Everyone stood looking at either the business end of Toby's waving hoe or the floor. "Well," cracked Constance Keyes at last, "he does work for the man."

He remembered shortly thereafter coming upon Curtis and Nesbit in animated exchange beside the bottomless eggnog bowl and then pausing momentarily at his approach. "Not every federal employee owes slavish allegiance to his commander-in-chief," Guy said, "wouldn't you agree, Ronan?"

The only thought in Toby's head just then was that there was Second Lieutenant Mitchell Nesbit holding a cup of alcohol-laced beverage in his sanctimonious little raccoon paws. "Is that a vice I see before me, Lieutenant?" he asked, nearly toppling into him.

"Watch it, will you?" Nesbit barked.

"I'm watching, I'm watching—and it's indecent and irresponsible behavior in my studied opinion, your sopping it up in public like that —dishonoring the uniform of the nation we all love and cherish till God uth dost part—"

"Lay off!" Nesbit warned as Toby's breath wilted his lapels.

"Sauce for the gander, Lieutenant," he slobbered, "speaking of which, the goose'd like to help himself to a teeny bit more—"

As he tried to reach past them for a fresh cup, Guy grabbed his arm in restraint, and Toby whirled on him. Curtis caved in under the sudden shift of weight, and as they went down together, Toby's hoe hooked the bowl of eggnog and brought it swirling and splashing onto the rug, dousing everyone within range.

He reeked the whole long, lonely, bone-cold walk back to camp and never thought to flag a hitch from the few passing cars. One of them had to belong to Mitchell Nesbit.

That sobering hike routed his grogginess, but nothing could have prepared him for the news at camp. Every light in the place was ablaze, creating a ghostly canopy, when he trudged onto the campus. The steady murmuring that drew him toward the Rec announced a vigil, no revelry, was being held within. Joe Calabrese was already dead, Skeezix reported, eyes hollow in his stubbled face, and half a dozen others remained in the hospital, where the captain and Dr.

Haseltine were standing by. The adjutant was down manning company headquarters and had promised to call them on the pay phone if there was news. Nearly half the company was away for the holidays, at home or visiting somewhere, but everyone who remained in camp milled inarticulately about the now-bleak hall, numbness medicating their too-new sorrow. A rare upraised voice or bleat of laughter meant no disrespect—only that those uttering them were glad to be survivors.

By four all the boys had turned in except Eddie and Skeezix, who walked Toby down to the office to wait with Nesbit for word from town. None came till six when the doctor called to say that only Bingo Barnes remained in a grave way. After Toby got on the line at Haseltine's request, the doctor said softly, "The captain wonders if you'd be kind enough to call Joe's family—considering your closeness to him." He paused just long enough to let Toby know it was an order, not a question. "You might say we'll get back to them later in the day about shipping home his remains."

He thought the captain was acting unmanly and, with the two boys out of earshot in the anteroom, told Nesbit so. "It's a hard thing to do from a hospital phone," the adjutant said.

"Then let him come back here and do it—it's his duty."

Nesbit went to the filing cabinet and took out Joe's folder. "It's a neighbor's phone," he said, writing down the number. "Who's going to do it—you or me?"

Having aired his opinion of Sparhawk, he felt no choice. It took a very long time for Joe's mother to come to the phone. She must have guessed, given the hour, that tragedy was beckoning. For someone who hated the impersonality of the telephone, Toby was grateful this once to be a disembodied voice, charged with bearing the saddest tidings a heart can know.

There had been an accident, he said as soon as she came on, and he was so sorry but her Joe was gone. There was an unbearable pause, and he wondered during it if she knew the language well enough to understand. Then came a short cry of such tearing lamentation as to end all doubt.

He did not know what more to say after that. Only soft sobs were audible as he tried to tell her how fond everyone was of her son, but the words were inutterably cruel, for all their intent, and he stopped, and soon there was no sound on the other end but the heavy knocking of a dangling receiver.

In the streaky, pallid light of the year's first daybreak, a few of them trooped to the middle of the campus and raised the flag to half-mast while Link Salter blew taps for his only real friend in the world.

That those long, sweet, quavery notes were unauthorized made them all the more plaintive as they lifted through the brittle air and wafted above the crusted white forest and into the timeless, gathering hills. By the bugle's last note, every man in camp was out in front of his barracks, hand over heart. Next to the officers' quarters, the captain and the adjutant saluted side by side.

Afterward, Link came to Toby's door and handed him the bugle, Joe's chemistry book, and a dog-eared copy of *Macbeth* he must have been reading for school. Link wondered if his bugle might be buried with Joe. Toby promised to ask.

TWELVE

Wednesday, Jan. 16, '36

Ambrosia from the gods!
Corps Area HQ advises we ranked third among 61 camps in Mass.
Dist. for 2nd half of '35 and eighth in entire Area I. Plus special com-
mendation for most improved camp in Dist.—and specific mention of
overdue estab. of satisfactory ed. program as vital contributor.
Whoopee.

Capt. floating with the cumuli. Called mtg of company after supper
to read glad tidings, dispense kudos & then add the inevitable joykiller:
"We're going for the gold ring this time around, fellas—which means
every last man among you pulls his oar between now & re-enlistment
or he won't be with us after March." . . .

THE BAUBLE from corps area concentrated Sparhawk's obsessiveness
wonderfully.

He looked almost dashing now astride the big bay roan he rode over
to camp each afternoon from the stable in Hancock and out into the
field to inspect his troops. The great steamy snorts from the stallion
and the flawless gleam to the boots of its rider lent a Napoleonic flair
to their fused image: gallant commander on rearing steed, rallying the
snowbound ranks against the enemy and the elements. The horseshit
was easier to overlook in all this keen posturing.

Until then, his command had been largely a private transaction;
finally, though, Gordon Sparhawk, Capt., U.S.A.R., was ready to cash
in his heavy psychic investment in Camp 127, openly pursuing the reward of recognition from his military and civilian superiors. Under
orders to propose higher goals and the means to meet them during the
ensuing six months, the camp high command assembled in the captain's quarters and, succumbing to his monomania, turned itself into a
scourge.

Ash Cummings offered only token resistance to the hopelessly ambitious agenda of work projects Sparhawk was determined to see completed that spring. Suddenly it was vital that the circuit road up and down the mountain be opened to the public in time for the June blooming of the azalea fields just below Berry Pond. "We'll make a big splash of it," he said, conjuring pavilions of dignitaries and multitudes of grateful locals to applaud the unveiling of this, his monumental gift to posterity—Pittsfield State Forest, the peerless bower, an American Arcady. And there would be ancillary projects to rush through for the occasion: a swimming area at the pond, foot bridges fording every stream, hikers' shelters, rest rooms, parking lots, a rustic lodge near the forest entrance to serve as a permanent haven once the camp was taken down, and a fire tower for monitoring the safety of that vast arbor.

"Now we don't want to go makin' the place into some kinda sleazy amusement park," Ash cautioned with the proprietary mentality he had adopted toward the forest. For him, those sweet hills and humming brambles, those limpid brooks and hushed hollows were all the recreation a yearning soul could ask; to "develop" this incomparable temple the Lord had bestowed and to make access to it too easy was to guarantee its early defilement.

"We're here to serve the needs of the public," the captain replied officiously, "not run a private country club. It's time we got on with it!"

Mitchell Nesbit was ready. His prescription for bleeding the turnip was to rate every man in the company, West Point fashion, on his weekly performance and post the score for all to see. Each enrollee was to be graded on a scale of one to ten in four categories—effort, initiative, achievement, and cooperation (the last counting double). The lieutenant and the barracks leaders would mark camp conduct; Ash and the Lems, field work, and Toby, classroom performance. Those at the bottom of these complex computations could anticipate constant harassment and would run the perpetual risk of discharge. To improve discipline, furthermore, the company would be required from then on to line up in orderly fashion and file singly into the mess and the Rec and for all other activities instead of trampling one another for advantage like a pack of hyenas. Meals were no longer to be shouting matches, and horseplay was to be forbidden in the barracks as well as on the job. "Tight control is essential for increased productivity," the adjutant asserted, metallic jaw braced against the likely storm of protest.

Sparhawk fussed with an agitating few follicles on the right flank of his mustache. "Will the men stand for it?"

"If their choice is made clear to them."

"I don't want a surly crew on my hands, Mitch."

"Caesar didn't force-march the legions by blowing kisses at them."

The captain turned to Toby for the expected dissent and was not disappointed.

Positive incentives were a better way than repression to improve the men's productivity, Toby proposed, and the obvious method in his view was to enhance their chances for post-camp employment by raising the level of their skills. Without a doubt, that would require a willingness by the Lems to teach on the job and much closer supervision of the work performed, but the investment was sure to pay off. The undeniable fact was that the enrollees spent most of their field time performing the meanest sort of unskilled work—digging ditches, clearing brush, chopping trees, uprooting stumps, hauling rock—and leaving all actual construction and precision work to the Lems. Little effort was expended in matching a boy's assigned job to his skills or interests. Job rotation was handled unsystematically. And upgrading of skills was an all but alien concept. With planning and resolve, all that could be changed—and the captain's targets achieved.

The work superintendent licked his thin, weathered mouth and gave his head a single vehement shake when Toby was done. Pressed by the captain for comment, Ash Cummings said only, "You want to turn this into a trade school, you'd best get yourself a crew from manual training to run it. We're just working woodsmen."

Wisdom no doubt dictated retreat, but Toby, relying instead on Sparhawk's new zeal, pressed the attack. While the forest enjoyed its winter sleep and the men had little to do but struggle ineffectually on the circuit road and try to stay warm, why not divert the most skilled enrollees in the company to begin construction at once on the projected rustic lodge—and make it a showpiece? It would give them a jump on the building season. And because the lodge was to be sited close by the camp, working on it would be relatively convenient, even in the cold. And because it was to be more sophisticated than anything else the company had built, it would be an ideal means for determining just what skills the Lems could readily convey to their raw apprentices. "And besides," Toby confessed, "the sooner the thing gets built, the quicker I'll have some decent classroom space."

"We can't build," Ash said flatly, "till the frost's out of the ground."

But the captain was antsy. Unwilling to hibernate a moment longer than necessary, he asked Ash how deep he figured the frost was. The heavy snows had helped insulate the soil, Ash granted and supposed the frost line was down about six inches, maybe eight. Foundation work might be begun by early April, or late March if they were lucky.

"Too late," said the aroused Sparhawk. "Why can't the boys dig out the frost right now?"

Every tributary on Ash's heavily seamed face came to life. "That's one helluva lot o' damned hard work you're talkin' about."

"That's why the boys are here."

The superintendent nodded. "Trouble then is that she'll freeze right back up on you—underneath whatever's taken out."

"Not if we keep the site warm enough—maybe a few oil-drum fires in there—and cover the exposed surface at night with tarps till the foundation is down."

It was a superb piece of carpentry. Everything in it came out of the forest except the casement windows, which were bought at a good price within the projects budget. Thirty-six feet long by twenty-one wide, the interior of the lodge was crowned with an intricate criss-cross of massive timbers that gave it the monumental scale of the great hall in a medieval manor house. An enormous split-log mantelpiece of white pine varnished to a high luster surmounted the stone hearth, and the walls were stained an inviting soft brown. More notably, not a single nail was used—every beam and board was pegged or dovetailed or joined tongue in groove or with mortise and tenon, all of it requiring infinite cutting and trimming and fitting and refitting.

The only trouble with this prodigy of craftsmanship was that the Lems performed it as if they were operating a closed guild in a fifteenth-century Hanseatic League town. While the enrollees broke their backs preparing the site and hauling in the raw materials, Ash's crew designed the building around the desk in his office, then repaired to the back of the work shed, where, warmed by blazing stoves, they toiled meticulously over the lumber on the big power saws and the jigs. It was undoubtedly a labor of love for the Lems, many of whom came in on the weekends to hand-hew the woodwork. But so far as the company was concerned—and despite the pledge to treat the lodge as a learn-as-you-go experience for the boys—it was the same old story. When Toby said as much to Ash, he grew snappish and resentful. "In case you ain't noticed, the mercury says seventeen degrees. Now I can't have my men standin' around with icicles hangin' off their balls while a bunch o' snots is tryin' to figure which end is up."

The captain, consumed by visions of Valhalla made manifest before his blinking eyes, was equally unconcerned. "Everyone's pitching in very nicely," he said. "Any of the fellows who want to observe closely can absorb the building techniques that way."

"Cotton absorbs," said Toby. "Boys learn by doing."

He drafted a memo to Sparhawk toward the end of February as the main structural work on the lodge neared completion. With only the kitchen and toilet installations left for the thaw, it was essential for the morale of the men, Toby wrote, that all but the supervisory work on the sanitary disposal plant connected to the lodge be undertaken by the enrollees. This was definitely not the same sort of high craft that the structure itself had required and so could reasonably be entrusted to neophytes. Perhaps the captain himself, trained as a civil engineer, would direct the operation, explaining to the men step by step why so vital a part of the facility could not be constructed haphazardly. He might begin with a topographical profile of the site, indicating how the disposal line had to slope downward from the lodge and the way the land contour affected the pitch and depth of the ditch. Then he could proceed to instruct them on what sort of piping ought to be laid and of what weight and length and strength, and how to carry it without breaking it or themselves, and how to fit the sections together, and mix concrete so it would not fall to pieces. And if the men mastered these simple skills, they could be shown more advanced ones. "There is a persistent and troubling tendency to give the work projects higher priority than the skill development of the enrollees," his memo ended, "and this misplaced emphasis does a disservice to the corps' overall objectives."

Sparhawk put Toby's ardent presentment to one side and pinched the bridge of his nose to relieve his eye strain. "So in short," he said, "you think the men should come before the work?"

"That might be one way to put it."

"And where did you get that idea—if I may ask?"

"I—just think—it's self-evident. Human beings matter more than inanimate objects."

"Generally speaking," he said, "but work is hardly an inanimate concept. We're dealing here with something very human, but it goes far beyond the individual. We're dealing with a massive, cooperative venture—a cause, if you will—a kind of crusade of the spirit. In that sort of effort, as it happens, the work matters more than the men. Men are expendable, Toby, but the work, if it's worth undertaking in the first place—the work must go on, at all costs—"

Fanaticism was implicit in his every word now. He was coldly, deadly certain of what he was after and how he intended to get it. Not only would the work routine not be changed, but Nesbit's harsh regimen, with its weekly ratings of the enrollees' performance, posted in numbers as hard and cold as the season, would be fully implemented as soon as possible.

"Okay, Captain," said Toby, reclaiming his brief in behalf of the boys, "but I think you're sitting on a time bomb."

II

Wed., 30 Jan. '36

Where would I be without Time? *Current number reports that Japan—*Time *does not like Japan—has done its best to torpedo London Naval Conf. & continues to thumb "its short nose" at the Occident for branding her racially inferior by imposing 5–5–3 naval ratio. Tokyo papers said to be full of claims Nippon can outbuild U.S.A. in warships due to our depression & lack of fighting will. (The Yellow Peril Meets Yellow Journalism: which is worse, Japanese racism or the* Time *slant?) . . .*

After several months of weekly one-hour assignations at Holly Curtis's austere Pittsfield studio—sessions almost totally devoid of tenderness—he began to come away with the feeling his hostess was little better than a classy courtesan. In slightly more discreet language, he told her how he felt. "It's all so—matter-of-fact."

"Yes—but that's what makes it so exciting! Don't you think it's exciting? You don't seem to be suffering, exactly, in the arousal department—if I may be so crude about it."

"That's not the point."

"Points bore me, sweetie. Woodrow Wilson had points, and look where they got him. Just relax and enjoy yourself—and do try not to feel cheap—though I'll admit the price *is* low."

"Your crude is showing again—sweetie."

"So sorry," she said, reaching for the ashtray, "but I'm afraid crudity and brevity are the best I can manage just now. Take it or leave it—and don't 'sweetie' me or I'll deball you."

All the affection of a condor. It wasn't that he wanted solemnity from her—just something more than mere mechanics. He backed into the subject anew a week later by remarking, afterward, that he couldn't believe their liaisons did not somehow intrude upon her relationship with Guy.

"Believe what you want," she said. "My thing with you is a private matter between me and my body."

"What happened to me in there?"

"And you—obviously."

"Or any other handy body—"

Smoke poured forth from her nostrils. "Are you asking me or telling me, sweetie?"

"In my opinion, you're using this—us—to punish Guy."

"Really? Why don't you just send your opinion in to George Gallup?"

"Or is it yourself you're trying to punish?"

"I hadn't realized the orgasm was a variety of punishment."

"Then you don't deny it?"

"The Crown neither confirms nor denies—it's above all that."

"Then I'll infer what I want."

"Infer your ass off if it makes you happy. Look, I don't give you a hard time about your using the Polish girl to get back at Temple—"

"*Wha-a-t?*"

"Oh, sure—Mr. Innocence. You know, that really burns me up! Just because you're poor doesn't make you morally superior, buster!"

"Who said anything about being morally superior?"

"Christ, it's written all over you—the pearly purity of poverty. And anybody who's rich and principled has got to be a bohemian or something—isn't that what you think? The impoverished have a monopoly on goodness, and all of us bluebloods are burdened with original sin the first day we lick our little silver spoons—right?"

"Is that a backhanded way of saying you've got your principles?"

"As much as you, sweetie! Now cut the inquisition, okay?"

But her impatience with his expressed dissatisfaction over their quick-and-dirty meetings seemed to turn to acknowledgment a week later when she told him, with some eagerness, that Guy was to be away in Boston the following weekend at some seminar and they might spend all of Saturday together.

It took rearranging plans with April and a few precautions about where to meet. In the end, it was easiest for Holly to pick him up as if by accident while he was hiking into town. He jumped into her midnight-blue Buick—that and pitch black were the only two colors she approved of on a motor car—and they went up to Bosquet's, where in relative seclusion she gave him his first ski lesson.

"Bend your knees, dammit!" she yelled the whole while, intolerant of retarded learners. "What I can't understand," she would say gravely each time they went back up, "is how anyone your size can fit so nicely on my sofa but can't manage to maneuver his limbs around out here."

It was nearly dark by the time they reached West Stockbridge. Holly honked twice as they drove up to Nimrod past the groundskeeper's cottage—"just to let them know it's us and not some Cossacks come to tear up the joint." She had called ahead of time to say she would be spending the evening and to have the heat turned up. He wondered if she wasn't concerned about being detected in their pending indiscretion.

"Not in the least," she said. The rest of the family was in the city, coming up only on holidays during the winter. And, after all, it was her house, too—"I can do what I choose in it. And the help doesn't talk—if it knows what's good for it."

He asked how she could be so sure. "Because," she said, parking under the porte cochere and drawing him along by the hand toward the front door, "I made the mistake of breezing in unannounced one winter while I was in college and found Daddy practically *in flagrante* with a delightfully pneumatic floozy." Father and daughter agreed, after some sharp words, it would be to their mutual advantage for the matter to go unreported. As to the grounds people, "Daddy said they were paid well enough to know when to keep their mouths shut." She unlocked the huge door with a couple of knowing twists and did a ballerina whirl across the Aubusson carpet. "Besides, I make it a point to give them each something unjustifiably expensive at Christmas."

After their earlier confinement, the house was like having all of Yellowstone Park to romp around. They drank and smoked and danced and lay down on anything handy including the floor in an endless succession of rooms until he lost track of the time and their whereabouts and the number of climaxes collectively achieved. Each location seemed to arouse her afresh and demand bliss through friction of one sort or another. Membranes raw with overuse, she began to taper off after their tumble about her father's study and turned muzzily philosophical. "You know," she said, "sometimes I actually wonder if I'd adore Daddy half as much if we weren't so—comfortable. I mean, he and I are so far apart about so many things that I'm not always positive I'm his legitimate little sugarplum."

Having shared almost no intimacies beyond bodily ones with her to that point, he grew uneasy at this sudden surfeit of revelation, including news of a licentiousness that appeared to be congenital. What the change signaled, he could not tell—whether her intake of scotch or his advancement to trusted retainer, at least on a par with the gardener, or perhaps even a genuine softening, a welcome lowering of her guard, a wish for a little connecting of souls as well as genitalia.

"Promise not to laugh," she said just when he was sure she had nodded off, "but sometimes I think of us as Bertie and Wallis—facing down the impropriety of forbidden love and all that. Tell me what you would do if you were King right this minute."

He had not devoted excessive attention to the romance between the newly crowned Edward VIII and his American friend. And it was not clear to him in the first place how a Prince of Wales could have

reached the advanced age of forty and remained unwed unless his tendencies were along other lines. "I'd either advertise for the ripest titled
arse in the kingdom," Toby said, "or proclaim the monarchy dissolved
and hie myself off to Tahiti with my American baggage. The latter,
probably, rather than remain a footling monarch in this day and age."

"Oh, God, no!" she moaned. "It's the only throne left in the world
worth mentioning."

"Well, there *is* the Emperor of Japan, my dear."

"That doesn't count."

"You're against the Yellow Peril in all shades and sizes?"

"It's not their color so much as their texture—they're so—oily.
Rather like the Jews, one might say."

"The better for burning, one might say."

Even half-bagged, she caught the chastening tone to his comment.
"Oh, I'm not down on the Jews all that much—except when they try
to take over things—like this Morgenthal person."

"Morgen*thau*, I believe—if you mean the Treasury Secretary."

"Are you sure? I thought it was like Rosenthal."

"You're thinking of Rosenvelt—he's half-Jewish himself, I hear."

"Mmmm, that's what Daddy says. He thinks we're being overrun
with Zionists. He says we ought to pay their carfare back to Palestine
if that's what they want—all of them, including Einstein."

"But they don't own Palestine—England does."

"Well, maybe Bertie'll sell it to them at half-price if they'll promise
to keep their grasping hands off of everywhere else."

He did not stay the night. There was a note to greet her when she
awoke, thanking her for their long, adventurous day together. But the
truth was that being with her for that sustained spell confirmed what
he had suspected about Holly Larrabee Curtis: Deep down, she had
no more redeeming virtues than were visible on the surface.

The following Wednesday, his loins depleted but head half-settled
on breaking off with her some time soon, he left Holly's studio and
caught a glimpse of Temple Keyes, or a remarkable facsimile, inside
the window of a pharmacy across the street. He waved. She looked
away. Perhaps she had not seen him. As he began to cross toward her,
she bolted out the door and hurried away with such urgency it was
apparent that her having been there was no accident.

He gave chase, no easy matter on that icy footing. She struggled to
maintain the gap between them. His legs, though, were too long and
sure for her uneven ones. He was nearly next to her when, heel
caught on an iced rut, she went over and howled in pain. "God
damn!" she cried as he knelt beside her. "God damn! God damn! God
damn!" It was plainly more than her ankle she was cursing.

He carried her into the drugstore to wait while he got her car and then drove her straight to the emergency room at the hospital. She was utterly still for most of the ride, but toward the end she relented long enough to say only, "This seems to be my favorite trick whenever you're around."

"I guess that's a good reason not to have me around."

"You've got your own reasons—that's fully apparent."

The x-ray proved negative. The hospital orthopedist, presenting her with an elastic bandage and urging that she go easy on the foot for the next several days, asked why she did not wear a built-up shoe on her shorter leg to even her gait and reduce the risk of falling.

Temple's look grew dark as she withdrew her bare, swelling, and now pitied limb from public exposure. "I don't require any prosthetic devices, thank you, Doctor."

"It's all done within the shoe, Miss Keyes—there's nothing at all visible on the outside. It all looks perfectly normal."

"Yes, *thank* you very much."

Her father was at work, her mother at some organization luncheon, and the cook off marketing when he brought her home and helped her into the conservatory. The linkage of their arms was distasteful to her in the extreme, he sensed from her stiffness. Recumbent in her favorite room in the house, she dismissed him with curt thanks, but he proposed staying with her until someone else arrived home. She agreed reluctantly, provided he put something on the Victrola to fill the bristling air between them. He asked what she wanted. "Anything," she snapped.

He sat across from her in a wicker rocker, hunched forward with his arms thrust between his legs and hands folded tight to keep from flying off in contortions of denied guilt. When the record ended, he did not rush to replace it. But by then she was composed enough to confront him. It was nothing artful. She waited until the needle had clicked perhaps a dozen annoying times and then demanded, "How *could* you? How *dare* you?"

He grasped at innocence. "She gives me piano lessons—"

"I *know* what kind of lessons she gives you!"

She spit out her wrathful tale. A few weeks earlier, she had come by the studio one Wednesday noontime, hoping to join Holly for lunch—her phone calls had encountered a steady busy signal. Hearing no piano-playing inside, she started to knock but suddenly detected faint and intimate-sounding murmurs within and so held back. Overwhelmed with curiosity, she stationed herself in the pharmacy to see who Holly's visitor was. Her chagrin was severe at the discovery.

Repeated observation disclosed their weekly ritual; inquiry of Temple's other acquaintance at the camp further disclosed that Toby did not practice the piano between appointments with his piano teacher. There was only one conclusion.

"And we're loathsome and despicable creatures, is that it?"

"You especially," she said. "Can't you see what she is? Do you think you're the first? She's corrupt—and corrupting—"

"Then why are you her friend?"

"Because—we used to be very close—and I don't think she can help herself—and I feel sorry for her."

"I don't have that impression—of her helplessness—"

"No—because you have an adolescent sensibility—for all your damned Harvard education. All you're after is easy gratification."

Her utter lack of charity toward him evoked a responsive bitterness. "I would have thought the least you could do is commend me for carrying on with a higher class of trollop."

She reached over to the phonograph, ripped the still-spinning record from the turntable, and, like a chairbound discobolus, sent it skimming at him with the shout, "You're a damned dirty bastard! Now you go, Toby Ronan, and don't ever bother coming back to this house!"

He studied the shattered black shards of Johann Sebastian Bach at his feet and listened penitentially to her grasping volley of sobs play itself out in anguish. At its end, still fixed in his seat, he said, "Did it ever occur to you that I've been with Holly because she was as close to you as I could get?"

She looked up through bleary, meanly slatted eyes. "And did it ever occur to you that Holly thought you would have stopped seeing that —other girl—if you really cared a damn for me?"

"If you cared a damn for me, you wouldn't have insisted that I stop. I don't take kindly to demands." He tried to subdue the rage rising in his throat. "Anyway, I'd have stopped soon enough if you'd given me half a chance."

"No one set you a deadline—it was just either/or," she said, turning aside, "and you made your choice—in fact, two choices."

Cook came in then. There was nothing more for either of them to say, anyway. He left with a perfunctory wish for her swift recovery.

That Sunday, he was called for by the Larrabees' chauffeur in a black Cadillac and driven to Nimrod for an audience with Holly's father. On the phone, in a voice so full of command it never had to arch or dip for emphasis, he had said he thought a short exchange between them would be useful. The offer of a lift down to West Stockbridge translated to the imperative mood. Still, lulled by a perfectly temperate tone and secure in the knowledge of the man's own transgressions, he went more curious than fearful.

"I wish the occasion were as pleasant as our last get-together here," Everett Larrabee said as soon as Toby was shown to his study, "but I won't pretend as much, so why don't we proceed right to business?" Even on Sunday, he was dressed like a man who was used to dispensing power the other six days and did not know how to turn off the juice. He wore a glen plaid suit with a dark knitted tie; a perfect picket of handkerchief points in his breast pocket served as a signpost to his mottled gray pompadour that lent him a whole extra level of authority. In between was a ruddy, well-tended face without a trace of levity to the eyes or mouth.

"Whatever you say, sir." He had seen that room only recently from a different perspective. Perhaps it was only better decorum the man had in mind.

"I'm not a prude, Mr. Ronan, but as a husband, a lawyer, and a parishioner in moderately good standing, I retain some respect for the sanctity of the marriage contract. One does not flout it with impunity. You, alas, appear to have a different view. It has been called to my attention that, for some time now, you've been on intimate terms with my daughter, Holly." He paused to see if Toby would concede the point.

"Perhaps when I hear you out, sir—"

"Yes. Well, for the moment I'll infer that the fact is not in dispute. What concerns me at the moment, Mr. Ronan, is not whether you are an unconscionable son of a gun—in fact, I'm assuming you're a fellow with the normal hormonal drives of someone your age who finds himself confronted by a tempting and, I don't doubt, quite willing young lady." It was Holly's behavior, he said, that troubled him far more. His daughter, in case Toby was unaware, was a willful, spoiled, and perhaps deeply troubled woman who, if her whims went unchecked, would drive everyone connected with her to disgrace, even ruination —"yourself included." There could be no doubt, for instance, that Guy Curtis would eventually initiate a most unseemly divorce proceeding, bringing infamy to the Larrabees and probably extracting damages for alienation of affection from a number of Holly's companions—"yourself almost certain to be included." Would Toby, therefore, as a prudent man and one presumably anxious to recover the status of gentleman, please cease and desist forthwith from accepting his daughter's favors? As a token of his gratitude for this admirable act of voluntary abstinence, Mr. Larrabee was prepared to use his

good offices and many connections to try to help him launch whatever
career it was he had in mind—"which is what, if I may ask?"

"I've done some writing—journalism, maybe, if I can find something."

"Very good. We've got ties to young Luce—he's doing very nicely
with *Time*, don't you think? And we see the Reids from time to time
—the *Herald Tribune* Reids—"

Regardless of whether he took advantage of that offer, Toby would
be receiving a money order in the next few days that Mr. Larrabee
hoped he would accept not as a crude payoff for his cooperation but
as a means of easing his financial burdens and those of his family while
he got started in New York or wherever it was he might choose to go
—so long, he did not need to add, as it was away from Berkshire
County and soon, very soon.

Toby thanked him for his generosity and cordial manner. "But
wouldn't it be easier, sir, if you just went into all this with Holly instead of me?" No doubt he would have little welcomed the ordeal of
the pot calling the kettle black—or scarlet, as in this case; still, family
was family.

"A fair enough question." He had tried a more direct approach
with her in the past, to no avail. "In fact, she rather delights in keeping me posted on her latest—peccadilloes—Lord knows why. Shock
value, I suppose."

Retribution, Toby supposed. "Are you saying she told you about—
us?"

"Actually not—which is really the answer to your previous question. I believe her uncustomary reticence may mean that she cares for
you as more than a distraction from what I suppose we all have to
concede is not a very successful marriage." But Holly was used to
seizing up and casting aside lovers as caprice moved her, and, whatever esteem Toby was enjoying at the moment, his days were surely
numbered. There would be great therapeutic value in it for his daughter, however, if, for a change, somebody she favored inflicted actual
pain by discarding her first. He was offering to pay Toby, in several
currencies, to hurt Holly. "The cure might begin from there," he concluded.

He left without any promises but having agreed to think hard about
everything his lordly interrogator had said—*sans-culotte oblige*. Next
morning, he biked into town first thing, marched directly into Temple's office at the library, and shut the door behind him. "How *could*
you?" he demanded, derision and anger competing. "How *dare* you?"

Bewilderment played roughly with her high forehead. She insisted that he explain. At the end, she sat back with crossed arms, absorbed but not displeased by his narrative. "The family employs a detective bureau to keep track of her," she said quietly. "She told me herself— she thinks it's laughable. But after all, they're worth a lot and can't risk somebody unscrupulous trying to use her to tap the Larrabee fortune." She stood and shook her head. "No, they don't need me to tell on her—although I suppose I can see how you got the idea."

She spoke calmly and with something approaching commiseration. He apologized for accusing her and the white heat with which he had burst in.

"It's all right," she said, "I understand." As if to prove it, she came over to the window and stood beside him looking out. "Naturally, you'll reject Mr. Larrabee's heavy-handed attempt to stifle your manhood."

"I—don't know."

"At any rate, you'll not accept his bribes—being the fellow of utmost principle that you are—"

"Naturally."

She sighed and touched him lightly on the arm. "You see, that's where he's got you. The Larrabees are very clever people." He said he didn't understand; she said that was apparent. "If he had just asked you flat out to stop seeing Holly—especially if he had stormed and threatened—he would only have gotten you angry—and so no doubt you'd go on your merry old way. But this way, by transparently trying to buy you off, he's giving you the opportunity to demonstrate your moral superiority to the rich and mighty Larrabees. You'll fling his largesse in his face, of course, and then turn right around and do exactly what he wishes, anyway—because you have so much bloody character." She took his hand, gave it a quick, fierce squeeze, and released it, adding, "Except when you don't, you dumb louse."

That was Monday. On Tuesday, the mail brought him a money order for one thousand Yankee dollars; the envelope bore no note or return address. He mailed it straight back the same way to Everett Larrabee's New York law office. On Wednesday, he did not go to Holly Curtis's studio. Or call to tell her why.

That Saturday, the Chevrolet dealer in Pittsfield telephoned camp to say that the coupe Toby's uncle had bought him was ready and waiting any time he wanted to come by for it. It was black and shiny, and the ownership papers in the glove compartment carried his name. He drove it back to camp long enough to pick up his bike and stow it in the trunk. Then he drove down to Nimrod, parked the Chevy in the driveway, endorsed the ownership papers over to Everett Larrabee,

biked back up to Pittsfield, left the Schwinn outside April's house
with a note saying he had had his fair share of its use, and hiked out to
camp as a fresh, light snow began to fall.

III

Sun., 10 Feb. '36

*Big turnout over weekend for first sessions of riflery "club"—latest
martial imprint on "civilian" conserv. corps.*

*Drills & target practice with firearms strictly against regs. in camp &
during workweek, so it's all extracurricular: Lems, led by Will B.,
provide hunting guns, army (via Carmichael) supplies ammo., & Nesbit instructs Sat. & Sun. at range set up in Goodrich Hollow with targets wired to hay bales. Participation completely voluntary—but word
is around everyone who qualifies as marksman gets standing bonus on
weekly grade. Also, capt. won't promote any non-gunner to rated
rank.* Vive la guerre!

As Toby's aide, David Schumacher proved marginally competent.
Typing up the stencils for the class dopesheets and the weekly issue of
The Lulu Bell, he had a tendency to punch the "o" and "e" keys too
hard and drill holes in the wax sheets, causing the ink to speckle. On
the mimeograph, his failure to keep the rollers spotless often produced
unsightly overprinting. And in logging the weekly grades for every
man in the company, the nib of his pen habitually scratched and splattered so that the roster appeared to have contracted a chronic case of
blue-black measles. However sloppy, he was unarguably diligent and
never abrasive. If there was a real fault to find in him, it was his reticence about himself and how he was enduring—all of that he saved
for his thrice-weekly letters home. Toby had the feeling David feared
that anything confided elsewhere would shortly be used against him.

The company still viewed him as weak, flabby, and effeminate. He
was tolerated now instead of being openly abused, but no one ever mistook him for "one of the boys." Yet it was exactly that he wanted
more than anything: to leave camp regarded as a man and rated as a
leader. In no one else but Link Salter would such aspirations have been
taken as the wildest of fantasies. In pursuit of them nonetheless, David
was among the first bunch to report for weekend riflery instruction.

The cold stiffened fingers and moistened eyes, badly skewing the
group's collective aim at first. Belly down on tarps, they persisted,
though, and soon the hay began to fly and the targets to be shredded.

David, however, continued to score consistently at the bottom of the class. Whether it was faulty hand/eye coordination, fear of the weapon's recoil, or plain deficiency of will, there was no telling; he simply did not improve much after the first few sessions.

Nesbit ordered him to have his eyes checked by the doctor, who found nothing abnormal. It was then proposed that David stop wasting good ammunition and quit the lists. At which point, he scored his first, and only, bull's-eye, which heartened him so greatly that he dug in and tried all the harder. He managed to put a couple of shots somewhere on the target every turn, mostly near the edge, but his usual trajectory ranged from a foot to a yard off the mark. "Hit the ground —Fatleroy's firing!" was the cry each time his turn arrived. Humiliation hardly abetted his confidence.

All this gunnery fired up the participants, drillmasters and pupils alike, to the point of taking a deer illegally at sunrise one Saturday. Will Bassett led the frigid party, impressing on all who wished to join it the need to remain absolutely motionless for up to ten minutes at a time without contracting frostbite. David went along, presumably more to demonstrate his talent as statuary than deerslayer. The result of the expedition was one scaly-coated, medium-sized doe that hunger had driven to browse the pine bark too close to human habitation. Will took her down with three clean shots. Everyone enjoyed the venison but the educational advisor and his assistant.

When Toby asked why it did not violate the code of the woods to shoot the deer out of season, Will explained quickly, as if primed for the objection no one else had wanted to register, that the Berkshire herd needed to be thinned both for its own sake and the good of the reborn forest. "Balance of nature's off," he said. "Us and bobcats are their only real enemies—and no one's seen a 'cat in these hills for years."

The justification failed to stay Toby from town the day after and placement of an anonymous call to the state police. He identified himself only as a Hancock resident miffed by all the shooting in the forest on weekends and powerfully suspicious that the hunting laws were being abused. The call prompted a visit to camp by a sizable state trooper who issued a stern warning against out-of-season hunting. After that, no further living targets were used until Pickles, the hound one of the Lems had donated as camp mascot, showed up on a late-February morning with so deeply imbedded porcupine quills all over her—a nocturnal battle with a den of the rodents in the ravine at the north end of the forest was blamed—that she had to be put to sleep to end her agony.

Since there were no restrictions on slaughtering porcupines, which

Will said did fearful damage to the hemlock foliage and tender inner bark of the sugar maples, an onslaught was organized against them in the name of avenging the late Pickles. A mixture of salt and strychnine was put out in wooden trays installed on sturdy maple branches about ten feet off the ground. The salt was an irresistible lure to the porcupines, while the poison was well under the dose required to kill them. For fun and practice, each rifleman was then allotted one of the enfeebled animals, which were brought to the shooting range and released one at a time. If the shootist failed to wing his prey with three rounds—i.e., if the porcupine was still moving—the rest of the class, positioned enfilade to the left, was invited to bang away until the creature was thoroughly destroyed.

Against the snow, the porcupine blood ran dark as the heavy-gauge shotguns tore the bulky animals to bits, regardless of the marksmanship of the primary gunner. So protracted and inhumane was the gory game that David was trembling with disapproval by the time his fat, sluggish target was released. Incapable of squeezing the trigger, he lay there just watching the wretched animal waddle off to its doom. "Shoot, you fuckin' fairy!" someone cried, and still David held back. As the thing tottered nearly out of range, the others opened up their raking fire.

"No!" David shrieked at them. "It's mine—it's mine!"

But since he had plainly intended to spare it, the shooting went on. The animal seemed to rise up off the ground and atomize into crimson chunks of meat and sinew. David screamed louder and kept on even after the dismemberment had stopped. Then he fell silent, stood up, turned his rifle toward the firing line, and loosed a blast well over their heads. So notorious was his aim, though, that everyone flung his weapon aside and hugged the ground for dear life.

That was the end of David's days as rifleman. He put his weapon down and left the hollow without a backward look. In camp later, Nesbit told him he would never earn rated status—and that if he ever again touched a gun while in the company, he would get his head blown off at once.

I V

Sat., 1 March '36

A red-letter day! Anton ("Call me Tony now") Sota materialized from nowhere at the camp gate this a.m., bearing me Bonnie's best & his own brooding heartiness. At first he claimed just to be passing thru & overcome by curiosity whether the C's have proven as Prussian as he predicted to me. I knew better.

Got treated to supper at the Berk. rest. & sev. hrs of bittersweet
memories—as if we'd had much more in common than the case hap-
pened to be. Over coffee (sparing me that long, at least) he asked if
I'd heard Cheska was getting married in June—to an asst. law prof at
Berkeley, supposedly very brilliant & "progressive." . . .

"She was remarkably bright and very courageous," Anton Sota
eulogized their girl of the golden West, "especially considering who
and what she was. When you got right down to it, though, she was
incorrigibly bourgeois—wouldn't you say?" He must have seen the
glazed look with which Toby greeted the news of her engagement.
"Or didn't you ever get right down to it—with her? I thought you
two were pretty thick for a while there."

"Get right down to what?"

"To—basics." He offered Toby a Galois from a mashed pack and
then helped himself. It seemed an odd affectation in a labor organizer
—unless the brand was to proclaim him a certified legatee of nineteenth-century socialism at its fount and thus the more incontrovertible. "Let's face it," he said, wagging the match out with admiring
gusto, "Cheska's body was as fine as her brain."

"When you got right down to it—"

"Yes. Unfortunately, I never quite did—though it wasn't for lack of
trying. We actually slept together one night—in a boardinghouse in
Knoxville—on our famous bus ride to liberate Harlan County—the
one you wouldn't come on?"

"I remember it vividly."

He shook his head with regret. "We were very close that night—
spiritually—but she kept her legs locked the whole time—and dress
on, too, now that I think about it. She was in love with my blazing
idealism—never me."

And what tortuous odyssey had that blazing idealism traveled since
Woonsocket? Mostly he had shucked it, he said. Non-ideologues made
the best operatives in the field. His whole agenda had simplified: Seize
control from the economic royalists and the bourgeoisie; their conversion or, that failing, their execution interested him far less than formerly. "Dialectics are grand for debating when you don't have the
power to act on them. Once you get some, the doing is everything."

"Which translates to communism is just socialism stripped of
ideals—"

"Just the opposite. A communist is a socialist who's so committed to
the cause he's willing to do whatever has to be done—"

"Guile? Force?"

"Of course."

"Which are one short step from deceit and terrorism—"

"Standard capitalist tools as well."

"But your way is supposed to be morally superior."

Anton edged into the corner of the high-backed, dark-wood booth, fondling his cigarette and trying to gauge if Toby's retrograde social thinking had altered any since he left Cambridge. "Yes," he said, "after we remake society." He folded his hands and slid them tentatively across the polished tabletop. "Your basic problem is that you still think Americans are a special breed of rabble. You actually believe there's going to be some great come-and-get-it day when everyone'll sit down like perfectly rational creatures and debate the whole bloody business in nice, logical terms and, at the end, choose of their own accord to redivide the pie and do all the other right and fair and decent things. It'll never happen, Toby—not in a million years."

"And I'm dumb enough to think Roosevelt's already made a start on it. But of course I work for the man."

He smiled grimly at the conceit. "Roosevelt's a creature of the system, and it's still the same old leaky tub underneath the paint job—rotten to the core—and Roosevelt's about run out of thumbs to keep plugging the holes. Anyway, I don't expect he'll be around after election day."

"Don't bet on it."

He smirked. "You're right—you've joined his claque. A full pay envelope does wonders to cement loyalty. Too bad the proles at camp are making only a dollar a day."

"The corps gives them other things."

"Sure—flag-waving, book-burning, and the goose step."

He had warned Toby before he joined that the C.C.C. was a fascist cabal to militarize the working class and make it heel at the command of its capitalist masters. If he had been half-right, he was also half-wrong. "There's security most of them have never had before—a chance to build up their bodies—and their sense of themselves—and even their brains a little."

"And their skills, too—getting trained in all those things so useful in the urban job market—like tree-trimming and ditchdigging. You know what percentage of these kids winds up holding a job a year after discharge from the C.C.C.? I've seen the figures at the Labor Council—between seventy and eighty percent of them can't find work. A lot of fat good these camps do—except to pacify what should be outrage."

"No one's claiming they're a panacea," Toby countered, trying to stave off those consuming jaws. "The boys are involved in worthwhile work while they're here—that's something that can't be taken away from them."

"Sure, they're involved—like the lamb in a lamb chop," he said and curled a mouthful of smoke toward the ceiling.

He was in town on a scouting expedition, Anton admitted during the lift he gave Toby to April's. The United Electrical Workers had received hush-hush inquiries from dissident elements at the General Electric plant—the most guarded, circuitous of contacts—and he had been detached from the New England Labor Council, a high-toned name for a task force of troubleshooters, to explore the Pittsfield situation and help the seeds germinate. The Wagner Act, in theory permitting locals to be organized now under the watchful eye of federal examiners from the National Labor Relations Board, was too new yet to be relied upon. And there was all sorts of missionary work to be done before the feds could be summoned and a vote risked on unionizing. What were the actual working conditions in the mammoth factory? What was the caliber of potential rank-and-file leadership? Into what bargaining units might the work force best be broken? How prone was management to reprisals and other means of repulsing the union threat? And would Toby help him get the answers?

"Me? I'm out there in Sherwood Forest all week. You're in big trouble if you have to rely on me."

"There are others—but we always need all the help we can get. You must know someone connected with G.E.—any capacity'll do."

"As a matter of fact, you may be in luck." He invited Anton along to meet April—"but don't start singing 'Solidarity Forever' right off."

Toby summed up for him what little he knew of the G.E. colony through the Keyeses and Janowiczes. Management was smug and the labor force cowed, with little sentiment for a union, from what he could tell. The local monsignor ran a social ministry as much involved with the workingman's welfare on earth as in the hereafter. "But he's not likely to start the bells chiming the minute the first picket hits the street."

"Our Lady of Holy Lip Service," Anton said. "Every tank town's got one. And the padre's convinced every organizer is a godless thug."

April shared that reflexive R.C. suspicion. "I mean what are you, exactly?" she asked Anton after they had picked her up and the three of them had settled into a quiet corner at the whitewashed roadhouse out toward Dalton.

"You mean am I a goddamned communist bastard?"

She laughed nervously at his understanding use of profanity. "Well, so long as you put it that way—are you?"

He softened his anthracite stare and began to lecture her ever so seductively. "April, the workingman—and woman—has been suffering injustice a lot longer than communism's been around. Plato was calling for the redistribution of wealth twenty-four centuries ago. He thought the richest man shouldn't earn more than four times the poorest—"

"Where did he say that?" Toby intruded.

"In *The Laws*." He cited chapter and verse convincingly.

"And are you for that?"

His eyes veered toward Toby while his head remained fixed on April, as if to say he wished not to be distracted. "Something along those lines strikes me as fair. I can see, though, where Harvard and the upper crust might have some reservations." And he winked shamelessly at April.

Toby would not subside, though. Arbitrary limits on wealth would no doubt advance social justice, he granted, but they also might smother incentive, the dirty little secret to America's success.

"Whose success? And with whose hands—and on whose backs?"

"I understand. So does Roosevelt. And he's making a liar out of Marx by not letting the workers sink deeper into poverty."

"But he can't change the leopard's spots. Labor is going to be exploited as long as profits and not need are what drive the system."

"Absolutely. The only moral justification for free enterprise is that it can deliver the goods—but I'm not sure any version of Marxism can without imposing an even more repressive form of enslavement."

Anton flicked April a look to make sure she was following the byplay like a verbal tennis match, and then he tried to put Toby away. "You know what Cabet said—'Nothing is impossible for a government that *wants* the good of its people.' And you don't enslave those you want to help."

"Who the hell is Cabet?"

His eyebrows soared. "Etienne Cabet—French lawyer, sage, visionary? You've never read *Voyage en Icarie?*" He turned to April, appalled at Toby's ignorance and assuming hers. "It's a novel, written a few years before the *Manifesto*—and full of the bravest prophesies— state regulation of wages, a progressive income tax, abolition of the right of inheritance, national workshops, public education—all unknown at the time, of course, and practically undreamt of." He raised an index finger at April to stress the point. "And that was less than a century ago. You see, things have been happening—and a lot more is still to come if courageous people pull together."

She was enraptured by the flow and certitude of his delivery—and not sorry to note the ease with which he deflected Toby's volleys. Not surprisingly, then, Anton turned up for mass the next morning at St. Mary's, where April introduced him to her parents and the priest as a touring young knight of labor. Assured of his benign interest in local conditions—Anton spoke vaguely of a doctoral dissertation on the coming of the industrial revolution to New England—the Janowiczes invited him home for dinner. A few nights later, he called to ask if Toby minded his taking April out for bowling and a beer. "Be my guest," he said. "She's more or less a casual friend."

"I know what you mean. They make the best kind of lay."

It was not at once clear to Toby what had provoked the remark. "Is that what they say?"

"Aren't you the authority?"

"That's very flattering but you must—"

"Not at all. It's that good Harvard heritage—all you wolves in sheep's clothing. In fact, I'd say you owe me one or two."

"You must have me confused with someone—"

"Oh, there's no confusion—Bonnie's told me all about your passionate summer together. She's not one to harbor dark secrets. She says you were very gentlemanly and good in bed, too—made up for what you lacked in size by a certain hyperactivity—like a violinist attacking a concerto, I think she said—she can wax quite lyrical at times, you know—well, I guess you would. Me, I'd rather be thought of as a percussionist of the mattress. But that's all beside the point—which is that I think I've figured out the reason behind your affinity for working-class girls. I'll be happy to take April off your hands, Toby, if it's all the same to you."

Before the month was out, Will Bassett was commiserating with him because his sister-in-law had turned sweet on his friend Anton. But he was sure she had not meant to send Toby packing and thought it would soon blow over between the two of them.

About a week later, Will dropped by his office one morning before the trucks went out and said that Anton had shown up at the Janowiczes' for supper the previous night with his arm in a sling and the rear window of his car shattered—the work, he implied, of company goons.

Toby put in a call to Anton's rooming house and roused him from bed. He was more amused than touched by the call. "Gambit Number Thirty-two in the *Union Organizer's Manual*," he whispered hoarsely, "but don't tell."

"You mean the company didn't do it to you?"

"Never laid a glove on me," Anton said. The ready-made sling was a standard part of his work tools. The rear-window demolition was an eight-dollar investment. Together, they usually generated priceless sympathy. With the Janowiczes, it had worked like a charm. The alleged attack so incensed April that she agreed to start listening in on phone conversations at the plant and feeding Anton whatever tactically useful information she could. And her father, finally informed of Anton's real reason for being in town, shared his daughter's outrage over the company's wicked ways and agreed to open his living room to a "purely informational" give-and-take between a dozen of his fellow workers in the transformer shop and the young union organizer.

Anton Sota, however unsmitten he still left Toby, knew his trade.

THIRTEEN

Fri., 23 March '36

Will sez the skunk cabbage grows right up through the snow patches because it generates its own heat. The bluebird is due to wing in shortly & will take offense if confused with the bluejay, among fiercest of the feathered flock. . . .

IN THE BARRACKS, the stoves lay cold and ashy, woodpiles went unreplenished, heavy underwear was cast off, and all the windows were flung open to receive the forest freshness. In reciprocation, the humming of harmonicas and love songs from uptuned radios rippled out over the dark, germinating earth. Every rain perfumed the air with the pungency of growth.

He had never been so close before to the greening process and felt himself an interloper amid its intimacy. Turf and leaf and fern sprouted in such profusion that he feared his every step would stunt some imminent shoots. The woods were slick with soaking moss, dank with fermenting mold, and teeming with the jeweled blossoms of hepatica, trilliums, violets, and all the other small, fragile beauties assigned to bloom in early spring while the sunlight can still reach them.

He was not the only one all but overwhelmed by the tidal turn that flung the hills and those who camped on them into internal uproar. Renewal sent its high spume through the spirits of the two hundred young men he lived among and not so lightly turned their fancy to thoughts of rebellion.

Gordon Sparhawk's master plan for pre-eminence among the several hundred camps in Corps Area I of the C.C.C. made no allowance for the spontaneous overflow of powerfully felt emotion among his charges. The camp's work had to accelerate at an exponential pace in the warming weather if the gala opening of the state forest was to be staged by June, in time for the close of the rating period. So relentless was the drive for order, beauty, and productivity that it supercharged almost every phase of the camp routine. Nesbit's never-ending rules, from the single-file chow line to the graded inspection of ears, beards, and cuticles generated steadily rising resentment. The company was being shepherded like a bunch of overage kindergarteners. In the field, the work tempo rarely slackened. The road crews especially, stripped to the waist and continually singed from the heavy applications of creosote, felt the Lems' lash as the circuit drive looped up around Berry Pond and began its downward spiral.

At no point during the earth-moving operations, or the construction of foot bridges, or the installation of sewerage and drainage facilities, was time taken to instruct the enrollees in any of the higher work skills; they still functioned primarily as choppers and lifters and haulers. The recreation program remained limited to pickup games of baseball at twilight; weekend contests were harder to arrange now with so many men on report for infractions that originated with the captain's crash schedule rather than any vernal outbreak of delinquency in the ranks.

This stifling purposefulness inevitably invaded the educational program as well. Everything yielded to the collective output and comeliness of the camp. Thus, the course in woodcraft, by way of example, was converted from instruction in cabinetry and other advanced woodworking techniques to a series of maintenance rounds, repairing loose floorboards, broken window frames, splintered steps, ill-hanging doors, and warped or otherwise unsightly porch and fence railings. When Toby pointed out the extreme exploitive nature of this assignment, performed in addition to the woodcrafters' regular work detail in the forest, the captain said only, "They want on-the-job training, they've got it."

It was this grievance of the woodcraft crew that ignited the uprising against the galley-slave existence being imposed on them all. In secret, behind stacks of supplies in the garage shed, they began making a totem pole.

They worked on it over the weekends after their forced labor was done. The twelve-foot log, trimmed down from a white pine taken out of the least trafficked part of the forest, was intended as a permanent monument to the camp and all who participated in the reforestation. That it was also to embody enrollee sentiment toward the camp authority figures became manifest soon after Boxcar Malone, the Leonardo of the project, set his team of artisans to their task.

With knives, hatchets, saws, chisels, drills, planes, adzes, awls, files, and practically every other kind of woodworking tool devised by man, they created a vertical gallery of caricatures closely approximating the basic sketch Boxcar had drawn. The captain topped the pole like some glowering Loki, his hair a tight bonnet of rigid rivulets running straight back from the scalp line, his all-seeing eyes half-hooded by lids in midflicker, his mustache more Chaplin than Chapultepec; between his teeth, in the manner of buccaneers swinging aboard a Spanish galleon, lodged a carved cutlass. Being a Sparhawk, he was additionally blessed with a menacing beak and a superb set of wings, fully extended in classic totem-pole style. Beneath him came Nesbit's unmistakable cubed head, with its bullet eyes and porcine snout and incisors lovingly fanged. Below him bulged the jowly mask of Denis Carmichael, sergeant chevrons for eyebrows, a dollar sign for his left eye, a cents sign for his right, and a lasciviously lip-licking tongue protuding from the corner of his gross mouth. Ash Cummings's likeness was longer and leaner than the rest, its planar lines intricately interlocking, eye sockets drilled deep and the pouches beneath in a sorrowful droop; the mouth was bowed into a double-edged ax. And Toby they had just begun on when he was invited to the clandestine studio, where work proceeded by flashlight behind a cordon of watchmen. The sketch of him they were following explained the invitation: It lacked the malevolence of the others. They gave him a mortarboard and tassel with a few curly tendrils creeping out from under. His eyes were a respectfully owlish pool of concentric circles suggesting either depths of vision or dizzying uncertainty to his wisdom. The other features—prominent ears, jagged nose, foreshortened jaw—were mercifully little exaggerated; verisimilitude was mockery enough. He laughed out loud.

They pledged him to secrecy and disclosed the whole plan. When the pole was done—painted, lacquered, and incised with the initials of every enrollee who served there—they would wrap it in a tarpaulin and bury it in the forest for a year. Assuming that the camp had been closed by then, the carvers would rematerialize for a day like a band of druids, disinter their monument, plant it on a suitable knoll, and advise the Massachusetts forestry department of the provenance of the relic. And why had he been selected from among the staff for this sneak preview? "Because," explained Boxcar, wood curls from Toby's pine likeness clinging to his pelt, "you're all right."

However pleasing the affection behind it, he was uneasy with their confidence. The bonding allied him with the resentments the totem pole revealed; tacitly he became mentor and patron to their mutinous iconography. But to call them off it would have been to lose his standing with them. To have reported the outsized bitter jest was still more unthinkable.

It was Nesbit, naturally, who found it one early May afternoon on a routine inspection of safety conditions at the garage. One end of the tarpaulin in which the pole was hidden had been improperly secured, and after a few minutes of tugging and grunting, the massive, scurrilous sculpture was exposed. Here was no minor prank but a major conspiracy against camp authorities and several of their most sacred strictures. Taking a tree from the forest for such an impious purpose was a heinous crime. Smuggling the tools out of the work shed for each carving session was a multiple transgression. And the savagery of rendering in those doleful graven images was practically a declaration of contempt.

Reprisal was swift. Every member of the woodcraft class was docked a full month's allowance and placed on weekend report until further notice. The rest of the company was commanded to stand to, water buckets at the ready, while the infamous pole was drenched with kerosene and turned to charcoal.

It was, against the glow of that bonfire, ordered by humorless petty despots who ruled them now under nearly lock-step formation, that the far more militant insurrection took shape in the minds of those whipped young regimentals. Only a weekend intervened between the pole-burning, with its promise of harsh repression for all forms of protest against camp authoritarianism, and the onset of the strike.

It began with a nucleus of the woodcraft class, which had felt itself unjustly used all along, and three dozen or so sympathizers, including two members of the Kangaroo Court—Skeezix Bloomgarden and Owen Guilfoyle, the extravagantly tattooed leader of E Barracks. All together, fifty-seven enrollees assembled in the middle of the campus after inspection on that sunburst of a Monday morning and refused to report to their work details. They sat in a circle around the flagpole until the adjutant sounded fall-in on his whistle. Then the signs came out of hiding in the barracks—painted on oak tag and stapled to dowels, they dared to declare "127 IS A SLAVE LABOR CAMP!" and "TEACH & TRAIN US, DON'T BRAIN US!" and "ALL WORK & NO PLAY GIVES JACK A DOUBLE HERNIA!" and "WE WANT A SQUARE DEAL, NOT A FAST SHUFFLE!"— and the picketing was on with a great shout.

Toby was in Sparhawk's office when the outbreak occurred. To maximize the company's performance, the captain had taken to meeting with the supervisory staff each morning before the workday began. Progress was carefully charted against tight schedules, and any unmet deadline brought penalties to those responsible. Toby's regular pleas for heightened incentives and not just stiffer lashings drew only impatient flickers from the captain; the men had too much pride, he claimed despite repeated petitions by the barracks leaders for relief, to need lollipops as a reward for sustaining loyal effort. Duty well executed was the noblest virtue. So saying once more, he looked up to see the picket line troop around the flagpole and then head over to block access to the trucks. "What in Christ's name," he said, "is all that?"

Nesbit went for particulars. Hurrying back from a short conference with Skeezix, he brought a list of the striker's demands. Because it had been run off on the mimeograph, of which Toby was nominally the caretaker, the captain flashed him a look that said if he were not in active cahoots with these upstarts, at the least he must have had foreknowledge of their intentions. "I suppose you've seen this?" Sparhawk asked, scanning the sheet.

Toby denied it emphatically. Then he read over the list and silently approved of every item. They fell into three categories: (1) improvement of work training by such means as job rotation, skill advancement, and an hour's field instruction each day; (2) reduction of military discipline in such forms as demeaning weekly grades, queueing up for every activity, and "back-door" work details like the maintenance chores imposed on the woodcraft class, and (3) an expanded recreational program, stressing sports and music. That he had supported each of these repeatedly at staff meetings and warned against the consequences of the captain's work speedup, the superintendent's indifference to enrollee skills, and the adjutant's draconian discipline was incontrovertible evidence of his role as spiritual instigator of the uprising.

Sparhawk balled up the sheet with one hand. All his hopes of glory for the camp were suddenly imperiled. If he could not restrain the springtime exuberance of his own men, he did not deserve his commission, much less recognition as overseer of the best C.C.C. camp in New England. "Tell them to break it up and we'll meet tonight with their leaders," he instructed Nesbit, "but we won't discuss anything under duress." The jumpy eyes betrayed his bravado.

The strikers, formed by now in a chanting oval around the trucks, were in no mood for lip-service conciliation. "No square deal, no work," Nesbit quoted Skeezix as declaring in answer to the captain's offer.

"Why did we ever make a Jewboy leader?" Sparhawk asked no one in particular. "There's always trouble when they're around." He glanced out the window across the field to where the jeering grew as the rest of the company approached the trucks and confronted their picketing brother enrollees with intensely conflicting emotions. "Give 'em fifteen minutes to blow off steam," the captain ordered. "Anyone who's not on the trucks by then will have to suffer the consequences."

And anyone interfering bodily with the boarding crews, he added, would be prosecuted.

The threat only added to the tinder. The insurgents, preening their courage, called out to the others to lay down their tools and join the circle of defiance. To one side, Kevin Dundy, rake on shoulder, stood in urgent conference with Bloomgarden and Malone. The camp's senior leader and stellar corpsman, officially admired by no lesser eminence than the President of the United States, Dundy commanded a respect second to none from the barracks and staff alike. His Hibernian good looks, marred only by that lopsided nose, clouded over as he tried to sway the strike leaders from a course he must have disapproved of in countless secret parleys earlier. The pain of irreconcilability was plain in every pleading turn of his head and caring flash of eye. But Skeezix, the toy bulldog, and Boxcar, a tight-sprung Doberman, were not to be budged. Tailed by hooting and booing, the trucks pulled out. None of the strikers had contracted cold feet.

Less raucous now, they filed back to the center of the campus and resumed their march around the flagpole. Uneasy over what lay in store, each of them glanced over toward the headquarters shed as he reached the edge of the circle nearest to it. "Take their names down," Sparhawk told the adjutant and, retreating behind his desk, lapsed into simmering silence. In the doorway, beholding the spectacle with calculated neutrality, Eddie Spain tolled off the names of the insurrectionists. Outside Toby's office in the supply shed, David Schumacher lurked immobile, half-longing to join the ring of pickets, half-hoping to gain by his allegiance to duty. At the corner of the mess hall, after noisily hauling out two cans of breakfast garbage, Link Salter paused to weigh the risks of freedom.

For an hour or so, the captain pretended to go about his business. Papers fluttered, forms got filled out, reports drafted, correspondence conducted, phone calls made and returned. But by midmorning, he was pacing the office, eyes in a constant fidget, as Doc Haseltine came by and observed that the camp seemed to have become a battle zone. At eleven o'clock, Ackermann served them all a second post-breakfast round of vile coffee. "It's gone on long enough," Sparhawk said after they had each taken an obligatory swallow from the heavy white mugs. "I propose to tell them that every man who doesn't report to duty by noon can consider himself dishonorably discharged. We can't pussyfoot on this. If we give an inch, they'll want a mile."

"And if you don't," said the doctor, "you may not have a camp left."

The captain rubbed a thumb hard against the underside of his chin in courteous contemplation, then answered, "I think most of them will cave right in."

"Not this soon," Nesbit judged. "I say don't feed 'em lunch, put the barracks off-limits, and see how they feel after marching around in that sun all day on empty stomachs."

"And if they're still going strong?"

"Anyone who doesn't report for work in the morning is out."

The captain considered the more temperate course and endorsed it.

"And what if they all don't report in the morning?" Toby asked.

"We'll get along."

"And if they take their case to the newspaper—and it makes the wire services—and district and corps area hear, as they will? What happens then to everything you've been trying to accomplish here?"

The situation grew at once more dire by that very reference to the unspeakable. Sparhawk's emotional investment in the camp and his overweaning ambitions for it had delivered him to the outskirts of panic. He drained his coffee manfully and cast Toby a slanted look. "And what would you recommend—short of our unconditional surrender?"

"One or two concessions would probably go a long way if you can—"

"Never!"

"It doesn't matter which ones, even, so long as—"

"*Never!*"

"Then I'd wait them out. You've got nothing more to lose."

"No deadline?"

"A deadline is only going to strengthen their resolve. And then the onus is on us for having forced the men out of the corps."

"*Us?* Oh, are you still on our side, Ronan?"

The leaden sarcasm only verified the deepening severity of the captain's distress. Without need to defend himself or to offend Sparhawk further after having been proven right, he withheld a reply.

Abstention earned him the assignment of conveying to the strikers the captain's revised conditions for sufferance of their continued rebellion. All camp facilities were barred to them for the duration. They were to sleep on the campus, using their blankets but no other G.I. supplies except the clothes on their backs. They could wash in the brooks and relieve themselves in the woods, taking care to bury their feces with a spade. They would be on half-rations, dispensed at the rear door of the mess. If it rained, they could take shelter in the forest; otherwise, not. When delivery trucks arrived at the compound, they were to refrain from picketing or any other overt displays of protest.

Fraternization with the loyalist enrollees was absolutely forbidden. Any straying from the rules would earn the violators immediate discharge. And naturally, strikers would be docked their pay for time away from the job.

"Sounds okay to me," Skeezix said on learning the terms.

"We got 'em royally pissed, huh, prof?" Wolfbait figured.

"Half-rations!" Farmer Jones complained. "What kinda fuckin' deal is that supposed to be? We'll starve out here!"

"Everybody getcher blankets outa da barracks—on 'a double!" Owen Guilfoyle bellowed. "Canteens, too—an' fill 'em!"

"They didn't say canteens," Skeezix said.

"Tough shit!" said Guilfoyle, assuming Toby's complicity. "It's hot."

By the time the work details returned, the strikers were still frisky enough to strafe them with abuse for selling their souls to the company commander. The taunting was returned in kind, and the Lems in particular displayed disdain for the picket line by breaking through it so as not to have a longer than normal trip back to the work shed. On his way through, Will Bassett somehow got his feet caught with Farmer Jones's—each charged afterward that the other had tripped him—and down they went in snarling entanglement. By the time they were separated and lifted from their rocky cockpit, Will had a three-inch gash high on his temple.

Doc Haseltine drove him into Pittsfield for stitches, no longer trusting his own eyes for such precision work, while Toby brought Will's car home and told Trudy what had happened. When Will got back mended, he was not pleased to see Toby. "This is all your damned fault," he charged the moment Haseltine left, "feedin' these kids all this radical crap of yours—just the way your friend Sota's turned April into a regular little union spy."

"April's got a mind of her own," Toby said. "It's high time she was encouraged to use it."

Will swiveled his bandaged head toward Trudy. "What'd I tell you —they're both a couple of goddamned Reds! And they're suckin' your whole dumb family in!"

"He's hurt," Trudy said during the ride she gave him back toward camp, "for April's sake more than ours. He thinks you palmed her off on Sota—and the guy blows in and out of town like a traveling salesman, expecting her to jump whenever he snaps his fingers. Will says he's probably married, too, and just likes a little companionship on the road."

"First of all, she wasn't mine to palm off. And—"

"Is he?"

"—second of all, if she doesn't buy the union line, she's got no need to do his bidding at the plant."

"Is he married, Toby?"

"I don't keep track of his marital status. We're not even friends, really—we just have some mutual acquaintances."

"He's been leading her on, you know. And April's very—impressionable—especially where college-educated men are concerned."

"It's because we've all taken the same course—'Wooing the Working Girl for Fun and Profit.' Look, I think you and Will ought to get over the idea that April is Little Miss Innocence, being lured to her ruin by scheming Casanovas. Besides, you haven't exactly been locking her up in a convent."

"What's that mean?"

"It means she's—well, even the boys at camp could tell—"

"She's *what?*"

"Available."

"You dirty son of a bitch!" Trudy exploded and threw him out of the car.

The strikers had four campfires going in different sectors of the campus when he got back, and Nesbit was in the midst of ordering them all doused. There was a night chill but nothing so sharp that the rebels could claim they needed the warmth for survival. It was more a matter of celebrating their embattled state with the special comradery that rings a crackling blaze. Toby helped compromise the dispute: They could keep two fires going till midnight, none after that. As soon as the adjutant left, the other two fires were killed with urine. "Lemme leak on the lieutenant next!" Wolfbait piped, buttoning up.

He stayed with them awhile as they huddled near the flames and assessed the likely endurance of both sides in the contest. Guilfoyle produced his harmonica and played "It's a Long Way to Tipperary" and "Stout-Hearted Men" and "The Minstrel Boy" to lend an eve-of-Armageddon poignancy to the dying day. The talk turned to speculations profane and sacred—from the width of Nesbit's anus to whether it was true a man was born with only so many ejaculations in him to why God seemed so close a friend by day and a cosmic menace by night. As darkness thickened, a handful of them slipped off to the barracks at their grave peril to try to do some proselytizing. Wolfbait, ever drawn to the site of maximum danger, glided past the Lems drafted as emergency watchmen and let the air out of all the truck tires.

When the work details headed out in the morning—nearly an hour late due to the truck sabotage—the number of enrollees staying behind had risen to seventy-three, an overnight gain for the strikers of sixteen.

"Wait it out, did you say?" Sparhawk hollered at Toby when Nesbit came in with the numbers. "I think you're masterminding this whole goddamned business—if you want to know what I think." His hair, normally a well-oiled mat, was mussed from steady raking by his nervous fingernails. Any minute, Toby thought, he might start tearing it out in tufts. "If you want to know what I really think, I think you're trying to take this whole goddamned camp away from me— that's what I think! I think you sat down and cooked up this thing with—"

"That's pure baloney, Gordon," Toby broke in on his ranting, "and you know it."

"I know what I know, all right! I know you're a genuine, documented Harvard pinko! And I know you've got a goddamned commie labor organizer buddy in town—and he's probably feeding you pointers as you go!" Sparhawk interpreted Toby's grimace to suit his case. "Oh, you're surprised I know about him, are you? Well, maybe you think General Electric is about to hand itself to these union sons of bitches on a silver platter—but you're wrong! Their detectives have been watching your ratty pal from the second he hit Pittsfield— and tipped me he'd been out here and other places with you. Now I wasn't born yesterday, Ronan—or are you going to stand there and tell me with a straight face this character didn't put you up to this?"

He managed to say that nobody had or could put him up to anything, and that every utterance or action of his since coming to the camp had been intended to advance its welfare, and that Sparhawk's accusations were unfounded and unbecoming a commanding officer. But the captain was so swept up by the apparently disintegrating situation beyond his office door that he was not interested in listening, only in lashing out at the nearest target. He had veered off into these tangents of near-hysteria often enough, but the issues had always been narrow and the episodes inflated by a textbook paranoia. Now, though, the crisis was authentic—and his character so obviously deficient in introspection that even untutored eyes could not fail to see how near the man was to the breaking point. The sooner he was separated from his post, Toby decided, the better for all concerned.

It took him four phone calls to find Anton Sota. He was in Worcester at some sort of labor coordinating session, from which he had to be lured. No one else he knew was capable of obtaining the information Toby needed in a hurry. He had connections everywhere in the state and, through the union hierarchy, in Washington. He appreciated the situation, if not its timing, and gave Toby a number at which to get back to him at the end of the day; meanwhile, he would see what he could do.

Anton's contacts in Springfield, Sparhawk's hometown, proved forthcoming. The captain's in-laws had been prominent citizens there for several generations; Sparhawk's entry was a bleak, recent chapter in the family saga. The short of it was that he had been taken into his father-in-law's prosperous realty and insurance brokerage firm, participated dutifully though somewhat perfunctorily, inherited it sooner than he should have, ran the enterprise nearly into the ground, sold it off shortly before the Crash—apparently the only astute act of his business career—and had been living boozily ever since off the salvaged receipts and his wife's dowry. Mrs. Sparhawk herself, curiously, had not been seen around town for some years. The surmise was that she had died of a disfiguring disease abroad or had been in the process of doing so closer to home for so long that it was best to think of her as already having passed. She was remembered as attractive, pampered, and frail. As to the captain's military record in the Great War, Anton's source in the Department of Labor tapped Sparhawk's revealing file at the War Department. Contrary to his periodic claims, complete with tales of titanic ordnance that turned the earth to scorched powder in the battle zone, he had not served with the Second Army in France but as a gunnery officer at Fort Iowa outside Des Moines. By war's end, he had advanced to first lieutenant but seen no combat.

Toby could conclude only that the man had asked to be activated for C.C.C. service in order to forget his failures and, through swagger he mistook for bearing and by sternness he confused with inspiration, earn the glory he had never known.

"I think you may be overstepping yourself," Doc Haseltine cautioned when Toby reported his findings, "and relying on hearsay to reach invalid conclusions." But he had put Sparhawk under mild sedation, for no doubt he had been reacting to the strike as a man unused to the stresses of command.

By the third morning, the strikers' ranks had grown to eighty-nine, including Link Salter, who was discovered smuggling them out a scrubbed garbage can of leftover supper in the middle of the night and told by Denis Carmichael not to show his ugly black face back in the mess till the thing was over. Nesbit told Toby much the same with regard to his disagreeable mug in company headquarters. The captain, no longer ready to drop on all fours and start chewing the carpet, was convinced the rebels had reached their high-water mark and now was the time for him to hold fast; appeasers like Toby drained his resolve. "If you ask me, we've given too much already," said the lieutenant. "You don't feed your enemy when he's holding you under siege."

"I know," Toby said, "you'd have fired the whole lot."

"They'd have backed off first—without a doubt. Now it's too late, though—they've got the bit between their teeth—thanks to you."

It was not the strike, or the captain's toleration of it, or all his soft-hearted Harvard ways he held against Toby half as much as his having reclaimed the attentions of Temple Keyes as spring ripened. Being jettisoned for so unworthy a rival hurt the lieutenant's pride without doing much for his soul. In another age, he would have proposed pistols at thirty paces. As it was, they each deferred to their mutual vested interest just long enough to promote its survival. "Get him to give a little, Mitch," Toby said, "and I think I can do something with them out there."

"Who are you kidding? They'll leap the second you say so."

Nesbit's estimate applied only to Toby's woeful assistant, and even then it was less a question of his superior's sentiments than the boy's own latent impulse. David hung about in the office doorway all day with nothing to do but stare out forlornly at the growing circle of pickets. The education program had been suspended since the strike began, on the unspoken theory that every class was a potential hotbed of sedition. David moped and brooded and pretended to read a little Dickens while watching Toby out of the corner of his eye for clues to guide his own behavior. "Do you want to be out there with them?" Toby finally asked him point-blank as Nesbit's whistle summoned the camp detail to lunch.

"Sort of," he said.

"Because you think they're right?"

"Sort of."

"That's all? You mean you don't know?"

"It's not that. It's that I don't have it as rough as them."

"So you've got less to complain about legitimately—and more to lose—than they do?"

"Yeah. But I think they're right, so I feel bad."

"But not quite bad enough to join 'em?"

He dropped his head. "Yeah."

"History in a nutshell," Toby said. "Priviledged characters sit on their hands because they have it so good—while everyone else struggles to endure. Finally, the P.C.'s get it in the neck themselves and die screaming betrayal."

David saw the point but grew uneasy at the direction it would propel him. "Yeah," he said, "but suppose we all get kicked out?"

"At least you'd have been right."

"Yeah—I guess."

"You mean somehow the principle of the thing doesn't seem enough?"

His eyes turned dark and hard against that milky face. "I mean, tne thing is to win—isn't it?"

"Some people think being right is more important. I'll grant you, though, they're usually the ones with nothing to lose."

"Is that why you're not out there with them, too—you need the job?"

Finally, someone who took Harvard with a grain of salt. His active participation, Toby explained, would have served only to confirm the captain's conviction that he was the architect of the strike—and thus to obscure the issues involved. He understood, David said, and that was another reason he was hesitant to join in—it might reflect on Toby. A sweetness born of sensitivity to needs other than his own was beginning to surface in that once whiny boy whose dumb, stubborn courage, belying his ovoid form, had been his only redeeming quality. "I appreciate all that," Toby said, "but don't worry about me. In fact, I'd take it as quite a tribute if you'd do what you think is right."

"You would?"

"I'll go a step further, even. If you do what you believe in and anything happens to you as a result—like your getting discharged or something—then I'll quit, too."

"You will?"

"Only that's got to stay our secret."

His trust was total, and touching. It said Toby's sharing his fate would make it bearable. Toby did not disclose that he already considered himself a dead man in camp—and that David's, in fact, was the greater risk. The boy smiled, blinked back a rush of happy tears, gulped, shook Toby's hand harder probably than any hand he had shaken before, then stripped his shirt off and trotted out to join the bare-chested boys circling the flagpole under the midday sun. The roar of greeting was immediate and sustained. In the mess, Toby ate alone.

The showdown occurred at the end of that third afternoon when the dwindling work crews returned to camp and suffered their severest barrage of insults yet from the pickets. Their tools still in hand, the loyalists marched three abreast in rehearsed formation across the line of strikers to the flagpole, where Kevin Dundy, at the head of the column, delivered the group's collective rebuttal. "Ingrates" and "crybabies" were the kindest words to leave his lips. The cursing turned cruder on both sides after that, and then the Dundyites, inflamed by the ridicule heaved at them for three days running by their rebel brethren, assaulted their detractors with the weaponry at hand. The punishing purpose of the attack spurred the startled and unarmed strikers to matching savagery.

Dundy went after Bloomgarden with a fratricidal arc of his hoe. The straight edge missed Skeezix's head by no more than an inch or two and lodged in the side of the spruce flagpole. Spared but stunned by the viciousness of his assailant, Skeezix wheeled heavily into action. They collided like a pair of furiously puffing steam engines, skulls cracking, shoulders piledriving, arms pumping, legs churning and stomping. In the slanting sunlight, with such ferocity that the rest of the combatants cleared out room for them, they punched and kicked and gouged at each other's manhood, drawing on reservoirs of strength and immunity from pain neither knew he possessed.

Before their potent musculature at last spent itself in bloody battering without a victor, their frenzy infected the entire company. They spilled off the campus and into the barracks, with devastating results. Doors got wrenched off hinges, flying boots shattered windows, beds crashed through fiberboard walls, and the very roof was nearly sent skyward in the tumult. So explosive was the fray that Nesbit had been blowing his whistle for ten fruitless minutes before the shrill could be heard.

Only then did Toby, Ash Cummings, and a couple of the Lems begin to unpry the exhausted belligerents. After a moment's numbed repose, the first of the walking wounded staggered across the compound toward the infirmary—adversaries an instant before, now becalmed and bewildered by the intensity of their strife. The intramural war was over; the camp, in splinters, physically and emotionally.

Nesbit and Toby worked out the treaty on a paper napkin in a corner of the mess after about twenty minutes of negotiation. First, the strikers would be granted amnesty provided they put in twelve-hour days until the barracks were restored to their former trim. Second, half an hour of every workday would be devoted to field instruction by the Lems, and jobs would be rotated no less often than bimonthly, except for Link Salter, who was to be liberated at once from the kitchen. Third, the weekly grading system would be replaced by a much simpler monthly posting, with only three possible marks—"Superior," "Okay," and "O.T.I." (for "on thin ice"); lineups were to be eliminated except for the flag formations and inspection. Last, the camp would avail itself of the services of a part-time W.P.A. teacher, as offered by district headquarters, to expand the recreation program—"fun for the feeble-minded," Nesbit called it.

Toby took the conditions to the limping Skeezix; they were ap-

proved and ratified in a matter of minutes. The adjutant then went off
to the captain's quarters to try to sell him on the settlement. As he entered, a stonefaced Ackermann came the other way bearing an
armload of empty brandy and bourbon bottles. On the grass outside
the officers' barracks, Toby sat in vigil, sympathetic with Nesbit for
the only time he could remember.

The hush inside was ominous. Thunder would have been more reassuring. But the lieutenant reappeared in an unimaginably short while
looking like a narrow escapee from disaster—grateful but still
horrified. "He's in his own world," Nesbit reported, showing Toby
the captain's initials approving their agreement. Without a handshake,
he headed off to pass the word, assess the casualty list, and announce
the back-to-work schedule for the morning.

Toby lingered in the shadows outside Sparhawk's meticulously
hedged doorway. Somehow the idea seized him that the healing process would be speeded if he told the captain that he understood and
respected his firmness of policy even if he himself had not always
agreed with it—and hoped Sparhawk would grant him comparable
sincerity. At any rate, what was there to lose now?

He knocked, feebly at first, then forcefully when there was no response. On about the eighth try, a croak sounded asking his identity.
When he gave it, there was a long, airless pause, and then a cry that
came with the full force of a biblical curse: "Never!" And another, almost supernatural in its rasping echo: "Ne-VER!" And a third, like
the last relentless spikes in a coffin: "NEVER-NEVER-NEVER!"

To the end of his stay at Camp 127, although they communicated in
effect through Nesbit and other intermediaries, Gordon Sparhawk did
not address another word to him.

II

Thurs., 10 April '36

*Baked ham, peach pie & high conviviality at the Keyeses'—as if I
were a habitué at their table instead of a 6-month absentee. Mr. K. as
bonhomme as ever, Mrs. K.'s wit still withering, but Temple detectably queasy over the lifting of my excommunication. I was all deference but no repentance.*

*T. played for us after in the conservatory, scene of our late hostili-
ties (thus confirming my rehabilitated status?). Bach concerti, summoning in me exquisite sadness & keenest admiration. Her intensity so
palpable in every physical aspect of performing—the posture, the
fingering, the mouthing, the breathing, the vibrato—that I suspect it is*

a sexual surrogate as well as spiritual rapture. No less than by her
fierce pride & quick intelligence, I am drawn to this controlled pas-
sion that is hidden just beneath her astringency of manner. . . .

His note requesting the pleasure of her renewed company was short
but not especially sweet. A clinical report that he had disavowed all
female companionship for some weeks and felt his impurities of body
and soul fled, it was answered a few days later with a very proper invitation to dinner. A saving postscript noted that spring in the
Berkshires was like no other on earth, her father's regional predispositions notwithstanding, and she hoped he would enjoy the unfolding of
the season to the fullest.

Much of it they witnessed together. If it was not precisely courtship, it was a warmer, franker, more nearly equal association than any
other he had known. Each new outing to those savory hills, on those
opalescent lakes, in those dreamy hollows, helped resurrect their prob-
lematic fondness. It was a greening time for all manner of life.

One Saturday she showed him her secret haunts at the southern end
of the county on a drive to Egremont that ended at the Bash Bish
Falls. En route, they abandoned her car for a hike down an old road
that no longer went anywhere. It took them up grassy ways and down
swampy reaches till they arrived at a procession of maples and the
remnants of several once-stately homes Temple would stop by each
springtime and try to imagine restored to sturdy grace and repeopled
with bluff gentry. At one of them, Toby breached the tumbledown
stone wall and, despite her decorous protest, violated the serenity of
its decay.

All that remained of the house was its foundation; a great stone
chimney climbing out of a mass of moldering brick, wood, and plaster
rubble, and a portion of one side wall with two glassless window
openings still intact. Their eyes were drawn, as they neared at his insistence, to the single standing relic of that time-gutted interior—the
frame of a corner cupboard, gray and mossed over, its base split away
by the collapse of flooring and yet standing, as if by memory. Its
lower portion must have once been enclosed by a door, but the upper
part had probably always been open, to judge by its four gracefully
scalloped shelves. Its fluted pilasters on either side and connecting cap
and cornice survived whole, or so it seemed, conjuring a full complement of porcelain bowls and luster pitchers and blue china to service a
snug domesticity long departed.

He suggested they scavenge the cupboard before the elements did
away with it altogether. Temple was inclined to leave it, but he proposed that the greater kindness lay in the continuity of its life. Doubt-

ful, she nevertheless assisted in the effort. With all possible gentleness, they separated it from the wall and the single rotted joist that held it up in back. For an instant, it clung together, a mournful, ghostly unit, and then, despite all their tenderness in handling, it fell to pieces. Temple gave a short, shocked yelp of despair and then knelt quickly to examine the fallen components. Rotted from above, the carved keystone cap and cornice had practically disintegrated into a brown powder on impact with the ground. And the curved shelves proved to have turned to a damp punk. Only the fluted side pieces appeared still usable. Toby voted that they carry them off for future use but the completeness with which the affronted cupboard had disintegrated left Temple with no heart for it.

As they retraced their steps over that nearly vanished roadbed, the cupboard incident, so tiny and private, filled her with dismayingly cosmic thoughts on the vicissitudes of time. How she wished for the power to float freely into the past and future so that all life in a given place could be perceived at once as if in a sort of single fused dimension. Alternatively, she prayed on days as gloriously bright and richly painted and softly scented as this that she might live forever. But then that, of course, was life's supreme irony; it drew its preciousness precisely from the rarity of its perfection and the brevity of its duration. Time must have an end of us, she said, or it is a prison, not paradise. "There are even moments," she added as the road rimmed a copse of chestnuts, "when I wish I knew just how long I have to live. Have you ever had that feeling?"

"I've thought of it. The benefits seem limited, though."

"Oh, no," she said, "it would make life so much more orderly. You could plan it better—all your finances, and trips, and whole career. And if you knew you were going to die young or soon, you wouldn't postpone contemplated pleasures. I think it would be awfully sensible."

She may have had no politics, but the Apollonians clearly were her tribe. His was less structured. "First of all, no one ever said life was orderly or sensible. And second—"

"But don't you think it would be better that way—instead of all the ceaseless *Sturm und Drang?* Why must life be such a trial—such unending combat? So much of it is wasted that way."

Now he had it: she was a utopian isolationist. "And would everyone enjoy the blessings of life equally under your regime?"

"Not necessarily. But they would learn to be pleased with their share."

"Frankly," he said, "I think your basic scheme would be very upsetting psychologically. If you knew when you were going to die and it turned out to be soon, there's an excellent chance of your lapsing into permanent depression and not enjoying any of the remainder. Isn't it better to live every day as if it may be your last—and cherish its wonders—and be thankful for the gift of it?"

"You sound like Reverend Brandt—brimming with unreasonable expectations of saintliness among the flock."

"Look who's talking!"

"Oh, your way's more poetic, I'll grant you, but don't you see the problem with it? You either wind up loving life so much that parting with it becomes all the more painful—which is avoided entirely under my plan—or you're likely to fall into some sort of sustained dissipation because that way you might not even notice that you've died. . . ."

There was a cheerful irresolution to all their dialogues. Neither of them was trying to convert the other so much as trading disclosures almost too intimate to risk sharing. Where they came out after each exchange did not really matter—only the pleasure born of indulged phobias, fantasies, and fixations.

Mostly they refrained from intellectualizing the countryside and surrendered to serendipity. This innocent wayfaring, which became more satisfying as they grew less judgmental of each other in their dealings, sometimes revealed depths—and shoals—that premeditation never could have.

One Sunday they picnicked at Burbank Park, a piney woods beside Onota Lake, and took out a canoe afterward for some leisurely reconnoitering. He had seen the lake often, starting with the first time he rode out West Street to the camp and on every visit to Doc Haseltine's house on its eastern shore, but he had not been out on it before. From its midst—you were never very far offshore, although it encouraged the illusion of removal from all earthly cares—the sailor's eye swam with scenic joy over the stalks of birch clustered like snow shoots at water's edge, the upland reach of lush meadow and untrammeled dell, Greylock presiding mistily over the immemorial Appalachian skyline. Why, indeed, could God not have alighted here in the form of a pure white deer?

Temple had brought along her flute. While he dipped and swung the paddle in long, feathering strokes that described a course to nowhere, she piped a soft medley of English airs. The sound was so sweet and clean and silvery it was as if the lake itself had generated it out of liquid sunshine and refracted sky. In fact, it was blended equally of rapture and discipline. He asked her how it felt to possess that gift in which he was so obviously lacking at the piano keyboard.

She said it was like plunging into the rhythmic flow of eternity. That was too poetic even for him, he told her, but she denied any romantic intent and said it was a simple observable phenomenon. All life was flux, alternating tempo, cycles of surge and surcease, movement more skittish than linear—and music captured that elemental current in more compact yet accessible form than any other man had invented. Mostly it made him cry, he said. "Because it touches the sublime in your soul," she said, "which suggests you may actually have one."

Along the south shore, they came upon a handyman laying out sectors of a large H-shaped dock. In pleasing Scandinavian inflections, he explained the property was a private camp for boys, a couple of years old, and pointed to the long, freshly painted bathhouse nearby to indicate the quality of its accommodations. Here was no charitable facility for gutter urchins, no retreat for feckless skinnydipping; here the progeny of the privileged came to play, hardly more than a mile from Camp 127, where the government tended in its fashion to youth at the other end of the economic scale. Such juxtaposition, he whispered to Temple, bred Bolshevism.

As they prepared to paddle away, the camp owners appeared around a bend in the shoreline path. A young couple, the husband bright-eyed and handsome despite a pair of baggy blue shorts that accentuated his stockiness, the wife dark and muscularly pretty in a revealing tennis dress, they said their name was Williams and complimented Temple on her fluting, which had carried into shore on the June zephyr stroking the lake. They asked if the canoeists were from the area and, on learning their proximity, urged them to come by sometime to use the tennis courts before the camp opened in July.

"Very gracious," Toby said after they had glided off. "Now if they had asked me to bring along all my boys, I'd grant their generosity."

"I wouldn't—they're Jews, I think."

"Really? I didn't catch the guttural intonation. You Yankees have an ear for it."

"Very funny," she said, "but the truth's the truth. It's not their speech that's the giveaway. You can tell by that soft roundedness in their faces—particularly with her. Anyway, there was talk around the library that some Jews opened a camp out here."

"What of it?"

"Nothing."

"Then why mention it—unless you disapprove?"

"Not really."

"Or not much?"

Her lips tightened and eyes narrowed. "I just wonder why they come to Pittsfield—of all places? A family of them here and there is fine—the community's never been restricted, really—but why a whole colony?"

"I can see your point. They'll pollute the lake with their infidel urine. They should stay home in the ghetto and stick to their usury."

"You don't understand. I've got nothing against them *per se*—"

"I understand it's sad Jews should be herded into special camps—because they're not wanted—"

"But they do it to themselves! Everyone knows they're clannish—and don't want to have any more to do with Christians than they have to. We're not the chosen people—we're just dumb, pig-eating Gentiles."

"Does it occur to you they're being defensive?"

"That's ancient history. They've gotten along fine in America—"

"Only not through the doors of your fancy golf club, I'll bet—or your father's company or—"

"That's a matter of private preference. You can't *make* people associate with certain kinds who make them uncomfortable. But that's very different from actively picking on them—which is inexcusable."

"I'm not sure I see the distinction. How are Jews who've had a chance to mingle with others really any different?"

"Because they make their Jewishness the central fact of their whole existence—like colored people their color—"

"Not the Jews I've known. Perhaps you know a different sort—or you listened too long to Holly Larrabee."

"Her name," Temple said, "is Holly Curtis. And it behooves you not to claim a higher moral ground by assigning me to hers, thank you."

The topic lapsed until later that afternoon when they stopped by Dr. Haseltine's for a highball. The makings were all on a serving cart in the corner of the porch. Toby mixed them each a drink while he and Temple recited for him their afternoon discoveries along the shore, including the Williamses and the proffered courtesy of their tennis courts. "Have you ever met them?" Toby wondered.

"The people who own the Jewish camp at the south end? Hardly."

Toby glanced at Temple, whose eyes found his over the rim of her gin and tonic, and then back at the doctor. "I didn't say it was Jewish."

"Oh," he said, "but it's known that they are. Quite a decent element, though, from what I'm told—for New York ones, especially." He took the drink Toby placed in his hand and nodded thanks. "Actually, a few of the neighbors were primed for trouble—noise, unsightly clotheslines, offensive cooking smells—that sort of thing. But aside from an occasional rowboat or canoe, or a bugle call when the wind's right, you wouldn't know they're there."

"The chastening effects," Toby posited, "of the diaspora."

On the drive back to town, Temple was subdued. "What was she like?" she asked, breaking silence as they came up under the railroad bridge.

"Who?"

"The Jewish girl you went with."

"Who said anything about that?"

"I figured it out. Your concern is beyond casual humanitarianism."

He weighed her question while they drove around the city hall oval and drew up near the fancy red popcorn wagon on East Street just off North. "She was very much like you in some ways—since you ask. Smart—proud—high-keyed—"

"Oh, my. That's the last thing I think of myself as."

"Yes, it's so degradingly Mediterranean—so exotically Levantine—"

She gave a subjugated sigh. "And you cared for her passionately?"

"More than was good for me, anyway."

"She didn't reciprocate?"

"Less than I had in mind."

"Because you were a Gentile, no doubt—though I'm sure that offends your high principles of universal tolerance. I'll wager you anything she marries within her faith."

"And won't you?"

She shrugged. "Our situations aren't exactly comparable."

He reached for the door handle. "How do you like your popcorn?"

"Plain," she said, "and as little as possible."

III

Wed., 21 May '36

Have been drafted to co-author "Lulu Follies of 1936," the camp show, scheduled for presentation July 4th. Rehearsals begin in a week. The director is unfazed by notable lack of local talent. "Anyone can put on a show with talent," he sez. "Only the greats can do it with clods." . . .

Wally Eichhorn bounded into camp like a rollicking little Pan, but instead of pipes, he played the piano, and instead of being goatish, he was decidedly pixilated. "Holy Christ," Wolfbait announced after his first glimpse, "a gen-u-ine, twenty-four-karat fairy."

Forced under the strike settlement to accept a W.P.A. teacher to improve the camp recreational program, the captain made it plain that Wally's stay would be as brief as possible. "Mr. Artsy-Fartsy," Sparhawk was heard to remark and assigned him to bunk in with Toby.

Balding, gnomish, so animated that his rubbery limbs seemed in motion even when he sat chain-smoking on the bed with his legs crossed under him, he exuded theatricality. Just being around him made you want to perform, if for no other reason than to get his hands clapping and feet tapping.

A couple of dozen boys would bunch around him in the Rec after supper to listen to his show-business adventures. Having studied serious music at Yale and somehow emerged stagestruck, he started his career as a piano player in Jersey dives, performed as an accompanist in silent-movie palaces at shore resorts, and then developed a one-man novelty act that he managed to sustain on the vaudeville circuit for five years of steady bookings. "Ike Horn," his billing card read, "The Singing, Juggling, Tapdancing Maestro of the Eighty-eights." So many things were happening when he was on stage that it was hard to notice he did none of them very well. The road led finally to exhaustion. After that came bit parts on Broadway, emceeing on cruise ships, barely surviving as actor-director in amateur and semiprofessional community theaters, and finally, drama coach at several New England high schools and colleges until the depression curtailed such extravagances. The W.P.A. had kept him alive since.

Toby relished having a kindred soul around. They would stay up half the night talking. Wally had been everywhere and met everyone, high and low, and seen human nature at its most generous and callous, yet he had garnered little by way of fame or fortune. But he declined to curse his fate; rather, he took an almost perverse pride in it, claiming to have found reward enough in the gaudy array and hyperkinetic beat of life. "The thing is to keep moving," he told Toby, "and never feel sorry for yourself—because you'll be the only one."

Such a fellow, nearing fifty, had no need or inclination to negotiate his role at the camp. Sparhawk never existed for him, and he hoped the oversight was mutual. Wally's whole job was to whip a decent camp show together; he couldn't be bothered submitting sketches for the captain's crabbed censorship. "When His Majesty sees the run-through, he'll love it to pieces," Wally predicted airily.

It was astonishing how much the little director could make out of such feeble material, including Toby's short stabs at camp humor, authorship of which he urged Wally to keep anonymous lest the captain scrap the whole production sight unseen. The run-throughs,

Toby warned, would be soon enough. Sparhawk came to watch a rehearsal as soon as the whole production was assembled. He sat on his hands in the back of the mess and watched stony-faced. Wally had never played to a tougher audience.

Vamping outrageously in a dress, blond wig, rhinestone eyelashes, and other amusing transvestite accessories, Alfie "Rubberneck" Poteete delivered a sinuous version of "Lulu's Back in Town" as the overture to the show. Eddie Spain followed with a stutter-free recitation that began:

> Hark! hark! The dogs do bark,
> The rookies have come to camp
> With pajamas and knickers
> And bathrobes and slippers
> And one darn fool brought a lamp . . .

After a sidesplitting skit on the primitive culinary customs of the C.C.C., billed as "Who Put the Formaldehyde in the Corned Willie?" Skeezix Bloomgarden came forth in all his homely earnestness and offered, to Wally's tinkling accompaniment, "The Dream Girl of the C.C.C." It wound up:

> . . . For she'd have to be an angel,
> Worldly goods indeed forsake,
> To maintain a monthly budget
> On the thirty bucks we make.

The showstopper was a deeply affecting monologue titled "How to Quit a Card Game as a Winner and Still Give the Losers the Impression You Wished to Hell You Didn't Have to," offered by Wolfbait Stubbs.

Wally's theatrical genius and Toby's comic muse then collaborated in a snappy blackout routine called "From Sap to Nuts," intended to capture the hilarity lurking just below the drudgery of the daily camp routine. It had the added virtue of providing speaking parts for a couple of dozen virgin thespians, appropriately costumed and tossing off lines like:

CAMP COMMANDER (*mounted on a broomstick*): The horse I was riding yesterday wanted to go one way and I wanted to go the other.
ORDERLY: Who won?
COMMANDER: He tossed me for it.

Wally paced the production so the dramatic high point came just before the finale in a narrated pantomime, "The Smackin' Down of

Tuffy McGrew," starring Kevin Dundy as the narrator and featuring Farmer Jones in the title role as a bullying older enrollee and Boxcar Malone as "a real rube of a rookie." Providing soulful counterpoint to the action was a harmonica duo of Owen Guilfoyle and Link Salter. At the end of it, the entire cast flowed onto the stage, linked arms, and gave out with a slightly doctored version of "The Rangers' Song" from a late 'Twenties Broadway hit in which Wally had appeared. The chorus went:

> We're all pals together,
> Comrades—birds of a feather,
> Rootin' pals, tootin' pals, scootin' pals, shootin' pals,
> In rain or sunshine, pals . . .

" 'Lulu' Rings Bell in Berkshires!" Wally proposed as the headline for the review in *Variety* as he gleefully commended his novice performers after the run-through. Toby's warning against premature celebration he brushed aside even as the summons came to the captain's quarters. Sparhawk, it was clear from his glower as he left, had missed the healing powers that suffused the makeshift stage.

Half an hour later, Wally was back, looking blasted. The captain had asked for a few changes. The opening "Lulu" number he thought distasteful. And Skeezix's amorous complaint about enrollee salaries left a sour taste, harking back to the strike. The blackout routine he found personally offensive in its reference to his horsemanship and many forms of ineptness on the part of staff and company alike. Wolfbait's monologue suggested the boys gambled incessantly. The Tuffy McGrew number furthered the impression the corps was full of hooligans who brawled at every opportunity. And the rousing grand finale, with its fraternal exuberance, smacked of pinko propaganda.

"What the hell's he talking about?" Toby yelled, angrier than Wally.

"The first word of the second line in the chorus."

"What—'comrades'? Oh, my God!"

Wally's perpetually bulb-bright face had gone out. "I told him we'd change 'comrades' to 'fellows' out of deference to his xenophobia, but the rest of the show stayed as is. He said no. I said fuck yourself."

Toby kept him company in the room while he packed. "I threaten a man like him," was all he said in dismissal of Sparhawk. Wally gave him the name and address of his sister on Hudson Street in the Village and said to look her up if he ever came to the city; she could tell Toby whether he was in town. Eddie, grateful to have been in the show cast despite a speech disorder, drove him to the bus depot. Back at the Rec, everyone agreed Wally Eichhorn was one terrific guy, fairy or no fairy.

IV

Tues., 4 June '36

Why does fire burn uphill so much faster than down? Heat, acc. to tonight's lecture in Conflagrations 201, creates its own upward draft whereas a downhill blaze burns against the draft, ergo slowlier. If terrain permits, better to position fire lines on the downslope.

Ash demonstrated use of principal firefighting tools at camp's disposal. Everyone assigned one of three but expected to know how to work other two. Mine is a Rich rake, a mean son of a bitch that rakes-cuts-digs & never fills up with leaves, thanks to moving steel blades (which also easily slices up yr hands/feet/legs/neighbor if you don't watch it). Other two tools are: rotary fire mop, kind of revolving flyswatter with 6 rubber flaps (vertical downward strokes no good, sez Ash, becauz they scatter burning material; idea is to push or sweep back flames toward burned area), and back-pack water pump, which works best misting (i.e., don't squirt right into fire but wet ground and air directly in its path to dampen fuel, slow spread).

Everyone in camp inc. captain also pre-assigned to firefighting crew consisting of Boss (usually a Lem wielding a Pulaski ax), 4 Rich rakers, 4 firebeaters, 1 tankman, 1 messenger/waterboy. I'm in Crew #16. Drills tomorrow night . . .

At the approach of the hot, dry season, Work Superintendent Cummings pre-empted the regular teaching program every night for a week to give his mandatory special course, "F.F.F. in the C.C.C." Fighting Forest Fires. Considering the nominal purpose of the corps and his own lifelong love affair with the woods, Ash was admirably serious about the lessons. Anyone who clowned around during them risked having his back massaged with a Rich rake.

The menace grew graver, Ash advised, the more the sun and the wind dried out the forest. September would be the most dangerous time, but they had to be on constant lookout from then on, especially once the public began using the forest at the end of that month. The arrival of outsiders would make it imperative to keep the forest floor clear of brush and to get the fire tower built as soon as all the recreational facilities were completed. In this last project, he added, not without a small scowl from the taste of the crow, the enrollees would work as full partners with the Lems. "Sure," Skeezix said on the way out, "so it's our stupid necks get broken, not theirs."

If Wolfbait Stubbs had been caught sneaking his regular afternoon smoke anytime but the week right after Ash had delivered himself of these stern precepts, he might have escaped with light punishment or even a reprimand. But Will Bassett, another dedicated woodsman, was not amused by Wolfbait's blatant defiance of the absolute ban on smoking in the forest or by the sass the boy gave him for being such a grim enforcer. Will reported the violation to Ash, who brought it to Mitchell Nesbit with the request for Wolfbait's hide.

The Kangaroo Court voted three to two—Dundy, Bloomgarden, and Guilfoyle forming the majority—to let Wolfbait off with a month on the beauty squad plus loss of allowance and weekend liberty. The minority wanted him dismissed from the company, as much for his offensive character as the specific infraction. The captain intervened, holding that Dundy should have disqualified himself in a matter involving the fate of an enrollee from his own barracks. The crime was too heinous to tolerate, Sparhawk ruled and was joined eagerly by his fellow review panelist, the work superintendent. Toby dissented. Wolfbait's carcass was cooked.

A dishonorable discharge had the practical effect for its sufferer of eliminating the corps as a job reference. Without one, in that economy, work prospects were exceedingly bleak for a young fellow. Before the sentence was pronounced at evening retreat, Toby went to Nesbit and pleaded for clemency in Wolfbait's behalf. "He's got nothing—no family, no job, no place to go."

"He's a crummy little delinquent—and you know it."

"A lot of that's a front. Besides, he's reformed considerably. He does his work—and obeys the rules—mostly—"

"He's been a problem since the day he showed up here."

"They've all been problems, to one extent or another, or they never would have landed here. Considering the severity of his, I'd say he's come a long way. You toss him out now, you're throwing him back on the scrap heap of life."

"Don't blame us—he did it to himself. He should have thought of the consequences beforehand."

"A lot of them sneak in smokes out there. Now all of a sudden, you crack down. Okay, punish him—he deserves it—but not this."

"An example's got to be made—and I can't think of a better one."

"And to hell with the rest of his life?"

"He'll get along. How is his problem, not mine—and not yours. Your problem, Ronan, is thinking human nature can be changed."

Wolfbait was characteristically philosophical on learning that Toby's mission had failed. "It don't matter—I been meanin' to blow this lousy dump, anyway. It's been drivin' me bats lately."

"Maybe if you worked up a sincere apology—"

"Forget it. I hate the whole fuckin' bunch of 'em. There's maybe five or six guys in the whole place I'd give spit for—and maybe you. Yeah, you treated me fair, Toby—real Harvard classy—"

Toby worked up a smile to go with the kindly slap he delivered to the miserable boy's bony shoulder. Wolfbait took the gesture as a cue to try extracting one last charitable act from this rare well-wisher. Was there any chance, he wondered, of Toby's letting him have maybe a dozen "most employable" cards, the printed certificates awarded to departing enrollees who stood at the top of Nesbit's grading system? Having them would make a big difference in his chances of landing a job. It was understood, of course, that Wolfbait would forge the captain's signature of validation.

"That would undercut the whole point of your discharge," Toby said.

"Yeah."

"It would also be unfair to the rest of the guys—the ones who earned it."

He gave his small, scheming head a shake. "I figured you to say that —except it's really your own ass you're scared shitless for, I can tell. That's okay—I unnerstan', perfessor."

Undeterred by this parting slur, which by now he understood to be a perverse form of affection, Toby wrote him a short note to Bonnie Sota in Boston, if he ever got there. It asked her to please give the bearer some help if she could because he hadn't ever had much of it. Then he walked Wolfbait out to West Street to get a hitch. "Which way are you going?"

"Whichever way the first car that stops for me is headed."

At the corner, he waved a final goodbye. Wolfbait kept both hands dug into his pockets, gave what Toby took for a small nod, and turned to look hard down the road in both directions.

V

Fri., 28 June '36

All in readiness for the morrow.

Townies by the hundreds and officials by the dozen due for ribbon-cutting ceremonies, after which picnicking, games, swimming & tours of What Sparhawk Hath Wrought in the Wilderness. Himself has been surpassingly obsessive overseeing every detail; Lems laboring overtime all week as well to apply finishing touches.

Every enrollee assigned tomorrow as guide, or traffic director, or refreshments counterman in lodge, or cook at hot-dog roast, or player in ballgame vs. G.E. all-stars, or lifeguard at pond. Only I am idle; my repeated offer to assist capt. with his prepared remarks for the occasion repeatedly ignored. . . .

Still smarting from the strike, Gordon Sparhawk had sought to salvage his pride of command by ordering the entire company to participate in the Memorial Day parade in Pittsfield. The C.C.C. rule against military training was held not to apply since the men marched with picks and shovels at their shoulder instead of rifles—"it's strictly a civilian recreational activity," Nesbit explained.

To most of the company, however, it remained involuntary servitude, and they formed up in slovenly array and drilled each man at his own tempo. The worse they did, the harder the officers pushed them both before and after work, until fatigue overcame resentment and the soil soldiers began to shape up.

Toby's antimilitarist bias, dating back to a freshman year of impressed service in the R.O.T.C., was stirred anew by all this columnar to-and-froing about the flagpole to the brass beat of recorded Sousa. They marched by barracks, eight men abreast, five rows deep, each leader on the right front of his column. Skeezix Bloomgarden, sweating bullets and dreaming mutiny at the head of the B Barracks platoon, listened attentively to Toby's tales of marching mishaps at Harvard and conspired to do likewise.

On the big day in town, B Barracks confused "Column right, march" with "To the right flank, march," so the back two rows plowed into the three front ones, and by the time the other platoons were smartly complying with "To the rear, march," the B boys were a hopeless clot of colliding bodies and tangled tools. The sight so rattled the rest of the company that all discipline fled, and they finished out the parade as a cheerfully floundering scrum of agrarian rabble. The crowd applauded their grit when the laughing finally stopped.

This hideously public embarrassment, which Sparhawk apparently never thought to link to the only time-serving pacifist in his midst, made him all the hungrier for esteem upon the unveiling of the forest. At the dedication rites in the little glade just below the rustic lodge, he bore himself like an imperial viceroy completing the stewardship of a crown colony and expecting to be garlanded for its continued subjugation. In his dress olive jacket, flawless boots, and jodhpurs, riding crop at the ready to disperse any close-breathing wogs, he lacked only a white horse to complete the picture of majestic inanity.

By Eddie Spain's count, taken in the little booth constructed to mark the official entrance to the forest, more than twelve hundred people came that Saturday noontime to celebrate the opening of Pittsfield State Forest. There were a few splashes of bunting, the high school band sent the local fauna skittering, and a confluence of church choirs sang "America the Beautiful" and "Trees" and one or two others as cloyingly apposite. Almost everyone Toby knew or had ever met in the vicinity was there, including the whole Keyes clan—father in his official councilmanic capacity, mother as the doyenne of municipal uplift, son as newly hatched college graduate, and daughter at the explicit invitation of the camp educational advisor. Among those in the sizable working-class contingent were the Janowiczes and the Bassetts, together despite Will's transparent disapproval of April's escort, the duplicitous Anton Sota, back in town and spreading the union gospel wherever G.E. hands congregated. "You know," April said when she and Toby exchanged greetings, "I've never even been out here before—it's very pretty."

"And that," he told Temple as they moved off to hear the speeches, "is the great blessing of democracy—it expands the horizons of the under classes."

"Some of them," she said, her mind on the bulging front of April's backless sundress, "would appear to be sufficiently expanded already."

Reaching for rhetorical heights as he supposed the ceremony dictated, the captain outdid himself. His polished baritone, rich and triumphant as a coronet, nevertheless failed to disguise the bankruptcy of thought behind it. Instead of style, substance, or simple soldierly earnestness, the crowd was burdened with grossly misconceived allusions to Gettysburg, hallowed ground, and, by hardly sly implication, the speaker's own epic heroism. "We can not dedicate—we can not consecrate—what God in His infinite goodness has given free of charge," he orated. "We can only protect and preserve His divine gift. The world will neither note nor remember what is said here today—it is enough for us to trust in our hearts that we have not striven in vain for posterity's sake."

He turned then to introduce his staff and nearly came unglued. After Nesbit stood in taut acknowledgment of the applause, the captain began to refer to his miracle-working superintendent of works, but as Sparhawk's luck would have it, this legendary woodsman had absented himself. The captain simply forgot to tell Ash Cummings his presence was required; having never hidden his distaste for turning the forest into a public amusement park, Ash chose not to grace the obscene event. His absence, sending a stir of dismay among the audience, unhinged Sparhawk to the point of forgetting the names of half the Lems as they rose in unison for a bow. Whether by oversight or design, he omitted mentioning the remainder of the staff and stumbled straight into his peroration.

After a few halting phrases, his voice grew husky and lips tremulous, as if surrender of his dominion over those fairest woods in all creation was too much to bear. As the blinking began, Toby feared all was lost and half-expected him to pitch forward into the crowd in a swoon of emotional exhaustion. His long, obscure assignment nearly done, he should have settled for understatement instead of ludicrous public posturing that demeaned the whole painstaking enterprise he had captained the best he could; even sham had its uses.

At the last instant, as if the resentment Toby was telegraphing to him for all their sake had reached and righted him, Sparhawk drew himself upright long enough to conclude:

> . . . but we do not seek your gratitude. Rather, we offer you thanks for the chance to have served—and thereby brought purpose to our own lives. I speak for both the young men in the corps, who have known hardship most of their brief existence, and for their supervisors, who have known disappointment no less than our entire generation. Like the land, though, we all heal —and await other seasons.

None of the other dignitaries who spoke managed anything half as affecting as those few words.

While the rest of her family, along with most of the crowd, drove up the road to the pond for lunch and swimming, Temple hiked up with Toby, though she was not dressed for the climb. It was warm and buggy in the low areas, and her pale yellow dress kept catching on the raspberry bushes. But she never faltered, and her face took on a glow from the effort that added its own festive luster to the day.

"I can understand him," she said when Toby explained how Ash Cummings felt that easy access to the forest would rob it of dignity and mystery and, far from assuring its survival, only hasten its destruction. Since girlhood, the place had been a kind of shrine to her, especially up at the pond, where the woods flushed pink with mountain laurel in the spring, and in the azalea fields just below, dappled vivid red and white in June, as they were that day, and raging in September with the deep blaze of sumac. "Melville used to wander up here, you know," she said as they came into a clearing that looked down on a great beveled hollow of sublime stillness and a green so undiluted by atmospherics that the pigment seemed indelibly fixed to the earth. "He wrote once about passing 'a most glowing and Byzantine day' roaming these very trails."

He thought how well the words fit her own looks just then as the wind ruffled her careful blond bob, the sun singed her inclined cheeks, and those wide, blue-gray eyes patrolled a sky specklessly soft and voluptuously inviting. It stole away from them on all sides yet hovered reachably close, like a light but serviceable mantle. "Those writer fellas," he said, "are nature's noblemen."

"Except you all think you have a monopoly on sensibility."

"Well—maybe just the better franchises."

Even that playfulness she would not tolerate. "Some of us, you know, feel a great deal more than we know how to tell—or care to." Part of it, no doubt, had to do with an unwillingness to let go, she said in barely coded allusion to her own reticence. "It's the fear of exposure, don't you see—to ridicule for fulminating, like your poor captain down there—or to lack of emotional reciprocity once the cat's out of the bag. Can you understand?"

His arm ringed her alluringly narrow waist and drew her hard against him. She was warm and damp and loving the day and being alive and him enough to return his kiss quite fiercely. "Reciprocity," he said, "is for trade agreements."

Berry Pond was thronged as it was never meant to be. Barely a thousand feet across and set down like a large, moss-coated dipper among those time-blunted ridges, it charmed by the very unlikelihood of its location. Toby went up to it by himself often that spring to skip rocks or compose a page or two beside the hushed reflections. Its radiant repose was what made it a place for contemplation and reverence; littoral thought there could never be mean. Crowded, though, its very essence was defiled.

The pond was normally too cold to swim in except at the height of summer, but the overflow of visitors pushed the season that first Saturday it became an official water hole. Tents for changing had been put up temporarily, and a pair of rowboats manned by enrollees cornered off a bathing area about 150 feet square. A steady cacophony of yelps and splashes drove off the trout with which the waters had been freshly stocked, and the air was weighted with the smell of frying meat. The sullied scene—strewn wrappers, trampled plantings, new picnic tables freshly incised with initials, urine-fouled camping sites, cars locked bumper to bumper—sent the captain into a frenzy. He flew about trying singlehandedly to restore order, but the tumult could not be stoppered.

By midafternoon, Toby and Temple had had enough of all this

dispiriting joy and were preparing to leave when a sudden silence seized the crowd. A fellow in his early twenties reported that a male friend with whom he had entered the pond ten minutes earlier was nowhere to be seen. Hope that the missing swimmer had ducked off to relieve himself in the woods faded quickly as searchers beat the bushes in vain. All other swimmers were ordered from the pond, and a cordon of two dozen or so of the ablest waded out from the shore to scour the pond floor inch by inch. After five breathless minutes, April Janowicz poked her white bathcap to the surface and cried for help. A dozen hands flew to the spot, but by the time she and the others could bring the body in, it was blue and beyond revival. Doc Haseltine and a pair of other physicians in attendance concurred: The fellow must have cramped massively in the cold water, swallowed too much fluid in startled reflex, and gone right under. Amid a hundred other madly paddling bodies, his distress had been too brief to draw notice.

The *Berkshire Eagle,* in its Monday editorial comment on the opening of the forest, wondered whether all that commendable effort was worth the price of one needlessly lost life. It faulted collective and anonymous "authorities" for careless safety arrangements—a dubious charge but one the captain took to heart. The drowning had cast a pall over everything he had tried to achieve in the way of public approval, even as the strike had effectively rendered him impotent within the camp itself.

Corps area command delivered the *coup de grâce* a few days later. In line with a presidential order to begin cutting back the number of C.C.C. units operating—it was, after all, an election year and the Republicans were hollering about a grotesquely bloated federal budget— the camp was to be shut down not at the end of the year as previously contemplated but at the close of summer. All at once the cricket's note became the brashest sound in the forest. No one from town went to swim at the pond—Pontoosuc and Onota lakes were more accessible—and those who fished it were the same ones who had always come there before the camp was built.

FOURTEEN

Thurs., 18 July '36

Lookout tower begun. When done, it will be 100 ft high, 22 sq at base, 7 ft sq on top, solid steel, to be raised entirely by hand. Half of company involved hauling materials up ridge to pt. now renamed Tower Mtn. Capt. and Work Supt. directing from Forestry Service plans, calling for tower to be secured by fox bolts set in ledge rock & embedded in concrete. Sparh. stripped to the waist & wearing baseball cap to stave off heat prostration. . . .

WHEN LINK SALTER was finally emancipated from the kitchen, it was supposed he would be assigned to a field detail like any other enrollee. But the sight of his lean, black, hairless torso under that baking summer sun inspired the invention of a new category for his special skills and station in life—waterboy.

As the crews trimmed the firebreaks and dug new water holes and cleared out the last stands of scrub growth, Link would scuttle along the work line with a bucket and dipper, offering refreshment to any enrollee who signaled. Link was not permitted, of course, to raise the dipper to his own lips, as his Lem foreman reminded him once an hour. It was the Lems more than his fellow enrollees who prolonged his degradation. It had nothing to do with the color of his skin, they said, fending off the fat, buzzing flies and creeping menaces—he was just too scrawny to handle a pick or shovel effectively. Anyway, keeping the white boys well watered was a valuable service.

This menial task, assigned him by their civilian elders, had the effect among the boys of countenancing their renewed persecution. It was one thing when Link was out of sight ten or twelve hours a day in the hot, smelly kitchen and mingling with them just a few waking hours at night. Then he was a mascot, a lowly unfortunate doomed by birth and social custom to a standing even lower than any of theirs. But when he finally joined them in the field, the picture darkened. Miserable themselves in the heat and closeness of summer, they seemed unable to resist taking out their discomfort on him. Toby saw Boxcar Malone, his chest and shoulders almost scarlet and blistered with sweat, once tell Link there was green slime at the bottom of his bucket and he'd better get it out before they all got poisoned. When the black boy bent close to examine the alleged foulness, Malone shoved Link's nappy head hard into the bucket, to the approval of his convulsed cohorts. At the washup back in camp, Link was made to wait outside while the white boys showered, as if the presence of his naked negritude would have curdled their Lifebuoy. When an *Eagle* photographer turned up to shoot the work crews in the forest, Link was posed down in front, sitting cross-legged while everyone else stood, with the empty water bucket overturned on his head like a blunted dunce-cap.

Things changed the afternoon Malone carved up an artery on the arch of his foot when the ax he was wielding bounced off a knotty tree trunk. As he lay howling with fear at the gush of blood, Link took off down the trail at the speed of light to fetch up a truck. Toby watched him race through the camp compound like a small, dark comet. By the time the truck got there, the worst of the bleeding had been checked, thanks to Kevin Dundy, using his shirt and belt as a tourniquet. At the infirmary, Doc Haseltine clamped the artery, and Boxcar was driven to town for surgical treatment. Though his career in the forest was over, he was spared grave injury by the swift reaction of his fellows, not the least of them the victimized black one.

As a reward, Link was transferred to the wheelbarrow detail on a crew reinforcing the reservoir behind Lulu Cascade. Thrilled at this acknowledgment of his at least marginal humanity, Link wheeled twice as many barrows of sand and gravel as anyone else. Only on being told his lavish display of energy made the rest of the crew look bad did he succumb somewhat to the lassitude held proper in that swelter. When volunteer crews were assembled to work on the lookout tower, he was among the most eager to enlist—and the first designated to ascend with the scaffolding.

Instead of disappearing forever inside a tunnel of despair, Gordon Sparhawk emerged from the far end with his hard edges all rubbed off, ready to preside with almost affable fatalism over the dismantling of his fiefdom. Only Toby remained on the outs with him, a crimson cross to bear till the end. The fire tower became his consuming passion, the last of the public works he would ever supervise. His Purdue slide rule unholstered, he spread open the stock Forestry Service specifications for a medium-height tower and assumed full command of the project. Ash Cummings, with nothing to gain or lose from the manner of its execution, indulged Sparhawk his reborn engineering ambitions. To bone up, the captain ordered a scale model of the tower to be assembled in the work shed from an old Erector set one of the Lems brought in. What they could not rehearse, though, was construction of the pine scaffolding to lift the steel legs and crisscrossing support struts, some weighing nearly five hundred pounds. The intricate gridwork, with its interlaced series of pulleys and winches, went up more by instinct than approved construction design.

Link Salter was chosen to accompany it as it rose. He won the honor by virtue of being the lightest and nimblest man on the crew; that he was also the most expendable went without saying. The ease, speed, and fearlessness with which he moved about that impermanent timbering high above the earth drew almost as many admiring words as attributions of his ancestry to the lower orders of African primate. The higher he climbed, the more intrepid he became, his raspy voice carrying down orders to the ground crew and confidently positioning the rest of the scaffold-climbers as each new steel element was swung into place and bolted tight.

Then one night, when the tower was half up, the wind blew down part of the scaffolding on the eastern face. Link surveyed the damage with a shake of his kerchiefed head. He had had a dream that this would happen, he said, and declined to take the lead in beginning the repair work. His sudden apprehension frightened the rest of the boys, and no one else volunteered to go up. All eyes swung to the captain. They were his plans and calculations the crews had been following from the start; now, when cold reason fell under the evil eye of voodoo, everyone looked to him to lift the curse.

For an instant, despite his age and obviously atrophied athletic prowess, Toby thought Sparhawk might make the ascent himself. No single act could have redeemed him more in the eyes of the company. You could see him toying with the temptation: If he risked it and prevailed, all his ideals of mindless devotion to country and commander would have been validated; if he was killed or maimed, the sterling effort would not have been in vain—only in worthy failure did man qualify as nobly tragic.

But Gordon Sparhawk, for all his postures and demented interludes, was not fixated on martyrdom. Commanding officers gave orders; they did not lead the charge—not for long, anyway. Perhaps if some miracle of rejuvenation had seized his body just then, he would have flung himself up the scaffolding, trusting God and his own righteousness to guide him. Instead, his blinking eyes took a quick accounting of every able body at the site and settled on one notable for its rare employment in the field. "Ackermann!" the captain hollered. "Get up there and show these infants everything is fine."

The orderly had been busy fanning himself in the shade ever since work on the tower began. His normal activities were limited to picking up the captain's bedclothes or a folder of requisition forms—by all odds, the cushiest assignment in camp. So far as anyone knew, he had not abused it since the breakup of his bootleg gin operation. Even so, and even assuming the captain's ignorance of his orderly's earlier waywardness, there was poetic justice, if not much judgment, in the choice.

Dazed, Ackermann rose from the captain's field chair and came forward like a condemned man, eyes straight ahead, mind filled with the fact of its imminent extinction. Sparhawk briefed him on his mission with quick sketches on a notepad. Though he nodded numbly, Ackermann's unblinking gaze disclosed the intensity of his fear. But he went, motor apparatus functioning by instinct, arm over arm, slowly, steadily, never looking down, dormant young muscle tissue suddenly activated by dread.

At the top, where the wind damage had occurred, he positioned himself in a corner joint just below where several timbers had snapped off and, with great care, tested the stability of adjoining beams. He clung for dear life to each successive section of the pine planking as it proved solid under his weight. When he completed circuiting the upper reaches of the scaffolding, he called down his satisfaction that it would hold others as well. A rousing cheer went up.

As he prepared to descend, however, Ackermann took a look below him and froze. For several moments, he hung there on the outer edge, paralyzed, his hurriedly summoned adrenaline pumped dry and the drawing of his next breath too exhausting to risk. Ash sent up soothing words to break the spell, but Ackermann appeared to be locked in place. Without hesitation, Link sprang up the poles, calmed the exhausted orderly, and led him down by the hand. At the tower opening a week later, Link was given the privilege of standing first watch with Ash Cummings and Kevin Dundy.

His exemplary courage and industry, Toby thought, deserved more enduring confirmation. When one of the assistant leaders left camp to take a job near home, speculation ran high that Bavasi, the adjutant's orderly, would be picked for the rated position, probably the last one to be awarded before the camp closed for good. Most of Bavasi's effort, to be sure, was paperpushing and nit-picking, whereas Link had performed near-heroics in the field. It was plain, though, as between the two, and considering their sponsorship, which one would receive the rating.

Toby appealed to Dundy to enlist his fellow leaders to petition the captain in Link's behalf. Granting a black the status of a full tribal brave was one thing; designating him a chief, or even assistant chief, was quite another. Kevin said no. Only Skeezix among the leaders was amenable to the notion, but ever since B Barracks' antics at the Memorial Day parade, not to mention his part in the strike, his stock with the captain had fallen nearly as low as Toby's. With no hope, and therefore little risk, he sent a note to the captain via David, endorsing Link's candidacy for assistant leader. The kiss of death.

At lineup two nights later, Sparhawk commanded Bavasi to stand forward. For his conscientious labors in support of Lieutenant Nesbit, he was advanced to the rank of assistant leader. Link was then ordered forward as well. "And you, Putnam Salter," the captain declared, "in view of your sustained effort above and beyond the call of duty in recent weeks, are hereby advanced to the rank of orderly to the commanding officer."

Ackermann, everyone learned shortly, had been caught by the captain chiseling on the purchase of his liquor and other sundries. This unpleasant practice earned the orderly permanent reassignment to the field. Selecting Link as his new personal servant was, for Sparhawk, tantamount to knighting the black boy. Link missed the ceremonial significance of the appointment.

"I don't wanna be no fuckin' orderly," he said.

Toby corrected his double negative and pointed out it was pleasanter around camp just then than out in the forest.

"Hot shit," Link said. Or, as his friend the late Joe Calabrese had said the first time Toby drove with him, it hardly mattered whether you were a houseboy or field hand—a slave's a slave.

Link ran away from camp that night and did not return. The only misspelled word in the note he shoved under Toby's door was "appreshiate."

II

Sun., 21 July '36

Temple joining bro. Carl in N.Y., after all, come fall. She said last night they may even share a small apt. on theory of compatability & mutual need—he for a monitor to help him survive law school, she for company so as not to get swallowed alive by barracudas of Gotham. Am dubious of such clinging siblinghood—as if Laertes & Ophelia

*packed off for Wittenberg in tandem—but envy them their strong
sense of direction (not to mention the wherewithal to pursue
same). . . .*

Denied admission to the Columbia graduate program in anthropology after her brother had been accepted by the law school there,
Temple registered so little peevishness that Toby suspected she was
just as glad to skip the challenge. Life in the Berkshires was comfortable; the city throbbed with unknowns and vast potential for heartbreak. It took more than normal fortitude and virtuosity to prosper
among the multitudes in those churning boroughs, and Temple Keyes,
he judged, was not sufficiently willful to attempt it.

And then she confounded him by licking her wounds and applying
for the graduate program in fine arts at New York University—"Jew
York U," Carl called it with less than endearing snideness—where she
was promptly accepted.

Everything about her quickened on receipt of the news. Instinct
told her phlegmatic smalltown ways would spell doom in the metropolis. Her reserve by no means disappeared, but she no longer held
back in the pursuit of social pleasures. With summer sifting through
the hourglass at different tempos for them—Toby was in almost motionless limbo; she was full of expectancy and heightened curiosity
about the whole world—Temple proposed that they spend both days
of their weekends together, for when they parted, it would in all likelihood be for good.

He was moved by both the warmth and coldness behind the suppo-
sition. She was merely noting the obvious—that their mutual fondness
was circumscribed by time and place—and suggesting that while these
defining factors lasted, they ought to take full advantage. That such a
futureless condition might have drained the heart from the one to be
left behind, she seemed not to have considered; males were notoriously
untender in these matters, or healed, at any rate, ever so much more
rapidly.

With muted appreciation, he took up her proposal, and his weekends that bright, mark-time summer became as eventful as the week-
days were slack and sultry. On one late July Saturday, Temple and he
together even got to the bottom—or closer to it, anyway—of the
mystery of Gordon Sparhawk.

A busy day had been scheduled. In the afternoon, they were to attend the opening session of the two-day county horse show, held on
an estate at Interlaken just south of the Stockbridge Bowl. It and the
dog show in Lenox, Temple advised, were the highlights of the summer social season, and Toby was to leave his anticapitalist soapbox at

home. Afterward, they would dine at the Red Lion in Stockbridge and then head up the street for the evening performance at the Berkshire Summer Playhouse. Temple had seen Ethel Barrymore and Katherine Cornell and Katharine Hepburn and other notables on that stage, she said by way of reassuring him as to its professionalism. Her mind was already adjusting to metropolitan standards.

His woolen jacket was too hot for the horse show, she insisted and lent him one of her brother's old seersuckers. Even so, he felt out of his element. The estate belonged to a scion of Mark Hanna, that bellwether of McKinley Toryism, and the crowd was mostly white-shoe and parasol. However widespread America's continuing economic distress, it was nice to know that recovery had progressed enough to allow such showy shindigs to proceed without inciting riot. Or perhaps the Berkshires were so insulated from the more savage social currents that summertimes there had never lost their fecklessness.

While surveying the dandyism among the spectators and the equally needless currying lavished on the horse flesh, Toby failed to notice a dapper gent standing near them along the railing at one of the jumper events. Temple directed his attention to him with a slight nudge. He thought she meant his outfit—a cream-colored linen suit with a tan foulard tie, brown and white wingtips, an off-white fedora with a beige band, and a furled black umbrella he used as a cane on that cloudless afternoon. "Ooo-la-la," Toby said softly.

"It's your captain," she hissed and stood at attention.

What more natural place for the presence of a devoted rider? Still, Toby was startled, partly from never having seen him out of uniform before, partly from supposing he spent every weekend with his recluse of a wife, holed up at home in Springfield—or somewhere off the beaten track. In finery and footloose, he looked like any slightly dissipated high-liver, the very antithesis of his calling as professional martinet.

Toby pulled away from the rail at the earliest opportunity, turning in the opposite direction, but Temple drew him toward the resplendent spectator. His eyes were fixed on the jumping course as they came abreast. There could be little doubt he had spotted them— everyone came there to look and be looked at—and by avoiding their passage was making his sentiments unmistakable. "Captain Sparhawk," Temple greeted him without pausing as they went by. He glanced over his shoulder, took them in as a single disagreeable unit, touched the brim of his hat toward Temple, and turned back to the horses.

"He looks lonely," Temple decided as they wandered off and managed not to run into him the rest of the afternoon. But over drinks later in the crowded lounge of the Red Lion, they saw him again, wedged into the corner across from theirs and addressing a cigar and tall glass of something doubtless alcoholic. Temple took his normal mirthless state for a profound mournfulness. "What's the poor man going to do with his life once the camp closes?" she wondered.

"Just how poor he is I question," Toby said as a waiter replaced Sparhawk's glass with a brimming fresh one. "And from the looks of it—and everything else I've seen and heard—I predict a future of protracted alcoholism and premature senility."

"I thought you pitied him. That sounds like unhealthy loathing."

Hypocrisy was wearing him down; he had almost no charity left for the man. "He's so insecure of himself and his values that he spends his life oppressing everyone around him—and then relenting just long enough not to have you think he's an out-and-out rattlesnake."

"But that's sad, not contemptible," she said, and before he knew it, she was on her feet and making her way across the room toward him. "I'm going to ask him over—you hold the fort."

It was for him, of course, that she was doing it, casting herself as peacemaker between them. This unladylike initiative he both appreciated and resented. Having been branded *persona non grata*, he wore the distinction as a campaign ribbon from a ceaseless war, but increasingly it seemed an endurance contest neither of them could win. Toby was ready, he supposed, to sue for peace with honor—or, at any rate, to settle for it if offered.

Sparhawk stood as Temple reached his table. They chatted animatedly enough for a few moments, but at the end, he glanced at his watch and shook his head with a thankful smile on his lips. She offered him her hand, which he took with the semblance of a continental bow. Then he left to settle his bill at the bar.

"He was very appreciative," Temple reported on rejoining Toby, "but he has another engagement that he can't be late for."

"I'll bet. That's why he left three quarters of his drink."

Excusing himself to go to the men's room, he trailed Sparhawk out the door by some thirty feet. What he expected to see—or to say if the captain suddenly whirled around and confronted him—Toby did not know; something was simply drawing him after the man. Sparhawk paused on the veranda of that rambling old inn as if to get his bearings, then crossed to a very large, stately, clapboarded white house diagonally across the busy intersection and went in. His stride was slow but its destination certain enough.

"Austin Riggs!" Temple whispered, sibilants aflicker, when he got back and conceded the apparent truth of Sparhawk's story. The name, Toby said, meant nothing to him. "It's a sanitarium," she said. "Very advanced and humane, they say, and quite exclusive—but still—"

"A loony bin."

She gave her highball a distracted stir. "Yes."

They each consulted their private thoughts and then looked up with almost simultaneous understanding. "I'm going to check it," he said when she went to freshen up before dinner.

On the telephone he identified himself as the patient's nephew and asked if it would be permissible to send a plant to her room in care of the institution. "But we have no patient named Sparhawk here," replied the matron or nurse or whoever it was on duty.

He said he understood her need to be discreet but that his uncle, Mr. Sparhawk—"the gentleman with the mustache in the white suit and hat"—had left him just a few minutes earlier to visit her.

"Oh, yes—I know the gentleman. He always visits Miss Jennie Thornton—his sister. Oh, yes—that would be your aunt. Perhaps I can fetch him to the phone for you?"

No, the plant was to be a surprise, he said and thanked the mystified woman for her trouble. Then he invested twenty cents more in a call to the city desk at the Springfield *Republican*. Claiming to be a long-lost relative of the Thornton clan, he asked if they might please check their clips for the insurance broker of that name who had died seven or eight years earlier to see if his survivors perchance included a daughter, Mrs. Gordon Sparhawk, with whom he needed to communicate. Saturdays historically being slow news nights except on the police beat, he was accommodated. Within five minutes, they had confirmed his surmise.

With obvious reluctance, as he stirred them up a lakeside omelette the following noontime, Arthur Haseltine disclosed all he knew of the Sparhawk syndrome in view of what they had uncovered. The captain's erratic conduct and propensity for the bottle had caused the doctor to embark on a little detective work of his own well before Toby had ever reached the camp. Through professional contacts, he had located and conferred with Mrs. Sparhawk's attending psychiatrist. "The story has several versions," Haseltine said, "with the truth probably somewhere in between."

Jennie Sparhawk's melancholia was likely related to her failure to produce children, although it was far from certain whether that was cause or effect. Whatever the origin of her condition, its growing severity had seriously depleted the emotional and financial resources of her husband as well. He was said to have tended her with loving devotion; diverted time, energy, and funds from the business he had been willed by his father-in-law, and spared no effort to see to her comfort when suicidal impulses required her to be institutionalized. His business naturally suffered from these distractions, the reasons for which

Sparhawk did his best to conceal from the world. There were shames worse than commercial ruin. To outsiders, he was an incompetent whose chief talent at the office lay in the brevity of his daily stay there. His decision to sell out was taken for a confession of indolence; in fact that obsessive nature of his concern for his wife's health underscored the prudence of his action in preserving the family assets before they were exhausted. He was prescient enough, furthermore, to invest the proceeds largely in government paper instead of flying high with the stock market, a national pastime that his low spirits discouraged. The interest payments, unabated by the Crash, allowed him to subsist while meeting the onerous cost of his wife's care. He visited her every weekend for as long a stay as her condition permitted.

This narrative greatly sobered Toby and vindicated Temple's instinctive sympathy for the man. "Unfortunately, the other version is not quite so favorable," Dr. Haseltine went on. Pieced together from the patient in her moments of lucidity, her husband's unwitting revelations, and certain external evidence supplied by the Thornton family and friends, it cast Sparhawk as a prime contributor to his wife's condition.

Having suffered as an obsequious footman to a despotic father-in-law, he vented his festering resentment after the old man died by subtly terrorizing the ogre's daughter, estranging her from the rest of the Thorntons, and reducing her to despair for failing to bear him an heir. Accusations that she resorted to contraceptive methods without his consent rather than nourish his seed prompted her flight from the matrimonial bed. Every plea by the family physician that he be tested for sterility, he dismissed out of hand. "So it's not entirely clear, you see," Haseltine concluded, "which of them should have been locked up."

Temple was stricken with second and third thoughts. "The poor thing," she murmured, in obvious reference now to the disordered woman. "It's a wonder she hasn't put a bullet through his head."

"I only fear," said the doctor, "that he may beat her to it yet."

III

Sun., 4 Aug. '36

Hail the fearless conqueror of Mt Greylock—assuming an overgrown hill not 3500 ft high qualifies as a mtn. Went with Temple, Carl & his summer flame Deidre Applewhite, a leggy knockout. For sneering at it, the mtn made me huff like a broken bellows the last few hundred yds up. The Keyes Kids took it in stride, this being their sixth ascent. Deidre, a veteran outdoorswoman & highly accomplished physically (she's leading her family down the Allagash in a couple of weeks), counted it as no more than a stroll.

What it lacks in rugged majesty, Greylock compensates for by exquisite location. Peerless vistas on every side, a visible world 100 miles in radius, compassed on the north by the Green Mtns and the Whites; on the west, by the Adirondacks; on the southwest, the Catskills. In the foreground, the rolling Berkshire valley, so green and dreamy, with its silver cordon of lakes stretching south. An unbroken calm partaking of eternity. . . .

"It is my full intention," Carl Keyes announced to him early in the climb, "to get into Miss Applewhite's pants under the stars tonight."

Miss Applewhite's long legs, lovingly gripped by her work pants, bounded up the brushy incline alongside Temple some hundred yards ahead of them. In the interest of sociability, they had agreed to switch hiking partners every half hour or so. "And where is Miss Keyes to retire to," Toby asked, "during your festivities with Miss Applewhite?"

"Why, to your bedroll, old chum—a decorous grove or two away."

"I see. And have you advised her of the arrangements?"

"Temple? She wasn't born yesterday, my good man. Oh, yes, she's very refined, I'll grant you, and discriminating as hell in these things, but she's no chaste little doily, if that's what you've been thinking."

He paused for a sip from a flask of chilled gin and bitters he had fixed for the climb and offered Toby a swig. He declined, more out of disapproval of Carl's tactless advisory than for the possibly debilitating effect of the liquor. Why needlessly devalue the family currency— unless, of course, he sought to embolden Toby and thereby spare his sister a desiccated old maidhood. "I don't question your accuracy on the subject," he said, "only that the young lady elected to share such confidences with an obstreperous kid brother."

"Hell, you don't think she told me, do you? I've got my informants. I even know who deflowered her where, when, and why."

That sounded more like prurient trespass than fraternal oversight. He did not intend to encourage Carl's notion of hearty male bonding if it came at Temple's expense. "Voyeurism is illegal in most states," he said, "and reprehensible in the rest."

"You know the guy, too," Carl ran on with a snort.

Insinuation was about to yield to graphic reportage, from the sound of it. "Spare me," Toby said. But his mind quickly inventoried the possibilities and was appalled. "You can't mean—the lieutenant?"

"Which lieutenant?"

He groaned inwardly. Was khaki her aphrodisiac? "At my camp—"

"Oh, good Christ, no. He was a stick—to beat you with, I believe."

"Then who?"

"Can't you guess?"

How many other males did he know who were in any way connected with the Keyeses? Reverend Brandt? That would have been too scandalous even for Carl to broadcast. Doc Haseltine? Too old and fatherly. Guy Curtis? Too—too—but of course! That explained a great deal.

He spoke the pitiable name. Carl confirmed it with a leer. "In college, while Holly and Sis were roommates." Guy had seen Temple a number of times, flaunting his Amherst learning and tennis-team sweater, and persisted to the extent of discovering the Keyeses' social and economic status to the decimal point. Provincial gentry might have been acceptable if amply landed, but a salaried professional for a father and a mother of modest merchant-class lineage were not high recommendations, and so Guy's interest wandered. To tether it, she yielded to his passionate importunings—"complete with pedantic allusions to the metaphysical poets, the dreadful ass!"—and did the deed in the spring of her junior year at an unheated cottage on the shore of Lake Wauramug, where the Connecticut Curtises summered.

It proved a bad bargain. By the time Temple had clearly read Guy's shortcomings of character and intellect, he was making a strong play for Holly, who took her roommate's warnings about his ulterior motives as purest jealousy. "Hell, anyone could have seen from the way he ran around his backhand that he was a scummy jellyfish," Carl narrated with relish, "but blind, bitchy Holly thought Sis was just trying to recoup her lost virginity—the flagrant Mrs. Curtis admitted as much to me at our last New Year's party—and then invited me by her studio for—you know—some lessons." He shook his head. "A tragic case."

The unvarying drum of a cicada played in their ears as Temple and he climbed together through the heart of the afternoon while her brother and Deidre dawdled and dandled behind. The cicada, his zoologically minded companion advised, put out its ceaseless sound for a solid week, or two at most, after having spent a nymphal career underground for seventeen years—and then it died. "Seems rather a profligate life," Toby said, "given its gestation period."

"I see it more heroically," Temple said. "It makes all that racket to let everybody know it's been around."

"But it might not die so soon if it exercised a little restraint."

"But then it wouldn't be a cicada, would it?" She was thoroughly approving of the insect's singleness of purpose. "The thing is to concentrate your strength and not spread it all over—the way I've been doing." It was that resolve that had directed her now to New York, that marvelous honing machine, where everyone came following their nymphal life and drummed away to beat the band. "But what about you?" she asked. "You've only a few weeks left out there—I don't hear any plans after them."

"I'm still digesting the experience."

She took that for contemplation of a life of vagrancy—and was probably not far off the mark, he conceded. All he knew for certain was that he would not return for the time being to the academic life; from the perspective of the woods it seemed too stuffy and sedentary a vocation. Newspapering retained its appeal to him still; it allowed you to be out and around, sampling life endlessly but without either the rewards or perils that went with taking a big bite. "Or maybe I'll just roam wherever I'd like and write about it whenever the spirit moves me. Thoreau managed that well enough—though I suppose times were different then."

Having apparently read every book in the Berkshire Athenaeum dealing with local subjects, Temple recounted Thoreau's wanderings through those parts as they rested near the head of the trail for the last dash to the top. "He came over these hills alone and on foot—all the way from Concord, I suppose—plucking raspberries from the roadside on the trip up here, where he spent the night once." She had been surprised to read, though, that he would stop by a farmer's house every few days to buy a loaf of bread instead of doing chores for it or living on whatever else the earth provided gratis.

"You've misread the man as the ultimate ascetic. He was really very domesticated—except that he thought chipmunks were more interesting than people—and definitely more trustworthy. The low side of human character was the only one he seemed capable of recognizing. God knows, there's enough of that—but not so much as to make a misanthrope out of me—or a naturalist, either, for that matter. It just won't do to claim the sunset looks as grand from the poorhouse as from a mansion. That's all right if you're Thoreau and prefer hovels, but not if you've got no real choice in the matter." He waved away a winged pest lazing about his ear. "The social context is everything— unless you're just trying to make a living off of aphorisms."

She listened closely and nodded at the end, then took his hand and gave it a long, hard squeeze before pulling them both upright for the final advance to the hightest point in the Commonwealth of Massachusetts.

Carl and Deidre celebrated till dusk and then his flask gave out. Temple and he grew at least as intoxicated on the rarefied air and the immensity of vistas. Mellowing colors filled in the valleys and chalked the toy buildings in the town of Adams on Greylock's eastern slope and the distant spires of Pittsfield. Transfixed, they watched the broadening bands of light above the western horizon soften from gold to saffron to salmon to streaked lavender to a soft flood of deep purple, and Temple offered a eulogy to the dying day by reciting a stanza Fanny Kemble had penned in her Stockbridge days:

> . . . A calm and lovely death seems to embrace
> Earth's fairest realms and heaven's unfathomed space.

"I have been listening to that sublime horseshit through four solid years of college English," Carl cracked as the last limpid syllable left his sister's mouth, "and I'm up to here with it. I'd rather a good traveling salesman story anytime."

Throughout the cookout supper of hamburgers and canned corn, he continued in that profaning vein despite Deidre's halfhearted efforts to shush him. By the time he picked up their two bedrolls and declared they would be moseying off to another site, Temple was openly offended by his boorishness. "And what is that supposed to mean?" she asked.

"It means, sister dear, that I and my lady fair wish a little privacy and are bestowing the same on you and your worthy swain."

She looked up at him with blazing eyes, a charge of abandonment unmistakable in the flame-reflected light. "That was—not my understanding—of how it was to be," she said, restraining her fury.

"I don't remember any understanding," Carl said coldly. "What did you have in mind?"

"That we'd—well, camp out together—all four—as friends—"

"Like kindergarten, you mean."

His sarcasm was a sour response for having miscalculated his sister's affinity either for Toby or for outdoor expressions of affection—possibly both. Whatever her contribution to his demonstrative lewdness, she was anything but amused by it. "Like decent people, I mean."

"Decent is as decent does," he shot back and drew Deidre after him. "Anyway, why don't you come off it and warm up a little? Toby's the best damned deal you'll ever come across."

"You rotten little swine!" Temple shrilled across the fire at him. "Don't you tell me when and where and who to be intimate with—I'll decide for myself, thank you!"

"Don't wait too long," came the disembodied response from the darkness, "or 'a calm and lovely death' will wither your organs of increase."

"You can just find yourself another roommate for New York, you—"

"Shithead!" came the cackling suggestion, and then there was stillness.

Temple sat there humiliated, doing a long, slow burn. Even for a roistering young libertine, it had been a crude display. Toby deplored it and told her not to worry about his own intentions, being nothing if not a gentleman of the least predatory sort.

"It's not you," she said, reaching her fingertips to his shoulder. "It's him—he can be so vulgar and childish sometimes." She wondered if it would really be possible to share an apartment with him in the city.

"Not unless you get your understandings in order first," he said. "Maybe Everett Larrabee can draft you up something ironclad."

She laughed and gave his shoulder a squeeze and then his cheek a refined kiss, and they drew closer, and one thing led to another until he began unbuttoning her sweater. She said it was turning chilly and he had better not, so he stopped and went to poke life into the fire and arrange their bedrolls beside it. But in the end she took him to hers and slipped inside and tugged him in after. He said there was no need to accept Carl's sneering dare, and she said it was all right and not like that at all and to come touch her and warm her.

It was awkward, all that wool and so many hooks and buttons and the confinement and fear that someone would intrude. And she was unpracticed and more than a little anxious, from the hardness and dryness and tautness of her flesh. But he was patient, gentling her until she grew pliant and moist and sufficiently possessed to unbuckle him and hold him and move against him and the swelling, enveloping need they shared in the fluid darkness. And yet, for all the hurrying breath and gathering tremors, her advance was circular and she whispered apologies that it took her forever and he might stop if he wished, but there was no question of that. Only the longer it took, the tenser she became until she said she had lost it and there was no point in going on with her. He said they could wait and try again, but she said no and that he should go himself, and she ushered him into her with mingled pain and pleasure that grew into a frenzied cry of perfect sublimation at the instant of his release. The blankets went flying as they lay there pulsingly impervious to the attacking cool of the night.

He slept without waking till just before daybreak when he found her already risen, almost as if she could not wait to cleanse away the staining night. She was perched on a little knoll nearby, vacantly regarding the glow in the eastern sky.

He tried to take her hand as he sat beside her, but it was cold and unresponsive. He asked if she wanted to be alone with her thoughts, but she said she didn't have very many just then and welcomed the company. The problem, he guessed, was that she did not know her own mind, or heart, with regard to him—and that an intensifying closeness would threaten all her newly hatched plans, so she had resolved on awakening to encourage him no more, certainly not in that fashion, and to start preparing them both for the impending separation. Her mood matched the morning air.

Beset on all sides by slowly swirling vapors, they waited in silence for the new day to coalesce. It came not with a sudden lifting of the mist but by degrees, the eastern light probing between thick folds in the celestial drapery. Out of that miasmic ocean there appeared below a country seen only in dreams—soft-edged hills and sheltering groves, dewy pastures too fragile to tread, the glint of lakes with shorelines still inchoate. "Does life need more explaining than—all this?" Temple asked as the drama of daybreak played itself out.

"There is life," he said, "and there is life—yours and mine."

"Isn't it all part of the same—process?"

"I don't know. We each have our separate anguishes."

She pondered that somber chord. "They seem so self-invented just now."

He nodded. "But no less real. If life were always serene, who would ever climb mountains and ask what it all means?"

"I'm not asking—I'm accepting. Why assume its moods mean any-thing—any more than we do ourselves?"

"I need to think there's a distinction—between it and me."

"Why is that?"

"Because if my life is meaningless, why am I bothering so hard to live it?"

"Because the alternative is no more attractive."

"That's not good enough. What I mean is, some people try harder than others—more caring goes into their lives, and pain. How can there be no meaning?"

"Why can't it just be beyond our comprehension?"

"That's too easy an out. Trust in God—and to hell with all the hard, endless speculation. To be honest, I don't think God's such a bargain."

She fell into a brief spell, trying to sort out her own thoughts and mesh them with his. "Look, maybe some people's lives have meaning and some don't—did that ever occur to you?"

"All the time. What I can't accept is that mine may be one that doesn't."

That was when she took his hand—more in commiseration, he sensed, than tenderness. Behind them, sharing that uneasy rapture, Carl and Deidre had stolen up soundlessly, uncertain of being forgiven.

Back in camp Sunday night, he found a message from Will Bassett, urgently asking him to call. While Toby had been dwelling in the upper realms of bliss, General Electric was informing April Janowicz and her father that their services were no longer required. Since the plant payroll was growing, not diminishing, the unexplained dismissal could have stemmed only from the company's discovery of the Janowiczes' union-promoting activities.

He expressed profound regret to Will, who was not about to settle for that. "You owe them, dammit!" his angry voice insisted.

Toby denied the charge and then lit into him. Will had repeatedly violated his pledge at the start never to question Toby about what went on between April and him. And now, when nothing more was going on, he was blaming Toby not only for that but for everything that had happened to her and her thinking since they met.

"Because you turned her head," Will said. "She wasn't ready for anyone like you."

"And who put us together?"

"And who put her together with Sota and the union?"

"You make it sound like a sin."

"Whatever it is, look what it's gotten 'em."

"Why blame me—and Sota—instead of the company? If there's a sin, it's theirs—for firing a couple of loyal, hard-working employees just for doing what they think is right." April and her father, he said, were genuine heroes, risking their necks so working-class people everywhere might lead more decent and secure lives.

"Sure, and now they got those necks chopped in half! Toby, you can't turn your back on them. If you're so fired-up certain they're right, then help 'em. Times are rough—and the company's gonna make sure they're blacklisted all around here."

"What am I supposed to do?"

"You know people at the company—talk to 'em, Toby—please!"

Toby tracked down Carl Keyes at the country club the next day. He had just finished a couple of hard sets of tennis and was not of a mind to fret overly about the casualties of the class struggle.

"Let me get this straight," he said, between gulps of a bottle of grape pop. "This bimbo you used to play around with and her old man have been given the sack as union agitators—and you want me to ask Daddy to use his pull up top to get them reinstated?"

"That's—about it."

He wagged his head mirthlessly. "But why? Even if he'd dream of doing it—which I sincerely doubt—wouldn't it look awfully fishy in Temple's eyes?"

"That's why I'm asking you, not her—I thought you'd be able to be lots less emotional about it. It's not the girl I'm concerned about—it's the injustice of what the company did. I don't like to see anyone shoved around like that."

He agreed to think about it overnight. But next morning he called at the camp and said he didn't think he could make a very persuasive argument to his father, considering the people involved. "Leaving aside the merits of the company's position—which he's constitutionally incapable of doing—Father would be sure to see it as an act of disloyalty to Temple if he intervened. She's the one you ought to hire as your emissary."

He knew Carl was right, but the prospect disheartened him. Delay, though, was not going to make it any easier. He went to see her at the library that very noontime. "And you really think I'm all that dispassionate?" Temple asked after he explained his mission.

"It's not that so much as your capacity for understanding."

"Understanding what—that you've got old debts to pay?"

"Understanding me—you know me better now—and what I believe —and can see the injustice of the company's action—"

"But Father never will."

"As a favor to you, though—"

She shook her head slowly. "I couldn't do that to him, Toby—not unless I believed what you do with all my heart. And even then, I'm not so sure I'd ever ask him to go against his convictions. He may be hopelessly behind the times in my eyes—and impossibly hardhearted by your social standards—but he's still my father, and I honor him for that." She touched Toby on the arm to say she trusted his motives to be primarily humanitarian but added, "You'll have to speak to him yourself."

Lawrence Keyes was still closeted with his secretary when Toby came by his office a little before quitting time. When the wan young lady finally emerged, scribbling down shorthand even as she retreated to her desk, it was a good twenty minutes past the closing whistle. Keyes followed almost at once, adjusting his straw boater and, unaware of the visitor, offering to drop the girl off at her home. The sight of Toby produced an abrupt pause in his departure. Less heartily than he had hoped, Keyes agreed to give him a brief audience.

He listened expressionlessly and at the end was plainspoken in response. Unions served a purpose at backward companies, he conceded but insisted they were worse than superfluous at an enlightened place like G.E., which paid well above the going wage and set a high standard for safety. Unions cut productivity by reducing every worker to the lowest common denominator—how could it be otherwise if there was no incentive for efficiency and good workmanship, any more than there was fear of being fired for lack of them? He appreciated Toby's concern for the Janowiczes and agreed it was too bad that an example had had to be made of them, but he was in perfect agreement with company policy.

His secretary had made other traveling plans by the time they emerged.

After he regretfully reported his failure to Will, Anton Sota appeared at camp and took Toby for a short car ride and a hard talk. He had no doubt been gentlemanly in his approach to Lawrence Keyes; now the time had come, Anton told him, to apply brass knuckles. In her capacity as switchboard intelligence-gatherer, April Janowicz had compiled quite a dossier of irregular work and social habits among plant personnel. Her findings included a highly suspicious relationship between Keyes and his secretary. He was often overheard speaking sweetly to her. They regularly worked late together. He was known to drive off after work with her in his car. And once when the girl called in sick, the eavesdropping April heard Keyes express keen concern and the hope that her illness would not upset plans they apparently had to see each other on the weekend. Such an accumulation of clues could lead to but one conclusion.

Anton urged him to approach Keyes again and advise him that unless he bestirred himself in behalf of the Janowiczes within a week, "ruthless characters" over whom Toby had no control would disclose to his wife and company superiors all the details of his extramarital career. Here was that rare case, Anton argued, when two wrongs could add up to a right. The company's malfeasance in firing the Janowiczes had led to the disclosure of Lawrence Keyes's evident infidelity; by playing the two situations off against each other, a positive moral result could be achieved.

"Bullshit," Toby said. "It's blackmail."

"Call it what you'd like," said Sota. "We have to use whatever weapons we can put our hands on—even if they dirty us a little."

For three days he held out. On the fourth morning, Will came to work and told him his father-in-law had suffered a heart attack the night before and the long-term prognosis was not good. Toby was left in no doubt that the episode had been induced by worry and despair arising from his firing. Being out of work at the time of the attack, moreover, Janowicz could not claim workmen's compensation for a job-related illness. Toby's course was clear now.

When he telephoned to ask him to a quick lunch in town, Lawrence Keyes was testy. "If it's about the girl and her father again," he said, "you're wasting both our time." Toby said this was more of a man-to-man matter and thought it would be to his advantage to join him. That Mr. Keyes did not question him further he read as a sign of vulnerability.

Over sandwiches at one of the big booths at The Berkshire, Keyes's obvious distress at the disclosures Toby woefully related struck him as a further confession of culpability. The man grunted darkly at each itemized charge against him and, while neither admitting nor denying them, did not cry out indignantly that this was a dastardly defamation of his character. And what was it, he asked when Toby finished, that his acquaintances meant to do about these awkward allegations? "They intend to inform G.E. and Mrs. Keyes of them in full unless you agree to help," Toby said and then paused a respectful moment. "I'm extremely sorry, sir—"

His fleshy face had by then taken on its ruddiest hue of suppressed rage. "I see," he said. "And assuming—just assuming—I were to do the bidding of this bunch of yours—"

"They're not *my* bunch, sir—they're just using me as a messenger."

"And you're obliging them, aren't you? And by bringing you into it, they're touching on certain—sensitive nerves—wouldn't you say?"

"That doesn't mean I approve of any of this for a moment."

"Come, come, Ronan—you may not be in open cahoots with them, but you're in full sympathy with their purposes. That's been established. My question is—let's call it curiosity about the criminal mind—what's to prevent them from hitting me up for something else if I were to consent to their threat this time around?"

The very question fed the inference that he was desperately calculating which of his options was the least unattractive. So benighted had Toby found the man's social and economic views that this apparent squirming moved him not at all. The fates were recompensing Lawrence Keyes. "I don't know, sir. My impression is they're after a particular thing and don't make a habit of this—ugly stuff."

"Then you're an exceedingly impressionable young man." He wiped nonexistent debris from the corners of his overworked little mouth, placed his napkin on the table, and rose to leave. "Tell your people," he said with majestic disdain, "they would be ill-advised in the extreme to pursue this plot of theirs. That's all I have to say to you."

"Yes, sir—I'll tell them. But I'm in no position to stop them."

"Well, you damned well better try, young fella!"

He let Anton Sota know the outcome of his efforts and urged him to be merciful in exacting retribution against the capitalists. "Just like they are," he said and told Toby not to flagellate his conscience. "You did what you could."

He heard no more on the subject for the better part of a week. Then Constance Keyes telephoned at camp and, with unrevealing cordiality, asked him by for a drink that Saturday afternoon. His already considerable wariness grew when he discovered on arrival that neither Temple nor her father was home; they had gone to New York to arrange for the apartment she and Carl would share starting the next month when they took up their studies in the city. On hand, however, were Carl, the lissome Deidre Applewhite and her parents, on their way to Maine for a canoe trip, and a young couple whose presence immediately declared the gravity of the mistake Toby had made.

"Evelyn, this is Mr. Ronan—I believe you've met before," Mrs. Keyes said briskly. "My niece Evelyn, Mr. Ronan."

He recognized the girl as Lawrence Keyes's secretary; Evelyn's escort was introduced as her fiancé. She gave Toby an unsmiling nod and glanced away as fast as courtesy permitted.

His discomfort was allowed to fester a full fifteen minutes or so during cocktail chat before Mrs. Keyes drew him off to the conservatory and closed the french doors behind them. In a black skirt and high-neck white blouse, hands folded demurely on the right arm of her chair, she sat for a moment gathering her thoughts while he cooked in his juices. "You seem to have gotten Lawrence in a bit of a pickle at the office," she said finally and unabrasively, "not to mention Evelyn."

"It wasn't my doing, ma'am, I can assure—"

"Well, let's say it may not have been your intention, Mr. Ronan, but the damage was done nonetheless."

"But I had no idea she was your niece."

"And neither did anyone else, Mr. Ronan." Evelyn's family, she explained, had been hard hit by the Crash but too proud to accept a handout from relatives—yet glad enough to have a job arranged for their daughter. Corporation rules frowning on nepotism required that the family tie be kept confidential. The young couple, hoping to be married at the end of the year and set up house temporarily with her folks, were frequent weekend callers at the Keyeses'. "Unfortunately, Evelyn has now been asked to leave the company's employment, and jobs are scarce for a young woman of her limited experience."

"And I'm to blame, is that it?"

She shifted her hands, clasp intact, to the other arm of the chair. "Well, aren't you?"

"I don't see that. If Mr. Keyes had only explained the situation—"

"Mr. Keyes saw the situation rather more in terms of your character than his, Mr. Ronan." Her persistent formality in addressing him disclosed the degree of distaste the interview inspired in her.

"I'm not sure I follow you."

"Mr. Keyes was exceedingly distressed to observe that, confronted by manifest malice in the form of these union agitators of your acquaintance, you were unable to put aside your social prejudices and follow the right and honorable course."

"But that's just what I thought I was doing!"

"How—by asking Mr. Keyes to side with the Polish girl when instead you should have told your labor pals you wouldn't be a party to their—revolting scheme?"

"But they didn't need me for their plan—"

"There wouldn't have been any plan, Mr. Ronan, if you weren't acquainted with our family. Your obligation was to send these radical hoodlums packing. But you've chosen to repay us—people who have befriended you from the first and asked nothing in return but kindness to their daughter—you repaid us by doubting Mr. Keyes's honor and circumspection and seeking to punish him for an economic philosophy alien to your own."

"I sought no such thing—I swear to God, Mrs. Keyes!"

She rose in her place and gave her head a demure shake. "You're a great disappointment to all of us, Toby—but to me in particular because I was your champion in this household when you declined to discard the Polish girl merely to suit Temple. I thought that showed spunk—and decency. Obviously I miscalculated you—even as you have us." Her extended arm and open palm directed him to the door. "Need I add that Temple's future plans from this moment forth do not include you?"

Dazed, he walked into town. Instead of a brain to rationalize his unmerited fate, there was only a violently scooped void and a terrible pounding. Nothing made any sense; every shred of self-justifying impulse was swamped by an equal and opposing wave of nausea. In this highly agitated state, he nearly walked right into April Janowicz's reportedly cardiac father coming out of the bowling alley.

When his identity finally penetrated, Toby's amazement over the rapidity of the man's recovery was glaringly manifest. "You gone to Harvard," Janowicz rasped, not in the least defensive, "how come you such a sap?"

IV

Sun. A.M., 18 Aug. '36

Still hot & hazy. The wind raises a fine film of dust whenever it deigns to blow. Ash has put up a fire alert & says the forest should really be closed till after the next rain.

Am beginning final week of full yr here—long enough. Tempus is not fugiting. Undoubtedly I am wiser & meaner for the experience. Is that a net gain? Is there any way to survive adverse circs. with unscarred character? What are permissible dosages of pain, giving & receiving? Shall I ever shape these rural ruminations into Waldenesque verities? And who put out the story that country mice are holier than city mice? Cheese is where you find it. . . .

Late that drowsy Sunday afternoon, out of the window of a car descending the circuit road from the pond, where the driver had been fishing for trout and perch and possibly salvation, flew a crushed but not yet dead stub of tobacco. Nestling in the parched weeds and litter that no amount of human tending could keep clean long, the ember planted its fatal contagion midway on the slope of Honwee Mountain ridge, backbone of that lately renewed forest.

The hot, dry days had milked the moisture from the trees and bushes, and the tissue of the forest was brittle tinder. The smoldering spot spread an inch at a time, famished for fuel and near extinction, till it happened on a patch of pine needles and ignited with a flash and puff of disintegration. Like a sentient thing that has consumed its first prey, it became bolder and ready now to pounce on whatever would nourish it. But the forest floor was unnaturally clean from three years of grooming. And the wind was too listless to part the boughs and breathe fiercer life into the slight combustion on the side of Honwee ridge, and so the flames snuffed out.

But did not die. The virulence of the thing directed it into the earth itself to feed on whatever was organic. Burning slowly and stealthfully through subterranean capillaries, it gathered strength from its arduous feeding until, like pockets of compact lava, it surged up a root length to the surface, found a surrounding island of dried moss, and struck in a devouring gulp. And yet subsided, nearly petering out along narrow trails of grass but always awakening at the scent of fresh pine needles and sustaining itself until the trails converged on a clearing of spruce seedlings, where the fire feasted. Then receded once

more before coming to a stand of old pine, scrubby but not quite
threadbare enough to have been taken down, and gorged on the needles and leapt to the parched bark and seized upon its rotted pores and
traveled upward with murderous speed till only a charred silhouette
remained.

The earth and air were inflamed on the side of Honwee ridge away
from the fire tower. But only now did the smoke billow above the
crest, and a siren moaned through the thickening dusk.

By the time Eddie Spain telephoned all the Lems and the first of
them began to arrive, the company had assembled into its pre-assigned
crews, fidgety with their firefighting tools and spraying one another
for diversion with the five-gallon water tanks they filled in the reservoir. No flames could yet be seen, no glow above the tree line, and all
reports of a smoky smell were premature. But the menace in the air
was real enough, even if more a child's thrill over the approach of war
games than a reasoned dread of something lethal and uncontrollable.
The captain, an hour back at his post, barked orders galvanically. Everyone had to be in boots and full fatigues, dampened before combat.
Sanctioned, the hoses went all out. Calmer than Toby had ever seen
him under stress, Sparhawk dispatched the adjutant and a pair of Lems
up the truck trail to assess the fire while he awaited the arrival of Ash
Cummings.

Minutes ticked away. Eddie phoned again, and Mrs. Cummings said
something about problems with the car. Will Bassett jumped in his
own and hurried off for the work superintendent. By the time they
returned, the first whiff of smoke was curling through the camp. The
captain and Doc Haseltine shoved into the back seat of Will's car, and
Toby and two more of the Lems hopped on the running board and
held on tight as they jounced up the trail, springs flying. At Will's
elbow, Ash was deathly still, as if just awakened from a drunken sleep
and whisked unprepared into a living nightmare.

At the trail's end, they scrambled by flashlight up a foot path, down
a hollow, shortcutting through a glen but avoiding thickets, thanks to
the Lems' knowledge of the terrain, and then all at once mounted a
rise and saw the jagged line of flame, about five hundred feet across,
eating its way down the gully opposite. For a moment they stood in
speechless awe before the terrible beauty of the thing, a great candela-
brum of helpless conifers driving off the darkness. Nesbit's party
rushed up in ten-alarm anxiety, trailing smoke that assaulted their eyes
and noses even half a mile from the flames. Everyone turned to Ash,
ready for him to declare a plan of action.

Every crease in the Yankee woodsman's long, drawn facial mask
was shadowed in a wash of hellish light. His eyes, unblinking bulbs in-

candescent with rage and grief and incomprehension, were bewitched by the sight. His lips parted yet emitted nothing but unutterable anguish. It was what he had foretold. And the swift, cruel fulfillment of his prophesy had reduced Ashbel Cummings to a traumatized mannikin. His woods were burning up, and he was incapable of effort to stay the horror. "It's shock," Arthur Haseltine whispered to the captain, who studied the seamed map of the forester's soul another moment and then assigned Will Bassett to take over.

Will talked on the fly as they ran back to the truck trail, except for Ash, whom Doc guided along behind unfrantically—the fire's first casualty. He had never been in a fire fight, Will said, and was going by the book, which said you had to slow the blaze before you could extinguish it. To do that you denied the flames their fuel supply, dampened what you could not eliminate fast, beat back the forward thrust of the header, divided it near the middle, worked down the flanks and in from the sides, letting it burn in on itself and finally pinching it out.

To play it safe, Will designated the truck trail, built to double for a firebreak, as the main fallback line of defense. But there was room enough and they had the manpower to make a stand before that. Besides, the wind was low and what there was of it was carrying the fire downhill. The night, moister than the day, also worked in their favor. Will assigned half the twenty crews to dig an emergency break at the bottom of the hollow, six crews to battle the flames along the fire line itself, one each on the sides, and two to clear away all litter between the header and the new firebreak. Tarpaulins were to be used to drag out the rubbish—"wheelbarrows'll get us nowhere fast." Lights would have to be brought in for the men working the break. Will specified a route off the trail for half a dozen trucks and cars—it might cost a few busted axles, but headlights were the only ready source of illumination. A field infirmary had to be set up at the head of the trail, portable pumps obtained from town—he asked Nesbit to call the Pittsfield fire department—and the C.C.C. company on West Mountain summoned on the double to help build the break.

"I doubt we'll need them," said the captain.

"We'll need everyone we can get," said Will. "It's killing work."

The captain was unconvinced. "I don't know how outsiders will respond to our orders, frankly." As to bringing in Pittsfield firemen, he was even more doubtful. "They'll try to take charge—and the last thing we're going to need is too many cooks." The infelicity of the image hovered in the air.

"It's a chance we have to take," said Will as they arrived panting at the vehicles and piled in.

Sparhawk ruled against it. "We can do it on our own, Will."

"It's no time for heroes," said Will.

"I run this camp," said the captain.

"We're not *in* camp, Captain."

"The company's under my command, wherever it is."

"Then get yourself another fire boss," said Will.

In the backwash of the headlights, Sparhawk's eyelids beat fast. Behind them, the fire advanced unimpeded. It was madness to debate protocol. "I just don't want us falling over one another," the captain said.

"We won't—if everyone follows orders. That includes you."

Grimly the captain nodded, his complete delegation of authority confirmed. Within minutes, a caravan of vehicles snaked its way back up the trail, bearing the first wave of the human counterattack.

Will Bassett was everywhere now, deploying, cajoling, reminding, a dervish of defiance against the oncoming wall of flame. Toby's crew was on the fire break at first, water tanks cast aside and everyone digging and cutting and trying in the confusion not to lame the guy next to him. "The axmen first," Will yelled to the crew bosses, "then the Pulaskis and the Rich rakes, and the shovelers after that. We've got to hit subsoil or the ground fire'll eat right through!"

They fell to with a lavish splatter of energy as a strip was cleared a dozen feet wide and the trenching begun. Early giddiness gave way to fervent beavering, and then, under the lash of imagined catastrophe that denied all pause, cursing set in. But the earth piled high before the trench, each shovelful a weapon to cool and smother the fiery mass that edged toward them without mercy. A surge of kinship marked their collective tribulation. Soon even the curses, which siphoned off too much effort, yielded to grunts of ball-busting exertion. Toby's poorly conditioned back and arms were already numb, but resting was unthinkable. He had not known such a sense of powerless entrapment since Woonsocket two summers before. All around him ax heads flew, rakes punctured flesh, ankles snapped in the disorder of semidarkness, and the trail to and from the field infirmary never emptied.

The first reinforcements trickled in at last from the West Mountain camp. Toby's unit got five minutes off to prevent muscle spasm. Mordant hilarity prevailed. Shorn of rank, he was a foot soldier with the rest of them. Democracy was born in the trenches. All pals together, grubbing in the dank, black earth as if carving their communal grave. He was too bushed to sustain even morbidity. But he had not begun to appreciate his own resources; word arrived that they were being rotated up to the fire line, into the raging hearth. He prayed as he went —to whom or to what, he was not sure, knowing you cannot pray only when it is convenient. Besides, who could expect mercy from a power that loves destroying its fairest creations?

Shovels and mattocks were replaced by water tanks and fire beaters. The crew boss said to call their names out loud for the head count he would take every fifteen minutes at the front. Watermen were to aim their nozzles in the path of the flames, not hopelessly into them. Wherever the fire hesitated, the beaters and moppers and rakers were to attack, not with downward strokes that spread the incendiary edge but brushing it backward, in on itself, fire consuming fire.

The light and heat intensified punishingly as his group took over their sector. The replaced crew staggered past them, sweat coursing from their chins in great salty drops. Some of them fell to their knees, all but overcome by a retching cough. Quickly that testament to human frailty receded as Toby was immersed in the cauldron of combat with this fiendish enemy, convulsing them with smoke, sizzling their nerve fibers, hissing venomously and cracking like rifle shot, roaring now forward, now back, now upward in a fury of convection currents that carried aloft branches and bark and forest debris and fouled the air with falling brands and embers that ignited your hair and clothing if you were not watchful. Everything was at once brilliance and blackness, lambent and scorching, vaporous and impenetrable. Sudden tongues of man-high flame lunged at him like bayonets, and it was hard remembering where you were supposed to go and impossible to linger more than an instant on scorched earth before falling back to not yet eroded turf and starting again. Front and rear and sides spun together, a dancing blur to eyeballs so swollen they might pop like boils if you did not break free from this roiling madness.

A dozen yards down the line, the captain beat at the fire—a dauntless windmill of maniacal ineffectuality. He had finally to be dragged from the fight and restrained against his own frenzy. But as a stout hardwood crashed down, pinioning Alfie Poteete, who screamed in mortal terror at the instant prospect of incineration, Sparhawk broke loose from his captors and wrenched an enormous burning limb to one side with inspired might that allowed the trapped boy to wriggle free. The rescuer stumbled back from the fire with a badly singed hand and was force-marched to the rear, protesting at a howl all the way. By the time they were relieved on the line and collapsed back toward the firebreak, now only a few hundred yards distant, the captain had returned, left hand bandaged, and was roaming the earthworks to steel his men and see that the battlement was secure.

Will, with the instinct of a man who has consorted all his life with nature, feared the wind might rise or shift on them at any time now.

He sent two crews from the West Mountain contingent down the truck trail to come up the circuit road behind the fire and smother its dormant rear. But their way up the mountain was blocked by a herd of engines from the Pittsfield fire department. Despite impossible logistics and without knowledge of—or apparent interest in—Will's overall plan, the firemen had been proceeding to lay hose for a direct assault on the header. Will advised that the pumper hoses were too short for a frontal assault and ought to be turned instead on the back end and sides of the blaze. The fire chief, though, cared little for the subsidiary assignment—and still less for taking orders from Will. His coupe raced around to the head of the truck trail, siren shrieking, and the helmeted chief confronted the C.C.C. high command with an ax on his shoulder.

"It wasn't an order—it was a suggestion," Will repulsed him. His face was glazed with grime from the heat, sweat, and breathless toil. "Anyway, what the hell took you so long to get out here?"

The diversionary complaint momentarily disarmed the chief. "No one turned in an alarm," he said. "All we got is a call for line and pumps."

Will looked disgusted. "What'd you think we were doin'—watering the goddamned grass?"

The chief glared hard at Will. "Don't sass me none, mister—every pissant first-grader knows to holler fire when there's a fire, but not you bird-brained boys! On top o' which, we happen to run a little short-handed on the Lord's day, if that's all right with you. Now just clear your kiddies out of the way so we can run our lines in from the pumpers. We could use a couple of guides, maybe, if it's not too much trouble—"

Unhappy at this scornful dismissal of all their efforts, Will repeated his request that the professionals tend to the rear and sides of the fire, nearest their equipment, and leave the header to the C.C.C. "We're doin' all right," he said. "I think we can hold 'er at the break."

"In a pig's ass," said the chief. "Your forest is burnin' up—looks like seven, maybe eight hundred acres gone already. You done your best, but this is man's work. We'll take it from here."

"Sorry, Chief," the captain intervened. "This is our territory—and we've trained for this—"

The chief's displeasure neared the volcanic. "You're inside the municipal limits of Pittsfield, Captain—that makes it *our* territory. Now I'm not gonna stand around here all night and debate while the fuckin' fire is goin' strong—"

The captain was stainless steel. "This is a military base—what I say here, goes."

The fire chief's patience was gone. "This is state property within city limits—either you order your boys to help us like we say or clear 'em out of here fast!"

"Don't talk to me that way!" The captain brandished his unburned fist aloft like a cudgel.

"You got thirty seconds to pass the word to your people," the chief snarled, "or I'm gonna have you put under arrest!"

"You've got no authority to arrest anyone out here!"

"We'll see who's got what authority!" the chief shouted and drove off, steaming.

Will and Nesbit conferred, agreeing the captain was about to come unraveled. Will made a show of giving him a new and vital assignment. He was to return to camp headquarters, send Eddie Spain up to the fire tower to monitor wind conditions, and relay word of any change. "It's essential we know that from now on," Nesbit soothed.

"You're just trying to get the hell rid of me," said the captain, arms slack at his sides, damp hair matted to his skull, eyes no longer pinwheels of Olympian delusion. He had fought, and not prevailed, and been relieved of command. Self-assigned disgrace slumped his shoulders.

"You've done everything any one human being could—sir," Toby said from the fringe of the proceedings, where he had lingered throughout.

Even in this utmost travail, Toby remained pure strychnine to Sparhawk. The captain looked over at and through him and surrendered with a grunt to Bavasi, who taxied him back down to camp.

Within minutes the wind rose, whipped the fire into a brighter torch, then turned and began driving it back on itself, up the ridge, feeding on its own draft now as the slumbering higher end of the burn, still undoused despite Will's order, sprang to angry life. It shortly attacked a clump of rotted trees and sent their broomed tops off like fireworks. Embers shot up the ridge and sprinkled spot blazes ahead of the surging fire wall. Flames hurdled the circuit road and threatened to crown, turning the whole mountain ablaze.

The fire chief had never faced an adversary of this magnitude. Most of his equipment, backed precariously down the mountain road, stood uselessly out of reach of the upswept flames. The smoke thickened with the feeling that the situation was running rapidly out of control. Reluctantly, the chief turned back to Will and Nesbit, in co-command of the company, which nursed its wounds in exhausted bewilderment while mechanically quenching the old header a hundred yards shy of the firebreak. Will and Nesbit proposed that most of the C.C.C. boys gang on a new fire break on the far side of the ridge, about a quarter mile below the crest. The firemen, meanwhile, augmented every few minutes by another volunteer unit from a nearby town, were to run their lines out of Berry Pond and whichever brooks were still running and saturate the upper reaches of the ridge. When wind and topography dictated, backfires would be set, the perimeter of the burned area steadily reduced, and the whole monster bastard contained between the two firebreaks.

They were parceled off into new crews, and Toby was made a boss. The trucks juggled their battered bodies and reeling minds on an end run around the fire. Everyone was functioning like a zombie by now, tools rising and falling in sodden counterpoint, but moving nonetheless, and they were thankful not to be on the fire line anymore. Toby smelled like an animal. His clothes and body reeked of sweat, soot, urine he had had no time or other place to deposit, and blood from a couple of nicks by his own rake.

Beyond their view, the flames churned up the ridge, glowing torrid neon above the picket line of hemlocks along the crest. Tension that had never left them rebuilt. They drove themselves harder, fearful the fire would bound over the crest and roll down upon them and out across the rest of the forest.

Some time past midnight the crisis came. Just short of the crest, the fire slowed with the dying wind. It crept over the top and began to reach hot tendrils toward them, but the firemen could cope with it now. The C.C.C. crews moved in massively with long strips of soaked burlap and beat the flames to a flicker and then out. Its rage was spent; the forest was spared, though hideously scarred.

Will Bassett asked those who still had the strength to stand patrol along the rim of the burn while the rest of the company got some rest. In a few hours, work would have to begin on a barrier ditch down to the mineral level of the subsoil so that no lurking embers in the earth could spread the devastation. When Toby finally went in for coffee and doughnuts at the field infirmary, he found Doc Haseltine slouched in a fold-up chair and carefully cupping a forbidden cigarette in a still-unguented palm. They had handled forty-seven cases of burns, gashes, fractures, and smoke inhalation, he reported, twelve of them winding up in the hospital. He, a fellow practitioner from town, and a volunteer nurse were ardently commended by Nesbit, whose face wore the strained lines of battle. "We could do with a bucketful of Purple Hearts," he said, "and a group citation for the medics."

Even as an ether of lightheaded relief stole over them by lantern light and they began to recline for a few moments of rest, a hideous thrashing and wailing emerged from the edge of the woods. They jumped up to see what the matter was and were confronted by a many-limbed apparition. All their flashlights played over it. Skeezix Bloomgarden, dirt-caked face riven by tears, knees buckling from his burden, chest heaving with anguish, collapsed in their midst and deposited at Doc Haseltine's feet the lifeless body he had borne on his back from the ruins of the forest. One side of it had been blackened by the fire, fabric and flesh crusted from the shoulder to the knees, leaking thick, dark blood and other congealing fluids. The rest of the once-milky skin was splotched where it was not raw. The chubby arms dangled leadenly, and the head lolled to one side, eyeballs bulging, tongue protruding, agony having contorted every inch of him. It was hard to look for long on the remains of David Schumacher.

Skeezix was beside himself. In the frantic effort of the fire fight, he had stopped taking a head count of his crew, and when the men were redistributed to dig the second firebreak, he supposed David had gone to another sector or to the infirmary or back to camp. His forgetfulness, Skeezix tearfully insisted, cost the boy his life.

Doc Haseltine examined the body and shook his head. In the consuming excitement, Skeezix was hardly the only one to have forgotten. None of them had paused to consider David's disease—its only prior manifestation seemed so long in the past—or thought to order him away from the smoke. No doubt seized by a spasm, he must have crawled off behind a bush or rolled down a slope, gasping for relief but in his extremity finding only a suffocating cloud. It was not clear, said the doctor, whether the boy succumbed to the flames or asphyxiation but probably the latter.

Toby told Skeezix that if anyone was responsible for David's death, it was he for having persuaded the captain to keep him in camp when prudence dictated his discharge. "And I," added Arthur Haseltine, "for letting you."

"It's what he wanted to do," Nesbit put in to brace them. "It's no one's fault what happened."

They loaded him on a stretcher, over which Toby drew a blanket, and they rode the truck with him back to camp. Haseltine and one of the Lems drove on to the hospital to deliver the body.

In the headquarters shed, Eddie Spain was alone. Nesbit at once feared the worst. "He's up the, uh—up the, uh—he's up the tower," Eddie said.

"He's *where?*" Nesbit roared.

"Up-up-up, uh—the-the, uh—up the tower."

"But you were the one who was supposed to go!"

"He never, uh—never, uh—he never said th-th-that."

"How the Christ could you let him go up there in the dark—and with only one good hand?" the adjutant demanded. His alarm was

contagious. They all imagined Gordon Sparhawk's inert body splayed
somewhere around the base of the tower or snagged lifeless and
dangling from one of the girders. Eddie said he had been powerless to
countermand the C.O. but at least he knew the captain had made it to
the top because he telephoned down wind reports for the first hour.
After that he said he would stand watch until he was sure the fire was
all out. "Jesus!" Nesbit whistled and looked at Toby with a grimace
that needed no elaboration. "Ring him up and tell him it's over," he
ordered Eddie.

"I've, uh—I've been. He stopped answering."

"Somebody better get him," Toby said, "while he's still there to
get."

Nesbit nodded. "I may need some help—and it can't be you."

"I'll go," Eddie offered. The other two looked at him and then each
other in astonishment. Conscience had come to the company clerk:
"Every, uh, every-uh—everyone else in camp r-r-risked his neck out
there—except, uh—except, uh—me."

Neither Eddie nor Nesbit volunteered what happened after that. On
their return from the tower they allowed only that the captain was all
right and resting in his quarters. By morning, he was back in the field,
overseeing the restoration of the burned-out face of Honwee ridge.
Beside him was Will Bassett, the interim superintendent of works.

In headquarters when Toby came in, the adjutant was on the telephone, sparing him a duty no man should be called upon to perform
more than once in his life. David's mother had already collapsed at the
news, and Nesbit was insistently telling the boy's uncle that he had
died a hero's death.

Toby nodded his thanks when Nesbit hung up. "I figured you'd
rather put your thoughts in writing," the lieutenant said.

As far as they went, Nesbit's commiserating words were true, for
everyone in camp had been a hero that night. But if it was right to reassure themselves that no one had killed David Schumacher, it would
have been at least as correct—and infinitely more honest—to concede
that they all had.

V

His diary remained empty the last dozen days of the camp while he
devoted himself, like a dutiful federal functionary, to the completion
of paperwork, all of which would go from his hand directly and forever into cold storage. Folders had to be closed out for two hundred
men, each of whom he felt obliged to interview and try to help decide
on a course of civilian survival. Some were much strengthened and

hopeful as a result of their stay in the corps. More of them understood the truth: They had been granted temporary refuge from the storm, which at last report had not yet abated.

He wrote letters of recommendation for anyone who asked. Several, like those for Dundy and Bloomgarden, were more admiring than the rest. He exchanged addresses, though, only with Skeezix at the end. "I'll be staying at Doc's house for a while," Toby told him on mustering out day, August 31, and scribbled the address on the back of his last "most employable" card. "Write some time and tell me what you settled on, okay?"

"Yeah, sure," Skeezix said, barely looking at him.

"You could do almost anything you want to, you know."

"Oh, yeah—right. Maybe I should go to Harvard then, huh?"

"Why not?"

"No reason—just 'cause I'm dumb—an' poor—an' a Jew."

He assured Skeezix he was dumb like a fox, that there were ways of working his way through college if he really wanted to, and there were lots of Jews at Harvard—and lots of colleges he could probably make it through handily. But Justin Bloomgarden insisted on his unbookishness and wanted to make his way as a workingman, maybe even becoming a labor leader since he had already led one successful strike. Toby offered to make reference to that triumph in a postscript to his letter of endorsement, but Skeezix laughed and said that might not go over big with potential bosses. Then the smile left his heavy, earnest face. "The thing is," he said, "there's such a lotta shit out there, you don't know where to shovel first."

They clasped hands warmly, and Skeezix stuck his small, handleless valise under one burly arm and headed out with Kevin Dundy. Keen rivals, better pals. Whatever was good about the corps, they embodied; whatever was rotten about it, they endured.

Only a handful of them remained for the final lowering of the flag. The adjutant did the honors while everyone else saluted and sang "My Country 'Tis of Thee." Nesbit and Bavasi folded the flag carefully and presented it to the captain, who took it without a word and went to his quarters to pack. Toby walked the lieutenant to his office to pick up his August pay. "It's a little less than you're expecting," he said and handed him a check for six dollars.

He knew at once it was no joke. Through no fault of his own, the education program had been all but nonexistent the last month of camp. His course in citizenship had been banned as subversive, and no one showed up anymore for "Self-Expression." A few boys stayed with the strictly vocational subjects he made sure were continued till the end—auto mechanics, radio repair, bookkeeping, and typing. He helped out with the sports program, umpiring ball games and running a track meet to correspond with the Olympic Games going on at the same time in Berlin, and made himself available to any of the boys who wanted to talk about anything. It was not much of a counseling service, but the price was right and the ear attentive. "Look, I did whatever I could," he told Nesbit. "What the hell was I supposed to do—quit right near the end?"

"Don't blame me," he said. "I'm just following orders. The captain doesn't think you earned your keep. Argue with him if you want—not me."

"He's got no right to pull a thing like this—after the fact."

"File an appeal, then. He'll probably put in a ten-page rebuttal trying to get your citizenship lifted."

He had very nearly persuaded himself that his judgment of Gordon Sparhawk all along was too harsh, even as at Harvard it had been too admiring of Jeremiah Travis. And then at the end, he was dealt this royal rooking. He told Nesbit that it only confirmed all the meanness and bitterness, however mitigated, that they had both recognized was consuming the captain. "When you get right down to it," Toby said, "he's just a lousy son of a bitch."

"Maybe so," the lieutenant replied, "but he's still a better man than you've ever given him credit for."

"Then why is he pulling this last-minute shit on me?"

"Because you've made a horse's ass out of him for the past year."

"That's genuine horseshit. I've shown him all possible respect—"

"Except by obeying him when you thought he was wrong." Nesbit tilted his chair back against the wall and propped his feet up on the desk. "Some things in life are more important than doing whatever it is you happen to think is right at the moment."

"I don't believe that."

"Oh, I know. You're very dedicated where your own principles are involved—too much so, if you ask me. Why don't you ease up a little, Toby—on yourself and everyone else? You'll get along a lot better."

A clear case of the olive calling the pimento drab. "What's the six bucks for?" Toby asked.

"The night of the fire."

"I didn't think he noticed."

"He didn't. It was my idea. I told him to dock my pay for it if it bothered him, but he let it go through."

"That's very goddamned decent—of you both."

"No hard feelings, I hope." He got up and wished Toby well and strode off to finish overseeing the equipment inventory. Denis Carmichael was said to have had a nice little side business going in filched silverware.

Toby went to the Rec to reclaim his books from the library, due to be dismantled in the morning for distribution among other camps in the state. Then he hurriedly packed his few things and walked the length of the officers' quarters for the final time.

At the end, he paused in front of the captain's door, contemplating the soft-edged trapezoid of light from within that flowed under it. A million words churned through his head as he searched for the proper mouthful. Fury and sorrow and forgiveness were warring within him. Finally, he took the six-dollar government check from his pocket, shoved it under his door, and walked away.

Next day, at the *Eagle* office, the personnel manager remarked that his employment application was interesting but their only opening at the moment was in the mechanical department—"and I don't suppose that would suit anyone from Harvard."

"I can run a lino, work on the stone, read proof—I'll even sweep up the whole place at the end of the day if I can just get a crack at editorial when there's an opening."

The managing editor reviewed his application, assured him of transfer to the news side at the earliest opportunity, and took Toby down to meet the composing-room foreman. An hour's tryout on the Mergenthaler proved him rusty but promising. He was hired at $22.50 a week, about half his C.C.C. pay.

The job lasted two weeks. The foreman said he didn't know why but his orders were to let him go. Neither the quality nor quantity of his work was at issue. He went straight to the personnel office, but the manager's secretary said he could not have an appointment. Toby was determined that he would. Noon passed without the man's appearance —he must have eaten at his desk or been fasting for his sins—so Toby waited all afternoon. Finally, at the end of the day, the manager appeared and said the paper had received information he was a labor agitator and a union organizer and that the *Eagle* was committed fiercely to an open shop. "It's the only way to run a newspaper. Sorry, son."

With five hundred dollars of his C.C.C. earnings in the bank and nothing better to do locally, he put on his jacket and tie the next morning and took the first train to Boston. Franklin D. Roosevelt, Harvard '04, was scheduled to speak that day at the concluding exercises of the university's three hundredth birthday. Having just worked a year for the man, Toby felt a certain affinity for him and the hope he had reawakened in the country. Besides, he owed him $159 in back pay—the least he could do was supply a creditor, fellow Cantabrigian, and ex-New Dealer with a little personal inspiration.

The chill and intermittent drizzle could not take the edge off the panoply in the Yard, converted for the occasion into a mammoth open-air amphitheater astir with students and alumni by the thousands. His return was greeted—he had not expected quite that much—by a great pealing of church bells relayed live by transatlantic hookup from the English borough of Southwark, John Harvard's birthplace.

Modesty, poverty, and lateness consigned him to the last row, an excellent position from which to watch as ambassadors from hundreds of universities and learned societies the world over marched across from Widener and down the aisle of flags in the center of the theater to their places of honor on the platform. For sartorial splendor, he awarded top prize to the Italian delegation of academics in their green-plumed caps, with runner-up to a chap in a brilliant orange gown who someone said came from the University of Bombay.

Nothing anyone said could have mattered to him half as much as just being there. An overdose of emotional succor did not rob him entirely, though, of his critical faculties. John Masefield, the poet laureate of England, delivered what Toby judged an embarrassment titled "Lines on the Tercentenary of Harvard College in America." The only piece of oratorical glitter came when the president of Yale glanced up through the elms at the leaden sky and chided the Harvard powers for their policy of "soaking the rich."

A dignified flurry on the platform set off a slowly rising and finally tumultuous ovation that brought the throng to its feet and blocked his view. By the time the proceedings resumed, he saw seated in the center of the front row, in silk topper and morning suit—would he wear them in January at his second inaugural?—the slightly fleshy but unmistakably magisterial features of the thirty-second President of the United States of America. It was as if he had materialized on the spot by magic. There was no wheelchair, no hint of crutches or braces, only an enthroned potentate, apparently ambulatory like any other, calmly surveying his subjects. He had on a black- and white-striped tie without even a hint of crimson to detract from the solemnity of his office. From his watch chain, though, a Phi Beta Kappa key conspicuously depended—he was not above declaring that he belonged among this august company of the learned.

For the rest of the morning the President sat there like the rest of them, getting rained on and feigning attentiveness as the university conferred endless honorary degrees on world-renowned scholars, including nine Nobel laureates and the legendary Carl Gustav Jung. The rain let up and came again, mildewing Toby's jacket and, for all the presence of the elect, inducing a touch of despondency over the current muddle of his life. All those celebratory rites and titanic achievers served only to compound the suspicion of his own towering insignificance. To what triumphant convocation would he ever be summoned as a guest of honor? He was a lonely, unloved, undirected troubador without a song to sing, getting wet in the rain while privileged Harvard congratulated itself. Then he looked up and saw Franklin Roosevelt reject the proffered protection of an umbrella. The two of them were getting wet together; for the moment that was consolation enough.

By the time his turn came to speak after lunch, it was coming down heavily enough to force the program to be moved into Memorial Hall, which could hold only a fraction of the crowd. A hurriedly rigged p.a. system piped the speakers' words into various lecture and assembly halls about the campus. Toby found an aisle seat in a chamber in Sever, where he had been taught history four years earlier during F.D.R.'s first campaign. Now some wag had hoisted a sign behind the lectern reading "Landon Headquarters."

The lordly larynx was in excellent fettle. "Liberty is the air Americans breathe," his national leader declared. "Our government is built on the belief a people can be both strong and free . . . and that civilized men need no restraint except that imposed by themselves against abuse of freedom." Harvard men were well advised, the President added, to hew to Increase Mather's teaching to make no man their master but, above all, "to find a friend in truth." Love of liberty and freedom of thought, Mr. Roosevelt observed, were not the exclusive province of the university but—the deft New Deal touch—as much at home in America on the farm and in the factory. And so on and so forth: resonant and unexceptionable, elevating but hardly incandescent. The words could not withstand close scrutiny. A. Tobias Ronan, Jr. required substantive vision, doctrine to guide by, a program for the will. What was one to *do* with freedom? What *ends* was truth to serve? But all he got was this elegant, ultimate pragmatist refusing to be his savior.

Yet at the close, he spoke to him. Many Harvard men leave the college, Franklin Roosevelt said, with inquiring, open minds: "They have been given much, and from them much is expected." Yes, yes, there was his problem—no piddling goals for Toby Ronan; he merely wished to remake the world in his own image. The President prayed that the university's proud alumni might come "to account the service of mankind the highest ambition a man can follow."

Ahhh. There he had been, trying for a fortnight to assimilate his experiences at the camp, seeing the time he had passed there as no more than prelude, still waiting for a signal to come and his real engagement with life to begin. All at once now, he understood the process was well under way.

As he passed through Meyer Gate into Harvard Square, a tousle-headed student of dark intensity skewered him with a petition. It was a new academic year, and the political activists were mobilized. Would Toby share in protesting the university's award of an honor-ary degree to C. G. Jung, whose well-known sympathies with the aryan views of his Nazi masters belied Harvard's allegiance to aca-demic freedom and universal toleration? Toby told the fellow he sym-pathized with his argument but was not familiar with the Jungian po-sition.

The student looked doubtful. "But everyone knows Einstein de-clined the university's invitation because they asked Jung."

"I hadn't heard. I've been a little—removed."

The student sensed, no doubt from Toby's unceremonial rags, that this was not the run-of-the-mill Harvard man. "Really?"

"Sing Sing," Toby said. "Grand larceny. We're the part of the alumni body they never tell you about. I just got sprung—but I wouldn't have missed this for the world." He signed the petition and grabbed the streetcar for Back Bay station.

"Freud probably put him up to it," Arthur Haseltine commented when Toby got back to Pittsfield and reported on Einstein's quarrel with Harvard. "The chosen people stick together."

Glaucoma was one thing, but there were forms of blindness for which he could no longer pretend to work up sympathy. His stay at that peaceful house on that lovely lake in that congenial town would have to be shortlived. He had his own resources to fall back on for a time, but there was no telling how long he might have to search for work. Employment dropped in cold weather; besides, from all avail-able evidence he was blacklisted in Pittsfield. Lingering where he was seemed even less tolerable than pocketing his pride to send off a letter to Everett Larrabee at his New York office. It noted that while he had turned down the attorney's earlier gracious offer to help him find em-ployment in journalism, circumstances now obliged him to solicit such assistance. Salary was no object; anything respectable in the city would suit him fine. If the offer no longer pertained, he was nonethe-less appreciative of Mr. Larrabee's past kindness. Exceedingly sin-cerely yours.

There was no word for a week. He sat around Doc's house reading him the *Eagle*'s latest dispatches from Spain on the civil war that had erupted with full force in August. It was not so much that they fa-vored opposite sides of the conflict but that the doctor felt it had been madness to impose republican government on a theocracy barely removed from the feudal age. Anarchy to him was the abandonment of humanity and worse than any repression. To Toby, the social revolution had brought Spain, at whatever price in turmoil, the first glimmerings of justice.

The issue was still in dispute between them when the phone rang one morning, and the assistant day city editor of the New York *Herald Tribune* wondered if Toby might be interested in a job. "It's on the rim—and the lobster trick, I'm afraid. It's like a tomb here then, and the work's not very stimulating for a young guy—but it's a job."

"Terrific," Toby said. "What's 'the rim'?"

Ominous pause. "You sure you've worked on a newspaper before?"

"Small ones—no lobsters, no rims."

Another pause, then a laugh. The rim, he was told, was the copy desk; the *Trib*'s lobster trick was from midnight to eight. The pay to start with was $37.50 a week, beginning the day after next. "We've got guys with Phi Beta Kappa keys lined up begging to work for half that."

On the way to the city, he stopped off to visit with his father. He had left the can factory after all those years and taken a job as a guard in the bank of which he had once been a director. It was a bit of a comedown, he conceded to his son with a rueful smile, but the people there were nice and, besides, he'd always had a yen to work in a uniform.

PART THREE

Fellow-Traveling

"We were, most of us, fleeing the reality that man is alone on this earth. We ran from the fact of solitude to a myth of community. . . ."

—MURRAY KEMPTON, *Part of Our Time*

FIFTEEN

IF YOU WERE NOT BORN in New York and are uncertain who you
are when you arrive, it is easier to lose than to find yourself there.
Its absorbency, in fact, is one of the city's most attractive features to
those less concerned with conquering it than surviving intact. For
those undecided about why they are there, the urban tide can be doubly treacherous—stunning with its immensity on the way in, fiercely
draining on the way out.

Alonso Tobias Ronan, Jr., reaching the unmerciful isle of Manhattan in the twenty-fifth year of his untriumphal existence (and the nation's seventh since the economy had gone all to hell) did not come
hunting fame or fortune. If pinned to the wall of a back alley redolent of frying onions and the urine of the drifting destitute, he might
have said, with some embarrassment, that he was after only truth, justice, and love. Their order was not important to him; indeed, the three
were more or less linked in his mind when he allowed himself to think
of them, as he did less frequently now than in the past.

Had he bothered to ask anyone living in the city longer than a
week, Toby would surely have been advised he had come to the
wrong place for those particular commodities. By then, however, he
himself had about concluded there was no right place to seek them.
Truth appeared to him, with each passing year, to grow more mallea-
ble and perspectival; it, even as beauty, resided in the eye of the
beholder. Justice was worse. It survived only as an afterthought to the
ambitions of men for whom private dominion was an achieved fact.
Attending the anguish of those they had dispossessed in the process
was more a subject for diversion than conscience. As to love, Toby
was most distrustful of all. It was not so much that other people had
let him down as his own tendency to respond excessively to those he
most needed to approach with caution.

This last trait was easily enough taken for a weakness of character.
In fairness to the young man, it might better have been seen as evi-

dence of his incompleteness on arrival in the great city. He was, to put it oversimply, not secure as yet in his own identity. This is a common enough problem, especially in large cities, but perhaps more acute in the case of Toby Ronan because he was so aware of it. Such self-consciousness, in turn, left him vulnerable to the appealing suggestion that no one is able to define his true being or place or purpose except in league with like-spirited others.

Sensing the irony and improbability of this claim—that one's life can achieve value solely in the act of fusing itself to a larger portion of humanity—Toby was nothing now if not wary as he began to sample the streets of the city. Whatever he was still missing, he did not want them to take away what he had already earned from life.

Newspapering, Toby felt certain, was the best way for him to bear witness to the sweep and beat and rage of the times. That was the purpose of the profession. On boarding the Central's West Shore line at the Sparkill station, he was resolved to bring to journalism the same stringent frame of mind adopted by the keenest practitioners of the craft. He would be unfailingly objective but not blindly neutral; he would be feeling but not sentimental—like an ideal juror, open-minded beforehand, weighing the evidence painstakingly, reaching a verdict based on the facts, moral criteria of his own as well as society's devising, and a measure of compassion. The train, he soon decided, was too slow.

He had never passed a night in New York, although he had visited it several dozen times in his boyhood to go to a show or a museum or a department store with his mother, yet Toby always sensed in his bones that he would one day come to it to stay. It lay there all the while he grew up, thirty miles downriver from his little factory town —a great sprawl of ganglia just beyond the horizon, at the junction of the Hudson and the sea, exerting some primal pull on him. But he would not go to it until he was ready, until there was the need. All his life had been one long diversionary maneuver, alternately toward and away from the terrible lure. He had described a single vast loop of avoidance since leaving home, heading northeast to Boston, then west to the Berkshires, but never entirely beyond the metropolitan orbit.

There were thrilling new landmarks since his mother had taken him there last. Despite hard times, they had put up the Empire State and Chrysler buildings and the new Waldorf-Astoria, assembled the towering granite cluster of Rockefeller Center, bridged the Hudson at Washington Heights with a single span unmatched for length or grace, and even now were tunneling under the East River to link midtown with the burgeoning if still arboreal borough of Queens. The slick, slight, foxy dandy of a mayor was gone, along with his whole tinseled era, swept out by a new broom. Despite a minimum of neck and maximum of torso, Fiorello La Guardia, himself a composite of the polyglot elements over whom he presided, had thrown the money-changers out of City Hall and was proceeding by galvanic indignation and infinite energy to remake New York as Franklin Roosevelt was transforming America. In each case the leadership was inspiriting and not a little abrasive. Gotham, though, was decidedly alive and recuperating as it did everything—at a pace ahead of anywhere else.

Toby was not inclined to live close by the *Herald Tribune*, situated as it was on Forty-first Street somewhat nearer Eighth Avenue than Times Square. Hell's Kitchen was known to be drab, noisy, dangerous, and otherwise uninviting to him, at any price. The East Side was too expensive and inconvenient for getting to work. Chelsea and the Village made economic and logistical sense, but the prospect of bohemia and its attendant dissipations was almost as repellant as it was enticing. So, without a firm destination in mind, he hopped a red and yellow Broadway trolley uptown, settled beside the window into a cane-back straw seat, and watched the West Side unravel.

Even above Columbus Circle, the avenue remained wide. There were no throngs, but the sidewalks were active, and on each block the benches at either end of the grassy island that bisected the thoroughfare and separated the uptown and downtown trolley tracks were full of neighborhood people, some talking, more reading a newspaper or just communing with the sun and automotive vapors. The sitters were not a stylish lot, but Toby took their becalmed presence, hemmed in by congregations of pigeons and the ceaseless vehicular flow, for evidence that frenzy was not a universal condition among the natives.

At Ninety-sixth Street, having counted up ten second-run movie houses since Seventy-second, he got off and began working his way back down the east side of the broad concourse. At a delicatessen, he stopped for a roast-beef sandwich that came with too much veiny gristle and a pickle of exquisite sourness. Next door he bought a banana for dessert, paused a few doors farther on for a haircut, and then tried to march off his lunch by setting a brisk pace southward. The traffic lights, though, kept on breaking his stride, and even when he did not have to stop for the crosstown flow of cars, he found himself looking sideways at every corner for turning drivers who seemed to bear down on pedestrians with practiced malevolence.

At Seventy-fourth Street, just above where Amsterdam crosses Broadway to form a small trapezoid in the city grid, he came upon a bastion of a bank building that took up the entire block. Inside, it had gleaming marble floors, a great vaulted ceiling, and an enormous compound of tellers' cages of wrought-iron filigree that bespoke both style and solidity. Without hesitation, Toby deposited his savings there. Then he wandered across Broadway, drawn by the imposing facade of the Ansonia Hotel. Its sculpted beaux-arts massiveness and artfully rounded edges proclaimed high comfort if not gross luxury within. For one night only, he took a room. Bathing at once, he relished the suds long enough for his fingertips to develop prune-like puckers. Afterward, he put on a clean shirt and underclothes, went down to buy that morning's *Times,* and sat in the little triangular park beside his bank to study the real estate listings. It was a buyer's market, he could tell from the volume of rentals offered. It made more sense to settle first on the area he wanted and then see if anything was available.

Instinct veered him off Broadway toward the river. Drifting north by northwest, past the bulky, suffocatingly respectable apartment houses that rose a dozen to fifteen stories on every corner, he concentrated instead on the attached stone and brick townhouses that filled the middle of the crosstown blocks. A few rooms on a nice side street would be about right, he thought, liking the bourgeois dignity of the neighborhood. No stores of any sort intruded west of Broadway. Between it and West End, the next street over, the blocks looked cramped, and the avenue itself, while wide and treed and fronted almost solid with apartment houses of impeccable unstylishness, seemed sunless and dead. The much longer block between West End and Riverside Drive was more appealing. Those streets offered vistas and light and wind at the end that came up off the river, the same one that flowed past him all his boyhood and would keep him company here while he got accustomed to the place. Riverside had plenty of benches and shade trees and decorative cannons near the war monument at Eighty-ninth, appropriately resembling a round Roman temple, and you could see the water below through the strip of park that sloped down from the hulking palisades of apartment houses to the shoreline. But there was no shore—the water just stopped and the city leaped up in lusty profusion.

The *Times* listed a fifth-floor walk-up "suite" on Eighty-eighth Street that drew Toby to an address near the middle of the block but slightly closer to Riverside. The centerpiece of three joined brownstones, its front was practically rococo in the richness of its decorative carving. He especially favored the grapevines that encrusted the bulging underside of the big bay on the third and fourth floors. It was amazing that the narrow building, mansionlike in its pretension, did not collapse of its own weight. If the inside was in decent repair and the owner civil, it would do nicely.

A telephone call from the drugstore on the corner of Broadway produced an immediate invitation to inspect the premises. The residents were named Wasserman. The lady of the house—a woman in her late thirties, Toby guessed, with emphatically waved hair that testified to a recent visit to the beauty salon—eyed him briefly at the door to certify he was no derelict and then lead him directly up the stairs. All the way, he sensed her resentment over the geometry of their climb—his looking up her bottom—and tried not to exploit it. Though softening and spreading now, her body and the upright way she held it hinted of a former statuesque voluptuousness not altogether fled. Her stockinged ankles and flexing calves ranked somewhere between sturdy and shapely. She kept smoothing her skirt just below her wide, flat behind, as if hoping the fabric would descend and cancel the peepshow.

The apartment consisted of a good-sized bedroom, an adjoining sitting room, a tiny pantry-kitchen and a bath and toilet across the hall. It was all spotless and in good order. With spartan furnishings, heat, and utilities, it went for forty-two a month. Toby looked agreeable. "Sometimes," Mrs. Wasserman confessed as they headed down, "it takes the hot water a few minutes to come up. The radiator is no problem—but maybe you could turn it off when you're out?"

Toby nodded, as if the transaction had already been sealed. But Mrs. Wasserman had a few questions first, if he wouldn't mind stopping by briefly in their parlor. She turned to him with a quick little smile before opening the front door and explained that her mother-in-law, a woman of the old school, lived with them and liked to approve of the boarder. "We never used to take anyone in," she added, "and naturally she doesn't want just anyone around." Not that the family business was bad—her husband owned a haberdashery on Broadway with his brother, just around the corner—perhaps Toby had seen it?— oh, well, it was quite a fine store, he might want to stop by someday— but times being what they were, it hardly seemed a disgrace to take in a respectable tenant. Her face, pleasant rather than pretty, disclosed a certain want of spirit in the downward slant of her mouth and small vertical ridge of pinched flesh between her tweezered eyebrows. Toby felt something caged and anxious in her look.

Mother Wasserman, a bony, baggy old Gorgon with warts and glasses and gray tendrils that sprang straight out of her scalp in all directions, presided over the interview from a wheelchair stationed in front of the heavily curtained windows. Lighted only by a single bulb each in a pair of lamps with oilpaper shades, the parlor had a somber cast that the younger Mrs. Wasserman tacitly apologized for by turning on the overhead fixture as soon as they entered. The old lady, frowning at the sudden brightness, beckoned Toby to sit in the center

of the plump, deep-green sofa. The younger woman did the questioning but it was plain to him who his judge was.

Mrs. Wasserman asked about his employment and whether he could
provide character references. Well, he said, he didn't actually know
anyone in the city, and since he was only about to begin work at the
Tribune, he could hardly supply names from there. But then he
thought to mention Harvard, a reference he used in only very select
instances, and said he could provide some names from there if that
would help. The two women exchanged a wigwag of brows that said
Harvard was reference enough, especially taken in tandem with the
Tribune, an eminently respectable paper, although it was the *Sun*
Mr. Wasserman brought home each evening after closing the shop, his
wife said—"and I'm afraid one paper a day is about our limit."

Her mother-in-law thereupon released a few dozen interrogatory
gutturals clearly not intended for Toby to grasp. The tongue, definitely of European origin, sounded more to him like the yield of an ex-
pectorant than an intelligible language. Mrs. Wasserman answered her
briefly, but her mother-in-law persisted long enough for the younger
woman to hold up a hand in surrender and tell Toby, with some sorrow, "She's a little concerned about the personal habits of newspaper
people. She says she's read somewhere that they sometimes—do a little
—drinking."

"I've heard that, too," Toby said soberly.

"But I suppose that's true in many lines of work."

"I suppose so, ma'am. They say creative people are a little funny, of
course, but I see myself as more of a social scientist, really—an observer rather than an artist."

"You don't have a drinking problem, then?"

"No, ma'am. Anyway, I couldn't afford to." He added a smile
meant to lend conviction. All it did was bring a new burst of mysterious dialect from the old woman.

Mrs. Wasserman sighed. "She wants to know if by any chance you
happen to be Jewish."

"Is that required?" Toby asked.

"Oh, no. She's just interested—"

"I'm more or less Protestant, though not much of a churchgoer," he
said. "But I'm a strong admirer of the Jewish people," he added, turning to the old woman and enunciating the words slowly and clearly to
help her get their drift.

She adjusted her wire-rimmed glasses to put Toby in focus, leaned
forward in her chair, and fixing him with a lethal squint, asked, "Vy?"

He glanced over uneasily at Mrs. Wasserman, who turned up her palms with a shrug and shook her head to signal he was on his own. "Well, their—their cultural heritage—and—and their wonderful moral code," he said, gathering now that she understood him well enough but retained the prerogative of speaking only her own tongue, "and the Jews—the Jewish people I've known—are all very—nice—and refined—and—"

The old woman nodded eagerly, offered a gummy smile, and instructed her daughter-in-law to close the deal: a month's rent in advance and a half month's security. "She's just a little uneasy with strangers," Mrs. Wasserman said, collecting the money from him near the door and handing him the keys. "The other boarders have all been Jewish."

"Well—I meant what I said—about—"

"Of course." Her mouth suddenly turned up at the corners, unfastening its frown. "Well, good luck—it's a hard city for a newcomer." Behind her, the old woman launched an emphatic supplement to the well-wishing. Mrs. Wasserman displayed forbearance. "She says it's hard for oldtimers, too."

"Well, her ears are fine, at least," Toby noted pleasantly.

The old woman, hearing that as well, loosed an extended farewell fusillade. Toby looked for enlightenment. Mrs. Wasserman hesitated. "It can't be that bad," he said, smiling broadly.

Mrs. Wasserman closed her eyes and translated. "She says you should know not to walk on the grass in the middle of Broadway—the dogs go on it. Also, you should keep your place clean, especially the pantry, and the toilet sanitary."

Toby promised.

II

Whatever romance was attached to newspapering had all but abandoned the building by the time he reported for work.

To begin with, the *Tribune* offices were devoid of distinguishing ornament. Their exterior had none of the streamlined magnificence of the new *Daily News* monolith across town on Forty-second Street. The interior, in contrast to the paneled if not quite elegant offices of the *Times* two blocks away, was severely utilitarian—which was to say one short step from drabness. Being charitable, one might have called the place trim and uncluttered, a condition notoriously foreign to most newspapers.

By midnight, the first edition had already run, and the lobby, its tan marble walls vibrating from the overhead presses a few minutes earlier, was astir now only with the remnants of the departing night-side. The city room, on the fifth floor, quick by day with a hundred writers and editors, housed hardly a dozen souls, whose muffled voices sounded lost in the sea of desks. In the wire room, the banks of usually frenetic teletypes operated fitfully; only the overseas cable, with a dispatch from the Spanish front, and the City News line, dutifully recording the evening's miscellaneous shootings in the Bronx, clattered away with disdain for the clock. In the library, a copy boy languorously clipped the other morning papers. It was not called the lobster trick for its gastronomic delights.

The overnight desk had two functions. It was on standby for any remakes necessitated by breaking news until the final edition closed at 3:30. And it moved the least exciting, most expendable copy—society, features without a time peg, standing obits, Sunday entertainment and real estate pieces—so the composing room would be kept busy in the morning. Accordingly, the desk was not a very animated spot, and Toby's arrival there might well have passed uncommented upon entirely if he had not blundered into the wrong seat.

It was a big, U-shaped desk with nine chairs around the outside—the rim—and the slotman in the middle of the inside, facing out. Only five rim-men came on overnight. The first of the others to arrive gave him a nameless handshake and told Toby he was in his seat. Why any of the seats, which were identical in design and condition and equidistant from the slot, should have been preferred was hard to imagine, but Toby vacated hastily. The next two arrivals also gave him the boot, so he finally asked Kirby, the oblivious slotman, where to settle. "Anywhere no one else is," Kirby said, shoving a late homicide story into a short, transparent tube and dispatching it pneumatically to the composing room on the floor below.

Toby took an end chair and obliquely studied the routine of the others. All looked grim-visaged, granular-cheeked, and at least twenty years older than he, and each came with his own set of idiosyncrasies. One kept his snap-brim hat on the whole time but rolled up his shirt sleeves. Another was equipped with an eyeshade and a coffee thermos that he never offered to share. A third worked with an unlighted cigar in his mouth—a habit traceable to his former employment on the old *Herald* after a new owner bought it and promptly banned smoking in the office on pain of dismissal. The fourth devoted much of his time to trips to the water-cooler and men's room with a stop at the pencil sharpener on both legs of the excursion. The fifth was Toby, peculiar only in his eagerness; he was therefore massively ignored at first. Mostly, when they were not editing, the others read the horse handicappers in the tabloids or talked sports. Opinion was divided whether the strong arm of the Giants' Carl Hubbell could tame the Yankees' sluggers in the impending intracity World Series. Of shoptalk there was none. Plainly these were men hiding out—who else would have worked willingly while the world slept?—and their indifference to him he took from the start to be purely professional.

He was enough inkstruck to jump at Kirby's invitation the first night to see the shop and the presses roll for the last run. Tall, softly spoken, sleepy-eyed but all-seeing, the slotman had a wide, ready smile for the handful of compositors still on the job. Only three of the linotypes hummed under their private pools of light. Six dozen others slumbered in the semidarkness. The first lino used by any newspaper was put in the old *Trib* shop on Park Row, Kirby informed him drily. "Helluva gadget," he added, "but don't ever touch the metal."

"Hot, huh?" Toby said, cloaking his familiarity with the invention.

"No, chapel rules—the union'll chop your hand right off."

Kirby told them to close the remake of page three and some mustfixes in the theater review, and in a matter of minutes, the presses were churning. Up close, the noise was thunderous. And they were not even going full speed because the paper had ripped on a couple of the earlier runs, so the printers would have to do some dismantling when the final got off. Still, the sound and the blurring speed and the mechanical coordination of it all were breathtaking, and the pervasive ink a musky stimulant to Toby's soul. The gigantic rolls of newsprint whirled through the two-story assemblage and emerged in folded perfection at the rate of four thousand copies a minute—a marvel of pure modernity, even if he did find the paper's doctrinaire Republicanism hopelessly outdated.

In an age when other New York papers, including Pulitzer's oncegreat *World*, were dying, the *Trib* was thriving if not exactly prospering. Its circulation had grown to 300,000, the highest since the *Herald* and the *Tribune* had merged in 1924, although it was still the smallest in the morning field of five. Retail advertising increases of late had allowed the paper to remain at least marginally profitable. And prosperity had brought improvement in the product. Foreign coverage expanded, with bureaus from London to Shanghai. Fine young writers had flocked to the staff, drawn in part by the knowing hand of its city editor, Stanley Walker. Its classic typography and decorous layout were the envy of the profession. It was more brightly written and tightly edited than the encyclopedic *Times* or the fusty *Sun*, more responsible and informative than the hard-hitting *News* and Hearst's gossip-mongering *Mirror* and raucous *Journal* and *American*, and altogether more substantial than the lively but gimmicky *World-Telegram* and the small, struggling *Post* with its lonely liberality.

All things considered, Toby would conclude after several weeks of closely scrutinizing the field, the *Trib* was probably the best-balanced newspaper in the city—in the nation, possibly. It was well written. It was comprehensive without becoming the dreary catalogue the good, gray *Times* so often seemed. Its editorials were readable and measured, if too often wistfully Tory. Its society pages were stuffily correct yet open to climbers with credentials. Its sports were supple; financial news, alert, and the critical departments, catering to a clientele drawn largely from Park Avenue, the suburbs, and the East Coast intelligentsia, were as sophisticated as a *pousse-café*. Only its Sunday comics, featuring Caspar Milquetoast and comparable drawing-room gadabouts, had the personality of wilted watercress.

If it had earned the accolade of "the newspaperman's newspaper," the *Trib* nevertheless remained more of an aesthetic than material success. The *Times*, its only real rival for greatness, had far outstripped it in the lucrative classified business and kept plowing its profits back into building a bigger and better paper. The *Trib*, with overhanging debts and narrow operating margins limiting its resources, made do with editorial finesse. The pay, in other words, was lousy, even for the newspaper business. It was a fine place for the gifted young to come and learn, win a name for themselves, and leave for greener pastures. Joe Alsop had gone off to a syndicate and Stanley Walker to the *Mirror*, St. Clair McKelway and John Lardner and Lincoln Barnett to the magazines, Joel Sayre and Nunnally Johnson to Hollywood, and John O'Hara to write novels. But learned they had, as Toby was determined to, however bucolic the tempo on the lobster trick.

Kirby was a deceptively gentle counselor, drawing easily on his pipe as he leaned halfway across the desk to instruct his avid new pupil. He showed Toby how to cut a lead paragraph in half without any loss in net information and an actual profit in literary effect. He taught him to slash the last paragraphs from most stories on the demonstrable premise that writers slackened and padded at the end. He scorned the flowery phrase, condemning adjectives as a greater curse to the journalist than alcohol, and praised the verb as nature's noblest storyteller. But he deplored the use of "stated," "asserted," "declared," and "opined" when a simple "said" would do. He explained the rudiments of writing clear headlines that fit—"Life Begins" worked as well for Genesis as "God Creates Heaven and Earth; Man Reported Bareassed in Eden" and took far less space on the page. He pointed out the difference between "ramshackle" and "dilapidated"; that referring in print to city residents as "New Yorkers" was gauche, and to "the Reverend Mr. Smith" as "Rev. Smith" was hillbilly; that "Congressman Jones" was ambiguous since Congress was bicameral—it had to be Senator Jones or Representative Jones—and that the position occupied at the moment by Charles Evans Hughes was, according to the Constitution, "Chief Justice of the United States," not "of the Supreme Court." Most abominable of all was the press's fondness for the "active passive" voice, as in: "Birdwhistle was presented a gold watch on his retirement" or "The boy was given a docile aardvark for his birthday." It was, of course, the watch that was presented, the aardvark that was given—and death to all debasers of the language!

In his third week on the job, Toby was tried on his first breaking story for the city final. "Move it in takes," Kirby said. Fast, Ronan, fast.

It was about a twenty-five-year-old creole woman caught earlier that evening for robbing a Child's restaurant with a cap gun; she confessed as well to two previous restaurant holdups in the vicinity with the same fake weapon. Toby ran a pencil over it speedily, broke up a couple of the longer sentences, caught all the misspellings, and headlined it:

Gungirl Seized
For 3 Holdups
By Toy Pistol

Out of the corner of his eye, he had seen Kirby reworking the copy behind him, cutting and fixing with measured strokes. At the end, Toby asked what he had done wrong. "Later," the slotman said, spiking the dupe and phoning the composing room to clear a news hole for the piece.

It was little things, Kirby assured him once the edition had closed. The scene of the crime, for example, was given as 583 Columbus Avenue. "Most people aren't sure where that is—say what cross street it's near. If you don't know, call and check." The story went on to report that police apprehended the woman "at the corner of Broadway and 70th Street." Most intersections had four corners, Kirby noted. "Either specify which one it was or take out 'at the corner of.'" There was a problem also with the reference to the woman's police record, which included, according to the story, "four arrests for prostitution." An arrest was not a conviction, the slotman said icily; it was libel on its face to attribute a crime to any man or impute inchastity to any woman, "especially one who might sue our balls off." It should have read, ". . . arrested four times on prostitution charges." Finally, there was the reporter's fondness for the dubious graphic detail. Of the accused's appearance at arraignment, he had written:

> . . . Her naturally dark skin was pale, and above her bright-red lips could be seen the small scar by which the other victimized restaurant owners in the area have identified their female assailant.

"How do we know the natural darkness of her skin?" Kirby wondered. "Maybe at the *Amsterdam News* they can tell a blanch from a blush with these people—but not here."

Which left the headline. What would Toby have thought of changing "Toy Pistol" to "Phony Gat" in the bottom line—they counted the same number of units, and the latter was nearer the flavor of the piece.

"'Phony Gat.' Isn't that a little—flashy—for us?"

"So is 'Gungirl,'" said Kirby. He had changed it to "Woman"; each counted 6½. And since it was unclear whether the "By" referred to "Seized" or to "Holdups," he changed the last line to "Has Fake Gun."

Between such witheringly instructive forays, Toby devoted himself to the newspaper as an art form, comparing and contrasting every sheet in town and how each played the same story. Of particular interest to him were the nuances of political coverage since he was about to cast his first vote for a President, and the *Trib*, for all its excellence, was known to be partisan in election years.

"Only on the edit page," Kirby insisted. Its chief political columnist, after all, was Walter Lippmann, erstwhile Harvard socialist, *New Republic* mainstay, and edit-page editor of the *World;* that he of the Olympian perspective was opposing Roosevelt this time as an antilibertarian did not detract from the *Trib*'s lofty motives in having hired him. And there were, as well, Dorothy Thompson's clear-eyed columns from abroad on the failing health of global democracy; the daily book pieces by Lewis Gannett, a known supporter of advanced social causes; the generous enlistment of liberal reviewers in the Sunday book supplement, and the gently leftward tilt of "The Conning Tower" under the hand of F.P.A.

But the more closely he read, the more skeptical Toby grew. On one particularly slow shift, he took a careful accounting of that morning's edition and presented Kirby with the hard evidence. The usual editorial sniping at F.D.R. was no doubt the publisher's privilege. So, too, probably, was the crude cartoon that depicted Roosevelt as flaunting policies attractive to communist sympathizers. But it was the news columns, or what passed for them, that seemed subtly and inexcusably slanted.

"Take the lead," Toby complained to the slotman. The paper had put a five-column, three-line head on former Democratic standard-bearer Al Smith's endorsement of Republican presidential candidate Landon and accompanied it with a two-column picture of the smiling renegade. The second line of the head dealt with the less startling news that the G.O.P. nominees and ex-President Hoover had gathered to discuss tactics. Only the third line of the head was alloted to a major speech by Roosevelt, claiming he would balance the budget not by higher taxes but by the increased prosperity his policies would promote. Four of the five columns beneath the banner headline dealt with the Republican campaign effort. The *Times*, too, gave Smith's defection the lead but only four columns, no picture, and the top line of the head—the second and third lines were about the Roosevelt speech. And the stories below were closely balanced between the parties.

"A matter of news judgment," Kirby said. "All stories aren't equal."

Then why, Toby asked, did the *Trib* make it seem that way inside? Every pro-New Deal item was offset by a negative one. If Harry Hopkins claimed the relief rolls were the lowest since '31, there was a piece, given exactly the same play on the page, headlined, "Boondoggling of W.P.A. Cited by Republicans"—as if the two stories were equally factual.

"Even-handed coverage," Kirby said.

Then what about the five-column spread given the latest findings of the *Literary Digest* poll, showing Landon with a nearly three-to-two lead over Roosevelt? True, it was based on more than 700,000 ballots sent in from around the country, but the polling was highly unscientific, Toby contended, drawing as it did on the volunteered preferences of people with enough motivation to fill out the form and mail it back. Gallup was showing a different trend.

"News is news," Kirby said.

Then what was that anti-Roosevelt propaganda that filled the better part of two columns under a byline identified as "Director of the Landon Volunteers in Eastern Seaboard States"? It had become a regular feature of the paper during the campaign.

"But it's labeled right at the top," Kirby said.

"That doesn't make it any more objective. She's shilling."

"Because Roosevelt's people crank out reams of real and phony stories by the hour. At least this is openly partisan."

"But we shouldn't run the Roosevelt stuff either, then, unless we think it's legitimate."

"Oh, I get it," Kirby said, turning away to read Walter Winchell.

"Objectivity doesn't mean giving equal space to every party line and leaving it to the reader to sort out the facts. That's spreading distortions. I think our job is to—"

Kirby, by then, was unreachable.

It bothered Toby that the slotman could be the consummate craftsman in screening an inconsequential police story yet so indifferent to the claims of truth and fairness in the presentation of politics. But pursuing the matter would only get him pegged as naïve and a radical, he settled for reading snatches of *The Big Money*, the new novel by John Dos Passos, Harvard '17, that he brought along for company during idle moments. "All you Harvards stick together, huh?" Kirby remarked not unpleasantly, nodding toward the novel with a yawn when it was time to go. Then he invited Toby to join him for a drink before reporting in the next night.

A few steps east of the back entrance to the paper on Fortieth, the place was formally called the Artist and Writers' Club, but everyone at the *Trib* referred to it by the name of the owner, John Bleeck. A thriving speakeasy during Prohibition, it catered to a hard-drinking crowd. *Trib* people, accounting for perhaps half the steady clientele, were its privileged characters. At lunch and before supper, newsmen were stacked three deep at the bar. Staffers from every echelon drank and ate elbow to elbow, and even Ogden Reid, the publisher, was said to show up regularly and mix with the troops.

Bleeck's was doing a modest after-theater business the night Toby first patronized it. The decor was English chophouse. Dim amber lighting, polished bare-wood tables, stucco walls of glazed oxblood, and vaguely Tudor timbering all contributed to a palpable mellowness, the chief charm of the establishment. Toby peered in vain about the front room, impenetrable from tobacco smoke and low wattage, but caught the eye of one of the bartenders who, without a word uttered, directed him into the next room.

Kirby was at a corner table, his back against the wall, nursing something called a rye gag. "It's an Old Fashioned," he said, "without the garbage. Have a beer—on me."

They had been drinking in silence for a moment or two when Toby glanced up at a noisy party of six or seven, led by a handsome woman with a foghorn voice, that swept by them into the back dining room. All eyes followed the leader and her entourage.

"Speaker Bankhead's daughter," Kirby told him. "She has a show on —a dog, I hear, except for her."

"Who are the others?"

"Press agent, probably—director—understudy—lover—who knows? She's in here a lot—probably because it's so unglamorous."

"Maybe to her it is—the way the theater is to us."

"And politics—to some of us," Kirby said, drawing on his pipe and stirring his drink with a finger.

"Look," Toby said, "I'm really sorry about last night. I guess I wasn't being too realistic."

"Forget it," Kirby said. "If you were a realist, you wouldn't be here. It's no life for a solid citizen—the pay, the prospects, the indignities. I don't know why college guys keep coming into it, but they do. It must be the excitement of it—till they figure out what makes news is usually someone else's misery." He shook his head gloomily. "And then they survive by turning callous. The best ones are all craft and no conscience—hell, they'd miss their own mother's funeral—the real hotshots would—if it meant not blowing a story." He took a deep swallow from his glass. "You talk about politics—let me tell you something before you pop off again. Nobody has any politics in this business—only publishers can afford to. All a good reporter cares about in his imbecilic way is seeing his stuff in type. I know—I was like that myself."

"You make it sound immoral."

Kirby cupped his drink in both hands and angled it toward the wall fixture, inspecting for viscosity. One day when he was working for the *Brooklyn Eagle,* he said, he was sent out to a hospital to gather color from the survivors of a terrible factory fire off Flatbush Avenue. "These poor bastards were stretched out half-roasted all over the emergency room and overflowing down the hall, and I wasn't supposed to give a damn about anything except getting enough out of them for a three-graph insert for the first edition. Then I looked over and saw this bastard from the *News* practically slapping the cheek of some woman who was still in shock just so he could gouge a quote from her. That's when I knew I was on the wrong end of the business."

"And you don't find it a little—tame—on the inside?"

Kirby gave a snort. Inside, he said, was where the real action was. "Hell, reporters are a dime a dozen. All it takes is good legs, a hard heart, a little nerve—and a small enough brain so you get excited by not much. It's the people on the desk and rewrite who make the paper happen. You need smarts and judgment—a good memory and wide background—and the tools of the language. Who do you think gets picked to be the editors? Not reporters." He reached for the check. "Oh, you'll give it a whirl outside, probably—you should, I guess. Either way, though, go easy on the moral indignation or you'll wind up a drunk before your time. Or, worse yet, an editorial writer."

On the way out, they brushed past a tall, fair young man arriving in formal evening attire. He invested Kirby with a lordly tap of his silver-handled cane.

"Lucius," Kirby greeted him. "Another winner?"

"Execrable, my good Ned—the purest elixir of goose guano!"

Toby was dazzled by the preposterous hauteur of the man. "Who's *he?*"

"Our second-string drama critic—and chronicler of the café set."

"That's—Beebe?"

"None other."

"Why did he call you Ned?"

"It's my name."

Toby flushed. "I thought—"

"Yeah, well I figured all you Harvards called everyone by the last name—except for Lucius. And he got thrown out of Yale first."

III

"What Saul's really dying to know is not who you're voting for," said Wally Eichhorn, head bobbing mischievously toward his brother-in-law, "but how anyone with a drop of social conscience in him can possibly work for a reactionary rag like the *Trib.*"

The Orloff living room, a clutter of drained coffee cups, soiled magazines, rushing voices, and tumbling thoughts, was momentarily frozen by such an unartful thrust at their dinner guest. Subdued inquiries, playfully pointed now and then with regard to his social attitudes but free of contentiousness, had accompanied the pot roast and apple sauce. Politics were avoided altogether until Wally told his sister Adele, filling his plate with seconds, that he had decided unalterably to vote for Roosevelt.

"It's a matter of animal gratitude," he explained. "Next to you, he's the person most responsible for keeping me alive for the past three years. I owe him."

Groans of disbelief and hectoring abuse of Wally continued all through the main course, especially from his niece, Nina, bending her thick, dark eyebrows at him with stagy menace, and abated only when Adele announced she would serve fruit, cheese, and coffee in the living room. It was there, quartering his apple with a knife while the others attacked theirs orally, that Toby was subjected to keener scrutiny, this time for his political allegiance. Before he could answer, he had to contend with Wally's slur. Saul Orloff intervened first, indicating he understood the difference between teasing and discourtesy. "I doubt if Toby had his pick of the litter," he said. "Besides, I wouldn't call the *Trib* a reactionary rag. Not a week passes that it doesn't take a position well left of Marie Antoinette."

There was a spill of laughter from his wife and daughter to help ease any strain Wally's remark had introduced. "It's a very fine paper —in its way," said Adele.

Toby smiled his thanks and, to show he took the defamation for puckishness on Wally's part, remarked, "Well, we did have Karl Marx in our London bureau for several years."

"Unfortunately, the man who hired him has been dead half a century," said Saul.

"Actually," Nina put in, having gulped down a bite of apple to free her tongue, "Engels wrote most of those columns for him—not that it makes any real difference."

"You also had the illustrious John Calvin Coolidge writing under your banner for a while," Saul added. "And to nobody's amazement, his column turned out to be extremely dull. I think Walter Lippmann was meant as his replacement. He's more literate, anyway."

The information distressed Toby. "Coolidge wrote for the *Trib?*"

"Right after he left office. I read him religiously."

"Saul reads everything religiously," Wally said, "except the Bible." He flapped a hand toward the tables, shelves, unoccupied chairs, and every other horizontal surface in the apartment, not excluding the floors, particularly in the corners, all littered with literature of the Left. "And he saves it."

"A fellow in my racket's got to keep up," Saul said, revealing coffee-stained teeth that were small and regular save for the two outside incisors overlapping the middle ones and giving a slightly fanged effect to his words. He pronounced them with the exaggerated care of a man who had taught himself refined elocution and feared that the slightest slipup would disclose his under-class origins.

Just what his brother-in-law's racket was, Wally had not mentioned on the phone—only that Adele insisted he bring Toby along to dinner at their apartment. "You'll enjoy yourself," Wally promised. "They're very lively people—a little strident, maybe, but hopelessly intelligent. Adele always puts a meal together on Sundays and makes me bring along somebody stimulating and presentable—it's my ticket of admission, so don't let me down. Besides, she's got a daughter I'm sweet on —the most it can cost you is a look."

Strictly speaking, Toby had lied when he told his landladies he could provide nobody in New York by way of a reference. He knew Wally Eichhorn a little, and surely Wally would have vouched for him on the strength of their short but close association at the camp. But who knew if or where the W.P.A. had booked him at the moment, and it was doubtful that the Mesdames Wasserman would look with favor on the character recommendation of an aging, elfin ex-vaudevillian, himself on the brink of impoverishment. Toby had not thought to look him up until after a few solitary Sundays in New York. Saturdays he enjoyed; the whole city was out in force then, and it was like a day-long festival. But Sundays he found depressing. Everything was quieter, the streets almost ghostly, and only lovers seemed to stroll the wide promenade along Riverside. Even the Automat, which he had quickly discovered served the best food in town for the price, lost its entertainment value on Sunday, so he took supper at a Broadway cafeteria in midafternoon before the forlorn regulars showed up. It was time, Toby decided, for a little company.

He had lost Adele's phone number but remembered her last name and that Wally had said they lived on Hudson Street. Saul being the only Orloff listed there, he rang up Adele, who somewhat wearily acknowledged the relationship and said yes, Wally was in town. He'd chucked the relief work for the C.C.C. and caught on with a small production group on Fourteenth Street. But he still had no phone, and it might be several days before she heard from him—unless something glorious came through for him in, say, Chicago, in which case it might be several months. "I'll do my best," she said, "but he's a little unpredictable—perhaps you know."

"Not really—our friendship doesn't go back very far," Toby said. "But I think he's remarkably talented."

"Right. That and a nickel—" The voice was both wary and caustic.

"Excuse me?"

"Oh, you *are* new in town. It's an expression. Forget I said it."

Wally called him at the *Trib* two nights later, delighted Toby was working in the city and insistent on an early reunion. Their conflicting work schedules made Sunday supper at his sister's the easiest solution. Toby thought that an imposition, but the appeal of a home-cooked meal was considerable and the invitation pressed so ardently that it would have been ungracious to refuse. At any rate, he had wanted to prowl the Village a little, and Sunday was probably a good day for it. When the place turned out to be even deader than the rest of the city—the avant-garde was probably in a drugged sleep, recovering from its unspeakable perversions of the night before—he showed up with brimming curiosity at the Orloffs' second-floor apartment overlooking the wide, cobblestone street. Wally, of course, was nowhere to be seen.

"He does it all the time," Adele said. "It's the perversity of his muse —he thinks bad manners are an artistic statement."

"Also a social statement," said Saul, offering his hand. "He claims he can't afford a watch. The fact is, he keeps pawning them every time he gets the sack. Helluva living for a genius."

The foyer to the apartment was a purposeful jumble. Beside the guest closet an old wooden desk stood stacked with working papers, many of them legal-length. Perpendicular to it was a typing table with an old office-model Remington, its carriage jutting out to the extreme left like a turnstile to the hallway that led off toward the bedrooms. Partially blocking the arched entrance to the living room, a pair of rickety card tables bowed under the burden of a mimeograph machine with an ink-saturated green stencil affixed. Whatever it was Saul Orloff did, he seemed not to be lacking industry.

While Adele fussed with the food, Saul offered him sweet sherry and tried to make Toby comfortable. A lithe man of medium stature, with small, bunched features and a laurel wreath of bushy, graying hair, he appeared to listen with his eyes to Toby's innocuous comments about work and the city. They were not quite like any other eyes Toby had ever seen. Light brown and exceptionally clear in a man near fifty, they had a long, narrow shape that tapered very gradually at the outer edges in an almost lupine way. Only the dark lower lids and puffy gray crescents below betrayed his age and wear. Toby felt the eyes surround and track every word as it left his lips, pry it apart and examine it, and dilate or retract with approval or disdain. They were judgmental eyes that flattered you with their attention and frightened you into thinking no secret was safe from their owner.

His wife appeared to run on a different set of batteries. More connective tissue than vital organ, Adele Eichhorn Orloff navigated her surroundings by indirection, moving laterally, absorbing amply, viewing encroachers on her space without irritation as long as they did not expect her to perform for them. The top half of her was powerfully constructed for a woman: broad shoulders, muscular arms, large hands with long, strong fingers and short nails. Her face, Toby thought, remarkably resembled—coloring aside—the sculpted, full-lipped Roman handsomeness of the Statue of Liberty, save for a fleshy curvature of the lower nose. She wore her somewhat thin hair pulled back severely from her forehead and knotted in the back. Joining the men in the living room without apology for its untidiness, she eagerly drew off her apron and tossed it over the back of an empty chair, as if glad to shed the vestments of compulsory homemaker and assume an identity of her own.

In fact, domesticity was decidedly a part-time interest of hers. Most of her energy was devoted to service as the assistant manager of, and minor partner in, a leather-goods shop on Christopher Street. She displayed the pair of classically simple sandals below her long, full denim skirt and said they were a product of her own hands. Indeed, the design, workmanship, and output of all the goods the place sold, including handbags, wallets, belts, "and an occasional customized whip for the sado-masochist crowd," were her responsibility. The family had thus come to accept minimal menus and chronic disarray about the house. Her husband, prime resident messmaker, identified himself as "a lawyer for social causes," of which the most prominent was the American League Against War and Fascism. Toby remembered the group from his Cambridge career as an offshoot of the Left-liberal action coalition and decidedly pink in the complexion of its leadership. Saul worked as well, he said, with the International Defense League, neighborhood unemployment councils, tenants' committees, roughed-over union organizers, "and anyone else getting shat on who can find me with a free minute or two."

"And he does mean free," Adele said without evident bitterness. "Sundays, though, he charges a dime for wills."

Nina Orloff, back from a student concert at N.Y.U., flew through the door with her Uncle Wally in tow, blaming incipient influenza for his lateness and wheezily promising not to breathe on anyone. He looked paler and frailer than Toby remembered him from camp, but the habitual buoyancy remained. His niece, shorter than her mother, was similarly constructed; her features, though, closely favored her father's, except that her eyes, more green than brown, lacked the accentuated taper and nearly unbearable fixity of his. Her look lingered an engaging moment, then modestly strayed. A froth of small, tight curls, like an overturned basket of chocolate-covered berries, added to her height and unaffected comeliness. Over supper, Toby established that Nina worked days as a salesgirl in a hosiery store uptown and by night pursued an advanced degree in social work at Hunter, of which she was a graduate. "Radcliffe, too, she could have made," Adele put in and won at once her daughter's reprimand.

They were a tight little ring, their cohesion born of and bonded by mutual need; the intramural ribbing seemed to grow out of affection, not any Freudian repressions. Toby, oddly, did not feel alien in their midst. It was as if he had always known them in some dim but recurring dream of an ideal family circle, so securely interlocked by love and conviction that no prying force on earth could undo it. By the time the talk turned, after supper, to the national election, he hesitated only briefly before conceding that, like Wally, he would be voting for Roosevelt.

Saul's eyes motionlessly nailed him.

"It's just a process of elimination," Toby felt obliged to explain.

"The Republicans haven't learned a thing from the Crash—still insisting lower prices are a surer cure than a living wage—which is the *Trib*'s reprehensible position, I'm sorry to say." He nodded toward Saul for not begrudging him his job with a heartless employer. "The radical Left I admire in principle, but I think Roosevelt's stolen some of their thunder." The New Deal, he granted, added up more to a bundle of pragmatic gestures than a concerted policy of sweeping reform. But in its way—the open acknowledgment that poverty and chronic insecurity were pervasive and intolerable features of American life—it had been revolutionary. "And frankly I'm afraid a vote for the socialist cause will only help elect Landon."

The Orloffs sipped their coffee in silence while Wally emitted a couple of soft huzzahs. "You sound almost apologetic," Saul said finally.

"Do I?" Toby asked. "Maybe I'm intimidated by knowing your disapproval. Why don't you show me the error of my ways?"

"Said Little Red Riding Hood to the big, bad wolf," Wally inserted with a snicker of anticipation.

"It's your assumptions that bother me, really—not your conclusions so much," Saul said, bending his head toward Adele for a light. She was leaning back, arms extended above her head, in the worn, lumpy loveseat in front of the window and luxuriating in an after-dinner Chesterfield. "My only gripe with Roosevelt," her husband started up with a puff of smoke, "is that he lacks the convictions of his courage. The man is consumed with the uses of power while paying lip service to the ends of justice. Which should hardly be a surprise to anyone— he's an aristocrat without Tolstoy's passionate guilt. Everything he does in the way of relief is halfhearted unless it can serve as a monument to himself. The government housing program, for instance, is scandalously inadequate, but oh boy! have we got nice new dams and city halls and post offices. Or you take the Social Security bill and please convince me why it should leave out farm workers and domestics, who need it as much an anyone—more, probably. And why, in the name of simple decency, finance it out of contributory taxes? That sounds a lot more regressive than revolutionary to me, Toby."

"Well, Landon's plan is twice as bad," Toby offered in defense. "He wants you to prove you're destitute first. A secure old age should be a universal right—recompense for having paid your dues in life—not a handout or a favor by the government."

"Landon isn't the issue around here—it's Roosevelt," said Nina. "Daddy's furious at him for what he just did to Browder."

Toby had followed the story in the paper. Municipal officials in Terre Haute, Indiana, had failed to grant the Communist Party a li-

cense for its presidential candidate to deliver a political address there—
in Gene Debs's birthplace. Hurrying to the scene to claim his right of
free speech and assembly, Browder was met at the train station and
locked up at once by the police for "vagrancy." Appeals to the White
House produced only an unperturbed response from Attorney General Cummings to the effect that no federal question seemed to be involved. "Only the First Amendment," said Saul, "and the credibility
of the entire Constitution."

"Maybe Roosevelt doesn't think people who want to destroy everything the Constitution stands for deserve to be protected by it," Wally
said.

"What it stands for is a matter of interpretation. What's done in its
name half the time is morally indefensible."

"Therefore, it should be done away with violently—"

"In the end," Saul instructed, "if necessary."

"He loves to revise Lenin," Wally explained to Toby. "Vladimir
Ilyitch prescribes violent revolution to free the oppressed masses, and
Saul Orloff expects Franklin Delano to roll out the red carpet for
them."

Saul drew unexcitedly on his cigarette. "Lenin's thinking was
framed by tsarist tyranny—not blessed American democracy. But let's
be realistic—how can truly progressive elements ever win power here
by the ballot if people like Toby—intelligent and compassionate people—keep thinking it's pointless to vote for a Marxist?"

"Maybe you'll just have to wait," Toby ventured, "until you've
convinced a majority."

Saul's eyes snapped directly on him now. "You're giving me the-
chicken-or-the-egg routine. Majorities are the obstacle, not the solution. They were the tyranny the Founding Fathers feared worst. Most
men are ignorant and cowardly when they're systematically
oppressed. Just ask yourself how many good people live in dread
they'll be scorned as radicals for voting their true beliefs. I say a lot.
And all they're doing is prolonging injustice—and denying respectability to the committed Left." He flicked his cigarette ash without
taking his eyes off Toby. "Me, I'd rather be on the side of humanity—
regardless of the numbers—than run with the masters of a discredited
economic system."

His voice never rose. The conviction was all in his look. What he
was saying, though, Toby did not fail to detect, was that the consent
of the governed was incidental to their own improvement. "Maybe
my real trouble," he responded, "is that I can't go along with the basic
socialist program."

"If you're talking about the Socialist Party," said Nina, tucking her

legs beneath her, "you're absolutely right. They hardly have a program anymore—or an organization worth speaking of—"

"Just their virtue," said Adele, "and even that's suspect when you
don't demand sacrifices from people." Her speech was thicker and less
measured than Saul's and suffered the dentilated *t*'s and dropped *r*'s of
the common Noo Yawka.

"Actually," said Toby, "I was thinking of collectivism itself, not
any of the refinements."

Saul reached for a twig of black grapes from the bowl in front of
him and fed himself one. "You mean it's hopelessly impractical?"

"In America. Maybe it was fine for rescuing feudal Russia—the way
you say violent revolution may have been the only way out of the
nightmare there, but—"

"I believe Lenin said it before I did. But your point is we don't have
comparable tyranny over here."

"Nothing like they had."

"Go talk to our mill workers—millions of them are tyrannized
every day. Or the auto workers who get thrown out on their asses
four months of every year so G.M. can make its model changeover.
Or the farm—"

"Wait, you're making me lose my point."

"Your point is that collectivism may be fine for grubby Russian
peasants, ninety-nine percent of whom never had a thing to begin
with, but lousy for the great land of free opportunity—where proud
individuals carved a prosperous society from the wilderness by their
hard work and initiative—right?"

"Well—more or less—yes—till everything went haywire."

"And do you know why that happened? Because once their survival
was assured, they turned into greedy pigs—enough of them, anyway."

"And how do you avoid pigs under collectivism? With guns and
barbed wire and regimentation."

Saul pinched off another grape and rolled it contemplatively between his fingers. "I think you've been propagandized. It's a matter of
re-educating people—altering their temperament—"

"But you can't do that here. Americans worship their freedom—and
privacy—and possessions—and the chance to make something of themselves. To them, collectivism is surrender."

"But most of them never make anything of themselves because they
can't—the system's stacked against them. You make the profit motive
sound wonderfully benign. It's not. Your profit is my loss. Your castle comes right out of my hide. Tell me why there have to be any profits and losses. Tell me why we have to have a society split between
exploiters and sufferers."

"Because America isn't utopia."

"How come no one told Jesus that when he handed out the Golden Rule? I'll tell you why—because nothing could be more practical and self-interested than treating others the same way you expect to be treated. It's only the greedy who have to beat the game, and I don't know for the life of me why the rest of us should give in to those bastards."

"Maybe because a little greed greases the gears a lot better than coercion."

"'A little greed' is like being a little bit pregnant. I also happen to think there's such a thing as a social spirit among human beings that doesn't have to be coerced. It can be brought out by precept and example—and calm reasoning—once you've commanded people's attention." Saul rolled the grape about his open palm like bait being softened for the trap. "But leave all that aside, Toby, and just tell me one thing. If ninety-nine percent of Russia was made up of wretched serfs before communism, what do you think the percentage of wage slaves is in the glorious U.S.A.? Ninety-nine percent are people just like you—"

"I don't think I'm a wage slave—"

"You may be better paid than most, but that doesn't change the fact any—which happens to be that you're under the lash of apologists for antiquated capitalism—you said so yourself. It's a herald of reaction—a tribune for the oppressors—"

"Oh, that's beautiful!" Wally broke in. "Did you hear that?" He turned to Adele and Nina. "Odets, move over, baby!"

"Hush," said Adele.

"Hell, no—I think he's entitled to a little applause—and Toby to a breather. The central committee's ganging up on him."

Afterward, Wally walked him to the uptown subway entrance at Sheridan Square. "Is he really a lawyer?" Toby asked. "Somehow I think of lawyers as arch-defenders of the status quo."

"Not if they never passed the bar—and spent a year in jail for being a pacifist in wartime. Not that he lets any of that interfere with trying to save the downtrodden by every legal means. I think he's very admirable, to be honest with you. And the scary thing is that his pilot light never goes out. You could wake him in the middle of the night and he'd start right in spieling advanced dialectics. My only real objection to the guy is that he has no use for anything without a direct revolutionary function—like art, for instance. It gets him nervous as hell. They're all fucking philistines, every last one of them—"

"Communists?"

"Communists, socialists, syndicalists—whatever the hell they call themselves—the whole Marxist bunch. At least the Schuberts only close down a show if it flops—they don't send for the firing squad."

IV

The second day after he began dropping off a copy of the *Trib* in front of the Wassermans' door on his way home from work, it occurred to Toby that they might not appreciate the gift and even take it for some sort of Christian imposition on them. Waking in midafternoon, he decided to knock and ask if they had any objection; what good was a goodwill gesture that engendered the opposite?

Sylvia Wasserman, on her way out to the market, opened the door an instant after his first few tentative raps. She flooded him at once with thanks for the paper and said she had been meaning to put a note of appreciation under his door but household chores kept intervening. "It's really not necessary, though, you know," she added, touching her permanent wave to see that it had not capsized. On the back of her head she wore a small, dark bonnet with an equally subdued feather.

"It's no trouble for me at all," he said, "and it's free. But please don't be polite if it's really not of any interest."

"Oh, no—it's a very good newspaper, I can see that even at a glance. I haven't had the chance to go into it in much detail yet—I have a lot to do around here, although it probably doesn't seem that way. My mother-in-law's been reading it—she has more time on her hands—and enjoying it a great deal. She says she agrees with all the editorials." This last information was offered with a thin smile that Toby took to mean whatever pacified the old woman was very welcome in their home. She noticed him glance over her shoulder for corroboration from the Gorgon's mouth. "She's napping—that's when I shop."

"Oh. Well, don't let me keep you," he said. "Or maybe I'll come along if you wouldn't mind—I need a few things myself."

"Why—no—that would be—fine. I don't often have company during the day—I mean besides—"

"I understand."

"There's Victor, of course—I know you've bumped into each other out front once or twice—but he's in school most of the time, naturally —though I do fix him a little something for lunch—he comes home for it—the school's only on Eighty-ninth—between Amsterdam and Columbus—across from the stable. Isn't a stable an odd thing for a neighborhood like this? You wonder who's got time or money to go riding these days—"

She rattled on as they walked, obviously uncomfortable at first with company that was neither geriatric nor juvenile. To calm her, Toby asked which stores she frequented in the neighborhood. The list came back with crisp authority. Pick 'n' Pay, across Broadway on the corner of Eighty-seventh, was the best grocery, though a little dirty for her liking; the Orange Grove had the finest fruits and vegetables if he didn't mind paying slightly more and going up as far as Ninetieth; Feldman the butcher was on Amsterdam—she paused and shook her head. "I don't think you'd like his things, probably—"

"Why—if they suit you?"

"We have certain—dietary requirements—because of Babette—Milton's mother. I'd just as soon not, of course, but she's very set in her ways—and it's not all that much bother—just a separate set of dishes and silver—and dish towels—and soap—and doing without a few things at some meals. Do you know what I'm talking about?"

"You eat kosher meat."

"Yes—because of my mother-in-law. It's not as tender, I guess—the cuts are different—and the way they prepare it—and no pig, of course —though I understand they're the cleanest animals of all—and smartest, too—"

When she finally stopped running on, he said, "You seem like an awfully devoted daughter-in-law."

Sylvia savored the compliment for a moment and then discounted it. "Well, she's old—and an invalid—and my husband's mother—"

"You mean you don't have much choice?"

"Oh, I'm not complaining. There are things in life you have to do whether you like it or not."

Toby asked the nature of the old woman's infirmities. She suffered from a little of everything, the answer seemed to be—no organ had escaped affliction, and her limbs, severely arthritic, could no longer carry her beyond very short distances. Sylvia got to push her around the block in her wheelchair five days a week, weather permitting, in addition to cooking, cleaning, laundering, and shopping for her and bathing her failing body. "That's quite a burden," Toby sympathized and wondered if there weren't relatives beyond the immediate family who might help.

"There's Ira," she said, "Milton's brother. My sister-in-law Irene— isn't that funny, Ira and Irene?—she used to come by once a week, but they moved to Jersey after the bridge went up." Her disapproving tone implied plainly that the old woman, not the scenic treasures along the Hackensack, had prompted the flight.

He bought a box of cold cereal, a quart of milk, and half a dozen eggs at the grocery, omitting bacon out of deference to Sylvia's sensibilities. The small bundle left him an arm free to help carry her larger bags. This uncustomary service inspired her to suggest they stop off for a moment and have a look at the Wasserman haberdashery, which Toby confessed he had not yet visited. It was just a few steps out of the way, she said, obviously eager for him to admire the swank and solidity of the establishment.

Small but tastefully appointed with polished wood display cases and warm gray carpeting, the Saville Shop appeared at a glance to be burdened with one proprietor too many. Milton Wasserman, a bit bulgy to qualify as dapper in his navy pinstripe suit, was busy in the rear with a shirt salesman. In his late forties, a good ten years older than his wife, he looked quite presentable, except for a habit of vigorously brushing off his shoulders every few minutes, as if in pathological dread that a sprinkle of dandruff had fallen from his thinning hair—and who would patronize a slovenly haberdasher? Ira Wasserman, less well-fed and more haggard than his brother, minded the front of the store. Total sales so far that day, he told Sylvia, had been four ties, a bathrobe, a couple of sets of handkerchiefs, "and the last half-dozen of those lisle socks you said we'd end up giving away."

"Well, it only took three years," she said.

"Two and a half," said Ira, "but who's counting?"

Toby decided to buy himself a tie. "Oh, you don't have to do that," Sylvia said, flustering.

"I know," he said, "but I need one—and keep putting it off." Hovering over the infinite rows of neckwear, meticulously arrayed in the lighted case that warmed his hands as he gripped its edges, he studied the patterns and shades with feigned fascination. "What about this one?" he asked her, finally selecting a silk number in maroon with small white dots.

She reached around, pulled it out of the case, and, holding it up in front of him, judged it somewhat conservative for a young man.

"I'm quite staid, really," he said. "And these happen to be my college colors, more or less."

"But I thought Harvard was blue."

"No, that's Yale."

"Oh, yes—and they have a lion for their pet."

"I believe that's Columbia."

"Oh, you're right. So what's Harvard's animal?"

"I don't think it has one—unless it's the bookworm, possibly."

Sylvia looked perplexed for a moment, then laughed tentatively. "That is a joke, isn't it?" Toby nodded. She smiled at him in a fragile way that said comedy was not a regular feature of her life.

Coming home from work the next morning, he found a note from her under his door inviting him to supper with the family the following night. "Do you like tongue?" the postscript asked. He scratched his acceptance on the back, added, "Tongue's fine—only I'm never sure if I'm tasting it or it's tasting me," and went down to attach it to the copy of the *Trib* he had left off for them.

Sylvia Wasserman was a much better cook than Adele Orloff. Her skills, though, were taken for granted by the family and drew no commendation beyond Toby's lip-smacking enthusiasm, received indifferently by his hostess as mere politeness. Most of the table talk was devoted to a debate between Babette Wasserman and her son about putting up signs in the haberdashery window during the impending Christmas season to proclaim featured items and attractive prices. It was a subject they clashed over every year, Sylvia explained. Milton thought the idea degrading. "Broadway still isn't Orchard Street, Ma," he said and, after offering Toby some more, took another helping of tongue and baked beans.

But the old woman would not give up the fight. She continued to mutter away about the need for more aggressive salesmanship and less worry about offending the carriage trade, which the store never attracted, anyway. "Ve ain't Saks Fit' Avenue," she said between grinding chews. When Milton made no response, she turned without warning on Toby and asked, "Noo, vat d'you think, sonny?"

Toby took longer chewing his spinach than nature required. Sylvia jumped in at once to say it was unfair putting a guest into the middle of a family squabble. Babette was unmoved. It was a free country, she said, and Toby had to answer only if he wanted to.

"Well," said Toby, "I haven't ever really thought about it, but I suppose if I were buying men's apparel as a gift, I'd be a little more interested in the quality of the shop than anything else, so the window, if it were nicely decorated, would be all the advertisement I needed." He placed his knife and fork together on his plate, indicating he was done. "On the other hand, if I had a severely limited budget—as a lot of people do—I might very possibly be attracted by good prices, provided they were displayed more or less discreetly on small signs."

Everyone pondered that profound evasion except Babette, who turned to her grandson and asked, "Vat did he say, Victor?"

Victor, a quiet, depressingly well-mannered boy of ten, with coffee-bean eyes that had been scanning Toby for cloven hoofs from the moment he came in, rephrased the speech with a directness that laid bare its perfect duplicity.

Understanding the answer for what it was, Babette shook her head toward Sylvia. "A Spinoza ve got here," she said, leaving Toby in doubt whether the reference was made in admiration or contempt.

There was no sprightly after-dinner talk or variation from the apparent family routine in deference to the guest. Victor cleared the dishes and went into the parlor to share the radio with Babette. They switched back and forth, more or less amicably, between "The Lone Ranger," which the boy enjoyed, and "Lum and Abner," which his grandmother favored out of fascination with the hillbilly accents. Sylvia attended promptly to the dishes, which Toby volunteered to dry, while Milton sat like a king in the corner, savoring a cigar and the newspapers. At eight, Victor departed to do homework, and Sylvia claimed the radio, tuning between the strains of Jessica Dragonette and Andre Kostelanetz while she knitted peacefully and Babette and Milton drifted into and out of consciousness. This collective trance-like state, inducing perfect uncommunicativeness among them, reminded Toby of the fatigued silence that used to overtake his own parents every night after supper. He sat there politely next to Sylvia and fought off impolite thoughts of her ample womanliness.

At 8:45, as if aroused by a siren, Milton bounced up long enough to switch the dial to Grantland Rice, discussing sports in a smooth Southern voice that interested Babette even more than its sweaty subject mystified her. At nine, Victor reappeared for milk and a cookie and listened with the grown-ups to the dolorous commentary of Gabriel Heatter on the irredeemable state of the world. Afterward, a suddenly sociable Milton asked Toby his preference in the presidential election. He had no party, Toby said, but he thought Roosevelt deserved another term.

"Us, too," Milton said. "We nearly lost the store in '32—no one cared about clothes, then—only food and rent. The New Deal saved us."

Babette bunched up her face at that reasoning and announced, with the righteousness of a recent convert to the *Herald Tribune*, that she was flat against deficit spending by the government or anyone else. "That's how Papa vent bankrupt," she said. "Bad business is bad business."

"You can't compare, Ma," Milton said. "Papa couldn't get credit— Uncle Sam owns the Treasury."

"Uncle Sam shouldn't be no *schnorrer*, neither," Babette insisted, "or the Treasury is from hunger, too."

"But Uncle Sam owns Fort Knox," Victor offered brightly. "There's all that gold and silver and diamonds—"

"Vat diamonds?" his grandmother asked. "Diamonds they don't got."

"I bet they do," the boy said.

"Diamonds they'd steal—"

"No, they got soldiers there, Nana—they're watching."

"Ha!" The old woman shook her head.

Victor looked baffled and turned to Toby for outside expertise. Sylvia, though, intervened. "Don't try to contradict Nana," she told the boy.

"But she means soldiers steal. I thought Mr. Ronan might—"

"And don't call Nana 'she.' Now let's change the subject."

His independence of mind, while squelched, earned Victor an invitation to be Toby's guest the following Sunday afternoon at the rodeo in Madison Square Garden. Sylvia thought Toby's generosity excessive. "But I've been wanting to go," he protested, "only I doubt if it's much fun without some company." The boy, used to playing Monopoly with his father and grandmother for his Sunday recreation or taking a walk with them along the Drive while Milton pushed the old woman in her wheelchair, was ecstatic at the prospect.

The two women of the house were arguing openly when Toby came to pick up Victor, and the presence of an outsider did not, at first, shame them into a truce. Sylvia had seen a Lord & Taylor ad in the Sunday paper for alligator shoes at under seven dollars a pair and, needing some smart, versatile footwear, pursued the matter with her husband within Babette's evidently limitless earshot. She at once branded her daughter-in-law a spendthrift for spurning the excellent buys to be had on Orchard and Rivington; furthermore, the shoes Sylvia wanted were ugly loss-leaders she would surely regret a week after their purchase. The intrusion stirred a blaze of resentment in the normally subdued Sylvia, who calmed herself only long enough to try to press a five-dollar bill on Toby to cover the afternoon's expenses. This Toby stoutly rejected, but he tried through an unspoken expression of alliance to signal his support for her standing up to the ungrateful old horror. Milton hid in the Sunday comics as the battle resumed.

Throughout the rodeo, Victor hung off the edge of his seat, transported by the free spirit of the long-jawed cowboys and the sight of wild animals charging about a dirt ring in the middle of New York. He had often seen riders high on their mounts leaving and returning to the stable across the street from his school and dreamed, he said, of joining them for a gallop around the park or even across the bridge to visit his cousins in Jersey, smacking his steed smartly on the flank and shouting, "The Wassermans are coming! The Wassermans are coming!" But the horses looked so large and unmanageable, and his parents had discouraged the idea as expensive and dangerous. Toby said maybe they could both save up and someday have enough for a few lessons and a ride together.

At first, Victor declined the offer of refreshments. Toby thought him inhibited by politeness and kept pressing the suggestion. Eventually, the boy yielded and had some peanuts. Which necessitated a soda to wash them down. Which left an aftertaste of sweetness for which a bag of potato chips was the only known antidote. Followed irresistibly by a Dixie cup, starring a blue Myrna Loy on the underside of the lid—"There's two Myrnas in my class," Victor said, preserving the carefully licked souvenir—a box of popcorn, a cone of cotton candy, a frankfurter, and a second soda. Only the frank caused Victor a twinge of conscience. "What kind of meat would you say is in it?" he asked. Porcupine was all Toby could think to say and then, fearing he might be believed, urged the boy not to worry because the government had laws against the sale of tainted foodstuffs. Victor said it wasn't the government he was worried about and wolfed down the frank at a rate too rapid for even rabbinical detection.

By the time they got home, Victor was looking decidedly queasy under his new cowboy hat. The first glance at the platter of smoked fish awaiting him for supper prompted a swift dash to the toilet and a round of noisy retching. Heavy indulgence in forbidden delights was soon confessed—"All that *chozzerai*, no vunder!" Babette muttered, casting dark looks at Toby as prime accessory to the transgression— and Victor was sent to bed with a sharp reprimand and his cowboy hat impounded.

"It's my fault," Toby said. "I lost track of what he had."

"You're not used to being a parent," Sylvia said forgivingly. "I think maybe the planetarium would have been a better idea."

"But less fun."

"He has the radio for cowboys," said Milton Wasserman, his testiness ill-disguised. He had missed having the boy around the one afternoon a week he wasn't keeping shop, Sylvia whispered to Toby at the door and apologized for her family's all-day rudeness. She, at least, was grateful for his having been so kind.

V

Toby's transfer in early December to the regular nightside copy desk was as unexpected as it was, in his own view, undeserved. He jumped at the opportunity, of course—the four-to-midnight shift may not have been a great deal more civilized than working through the night, but it coincided with the period of peak activity in the assemblage of the paper. Still, he wondered about the promotion. On the lobster trick, he had worked with diligence, certainly, but not much distinction; the nature of the work precluded it. Perhaps it was simply that nobody else on the overnight desk coveted the added work pressure that accompanied the move. The night before Toby's swingover, Ned Kirby ended the mystification by confiding that the real reason was several extracurricular samples of his writing Toby had left by his place at the desk and the slotman, in appreciation, had taken the liberty to circulate.

The pieces were composed out of revenge. A regular part of Toby's chores had been to oversee the proofs of the society pages, a compote of wedding news, engagements, comings-out, tea parties, garden club meetings, charity balls, and the very latest on the fashion and beautification fronts. Layouts were always having to be altered, stories cut, headlines rewritten, so he looked on the task more as an exercise in honing his editorial skills than as neophyte's scutwork. But in his heart he felt it a waste of his energy on the most absurd, space-squandering drivel imaginable. And so one morning, as quitting time neared and he had nothing at all to do but nurse his coffee and doughnut, Toby began to toy with one of the rewrite typewriters nearby. What came out was his own version of the fatuous female copy he superintended every night. The first effort went:

> The Westchester Women's Wildlife and Game Preservation Society will inaugurate its indoor season next Thursday at the Billingsgate Country Club with a buffet supper of smoked bison and a diced pimento garnish. Afterward, the renowned safari director and snakecharmer, C. Percy Frothingtusk, will speak on "Anthrax and Your Pet."
>
> Mrs. Otis Spooner McLush, 300-pound president of the Southeastern Westchester Virginia Creeper and Pie Crust Club, announces that entries for the annual floral/bake sale may be submitted starting . . .
>
> Monthly meetings of the Girl Scout Leaders Association of the Pelhams convene weekly at the home of the otherwise purposeless Miss Aurora Languor . . .
>
> The Allied Arts, Crafts & Devil-May-Care Council of Bedford and Bronxville is in rehearsal for its winter production of the Greek musical tragedy, "Tyrannosaurus Rex, Son of Oedipus," to be staged in modern dress and in the round at Flooding Brook Farm in February. Running concurrently with the show will be an exhibition by artists working in papier-mache and beeswax . . .

Toby followed up with a beauty-care column on eye makeup, "that delicately subtle ritual," which recommended regular cleansing ("After carefully removing the eyeball, rub it gently into a compound of baking soda and epsom salts to get out the grit and add sparkle") and liberal application of eyelash thickener, "composed preferably of Belgravian Chimney Soot No. 6 and high-octane petroleum jelly." Another piece he headlined, "Tight Tunics and Pert Peplums Highlighted in Fur-Trimmed Suits," and concluded, "Remember, nothing is smarter than the brightest red you can find accented by coal-black persian lamb—or, failing that, banana-yellow trimmed in chest-beating gorilla."

Intended as no more than a private time-killer, the pieces produced enough amusement as they were passed from hand to hand to attract the attention of the night city editor and the nightside slotman. Budding satirists, they agreed, had the makings of natural rewritemen and copy editors, and drafted Toby for the first opening.

Not everyone who read his parodies, however, was equally enchanted. His first afternoon on the new shift, an in-house call came to him from a woman with a heavily frosted voice. "Is this Mr. A. Tobias Ronan," she asked, "the new Harvard gentleman on the staff?"

"Well—yes. And to whom do I have the pleasure of—"

"Your pleasure is my displeasure, Mr. Ronan—if you are in fact the author of those unfortunate mockeries being spread around the paper slurring the work of a good many dedicated people in the society section."

"Well—I did do them, but they weren't meant to be circulated."

"Then you should have had the decency, Mr. Ronan, to tear up your indecent scribblings when you'd had your little fun with them. They are cheap, ignorant, supercilious, and sophomoric—and aside from being hurtful to people too gracious to tell you so, they aren't the least bit funny."

The voice was young, almost squeaky in its stridency, and so wonderfully indignant that Toby thought for a moment that its wrath was staged. "Well, I'm really sorry if I offended anyone," he said. "It was the last thing in the world I intended. I'd be glad to apologize—if I just knew whom I was addressing."

"The whom you are addressing is Eden Chafee in society—and I happen to be in charge of the Sunday Westchester page."

"Well, all I can say, Miss Chafee—or is it Mrs. Chafee? I don't want to get in any worse trouble over there—"

"Miss Chafee will do—and if you have any apologies to offer, you might address them to the entire women's staff, starting with Mrs. Fitzwater, the fashion director."

"Would that prove I'm not a cad and a bounder?"

"It would be a start, Mr. Ronan. And a little humbling would probably do your soul a world of good. This isn't Harvard, old chum."

Toby took the advice in the form of a properly abject memo to the queens of the women's pages and was duly exonerated. He followed up with a note to the tart-tongued Miss Chafee, asking her to lunch with him at Bleeck's so he might thank her in person for her good counsel and allay any doubts that remained of his sincerity. "Bleeck's is fine for all you tough news guys," she wrote back, "but to us rose-buds it's a booze joint. Shall we say Sardi's next Tuesday at noon? No need to rsvp if okay. Ask for my table."

They were wedged between theatrical types not at all bashful about calling attention to themselves and a circumspect publishing tweed re-warding an author with cannelloni in place of an advance against royalties. As it filled up, the place took on an almost conspiratorial vibrancy; the diners were all people full of plans and talent and self-importance, dying to share confidences and plant rumors that might eventuate from those very seeds. Toby found it hard to hear and harder to think, possibly because, tumult aside, he was at once fas-cinated by the punishing personality of Miss Eden Chafee.

She had a snappy look about her: short, light-brown hair, streaked prematurely gray at both temples and done in neat marcelled waves that curled up at the end of their travels; wide-set sapphire eyes that knew their own worth, and a small, round, lightly lipsticked mouth that was quick to smile. "I don't believe a word of your apology, I might as well tell you," she said in a voice modulated to remain pri-vate yet cut through the surrounding clamor. "You still think the soci-ety pages are by and for a lot of silly twits—either that or you're a bogus Harvard man." She had gone to Wellesley and knew the Cam-bridge mentality, she insisted, so there was no point in his pretending otherwise. "Admit it," she said, pausing to order herself a daiquiri and niçoise salad and urge the crabmeat coquilles on Toby. He accepted the suggestion and had begun to answer her charge when she pulled a cigarette from her bag and asked, "Do you mind? Some men have an aversion to women smoking in public."

"Suppose I said yes?"

"Then I wouldn't, of course. At least one of us is sincere."

"Now who's being supercilious?"

"Never in my life," she said, taking small drags and expelling small puffs, as if undergoing a hateful tonic. "I know I'm right about you, though, because your satiric style is a dead giveaway. I mean it's lousy but vicious."

The aggressive little smile was asking to be wiped away. "My only actual objection to the society pages, as long as you've got me con-victed already," he said, "is that they deal with a single narrow stra-tum of the social order. They reinforce totally outmoded values, of which you ladies set yourselves up as high arbiters, and a rigid class

structure that has no place in a genuine democracy." He took a sip
from his water glass. "Otherwise, I think you're doing a bang-up job."

Miss Chafee drew heavily on her cigarette, seeing a skirmish on her
hands, and without inhaling let out a long, enveloping cloud behind
which she mounted a fresh assault. "It's obvious you know nothing at
all about what's happened to society since the Crash," she said. "It's
become so much less stuffy, so much more diffuse. People from
families of high social standing have actually been forced to go to
work. It's no longer just Vincent Astor and the international set that
matter, or old Newport and the '400,' or even entries in the *Social
Register*. You take Long Island nowadays. Society isn't just the horsey
set—it even includes Jews—of the right sort. There's a whole Sands
Point bunch of them—very quiet, very respectable, all immensely
wealthy financial tycoons—and of course half of them are hell-bent
on their children intermarrying. Why, it's practically impossible to distinguish them from Gentiles. And, my Lord, there's nothing at all exclusive now about café society—which is more fun than the old kind.
Why do you think the paper gave Lucius Beebe his column? Not for
his outrageous prose style, I can tell you. Anyone can crash society
today if he's of a mind to—even spongers, provided they dress well
and are amusing enough. Being amusing is essential—" She stopped
herself and eyed his clothes critically. "Since we're on the subject, Mr.
Ronan, and if you'll forgive me—you must do something soon about
your wardrobe if you expect to have a career in New York. I know
newspapermen have a tradition of down-at-the-heels dress, but I think
you're pushing it. Harvard men have their own traditions to uphold,
don't you think?"

"I thought you didn't care much for Harvard's traditions?"

"I didn't say that. I said I know Harvard attitudes for what they
are."

"Well, I'm not your standard Harvard sort, I'm afraid."

"Oh, I know. You're poor as a church mouse—no family—no club
—worked for the government at some wretched camp in the woods—
landed this job through some sort of mysterious pull with friends of
the Reids—probably got their daughter in trouble. Oh, don't look so
surprised. That's my job, remember—to know all about people who
count. I've got connections, too—how do you think I got my job?
Not by submitting the exquisite sonnets I wrote for the Wellesley literary magazine. So I know all about your impoverishment, but you
have to think of clothes as an investment—clothes may not make the
man, Mr. Ronan, but they can definitely unmake him. You go to
Brooks or Press or someplace decent and buy yourself a couple of
good suits. Believe me, you won't regret it." She tapped his wrist reas-

suringly. "Actually, your tie's not half-bad if you like maroon, but it looks like one of my grandfather's."

She picked at her salad and sipped at her drink, leaving half of both, while he tried to slow his racing insides and get down the expensive lunch. "Anyway," she said, when he failed to blunt her assault, "I think the women's pages are every bit as important to those reading it as the war in Spain or Ethiopia or some other God-forsaken place. And I don't see a blessed thing wrong with covering the elite—elites are exciting as long as they're not hidebound—they're something to aspire to—along with money and graciousness and taste. I'm for anything that improves the breed." She reached for the last of her nonstop cigarettes. "And even if I didn't absolutely believe all that, I'm doing what I know—there were Chafees in Westchester long before Horace Greeley moved in—and I do it damned well. But I'll be honest with you—I am a terribly honest person, as you may gather. A lot of the stuff we handle isn't very exciting. In fact, it's boring as hell. There are plenty of times I wish I could move over to the city staff and become the next Nellie Bly. I happen to think I'd make a marvelous reporter. But do you know how many female reporters the *Trib* has? A grand total of one—and if she weren't palsy-walsy with Eleanor Roosevelt, she'd probably be in trouble, too. It's very degrading." A small sigh of resignation escaped from her with the last puff of her cigarette. "So I have to compromise my principles—professionally, I mean—to keep going. Maybe everyone does, though. I'm sure you do—working for a paper whose editorial policies you obviously despise—"

"I can make the separation."

"Right," she said, "and that's your compromise." She reached for the check the moment it arrived. "This was my idea."

He put his hand on top of hers. "I'm not that poor."

"I want you to save up for your suits," she said and wrenched the check out of his grasp.

Only then did he fully understand that his little parodies of the women's page had probed a raw nerve in Eden Chafee. So dubious was she of the worth of her work and so resentful of the tight limitations slapped on her by the male hierarchy that she lashed out at Toby as the latest brutish slanderer of her sex; he had, innocently or not, perpetuated the myth of brainless femininity. In her furious defensiveness, she had gone after him with almost sadistic pleasure, partially disguising her effort at humiliation under a guise of personal concern for his well-being.

Toby squared his shoulders and leaned confidentially toward her. "If, deep within my soul," he said, "I did not understand that you are suffering from a severe persecution complex, I would have come to the ungenerous conclusion you were one of the most overbearing, condescending, thoroughly bigoted people I had ever met. But I see that it's your deep insecurity that makes you so aggressively unpleasant—and smoke like a kindergartener trying it out for the first time— so I've restrained myself and accepted your abuse like a perfect gentleman."

Eden Chafee's jeweled eyes turned to hard, narrow stars but did not flinch from his. "Well," she said, "perhaps we should go dutch."

He walked her back to the paper in silence. At the lobby entrance he said, "I'm sorry, but—"

"I had it coming—I know. I was being terrible. But I thought you deserved as much. Well, bully for you, Mr. Ronan—you put me in my place, all right."

"Toby—I'm Toby."

"Yes, all right—Toby."

"May I see you again?"

Her upturned lips pressed together. "Thank you, Toby—but I'm practically engaged."

"Oh." It was a social category unfamiliar to him. "What does that mean, exactly?"

"It means he's in his last year at law school, and we plan to marry after he passes the bar."

"Oh. But that's a ways off yet."

"I can count—as well as be insulting."

"Sorry. It just seemed to be a long—"

"That's how it is, though."

"And you're hopelessly in love with him?"

"There's nothing hopeless about it. Anyway, I think you're getting a little personal now."

"Well—I'd still like to try—if I may—to see you sometime." Any shred of encouragement would do.

Her eyes had lost their hard look and turned playful. "In this town, Mr. Toby Ronan, if you have to ask for something, the answer is always no. You just reach for it." She headed for the elevators, then whirled her head back toward him and said, "Try Rogers Peet, maybe —something in gray worsted would be good."

SIXTEEN

TOBY'S DISTASTE for Harris Becton set in the moment he saw the jowly night slotman noisily slurping up his coffee, which he consumed by the bucket, and straining it through his sinister drooping mustache. He also kept getting particles of bread, from cheese sandwiches mostly, caught in it and picking at his teeth and flicking at his nose, all the while supervising a dozen pieces of copy simultaneously with an uncanny feel for their soft spots.

It was not so much what went into Becton's mouth as what flew out of it that was unpleasant. He had a rotten tongue and a lecherous mind. His chief pleasure on earth appeared to consist of reading aloud from the sex stories in the first edition of the tabloids—the kind of thing the *Trib* rarely touched or, if unavoidable, buried with a few paragraphs ("The house rule," Becton recited, "is nothing with lace on it before page twelve"). He also had a gift for personal invective, delivered out of the side of his mouth like a back-alley tough but with his head angled away from its victim as if to disavow connection with the calumny.

Toby fell afoul of Becton early on while editing a story about $5,000 worth of jewels stolen from the wife of a wealthy East Sider named Fletcher, a man of no apparent attainments beyond having been born to rich parents. The victim herself, however, was identified at the end of the third paragraph as the fashion editor of *Harper's Bazaar*. Toby told the slotman he thought that fact should be in the lead and wrote the headline accordingly. "Who are you, Ronan—the last of the fuckin' suffragettes?" Becton snarled and rewrote the head to read: "Jewels Stolen/From Wife of/Allan Fletcher."

The next night, professional curiosity prompted Toby to query a U.P. dispatch from Spain that ran at the top of page three and said Franco had pledged "fullest rights" to the workers. The last paragraph of the story reported the further disclosure at rebel headquarters that if Franco's nationalists won the civil war, "El Caudillo" was to be a dictator comparable to Mussolini and Hitler, his rule absolute, with military men as chief advisors. Why, Toby wondered respectfully, was that part of the story buried and the alleged humanitarian angle about the workers featured? "Holy shit, we got a ravin' Bolshevik here!" Becton proclaimed to the rest of the rim. "Meet 'Lefty' Ronan, everyone—our comrade from the Harvard Soviet." Then, addressing Toby sideways, he said the foreign desk processed overseas copy as it saw fit and the rim kept its nose clean.

By the night Becton bounced a story he had handled about an apparent suicide police had "fished out of the melancholy waters of the Hudson River," Toby could no longer resist trying to parry his detractor. "The properties of water are volume and wetness—it doesn't get melancholy," the slotman growled, flinging the pages rudely back at him. "And what makes the Hudson more melancholy than the East River—or the Amazon?"

"They don't have to flow past Yonkers," said Toby.

Daniel Jonas, the youngish copy reader on Toby's right, struggled unsuccessfully to stifle a laugh. The slotman, though, was unamused at being sassed. "Don't be a wise-ass bastard," he said, "or they'll be fishin' you up next."

Such habitual abusiveness aside, Becton kept feeding Toby progressively bigger and trickier stories in a testing regimen the new deskman thrived on. Among these thorny training exercises was a tongue-in-cheek account of a garish gangland funeral written by one of the paper's gamier veteran reporters. The slain mug, who ran a big racing book and a distinguished Third Avenue crap game that had earned him the nickname of "Mr. El," was described in the piece as a close associate of the late Arthur Flegenheimer and thus rated a lavish burial of the sort long thought to have gone out of style; even the underworld had not escaped the ravages of the depression. His five-hundred-dollar pearl stickpin in place, Mr. El was laid out in a casket said to have been made of fourteen-gauge German silver. The Bronx vicars of Christ pronounced a solemn requiem mass for the hood, according to the story, and his last earthly remains were gladdened by a thirty-seven-car caravan of flowers bearing such condolence cards as "Sympathy, Friend," "Love, Pal," "We'll See Them, Kid," and "Goodbye, Oldtimer, from The Boys." The bier was flanked by a nine-foot-high broken column of roses and Easter lilies and a ten-foot-high floral clock with snapdragon hands pointing to the exact time Mr. El was rubbed out. The story added, "A spokesman for the attending florists revealed that an order had been placed for a giant bro-

ken heart to be fashioned of pink carnations bleeding drops of red tulips but was canceled at the last minute on grounds of excessive
mawkishness." Burial was in a mausoleum that reportedly set back
"The Boys" $20,000.

Becton read over Toby's edited version and summoned him with a
playful tug on his necktie. "First of all, I think the Mother Church is
out of the business of saying solemn requiems over the scum of the
earth—for any price," said the slotman. "Check it out. Next, I'd be
amazed if the casket was really solid silver—the mob wouldn't bury
him in it, they'd melt it down for pinky rings. Check that out, too.
And then this quote from the florists about the bleeding heart—I think
it's piped." Toby looked puzzled. "A fake—he made it up," Becton
said.

Toby was startled. "Does anyone do that?"

"All the best reporters—and Metcalfe's one of the best. They think
it's creative license. Go ask him—he'll be at Bleeck's, probably. And
who was this Arthur Flegenheimer?"

"I—I'm not sure. A major mobster, I suppose."

"You suppose? You're not supposed to suppose—you're supposed to
know. Go find out the name he goes by."

"How will I do that?"

"Try the library. If they can't help, call his widow and talk real
pretty."

Bleeck's was its usual late-afternoon bedlam of newspaper, magazine, and public-relations boozehounds, about half of them ardently
playing the match game for drinks. Metcalfe was in a group clustered
at the far end of the bar and did not look as if he wanted to be disturbed. A big, loud bruiser with short, iron-gray hair and a radiant
whiskey complexion, he spotted Toby coming for him halfway down
the bar. "Oh, it's Harry Becton's messenger boy, already, is it?" he
bellowed. "Tell the son of a bitch I died and went to Union City."

Toby waited politely at the fringe of the group while it finished up
the round. The match game was a Bleeck's pastime that added sporting spirit to simple dissipation. Any number could join in. Each player
tucked one, two, three, or no wooden matches into his fist and
presented it to the group; whoever guessed the exact total of matches
being held won the round and retired from the competition. The last
survivor paid for everyone else's drinks. The action was enlivened by
heavy side-betting over who would get out before whom. Metcalfe
was doing better than fair, to judge by his hearty disposition. "Have a
belt on me, sonny boy," he told Toby, "and I'll be with you anon, as
the Bard says."

Toby passed up the invitation as injurious to his on-the-job alertness and hovered uneasily. When the game broke, Metcalfe put an arm around him and, ripe with the sauce, said, "I'm glad to see you, sonny boy, 'cause I wanted to fix that quote from my 'spokesman for the attending florists'—oh, I love that. I got him saying they canceled the bleeding heart 'on the grounds of' et cetera—it oughta be 'ground,' singular. Got it?"

Metcalfe's hot, offensive breath nearly caused him to recoil. "He thinks the whole quote is a fake," Toby said, deciding to deal with the most sensitive issue first as long as Metcalfe had raised it.

"Oh, he does, does he—the ungrateful bastard!" He reached over Toby's shoulder for a refill. "Well, you tell him for me he's got one helluva nerve—questioning the integrity of a man who's been in the field thirty devoted years."

"That means the quote's legitimate?"

"Absolutely authentic—in spirit." Metcalfe gulped half a shot of scotch. "You got my meaning?"

"I'm—not sure. You mean they didn't say it but could have?"

Metcalfe's great melon of a head fell back in distress, then pitched forward intimately and said, "Now listen to me, sonny boy—what's your name, anyway?" Toby told him. "All right now, Toby boy, I want to tell you a little story." Toby closed off his nostrils and breathed through his mouth. As a young reporter for the *World*, Metcalfe narrated expansively so everybody around them could hear, he had been sent out to do a color piece on the St. Patrick's Day parade and the accompanying Hibernian hijinks. When he wrote it up, it all sounded pretty dull, so he stuck in a paragraph about a wizened son of the Old Sod tottering along the curb on Eighth Avenue while drinking a bottle of green beer. Suddenly the bottle slipped from the geezer's hand, Metcalfe wrote, and splattered the street a foamy emerald. After a stunned pause over his loss, the Irishman looked up and reportedly said, "I'd rather seen a church burn down." Metcalfe gave a gross cackle. "Now that, Toby, my boy, is good bright copy—and that is what the public wants—and Harry Becton knows it, so you tell him to go nitpick someone else's ass. Now what else is botherin' you?"

There was the question of the silver casket. Metcalfe had seen it, and it was silver, all right, but he couldn't vouch for how pure it was —"unless Uncle Harry wants me to dig it up and have it assayed." As to the highness of the mass pronounced over the deceased mug, Metcalfe conceded he had not attended the rites. "But the boys in the lead vests usually drop an M or two in the collection box and the priest'll do a jig on the coffin for that if they ask him to. Resurrections cost more."

Toby grinned. The guy was a better raconteur than gatherer of hard facts. "And who was Arthur Flegenheimer?" he asked finally.

"You gotta be kidding—a college-educated boy like you?"

"We only did Chaucer—and I don't remember anyone named Flegenheimer in *The Canterbury Tales*."

Metcalfe croaked with rotgut laughter. "Well, you go look it up— it's part of your graduate education."

Just then a busboy wormed through the crowd and handed Metcalfe a wad of bills and some change. The reporter, full of warm chuckles, gave him back a single and the silver. Toby could not hide his curiosity over the transaction. The third at Bay Meadows—"on the Coast," Metcalfe said; he'd had two on the nose at the horse parlor behind the barber shop across the street. Toby swallowed his dismay at such blatant consorting with the criminal element by a guardian of the public morals. At least Metcalfe tipped when he won.

Back upstairs, Toby got on the telephone. It was not a machine he ever liked much, but its aggressive use, he had been pointedly advised, was essential to his duties. It took four calls to track down Mr. El's funeral director, who advised that only the drop handles on the casket were real silver; the rest of it was bronze painted over. "They wouldn't settle for the plain solid bronze," the undertaker confided, "because it wasn't flashy enough—but don't quote me on it."

It took three more calls to trace the proprietor of the firm that handled the floral arrangements; the man had never heard of any order for a giant bleeding heart of carnations and tulips, though it was well within their artistic capability. And after five calls to find the number and eighteen busy signals, he finally got through to the rectory of the monsignor who had presided at the funeral—only to be told the cleric was in his room and unavailable. In desperation, Toby called over to the slotman for advice.

Becton picked contemplatively at his molars and shrugged. "Tell 'em to tell His Holiness it's God calling, and He's on deadline."

Toby tried a less sacrilegious tack—he pleaded for mercy. They would fire him, he told the rectory, if the monsignor would not come to the phone, so would they please, please try? A ten-minute silence was broken by a hollow voice, notably devoid of benevolence, that turned yet more aggrieved on learning the nature of Toby's question. He had sent the hoodlum's soul to its life everlasting with the usual mass for the dead, said the priest; there was no exalted ritual. Consumed by wonder whether any quantity of evildoing was enough to deny a son of the Mother Church her final forgiveness, Toby restrained himself and clicked off with thanks.

He fixed the errors in Metcalfe's story, cut the fake quote and substituted the undertaker's remark to him about a solid bronze casket not being flashy enough for gangster tastes—attributing it to "a source close to those planning the funeral"—and, after a quick trip to the *Trib* morgue, inserted directly following the name of Arthur Flegenheimer, "better known as Dutch Schultz." Then he handed it back in to Becton with the headline "Mr. El Takes His Last Ride in Style" and an apology that it had taken him so long. "For a great reporter," he added unthinkingly, "Metcalfe's a little casual with the facts."

The slotman hurriedly checked over the fixes, relayed the piece to the composing room, and, without an approving word, issued Toby a withering look. "We got three cardinal rules on this paper, Ronan," he said from a slit on the side of his mouth. "One is never reveal a source. Two is no story's worth ruining a woman's life for. And three is never shit on a buddy. Now go get your lunch—and bring me back a coffee, regular, like a good boy, huh?"

In bed that night, Toby tossed for hours, fretting whether it was worse to fake a quote or use one you weren't supposed to. All the funeral director had said was not to quote him on it—and he hadn't, not exactly. But who else besides the undertaker could have been the source? Hadn't he violated the man's confidence morally if not literally? Suppose the mob was offended and decided to erase the undertaker for a loose lip? The man's fate would forever be on Toby's conscience. Still, he consoled himself to the distant wail of fire engines, the quote made good, bright copy.

II

He decided to try out his new oxford-gray suit in church. And as long as he was being elegant and his motives were economic rather than spiritual—the paper paid three dollars apiece to staffers covering the Sunday sermon at "selected" churches—why not go where the finery would be most abundant? That way, even dressed up, he could feel humble.

The low ceilings on the top of the new double-deckers forced anyone his height to stoop before reaching a seat, but the mobile view they afforded of the river was well worth it. The zigzag route of the bus landed him at Park and Fifty-seventh. The last half-dozen blocks down the avenue he nearly jogged to be sure of a seat close enough to hear well. The Byzantine grandeur of St. Bartholomew's awed him as he slid in among the fashionable parishioners and fell beneath the seductive calm of the soft candlelight and swishing vestments and high liturgy and blessed sacrament of the Episcopal service which he had all but forgotten from childhood. Only the sermon intruded man's fallible word into this orgy of religiosity and renewed his suspicion that faith was propagated more by theatrical hocus-pocus than divine immanence.

Warding off the glances of his neighbors, Toby took out his pad and pencil and scribbled down the pearly wisdom of the rector, unearthly in his immaculate white robes and kettledrum delivery. He had recently returned from Europe, where declining Christianity, he said, was yielding to pugnacious nationalism and the worship of dictators. It was no place for America to join in any clash of arms, then or ever, unless in response to a transcendent moral issue. "And there is no such issue in Europe that I can find," he revealed. "The highest use of our blessings—and our greatest benefit to Europe and the world—will be to keep out of war made by godless men of disfiguring pride."

Yes, but why did God let tyrants prosper? The rector did not address the question, and that was what interested Toby. If tyranny, moreover, was not a transcendent moral issue worth warring over, then presumably its victims were getting what they deserved. The only way he could imagine accepting such a cruel world was through an unshakable faith that the Lord would without fail mete retribution to sinners and salvation to sufferers in the hereafter. In which case, given the relative lengths of the mortal span and all eternity, it followed that sufferers under tyranny had a vested interest in their own enslavement. Only the unbeliever and the earnest doubter, without an afterlife to count on, thus deserved to be ranked as truly virtuous since none but they risked their all against oppressors—with every likelihood their ultimate sacrifice would earn them nothing beyond the abyss.

The rector reached a different conclusion. In the face of Europe's moral bankruptcy, he said, "It is time for all of us to look toward our foundations, both as Christians and citizens, and to know where we stand and what we stand for, where we are going, and what our guiding principles are." Toby put it down, word for inspiring word. But what *were* those principles, exactly? How long *did* we turn our Christian cheek, enduring tyranny at home or countenancing it elsewhere? Where *did* we stand, exactly, and where *were* we all going? And why *were* there still so many wretched and desperate people in this blessed land, and why were those who bemoaned the fact and called for its lasting cure thought the lesser patriots for it? And finally—did he have to put a quarter in the collection plate if he was there as an objective observer and not a part of the flock?

On the front steps, a chilly drizzle was threatening to turn into snow. In the departing throng, Toby found himself directly behind Miss Eden Chafee, looking snug in a camel's-hair coat with a fuzzy fur collar. He tapped her on the shoulder, and she glanced back vacantly for a moment before lighting up in recognition. The tall, bony, older woman beside her she introduced as her Aunt Winifred. "We're roommates, after a fashion," Eden said. "I live with her. Can we give you a lift somewhere? We're headed downtown."

Aunt Winifred bolted ahead to the curb to flag down her driver. Eden, in her long, clinging coat, looked as appealingly sleek and high-waisted as a bud vase. Toby struggled for an excuse to accept her offer.

"Better yet," she said, seeing him hesitate, "come home and have coffee with us. You shouldn't be running around without a coat."

"It was warmer when I left—"

"It was not. It was colder. But you didn't have enough for a new coat after you bought your nice new suit, and you didn't want to wear your tattered old one over it to St. Bart's—I can see through you."

She could, too, and probably to the label on the inside of his jacket. He confessed before she caught him in a lie. "It's from Macy's—I don't go in for the prep-school models."

"I can see. Well, I'm sure it was a very prudent choice, even if it does make you look a little like a train conductor. Oh, there's Ralph now with the Olds—" She shoveled him along in front of her directly into the middle of the backseat beside a semi-startled Aunt Winifred. "I've asked Mr. Ronan back for coffee—and we have all that marvelous apricot cake I'm sure he'll loathe but politely help us finish."

"No doubt you'll force-feed him if he refuses," said Aunt Winifred, smiling brittlely. "Our Eden is a most persuasive girl."

Aunt Winifred lived in a spacious apartment, full of fine old furniture with faded velvet, on the north side of Gramercy Park. It was too big a place for a widow, her maid, and three declawed cats, so she had offered Eden lodgings when she went to work at the *Trib*. It was only a short cab ride from the office, Eden noted as her aunt made off to put up the coffee with a doughty, "Maid's afternoon out, I'm afraid."

Toby felt awkward there, and the more domestic Eden's chatter became, the uneasier he was, as if he had crashed a tea at Buckingham Palace. Only Aunt Winifred's return calmed him. "And how did the rector's sermon strike you, Mr. Ronan?" she asked, apportioning him more apricot cake than the other two pieces combined. "He's awfully commonsensical, wouldn't you say?"

Toby rapidly inserted an ungenteel chunk of cake into his mouth and, with a great deal of head-bobbing, said, "Mmmmm pretty much mmmmm."

"Mr. Ronan thinks he's a sententious old reactionary," Eden interpolated, "a spokesman for a smug, self-righteous elite—but he'd never let on now that he knows how you feel." She turned to Toby. "Aunt Winnie dotes on the rector—she has from the day she converted." Her aunt had been raised a Catholic, Eden casually disclosed while Winnie chomped seriously away on her pastry, and had stayed one until a few years earlier when her husband contracted cancer and the priest kept assuring her that a long-suffering death was a blessing because true believers were meant to share at the end in Christ's agony on the cross. "That was too much for Aunt Winnie," Eden said, as if discussing a distant third party, "and so she shopped around for a new church. . . ."

The social ended prematurely when Eden announced she had to run and meet her near-fiancé; they were headed for the Brooklyn Museum to see a new collection of pre-Columbian things, she told Aunt Winnie, and would be having supper in the Village. Toby was let out like the cat, to slink about the neighborhood and find his way to wherever it was he might be going.

Away from the blaze of that unattainable princess and all her corrosive charms, he felt doubly riddled by the cold and the damp of the gray, empty streets. It was unfair, utterly, for her to pick him up that way and stroke him intently, as if he mattered, and then thrust him aside with no more caring than she would bestow on a misfortunate stray that had momentarily captured her fancy. The wind pasted his pants to his legs with a chilling mucilage. She would be driven everywhere, door to door, on a day like this. What would he give to yank that arrogance out of her? If she would only hold still.

His head was so full of Eden Chafee that he did not notice, until reaching the newspaper office to write up the sermon, that he had left his notepad at Aunt Winnie's. Returning there was out of the question; with her gone, he could hardly cross that enchanted threshold. His only course was to reconstruct the rector's paean to isolationism from memory. He took pains not to offend Aunt Winnie, who would no doubt examine his account closely.

Eden had left his notepad for him at the desk when he reported to work the next afternoon. An attached note urged him to buy an overcoat before he caught pneumonia. He took her continuing solicitude, however playful, for a tender spot in her nettled heart and called her at Aunt Winnie's during his luncheon break that night. Miss Eden was out, said the maid. He left no message but tried again the next night; she was out once more. When his third try produced the same result, he dropped her a note care of the society desk, asking if she would go to the theater with him some night the following week.

"You're very sweet to ask," she said, telephoning him at work the next night, "and I do like you, Toby, but you know my situation. I can't see you if it's as prearranged as all that. It would have to be casual, like on Sunday, if you see what I mean."

"Sort of accidental-on-purpose?"

"Well—yes."

"I could loiter around the park in front of your apartment each morning, panhandling or maybe selling the *Hobo News*—"

"Well, no," she said with a laugh. "Besides, it's locked."

"What is?"

"The park—you need a key. We don't permit loiterers."

"I thought parks were public places."

"Not this one," she said. "Ta-ta—and take care of yourself."

But the following week, when he had half-succeeded in putting her out of his thoughts, she called to invite him and a friend to join her and her intended as their guests two nights later to see the Tallulah Bankhead play. Eden's parents had planned to take them, but her mother had been fighting the flu and had to beg off. "They say the show's not much but Bankhead's a bombshell—it should be fun. Oh, do come, Toby—and I'd like you to meet Richard, anyway."

"Why?"

"Why? Because—you're both very nice—and I think you'd like each other. Did I tell you he's a Yale man? Varsity crew and so forth."

"How nice," he said. "I think we're different types, probably—"

"So what? The whole world's different types—that's the fun of being alive. Oh, don't be peevish—and bring a date." She paused. "Or maybe you haven't had a chance to get around much yet. I could fix you up if you'd like—or at least try—it *is* short notice—"

He called Nina Orloff, apologizing for the lateness of the hour and the invitation but explaining the fortuitous circumstances. "I suppose you don't have much use for the bourgeois Broadway theater," he said, his voice tailing off.

"That's silly," Nina said. "A free ticket's a free ticket—and everything's a learning experience—so yes, thank you very much." The only problem was that after work she had a class at Hunter until eight and would have to run straight over to the theater without a chance to change or freshen up. "But I don't mind if you won't."

To free himself for this grand occasion, he arranged to swap shifts with someone who normally worked the desk weekend nights. The play, called *Reflected Glory,* was a protracted piece of fluff about a temperamental actress who pretends her true passion is for offstage domesticity when in fact she requires flamboyant exhibitionism to survive a life in which the curtain is always up. It was, as all the world concurred, a splendid vehicle for the star's bravura showmanship and flair for bitch-comedy. Toby, though, was more mindful of the two young women who sat flanking him than the glamour girl strutting the stage. The contrast between them was vivid: on the right, Eden Chafee, slim, fair, Nordic, hair carefully coiffed, brows plucked to an aristocratic fineness, chic in an accordion-pleated silk print, and voluble to a fault; on his left, Nina Orloff, broad, almost robust across the top, swarthily Slavic, hair naturally coiled, brows emphatic, drab in a graceless skirt of corduroy and button sweater not of cashmere, and reticent to a fault, at least with strangers. He and Eden's consort, Toby noted, were a comparable mismatch. Richard Townley Crandall —Eden used all three names in her introduction—looked like whatever Frank Merriwell must have three years out of Yale: geometrically approved profile, teeth out of a Knabe ad, obscenely developed thorax, tailoring ordained by the Brothers Brooks, and the preoccupied air of a *Town & Country* squire gravely contemplating the state of his tack room. Perhaps it was the company, Toby thought, that was beneath his interest. Or perhaps it was his defense mechanism against the indefatigable Eden, apt to usurp his every semblance of thought the instant it awakened his tongue.

Nina, hardly immune to all this incongruity, tried to hurry off home right afterward, telling Toby there was no need to escort her that far downtown. Eden, though, would not hear of their making so short an evening of it and insisted on coffee and dessert at some nearby inexpensive place with music—she had to have music, she said. Richard morosely complied, piloting them through the Broadway crowd, which for all its dishevelment warmed them against the cold. The Hickory House, a large, unpretentious club on Fifty-second a little east of Seventh, offered a small swing combo that played fluidly on the long platform in the center of the low-lit room. Eden ordered rye and ginger ale and chocolate cake; Richard, a bourbon and soda; Nina, tea, and Toby, coffee, regular.

Before finishing her dissection of the play, Eden made multiple allusions to the rich diet of entertainment she and Richard had taken in so far that season. Whether it was simple insensitivity or some deeper lacuna in her character did not matter; the recitation smacked of contemptuousness. Tallulah's performance, said Eden, could hardly be compared, of course, with those by Helen Hayes in *Victoria Regina* or Gielgud's in *Hamlet* or Maurice Evans as Napoleon in *St. Helena;* Bankhead had to be rated more as a barnstormer against, say, Ethel Merman in *Red, Hot and Blue* or the young comedienne Imogene Coca in *New Faces of 1936,* both musical revues. Actually, she and Richard preferred their music serious. That season they had heard Stokowski, Koussevitzky and Ormandy conduct and Heifetz, Elman and Kreisler play at Carnegie—and seen Martha Graham dance there to the Hall Johnson choir. And the D'Oyly Carte give a rousing *Penzance,* and the Ballet Russe, a somewhat sluggish *Swan Lake.* "Richard is really a jazz fanatic, of course, and puts up with longhair on my account," she said. "He's much happier with Benny Goodman—who's at the Pennsylvania, by the way, if you get the chance—or at the new Cotton Club—we saw Bill Robinson there the other week—it's not in Harlem anymore, you know—at least they let the Negroes in now, too—although we didn't see many—and Cab Calloway's band is marvelous—only to be honest, Eddy Duchin's more my style, except that the Persian Room's so awfully chichi—if not quite as preposterous as the horse show, which they still make you dress for—" Eden stopped short and misread the dark look on Toby's face. "Say, have you been to Madison Square Garden yet? It's quite a—"

"To the rodeo," Toby said, hiding in his coffee.

"The rodeo? You went to the *rodeo?*"

"Yes. The manure was very chichi."

"I thought the rodeo was for children," Eden said, impervious to ridicule.

"Of all ages, as they say."

"Oh. And was it great fun?"

"Very great—especially when they killed the bull."

Eden's eyes narrowed. "They don't do that—"

"See what you've missed? The cowboys all rope it and then take turns spurring the brute to death. It's most amusing—though this particular one cried a lot."

"I never heard of such a—"

"He's putting you on, baby, for putting him down," Richard advised her, emerging from his trance. "We'd better blow—I've got a lecture at nine." His big hand enveloped the check as Toby reached for it, insisting it be his treat since they had provided the tickets. "It's on us, pal," Richard said, waving him off like a hunter his mastiff, and left a five-dollar bill without waiting for change. There were stiff handshakes at the door before Richard dumped Eden into a taxi. Toby and Nina walked to the subway at Fiftieth.

Gloom claimed him for having inflicted the whole evening on her. "Well, that's how the other half lives," he said on the ride down.

"It was a better show than the show," Nina said. "Don't feel bad."

III

Nina reciprocated on an icy Saturday night right after the turn of the year. "Now this isn't Broadway," she stressed, "so don't come expecting to be entertained. You're here to be stimulated." She pulled the shawl tighter around her head as they turned off Fourteenth on to the avenue with its lofts and factories and warehouses bunched somberly between inelegant office buildings. "Anyway, my father thinks you're something of an intellectual tourist and this'll do your soul some good."

"My soul doesn't like being preached at for two hours at a time," he said. "And I think your father's a bit of an intellectual bully, so maybe we're even."

She tilted her head against a blast of wind. "It's only an hour play, if that—and it's not preachy. Odets says new works of art should shoot bullets, and that's what his do." Just turned thirty, Clifford Odets was the first authentic genius of the revolutionary theater, she felt; no one more exciting had come along since O'Neill.

Her words were offered with such unstinting conviction that Toby could not doubt their sincerity. Her judgment he would determine soon enough. She had seen *Waiting for Lefty* no fewer than five times, including a production her Uncle Wally had directed for the Workers Laboratory Theatre. Wally had since grown disenchanted with the so-called social realism of the revolutionary theater, branding it cheap, strident, and corny, and was doing something now for the Federal Theater Project without any sledgehammer messages in it. Nina loved him dearly and went to see everything he did, but she thought Wally had revealed his limitations in this flight from social content. It was one thing to spurn the hortatory heroics of the Theatre Union, she said, or the unrelieved gloom of the editorials of the Living Newspaper troupe that the W.P.A. was financing on Broadway, but Odets and his Group Theatre generated authentic passion and anger and moved anyone who came to watch with an open mind. "Wally's trouble is he's too much of an aesthete at heart."

"Since when is that a handicap for an artist?" Toby asked.

"When it makes him forget the worth of art is all in the intention of the artist, not its execution." She did not say it pugnaciously, but it still came out like an incontrovertible law of the cosmos.

"Oh. I hadn't realized that."

Nina Orloff did not go in for repartee. "Well," she said, "it's what I happen to think. You can scoff like Wally if you want, but to me art for art's sake is among the more corrupt forms of self-indulgence."

The theater was a drafty second-floor union hall, lent three nights a week by the Amalgamated Sheet Metal Workers for semi-professional productions. The actors worked for lunch money, with the bulk of the proceeds going to the union movement. Toby had never seen such a stark theater setting: perhaps two hundred folding seats scattered about the barren room, no proscenium arch, no scenery, no costumes; it was all done with lights and shadows and the projected power of the players.

Waiting for Lefty was one sustained howl, six scenes long, about the prelude to a taxi drivers' strike. From the first word, there was nothing nuanced in its indictment of the killing cruelty of capitalism. Edna, the beleaguered hackie's wife, moans that there is hardly enough to pay the rent, and the children are always hungry, and the furniture has just been carted away, and there is no prospect but squalor if the drivers do not rise up and demand just wages. It went on that way, a piece of living tissue torn from the underbelly of life and throbbing with pain, blatant and compact, its message of rage inescapable. Actors jumped in and out of the audience, breaking the barrier between passionate performer and impassive spectator. The language, for the most part crude and direct, at times managed a disarming piquancy. "My God, Joe," says Edna, sending her husband out to do battle, "the world is supposed to be for all of us." The class struggle was no idle rhetoric on the lips of Clifford Odets' characters; it was a fight to the finish. At the curtain, the audience was screaming for the strike every bit as vehemently as the cast.

Caught up in the raw frenzy of the spectacle, Toby said nothing afterward until they found shelter in the booth of a Sixth Avenue coffee shop. "But why," he asked finally, grateful that she had not pushed him sooner for a reaction, "does it all have to be set in a communist context? Why can't reform come along other lines as well?"

"Because the communists have assumed the moral leadership of the Left," Nina said. "Is that so hard for you to accept?"

"It's not easy. It seems so foreign—and un-American—"

"So was democracy—and capitalism. The Indians didn't invent either one. What makes you so afraid of communism? It's given meaning and hope to a lot of people whose lives have had neither."

"People like you?"

"I wouldn't put myself in that category." She had grown up, she said, in a family with strong roots in the labor movement. Her mother had worked in a shoe factory for a while after grandfather Eichhorn, a thriving furrier, died and the family business collapsed; Adele Orloff knew the depredations of the sweat shop. And Saul Orloff had worked for union causes practically since he was a boy, with particular commitment after two of his cousins leapt to their deaths in the Triangle fire. So her parents had oriented her toward Marxist thought, but by herself Nina had come to feel the fullness of its promise— "especially with so much evidence all around that the rest of the world is a moral vacuum."

"And you've got the sure cure for it?"

"Surer than any other."

"Why—because you want it to be? Wishing doesn't make it so."

"Because it's a moral system at its very foundation—that's worth everything. It's too easy to despair over the awfulness of how things are now—that's what *Lefty* is all about. The thing is never to doubt—you have to believe with all your heart that you're on the right side—on history's side—and that life was meant to be better than it is for most people. Is that too much to hope for?"

"Not if you think human beings are basically good."

"Don't you? I mean if they had a chance to be?"

"But people don't live in test tubes. They're social creatures—and society runs on economics—and economics works on the premise that human nature is basically selfish."

"Capitalist economics, you mean. And that's what's wrong with it."

"But if you don't give people incentives, you don't have a functioning society for very long."

"There are other incentives besides wealth, Toby."

"But most of them are still forms of self-interest. That's why I can't sit still for slogan thinking—like 'From each according to his capacity, to each according to his need.' What does that mean except that the ablest people should do the most, and everyone else benefits regardless of merit? Why is that fair? I really don't understand. That sounds like mass parasitism to me."

Nina stirred her coffee slowly, reflecting on his words as if trying to sift for clues whether he was friend or foe at heart. "You don't understand because you don't really want to," she said, "and because you're a victim of your own prejudices." Her eyes connected with his and lingered long enough to register a warmth beyond politeness. "Stop reading it literally—it's the moral content that matters. All the first part of it means is that men really aren't created equal in terms of their gifts—their brains and beauty—their strengths and talents—but whatever you've got, you have to contribute to society—the most you can—and be the best person possible—as industrious and giving as you know how. What's parasitic about that, I'd like to know?"

"Nothing—but the second part doesn't follow from it, that's all."

"Why not? It just means nobody should have to starve to death—or go without a roof over his head—or clothes or medical treatment. It means having the compassion not to let everyone else suffer while the strongest and bravest and cleverest prosper. It doesn't mean everybody should have exactly the same rewards—that the ditchdigger and the plant manager and the research chemist have to live in identical surroundings with identical creature comforts. There's room to differentiate so long as society admits there's dignity in digging a ditch well. All Marx was saying is that life shouldn't be either feast or famine, whoever or whatever you are." She blew softly on her coffee before lifting it to her lips. "That's good enough for me."

She was not altogether persuasive—collectivism still seemed to him more witless than classless, a sure formula for dissension and disorder, once the pure flame of altruism died—but the earnestness of her faith was appealing. Contagious, almost. "And how do you get the top dogs to go along with all that?" he asked.

"By convincing them they're going to die otherwise."

It came out like a diamond knife, flashing all the colors of the spectrum for a lethal instant and then hurriedly recessed into the folds of the assassin's robe. Either the words were conditioned bravado or her whole moral posture was irretrievably skewed. "Why is that?"

"Because they deserve to."

"Why—if they've earned it?"

"Nobody earns the right to oppress anyone else."

"You mean anyone who's successful has to be an oppressor?"

"Successful in terms of money? Yes—pretty much." She fussed with the fringe on her white shawl, avoiding his disapproving look. "I can't help it if you think that's extreme, but it's what I believe."

"And democracy can't change any of that—by redistributing the wealth and so forth?"

"Who's going to make them redistribute it?"

"The legislature. That's why democracies have them—to resolve differences without bloodshed."

"The propertied class buys the legislature as soon as it shows the least inclination to dispossess them."

"It hasn't bought off Congress."

"Not yet—which is proof Roosevelt hasn't attacked anything basic. He's just running a big soup kitchen."

There was definitely a hardness in her, he decided, that went beyond mouthed phrases learned at parental knees. "So the American system can't possibly reform itself—and you scorn Roosevelt for trying—and people like me who believe there's a middle way?"

Nina placed a warm, soft hand on his. "Nobody scorns you, Toby. But you're too smart to stay innocent. You can't change the world without struggle and sacrifice—and killing, I'm afraid, unless the owner class surrenders. And in all history, it never has."

It was becoming clear that there was nothing he could ask or say for which she did not have a ready answer. All the points had come up many times before; no doubt she had been the star of the Hunter Y.C.L., with a precocious affinity for dialectical debate. It was like trying to have a dialogue with a steel trap. In frustration, he said, "I hope the party appreciates your devotion."

"The C.P.? Oh, I'm not all that involved," she said. "I've got my job and my studies—"

He sensed a trace of evasiveness in her for the first time and tried to probe at it. "Why do I have the impression they hold their meetings after midnight in the corners of remote subway stations or down in the ground somewhere—?"

"Somewhere smelly?"

"Well—yes, now that you mention it."

"Sure—because the owner class is afraid. It's to their interest to paint us all as shadowy fanatics—too cowardly to show our faces in daylight and therefore all the more contemptible."

"Which is ridiculous, of course—"

"It's more than that—it's hateful. And it misses the central point. You have to understand—the C.P. isn't just another hack political party—or some misty social movement. It goes beyond petty partisanship. It's a whole value system—an entire way of thinking about life and the world. And if you subscribe to it, it goes on inside you all the time, day and night, seven days a week, not just when there's some official function and you're expected to demonstrate allegiance."

"What room does that leave for anything else in your life?"

"But that's the point—everything else is caught up within it."

"Sounds cruelly demanding—almost inhuman."

"No! It's human as hell. It's more intensely human than any other kind of life I can imagine." She studied his attentiveness and risked opening more of herself to him. "Shall I tell you what it really is for me? It's a loving feeling—very deep and very wide—toward life and people—all of them—except the ones who want to chain me. It's just exactly the opposite of the feeling capitalism promotes—"

"I don't believe much in abstract love," Toby said.

"It's not abstract."

"What else is generalized love?"

"But it's very specific at the same time, too, don't you see? It's the kind of love my mother and father share. It goes beyond themselves.

Marriage isn't just loving each other—it means coming to love a lot of the same things—people—places—ideas—values. Their politics became their marriage vow somewhere a while back, and they're bound now by a very real pledge to try to reduce the misery in the world—they don't think there's anything divinely ordained about suffering. And if there was, who'd want to pray to a God like that?"

By the time they reached her front door, he was congested with the spiritual visions of Nina Orloff. Her ideas, reducing large abstractions to private passion, were definitely worthy of his further thought. He took her hand and thanked her for the instructive evening. She smiled and said she would ask him inside except that her father was almost certainly still working. "On Saturday night?" he asked.

"He goes at it all the time."

"I guess he's pretty important—to the party, I mean."

Her eyes skipped away reflexively. "I don't know—he doesn't talk a great deal about what he does. He just does it."

"And you wouldn't say if he did. I'm sorry I pried."

She pressed her lips together and nodded. "With all the misunderstanding, you can see how being cautious is important."

"Sure. Well—anyway, I hope I can see you again," he said and gave her hand a more ardent squeeze.

"You're allowed to kiss me, you know."

"Oh." He grinned at his needing to be goaded. "I wasn't sure you went in for any of that."

"Why not?" Her hand still rested warmly in his.

"I don't know—I just thought—that comrades think there's something indecent about it."

"Is that a joke?" Her hand fell away.

"Not really. It's just that you seem to have so much more on your mind than—personal things."

Her eyes sparked in the dim hallway light. "They aren't two different things," she said, sharpness entering her tone for the first time. "I don't think you followed what I said—or believe much of it—or me." And she was gone, unkissed and unkissable.

He half-ran to the subway, wending amid Saturday night revelers and trying to sort through a headful of warring emotions.

IV

In Bleeck's perpetual twilight, Buddy LaRusso's heavy beard gave him a menacing cast entirely at odds with his easy, demonstrative manner. He talked freely with his hands, not troubling to hide—or perhaps no longer noticing—the dirty fingernails that came from running a thick, black pencil and gum eraser with censorious rigor through reams of overblown prose. A onetime sportswriter now on permanent assignment to the Sunday desk, he obtained job satisfaction, he explained to Toby, mostly by trying to improve the working conditions of craft. "And on this paper," said the *Herald Tribune*'s guild unit chairman, "that's no easy trick. Management's conservatism is very catching. They pay peanuts and make you think it's a privilege to work for a pillar of the profession."

But things were definitely coming along lately. The *Daily News*, of all papers, had signed a guild contract just a few months before, with the highest pay scale in the country. The liberal *Post* had come in earlier, more in principle than with material gains. The *World-Telly*, Heywood Broun's home paper, was flirting seriously with them—Roy Howard was on record supporting the guild concept—and Hearst was reluctantly granting recognition and better terms since the guild had struck him in Milwaukee and Seattle over the firing of enlistees in the cause.

The *Times* and *Tribune*, however, remained strongly opposed to the guild on the sanctimonious ground that the professional objectivity of the newspaperman would be fatally compromised by his enlistment in a labor organization. And there was no longer any doubt, since it had affiliated with the A.F. of L. the past June, that the American Newspaper Guild was a good deal more than a benign lobbying fraternity. Even the *Trib* was being forced now to acknowledge the growing strength of the newly active guild unit on the premises by spreading around unsolicited raises of up to five dollars a week to discourage defectors. "We got 'em scared," LaRusso said, raising both arms and feigning a nervous tremor with his splayed fingers. "But there's a long way to go yet here, which is why we're so anxious to get new people like you on our side—before they become Reid family retainers."

Toby cradled his beer and pondered the moral dilemma LaRusso's forceful entreaty created for him. It was one thing to sympathize and ally himself with the legitimate aspirations of the laborers of the world; it was a far larger thing to concede he was one of them. "It's just that I've never thought of myself that way," he said, "even when I've worked in shops. I don't mean to sound stuck-up or anything, but it's—"

"It's the Harvard influence—and don't apologize. We're full of Harvard people. Broun was class of—what was it?—1910, I think, and he launched the whole shootin' match—and he's still the spiritual captain of the ship. And hell, the *Trib*'s top two literary lights—Lippmann and Gannett—are both Harvard men and guild stalwarts. It doesn't take a proletarian background to recognize the shit most news guys have always had to put up with."

But Broun and Walter Lippmann and Lewis Gannett were all luminaries, Toby thought, with famous bylines and regular columns, invulnerable to the suspicion that they had joined up because there was no other route to their material advancement; for them, guild membership was *noblesse oblige.* "It does seem to go against the grain of the profession," he told LaRusso. "Isn't the whole point of it to be above the battle?"

"No," said the guild operative, scissoring his hands over each other, "it's to be there and report it fairly—and well. Hey, look, we all know the legend of the Glorious Fourth Estate—we all grew up believing in it. The gentleman of the press is your classic American individualist, as good as any man on earth, and he'll give up health, wealth, family, sex, and all hope of heaven for his love of the game—to see his stuff in print and his name on top of it—and hobnob with the powerful and famous—and if he's any good, he'll become rich and a celebrity in his own right. Who needs unions? Unions are for lunkheads, guys who do dirty, boring, physical work, who can't hope to—"

"I don't look down on them. I don't look down on anyone."

"Sure, I know—but you got all the classic symptoms without knowing it. Let me tell you something, though, Toby—we're technicians, most of us, not Shakespeares. One guy in a thousand becomes a star, maybe, and good for him. But the rest of us burn out after a couple of years and do the job from habit, not inspiration, and hope management doesn't notice. You become grateful for crumbs and don't mind getting your ass kicked around so long as there's something in your pay envelope every week. The ones who can't face the truth drown their sorrows in booze, or the ponies, or, around here, in both of them and the match game."

The depression had stripped the legend of its last pretensions. For a lot of reporters, pay sank to under twenty dollars for a six-day week, with ten- or twelve-hour days and no overtime pay or the slightest job security. And those who hung on, LaRusso recounted, sometimes had their salary slashed 30 percent at a time without recourse of appeal. The printers, meanwhile, thanks to their union, earned a lot more, worked a five-day, forty-hour week, with time and a half for overtime, and didn't get fired without a cause or have their pay cut without a full-scale negotiation. "It used to be a badge of honor for a reporter or deskman to have been fired from five or six papers because the city editor didn't like the way you combed your hair. Well, I can tell you it's no honor if you're trying to hold a family together in this day and age on a newsman's pay."

When the New Deal arrived and signaled its concern for the plight of the working stiff and all the ones being denied a livelihood, Broun's call for a nationwide union of newspaper writers—all those unorganizable egoists—brought an unimaginably broad response. And when the publishers fought furiously for exemption from the N.R.A. codes on the claim they would infringe on a free press, a lot of staffers saw through the transparent allegation. "All they were worried about was losing their delivery boys to the child-labor provisions—and having to pay us halfway decently even when their own revenues were down—as if the glorious free press should have been subsidized forever by practically free labor. But it's all turning around now, Toby. Every paper in the country's going to have a guild contract before not too long if we can just keep up the momentum. You have to decide if you're going to help make it happen or you're one of those who comes along for the ride afterward—there's nothing in between."

Toby brooded. His course should have been clear—the justice of the thing was unarguable—but something in him resisted, as it always had. He could feel his whole being bend. That native impulse for the underdog, for the degraded and disowned, had till now been a philosophical and emotional preference rooted in conscience rather than perceived self-interest. Was that highmindedness anything other, though, than his private version of the mythic journalist-as-Galahad? In the back of the main dining room at Bleeck's, a suit of armor left over from the old Metropolitan Opera costumery stood watch in a lighted glass case, like a protective knight errant on guard over the writing clientele. The suit was much too small for him, Toby decided, and probably as rusty as the legend. In fact, the journalist was probably twice as susceptible to exploitation as mere mortals because of his very romanticism, however he veneered it with caustic worldliness. Sensing that, Toby still felt prudence required him to weigh all the factors before deciding. He had to ask the one man he knew at the *Trib* who was most certain to serve as counterweight to LaRusso's proselytizing.

"Don't sell your birthright for a mess of pottage," Harris Becton said sideways after the city edition had closed. He scraped a coffee-cake crumb from his mustache and leaned back, obscenely massaging his belly. "The good ones don't need any guild," he told Toby. "It's the misfits who need all the help they can get." Unions meant the triumph of the lowest common denominator, whereas newspapers demanded the highest productive talent. Besides, how could a newsman serve two masters? Or a publisher with any pride run a closed shop of writers all drawn from the same political sector or with the same social viewpoint? Sure, printers were unionized—because they would al-

ways be printers, never editors or columnists or front-page byliners or
foreign correspondents. Newsmen were the heart of the press, with a
sacred calling, not just mercenaries who'd as soon be stock brokers or
shoe salesmen. "The guild's a crock, Ronan—and half of 'em are
fuckin' communists. And Broun—Broun is a buffoon, and a sot. He
used to go around sippin' hooch in public, you know, when he ran in
'30 as a Socialist for the East Side seat in Congress. The guy was a
laughingstock. Some union man—he makes nine hundred a week and
lives in a penthouse. Every time there's a strike somewhere, he shows
up on the picket line for an hour and he's a hero. Then it's back to
feedin' his fat ass and the good life in the joints." The slotman slapped
his thigh and grabbed the top copy of the first run from the stack the
boy had brought up from the press room. "You want my advice,
Lefty, you keep the hell away from the Reds and maybe someday
you'll have a future here. We got no lasting prejudice against Harvard
men."

He went for a beer after work that night with Dan Jonas, a Columbia Journalism School graduate a couple of years Toby's senior, who
sat next to him on the nightside rim. Jonas had high technical skills,
compulsively orderly work habits, and a well-repressed loathing of
Harris Becton. "He's the last guy on the paper I would've told you're
messing with the guild," said Dan. "He'll hold it against you forever—
he uses whatever he can get his hands on. The man's a savage."

"I thought I might as well hear the worst," Toby said. "LaRusso
makes a pretty good case."

Dan's low, fretting brow rippled. "You're not actually thinking of
joining, are you? I mean that's sheer suicide."

"I think it's probably the right thing to do, though."

"They'll bury you here, you join the guild. If you don't get axed
outright, they'll have you editing pissant cop stories or writing obits
or covering Kiwanis conventions till you drop."

"I thought the *Trib* was a beacon of enlightened social thought."

"Oh, sure. Do you know who the guild's arch-enemy is? It's the
American Newspaper Publishers Association. And would you like to
know the name of its outgoing president? It happens to be one Howard Davis, who also happens to be the business manager of the *Herald
Tribune*. Does that give you a clue as to the paper's openmindedness
on the subject? Now it's conceivable, being one of the few identifiable
Jews in the place, that I'm extra sensitive about things I think are going
to get people's back up, but if you want to get ahead here, Toby,
don't cross 'em."

It had not occurred to him that a Jew working in New York might feel uncomfortable in his place of employment. That interested Toby more than Jonas's expedient view of the guild. His caution was inextricable from his Jewishness—which made it that much more incumbent on Gentiles there, particularly those with a Harvard pedigree, to act in principled fashion. "The *Times* isn't any more sympathetic to the guild," he mused. "Are the Jews there any more active in it?"

"There aren't many there—it's practically as bad as the *Trib*."

"But I thought Jews owned it."

"Yes—of a highly recessive sort. And they're so afraid of being labeled a Jewish paper that they're almost rabidly anti-Zionist. You think it's an accident that the most eminent columnist on each paper—Krock and Lippmann—is practically an anti-semitic Jew? They know which side their bread's buttered on."

A week later, LaRusso took him to hear Heywood Broun address a conclave of the guild's New York City chapter in one of the Astor's smaller ballrooms. Hundreds were on hand representing two dozen units, from *Time* and the *Times* to the Bronx *Home News* and the Yiddish *Forward*. Harry Bridges, the West Coast leader of the longshoremen, was the featured speaker, but Broun was the draw—Broun the zany, Broun the reprobate, Broun the most widely read liberal commentator of his generation.

He was a giant humpty-dumpty, with a face that looked like freshly kneaded dough, a gait that never exceeded a shamble, drawling speech to match, and a getup that came straight out of Central Casting's notion of a hard-boiled crime reporter. The suit bagged, the shoes were shoddy, the tie knot was at half-mast and askew, and cigarette smoke spilled out of both sides of his mouth. Since the gathering was intended in large part to attract increased membership, many in attendance were getting their first look at the original and still reigning president of the American Newspaper Guild. From the stir of disbelief greeting Broun's heavy tread to the microphone, few of the uninitiated were prepared for the sight.

"I have been described by people knowledgeable in these matters," he began, "as looking like an unmade bed. And if you don't think I'm a fashion plate in civilian clothes, you should have seen my army outfit during the war. I wore a uniform so badly that General Pershing asked me once if I had just fallen down." The laughter billowed. "But let me tell you something. Show me a newspaperman who's well-dressed and I'll show you a guy on the take."

For newcomers to the field, he had some terse advice: "Get in, get wise, and get out while the getting's good. You know when you're over the hill the same way a ballplayer or a dancer does—the legs go first. If you hang around after that, sooner or later you'll succumb to alcoholism, insanity, or—if you've really crossed the good Lord—a fat salary in public relations. The first two are no barrier to joining the guild; the last is a definite blackball."

But he was a very serious clown. Rumors persisted, Broun boomed with the relish of a seasoned stump speaker, that the guild membership and especially its leadership were a pack of wild-eyed radicals. The truth, he said, pivoting slowly and dropping his voice, was that most newspapermen came from educated homes and middle-class backgrounds unsympathetic to the labor movement. They grew up thinking unions meant violence and desperate men trying to throw a monkeywrench into the machinery of capitalism. "But something changed for a lot of us between then and now, and it's no mystery what. They let us go around and see what's happening out there—and if we're even halfway observant, which is what we get paid to be, pretty soon we begin to figure out that, by and large, the facts of life are not very pretty. If you're alive and kicking in this business, you can't miss seeing one helluva lot of injustice every day. Is it any wonder that the average informed newspaper Joe on the *Daily Whosis* is to the Left of the average isolated citizen? Or that the publisher of the *Whosis* wants everyone in town to think he's got an exclusive claim to the First Amendment? Well, I say to hell with that!"

He wound up with a rousing call for all the units in the city to hang together and weather any crisis that might hit the major dailies in the near future. "We're building," he said. "Come help us—and yourselves."

They went to Bleeck's afterward with a short, peppery courthouse reporter named Gutwillig, who was secretary-treasurer of the *World-Telly* unit and LaRusso's neighbor in Kew Gardens. "He's no bathing beauty," Gutwillig conceded when Broun's name came up, "but he's something. They may tell you he's a gin-swilling, poker-playing bum —and such a lazy bastard he takes a cab from one side of the street to the other—but I'll tell you one thing—he's no phony. He risked his career going to bat for Sacco and Vanzetti. When the bad times hit, he'd walk the breadlines and hand out whatever he had in his pockets —twenty-dollar bills even, sometimes. And when the guild started, he was always there in the crunch. I saw him out in Newark during the *Ledger* strike, in the freezing cold, cracking wise to keep everyone's spirit up, making sure there was coffee and rolls and the pickets had enough clothing. The rest of him may be a mess, but his heart's not."

Toby was 90 percent persuaded. There were a few things still troubling him, though, he confessed to the two guildmen. The argument that union membership compromised the independence of a newsman they rebutted eagerly. "It's just the opposite," LaRusso said. The added economic security the guild gave a man armed him against illegitimate influences; he could be that much more skeptical and less vulnerable to press agency, bribery, the blandishments of politicians, and service as the publisher's lackey.

"And how come they've always trusted us," Gutwillig added, "not to bring our own biases into the story while covering every other kind of news, but now all of a sudden that there's a guild, we're all going to turn into propagandists for labor? That's unadulterated bullshit." The alleged intrusion into hiring practices that the guild shop was supposed to constitute, they said, was just another of the publishers' dodges. No paper would be restricted to hiring just from the guild membership list; it would work the other way around—whoever was hired would have to join the guild within thirty days. "No matter how they slice it, management's peddling you baloney."

As they satisfied the last of Toby's reservations, into the nearly empty back room where they were huddled strode that utterly anomalous vision of elegance—Lucius Beebe, in white tie and tails. Tall and trim, he gained stature and wing spread from the top hat and opera cape he also affected. "Ah, a passel of Luddites, if I'm not mistaken," he said, slumping into the large booth against the front wall and looking over toward their table. "And how did your nefarious affair at the Astor go this evening, gentlemen? Wretchedly, I trust. Come join me for a touch of the grape before I am obliged to plumb the gaping maws of the El Morocco menagerie."

His whole Bourbon manner reminded Toby of his late Harvard tutor, the doomed Graham Halyard, but Beebe's exhibitionism was so flagrant that the temptation was to believe he could not possibly be serious. The man was a walking parody of all society's posturing. But he carried it off with such élan that his command to join him was irresistible. On being introduced to Toby, he sensed at once the nature of the discussion he was interrupting. "Ah," he said, "they are trying to lure you into their insidious web—every new little comrade hastens the revolution."

The man's towering disdain seemed less comical when aimed his way. "I'm just listening," Toby said and was at once sorry he sounded apologetic. "Actually, none of it sounds very revolutionary to me. You don't belong, I take it?"

"I? To the Newspaper Guild of America—or whatever the vulgar thing is called? How very perceptive of you, Mr. Ronan." He sniffed the wine bottle the waiter brought and with a wiggle of his fingertip

instructed it to be poured. "No, I do not belong and will never entertain belonging unless a closed shop eventuates—in which case it would
be a nearly even choice between my integrity and my job."

"I think joining takes some integrity," Toby said.

"Do not bandy words, Mr. Ronan, with the great bandier. What I
am saying—lest you are more opaque than you seem—is that I do not
believe in gangs of any sort, and a union is just that—organized for
the benefit of the worthless, discontented, and incompetent to harass
their betters and to prevent ambitious, hard-working people from getting ahead. The guild, of course, is nothing but a racket of the most
patent order, and why newspaper reporters should want to associate
themselves with anything so shabby, degraded, and spurious, I'm
damned if I know."

Eden Chafee came through the city room on her way home from
work one afternoon a few days later and whispered into Toby's ear
that she had to have lunch with him—the following noon if possible—
and for him not to do anything rash till then. Toby, mystified, agreed.

They met at a Greek place on Eighth a few blocks above the paper.
She ordered him a bowl of lemon soup and shared his portions of
stuffed grape leaves and baklava—all fresh delights to his palate. "Rash
like what?" he asked, midway through the thick, delectable soup.

"Like joining the guild."

It was the best soup he had ever tasted. "Who told you that?"

"It's a small place—and you have a big mouth. Besides, I told you
once—it's my business to know things about people who count."

"Since when do I count? I'm about the lowest of the low up there."

"You're not low—you're new. It takes time. And you started to
count the day they let you in to Harvard. People know who you are.
And they know everyone who's in the guild. Most of them are
nobodies, Toby, or zealots. You don't need it."

"I may someday—who knows? And it's more than my own skin
that's involved. It's a question of social responsibility."

"Whose—to whom? Your responsibility is to yourself—not to do
things in the name of some fancied principle that's going to hurt you."

He put down his spoon and wiped the residue of soup from his lips
with the cloth napkin. "Why does it matter to you?" he asked. "I'm
not your ward."

Her eyes danced over him quickly and then settled on his empty
bowl. "I like you," she said, "that's all. And I don't enjoy seeing people I like make fools of themselves."

It came out of her like a slip of the tongue, a kindness you would
toss at a dumb animal, with nothing invested in it. She *liked* him.
Good Christ, but could she *feel* for him? Could a sleek creature like

her feel for anyone? Her flow of words was second nature; neither harm nor benevolence was intended. It just amused her to have an audience.

"I see," he said. "That's very considerate of you."

"Now don't you be lousy when I'm trying hard to be a good girl."

"Maybe I don't much enjoy being thought a fool."

"But that's why I'm trying to head you off. You can't be expected to know the whole score, coming in here cold like this. The guild is a test of loyalty in management's eyes. I'm just letting you know—for your own good. If that makes me a busybody, well, *tant pis.*"

There was something there, he could tell—there had to be. Something in her that was responding in contained measure to the pull on him the very sight of her exerted. She did not have to do this. Or be as kind as she had been to him since Sardi's. It was beyond kindness, he was sure, yet he could not name the intensity of emotion. Less than his own, was all he knew. "I'm not unappreciative," he said, "but I could hardly expect you to understand my situation."

"It so happens I voted for Roosevelt—and so did my father, if it's of any interest. He manufactures paper bags for a living, which no doubt makes him a bloody oppressor of the masses in your eyes, but we're a quite enlightened bunch, it might amaze you to know. Why wouldn't I understand, Toby?"

"Because—of the way you live."

"How? You mean doing things?"

"Every night—and without regard to the expense. I guess it's fine if you can pay, but it's not the real world—not mine, anyway."

She folded her hands in front of her and, head bent but eyes upturned to his, said, "I'm sorry everyone doesn't have my advantages, Toby—but they don't—and they can't. And I don't intend to flagellate myself because of it. I'm determined to enjoy life even if the world wants to make me feel guilty—because I didn't make that world, and I can't cure its ills—though I'll give what I can back to it someday, somehow. The fact is, I am honest, loyal, industrious, respectful to my elders, have the highest personal morals—and my stocking seams are always straight. If all that doesn't count and I'm nothing in your eyes but a rich bitch, then I'm sorry I bothered."

She could turn on a dime from insufferable to embraceable. There was nothing to her—and everything. She was all glitter and breathlessness—yet quite touchingly genuine. She made him feel worthless one instant and passionately prized the next. Like the buoyant ravages of a fever. "I like you better than I do Richard Townley Crandall the Eighth," he said. "What's he got besides money?"

"The taste not to do things beneath his dignity. You should learn."

V

He began to go shopping with Sylvia Wasserman almost every afternoon, even if there was nothing he really needed. He could always think of something to get—a bar of soap, a quart of milk, pencils at the five-and-ten; she never questioned the minimal nature of his errands and was clearly glad for the company.

They would leave after she had served Victor his lunch and Babette had gone off to her nap. It was the warmest time of day, but still they walked fast to ward off winter's sting. Every few days they would stop for fifteen or twenty minutes at Ellman's, the fancy coffee shop a few doors from the haberdashery, and have a little something. Those were the times when Sylvia unburdened herself to him.

She was almost but not quite resigned to the narrowness of her life. There was so little space within it for herself, she told him, and no pleasing her relentless mother-in-law. She nagged incessantly—why weren't Milton's shirts ironed better? Why did she let the boy pick at his calf's liver when it was good for him? Why did she waste her money at the beauty parlor every month? The only relief Sylvia got from her all week was when she marketed, when Milton took the old woman to the Friday-night service at the big synagogue on the next block, and when she herself went to do the Saville Shop bookkeeping after closing on Saturday.

"But it's your home," Toby said. "Why can't you stand up for your rights in it?"

"It's my home but not my house," said Sylvia. "That's part of the problem. We couldn't afford it by ourselves, so Milton asked her for a loan. She came in the bargain."

"But if you let Milton know the advantage she takes, wouldn't he—?"

"Any time I start in, he says it's ingratitude—or that I should remember the frailty of her condition. He even calls Ira's every other day when we take our week vacation in Asbury over the summer—just to see how she's getting along."

Toby sighed, not wanting to offer anything that would add to her frustration. "For your sake," he said, "I only hope Victor turns out to be half as dutiful a son."

"God forbid! I'd rather he shoot me first than let me be a burden to him." Sylvia's round, ruddy face grew grim and overcast. "To tell you the truth," she said, flicking absently at a piece of pie with her fork, "there are days I want to murder her myself." The horrid confession hung in the air for a painful moment as she looked up at him with suddenly pitiless eyes. "And nights when I go to sleep praying she'll be dead in the morning." She pushed the pie plate to one side. "But if it ever happened, I'd never forgive myself."

"Why? She's put you through enough torment. Besides, you could go into business then as an authentic witch."

"Oh, you're awful," she said, smiling at his effort to jolly her out of the dumps. "But so am I for bothering you with all this."

"I'm glad to be of service. Anyhow, all life's a learning experience."

Remarks like that made her think him wise beyond his years. Such an impression, coupled with his kindness and availability, began to deepen her gratitude toward him for lifting her temporarily out of the imprisoning rut her life had become. In short order, she grew dependent on their little outing as the highlight of her day; the disappointment reflected in her face when some other activity of his intruded.

One afternoon, after he heard her telling the old woman that she was off to the beauty parlor, Sylvia took him instead for a lunch at Steinberg's, the dairy restaurant in the block between Loew's and the R.K.O. Toby had passed the place often, wondering what the kosherers did to sanctify their non-meat cuisine—and why the restaurant's name on the neon sign in front was all red except for the "i," which was green. Sylvia said she had never noticed the irregularity but assured him the food was excellent. She ordered him borscht with a boiled potato and sour cream followed by cheese blintzes also with sour cream. The borscht had body, and he liked the contrast between the hot potato and the cool pink soup that dyed it to look like a piece of rare beef. The blintzes were midway between a fritter and a crepe and far too rich for him to finish. Even so, she was pleased with his favorable verdict.

They went afterward to the big toy store across the street so she could buy Victor a present for his birthday. "I want to get him something, too," Toby said, but she objected that he had been more than kind already to the boy. "Something very small, then," he said. While she searched among the board games in the rear, he settled on a two-dollar penknife and hid the box from her after it was gift-wrapped in case she would think he had splurged.

At her door, she hesitated a moment, as if remembering she had made up the story to her mother-in-law about the beauty parlor and not bothered till then to figure out an excuse for not having gone.

"You could just say you got the appointment day mixed up," he said, guessing her thoughts.

She welcomed his complicity with a soft smile. "Yes," she said, "that's what I was thinking." Her hand reached up to his face and gave it two small pats of thanks. "We're having a little party for Victor on Sunday—cake and ice cream and the presents. Come if you can —he'd like that a lot."

"Me, too."

"Me, three." She gave a girlish giggle and unlocked her door.

The party began at three, when Toby came, with everyone joining in a game of Monopoly. Because it was his day, Victor was allowed an extra five hundred dollars in play money. His grandmother was nonetheless keen in her pursuit of victory, following her usual strategy of trying to snap up the side of the board with the maroon and orange properties, which she instructed Toby were the very best buys, considering the building costs and the rents they yielded. The game was declared over at five-thirty with Toby pauperized, Sylvia hanging on with the yellows, Milton doing well with the light blues and greens, Babette refusing at any price to trade her son Park Place to go with his Boardwalk, and Victor narrowly but exultantly leading with hotels on the cheap purples, houses on the reds, both utilities, and three of the four railroads. "Finally," said his grandmother, "'ve got maybe a businessman in the family."

Sylvia put out a light supper with birthday cake à la mode for dessert while the boy opened his presents. There was a game of Camelot from his mother, a brownie camera from his father, a dress shirt and tie from Babette (courtesy of the Saville Shop), one of the Terhune dog books from his Jersey cousins, and the penknife from Toby. "*Guttinu!*" his grandmother exclaimed on seeing the knife and added other Yiddish lamentations.

"She's afraid he'll cut off his thumb," Sylvia explained, even as Victor was gently touching his index finger to the blade and thrilling at its sharpness. It was his toes she worried about, said Sylvia, having seen the children on the block playing "territory" in the islands of earth where each tree rose up out of the cement. "It's a boy thing, Ma," she added with resignation.

"For *schgutsim*," the old woman said, shaking her head darkly.

"Who's that?" Toby asked, fearful he was newly corrupting Victor.

"Never mind," Sylvia said. "It's a very nice gift."

One March afternoon with intimations of spring in the air, she was in a buoyant mood so they stopped after the butcher's on Amsterdam for sugar buns at the bakery next door and, on the way back, at the lending library on Broadway. She had been laboring all winter to get through *The Brothers Ashkenazi*. What sort of novels did he enjoy, she wondered—she would like to read and understand what a Harvard man chose. He should not suppose, she said, that because her education had been limited to high school and a year at a business academy, she was illiterate. She loved to read in bed, though Milton was always dropping off right away, and soon she would begin feeling guilty that the bed lamp was somehow denying him the full benefits of Morpheus.

He picked her out *The Big Money*, saying Dos Passos was socially significant; Huxley's new novel, *Eyeless in Gaza*, noting that the author was a greatly gifted wit and stylist, and *Absalom, Absalom!*, the literary event of the previous fall among the cognoscenti. "Now Faulkner's prose is a little dense," he explained, "and some people think he's just a regionalist, but his themes are universal and his characters archetypal so what emerges attains an elemental and almost mythic power—if you see what I mean."

"I think I'll do the Huxley," she said, looking more puzzled by than grateful for his instruction but promising to report back to him, though she could not say when.

Sylvia's airy spirit prompted him to turn the tables and enlist her taste at the antique shop on the corner of Eighty-ninth. It was time he got something to decorate the walls of his apartment—nothing very expensive but enough to break up the blankness. They examined the entire stock of the place before settling on a framed old mezzotint of a hay wagon at an English country crossroads. Giant overarching oaks cast a caressing shade upon the scene that transported Toby to a dreamland devoid of subways and slotmen. Sylvia, admiring the flaking gold frame more than the composition, judged it a bargain at three dollars.

So caught up were they in domestic considerations awakened by the tranquil picture that they rushed right by her front door and were halfway up to the second floor before realizing. Sylvia halted abruptly and began to explain the mindless impulse: "But where will you put it?"

"In the sitting room."

"Of course," she said. "Which wall, though?"

"I—hadn't really thought." He dropped his eyes, shielding himself with the frame. "Would you come up and give me your advice?"

"If you like," she said. "Just for a minute or two."

They resumed the climb, less spontaneously now. "It's not all that neat, I'm afraid," he said, "but nothing unsanitary."

Once inside the door, which he left wide open, he set the picture down with care and surveyed the walls for a likely hanging spot. When he turned back toward her, Sylvia was close beside him, arms full of packages that were the only barrier between them. Slowly, as if of their own weight, the packages fell away, books and beef and buns

and the rest, and they touched, almost imperceptibly at first, then unmistakably, leaning against each other, arms still at their sides. Her
face nestled under his chin, warm and smooth on his neck, and her
breasts made full, definite contact. They latched together that way for
a noncommittal moment before he slowly reached his arms up and
surrounded her open coat in a silent, confirming embrace. Their faces,
though, stayed apart. Finally, her head against his chest, she whispered, "Are you lonesome, Toby?"

"Not around you," he said, throat sticking.

"That's what I've been thinking—lately." She brushed her face
against him in a tender, rocking motion. "I shouldn't be here like this."

"The landlady's allowed to check up on the tenant."

"I'm not that sort of woman, Toby—"

"I know—I was kidding. I shouldn't have—"

"Whatever else is wrong, I wouldn't—I couldn't ever—it's not—"

"I know."

"I have to go," she said, not going. "I'm expected—Victor's due
home from school soon—I'm a married woman—we're very—I mean I
couldn't even—"

"I know," he said, stirred by the warm mass of her upon him, feeling wanted, and wanting. She was not really old enough to be his
mother.

VI

"Boychik! Boychik! You got the right place!" Wally Eichhorn
yelled over to them as Toby and Dan Jonas, his ticket of admission,
hesitated at the door to the mob scene. "Come help us break the fire
laws—it's all for the good of the cause!"

Wally, in a thick, oatmeal sweater that billowed about the top of his
wispy torso and a pair of floppy dungarees, had to fight his way to
them through the crowd that threatened to elbow down the whitewashed walls of the packed studio-loft. Perhaps sixty feet long and
fifteen or so feet high, it was a stark hollow except for two daybeds
shoved into the corners, a couple of canvas chairs, a long, low table of
pine boards stretched over cinder blocks, and a great diaphanous scrim
in cheesecloth painted with flowers and hung from the ceiling. That
left room for tons of people, all trying to make themselves heard
above the anguished wail of Bessie Smith on the phonograph behind
the lacquered Chinese screen at the far end of the enormous chamber.
The sink and stove were back there, too, judging from the spicy
aroma of cooking paella.

"We roll up the rugs now—people kept burning holes in them and spilling wine," Wally explained, ushering them through the throng. "The plants, too, we have to hide—they kept getting pissed on. Oh, it's a very civilized bunch." They were mostly legitimate artists and intellectuals, with a nice interlarding of poseurs. "The louder anyone is," Wally offered as a guide, "the less important. The shouters, ignore altogether." Theatrical people were strongly represented, given Wally's connections and those of his roommate, whom he introduced to Toby and Dan at the top of his lungs. "This is Kenny Lomax, who aside from his other virtues is the best set designer in town, bar none. Kenny, meet a couple of not-so-loyal stooges of the capitalist press."

Hipless and long-haired, with a touch of blue eye shadow to add drama to boyish good looks just beginning to erode at the edges of each pretty feature, Kenny used both his hands to grasp their extended ones. "You're angels to come," he said, "and don't let anyone browbeat you into giving—we just let them use the place. Actually, we're with the Falange." His smile disclosed almost as much silver as enamel. "Go get yourself some beer and pretzels—the divine Nina's *pièce de résistance* won't be along for hours."

A young black man in a blacker turtleneck and coral necklace sat cross-legged beside the serving table, passing out paper cups of white jug wine and dispensing beer from a keg into glasses he seemed to take perverse delight in filling with the tallest possible head. "An amateur barkeep," Toby said, sucking up some of the surplus foam before it spilled.

"On the contrary," said a female voice behind him. "He's told to pour into the middle of the glass—the keg lasts twice as long that way."

Toby turned into the incandescent face of Nina Orloff, who brushed a kiss off his cheek and took Dan Jonas's hand with gusto. She had on a handsome suede skirt that Toby assumed to be her mother's handiwork and an embroidered blouse under a long-sleeved black sweater that covered but hardly hid her womanly form. "I hear that's why the Loyalists aren't winning," he said. "They fill their guns the same way."

"Too true, I'm afraid. But we're trying." She put her hand on his wrist to keep him from being borne off. "I'm really glad you showed up—it was Wally's idea, I want you to know. You shouldn't think I've made your moral redemption the consuming mission of my life." The smile was tentative. "Look, just make yourself at home—nobody here's intimidating except the phonies. I wish I could stay with you awhile, but I've got to watch the food—and everything else—I'm sort of the den mother. Don't forget to sign the register—you'll get invited automatically next month if you survive this one. And guess who gets to send out all five hundred post cards?"

The talk was a melange of art, politics, sex, money, name-dropping, and self-promotion. ". . . And if you have a talent—real talent—the problem is worse," a lean woman in a long dark beaded dress was telling the group beside which Toby and Dan drew up. "I mean, how much can you sacrifice for your social beliefs and still have enough left over for your creative work? When I'm practicing, I feel guilty as sin for all the oppression and injustice in the world and think I should be out there working my behind off for the revolution. And yet when I do my bit for it—I'm not even a regular, you understand, just sort of a camp-follower—and I don't even do what I do for them very well—hell, then I'm wishing selfishly all the time that I could be playing my fiddle. It's enough to make you certifiably schizophrenic. . . ."

Passionate phrases and shrilled snatches rose on all sides of them but never intersected: "Thunder Thighs, he calls me—I don't know whether to hit him or hug him!" "The British Cabinet's been talking blockade for months, but they've got no balls for it. . . ." "If you don't count the Hollywood people, the only high-salaried female in the country is the Mars woman—and she inherited the candy business. . . ." "Trotsky's warning there's a seventy-five percent chance of war, but who's going to hear him from Mexico?" "They say Mae West goes to church every day because her mother was a Jew. . . ."

Through the din, a paunchy, bearded basso profundo in thick glasses was insisting to a ring of listeners that it was not necessary to be a communist in order to subscribe to the Marxist interpretation of history. "You've got Veblen and Beard as clear cases in point—loyal American economic determinists," he argued, "and you know Columbia is no hotbed of Muscovites. To recognize class warfare as the universal condition of man—or that George Washington and the Founding Fathers were the plutocrats of their time and so naturally devised a political system to feather their own nests—I mean that's not Bolshevism, those are hard facts."

The voice was familiar. Toby studied the face for a moment, trying to debeard it. The fellow felt his stare, glanced up, and beamed in instant recognition. The two had not seen each other, Melvin Kantor exclaimed, since their days together in the Harvard cell of the National Students League. Precocious then in his warnings against the maniacal strain in German culture that was feeding Nazi brutalism, he held forth now as an instructor in philosophy at N.Y.U. and wrote occasional pieces for the Leftist press. "I don't know what I am anymore," Melvin said, breaking away from his group and joining the two of them against the wall. "Everyone's a social democrat, and everyone's for the Popular Front—and meanwhile we're all being manipulated by the party because Spain's going down—of all places. Good Christ, Spain hasn't been up since the Armada was sunk."

"What party?" Dan asked. "I thought this thing was nonpartisan."

"Nothing's nonpartisan now—not even the Red Cross." Paella suppers like this one to raise money for the Spanish Loyalists may have been a specialty of the nominally unaffiliated League Against War and Fascism, Melvin said, but everyone knew the Communist Party supervised the effort and took in the money. The two queers whose loft it was were only sympathizers, he confided, but it was common knowledge they had close family ties to the party. He directed their attention across the room to a stocky, balding man in a leather zip jacket with a dark scarf hanging loose around his open collar. "That's Pete Lomax—the C.P. section organizer for the East Side from Twenty-third to Houston."

Dan looked uncomfortable, suddenly fearing he had fallen in among a band of revolutionaries. Melvin reassured him that while there may have been a dozen party people or affiliates in the room, Kenny Lomax's brother was the only *apparatchik*. A City College graduate and son of a prominent trade unionist, Pete Lomax was known to have converted from socialist ideologue to radical activist in the early 'Thirties. The turning point came, as Melvin heard it, after a couple of scab painters had taken a job in old man Lomax's neighborhood, and he and Pete decided to put a stop to it by themselves. One of the scabs tried to run, but Pete's father stuck his foot in the way and the painter went sprawling head-first down two flights of stairs, splitting his skull and breaking his neck. The other one tried to scramble down from his ladder, but Pete kicked it out from under him, then landed on the fallen scab, smashed him senseless, ripped his clothing off, painted him from head to toe, genitals included, with his own brush, and then shoved the brush handle up the guy's ass. By the time the cops came, the Lomaxes were nowhere to be seen. Ever since, Pete had the reputation for being as strong-armed as he was iron-willed and silver-tongued. "You'll hear him," Melvin said.

Bessie Smith went off, and the intense violinist who had been registering her torment over the opposing pulls on her of art and politics—she was introduced as Sandra Something—performed Mozart and Mendelssohn above the murmuring crowd. Then a young actor with a haunted face probably earned by malnourishment recited some verse by Rupert Brooke and Walt Whitman before Nina marched the paella to the center of the room and began serving modest portions with

Italian bread and cole slaw on paper plates. Toby ate in a corner with Dan and Melvin, who soon interrupted his eating to befriend Wally in a clash on the merits of the revolutionary theater. Depression realism, argued a heavy-lipped radio writer and would-be playwright named Meshantie, deserved ranking with European modernism because the two shared the essential quality of social consciousness. "But being furious is not enough!" Wally yelled, displaying the effects of too much wine. "Art isn't just an engorged piece of life. It has to distill it—it has to transform it—the way the Europeans do—"

Meshantie coolly stood his ground. "The theater, by its very nature, is a social transaction. Registering fury *accessibly* is the essence of dramatic art."

"That's horseshit!" Wally shrieked so that the whole room heard him and stilled to listen to the exchange. "Histrionics don't become art just by virtue of being understood—"

"No, but being understood is a precondition of all art that aspires to be affecting. And the plainer the point, the more likely it is to serve society."

Melvin Kantor jumped on Meshantie's dialectics. "So Odets and Lawton and the others are every bit as valid as Pirandello and Brecht and Lorca?"

"Every bit as meaningful and useful, certainly."

"Useful how?" Melvin asked hotly. "Telegrams are *useful*, too—and they're better than plays for sending messages—but they're not art."

When the tempest finally receded, Pete Lomax arose like a pillar of civility in the center of the room and broadcast a calm, steady look meant to heal the doctrinal breach. "There may well be issues that divide us," he said in a voice full of command and ragged with the grain of city streets, "but one thing we're all agreed on—if Madrid falls, we fall, too. Some of us may find it hard, in following the war over there, to keep it all straight—to tell the U.G.T. from the C.N.T. or the P.O.U.M. from the Basque Nationalists, just as over here it's not easy at times to separate the elements of the Leftist coalition and what each stands for. But we all recognize one thing—if Spain dies as a social democracy, liberty dies everywhere, and tyranny tightens its terrible hold on the globe."

With little rhetoric, he updated conditions in Iberia. True, Franco's armies held thirty-three of the fifty provincial capitals but not the more populous and industrialized areas—and not the metropolitan heart of the nation, so long as Madrid and Barcelona and Bilbao remained in Loyalist hands. And it was not only a defensive war the republic was waging; a large Italian contingent had just been routed near Guadalajara. But in a distressing sense, the Loyalist effort was indeed a holding action, for while Italy and Germany supplied men and weapons to Franco's fascist forces, London and Paris dithered, favoring non-interventionist pieties to reinforcing beleaguered Spanish democracy, and America formally insisted the squabble was Europe's, as if having learned nothing from the Great War. Only the hard-pressed Soviet Union was doing what it could to uphold the cause of humanity and social justice in Spain—and that, sadly, was not enough. So the Loyalists sent untrained and underequipped men into combat, and the results were all too predictable. They were fighting with defective rifles, Lomax told the room, thoroughly hushed now except for the soft hissing of exposed steam pipes, and many soldiers had to abandon ill-fitting helmets for cloth caps, frail comfort against field bombardments and murderous German air assaults. Money from America would help train and arm and dress them. "We do not applaud needless death," he said at the end, his legs apart and arms at his sides and head high, "but better for a man to die young in a noble cause than to live a long life without one."

To hold the mood of tragic urgency, a guitarist performed classical Spanish pieces while Nina, Kenny Lomax, and one or two others circled the room, soliciting donations with a breadbasket instead of a collection plate. Afterward, Wally rolled out a spinet piano from behind the Chinese screen and joined Sandra, the violinist, and the guitarist in a string trio as the loft turned into a dance hall. Groups of ten formed into handholding circles all over the room, and Wally, standing while he played, called out the turns to the Big Apple with perspiring exuberance.

Big-bottomed Melvin Kantor joined in, glasses steaming, and even Dan Jonas, caught up in the communal gyrations that dashed them together like a giant bowl of whipped protoplasm. Toby, though, hung back, telling himself he felt about dancing the way he did about marching. Then, out of nowhere, Nina grabbed his hand and organized a circle of wallflowers. Her face was wet and eyes gleamed and curly hair seemed to come unsprung as she showed him how to follow Wally's hoarse, frenetic calls: "Truck to the right . . . reverse it . . . now to the left . . . and in place . . . stomp that right foot . . . swing it . . . all right, every-body, shine! Suzi-Q to the right . . ." Bodies floated and fannied and flew around him while Wally kept reeling them off—the shag, the Charleston, the Lindy, the Black Bottom, London Bridge and a dozen more square-dance turns, and even some sort of Indian rain dance—and Toby grew hotter and dizzier and ludicrously farther from the called step till it was all one consuming swirl Nina was lashing him through. Finally, everyone was leaning back and raising arms high to the ceiling as Wally, a distant croaking dervish by now, sang out, "Everybody, praise Allah!" whereupon they all collapsed in place and howled their sated pleasure.

Nina lay there panting beside him, drained of the manic energy that had driven her nonstop through the evening. "What did you think?" she asked him after catching her breath.

"That I dance like a whale," Toby said. He offered her a sip of the wine at the bottom of his cup.

"No, thanks—I've had a ton." She drew her sweater back on and blotted the moisture from her hairline. "I meant about Lomax."

"He's—very dynamic."

"Can you understand now—what he said about having a cause to die for? I feel that. Sometimes I wish I were a man so I could go join the Brigade—but then I tell myself this is helping—what we're doing —in some small way." They were singing "Solidarity Forever" now, and then it turned into "The Internationale." Nina joined in for a few phrases. Toby's stony silence made her sit up. "How can you bear not having a cause in life?" It was an accusation, not a question.

"I have a cause," he said, gulping the last of his wine and crumpling the cup. "I want to survive honorably, not die young. Causes are someone else's idea of virtue—a way out of loneliness." Lubricated by more wine and beer than he remembered, the words came out of him like crisply parsed aphorisms. "But there is none, Nina—political causes are as delusionary as religious ones—though maybe more frankly expedient—"

"God," she said in disgust, holding her head with her hands, "you sound like a dried-up old fart." Wearily she climbed to her feet. "I've got to clean up."

When the anthems of the Left were over and the crowd began to empty out onto the stairs and down into Lafayette Street, Toby felt a sudden surge of revulsion. Positive he had been used to dishonor his country and pay homage to the compassionate Soviet soul as defender of freedom and justice for all, he stood up and began to sing "America the Beautiful." He sang at the top of his lungs, indifferent to his semidrunken state. His voice had the tonal purity of sandpaper on a Mason jar. People turned on their way out and joked about tossing him a coin. But he kept on singing until Wally mercifully picked it up on the piano, complete with rippling arpeggios to signify all those fields of grain. And then the room was empty except for them and Dan, and Nina and Kenny Lomax, picking up the litter.

He went to say thanks to Wally, who lay folded on his bed in the corner, drinking directly from the last wine bottle. "Givin' you a tough time, huh?" Wally said, wiping away some wine that had sloshed over his chin and neck.

"Who?"

"The kid." Wally turned his head over his shoulder toward Nina, who was scouring the stove with mindless devotion. Toby conceded their rift and reported with a laugh what she had called him. "She's a real pisser, given half a chance," Wally said. "And the sad thing is, she doesn't see it any more than Saul and Adele do—all this living for and through the party—"

The words carried, as they were meant to. "Doesn't see what?" Toby asked, drawn in by the little man's powers of provocation.

"That they're using it to hide from themselves. Nina can't see it anymore—if she ever could as a kid. But Adele's my baby sister and I know what her life's been, Toby. The party fills in all the gaps—all the shortcomings. It's a thing they can love without worrying it won't love them back, so they give themselves to it body and soul. They're not idealists or dreamers, most of them, and certainly not serious revolutionaries. What they are is misfits—square pegs—failures—nonentities—and can't face up to it—that they've got nothing to offer society —and society's repaid them with nothing, so they decide the fault's not in themselves or the stars but in the whole fucking system, which they have to tear down—*Vive la révolution!* And heaven help anyone standing in the way—"

"Stop it!" Nina shrieked, wheeling on them from the stove and hurling her scouring pad. "Stop poisoning him, you—you—"

"He's my friend—he's entitled to know my opinion—"

"—dirty little prick!" She clapped her hands over her ears as if to keep out her own profanity and screamed, "Stop it! Stop it! Stop it!" She stood sobbing uncontrollably for several moments, flooding the room with her vehemence, then crumpled, as much from exhaustion as fury, and passed out.

Her forehead felt fevered by the time he and Dan brought her home in a cab. In the morning, when Toby telephoned to find out how she was, Nina answered herself, sounding like death with a hangover. She was all right, she said, but Wally was not; he had suffered a stroke about an hour after they left—and there was no telling yet how bad it was. Her parents were with him at St. Vincent's. "I guess it all caught up with him."

The news knotted his insides. Wally Eichhorn was hardly more than a stranger to him, but he had never met anyone more alive, or compassionate, or feeling, or brave in the teeth of a life that had not much favored him. The little man's unexampled verve bore no relationship to his years. To think of him reduced to inanimate tissue, perhaps never again to exclaim or exult, saddened Toby to the brink of hollering "No!" at whatever power ruled heaven and earth. Some losses were irreplaceable. "You can't blame yourself," he said finally, sensing through his enfeebled rage that she felt implicated. "It was all that exertion—"

"I didn't help any."

"He was being—a little abusive—"

"But he's always that way. I shouldn't have let go at him."

"Look, I was the one who stirred him up—telling him what you said."

"Toby, you don't understand him," she said, struggling to control her voice. "That was just an excuse. He has to mock what he doesn't know how to deal with—or feel. It's his way of punishing the rest of the family—because—I mean we've always accepted him, but he's always had his doubts, don't you see? And the thing is, what he told you was garbage. He believes in the same things we do—only he's never been willing to give in to his better instincts. Commitments make him nervous—maybe because no one's extended him any— besides us." She was crying now, he could hear. "You're that way, too."

Was that their link? He felt his eyes filling in response to her choked sounds and fond indictment. "Maybe," he said.

She was too weary to pursue the point, yet hung on the line, trying to swallow her grief. "By the way," she said, with momentary pluck, "you sing worse than you dance." Then the mordant mood over-whelmed her anew. "Oh, Toby!" she cried and wept openly into the receiver.

When he got to the apartment, nobody answered. At the hospital, he would be an intruder. He walked away the afternoon alone.

SEVENTEEN

HIS FIRST OFFICIAL FUNCTION for the guild was purely philanthropic.

Buddy LaRusso asked him to help pass the hat around the paper for a memorial fund being established in honor of a charter guildsman named Ben Leider, who had been shot down in February on the Madrid front while flying for the Loyalist side. A major force in the New York *Post* unit and a guild activist, he had picketed in four strikes against metropolitan area papers, and in a grim confrontation with the Hearst empire at the *Wisconsin News*, Leider had given up his vacation to fly his own plane out to Milwaukee and drop leaflets presenting the strikers' story. The feat won him renown as "the sky picket," and few who knew of him were surprised when the Russian-born newsman, himself a childhood fugitive from the tsarist pogroms, volunteered to fight fascist tyranny in Spain.

"Now you don't have to do this if you don't want," LaRusso told Toby and said no more. But the implication was plain: Having signed up with the guild, he was obliged to show his good faith. Here was a chore that, while irksome, was neither difficult nor time-consuming. And, after all, the cause was humane as well as just; all contributions to the Ben Leider Memorial Fund would go to buy food, medical supplies, and technical equipment—no guns—for the Loyalists.

Toby was nonetheless hesitant. Identifying himself openly with the guild by soliciting for it invited a devaluation of his standing on the staff that he had not bargained for so soon. In fact, LaRusso's untimely request left him wondering whether it had not been a mistake to join. If militancy, or its appearance, was likely to land him in the *Trib* doghouse, passive membership made scant sense; better to have steered clear altogether. He consulted Dan Jonas about the charitable undertaking.

"Oh, that'll be a very popular cause around here," said Dan. "Let's see—the guy was a Russian, a Jew, a union agitator, and a staffer on the beloved *Post*, beacon of American liberalism. I'd say you might raise as much as—oh, at least a dime if you asked everyone very nicely —and get yourself laughed right out of the city room. Toby, think what you're doing!"

He dodged Buddy LaRusso for a week. He could not bring himself to say a simple yes or no. When the guild unit chairman finally caught up with him at the water-cooler, Toby said he would let him know for sure the following week.

Monday a force of German Junkers and Heinkels appeared in the sky over the ancient Basque capital of Guernica, undefended and far behind the front lines. It was market day, and the peaceful town's entirely civilian population was swollen by shoppers from the countryside. With unswerving German methodicalness, the planes attacked the helpless community for more than three hours. First they dropped bombs and grenades to stampede the people. Then they flew in low and machine-gunned the throngs screaming through the streets and lurching out into the fields. Finally they dropped heavy incendiaries to wreck the houses and bury those who had sought shelter indoors or underground. When they flew off, all of Guernica was in flames, eight hundred were dead, many more maimed, and no military target touched. Franco's radio that night denied the atrocity, charging that the act, without precedent in military history for the manner and scale of its devastation, had been carried out by Republican forces.

The next day Toby took up the collection in memory of Ben Leider—and now the victims of Guernica as well. The logistics of the operation, however, required thought. To go from desk to desk around the city room, badgering staffers at their work, would hardly ingratiate him or his cause. More than likely, it would also get him bawled out for mixing private business with the paper's. Instead of soliciting on the premises, he elected to establish his headquarters at Bleeck's.

Among the late-drinking crowd he needed a patron—someone who might have had no use for the guild or Ben Leider but who had been moved by this latest and gravest barbarity in Spain. Undisputed titleholder as bluffest mainstay in the place was the expansive Metcalfe, who was presiding in the oversized booth beside the front door when Toby arrived. He took a chair at the end of the bar and hung off it sideways, trying to insinuate himself into the conversation that surrounded the ever-ongoing match game. The bombing of Guernica had apparently been under discussion because Metcalfe was saying how the krauts had never worried about the sanctity of civilians, witness the assault on the *Lusitania* and the Black Tom munitions explosion on the Jersey docks in '16, an open-and-shut case of sabotage, even if the charge never was substantiated. The dissection of national character traits wound down, only to give way to still grosser ethnic stereotyping. Much ire was voiced over the decision just announced by the city's licensing commissioner, a La Guardia reformer named Moss, to close all fourteen burlesque houses in the city as detrimental to public morals.

"That's the biggest trouble with Jews," Metcalfe said. "They feel so guilty when they have a good time that they try to stop everyone else from doin' likewise." He felt Toby hanging over his shoulder and spun his large red face around. "What do you say, sonny boy—let's shove 'em all back in the ghetto and save us our pretty titties and grinding Gerties. Kee-rist, the striptease is a gen-u-ine art form—or haven't you ever seen the exposed female anatomy?"

Toby managed a disingenuous smile. "Once or twice."

"I mean what gives this fuckin' Hebe the right to ban an artistic exhibition?" Metcalfe demanded, sliding over and patting the leather booth seat beside him as a signal for Toby to join them. "That's freedom of feminine expression he's violatin'—it's gotta be unconstitutional—isn't that right, sonny?"

"Toby—Toby Ronan."

"Right. This is Toby Ronan, everyone," Metcalfe said, interrupting the match game that was about to conclude on the other side of the table. "Harry Becton's newest baby bloodhound. Give us your learned slant on the ethics of artful exposure."

The rest of the table glanced up at the challenge. Metcalfe was a past master at baiting *Trib* tyros. Toby wished neither to toady nor offend. "I think it all depends how dirty the shows were," he said.

"Dirt's in the eye of the beholder," Metcalfe persisted. "You're not comin' to grips with the principle of the thing. A man wants to make his living off of female nudity and dirty jokes, he's got a perfect right in a free country."

Toby tried to thread the needle without provoking. "I think intimate pleasures become a vice when they stop being private and the public gets charged for them."

"The public gets charged to hear an opera—what's the difference?"

"You can't put on an opera in bed," Toby said and drew a laugh, deflecting everyone's interest back to the game. It broke up a moment later, and most of the players headed home. Metcalfe, though, stayed on, an addicted barfly, and asked Toby to join him for supper. The ox tail was particularly good, he said, if Toby had never tried it. Ox tail he ordered with a rye gag, to Metcalfe's nodding approval. Over coffee he confessed to the blowsy veteran that he needed his help.

"I think you're after blood from a turnip," Metcalfe said, glad to **be** of counsel. "The guild's poison around here—and on top of that, the guys hardly know you." Toby suggested that the cause transcended politics and personality. Metcalfe thought the opposite; the cause mattered less than who was doing the asking. "Why don't you come by tomorrow and join the game?" he said. "That'll get you in with the boys some. And bring money."

He was like a sailor crossing the equator for the first time—at the mercy of nature and his crewmates. Everyone gathered around for the rite of passage. There were nine in the game, and according to the house rules, the inductee always guessed last. They all knew the routine but him. Starting at the newcomer's left and going clockwise around the table, the players hid matches in their fist in the sequence 3–2–1–0 (i.e., the first man held three; the second, two, etc.). That meant a total of twelve matches, excluding Toby's, was held in the first round; depending on how many he hid—within the permissible range of none to three—the correct total had to be between twelve and fifteen, numbers that were all guessed well before Toby's turn. There was no way he could possibly win until the last few rounds, and even then the odds were against him. Letting himself be goaded into side bets as play continued, he professed amazement at his run of bad luck and wound up paying with a smile for everyone's drinks.

By the second day he knew the fix was on. But in view of his mission, he continued to suffer his setbacks in good spirit, consoling himself that the accompanying shop talk was all part of his professional indoctrination. Principal topics included who was the best city editor in memory—the wrathful Charles Chapin of the *World*, electrocuted at Sing Sing in 1930 for murdering his wife (not to mention liquidating reporters by the hundreds), or the genial transplanted Texan, Stanley Walker, formerly of the *Trib* and now pining away, if better paid, on the *Mirror;* who was the finest sportswriter in town ("Runyon," insisted Metcalfe, "because he made poetry out of the ponies— 'Never a handy guy like Sande bootin' them babies in'"), and which mayor was better copy—Jimmy Walker or the Little Flower ("His Nibs lied classier and dressed flashier," one of the city hall men summarized, "but His Nubbin screams louder and chases fires quicker"). On the third afternoon, by which point Toby's losses were earning him some guilt-edged sympathy, the subject was the natural unfitness of women for the newspaper game. "They're okay maybe covering a trial, where the story's all laid out in front of 'em," one of the police reporters charged, "but let 'em have to dig into somethin' and get a little dirty, they expect you to make like Sir Walter Raleigh for them. But God forbid you ask them for anything! Let 'em stick to society shit and keep swiggin' their Lydia Pinkham."

Toby snickered along agreeably with the others and tried not to stop when it came time to pick up the tab again. By week's end, though, he was more than thirty dollars in the hole and sure he had been taken for a ride. Having decided to cut his losses and just pass the hat at Bleeck's come Monday, however meager the take, he went instead on Friday to pay his weekly visit to Wally Eichhorn, recuperating in a nursing home in Chelsea. His speech was still thickly slurred and his right side mostly not working, but Wally listened with apparent gratitude to Toby's diverting account of his misadventures in the match game. Also listening were Wally's other visitors, Kenny Lomax, who came every day to see his stricken roommate, and Saul Orloff, who visited his brother-in-law nearly as often. "If you want a little unsolicited advice," said Saul as they stopped outside the home to buy hot dogs from a street vendor, "I'd say it's a mistake to ask anyone else to make your pitch for you unless you've got the goods on him. Just ask Miles Standish. Your pal Metcalfe's a bastard."

"The whole thing is you've got to dramatize the situation," Kenny added. "Everything depends on how exquisitely you present it."

"It takes conviction," Saul waded in, wolfing his hot dog. "You can't be halfhearted yourself about the guild and its causes and expect anyone else to care. You've done a fine thing in joining—be proud of it! I'll tell you what to do—you come march with us tomorrow. Kenny'll be with the Theatre Guild contingent—the Newspaper Guild's right in the middle there somewhere—" He rummaged in his pocket for a list.

"Saul's a *gonsa macher* on the May Day committee with the cops and the unions," Kenny explained, "to keep it all sweetness and light."

Saul separated some stapled sheets from a collective ream of papers he had tucked away in his various pockets. "Let's see—the guild people form up at two o'clock on Thirtieth just west of Ninth. Everybody helps."

"Thanks, but I'm not much for marching," Toby said.

"Hey, it's not anything like you probably think." Saul slid the list back inside his jacket. "It's got practically nothing to do with communism as such anymore. In fact, it's mostly an A.F. of L. show—which is about as far from Marx as you can get and still be in the American labor movement. There aren't any speeches or demonstrations—just a polite sign here and there and maybe a little singing. It's all disgustingly respectable these days, Toby, with no chance of violence. There'll be an army of cops standing by—"

"I'm really not interested."

Saul met the rebuff with a prosecutorial look. "Okay," he said, "so you're afraid to stand up and be counted. You wouldn't be the first."

"I already count—I don't need anyone else to count me—"

"Sure. I get it. Joining the guild was a private act. It did wonders for your conscience. No obligations or responsibilities are involved—just like any cheap, empty gesture."

"I don't have to prove what side I'm on—"

"Oh, have you got a side?" He raked his gray, lupine eyes over Toby. "Well, I suppose it's hard being a vicarious victim."

Toby was determined not to be bulldozed into it. He thought hard all night, and when May dawned warm and bright, he was still thinking. Labor's legions had been on the move all that spring as never before. The great American industries were being brought to their knees as John L. Lewis and his Committee for Industrial Organization rebelled against the timorous American Federation of Labor and, with federal complicity, forced mass unionism on the diehard makers of steel, rubber, textiles, and that most basic of all American produce, the automobile. In Flint and Detroit, boyish Walter Reuther had humbled lordly General Motors and inspired workers by the tens of thousands across the land, from dime-store clerks to steel-mill smelters, to sit down and refuse to budge till their rights to collective bargaining and humane conditions of employment were recognized. On so clear and hopeful a morning, the tide looked inexorable to many young unionists, of whom Toby Ronan decided, narrowly, he was one.

He wore a white shirt with the sleeves rolled up and no tie, the pair of green fatigue pants he had salvaged from the C.C.C., and his old sport jacket that seemed to go better when slung over his left shoulder. It surprised him to see children among the gathering marchers backed up along the factories and tenements of Thirtieth Street from Eighth to Tenth. There were, as Saul promised, no floats of the proletariat in chains or effigies of Uncle Sam with dollar signs all over his high hat and tails. Displays of partisanship were restricted to signs and placards decorously calling for abolition of child labor, the right of everyone to organize free from terror, release from jail of the long-suffering Tom Mooney, and resolution of more parochial disputes ("End Slavery for Brooklyn Hospital Workers!"). The only outspoken protest was against the dark powers of Francisco Franco and his German and Italian accomplices in savagery. "Drive the Fascists Out of Spain!" a flock of signs declared, and red berets of the sort worn in the International Brigade were spotted by the dozens all along the swelling column of march.

The route went east along Thirtieth to Fifth Avenue, down to Madison Square and its convergence with Broadway, south to Seventeenth, and then east into Union Square. The Newspaper Guild marchers, perhaps seventy-five strong, came—for no reason Toby could fathom—between the Brotherhood of Painters and Plasterers and the Cafeteria Workers Union. The bands were well to the front and rear of them, so they marched to their own unsynchronized tread, in lines badly undulating, through streets nearly empty except for the cops, and yet great good humor held sway. LaRusso and Gutwillig strode side by side in the row behind him, chiding Toby not to dog it. He did not feel much uplifted or daring in the least—only a little silly and self-conscious, especially on the crosstown streets where they were shunted like pariahs infected by foreign dogma, not like the lusty yahoos allowed to celebrate truly American festivals marching the great north-south thoroughfares of the city. There were no thoughts of revolution in his mind or anthems of protest on his lips, although he welcomed the spirited strains wafting back from the ranks of singing schoolteachers well up ahead. He just marched, dutifully but mechanically, in outward accommodation of his unresolved inner quarrel.

As they neared the square, his excitement rose. Spectators massed five and six deep now, bands played with sweaty gusto that somehow coordinated the marchers' steps, and the blurry emanations of a loudspeaker heralded each new unit on its arrival. Union Square throbbed and echoed with cheers and chants, and bulging crowds narrowed the passageway to the reviewing stand. The cops, on foot and horse, stayed to the rear as labor's own marshals, white-shirted men and white-sweatered women in red armbands, good-naturedly drove back the masses to the unctuous importuning of the public-address announcer: "Let's show that workers can maintain discipline!"

Toby was within twenty feet of the reviewing stand when a whistle sounded and the line of march halted. A speaker identifying himself as a state committeeman for the Communist Party took the microphone to introduce Earl Browder, the remarkably unferocious-looking chief of the American *bolsheviki*. He might have been taken for a clerk as easily as the clarion of the revolution. His words, brief and temperate, were followed by a comparably innocuous greeting by proxy from Norman Thomas, cabled from Moscow, where the Socialist Party chieftain was observing May Day at the fount. The whole event was so subdued and conciliatory that Toby thought it more a bloodless charade than a mass rally in the class war.

But then, and only then, flashed a jagged charge of red lightning. The C.P. committeeman raised his right clenched fist in the Leninist salute and beseeched the assemblage to take a solemn oath "to assist the united labor and antifascist movements of heroic Spain." As in a vast game of Simon Says, fists rose in instant obedience along the whole northern edge of the square and all over the reviewing stand, where

Pete Lomax stood in the row behind the speaker and, nearby, Saul Orloff looked down with monitoring intensity. So fierce and swift was the updraft of moral suasion that it felt as if ten million of them were there, fused from every nation and race and faith, drawn from ages past and living and yet to come, thunderously proclaiming the oneness of man and calling down heaven's retributive wrath on all who would deny it. But in that mote of time between the demand that he comply and the onset of his motor response, his every instinct constricted. The outlines of his entire being, the very barrier between him and all the rest of creation that was not him, threatened to tear away irreparably. Toby Ronan would not raise his arm or clench his fist.

Sunday, though, he phoned Saul and arranged to get hold of one of the red berets left over from the parade. With an embalmer's macabre artistry, he ripped it and muddied it and soaked it in beef blood he obtained Monday morning from a neighborhood butcher and then stuck it in the oven to turn caked and charred. At the office that afternoon, he presented it to Metcalfe at his desk: "This is what Ben Leider was wearing when they dug him out of the wreckage. If you'd like to pass it around till it's full, that's fine. If not, you know what you can do with it. Either way, I'm done playing fall guy."

The beret sat atop his typewriter like a sacred relic from Calvary. Metcalfe, looking as if he wanted to cross himself in the worst way, started to sputter apologies: "It wasn't somethin' personal, Toby. But you gotta pay your dues around here first before you can expect—"

"I'm done paying—and thank you very much."

He did not go to Bleeck's at his lunch break that day. But when he came in to work on Tuesday, a man's hat box was sitting at his place on the copy desk with his name on the tag attached. As he undid the bow carefully, half-expecting it to detonate, he sensed every eye in the room on him. Inside the box, wrapped in tissue paper, was the red beret. Underneath it was $137.65 in cash and a note. The note, typed but unsigned, read, "With admiration from the Trib Brigade to the loyal defenders of Spanish liberty. P.S., don't ask us again—the well's dry."

Toby, eyes flooding, glanced around and saw half a hundred heads look away in unison.

This unthinkable feat, coupled with his appearance in the May Day parade, catapulted Toby overnight onto the executive council of the guild unit and caused Becton to rechristen him "Robespierre." As a concomitant of his new eminence, he was prey to Buddy LaRusso's urgent request of the unit leadership to intensify recruiting efforts before the guild's national convention the following month in St. Louis. The meeting would determine whether, as Heywood Broun and the left-wing officers strongly favored, the guild would bolt the pussy-footing A.F. of L. for the militant C.I.O. and open its ranks to advertising and circulation department employees as well as editorial personnel. The loss in exclusivity would be repaid several times over by the growth in bargaining power—enough to bring newspaper management to heel everywhere. "New York's the key," LaRusso told Toby. "Every vote we can get out of here improves our chances in St. Louis. Get cracking."

He tried Dan Jonas the next day.

"I wouldn't join," said Dan, "if Leon Trotsky asked me."

Then he tried Eden Chafee as she was leaving work. "Just think about it—as a personal favor to me—okay?"

"Me—in the guild?" Her eyebrows soared. "You *are* a funny fellow."

"Why not? It's the right and humane thing to do—and you know it."

"All I know is what my father taught me—labor is a commodity."

"I thought he was so enlightened."

"Oh, he is. He takes very good care of his commodities."

"But most bosses don't. They exploit the hell out of them."

"Then they should work somewhere else."

"Did you know that at Stouffer's they inspect the waitresses to make sure they're wearing the right brand and shade of nail polish?"

"A very sensible arrangement. Probably improves their looks and hygiene both. Anyway, I'm not a waitress, so it doesn't really—"

"But you can take a little wider view of the thing—"

"Each class has to look out for its own interest."

"You can't believe that, Eden!"

"I can, and I do. That's how social progress occurs."

"That's how society destroys itself."

"I have to go," she said. "I can't stand in the corridor debating social profundities. Some other time, perhaps."

Direct confrontation was not working out very well. He decided to restrict the rest of his recruiting efforts to an eloquent leaflet he would compose and ask Saul Orloff to run off for him on his mimeograph. During his lunch break at Bleeck's, he had begun to sketch out the tract in his mind when word circulated that the German dirigible *Hindenburg*, the world's biggest airship, had just exploded while landing in Jersey. Everyone who could manage to get himself vertical was wanted upstairs, and fast.

The city room was a study in centrifugal frenzy. The whole paper had already been pulled apart and the first seven pages given over in their entirety to reporting the disaster. Becton and Ward Stakesing, the stoop-shouldered night city editor, were deploying troops as fast as they appeared. The phones were going off all over, the teletypes were exploding like a battery of machine guns inside the wire room, and every pulse in the place was racing against the clock.

Toby picked up a dupe of early A.P. bulletin copy out of Lakehurst and read how the 804-foot zeppelin, giant swastikas painted on its tail fins, flamed spontaneously five hundred feet in the air and tumbled into a heap of molten girders within half a minute. The dead, it was said, were expected to number at least fifty. Handing the wire copy to Dan, he remarked, in a voice he supposed all but inaudible above the office tumult, "Maybe there is a God, after all."

Harris Becton's supercharged features grew taunt. "What did you say, Ronan? Tell me it wasn't what I thought."

"I—was just—reflecting—after what they did at Guernica—"

"Like the Heinies deserved this, you mean?"

"They killed a lot of innocent people over there—"

The whites of the slotman's eyes seemed to swell in ghastly dilation. "You're off this story!" he bellowed. "You'll do police stuff the rest of the night—everyone else does the *Hindenburg*."

"Why? All I said was—"

"I heard what you said—and then you explained it clear as a bell."

"Look, I'm sorry if you—"

"Don't be sorry, Ronan—be smart! You learn to keep your goddamned politics outa this newsroom or they'll be warming up a chair for you at *The Worker*. And nobody worries about God down there." He spun away and began to log in the first copy on the crash.

II

The note inviting him to cocktails at Aunt Winnie's was sufficiently casual to arouse his worst suspicions. "This little shindig wouldn't provide the occasion for you and Richard to announce your engagement, by any chance, would it?" he asked Eden by way of a response.

"What a perfectly tacky notion," she said. "You do those things right or not at all. Anyway, neither Richard nor I believe in long engagements. The fall's soon enough for announcing a Christmastime wedding."

"Too soon, I'd say—in some cases."

"I'll ignore that. I'm not going to try to sell you on Richard's virtues—you're not the one marrying him. But he happens to be extremely bright and competent—and highly attentive and considerate—and quite handsome—and—"

"Well-heeled."

"That, you may rest assured, is not a basis of our friendship."

"Heaven forbid!"

"If you find him so distasteful, Toby, you really needn't bother to come. It's just a little pre-graduation get-together for Richard's law-school chums and some of mine. I thought you might enjoy widening your circle of acquaintance. But if you're determined to keep taking childish potshots at Richard—and me, by implication—you might as well—"

"Sorry, it's just my impetuous youth—and orphaned upbringing. I never learned proper manners or respect for my betters. I'd be delighted."

"Good," she said, "and bring what's-her-name if you'd like—if you're still seeing each other." Disapproval was thick in her smoky voice.

"Nina? Yes, I see her. We're not really romantically attached, if that's what you mean. It's more sort of circumstantial—"

"I won't begin to guess what that means. If you bring her, though, you might suggest a dress this time—charming as her theater outfit was. See you then."

He went alone. The crowd was expensively clothed, merry as the season, and, to judge by the prevalence of cigarette-holders, straining for sophistication. He recognized nobody but the host and hostess. As the bartender fixed him a drink, he considered which was the greater mystery: why he had been asked or why he had come. Perhaps Eden simply needed to fill up the room; perhaps he was drawn simply by the hope of social advantage. Or perhaps the very sight of her fed his bewitchment, and she was pleasured by entrancing.

He gravitated to the edge of a group of Columbia lawyers-in-training. Opinion within it was hotly divided on the merits of impeaching the President for his recent effort to stack the Supreme Court with supporters of his brand of social reform. "He doesn't like the Justices' rulings," said Richard Townley Crandall, smart in tan whipcord, "so the solution is not to question his own policies but to alter the Court. That's your basic despotism in sheep's clothing."

"But there's nothing in the least extralegal about any of it," parried a loyal New Dealer. "It's not as if he's usurping Congress."

"Roosevelt *owns* Congress," Richard dismissed him.

"It's all basically academic, anyhow, since Roberts reversed himself in *Parrish*," another classmate contended. "With Van Devanter retiring now, the President'll have his Court soon enough. The whole business was a transparent ploy to make them come around—that's politics."

"That's conspiracy to subvert the system," Richard declared, "and to give nine old men heart failure. His re-election has turned the man into a cold-blooded tyrant."

"Reactionary twaddle," someone behind Toby whispered in his ear. He turned to confront a grinning Carl Keyes. "Don't you just love these closet fascists calling the kettle black?"

He had grown a tidy little mustache and looked somewhat drawn but there was no mistaking Temple's obstreperous kid brother for a city slicker. There was still something of the pup in his immediate warmth and openness. He had not counted on law school being quite the ordeal it was proving, Carl said in explanation of his presence. More for kindness than cash, Richard Crandall had been acting as his tutor the spring term, and not only in matters legal. He might not make the *Columbia Law Review*, Carl conceded, but at least he knew his way around the Village passably well by now.

Temple had come, too. Carl ushered him over to her without hesitation and, manners improving, discreetly evaporated. She looked stately and bored in a black shantung suit that was too old for her—a slavish tribute to her mother's taste. "Well," she said, with her cool smile, "fancy meeting you here."

"Yes—fancy."

"I—we—you're looking well, Toby. I hope that means your work agrees with you."

"More or less. There's a certain amount of tedium in the beginning."

"Naturally. But I'm sure you'll do fine."

The sight and sound of her, so formidable yet so vulnerable, brought a rush of renewed and convoluted feelings within him. He could detect traces of the welling elements—respect, admiration, understanding, regret—and an abiding anger for having been dispensed with harshly. "Are you?" he asked.

"Perfectly sure. Oh, I knew you would the moment I heard you'd settled on a firm direction."

"So long as it was away from Pittsfield."

"Well—yes—for your own good."

There was to be no concession of regret on her part, that much was clear. She turned at once to the rewards she had been deriving from the city and her studies; her parents had been generous in seeing to it that she and Carl made the most of the opportunities in which New York abounded. She feared, though, that her brother had been pursuing the noncultural aspects of his education too ardently. It was fine that he had Richard to help him along—she had come to the party at Carl's insistence that she meet him and his crowd—but she had her doubts the tutorial influence was positive, all things considered.

"I'm worried to death, to be honest," she said, pulling Toby into a corner. "He's out two or three nights in a row sometimes—all night, I mean—and relies on Richard to pull him through. And when exams come, he goes on Benzedrine—he says no but I've found the bottles, and the symptoms are unmistakable. He's insomniac, he passes out for no reason—he looks—well, you see how he looks. He pulled himself together for this little show, but frankly I think he's falling apart—and his fear of the finals will do him in." She fidgeted with a small silver pin on her collar. "Toby, he won't listen to a word I say."

"And you are your brother's keeper."

"A pretty poor one." She moved closer to him. "The thing is, I don't think Carl wants to pass—I'm afraid he's got self-destructive tendencies. He keeps talking about going off to Spain to fight—he has no idea for which side or what it's all about." Her chin lifted in direct appeal to him. "I hate to ask you, Toby—after everything—but would you speak to him? He's always respected you—and your ideas."

Toby smiled. "And I thought I'd struck out with all the Keyeses."

Carl adjourned with him willingly to the street, where they began walking around the fenced park while Toby attempted to explain his presence at the party as something other than rank social-climbing. In the telling, his distaste for Richard Crandall was badly masked. "Oh, he's not all that bad," Carl assured him. "You've got to consider that his uncle is an ornament of the New York bar while his father made his bundle as a bootlegger. I think Richard thinks he's got something to prove—you know, that the bar-sinister branch of the Crandalls is up to the legitimate one."

Toby looked up in disbelief. But Carl fortified his indiscretion with an assurance that Richard's disclosures were made to him late in their marathon tutorials, generally over the third brandy when the truth would always out. In fact, it was a point of honor with Richard that his father's enterprise—founded on a nightly air run of bonded scotch from Nova Scotia to a landing strip in a Rockland County pasture—had for ten years eluded both the law and the mob. And what immorality had there been, after all, in defying a medieval statute? Richard thought the business comparable to the operations of the merry men of Sherwood Forest and the profits hardly worse than old Boston fortunes extracted from the slave trade.

The news at once lifted Alonso Tobias Ronan, Jr., in his own mind, to social parity with Richard Townley Crandall. His hangdog mood dissipated, and he was all brotherly advice to the self-victimizing Carl Keyes.

"Father says lawyers run the country and always have," Carl began, tracing his disaffection with law school, "and that's what he wants for

me—or at least to run our part of it. He says to look at the big headstart I'd have."

"That's certainly true."

"Sure—except Pittsfield's noplace. And, anyway, who says I ought
to run anything?"

"What is it you want to do?"

"Who knows? Right now I think I'd rather go over to Spain and
shoot the brains out of a lot of fascists—or even Reds, for that matter
—I'm not particular."

"The ideal mercenary," Toby said, hoping to make light of the agitation so evidently gripping Carl. "You'd probably be better off with
the American army, if you want to be a soldier of fortune."

"Hell, no—they march around with brooms all day."

"Yes, but they live longer." Whatever his uncertainties, Toby added
as offhandedly as he could manage, Carl was dooming himself by his
dependence on pills. "Keep it up and you'll flunk out for sure—and
lose your father's confidence—and all the advantages in life it gives
you. Is that what you want, Carl—to be like everyone else?"

"It doesn't seem to have hurt you any." At once Carl reconsidered
the two-edged nature of the remark. "Not that I think you're ordinary—with that brain. I just meant in the way of connections—"

"You're right—they are a little tenuous."

"But that's your big advantage over me—no one's telling you what
to do with your life and arranging it all for you. I've got these
damned marvelous expectations over my head, and heaven help me if I
don't deliver on them." He brushed a hand over the top of a fire hy-
drant as they passed. "The truth is, Toby, I'm not a genius and never
have been. And I don't want to be a millionaire or a captain of
industry—I haven't the ambition or the discipline for it—or the
toughness, either, when you get right down to it. No, Temple's the
one with the brains and initiative and perseverance, but she's too lady-
like to admit it—and too nice a sister to try to step over me."

Toby prescribed a temporizing regimen. First, Carl should kick the
Benzedrine. Second, he should kick Richard Crandall. Third, he
should keep his options open by exerting himself mightily and passing
his first-year law finals. Then he should go somewhere besides the
Berkshires for the summer—anywhere but Spain—and think through
what it was he most wanted from life. Spain was only for if he decided life was worthless.

"Why? I thought that was just the place for flaming idealists."

"If they can tell the sides apart. Your war's inside you."

Carl pondered that analysis. "Is that so terrible?"

"I don't know—I'll tell you when my own's over." He stopped at the locked gate and gave it a testing tug. It would not budge. "You know, maybe that's both our advantage over Richard—suffering doubts instead of compulsions. Not a bad one, either, if you think about it."

Temple sent him a note care of the paper toward the end of the following week, full of thanks for his efforts to steer Carl back to the primrose path. Whatever he had told her brother seemed to be working. He was studying hard, "and without artificial stimulants or prepossessing tutors. And if he doesn't pass, he threatens to do no worse than join the navy—ours—and see the world without benefit of parental dole. I am greatly in your debt."

He waited a seemly three days before writing back on *Trib* stationery. His powers of persuasion, he said, could hardly have been the decisive factor in Carl's welcome reform; it had to be her brother's own native good sense surfacing. "But I will not reject your improved opinion of me," he added, "if it inclines you to consider renewing our friendship. Should such a suggestion cause you the slightest discomfort or sense of disloyalty toward your family, then naturally you ought to dismiss it. But in that event, I hope you may find it in you to tell your parents of my help with Carl so they will not think ill of me forever. I never intended them—or you—the least disrespect in anything I did."

A week passed before her reply came. The interval boded no good. He took it into the wire room to read in privacy:

Dear Toby,

I never thought you had unworthy intentions toward any member of my family, so there can be no question of disloyalty at my end in weighing your suggestion. Your fault, if any, was in failing to deal directly and forthrightly with an ugly situation not of your making. In trying to split the difference between the parties, you showed, in my opinion, faulty judgment rather than bad character.

That episode, at any rate, is ancient history to me. My chief reason for not encouraging you at this time is unrelated. The fact is, I go out with a very nice fellow whenever my happily crowded calendar permits, and I am not as good as some people at dividing my affections, even if time would allow.

As to your other request, I could say yes and you would never be the wiser, but you deserve the truth. However imprudently, I have kept word of Carl's difficulties from my parents, thinking this would only aggravate the problem. Your kindness, I'm afraid, must go unreported.

I hope, however, despite failing you on both these counts, I can leave you with at least one useful thing—a little free advice. Please, Toby, don't fall in again with that same dreadful bunch that took you over back home. For all your intelligence, sensitivity, and idealism, you are very impressionable about worldly things and easily led astray. You have to look out for your own well-being!

You will always be—believe me—a special memory of mine.

Your friend,
TEMPLE

He walked along the river the next morning as far as Seventy-ninth Street, where he stopped to look over the boats. Balling her note into the tightest possible mass, he pitched it into the current and watched it sail off the earth. Becton was right; waters were never melancholy.

III

When he found a sexual collaborator under his very roof that June, Toby at first was wary in the extreme—the likelihood of exposure and recrimination seemed strong. But their fondness evolved into an attachment so suitable to both of their needs that he was as incapable of shunning it as she proved of surrendering forever to the mean demands that had nearly torn all the love from her life.

The relationship was vital to Toby because the other aspects of his life in the city did not precisely abound with sources of emotional sustenance. He had no family he could turn to for that purpose, no friends of either sex he could truly confide in. His work, while worthier than most, hardly taxed his full creative capacity. And his yearning to have a hand in the betterment of mankind entailed risks he was not ready to assume and renunciations he did not yet feel himself in a position to make. He was therefore in all the more urgent need of sexual intimacy, both for the outlet it provided and other longings it might, for a time, replace.

Ideally, of course, Toby would have exercised his sexuality in the company of a woman to whom he was strongly, if not altogether lovingly, attracted. With the removal of Temple Keyes from the list almost as soon as she had been rediscovered, the number of such women of Toby's acquaintance remained at two. And neither was accessible to him in that regard. Eden Chafee was an entrancing enigma, near but very, very far—in another universe, practically, but still maddeningly visible. Nina Orloff presented him with a somewhat different situation.

Much about Nina appealed to him—her intellect, her seriousness, her idealism, her obvious physical ripeness—but she came in a package

so crowded with other commitments that pursuing her beyond a casual pace would have got him nowhere. She had a fulltime job. She
studied nights at Hunter. She helped her working mother with the
apartment. Weekends she did what she could to advance the revolution, played nursemaid to her recuperating Uncle Wally, and saw
other young men besides Toby. His physical relationship to her, to
the extent he could be said to have any, was not quite platonic but had
scarcely advanced beyond the stage of adolescent fumbling. For one
thing, there was no suitable private place to be with her. One or the
other of her parents was always at home or about to be. His own
place was theoretically available, but the one time he hinted at it, she
closed off the option as indecent. That left the movies, which she
found both extravagant and silly except for the Soviet films, with all
their "natural faces," at the Acme, the boxy little firetrap on Union
Square, where she was too rapt to mind, or probably even notice, his
probing hands and brushing lips. Otherwise, he had to settle for a few
moments of clandestine necking at the Orloffs', with Nina poised to
leap at the first click of the door lock, or a little hurried petting at
Wally's studio-loft while Kenny Lomax was out walking the patient.

Given these realities, Toby had no choice but to feed his erotic appetite as he had in the past—wherever chance presented him with a
marginally agreeable partner. He was by no means indiscriminate in
this activity but, rather, too realistic and needy to remain hyperselec-
tive. He was able, as a result, to tame his libido sufficiently to pursue,
without impatience, women who aroused his deepest emotions. Earlier,
the only trouble with this sensible arrangement was that convenience
and not discretion had governed his choices so that his surrogate
lovers eventually proved an obstacle to his quest for a real one. He
was determined now, in taking a new partner, not to grow incautious
once more.

The very peril of discovery, exaggerated by the constant scrutiny
under which Sylvia Wasserman lived, added immeasurably to the excitement. Their confining circumstances imposed certain logistical requirements. She could come upstairs only under a confluence of conditions—when her husband was at the store, her son was at school, and
her mother-in-law was napping—which reduced them to a single hour
on the one day a week, or sometimes two, chosen for their liaison.
Since Sylvia was ostensibly shopping during that time, it was necessary for Toby to go out earlier in the day, with a list she would leave
for him under the lamp on the outside hall table, and do the marketing
for her. The burden was not to be all on her end. At half past one or
so on the designated day, after Babette had gone off to her room, Sylvia would take up her handbag, leave the apartment, give the front

door a slam while remaining inside the vestibule, and then, removing
her shoes, tiptoe up to the top floor and her young Gentile lover.

The whole experience was so nerve-racking for her at first that the
act itself was anticlimactic—and, in fact, impossible to consummate.
Even safe inside his door, she was afraid to speak out for fear her
voice would somehow resonate familiarly four flights below. She
risked only whispers and cautioned him against anything louder. In
time she relaxed enough to talk normally in his sitting room but not to
yield in bed to any outcry beyond a low pant. The result was less than
fulfilling for each of them; his gagged release, after heroic but fruitless
cultivating of her clenched vulva, had to do for them both.

Still, she came undaunted to his door and kept trying. Only when
he convinced her she was more sinned against than sinning did she
start to experience the first spasms of satisfaction. Progress was relatively rapid thereafter. Her needs dictated their pace. Moans and even
cries of pleasure escaped regularly from her now, and afterward,
curling the hair on his forearms, she would openly admire the length
and leanness of him, the tenderness of his touch, the duration of his
tumescence, and a patience she thought remarkable in a lover so short
of experience. Her enjoyment naturally multiplied his own. He could
sense, in the fierce abandon with which she ground her whole irri-
gated bottom against him, the voluptuous delight she had all but forgotten—if she had ever known it.

The very constraints upon the affair helped it prosper. There could
be no pretense that it was anything more than a mutual convenience,
to be grasped and savored as time and the separate flow of their lives
allowed. Having been party to earlier adultery, Toby grew introspec-
tive about his utter absence of guilt over the practice—surely a questionable trait in a young man of professed principle. Guy Curtis's fat-
uousness had no doubt inspired Toby to help the former Miss Holly
Larrabee cuckold her husband, but Milton Wasserman was a pitiable
soul, grubbing his gray life away in a marginal shop on unfashionable
upper Broadway; why was Toby immune to shame for conspiring in
the infidelity of so defeated a man's wife? Because he had abandoned
her emotionally. Because he took her for an object, and his conjugal
rights to be a life sentence on her to serve, honor, and obey him while
he returned nothing beyond her material needs. A wandering wife was
testimony, Toby decided, not to her own promiscuity but to a husband who was selfish, callous, or at least grievously indifferent.

Sylvia's own apparent lack of remorse worked to strengthen this
assessment. Her relish of their lovemaking even suggested, he began to
believe, a strongly punitive motive. She was paying Milton back for
inflicting his mother on her nearly every waking hour of her life. This

ancillary satisfaction, perverse less for its form than the fact that knowledge of it was scrupulously withheld from the objects of her vengeance, Sylvia made sharply manifest to him by spewing out laughter only seconds after they had completed the act with particularly hungry energy. "If only they knew!" she nearly sang.

Toby was less confident that the old woman did not, in fact, know. During Sunday-night suppers, at which he had become a more or less regular guest of the family, Babette would cast her crone eyes over him as if working some Old World spell that would rot his soul. No doubt she could see right through his underpants to his ravaging *goyisch* member. His sociability under such conditions was hypocritical in the extreme, and he would head for the door with thanks the moment the Jack Benny program ended. But when he proposed to Sylvia that these dispiriting Sunday visits should cease altogether, she argued that it was his absence rather than his brooding presence that might arouse suspicion. As to his fears of Babette's occult powers, Sylvia herself would have fallen victim to them long before, she said, had her mother-in-law been able to read minds.

"You and I aren't all she doesn't know about," Sylvia told him one mid-June afternoon. Toby, ensnared, urged her to explain. For all his filial devotion, it seemed, Milton Wasserman kept two dark secrets from his mother that could not be hidden from his wife. One was that his brother Ira stole from their haberdashery business. It was perfectly evident from the books, Sylvia said; there should have been more left in the till each week, and when she confronted Milton with the charge, he conceded it. "He resents it I'm the boss," was how Milton tried to explain away the disgrace, and he would not hear of calling Ira on it. Less tolerable to her was his other secret: Every month Milton paid a gangster $150 in cash for protection. If the money had been withheld, he was sure, the store would have been smashed up, its stock looted, and the family injured—or even done away with.

"But that's extortion!" Toby cried. "He shouldn't put up with it."

"Try telling Milton that."

"He should go to the police—that's what they're there for."

"Don't you think I've told him a dozen times? A hundred, even. He says the mobs have connections with the police—they buy them—so they know who tells on them and take care of them good. He's scared, Toby."

"But that's exactly how the mob takes over—by terrorizing innocent people who don't have the guts to complain. That's a crime in itself—surrendering to evil."

Sylvia lay quietly next to him. "You're young sometimes," she said. "And you don't know a lot about New York."

"I know it'll be corrupt through and through if people don't fight."

"Some fights aren't worth the risk involved."

"You sound as courageous as Milton."

Her head pivoted toward his on the pillow. "I'm here, aren't I?"

Telling himself he owed it to Sylvia, he set out the next day like a knight errant to drive the dragon from the Wassermans' cash register. That the effect of his quest would be to dramatize Milton's impotence and his own virility was incidental to justifying it in Toby's mind. Evil unhorsed was gain enough. He made guarded inquiries at the paper of the men on the crime beat and, after a few telephone calls to pave the way, presented himself at the Woolworth Building offices of that scourge of the underworld—Thomas E. Dewey.

For two years, the state's scrappy young special prosecutor had been investigating the rackets and achieving remarkable results. The dapper Dewey, heading a strike force of fast-moving assistants and two-fisted detectives, had dealt sharp blows to prostitution and policy operations and netted many other fish ranging in size from neighborhood loan sharks to Lucky Luciano. Dewey's raiders struck suddenly, assembled airtight cases, and brought lifelong criminals to their knees in open court. From his picture in the papers, the prosecutor looked innocuous enough—small of stature with slick, jet-black hair and a severely cropped mustache that might almost have been pasted on—but after chief G-man Hoover, Tom Dewey was the country's most celebrated crime fighter. Toby would try him in preference to the precinct stationhouse.

The assistant whose name he had been given was away and his return uncertain, so Toby waited nearly two hours outside that den of eager-beavers until a bright but brusque young man in a dark suit vest and shirt sleeves granted him a five-minute interview. Since he was acting only as an intermediary and had himself not been victimized, Toby was directed to the Civic Vigilantes, a new effort organized by private citizens aimed at gathering tips and calling suspects to the attention of the Dewey office. "This isn't a question of suspicion," Toby protested. "This is a clear-cut case of protection racketeering. Besides, I don't happen to believe in vigilante justice."

The lawman was too busy to debate the matter. As a uniformed officer politely but firmly escorted Toby toward the door, through it from the opposite direction burst the tall, husky form of Rupert Perry Donovan, Harvard '34. "My God, Toby Ronan!" he exclaimed, spotting his old roommate's disconsolate expression before it brightened at sight of him. "What have they got you for?"

After a hurried explanation freed him from the cop's grasp, Rupe led Toby to his jumbled desk and sent out for coffee. He was an hour behind schedule and had eight phone calls backed up, he said importantly, but all that would have to wait a moment. From the ebullience of his greeting, Rupe's genuineness could not be doubted. He had been on the job for only a couple of weeks, Rupe explained, but he could not imagine a better use for his law-school training. Gone was the sneering pedantry that had so repelled Toby his last year in Cambridge, and reactionary tendencies had been supplanted, from all appearances, with those of the rekindled young social reformer. It was a cheering reversion. He was married now, too, to a hometown flame—"daughter of a steel magnate, as they say"—and living in the east Eighties. Toby would have to come by for a visit sometime soon. Any weekend would be fine, Toby said gratefully; he could always be reached at the paper weeknights. Rupe noted down the number with a show of firm intention.

He was equally obliging in the matter that had brought Toby to the office. Their backlog of mobsters ripe for the plucking was vast, but they were always on the lookout for promising cases. Two qualifications were essential: The hood had to be a journeyman at his trade—two-bit punks were not worth the effort and expense required to prosecute them. And his victim had to be willing to testify in court. "Dewey isn't batting a thousand with mirrors," Rupe explained. Toby wondered about the risk of reprisal attendant in testifying against organized crime. The bulk of the office budget went toward pre-trial protection of witnesses, Rupe assured him, and no known cases of a revenge attack had been reported once Dewey put the miscreant away. There could be no guarantees, of course—the public would have to be willing to substitute confidence in the law for fearful submission to terrorism if the mobs were ever to be stamped out. "But if your friend is willing to come forward in court—and we find out the mobster is somebody worth our while—maybe we can do business."

Sylvia became anxious on learning of Toby's uninvited initiative, though he swore to her he had not mentioned Milton by name. At first she accused him of being meddlesome but acknowledged soon enough that his motives were only the best. Promises of police protection might sway Milton, she thought, but it was surely wiser to find out if Dewey's office would get involved before she dared to broach the subject to Milton—and thereby reveal Toby's role. "Just tell me this mug's name, then," Toby said.

"I don't know—Milton doesn't exactly write him a check. And I'm sure the man doesn't leave his card. All he does is always buy a shirt."

"Is there some way you can find out from Milton?"

"How—without letting the cat out of the bag? Anyway, I'd be surprised if he knew the man's real name."

But she herself was aware that the gangster came by for his payoff on the morning of the first working day of each month. Milton used to get jittery in anticipation of his visit, and when Sylvia pressed him for the reason, he confessed it.

That was lead enough for Toby, who, as instigator of the countermove, recognized that he could not remain immune to danger himself if the project was to advance. Borrowing Dan Jonas's father's car on the pretext he had to attend a funeral in Jersey, Toby cemented himself behind the wheel at the northwest corner of Broadway and Eighty-eighth Street, a few doors below the Saville Shop, just before nine on the morning of July 1. Not many thuglike customers were likely to patronize the store before noon—and still fewer probably would emerge with a package the size of a shirt.

Eyes locked to the rear-view mirror he had angled severely sideways, Toby sat in rigid expectation. Would there be a giveaway lump under the mug's shoulder? Would he spot a tail the moment Toby started up the car and dart down an alleyway never to reappear? Or would he lead him on a goose chase to some deadend street by the river and then fly at him with brass knuckles and a gun butt? What was he doing this for—it was not his money they were stealing. No, but he had to prove a point to Sylvia. And what was it—that it was high time Jews stopped letting themselves be victimized? On what empirical basis, though, could he generalize that Jews were so inclined? The Orloffs were surely not shy about fighting for the rights of the oppressed. Then again, Dan Jonas was a study in compliant circumspection. But Skeezix Bloomgarden had hardly been lacking in courage, nor was Melvin Kantor. And Cheska da Silva, as he remembered her, knew no fear. Jews were, in all probability, as statistically prone to act cravenly or with valor as any other group. Perhaps, then, it was because they were so unfairly reviled that he resented Milton's yielding. . . .

It was just past eleven when his man entered the haberdashery. As he left a few minutes later, there could be no mistaking the muddy shade of his suit, the heavy shoulder padding, the cocked oversize fedora, the coarse puffy face, the quick uneasy stride—and the package containing his monthly shirt purchase. He cut directly in front of the car without glancing at its popeyed driver, crossed Broadway against the light, and grabbed a cab going uptown almost before Toby could hit the ignition. All senses screeching, he U-turned the car around the grassy island in the middle of the avenue seconds before a clanging trolley would have cut him in half, and sped north in pursuit.

Traffic was scarce enough for him to hang a block or more behind. The very fact the mobster had jumped a taxi suggested it would not be a long trip. Still, Toby was primed to start ducking and swerving the instant the first whine of a bullet rang in his ear. Fantasies of splintering windshield glass and hot splattering blood were beginning to assail him when the taxi pulled up at a bar on Broadway near 105th Street and discharged the hood. Toby cruised to a halt a block beyond, looked back to see that no one was watching before he parked, and waited a good ten minutes till he decided to follow his prey inside.

On the way, he thought to stop for a copy of the *Daily News* to camouflage himself. Then he pushed in the curtained glass door not at all tentatively, though fearing greatly for his life. On the street, in a car, he had a fighting chance; indoors, they could ambush him without a witness, tie a beer keg to each ankle, and drop him in the ocean. The place, called Cisco's Tavern, was distinguished by a large mirror behind the bar with recessed pink neon lighting and a sign across the top saying: "KEEP YOUR WORDS NICE AND SOFT—YOU NEVER KNOW WHEN YOU'LL HAVE TO EAT THEM." Black and white mosaic tiling covered the floor and part of the walls, lending the establishment all the warmth and elegance of a "Y" men's room. Even that early in the day, a dozen customers were spread around the dive—half of them rummies, Toby guessed, and the rest probably divided equally between crooks and undercover agents. His racketeer was sitting at the back end of the bar next to the cash register, gabbing with the aproned bartender and attacking a pickle, whole, and some sort of cold meat sandwich.

Toby sat at the opposite end of the bar, near the door, and busied himself with the *News* while trying, and failing, to overhear the mug's conversation. He ordered a beer and hamburger, and when told the kitchen would not open till noon, said he would wait if that was all right. The bartender shrugged permission and tapped him a beer before resuming his talk with the hungry racketeer. None of the words in the newspaper registered but Toby crackled the pages conspicuously by way of declaring he was just an average slob of a *News* reader and not actually a stalker after gangsterism. The thrill of the chase vied inside him with the churning dread that he would be waylaid from behind momentarily.

Milton Wasserman's tormentor smoked a leisurely cigar and left just as Toby's hamburger arrived. He chewed it endlessly, and tastelessly;

even so, it kept sticking in his throat. When the barman came for payment, Toby glanced around to be sure no one was nearby and, eyes averted, asked prayerfully for the name of the gentleman who had eaten at the other end.

The bartender took Toby's plate and glass and mopped the counter where they had been sitting. "Which gentleman was that?" he asked.

"The one in the brown suit and felt hat."

"We get a lot of guys in here all day and all night. I don't know one from the next—you know what I mean?"

"You know which one—you were talking to him a lot."

"So maybe I do and maybe I don't. Who wants to know?"

"Just—me. He looks like someone I knew once."

The bartender laughed. "If you knew him, you wouldn't have forgot."

"I'm dumb," Toby said. "Remind me."

"I forget his name, too, now."

Toby reached into his pocket and put a five-dollar bill on the bar top. "Will this help you remember?"

The bartender locked his elbows together on the counter to shield the money and leaned across. "Not enough."

Toby fumbled in his wallet for another five.

"You're not close yet."

"Look, I just want to know his name."

"I got that. Everything has its price, though."

"Okay—what's yours?"

"Fifty."

Toby's jaw sagged. "I don't have fifty."

"Thirty."

"Just for his name?"

"Take it or leave it."

"How about twenty?"

"Twenty-five or forget it."

"Shit," Toby said and dug out fifteen more dollars, all he had left.

The name of the gentleman in question was Earl Cooney—"and lemme tell you somethin'," the bartender said, pocketing the bills. "I seen him in here grab a beer bottle, smash the bottom against the counter, and take a guy's ear right off with the jagged edge. I don't know what your business is, mister, but mess with Earl an' you better watch your step."

He called the name in to Rupe Donovan and two days later got the lowdown. Earl Cooney, alias Paul Carberry, alias Patrick Coyle, sported a long string of arrests for assaults and killings of studied cruelty, but he had been put away only once—when he attacked a total stranger whose car had stalled in front of his on Ninth Avenue and police caught him pounding the life out of the driver with a tire iron. Once a force in the Jersey City beer wars, he was now reduced to Broadway bagman for the rackets between Eighty-sixth and 110th Street. "He can lead us to big stuff," Rupe said. "We'll go after him if your guy'll testify for us."

Sylvia, more fearful of a reprimand for having divulged family secrets than of the consequences of cooperating with the state prosecutor, hesitated a week before bringing up the subject with Milton. Her story went that when Toby told her about his friend in Dewey's office and how high a premium they placed on protecting witnesses, she took it on herself to ask if they would go after Milton's protection racketeer. She thought it their only opportunity to rid themselves of the leech. Glad of her concern, Milton was nevertheless peeved with her for enlisting the help of strangers and intruding on the business in a way that disparaged his manhood and disputed his judgment. He would not even consider cooperating with the authorities.

But Sylvia kept working on him, as Toby did on her. "This is the scum of the earth we're talking about," he said. "And Milton would have the best law-enforcement office in America behind him."

"I'll tell him again," she said, "but he's sure this man has his connections and would do something awful before the cops could stop him."

"You're not being forceful enough with him."

"What do you want me to do?"

"I don't know. Try telling him you won't go to Asbury with him next month if he doesn't show some backbone."

"I couldn't do that."

"Why not? It would show him how much this means to you."

The prospect of their annual summer week at the Jersey shore, with her mousy husband and away from her lusty lover, had been greatly depressing her. Toby's provocative suggestion was therefore sure to accomplish one of two desirable results: It would either spur Milton into action against the powers of darkness or allow her, with perfect indignation, to remain home while he vacationed.

Milton decided that Asbury Park by himself was intolerable. "He promises he'll take care of the thing his own way," she reported back to Toby, "but he won't tell me how exactly."

On the first of August, they had their answer. When the gangster came to the haberdashery for his monthly payment, Milton told him to go to hell. Sylvia was astonished, and not a little pleased. Toby told her Milton was definitely no longer a coward—just stupid. She looked confused.

On the second of August, shortly before dawn, two large rocks were thrown from a passing vehicle through the plate-glass display windows at the front of the Saville Shop. A muffled voice on the phone advised Milton that far worse would happen if he withheld further payments or even dreamed of going to the police. He reported the message to Sylvia and, as if to leave her in no doubt who was to blame, added, "See?"

She went to Asbury with him, anyway; a deal was a deal.

Toby left word for Rupe Donovan that things had fizzled at his end. Rupe never called back to invite him home. It was a big city, Toby decided, and people were very busy.

IV

His third day on rewrite, Toby was fed a story about how the animals had broken out of the Central Park Zoo.

Three different legmen phoned him their reports, which had all the makings of a front-page piece. Somebody had allegedly opened the locks in the monkey house and on the flying cages, releasing hordes of gibbering primates and flocks of exotic birds. Aside from a missing infant that was claimed to have been snatched from its carriage by a swooping bald eagle last seen headed toward the Tavern-on-the-Green, the animals' antics appeared harmless enough. Several of the ringtails were said to be pitching apples to Rosie the hippopotamus; some chimpanzees, to be riding piggyback on the sea lions in their pond, and at least two red-bottomed baboons, to have swung in through the open windows on the top floor of the neighboring old Arsenal, where the Parks Department was now quartered. Among those under questioning in connection with the incident, according to the phone reports, was former Governor Alfred E. Smith, honorary night superintendent of the zoo and possessor of a key to all its locks.

This last item especially gave Toby pause. What angle could be more to the *Trib*'s liking than a hint of madness in the archetypal Tammanyite? A hurried examination of the library clips disclosed, however, that the "Happy Warrior" had indeed been one of the inspirers of the rebuilt zoo and, for his efforts, been rewarded with visiting privileges any time of day or night. And he lived right across Fifth Avenue from the menagerie. With this reassurance and the City News wire copy in hand for documentation, Toby wrote at top speed, prevented from whimsy only by the putative sortie of the bald eagle. He handed it in with vague hopes for his first by-line.

"What's the name of the missing baby?" Ward Stakesing asked, summoning Toby to the city desk several minutes later.

"He—didn't give it to me."

"Did you ask?" the night city editor wondered.

"I—just assumed—he'd give it to me if he had it."

"I see. And you don't know whether it weighed five pounds or twenty-five pounds, right? Our readers might be interested."

"I—didn't get that, either. Sorry."

"Look into it, will you? Now about these amphibious chimps frolicking with the sea lions—who taught them to swim?"

"I beg your pardon, sir?"

"I say, monkeys, to my knowledge, don't swim—they climb."

"I—didn't think to ask that. It all sounded so bizarre."

"Then why did you write it up?"

"I—was told to."

"You were told to take down information. We pay you to think, Ronan, not take notes and type them up. Go back and think what kind of paper we'd put out if we fell for every joker or nut who called in with a fish story like this."

A light slowly flickered on. "But they were our legmen—"

"How do you know?"

"They—told me."

"And if I told you I was the crown prince of Patagonia, would that make it so?"

"No. But—but there was the City News wire copy—"

The editor finally flashed a grin. "Yeah, I guess that was a bit of a curveball. We had it put up special for your attention. The point is, though, that you're the main line of defense here—use your wits all the time." The story sailed on a pretty arc directly into the wastebasket.

V

From the freshly mown slope below the patio of jigsaw flagstone, Nina scanned the perfection of the Chafee place—the lush lawns and clipped hedges, the flower gardens in complementary bloom, the ovoid pond just big enough to row a boat about, the pool, the tennis court, the flashing thread of a brook with its little bridge into the woods, the gazebo and greenhouse, and presiding over all, the fine old manor house of fieldstone and aged white clapboard—and announced, "God, how I hate this."

"You wouldn't," said Toby, "if it was yours."

"It couldn't ever be mine—I'd turn it into an orphanage."

Eden had made it sound like an irresistible weekend. "We do it every Labor Day—and everyone always has a smashing time. My folks chaperone, of course—I'd like you to meet them, anyway, Toby

—you and my father especially would hit it off, I know—better than you and Richard, I promise. Father thinks Richard's social views are antediluvian—"

Nina was only slightly more mystified by Toby's invitation to her than Eden's to him in the first place. "I just don't see what you have in common with them," she said, not quite rejecting the proposition out of hand. "And I certainly don't belong sunning myself on a Westchester estate, chitchatting over brandies with a bunch of spoiled girls who wouldn't even spit on me in any other circumstances."

"Eden says it's not much of an estate, as estates go. And I think you're just prejudiced against Christian capitalists."

"That's ridiculous. You're just flattered you've been included as a representative of the great unwashed—and want some company that's even less socially acceptable. You've got your Harvard diploma, at least."

"Do I detect a lurking pinch of self-pity?"

"Not on your life," Nina said, her opposition softening. School, after all, would not begin for another two weeks, and the shop where she worked closed up for the long weekend, and Eden had promised that the whole thing was strictly informal and casual old clothes entirely in order. She drew the line, though, at passing Labor Day itself cavorting among the filthy rich. And she could not bear the idea of sleeping more than one night at the home of people she didn't know and was certain to dislike—they would have to come home late Sunday. But yes, she would go, if Toby wanted her to so badly; she was always eager to broaden her knowledge.

Eden, in navy slacks and a short-sleeved linen blouse, met them at the Chappaqua train station with a shiny black Packard. An Irish setter was in the back. "What—no chauffeur?" Toby asked, helping Nina into the front seat and then joining the dog.

"I'm afraid only Aunt Winnie can manage a chauffeur these days. But we've an actual gardener—he's a marvel—who always tinkers with the cars, but my father's dead against chauffeurs in this day and age—he says they make for revolutions." She swung on to the street without bothering to look around, as if any approaching vehicle was bound to defer to hers, and accelerated nearly beyond the endurance of the gears. "The pooch is named Jefferson," she told Toby. "He's a love."

Perhaps it was the rusty hair coloring they shared, but for some reason, the animal, perched like a person on the seat beside him and swaying adroitly around the turns Eden took on the fly, struck him as immensely likable. Toby stroked its softly radiant coat and rubbed it playfully about the neck, earning many pants of gratitude and several soulful looks in the eye. At the house, where sandwiches were already being served for lunch on the patio, Jefferson decided to tag after him. Toby, thinking to solidify what friendships he could in foreign parts, removed a small corner from his roast-beef sandwich and slipped it to the dog.

"I really wouldn't do that if I were you," Richard Townley Crandall cautioned, tilting backward in his chair. "The family's awfully fussy about his diet—and they don't encourage him begging for scraps."

"He didn't beg—it was my idea. And I wouldn't call it a scrap, exactly." Jefferson sat waiting for more. "But I see your point."

Richard shed his white tennis sweater with its sporty red and blue piping around the V-neck. "Do you play?" he asked.

"Not much."

"Well, come down later, anyhow—everybody gives it a whirl."

"Don't let him bushwhack you, Toby," Eden said, arriving with a trayful of iced coffees. "He's voracious on the tennis court—a total loon. Claims it cures all his aggressions—except toward me."

"If I'm so aggressive," Richard asked, giving her a small pat on the rear, "how come you're the one wearing the long pants?"

"What do pants have to do with anything?"

"They're very revealing—in more ways than one."

"One of which is the beholder's degree of fossilhood."

"Would you say that if I took to wearing a skirt?"

"That's different—pants are practical. Also emancipating."

"But not very feminine."

"They look feminine on Dietrich—and she wears them all over town. It's a matter of attitude."

"It's a matter of fannies." Richard stirred a single spoon of sugar into his coffee. "She can get away with it."

"And what's wrong with my fanny, I'd like to know?"

Richard squinted at the blazing sky. "I was speaking in general," he said, mugging to the other couples. "I'm not sure we ought to get down to cases in front of mixed company."

Debate on the manifestations of feminism altered course with the arrival of Eden's mother. Whatever misgivings Richard might have harbored about the demureness of Eden's caboose, Rae Chafee could not have borne genetic responsibility. A tidy champagne blonde with gray streaks like Eden's, she appeared to have no misplaced curve or fatty deposit anywhere upon her excellently preserved form. With gushless grace, she greeted each young guest, by name when she knew it and right after Eden's introduction when it was someone new, and told everyone to have a grand time and not hesitate to ask for anything at all.

Ablaze with daughterly pride, Eden insisted she sit with them awhile and describe the flying lessons she was taking at a field outside of White Plains. "Really, dear," her mother held out, "I'm sure everyone has more gripping topics to engage them."

"Mom's going to fly Dad to the paper mill in Quebec next time he goes up to buy," Eden said, tugging her into a chair next to Nina.

"I think that's a bit premature, dear. First let me learn which way is north, if you don't mind."

Everyone laughed, but that could not rout the fresh specter of Amelia Earhart from occupying all their thoughts. Hardly six weeks had passed since the aviatrix had been lost over the Pacific. Mrs. Chafee sensed their unspoken concern and brought it up herself, noting that Earhart, for all her skill and courage, had flirted with disaster by electing not to take along certain radio equipment and other safety precautions.

"What probably got her into trouble," said Richard, presumably to make light of the grim turn the talk had taken, "was not so much hubris as immorality. I don't think any woman should fly around the world with someone else's husband."

"Good God, Richard—it's not as if they were snuggling up there together," Eden railed. "The man was Pan American's ace navigator. And they went for science—you make it sound like some cheap little fling."

"Cheap it wasn't. It must have cost a fortune."

"Very funny. But you can't measure a scientific expedition like that as if it were a private safari. And frankly, I don't think they made a proper effort to find her. If it were Lindbergh, the entire U. S. Navy would still be out looking. But a woman's only an adventuress, right?"

Nina, who had said nothing to anyone so far, turned to her hostess suddenly and asked, "Didn't I read that the search for her cost fifty thousand dollars a day? You can't keep that up forever, no matter how admirable someone is. After all, she wasn't God."

Eden's blue eyes sparked disagreeably. "If you'll excuse me, I think it's obscene to put a monetary value on any human life—especially one that inspired so many people. She had tremendous spunk—a rare spirit. I'd say heroes like her are a bargain at any price."

"But someone has to wind up paying the bill," Nina replied. "Anyway, I'm not sure I'd place all that high a premium on heroes and heroines in terms of human progress."

"Yes, I'm afraid Eden takes rather too romantic a view of flying," her mother said, rising to excuse herself. "It's just a big damned machine. Cars are more dangerous, especially the way she drives them."

Richard capped the discussion by attributing to the missing flyer a baleful influence on American womanhood, filling the sex with as many antibiological heresies as Margaret Sanger. "And if you want my opinion," he told Eden, hardly troubling to lower his voice, "I'd try to call your mother off this madness instead of encouraging her to become the world's oldest flying daredevil. It's unbecoming in a woman of her quality."

"It's plain," she aaid stiffly, "they never taught you gallantry at Montclair Prep."

"Academy, my dear—Montclair Academy. It's actually quite well-known in New Jersey "

"New Jersey is uncouth."

"Ah, it's too bad," he said gaily, "that you never had the bracing benefits of overcoming a deprived childhood." And before she could get off a squelching reply, he was leading a parade of guests down to the tennis court, where he set about at once to measure the height of the net with his expensive racquet.

Richard's charms were continuously exhibited throughout the afternoon. He hogged the tennis court under the edict that winners retained title against a limitless succession of challengers, until finally his mixed-doubles partner, a Wellesley friend of Eden, nearly dropped from sunstroke. Then he wandered over to the archery target, where Toby, Nina, and Jefferson were casually engaged, and proceeded for three quarters of an hour to give an intimidating demonstration of his marksmanship. Thereafter, he sailed through the three-hole pitch-and-putt course at the far end of the property, readily outgolfing Garrett Chafee, Eden's father, and wound up at the pool in woolly black swim briefs that allowed prominent display of both his diving form and genitalia.

As he and Nina roamed the Chafee estate, open poachers among the gentry, Toby peripherally tracked the movements of Eden in her lair, easy at her entertainments, gliding with laughter from one set of friends to another, trading on private jokes and extracting pleasure from every encounter. So relentlessly engaging was she in her rounds that her discharge of nectar nearly neutralized Richard's trail of vitriol. But having fetched Toby there, she showed him no special favor, as if he and Nina were to mix like any other guests despite their obvious distance from these inbreeding heirs to the realm. In a way, he supposed, it was a compliment—that he was in need of no helping hand across the social boundary. Still, her flighty path, barely crossing theirs, seemed unkind, a sin of heinous omission. Her presence, her thereness, exerted a gravitational tug on him out of all proportion to her compact mass. A minute with Eden Chafee was more consuming than an hour with any other girl he had ever known.

"You've been edgy since lunch," Nina said, taking his distracted state for social unrest. "Too ritzy for you?"

He wrapped a playful arm around her shoulder as they made their way slowly up the slope toward the stately house. "Did Moses miss the bulrushes?"

Without recourse, he joined Richard, Mr. Chafee, and several of the others on the patio for a late-afternoon drink while Nina went in to put on something fresh. Richard was making a show of mixing them all perfect gin rickeys in a shaker of his own he had brought along for the purpose. Mr. Chafee turned a puckish eye on Toby as he sat and said, "Rumor has it, young man, you're convinced all capitalists are bloodsuckers."

The remark was plainly intended to invite an engagement, not ridicule the sentiment. Though he had the stringy muscularity of a sportsman, with a Western windburn and peninsular jawline that stamped him a man of direct action, Garrett Chafee's aging movie-hero looks were dashed by a veritable Gobi of a scalp. The high, oblong forehead gave him an appearance almost quizzical in its fixed proportions; all in all, the effect was benign. "And I'm led to understand, sir," Toby replied, "that you regard all labor as a commodity."

"Well, of course—in a manner of speaking. Just like capital. I was explaining the economic facts of life to Eden, not making a value judgment. Labor's no better or worse than business—we all put our own interests first."

"But you'll grant that labor, at least, is animate?"

"Oh, very. But that doesn't deter business from pretending it's not. As I keep trying to tell Richard over here when he lets me get a word in edgewise, that's where his worship of *laissez-faire* is sinful—it claims enlightenment for selfishness. I say call it what it is."

"Don't blame me," said Richard, poking a frothy highball under Toby's nose, "blame Adam Smith. I'm only a brilliant disciple."

The self-advertisement seemed to amuse Chafee. "Adam Smith's not around to correct, so you'll have to do. No businessman alive believes the invisible hand of the marketplace should be allowed to control supply and demand. Hell, who wants a really free market—we're all natural monopolists at heart. Give me half a chance to corner the paper-bag market, and I'd jump at it."

"And cut wages to the bone?" Toby asked.

"That's what you do with commodities if you're the buyer—pay as little as possible. But don't blame me—blame labor. It invites exploitation. Instead of mobilizing itself massively and monopolizing the force so it can command a decent wage in every industry, it stupidly divides itself into a hierarchy of skills—as if we're all still back in medieval Europe."

Toby nodded emphatically, delighted with the discovery at last of a candid capitalist. That was precisely why the Newspaper Guild had quit the A.F. of L. in June, he said, and joined the C.I.O. "I think you're right—unionization has to be an all-or-nothing proposition."

"Eden's told me all about your guild," Chafee said. "In fact, I urged her to join up after your switch. I said if she's determined to be a workingwoman, she ought to act like one and not be afraid to show a little moxie. But she's too much of a self-styled aristocrat for that—it's the privileged delusion of capitalists' daughters."

"Abetted by the unswerving instruction of her clear-eyed suitor," Richard inserted. "I keep telling her once business is at the mercy of labor, we're cooked. No society can stay free unless its commerce flourishes. Why do you think Hitler came to power? Not because he crushed the unions—times were bad to begin with, and that's when tyrants thrive."

"You mean only a rich people deserves freedom?" Toby asked.

"I mean," Richard said, "they're the only kind who can afford it. Liberty and prosperity are indivisible. And you don't achieve high productivity without high profits—there's no incentive otherwise. And the more output, the more jobs—and the higher the wages. It's really got nothing at all to do with unions or collective bargaining or militancy of any sort, don't you see?"

"Richard's an unreconstructed Hooverite," Chafee teased. "He thinks the sole function of government is to promote conditions favorable to free enterprise." He himself was a Keynesian to the extent of believing governments existed to supply those functions private individuals either couldn't or wouldn't perform for themselves. "I see nothing wrong with a state that limits our extremes of misery and cupidity."

That was so entirely sensible a view that Toby wanted to shake his hand when Mr. Chafee rose to go in for a shower. In his wake, the ever-captious Richard Crandall remarked, "There goes the only unforgivable kind of plutocrat—a guilty one. I think he weeps all the way to the bank."

Toby and Nina sat at the outer edge of the patio during the buffet supper, a hearty spread of hamburgers, barbecued chicken, and spare ribs. With a hand carefully shielded by the tablecloth, Toby broke off juicy chunks of his ground meat and fed them to Jefferson. Afterward, before the singing and dancing were due to begin indoors, cigars and port were handed around to the young men, who were invited to join Garrett Chafee on the sun porch.

Trailed by the Irish setter, Toby moved sluggishly to comply. When he got there, the talk was of Joe Louis, newly enthroned as the first colored heavyweight champion in more than twenty years, and how the crown would not be a true fit until he again met the German Schmeling, handy victor in their earlier bout. "I hope Louis flattens him," someone said. "Over there they don't consider Negroes human."

The comment led to remarks about others the Nazis regarded in similar fashion. Richard was inclined, he said, to blame the Reich's undoubted anti-semitism less on inherent malevolence than a poverty-induced psychopathology—"although they do say every country gets the Jews it deserves." America, on the other hand, had been Europe's dumping bin in that regard for fifty years, and what with Professor Frankfurter soon likely to join his two Hebrew brethren on the Supreme Court, Richard thought, "It's only a matter of time before Zionism is enshrined as our national policy."

Toby had had enough of Richard Townley Crandall for one lifetime. He pushed himself back from the glass-topped table and said as he rose, "I think your comments are out of line."

Everyone else sat frozen in place. "Sorry," Richard said calmly, "but I'm entitled to my reasoned opinion."

"You're not entitled to be rude."

"How was I being rude?"

"You were speaking of Jews as if they were some sort of plague."

"It's an arguable position. And even if it weren't, there aren't any Jews out here, so what of it?"

"Nina's a Jew, and you damned well know it."

"That's not my problem. Anyway, she's not among us—"

"But I am—and you're insulting both of us."

"That's not my problem, either," Richard said and turned away.

Toby groped for punishing language. "Crandall," he said, the loathing explosive within him, "you're a damned arrogant—repulsive—bastard."

Without a word, Richard sprang up and unleashed a powerful fist across the table that fell just short of its target. In the process, however, he managed to cascade the wine he had been holding all over his own beautiful white tennis sweater. The sight of it doubly enraged him, but as he began to uncork another swing, a brownish red snarling blur interposed its protection between Toby and his assailant. "Down, Jefferson!" Mr. Chafee roared. The setter subsided only when Richard did.

"Hey, I was just beginning to enjoy myself," Nina hissed when Toby came to collect her and their things.

Eden rushed out into the foyer after them. "Toby—you're making a terrible scene! What on earth's the matter?"

"Nothing," he snarled, "except your goddamned snotty boy friend."

"Oh, good lord—that's just his manner. He doesn't mean any harm."

"I don't care what he means. Every other word out of his mouth is disparaging. I don't understand why you put up with it."

"It's not anything you have to concern yourself about."

"Oh, I'm not—believe me! I'm leaving. But just tell me what gives him the right to strut around here like—like—like King Shit? He's nothing but a bootlegger's son hoping you'll make him legitimate."

Eden's arms dangled helplessly at her sides. "All right, Toby—I guess you've had your say. You can wait out front for the cab—I'll call."

Nina let him brood by himself until the train passed White Plains. Finally she said, "I think you're stuck on her."

"Who?"

"Who do you think?"

His frown was a prodigy of protest. "That's—ridiculous."

"Maybe. It's also the only reason I can think of why you ever went up there in the first place—and then made such an ass of yourself leaving."

"That's—still ridiculous."

His disclaimer hung hollow in the almost empty train car as it clacked south toward the city. "Don't worry about my feelings—if that's what you're thinking," Nina said, with a consoling pat on his arm. "I'm just sorry I can't say any more for your taste than you did for hers."

EIGHTEEN

WHILE HIS HEART was tugged in three different directions that fall, Toby devoted his soul to the exclusive service of Fiorello La Guardia, seeking re-election as the mayor. In the course of the campaign, Toby came to conceive of the tempestuous little man with the coal-black hair and the burning dark eyes as the most admirable American politician since Lincoln. This investment of excessive partisanship was traceable almost wholly to a growing conviction in him that the *Herald Tribune* was no longer worthy of his highest allegiance.

His disenchantment with the paper grew not out of his own work status—he continued on evening rewrite, turning out copy swiftly and smoothly enough to suit the editors—but the *Trib*'s complicity in a last-ditch, nationwide war by the newspaper publishers to break the growing strength of the guild. There was nothing subtle about this campaign of attempted repression. After the guild had bolted to the C.I.O. and doubled its size almost at once by admitting members from the business departments, publishers gathered behind closed doors in Chicago to map a coordinated counterattack. Nowhere was this resolve to defeat or paralyze the guild carried out more determinedly than in the communications capital of America.

The wily Hearst, who elsewhere diverted his papers' business personnel into unions other than the guild, discouraged organization in New York by the yet more drastic expedient of closing down his morning *American*. The resulting overflow of job applicants detectably dampened guild militancy. Activists on the surviving papers faced an implicit threat of getting fired. The *Times* moved more discreetly, encouraging a group of its editorial hands led by one of the makeup editors to form something called the American Press Society —a transparent vessel to siphon off enthusiasm for the guild. Such hectoring by the nonpareil of American newspapers prompted the union to file charges against it with the National Labor Relations Board for "coercion and interference with the organization of employees." At the *Brooklyn Eagle,* management chose to accept a strike in September rather than yield to guild demands for better pay and work conditions. And at the *Trib,* the ownership played a stalling game.

"It's a war of nerves," Buddy LaRusso, unit chairman and head of the negotiating team, reported back to the executive committee, of which Toby was the lowest ranking member. "The bastards are bargaining in bad faith." There had been seven drawn-out conferences so far with the *Trib* business manager, who was nitpicking to pieces the language of the proposed guild contract. When LaRusso made what he felt was a key concession—waiving the demand for a guild shop—management insisted that the promise be endorsed in writing by the guild's national executive board, which met infrequently and was likely to wrangle over the surrendered point. By summer's end, the business manager was reported ill and unable to resume negotiations. An indefinite delay was in prospect.

Thus frustrated, many guild members turned their off-hours energy to the politics that would determine their city's stewardship. The disarray of New York's party system had been accelerated by La Guardia's reformist administration. On the outside looking in were diehard Republicans, the discredited and bitter Tammany regulars, futile independent Democrats, and the fast-withering Socialists. Only the *ad hoc* Fusion movement prospered with the mayor, and it was more a whim of the exalted civic spirit than a viable political mechanism. In the midst of this degenerative process, the vigorous young C.I.O. devised a direct-action weapon ideally suited to the New York political wars—the American Labor Party. Instead of putting up a slate of its own, the A.L.P. backed candidates it judged most supportive of the aims of its constituent unions, of which the Newspaper Guild was now one. And there was no doubt in the autumn of 1937 which of the candidates for mayor of New York, in the view of organized labor, was the best friend of the workingman.

From what Toby had heard in the city room and at Bleeck's, in many ways La Guardia was a perfectly terrible person: irascible, insolent, cunning, forthright to the point of abrasiveness. There was no excuse for his volatile and often cyclonic temperament—except that he was a genius at governing. It was not merely that, despite a legacy of depression, rampant organized crime, Jimmy Walker's jaunty debasement of City Hall, Tammany's bottomless tin box, and a public unmanageably vast and discordant, he had restored the city to financial health; the remarkable thing was to have done so even while measurably improving its police, fire, hospital, sanitation, and other vital services. It was not only that he built schools and colleges in excess of

all his predecessors, and bridges and tunnels and highways and housing, in the bargain adding five thousand acres of parks and playgrounds, but that he got it all done without payoffs and kickbacks; no
greasy political palms intruded as usual between the city treasury and
the building contractors, denying construction workers their full
wages. Merit became the sole criterion of municipal job-holding, to
the chagrin of displaced grafters and practiced clock-watchers.

What appealed most to Toby about this one-man revolution was
that it had no dogma, no doctrine—it just performed. La Guardia
craved power not to own it but to spend it. The outlay crunched toes
and crushed egos and awoke enmity under many a rock, but even if
his own sledgehammer did him in, there were worse sins than the indignity of a self-inflicted wound. "Sure," Toby replied eagerly when
Nina first proposed he join the campaign. "The man proves democracy can still really govern."

"What he really proves," she said, "is that you need socialism now
to pick up the pieces and rebuild the city—and the country." La
Guardia had mollified the masses only with hundreds of millions in
federal funds for public works. And his most ardent constituency was
the million and a half New Yorkers on welfare, whose needs he had
been knowing enough to meet by staffing the Emergency Relief Bureau with honest and compassionate civil servants. Because these were
selected on a nonpolitical basis, they included a sizable number of
communists and their sympathizers. The fact had been seized upon by
La Guardia's Tammany opponent, a judge named Mahoney, for an
orgy of Red-baiting. "No citizen of New York is going to come humbly with hat in hand to a communist-led organization," the judge declared, "and beg it to intercede for him so he can get food and clothing for his children. I am going to toss the Reds out—there will be no
minor-league Moscow controlling the administration of relief under
me."

Preventing such a reactionary purge was one of the pressing reasons
Nina asked Toby to help man the A.L.P. storefront headquarters that
Saul Orloff had been put in charge of on Christopher Street just west
of Bleecker. Whatever his political differences with the Orloffs, Toby
did not take much persuading; Fiorello La Guardia defied dialectics as
he did everything else.

The ruffled café curtains on the windows and door were the only
remnants of the pastry shop that formerly occupied the premises.
Wedged between an upholsterer and a florist, it was just large enough
to house the American Labor Party's temporary operations in the west
side of the Village. Toby supervised the day shift of volunteers who
dispensed literature on the street, hand-addressed envelopes stuffed

with campaign fliers, and rang doorbells to pitch the La Guardia slate. A welfare worker's wife headed the afternoon shift, and Saul and Adele Orloff were in charge on weeknights, when the place offered free cider and doughnuts and served as an open house for anyone who wanted to wander in and debate the issues. Saturday nights, from six to ten, Toby drove a soundtruck with an open back from which Nina and Melvin Kantor took turns delivering short curbside speeches and fielding questions from the crowd.

Nina, too tentative and nervous in her delivery at first, would go into the bathroom at the back of the shop to feed herself a shot glass of scotch and then brush her teeth vigorously before going on. The effect was so bracing that at times she ignored the microphone altogether. Between turns, she sat in the truck cab beside Toby, smoking for the first time in her life and studying her lines for the next speech. Her pitch varied slightly with campaign developments and the economic composition of the neighborhood. At every site, though, A.L.P. workers were in the crowd, yelling up planted questions that allowed her to spiel off statistics too tedious for inclusion in the speeches themselves.

Nina's earnest, beseeching tone, which attracted small audiences that listened politely to the end and rarely heckled, served as a warm-up for Melvin's far more flamboyant and often sarcastic style. "When the mayor's opponents call for the return of law and order to the city," he would thunder into the mike, "they mean there's too much social protest being allowed. What they want to do is nightstick the workers of New York into submission so they'll accept starvation wages with a smile." Or: "You hear Mahoney talking about graft now! Why, four years ago prostitution was a flourishing business in this town, with a booking office and booking agents and a distribution center—and direct links to the leaders of Tammany. And the honorable judge was one of those leaders and remains the creature of Tammany, which can hardly wait to get back to purveying flesh!" He drew bigger crowds and far more heckling, most of it directed not against the mayor but the pink tint of the A.L.P.

Toby, who had always dreaded giving speeches for fear he would forget his lines or make a fool of himself with clumsy phraseology so easy to avoid on paper, admired Nina's courage and Melvin's panache on the stump. He coached them each a bit, urging Nina to avoid a tendency to rush her speech, as if eager to be done with it, and Melvin not to wax quite so eloquent. But when they invited him to take his turn at the makeshift rostrum, Toby declined, citing professional ethics. An off-duty newspaperman was perhaps permitted to lick stamps and drive a truck for a political cause, but it was something else to stand up in public and identify himself with a candidate. "That's a fine line," Nina said, "but suit yourself."

What suited him, actually, was being with her every Saturday night and afterward walking her home and talking and necking circumspectly to band music on the living-room radio after her parents had gone to bed. One Saturday early in October, however, as he was working up to suggesting that she stay late with him to clean up the headquarters after everyone else had gone—the curtained darkness would have provided them a rare privacy—Nina left instead with Melvin and not even a backward glance of apology.

Toby rationalized. She had, after all, no standing Saturday-night commitment to him; they had just fallen into the habit. And Melvin, exhortations flying from his tongue as if forged at Lenin's own sparking crucible, held an undeniable attraction for her, despite his bottom-heavy shape and pedantic tendencies. Still, Toby fumed at demotion to second place behind a blowhard, even if of the right persuasion.

The following Saturday, the three of them locked up headquarters together at midnight, and Nina invited him, with perfunctory courtesy, to join her and Melvin for a drink. Toby barely acknowledged the offer. Leaving them at the door, he walked over to Seventh, picked up the Sunday papers at a newsstand, stopped at a take-out delicatessen for a sandwich, and decided not to wait till he got home to eat but to go back to headquarters and wash down the ham-and-cheese with apple cider, of which there were ample stocks in the supply closet. Traffic on Christopher had slowed by then, and only a few pedestrians were in sight. No one was likely to disturb him at that hour even if the shop was lighted behind the frilly curtains.

As he turned the key and reached around behind the door for the light switch, he heard a frantic scrambling in the darkness. Retreating to the threshold, he asked at a shout who was there. "Who the hell do you think?" came the disgusted voice of Melvin Kantor from the old sofa in the corner. "Just leave the light off and go home."

"Oh," said Toby, "oh, sure. Excuse me—I didn't know there was a party going on."

He was so burned on the ride uptown—to think that fat, four-eyed Mel Kantor had beat him out for Nina Orloff's longed-for carnal favors!—that his train was pulling into the 103rd Street station by the time he remembered to look up. He backtracked the fifteen blocks along Broadway on foot, trailing flames of envy all the way. In bed in the morning, surrounded by thumbed-through sections of the papers, he was still smoldering when Victor Wasserman thumped on his apartment door to say there was a lady down in the vestibule waiting to see him.

She wore her fringed white scarf over her hair and a look of such petulance that he saw at once the mortification his untimely return to Christopher Street the night before had caused her. "Look, it wasn't what you think it was," she said after they had battled the wind along Riverside for half a block of icy silence. "It was just—not that—okay?"

"Whatever you say."

"I'm telling you the truth!" Vehemence endorsed the claim.

"Sure—okay. Now let's forget it—I didn't see or hear a thing. And you don't owe me any explanations. You go do what you want with whoever you want—what difference does it make what I think?"

"Shit!" She looked straight ahead. "Stop being so damn nobly sanctimonious. You know how much I care what you think."

"But not enough to be with me instead of him."

"I'm with you a lot—I'm entitled to see other people without your becoming a crybaby. And there's nothing wrong with him. He's very nice—and very brilliant and dedicated—"

"If he's so goddamn brilliant, why was he trying to lay you on a greasy sofa in a grubby store? And I thought you were so big on decency? The least you could have done was insist on a real bed—"

"Nobody was *laying* me, as you so elegantly put it! It was just a spur-of-the-moment thing. You left, the place was all empty, so we went back in just to—to—"

"Do a little hot groping?"

"Is that so terrible? You want to do it all the time."

"You're not sorry you did whatever you did with him—you're just sore I know about it."

"I'm sore that you think it was more than it was."

"How do you know what I think?"

"Because—of the circumstances. I know how it must have looked."

"Okay, okay—you were playing tiddledywinks. You came all the way up here to tell me that, so it must be true. What else?"

"I want you to believe me, Toby."

"Why?"

"Because—I care for you—and I don't want this to affect the relationship among the three of us. We're a good working team—and the campaign doesn't have that long to go—and you've been very valuable."

"Swell. Good soldier Ronan will report for duty as usual tomorrow."

"And not be mean to Mel on Saturday?"

"Why would I be mean to Mel? All he was doing was trying to ex-

ercise his normal biological instincts. You know all us men are alike—
and if it's not one girl, it's another."

To cultivate the peculiar emotional advantage that knowing of her
dalliance—whatever degree of wantonness it was—gave him for the
moment, Toby spent all week secretly working up a speech for delivery the next Saturday night. It was only seven or eight minutes long,
but he wanted every word of it to be just right. He wrote it and
rewrote it and practiced it to perfection. By the time that Nina
finished her usual shotgun delivery from the rear of the soundtruck to
the usual smattering of applause at their first stop, he was nearly liquid
with apprehension. Almost in a daze, he relieved Nina of the microphone, much to her surprise, and before Melvin could come forward,
Toby introduced himself in a thick voice and told the gathering of
scarcely three dozen that he had lived in New York a little more than
a year but, even so, wanted to explain why he was for La Guardia.

He came from a small town up the Hudson, he said, where almost
everyone knew who everybody else was and the most trivial happen-
ings in all their lives were written up in the newspaper. Like almost all
such towns, he said, his took too much pride in its meager self, boasted
unduly over any accomplishment of its residents, and received criticism very poorly. But it did have one thing—an undeniable sense of
community, of civic cohesiveness, of a shared destiny that bred a
collective conscience. They cared for their town, and for one another.
When he left for the city, he said, everyone told him New York was
nothing like that—in fact, that it was just the opposite. It was so big
and so busy and so hard that caring for themselves was the only thing
people there had time for. Nobody knew anybody more than a few
doors or houses or, at most, blocks away, and you had to be murdered
—or close to it—to make the newspapers. And there was no such
thing as civic pride because you could never think of the city as your
own, and there was almost total indifference to graft and crime and
whatever else ailed the place because nothing could be done about it.

"But when I arrived here," he said, his throat unclogged now and
his voice driving, "that's not what I found at all. I found a lot of people proud of where they lived—and caring greatly about making it
cleaner and safer and healthier and more honest—and glad it was getting new places to work and to learn and to play. Instead of everyone
feeling lost and alone, they had all somehow been linked. Now one
man can't make all that happen by himself. But one man can be the
spark. Even in an enormous metropolis, one man can be the highest
common denominator of the people by bringing out the best in them."
He paused, and no one moved, as they had not since he began. Then

he said, "That's why I'm going to vote for Mr. Fiorello H. La Guardia on election day," and sat down.

The street was silent. Finally Nina clapped. And then the little crowd, slowly at first, gradually louder, and with real fervor at the end, for themselves as much as the speaker. Toby sat with his head bowed. Nina reached over and took his hand. "I think you're about to join the troupe," she whispered happily. But he shook his head and said he was retiring then and there. It was just something he had made up and wanted to deliver—had to once—but a performer he was not.

Back at headquarters, when the evening's speechmaking was over, Nina kept pushing him to relent and give his "hicktown pitch," as she approvingly called it, the last two Saturdays of the campaign. "Don't you think he should?" she appealed to Mel Kantor. "Didn't you think it was marvelous?"

"I think he should do what he wants to do," said Mel, revealing his distress that Toby had not spoken a word to him or even looked his way the entire night. When it was time to close, Melvin Kantor knew which of them was taking Nina Orloff home.

Toby did not try to neck or do anything else with her that night, did not even accept her invitation inside. Instead, he asked her to the guild benefit for the *Eagle* strikers, to be held the following week at the Manhattan Opera House; the mayor was to be there. She said yes and kissed him goodnight long and warmly.

Of the two personalities featured at the guild gala, Miss Gypsy Rose Lee had the better figure. The mayor, appearing prior to the chilly chanteuse, had the better lines. Toby had never seen him before. He was short and chunky, and his thick dark eyebrows met, and he bounced up to the lectern at a quick, choppy gait, and he had a funny, arching voice. "I came for one reason," he confided to the thronged house. "They told me Gypsy Rose Lee was going to be here." A wave of anticipatory laughter. "Now, you know, Gypsy and I are doing the same act—only she strips herself and I'm stripping Tammany." He had them in his hand after that.

Whatever else newspaper people were, he said, they were wage earners, and he was on their side. He wanted to turn the phrase "Made in New York" into a hallmark that stood for decent wages and good working conditions. He was sorry that not everybody loved him, especially the six thousand political appointees he had fired from city government—"though I hear some of them for the first time in their lives are working for a living." As to the charge that his political base consisted of welfare families by the tens of thousands and other unworthy elements, he was testy in the extreme. "The word 'charity' has absolutely no place in modern government," he shrilled. "It is the duty of government to take care of all the helpless citizens who are in need —and I mean to see that those needs keep being met until they carry me out."

The whole occasion had left her exhilarated, Toby could see in Nina's glowing eyes as they neared the subway station. "You know," she said, within a few feet of the glass-domed entrance, "your place looked very nice from the outside the other Sunday."

He stopped short and smiled excitedly and then steered her across the street to the uptown station. She hoped no one else had the key to his apartment, Nina said with a barely perceptible grin. "Just the land-lady," he said, gathering her closer to him as they ran down the steps at the approaching rumble of the train.

Of the seven women he had now made love to, Toby calculated after their last spasms had stilled in the lamplight of his sitting room— the bedroom he had kept reserved for Sylvia—Nina was the most expressive. Bonnie had taught him most. Holly's aggression had roused him most. April's bosomy passivity soothed him most. Sylvia appreci-ated him most. Cheska and Temple—them he had cared for too much and lain with too little to make a clinical assessment. And now Nina. It could not have been her first time. Only Cheska, of them all, had been inexperienced, technically. Nina thrashed her head from side to side, mouth contorting in soundless ecstasy below his, and then he locked his fingers into her tensile hair with taming force and surged within her. Their joint energy expenditure was massive, the joy magnified by its long repression. A delight in sexuality added to her other passions made a formidable assemblage. She lacked only humor to leaven her rectitude. But wasn't that the one ingredient fatal to redeemers of the species?

"I'd just as soon stay the night," she said in sleepy detumescence, "if I'm invited."

Her suddenly demonstrative warmth pleased him no end. His only hesitation was over Sylvia, who might hear their tread on the stairs in the morning and throw open her door in greeting. "If you're sure it won't upset your folks," he said.

"It won't be the first time," she said. "I'm nearly twenty-three."

"Right. Well—maybe you want to call them so they won't worry?"

She slid a leg over his, brushing against his depleted virility. "I told them not to expect me—if you must know. Now can we stop talking about my parents?"

By Saturday, their ardor was a memory. At headquarters, she was all business. Word had filtered down to Saul Orloff that Mahoney's peo-ple, in the homestretch of a race that it looked increasingly as if they were going to lose, were pulling rough stuff all over town. Tammany was exercising its residual power every way possible just as its mayoral nominee was growing more reckless with his charges against the incumbent. No lie was too big. Meanwhile, Fusion and A.L.P. headquarters were being rifled, literature confiscated, and workers harassed. Union toughs had been assigned to protect La Guardia outposts whenever available. Saul obtained a couple of longshoremen to stand watch at Christopher Street; one of them went out with Nina, Melvin, and Toby in the soundtruck.

At Sheridan Square, their second stop of the night, a Tammany truck pulled up across the street from theirs and began blasting its message at twice the amplification. The speaker claimed to be a member of the Welfare Workers Association, an anti-La Guardia faction within the Emergency Relief Bureau. "Every morning when I come to work," he bellowed, "our desks are cluttered with pamphlets published by the Communist Party—and I don't like it one damned bit. But who can I complain to when City Hall has a direct line to the Kremlin?"

Toby and the longshoreman went over to the Tammany truck to tell them they were poaching on A.L.P. territory. "No one owns the streets, Mac," the Tammany driver said. His hefty partner, massaging a lug-wrench, agreed. Toby said he had a police license to be there. "We got a license, too, Mac—big deal," Tammany said. "You wanna call the cops, go ahead. You wanna be smart, go home."

For the rest of the night, the Tammany truck shadowed theirs, putting out enough decibels to drown the La Guardia crew. By the time they got to Nina's, she was in a remarkably unromantic mood.

Toby stopped by midweek at the store where she worked and they had a quick lunch to plan how to avoid another noise blitz on the closing Saturday of the campaign. Her father was trying to arrange for police protection along their route, but the internecine struggles on the force made the prospect far from certain. Without fail, though, at least half a dozen union heavyweights would accompany them on the back of the truck this time, using whatever forms of suasion were required to send Tammany intruders packing.

The sides collided at the northwest corner of Washington Square, just off Waverly Place. Tammany came not with a truck this time but a gang of severely disruptive hecklers. Nina had gone about halfway through her speech when the interlopers, spread throughout the crescent-shaped crowd, began to assault her with catcalls. The hooters charged, among other things, that La Guardia was a communist stooge and had tried hard at least three times to get the subway fare raised from a nickel. As soon as it became clear the hecklers intended to let Nina neither answer their charges nor finish her own remarks, the union heavies piled off the soundtruck and fell upon the enemy. Shrieking bystanders yielded like waves of wheat as agitators and their avengers clawed and clubbed at one another under the pale yellow streetlamps.

The strife was brief. A whistle blasted somewhere, and from around every corner of the square cops appeared and converged on the scufflers. Toby, in the cab of his truck, watched with brimming admiration for Saul Orloff's municipal influence. This once, the massed forces of order were arrayed on the side of justice. But even as the thought flicked through his mind, a group of the police detached themselves from the main contingent and stormed up onto the platform of the soundtruck, taking the speakers into custody. "But we have a license!" Melvin Kantor screamed over and over as they bore him and Nina away for disturbing the peace and inciting to riot.

Trapped in the truck cab, Toby sat frozen by indecision. Resistance would have been futile; flight, impossible and unmanly. Surrender, though, would mean only arrest and getting sacked by the *Trib* for unruly political partisanship. So instead of just waiting for the rough grasp of the law on his collar, he slid down below the window level out of view from outside the truck. In the uproar and the half-light, nobody spotted him. As soon as the din began to recede, he reached up a hand, slowly unlatched the door on the passenger side, and slipped out. Not a cop in sight. He hurried over to Christopher and reported the news to Saul, who was on duty at the A.L.P. outpost in the event of just such an emergency.

It was four in the morning before Nina, Melvin, and the union men were released on bail that Saul had to rummage up all over town. Toby served as his errand boy throughout the process, shuttling among bearers of ready cash once Saul had solicited them on the phone. His very usefulness helped him rationalize the cringing expedient he had instinctively chosen in the instant of maximum peril.

Nina, though, was less forgiving. After Toby had walked them from the Women's House of Detention at Greenwich and Sixth to the Orloffs' apartment entrance on Hudson—a trek on which the most dire imprecations were loosed against the American notion of justice—Nina turned to him privately, as she had avoided doing the rest of the way, and said, "I'd rather you didn't come up, okay?"

He could sense her displeasure but not its cause. "Sure," he said. "I guess you're exhausted from the whole thing."

"I'm not exhausted—I'm disgusted."

"I can understand—after all the—"

"With you, Toby!" Her tapered eyes were narrow and her mouth tight with the intensity of revulsion that had seized her. She turned to her parents and Melvin and ordered them to go upstairs so she could deliver her indictment without an audience.

"I don't understand," he said when they were alone on the sidewalk.

"Yes—that's the problem!" She shook her head in a spasm of disapproval. "How on earth could you have done that, Toby?"

"Done what, for crissakes?"

"Hid inside the truck that way—like a rat deserting the ship. How could you have? I thought you were good—and brave—and principled—"

His head spun at the charge. Did it stem from the ordeal she had just been through or from a deeper well of fanaticism than any he had imagined at the source of her strength? "What was I supposed to do—start swinging at the cops until I got myself knocked cold?"

"You were supposed to stand up for your rights like a man—next to me—not slink off like a dirty coward."

"And get myself arrested—unjustly—and fired from the paper?"

"You have a duty to dramatize the corruption of the system. How else is it ever going to be changed?"

"I—hope to write about it—sooner or later."

"Not for your paper! And that's just a damned excuse, anyway. You were already in this thing. You can't always stop to worry about your own precious skin, Toby—there are bigger things in the world."

"Hey, pal, I don't have anyone to look after my skin like you do—no nice mommy and daddy waiting to bail me out of jams or feed me and nurse me and—and all that. And why are you taking all this out on me, I'd like to know? Why isn't your father to blame? I thought he was supposed to get us some friendly cops? As long as you're tossing blame around, try to be fair about it."

She looked as if she wanted to scream back at him but drew a deep breath instead. "When are you going to figure out there aren't any friendly cops?" she asked, dousing him with scorn. "Cops are oppressors, no matter who's mayor. The only side they're on is the one that pays them—and Tammany must have paid off—got it?" She turned away from him and began to shake with sudden, tearless sobs, the excoriation too much for her on top of everything else the night had witnessed. He tried to loop a comforting arm around her, but she recoiled at his touch. "Don't you understand?" she blurted. "I expected more from you—of all people—I expected more—"

"I thought I was doing the right thing—going for help—"

"The help would have come—what difference could an hour have made? I wanted you there with me—" Her head snapped up and confronted his. "I gave you part of me because—because I thought you were worth it. But now I see all you're worried about in life is protecting your own sweet ass."

Three days later, Fiorello La Guardia polled 483,000 votes on the American Labor Party line; his winning citywide plurality was 450,000. The celebration at the Christopher Street headquarters went on past midnight. Saul Orloff gave him a warm handshake when the final results were received, and Adele Orloff added a kiss and a hug. Nina offered nothing but a cold smile of thanks and left early with Melvin Kantor.

He called her vile names in bed alone that night and wondered what it took to wring justice from the just. She was someone he might have come to love.

II

The letter from Justin Bloomgarden, forwarded with a well-wishing note appended by Doc Haseltine in Pittsfield, seemed like a palimpsest of a long-fled folk culture, a runic artifact of some forgotten world he had visited once under the spell of druids. New York, voracious consumer of lives and feelings, was unkind to memory; it operated entirely in the present tense.

After saying he hoped things were good with Toby and all was fine in New York, Skeezix got right to the point. At his end, things were not so hot, and he thought they might go better for him in New York, where he had some relatives. He had written them to see if they knew of any jobs in the metropolitan area but so far no luck. Maybe Toby had heard of something or knew of somebody who could offer a lead. "I'll do anything that pays," Skeezix wrote, "and am a good worker, which I think you can vouch for."

He asked Buddy LaRusso to check with the craft unions at the paper, thinking Skeezix had the makings of a good pressman, but there was nothing doing and probably would never be; an inexperienced man without a legacy had to learn the trade somewhere else. Toby then telephoned Saul Orloff, who promised to give his request some thought but advised there were four jobless men in the city for every opening that paid more than subsistence. "Tell your friend they stopped paving the streets here with gold about twenty years ago." At Sunday supper, Toby even asked Milton Wasserman if he knew of anything—or if he would ask Ira to keep his ears open for anything in Jersey. "Vat kind of a Bloomgarden," Babette wanted to know, "is called Justin?"

His last resource, which he mined most reluctantly of all, was Garrett Chafee. Hoping the memory had faded, Toby offered no regrets in his letter for his behavior at Eden's Labor Day party and stressed instead the work strengths Skeezix could bring to the Chafees' paper-bag factory—honesty, conscientiousness, and enough intelligence and leadership aptitude to qualify eventually for managerial rank. "Your superintendent," Toby concluded, "would find him a very valuable commodity, indeed."

Probably the man would not answer him. Probably there was a surplus of paper-bag workers. Probably the Chafees were preoccupied with plans for Eden's wedding—the house and grounds would make a storybook setting for it. Odd, though, that there had been no engagement announcement in the paper yet; Toby looked every night as soon as the first edition came up. It would be any day now, certainly. They deserved each other.

Mr. Chafee acknowledged the inquiry almost at once and with the utmost courtesy. He telephoned at the paper to say there was a small but constant turnover at his plant in North White Plains, so that if Toby's Mr. Bloomgarden would present himself at the manager's office, there would be a position waiting for him. The work was pretty monotonous at first, he felt compelled to warn, but if Bloomgarden was both diligent and patient for six months or a year, he would probably advance rapidly and earn a decent enough living. Toby thanked him warmly, told Chafee he would not regret this kindness, and, conscience-stricken at the end, added apologies for the display he had made at their home.

"That's quite all right," Chafee said. "And you weren't all wrong."

"Sir?"

"I say, you weren't all wrong with regard to Richard."

"I'm not sure I follow, sir."

"I think the fellow's got some deep problems to work out."

"I—wouldn't be surprised, sir."

"You sound as if you don't know they've broken off."

"Who, sir?"

"Eden and Richard."

His whole world stopped rotating. "I—no—no, sir—I didn't know, sir. I don't see much of your daughter here, I'm afraid—since—that night—"

"Yes—well, it's done with, and for the best, I think."

"Yes, sir. Well, thank you again, sir. My best to Mrs. Chafee, sir—and your dog, too, sir—he's a fine animal—"

Rapturous the rest of the workday, he did not pause to separate the rush of vindication from the far sweeter scent of sudden possibilities he had so long relegated to daydreams and anguished nights empty of all feeling but envy. That evening, though, incontainable with wild hopes and furious desire, he paced Broadway and kept battling the intrusion of reason. What preposterous theory of countervailing fates had planted in him the notion that Richard's plummeting star would signal the ascent of his own? What conceivable justification was there for such a sequence? Which of his sterling qualities could commend him to such a girl—who lacked for nothing but tenderness?

The night air cooled his mania and bent his resolve. Now that she was no longer at an encased remove, he weighed the reality beyond his infatuation. What did he really know of her? Propriety had denied him any touch of Eden Chafee beyond the merest grazing. He could conceive of her only in terms of fleeting sensation—the dart of her unsparing tongue, the mineral luminosity of her glance, the burst of graceful laughter so attentive that its equally swift withdrawal left him pained. . . . But her essence grew more elusive with each sensory strand. It was like trying to render a sunset by reciting the properties of light and the principles of refraction.

Yet he could not help himself. By morning, he was ready to approach her at the paper—saying what? He had heard and was sorry? A heinous lie. Had heard and was delighted? Infelicitous in the extreme. No, he could not plan it. Yet he would not trust to spontaneity in so fragile a circumstance; the wrong word, or phrase, or nuanced look was odds-on to infuriate.

He was spared the dilemma that afternoon by one of her now rare appearances in the city room. She was talking earnestly to Stakesing when Toby noticed and, with angled steps and averted head, managed to overhear the gist of it. Eden was after an assignment with the big boys. She had picked up a lead from the editor of the fashion page. One of the strikers from the *Eagle* had been dressing up in a gorilla suit and running up and down the escalator at the Abraham & Straus department store in Brooklyn, urging customers not to buy there so long as it kept advertising in the struck paper—and wouldn't that make an amusing feature story for her to handle? Stakesing thought not. Eden came away from his desk with blood in her eye.

Toby intercepted her at the water-cooler. "Goddamned dictator," she swore within his hearing only. The editor had ruled her ineligible for assignments outside of her lovey-dovey department—and furthermore, the *Trib* was not in the habit of publicizing newspaper strikes. "How the hell did Nelly Bly get a break?" she snarled, barely noticing him in her anger. "Sleeping with the slimy bastards, I'll bet."

It had to be one of the few times in her life she had been thoroughly thwarted. She might even be experiencing a glimmer of compassion for the world's downtrodden, a momentary grasp of the meaning of oppression. He called her aunt's apartment that night and proposed that she keep him company the next day while he discharged his moral duty to march in the *Eagle* picket line. "Come on," he said, "it's time someone showed you there's more than peaches and cream out there."

"That's dumb," she said. But her usual snappishness was missing.

"Come on—you'll learn things."

"I've got work."

"Me, too—but you can play hookey for once. Call in sick like I'm going to."

"Why should I? I don't give a damn about the strike."

"That's exactly why. It's not just guys running around department stores in gorilla suits." He paused while she considered. "How can you expect ever to be a reporter if all you care about is the light side of life?"

There was a vast, heavy-breathing stillness. Then she said, "All right."

She showed up in her lobby in gray wool slacks, a man's checkered hunting jacket, and a silk scarf over her coiffed head, all intended to ward off the cold as Toby had prescribed. Whether it was just her mood or the bleakness of the day or her misgivings about the cathartic value of their expedition, she was uncharacteristically silent on the subway ride to Brooklyn. It was the only time he could remember being with her when she had not at once made him feel at a disadvantage. She wore the vexed look of somebody who had just had the air let out of her tires in the middle of a prairie. "Do you want to talk about it," he finally decided to risk, "or shall I pretend not to know?"

She studied the advertising placards across the aisle. "I'm sure I don't know what you have in mind."

"Forget it, then—I'm in no mood for games, either."

"Fine by me." But plainly it was not. She let another station pass before half-turning toward him and unburdening herself. "He's full of hate," she said, "mostly of himself."

He only nodded and let her explain at her own pace.

The breakup had begun with an untidy row at a restaurant between Richard and Eden's married sister, Alicia, and her husband, Rem Pelham, who directed sales operations of the Chafee manufacturing enterprises. Rem and Richard had been cast as close future associates, but they had never exactly hit it off. And then, at the fateful lunch, Richard had passed a remark about Mayor La Guardia's "mongrel ancestry" that Alicia found distasteful in substance and unduly loud for public utterance. "And what with Rem's long-standing disapproval of Richard's mannerisms—the ones I thought were playful he told Lish he found actively unpleasant—the two of them up and left in the middle of the meal."

On a visit to the Chafees' soon after, Richard was seen by the gardener delivering a swift kick in the flank to the startled Jefferson, their Irish setter—"something about its sniffing up his pants leg too determinedly," she said. "Ever since your memorable appearance, I think Richard took it into his head that Jeffie was the enemy." Nobody called Richard on his outburst, but her father let Eden know he didn't hold much with dog-kicking. "And finally there was this little bombshell." She dug into her change purse and drew out a much-folded news clipping.

He had seen the item when it ran and thought nothing special of it. The grand jury, at Tom Dewey's behest, had returned indictments against four men for racketeering in the bakery industry. Toby recognized none of the names. "What about it?"

"The third one—that's his father."

"Nathan Kronisch?"

"Better known as Norbert Crandall for the past twenty years or so." She had been apprised of his bootlegging activities—Richard had made them sound quite sporting; after all, probably half the country had flouted Prohibition. And by association, Richard became vaguely notorious and all the more exciting to her. At any rate, he assured her that outlaw booze had never been more than a sideline for his father, whose principal business was importing luxury goods—fine wines, perfumes, rugs, animal hides. More to the point, Richard insisted the Crandall interests had gone entirely legitimate since repeal. "When this indictment thing hit, he swore it was all news to him and begged me to believe him."

What had reduced Richard Crandall's credibility to the vanishing point, of course, was not his father's devious doings, of which a son might plausibly have been ignorant, but the withholding of his family's religious antecedents. Still more troubling to her than the dubious social rewards of marrying the son of a Jewish racketeer were the implications of the pitiable anti-semitism and related displays of malignity he wore as a cloak. These bespoke a character so devious and unworthy, and a personality so obviously ill at ease with itself, that she was left with no option in their relationship but to end it unconditionally.

"I'm sorry—for you," Toby said.

"Oh, well," she said, looking up at the ceiling fan, "you have to admit the timing was exquisite—we had all but set the date. I actually thanked God in church the Sunday after it happened—and Aunt Winnie was practically down on her knees. She's never been high on Jews." She tucked the bitter memento back into her purse, gave a couple of uncertain blinks, and then looked up at him brightly. "Now remind me why it is I'm going out to this awful place to lend comfort to the proletariat."

"Because," he said, "they'll kill you eventually if you don't."

Like the *Trib*, its artistic qualities did not spare the *Brooklyn Eagle* a reputation for miserliness. For eight weeks now, the guild had thrown its whole weight against the paper, picketing from six in the morning till midnight. It had even pulled out six hundred delivery boys in a wholesale effort to strangle circulation. But though its sales were slashed almost in half and ad revenues were off sharply, the *Eagle* would not go down.

The crippling flaw in the guild's assault was the International Typographers Union—the printers. Neither the I.T.U. members nor those in any of the subsidiary mechanical unions at the paper, all of them A.F. of L. affiliates, were willing to go hungry out of sympathy for the white-collar guildsmen, who belonged to the archrival C.I.O. The guild picket line was crossed with impunity, scab staffers were hired to write the paper and lay out the ads, and the presses kept right on rolling.

"But why do the printers do that?" Eden asked. "Aren't the workers all on the same side?"

"If the *Trib* pressmen were striking," Toby said, "wouldn't you cross their picket line and go to work as usual?"

"I never thought about it. I might not—if I knew they were really being underpaid."

"You'd give up your salary, however long it took, to help them?"

"I might. But then of course I wouldn't go hungry, would I?"

"You're catching on."

"But if they don't all pull together, it can't work, can it? I mean, if the printers don't help the guild, why should the guild ever help the printers?"

"You've just analyzed why communism is a dud in America. The printers figure they're the princes of the labor movement. And if they strike and the guild crosses their lines, they'd beat our heads in with large, heavy pigs of lead."

"So why don't you guys do it to them?"

"Because," he said, "the guild is dedicated to the absurd notion that you can be a workingman and civilized, too."

The battleground was an unpicturesque canyon of gray buildings, patrolled by more cops than pickets. Around the corner, the strike high command operated out of a rickety tenement, overflowing with haggard guild members, relatives, and camp followers. Secretaries churned out letters to friends, civic and church groups, and everybody else anyone could think of, asking them to stop taking the *Eagle*. Bookkeepers doled out meager benefits from the shrinking strike kitty. Reporters in slouch hats pounded away on old typewriters, composing the daily strike bulletin. Classified saleswomen worked the phones, urging advertisers they had once solicited to pull out their insertions. Circulation men in derbies hammered fresh picket signs together in the back room. On a big bulletin board, the picketing schedule was posted and consulted. Volunteers from other guild units in the city hung around, waiting to fill in for those who failed to show up.

There were tales of hardship on every side. A married young police reporter who covered Canarsie said he could not take care of his family on thirty-three a week; the humiliation of having to borrow all the time from relatives had pushed him into the guild. A layout artist in display had been furloughed twice and fired outright once without severance after advertising volume took its seasonal dip. A fourteen-year-old who used to deliver to homes in Gravesend passed off his school truancy that morning as kid's stuff and griped about having worked the streets for pennies an hour in all sorts of weather.

This cumulative threnody, offered less in complaint than in petition for understanding, brought a look to Eden—glazed eyes, pale pinched lips, hair mussed and for once forgotten—that Toby took for confession of past obliviousness. She had always known the world was not all Chappaqua and Wellesley and Gramercy Park, but as long as she could repair to them, other people's woes were basically their own. Over a sandwich and coffee at a diner of unredeemed fetidness, Eden announced she would join him on his midafternoon tour of picketing.

It was chilly by then and blowing, but she did not back off, even on seeing she was the only woman out there. The men on duty declined to soften their militancy out of deference to her; they yelled their usual obscenities at everyone who crossed the line. She would not degrade herself by joining in the name-calling but marched beside him, shoulders straight and head up, slackening only toward the end of the hour and then just long enough to light up a cigarette with the others. "Proper women are never seen smoking in the street," he taunted to keep her feisty.

"I have my own rule for that," she said, fighting off fatigue. "So long as you know a thing's wrong—and it doesn't hurt anyone else—you're allowed. Like putting your elbows on the table or saying 'ain't' in polite company." And she puffed her cigarette defiantly down to its last inch.

The oppressively protracted afternoon had at last turned dark by the time the daily meeting assembled at strike headquarters. Afterward, the evening shift was due to take over the long picketing vigil till midnight. Guild morale was at its low for the day, riddled by wea-riness over the cost of the struggle and the uncertainty of its outcome. They needed bolstering badly about then.

But no outside reinforcements from other unions seemed to be com-ing that night as they had on other evenings. Somberly, the negotiat-ing committee, with no movement to report, yielded the floor to the medical committee, which gloomily began to advise there were not enough volunteer doctors to treat all the strikers' families who needed them. The whole room sagged in spirit. Toby looked over at Eden, who was sated with the whiff of despair and eager now to flee the scene.

The next instant, though, the whole building started to shake with the tread of arrivals pounding up the narrow staircase and bursting in upon the dispirited setting. They were brawny men in pea jackets and dungarees from Joe Curran's National Maritime Workers, and there was no end of them. They filled the room and backed up along the staircase and out into the street—more than a hundred able-bodied seamen, their leader reported, as the guild people clapped and cheered and whistled and took heart anew that their cause might yet prevail. Odets himself, Toby thought, could not have staged it better.

The seamen made wonderfully truculent pickets, rippling their tat-toos and bellowing in their foghorn voices, slowly at first and then building into a chant that only the stone-deaf among the printers in-side the *Eagle* could miss: "Don't set scab copy! Don't Set Scab Copy!! DON'T SET SCAB COPY!!!" On this ringing note of hope, Eden and Toby headed for the subway back to Manhattan. The whole day had confused and moved her.

En route to the station, they turned down a side-street shortcut and passed a fenced lot. Gruff voices and violent sounds jumped the bar-rier. Toby ran to a narrow slit in the worn fence planking and peered in. Just enough light from the streetlamp on the corner fell over the lot for him to make out the mayhem. Three or four of the union seamen, supervised by derbied guildsmen hovering in the shadows, were pounding away at the guts and groin of a pair of apparent scabs, waylaid on leaving the *Eagle* for home.

Toby looked at Eden in mute frustration. It was an inexcusable act —the work of brutes—but what could he do? She pushed by him to the fence, looked on with horror, and whirled around on him. "Well, don't just stand there, for heaven's sake! Make them stop it!"

"How?"

"Go in there and tell them they're animals!"

"They'll knock my block off—"

She spun away from him furiously and started to scream for them to stop at the top of her voice. She screamed murder, she screamed for the police, she screamed for neighbors to help. The beating in the lot broke off almost at once as her shrill alarm rang down the street, and doors and windows flew open in response. Within moments, a siren wailed in the narrowing distance and a protective ring of onlookers had formed about the beaten scabs.

Nerves frayed, Eden hailed a cab for the trip home. She sat in a corner, as far from Toby as possible, smoking rapidly and making her displeasure with him unmistakable. "Were you really just going to march right by there," she demanded finally, "as if nothing horrible were happening?" She did not care if the driver heard.

"I couldn't have done any good against all of them—"

"I did—and I'm lots littler than you."

"Men aren't supposed to scream—"

"They're also not supposed to run away from a fight!"

"I wasn't running away. I just—wasn't—running into it—"

"Oh, what's the damned difference? I thought you were so honorable?"

"I never claimed that. I try to do what I think is right—"

"Wasn't it right to stop that—that—beastliness?"

"If I could have thought how—without getting my neck broken—"

"You think too goddamned much, Toby—that's your problem! Sometimes you just have to do what your instincts tell you to."

"I do—all the time. You should know—weren't you around when I told your ex-boy friend what I thought of him? You practically shoved me out the door."

She fell silent, replaying the episode in her mind. "That was different—you had nothing to lose."

"Nothing," he said, "except you."

"Me? What did I have to do with it? I thought that was all about Nina."

"You thought wrong. I was also sending you a message."

She pulled deeply on her cigarette and sent the smoke curling to the cab roof, seeking madly for escape. "Then you're even less principled than I thought."

For an instant he wanted to grab this merciless girl, this implacable cunt that she was, and pitch her in the river. He said nothing until the cab swept up the approach ramp to Brooklyn Bridge. "Has it ever occurred to you, baby, that maybe those fucking scabs got what they deserved?"

She watched the soaring filaments of bridge cable whiz by like giant harp strings serenading returnees to the heart of the city. "I thought, *baby*," she said wickedly, "yours was supposed to be the civilized side."

It took till the Friday after Thanksgiving for his anger to subside. This sudden vicious streak of hers made no sense. Probably it had more to do with her own disquiet than any failing of his. Having narrowly avoided marriage to a man severely short on scruples, she was overquick now to find fault with him—even as Nina, casting herself as the embodiment of retributive justice, had demanded the sacrifice of his hide for the gift of her precious intimacy. Bitches, the both of them.

In the society department, they told him she was gone—resigned from the paper, hadn't he heard? Something about personal problems she had to work out. Such a shame for the staff to lose so able and hard-working a girl. . . .

On the phone, the maid told him Miss Eden and her aunt had gone south for the winter. No, there was no message for him. He thought of asking for a mailing address but decided against it. Instead he sent her an early Christmas card care of the apartment. "My side says taking a powder like that is also not very civilized. Please write to me—I miss you and want you to know how much."

But Eden Chafee did not write.

III

If his relationship with Sylvia Wasserman had no possibility whatever of growth, it had the virtue, at least, of being undemanding—a quality on which his reeling emotions placed a high premium at the moment. Still, it bothered him to think of her as just an easy lay at a time when little else in his life seemed easy.

She was not altogether simple. In comparison with the two younger women who had brushed him off so shabbily, she plainly suffered from an inferior education and narrow range of experience. Within those limitations, though, her mind was as capable of being aroused as her body. Not surprisingly to Toby, she tended to fix on elemental questions rather than the great socioeconomic issues of the day. She would pursue them with a childlike curiosity that, even while risking his esteem, touched him.

One afternoon she asked him why he thought men had nipples. The question, coming as they lay side by side naked and spent, made him laugh at first. But she was not just being playful. Men's nipples, without function or beauty, genuinely puzzled her. How could nature have made such a mistake?

"Would you feel happier if they were rhinestones?" he asked. "Or maybe coat hooks? Hooks would be good—men are so sloppy, always tossing their clothes and things around—"

"You're just joking," she said, "and I'm serious. Don't you think it's strange, really? Everything else on you has some purpose—except maybe your body hair—and I guess that's left over from when men were monkeys."

"Apes, I think it was." But he restrained himself from patronizing her when he saw, as then, that she was truly taken with some less than cosmic mystery. "Maybe it's the same with nipples," he offered. "Maybe sometime way back, men could nurse, too."

His speculation interested her. That it was an utterly idle one did not diminish its value to her. And her way of soliciting his views and engaging his casual answers was as flattering to him as his continuing sexual attentions were to her. There were times when her questions caused him to think through a thing he had never bothered to pose to himself before, and he would return to her a few days later with elaborated thoughts, as if discharging a school assignment.

Earlier that fall, he had presented her with a copy of Hemingway's new novel, *To Have and Have Not*, thinking she might be taken with the feral masculinity of Hemingway's latest and most ruthless hero. Toby had found something oddly sympathetic in the character and plight of Harry Morgan, particularly as manifested in his dying words: "A man alone ain't got no bloody . . . chance." Sylvia was repelled by the book and wondered what made it literature.

"The language," he said, "the feeling, the thought—it's hard to separate them. I guess you didn't think it was very refined."

"Not very." Few American novels of literary pretension had dealt with sexuality as advanced and varied. Sylvia was more confused than stimulated by its inclusion. "Why does he have to write about it that way?" she asked.

"What way?"

"So much—and so openly."

"Why not? It's an essential part of life."

"But it's so—so private. He makes an exhibit of it."

"That's what writers do—exhibit our secrets. Hemingway's always writing about love and courage and death—they're private, too."

"Not the same way."

Not to her, anyway. Sex was the prime adventure in her life at the moment, and he would say nothing to make it seem commonplace. Instead, he considered the question she had not quite articulated and came back to her not long after with a fresh thought he hoped would satisfy her. "Sex belongs in literature because they share something basic," he proposed. "Each is more intense than normal life. Each is supposed to be more exciting than ordinary experience—and so more beautiful and powerful and affecting—"

"But some things become less beautiful when you write about them," she answered. Then, hesitating, she added, "And if you were a woman, you wouldn't think of sex as so wonderful and intense. A lot of the time it's very—unpleasant—when you have to, no matter how you feel—" She looked puzzled by the sudden furrow of his brow: was it due to her swift rebuke of his exquisite insight or an inference that going to bed with him could be an ordeal? The latter seemed more likely. "Oh, I don't mean us," she said. "I meant—before. With him—" She ran her hand over his ridged forehead to wipe away the distress.

"Did you ever try telling him?"

"What?"

"That you didn't feel right sometimes—or that you had needs, too."

"I couldn't do that."

"Why not?"

"He's not like you—he wouldn't understand. He'd think I was—either oversexed or undersexed, depending on—you know—"

"I think you should risk it. It's your life, too, not just his."

There would be moments like that, when their minds and feelings as well as their bodies drew close. It was then that she was most likely to become not quite possessive but deeply concerned about his future—almost perversely so, he thought, since it was plain she would not be a part of it. To her he was so smart and personable and well-mannered and, judging from the things of his he showed her in the paper, so talented that she supposed he could do almost anything in life. The *Trib* struck her as a way station for someone with his blessings. "Don't you ever want to have money," she asked, "and position and—and influence? Maybe you just need the right connections."

"I'm afraid it's my connections and not the rest that got me this far," he said. His ambitions at the moment, he added, did not extend beyond trying to stay solvent and hoping somehow someday to make the world a more decent place. She asked what he meant by that. "Nice people," he explained, "ought to be better off than lousy ones."

"Oh," she said, closing her eyes and placing a warm palm against his cheek, "oh, you poor boy."

He wanted to do something special with her over the holidays, but it was obviously impossible, so he did the next best thing, hoping she would understand. He invited Victor to Radio City for Chanukah to see *Snow White and the Seven Dwarfs.*

More than a year had passed since he had taken the boy to the rodeo. Toby's relationship with Victor's mother made this outing a more trying prospect, as if it profaned the very idea of family and fidelity, but he mustered an extra ration of cheer to hide his uneasiness. Victor was much too enchanted by Disney's sugar-plum shenanigans and the whole festive air of the great movie palace to notice Toby's solicitude. Only when the stage show came on, offering an outsized Nativity scene followed by a colossal "Ave Maria" on heaven's own organ, did the boy slip into a somber study of his own. Jesus had been on his mind lately, he told Toby on their walk to the subway. He had heard his parents and grandmother talking about an article in the newspaper that said the Nazis approved the celebration of Christmas in Germany even though Jesus was nominally of Jewish parentage. According to the Nazi version, Jesus had actually been sent to earth to save it from the Jews, and anti-semitism was one of the cardinal tenets of authentic Christianity. "That's stupid and hateful," Toby assured him, "like everything else about the Nazis."

"Then why was Jesus sent to earth?" Victor asked.

"To purify it, I think the Bible says. A lot of people—Jews among them—had lost faith in God and become corrupt."

"Like caring about money and stuff?"

"And not much else—except maybe having a good time."

"Is that what you think, too?"

"I—I'm not sure, exactly. I wasn't around then."

Victor's suspicions were alerted. "Don't you believe in Jesus, Toby?"

"Well—yes—there was a Jesus. And he taught wonderful things. But I'm not so sure God sent him—or who or what God is Himself."

Victor's eyes widened at the enormity of the confession. "You don't believe in God, either?"

"I didn't say that. I said I don't know what God means, really, except some thing or some body lots more powerful than people."

Victor pondered that on the ride home. "If you don't believe Jesus was related to God," he said prescriptively, "you might as well be Jewish."

Toby smiled and said he thought all the world's religious denominations would do more good figuring out what they agreed on than arguing.

Victor nodded and thought some more. "Do you think the Seven Dwarfs were German?" he wondered as their train pulled into Eighty-sixth and they got up together to get off.

"I think they were sort of international." On the short walk home, they rehearsed the names of the dwarfs. Victor kept forgetting one or another. Toby provided them with rhyming aliases. "Let's see, there's Bumpy, Mopey, Sleazy, Sappy . . ." Victor was convulsed with giggles by the time they got back to the house.

His grandmother, however, was not when, several days later and in a somewhat garbled version, Victor recited Toby's articles of agnosticism to the family and sought their opinion. "Did you really tell him Jews cared only about money when Jesus came?" Sylvia asked him on their walk to the store the next afternoon. Toby denied he had said that and was afraid Victor had misunderstood everything else as well; he would be glad, though, to straighten the boy out. "I wouldn't," his mother said. "He's still too young. And Babette thinks you're trying to convert him as it is."

"To what? I told him I had my doubts about Jesus."

"I know. Babette hears only what she wants to hear. Sometimes I think she's got it in for you—though I can't imagine why."

Shortly after the year turned, clues emerged to the old woman's animus. On one of their assignation days, Babette found the shopping list that Sylvia had left for Toby under the lamp on the vestibule table. The only time she regularly got up from the wheelchair each day, other than to use the toilet, was after the mailman poked his delivery through the front-door slot at about ten in the morning. She watched for him through the parlor curtain, with special eagerness on days she was expecting something from relatives on the other side. Charged with anticipation, she would then shuffle to the door, painfully negotiate the little flight of stairs in the outer hall, and devour the day's post. It was on this regular mission one January morning that she spotted Sylvia's shopping list awaiting her lover's retrieval.

"I told her it was yesterday's list," she reported to Toby on their walk, which by pre-arrangement replaced their upstairs rendezvous if the list was missing. "I said I must have left it there with the grocery bags so I could get my key out when I came back."

The incident would not have been worth a second thought had the old woman not noticed that the list included lamb chops when Sylvia in fact had brought home a brisket the day before. Sylvia explained that the butcher was out of lamb chops, but the interrogation hinted at a pattern of heightened surveillance. One afternoon the previous week, Babette had watched her daughter-in-law go out shopping in a coat too light for the season and—she told her after, amused by the futility of the gesture—wrapped a knuckle vainly against her bedroom window to summon Sylvia back inside. What bothered Sylvia about this earlier incident was its disclosure that Babette did not always nap in her room after lunch even though that was her announced intention. Neither development, however, or even the two together, could necessarily be taken for intensified scrutiny of Sylvia's activities. "Some times are worse than others," she told Toby, "but it's always been more or less like this."

Even so, they decided out of caution to refrain from their appointment in his room that week. And Sylvia would make sure thereafter that the shopping list was well hidden under the base of the lamp in the hall.

Their sexual activity resumed without further disturbance until the first week in February. On the appointed day, Toby went down to do Sylvia's marketing but found no list waiting under the lamp. Assuming there had been some hitch again at her end, he stayed in that wintry day until just before it was time to meet her for their walk. But then, a moment or two early and as if nothing irregular had interrupted their arrangement, Sylvia tapped lightly on his door and came in flushed as usual from the four-story climb and the prospect of imminent delight. The surprise on his face, and the reason for it, set off an immediate shared alarm. Could she have been careless enough to have left a tiny corner of the list exposed? If so, Babette must have been examining the area with a magnifying glass. Or was it possible Milton or Victor had taken it? But why? Or was it possible Sylvia had somehow been distracted and forgot to put out the list? "I don't forget you," she said and clenched her fists in suppressed panic.

They sat and planned her explanations step by step:

1. On certain days, especially when the weather was raw and she had other errands, Toby did Sylvia's marketing along with his own as a courtesy to her and a way of repaying the family for the Sunday suppers he took with them.

2. The note was left secured under the lamp so it would not blow off the table when Milton and Victor went out or the postman pushed in the slot.

3. Sometimes while Babette slept and presumably did not need her, Sylvia would drop up to Toby's sitting room for a cup of tea and a little socializing. She was most likely to do that on days like this one, when he had shopped for her and she had a little extra time on her hands.

4. None of this had been revealed to her mother-in-law earlier because Babette, being of the old school, might get the wrong idea. But she could be sure Toby was a perfect gentleman at all times.

With this lawyerly defense worked out, Sylvia's courage and carnality revived together. She had no intention of being bullied out of the only steady source of pleasure in her life. Boldly she drew Toby up by the hand and led him into the bedroom. The threat of detection, however remote, worked as a powerful aphrodisiac on them. Her passion in particular flung him up and askew of her fleshy limbs and nearly smothered him in viselike caresses. She was never a pliant lover, and torrid moments only emphasized her density, but there was nothing ever mechanical about the motions she went through on his steamy bed.

As he sat on the edge of it afterward, watching her draw on her garments with distracted precision and admiring her defiance of whatever lay in store below, he heard the noise. It was a dim thump but close by enough for them to look up in unison toward the door. Toby dressed quickly, catching up to her, and poked his head cautiously into the hall. He saw nothing out of order at first. Then his eye wandered down the staircase. There, sprawled crookedly across the steps midway to the fourth floor, lay Babette Wasserman's wasted body.

They exchanged a horrified glance as Sylvia rushed up behind him to the head of the landing. The look alone sealed their tacit concurrence: Nothing could have pushed the old woman to that expenditure of effort, with its attendant pain, except the hope of catching them in the act. And she had very nearly succeeded.

Sylvia slumped against the wall in soundless shock. Toby, swept up in fright yet oddly insulated from panic by an almost pleasurable sensation of detachment, went to examine the crumpled body. Though she was still warm, Babette's eyes and mouth hung open in ghastly accusation; Toby could detect no breath or pulse. Beneath her sat a small puddle, where she had voided, and nearby, the telltale grocery list, creased from fierce fingering. He looked up at Sylvia and shook his head. She uttered a single gasp and slipped to the floor, conscious but momentarily paralyzed.

He calmed her and said they would have to call at once for an ambulance. After a moment down some dark, bottomless shaft, she raised her head, panic in retreat and the first flicker of relief in her unfocused eyes, and asked him what they should say had happened. His mind tumbled after order. Nothing could undo the damage. The thing was to minimize it as perfectly natural. While Sylvia telephoned, he would carry Babette downstairs to the parlor sofa. Sylvia would say she had found her at the bottom of the landing when she got home after the old woman had presumably tried to climb to the second floor on some errand as she would occasionally do rather than await her daughter-in-law's return. The noise of her fall would have been too remote for Toby to have heard from his room.

Sylvia nodded numbly and drifted down the staircase, stepping over the remains of Babette Wasserman as if they were already carrion. Toby bent almost worshipfully and hoisted the body with the utmost care, trying not to look at the Gorgon head and instructing himself he was in no real way culpable for her unfortunate end. She weighed more than she looked. Struggling with the leaden load, he called after Sylvia for help. She stood frozen at the foot of the landing, watching his wobbly descent. "Suppose she's not dead?" she called up in alarm.

"What about it?"

"She'll tell—"

His mind had fogged. She was right. They could not chance a return from the dead and a contradiction of their account. They would have to revert to their previous story, he said as she helped him lug the ghastly cargo down—Sylvia had been up in Toby's rooms taking tea when it happened. He worried about stirring Milton's suspicions. His anger would be aroused, Sylvia guessed, only by her temporary abandonment of his mother's service. Indifference had precipitated the tragedy, he would charge, adultery never entering his mind.

But it was never far from hers, even after the mourning period had passed and Babette's broken bones and burst heart were one with the earth. She would not resume their sexual relationship until he had persuaded her that the old woman might have died at any moment and, if any blame had to be assigned, her own wickedness was at fault ten times more than Sylvia's justified infidelity. But she lay beside him cold and inanimate, as if the harridan's scolding phantom still stood watch outside his door. He consummated the act despite her rigidity, and she abandoned any pretense of effort, leaving his room sorrowful that she had let him convince her to enter it.

When Victor contracted pneumonia soon after and worked up a blazing fever, Sylvia left Toby in no doubt, by barring the door when he offered to help her with the nursing, that she took the boy's illness for divine retribution. The severity of his condition put Victor in the hospital for four days, during which his mother was in almost continuous attendance. After he was better and back home, she climbed up to Toby's room at the first opportunity to say that she could never sleep with him again and their friendship and its confidences were over. He did not argue, thinking she would change her mind soon enough. Instead, she came up to him again one morning the following week and said she could no longer bear the thought of his being up there—and had decided she must tell Milton everything. She was terribly sorry, but Toby would have to move out by the end of the week.

"But why?" he asked. "You think God's punishing you?"

"And won't stop until I do this—"

"Sylvia, God's not a bookkeeper! It's all in your head."

She stood in his doorway, fleshy arms folded. "Yes, I knew you'd say something like that. But it's what I feel—you have to understand—"

"And telling Milton about us—is that supposed to make him feel any better? Does making your husband miserable help you much with God?"

"I—don't know. I just—have to. Milton has to understand, too."

"And if he doesn't?"

The sternness drained out of her shame-haunted look. "I can live with that better than trying to hold it all in."

Victor watched him pack in grieving silence. It seemed funny for anyone to move just to get a little closer to work. At the end, he asked Toby if he would come to his bar mitzvah the next year. "If I'm invited," Toby said, looking up fondly and trying not to let his own sadness show. Then he gave the boy a firm handshake and the house key for his mother, who was out at the beauty parlor. The country English mezzotint she and he had bought at the antique shop he left behind on the sitting-room wall.

The trolley took forever to come. The long wait made him feel doubly exposed by his eviction. Nobody he wanted wanted him. The fault could not reside entirely in the stars. Yet he did not understand what he had done wrong—to have been rejected so utterly and in such short order by all three women. Whatever it took to win a sustaining reciprocal love in this life, he had been unable to discover. It began to occur to him that day that perhaps he never would.

When the trolley came at last, it was a short ride down to Lincoln Square and the small room he had rented in a cheerless residential hotel just east of Columbus. You couldn't beat it for convenience, he told himself, unpacking.

IV

Sundays threatened a return to the loneliness he had shed after the first few months of tenancy at the Wassermans', so he planned to pass at least part of his first one away from them by visiting Wally Eichhorn. Wally's devoted roommate, Kenny Lomax, welcomed his call and urged him to come by for a light lunch they had planned for a few friends. To ensure against a blue stretch thereafter, Toby rang up Dan Jonas, who suggested they take in an afternoon movie and have supper at the Jonases' Grand Concourse apartment. Glad of the offer, Toby proposed as an afterthought that Dan join him on the visit to Wally's.

They brought bagels and whitefish to supplement the small spread Kenny had put out for the guests, who included a couple of theater people and Kenny's brother, Pete. Wally's stroke left his speech only slightly impaired, but he had lost his speed on the uptake and was more inclined now to be a listener than the flippant foil he had always relished playing. The lead part, somewhat altered in tone, was taken for him by Pete Lomax, whose sobriety was leavened by flashes of warmth that Toby supposed uncommon among higher functionaries of the Communist Party.

There was little of the firebrand to his rough-hewn look, which, on a cold, quiet Sunday, was just the civil side of ill-kempt. His sizable homely head suffered from a spareness of hair, concentrated in puffy arcs of grayed black above his long, narrow, nearly lobeless ears. A bulbous nose added to a certain coarseness of appearance. Only when he unlimbered his balladeer's voice did he convey a more than physical largeness of presence. Yet his private conversation was ideologically lean, almost devoid of rhetoric, and the more persuasive for it.

He was saying that the war in Spain was still in doubt but the Western democracies were content to let the Republic bleed to death. It had come down now to a contest of morale—"which is why the bastards are bombing the hell out of the civilian population up and down the east coast. It's Guernica times ten."

Toby said he was not entirely sure the bastards were all on the other side. In Loyalist-held Barcelona, where the fascist "fifth column" had induced serious internal hemorrhaging, pro-Franco sentiment was reportedly cause enough for arrest and detention and, in a growing number of cases, execution. "That's not exactly a ringing endorsement of liberty and democracy."

Pete Lomax looked across his end of the table at the polite young challenger and, correctly gauging his general sympathies, was disinclined to argue. "But you can't think we like doing it."

"I don't know if that matters," Toby said. "I'm just saying it costs you your moral advantage. Once violent repression begins, there's no end to it. It's never stopped in Russia, and the revolution is twenty years old."

Provoked more pointedly, Lomax remained unfazed. "I have a little secret, Toby, I want to share at no expense." He leaned forward in mock confidence, bulking his shoulders. "War is shit. People are shit. The whole world is shit. And my side isn't a whole lot better than the rest because it's only human. But it also happens to be man's best hope for salvation, so take care how you knock it."

Toby said he was openminded on the subject, but the evidence from Russia was not overwhelming. That very morning, he had read an article in the new number of *Partisan Review* that left him particularly doubtful. Titled "Second Thoughts on the U.S.S.R.," the piece was by André Gide, among the world's ranking men of letters and a pro-Marxist. Russia had cast open its arms to him recently, recognizing a potential bridge builder to the Western intelligentsia. Gide was appalled by what he found: on every side, political terrorism, profound poverty among the workers, gross disproportion of incomes, re-establishment of the class system with party membership assuring high privilege, and liquidation of the soviets—and thus all semblance of legitimate democracy. The Soviet Union had utterly betrayed his hopes that socialism was the antidote to capitalist oppression.

Pete Lomax listened, hands clasped over one elevated knee, and nodded at the end in acknowledgment of the charges. He had not read the article, he said, but was certainly familiar with such criticism. It was necessary to bear in mind, however, that people like Gide, even if well-intended, were products of a highly developed bourgeois culture and had next to no firsthand knowledge of conditions under tsarist Russia. Without a doubt, the Soviet state practiced a degree of authoritarian control, but this undesirable policy was an absolute historical necessity. Centuries of depraved despotism had crushed the Russian masses and left them desperately selfish and smallminded. It took the Revolution to start convincing them of their own better natures—and that their only real prayer of escaping a life of perpetual degradation was to pull together. Sometimes the lesson had to be taught ruthlessly to discourage counter-revolutionary elements.

"In other words," Toby translated, "all dissent is treason. And what else can you call that but totalitarianism?"

"They call it patriotism," Lomax said with a tolerant smile. There seemed to be no hidden menace in the man.

Perhaps spurred by his exchange with the Communist operative on the ambiguities of social reformation, perhaps shamed by the rebukes dealt him for cowardice by Nina and Eden, he did not shrink from what he conceived to be his duty on learning at the paper the next day that Buddy LaRusso had been let go.

After the *Eagle* strike had been settled at the end of the year on terms close to the guild's demands, LaRusso renewed his push to get the long-lapsed contract talks with the *Trib* management going again. In response, word was circulated that LaRusso was merely a puppet carrying out instructions from the guild's Red-lining New York chapter. When the paper said it would consider resuming negotiations only if the *Trib* unit elected a new chairman, LaRusso protested the condition as a transparent tactic to divide and conquer guild ranks and refused to relent. Low on-the-job production was given as the reason for his dismissal, but few doubted what was behind it.

Fearing further management reprisals, no one else in the *Trib* guild unit was willing to circulate a petition protesting LaRusso's firing and demanding his reinstatement in the name of fair play and free speech. The cause, for once, seemed utterly unambiguous to Toby; the risk, while plain, worth it. It was not merely a matter of somebody's having to do it—he believed that the pivotal moment in the fight to win a guild contract was at hand, and if a moral example were made of management's intransigence, the outcome of the battle could be changed. Once he had faulted his father for a failure of character in a matter of comparable self-interest; was the difference between them to be only the size of their worlds?

"They'll kick you the hell out of here for sure," Dan Jonas told him when Toby presented the petition for his signature.

"Not if the staff stands up for what's right."

"The staff'll sit on its ass and protect it."

Toby regarded his friend with the resignation of a shipwrecked sailor watching the last timber float by.

"Dan, I really need your help on this. It's for everyone's good—"

"Not mine," Dan said. "I'm sorry, Toby."

He tried to buttonhole people on both shifts in front of the lobby elevators as they arrived and left, but everybody kept waving him off like an annoying insect. During the lunch break, he pursued them at Bleeck's and got an even colder shoulder. Finally, he took up a position just inside the lobby doors, where he was hard to miss, and stood there all day with his petition on constant view, in silent accusation of management's iniquity and the staff's complicity in it, until it was time for the nightside to report upstairs.

After three days of this conscience-pricking vigil, meeting the eyes of every passing staffer who dared to face him—whether with admiration, pity, or contempt made no difference—Toby was summoned to the office of the managing editor, a potentate with whom he had exchanged not more than six words since joining the paper. His vocal cords constricted as he hied himself into the dock. He had done nothing he was not proud of or was afraid to answer for. Still, doom was in the air.

The managing editor looked like a clergyman, with his punishingly starched collar and steel-framed glasses and well-fed face and fine white head of hair. His voice, directed into the phone at the moment of Toby's arrival, was remarkably placid, as if used to no greater effort to gain its sway. Having motioned Toby into a chair, he was in no hurry to ring off. After a few exchanges, it was plain that the party at the other end of the phone was Walter Lippmann. They were talking about the situation in Austria, on whose borders Hitler's troops were massing. All at once the world seemed extraordinarily large to Toby and his place in it infinitesimal. He sat and stewed, contemplating his fate and Austria's, linked only by their joint powerlessness.

The managing editor of the New York *Herald Tribune* finally hung up on the paper's most celebrated retainer and turned his attention to perhaps its least celebrated. "Mr. Ronan, you are either about to be promoted to our City Hall bureau because you've shown such high promise since coming here," he said with awesome crispness, "or you're going to be dismissed for demonstrating no talent whatever after a fair enough trial period. The choice is entirely yours."

"I—don't quite understand, sir."

"This is not the moment for ingenuousness, Ronan." The forbidding figure picked a sheet of note paper off his desk top and consulted it briefly. "By a wide consensus of your superiors on this paper," he said, as if dictating a flawless lead, "your editorial skills are matched only by your misguided social idealism. No one questions your right to this alleged highmindedness in the privacy of your conscience—or perhaps your prayers—but once it manifests itself overtly, your value as a professional newspaperman all but vanishes." His eyes strayed from the paper for an instant, locking onto Toby's by way of assurance that the judgment against him was not disembodied. "Almost from the day you were taken on, you've worked tirelessly to advance the efforts of the Newspaper Guild to organize this paper in the face of management's known disapproval—"

"That's not really true, sir—"

The man flicked another look at him over the tops of his rims. "Let's not quibble over a month one way or the other, shall we? The charge is essentially valid."

"I'd question your word 'tirelessly,' sir—just as I would your use of 'misguided social idealism.' I thought it was my professional obligation to try to help win better working conditions for news people."

"Your professional obligation," the managing editor said, chillingly now, "does not include functioning as a union agitator at your place of employment or as a political radical in your off-hours." Among Toby's offenses, according to his extended indictment, were attendance at Leftist fund-raising events, marching in the May Day parade, campaigning for the American Labor Party, picketing the *Brooklyn Eagle*, consorting with known members of the Communist Party, and, of course, continuing acts subversive of *Trib* management. "Now you can either be a newspaperman here, Ronan, or you can be a Red, but you can't be—"

"I'm no Red—sir—"

"Well, from all the evidence, you're certainly a fellow-traveler,

which around here is a distinction without a difference." He replaced
the damning slip of paper on his desk. "Now you can either tear up
that petition of yours for Buddy LaRusso—what's done is done where
he's concerned—and promise us you're through with all such childish
and unwarranted agitation—in which case you begin at City Hall next
Monday with our full blessings. Or you can take a walk out of here
with our profound regrets and not expect to find another newspaper
job in this town—or probably anywhere else."

It was a face wrapped in the eyeless mask of obsidian authority,
human in form but titanic in might and preternatural in purpose, compacting behind its scaly shell all the malignity on earth. The choices it
dangled before him were to recant for no wrong and conform with
iniquity—or to purchase his own professional oblivion.

"You told them everything," he charged, more in sorrow than in
anger, as he pulled Dan after him into a corner of the wire room. "I
thought you were my friend—"

"I didn't tell them anything they didn't know already—mostly,"
Dan said, swallowing hard.

"No one else knew all that about my personal life!"

"You're wrong—a lot of people did—and they asked everybody.
And you don't exactly have a button for a mouth. I've told you all
along you were digging yourself into a hole—"

"I haven't done a damned thing dishonorable!"

"They think you're a communist, Toby, or about to become one—"

"So why didn't you set them straight?"

Dan fell silent, struggling not to cry.

"You mean you think so, too?"

"I don't know what you are—I don't think you do, either, if you
want the truth." He confronted Toby with watery eyes. "They said
either I told them what I knew and they'd make me a reporter, or
they'd put me on the lobster trick and leave me there." His eyes
dropped to the floor. "What choice did I have?"

Over and over, in mindless refrain, the curse blazed through his
brain, taking temporary possession of his reason as he battled the rush-
hour hordes in the Times Square subway station. He had never met a
Jew he could fully trust. They always had some excuse for their rubbery behavior, as if survival among the Gentiles justified a license in
dishonor. And Jonas was a Jew, and his spineless treachery congenital—

By Columbus Circle, the fever had receded, leaving him in flushed
awareness he had been re-enacting two thousand years of history.
Calmer now, he tried to distill instruction from disaster. Tumblers
whirred, hunting for a mesh. Life was an endless series of delusions

from which a man had to disenthrall himself to survive. There was no God to grant his soul grace. No Truth to guide his mind to serenity. And, most especially, there was no Justice on earth worth struggling to enthrone. There was only an abyss men dreaded to approach. He crept to its edge unaccompanied—his abandonment was complete now —and peered over. With cold detachment, he contemplated his own obliteration, wondering only why eternity had bothered to create him in the first place.

On the seat next to him, a little girl drew her mother's attention to a placard across the aisle advertising *Snow White and the Seven Dwarfs*. The child began to recite the gnomes by name and then hesitated: "Happy, Dopey, Doc—"

He completed the roster:—Grumpy, Smelly, Shitty, and Despondent. And Snow White was a whore.

NINETEEN

HE RAN OUT of curses and melancholy at about the same time and
then was mostly in need of balm. But in the entire city, whose shoulder could he cry on? Or in the wide world, for that matter? His own
would have to do—no easy trick with a neck as stiff as his.

His options, he saw on cold reflection, were three: self-extinction,
flight, or renewal.

The first was not without its momentary appeal. He was exhausted
by defeat. But there was no getting away from the irreversability of
the step. Life was not very long, anyway; only misfortune made it
seem so. He had reason enough to dwell in gloom, he told himself, but
not yet to despair. Being up the creek without a paddle was not nearly
as bad as being there without a boat. And in his own mind, anyway,
he was still seaworthy.

Perhaps voyaging somewhere else was the answer. But he had already been there. No, New York was the crossroads of humanity; if
he was to thrive anywhere, his chances were better here.

That left a fresh start. Well, he was young enough and strong
enough for that. But how could he reverse his abominable luck? If he
had been cast as misery's child, maybe the reason was that he had been
more at the mercy of events than their shaper. He could reverse the
sequence by the exercise of will. As long as the world kept rewarding
him perversely for his principled behavior, what point was there to his
playing by the rules of righteousness? No one else did.

Having been discarded by his last two employers for a cause entirely unrelated to his performance, Toby now suffered only the
briefest stabs of guilt over doctoring his job résumé. The deceit was
justified by his estimate that, given the cutthroat competition for editorial work, he had more to gain than to lose from it.

He had contributed regularly to the *Lampoon* at Harvard, he lied
on his meticulously typed *vita*, and been an editor on "the undergraduate daily," omitting that it was a short-lived rival of the *Crim-*

son. After that, he claimed two summers as a staff reporter for the Nyack *Journal* and six months as a police reporter for the *Berkshire Eagle* before coming to the *Herald Tribune,* from which he said he had resigned over a philosophical disagreement. For references on the out-of-town papers, he made up names, figuring nobody would bother to check. For the *Trib,* he listed Ned Kirby, the lobster-trick slotman, who he prayed was kindly disposed toward him; every other editor, he supposed, was certain to hew to management's line and brand him a troublemaker.

He sent out exactly one hundred lying letters—thirty to newspapers, of which the Trenton *Times* and Stamford *Advocate* were the most distant; thirty to magazines, especially recommending his gift for prose condensation to the *Reader's Digest,* and forty to publishing houses, stressing his graduate work in literature. In his first sustained go at it, however, dishonesty yielded him no more than virtue had. He got back only two inquiries of interest. Harper & Brothers interviewed him for an opening in its copy-editing department but hired someone else. And the *Record* in Hackensack asked him out to Jersey and liked his credentials—until they called the *Trib* for corroboration, and Ned Kirby said he hadn't seen enough of Toby's work to judge it properly.

After a month on an emotional rollercoaster, living off his bank account and beginning to fear fear itself, Toby went one night to seek counsel from Wally Eichhorn, a past master at survival in the arts. With his special knack for uncovering submerged talents, Wally soon established that Toby had training as a printer as well as a *litterateur* and urged him to seek something temporary in the mechanical trades; meanwhile, he could write on his own and collect unemployment insurance from the state.

Only the last part of the suggestion did he find distasteful; he would not go on relief without being really destitute. Three quarters of a million people in the city needed help worse, and the state had just announced a 10 percent cut in the welfare budget. It was not a matter of his being excessively moral, he told himself, spurning a fresh chance to cheat on the system; it was a question of self-respect. Lying a little to get a job was different from taking bread out of someone's hungry mouth. "You, *boychikel,*" said Wally, "are what the locals call a first-class *schmeggege.*"

For a change, though, his incorrigible rectitude actually did him some good. Wally's roommate relayed word of Toby's plight to his brother. And upon learning of Toby's courageous stand, and fall, at the *Trib* and his refusal to take relief he did not yet need, Pete Lomax was moved to offer him help in finding work as a printer. Toby's pride readily accommodated this kindness from an official Communist so long as no strings were attached. When Lomax phoned a week later about "an unusual situation," he promised Toby the only recompense that would ever be asked was to spend one day in the field alongside him, observing a C.P. officer in action. On that understanding, Toby became the sole hired hand of the Sunshine Press, a comically cramped job shop in a Lafayette Street loft.

Isidore Sonnschein and Benjamin Rafalsky had eked a living out of the place for twenty-two of the thirty-five years since the distant cousins had emigrated together from Galicia—and fought with each other all the while. Bennie, a bachelor, was the more apoplectic of the pair. This condition, according to Izzie, traced back to their initial decision to call the business after his name instead of Bennie's or some combination of the two. "Could I help it everybody is happy from the sun shining," Izzie asked, "and nobody cares from a Rafalsky?"

"He's *meshugge*," Bennie rebutted after Izzie had gone home for lunch. "Also a *draykop*—you know vat dat is?" He poked the side of his skull with his finger in imitation of a woodpecker on the job. Bennie's real complaint was that Izzie was good for nothing but fixing the machines; when they were running fine, Izzie ran like molasses. Bennie put up with it, he said, because their business was rarely heavy enough for Izzie's phlegmatic ways to hurt much, and when orders piled up, they hired part-timers for a few days. It was true that Bennie moved at about twice his cousin's pace, but neither of them thought to mention, until after Toby had been there several weeks, that Izzie had suffered a heart attack five years earlier and probably should have been exerting himself still less.

Izzie's reduced capacity and Bennie's advancing years explained the unique nature of Toby's apprenticeship. Neither partner had an heir apparent to groom; Izzie's daughters were married, one to a dentist, the other to a butcher, and Bennie had no close family except a *schmendrick* nephew who was barely literate. If Toby proved efficient inside the shop, they would eventually cut him into the partnership. And if he could bring in new business, especially from the Gentile world, where the two principals rarely ventured, his percentage would grow accordingly. Meanwhile, much of their volume came from Leftist sources—union letterheads and newspapers, C.P. pamphlets, A.L.P. campaign literature—that they supplied almost at cost to appease their socialist souls, so Toby would have to settle for thirty a week, whether the work took him ten hours or sixty. And no bonus for turning all the copy that came in into creditable English.

Toby convinced himself there was nothing humiliating in the obscurity of his new labors. He could not have just sat around waiting for an editorial job to turn up. And who knew where this opportunity might lead? After all, Ben Franklin and Sam Clemens had started out as printers and wound up celebrated. Here was the chance to create his own franchise. And with a little judicious budgeting, he could get by on the pay and still put a bit aside.

By the time he arrived in the mornings, the fumes from the cooking lead pot told him Bennie had already been at the linotype awhile. Bennie was a demon on the lino (aside from a tendency to drop the articles from his setting copy when he went too fast), so Toby was assigned mostly to the composing stone and operating the smaller presses. His rustiness showed most when he had to set display type by hand, but he savored reacquainting himself with the distinctive character of the faces—the grace of Caslon, the clarity and dignity of Bodoni, the crabbed fussiness of Cheltenham, the proletarian bluntness of the sans-serifs. Breaking down the handset, though, and resorting it was another matter, mindless and boring. Gingerly he asked Bennie if there was any prospect of their getting a Ludlow machine; it would improve his work output considerably, Toby said. "I ain't no capitalist," Bennie replied, "and God didn't give you hands so you should be a pickpocket."

Blistering heat and ragged metal soon calloused those soft hands, and ink rimmed the pores of every exposed centimeter of his body, eyelids included, from the feel of it, as production at the Sunshine Press rose steadily. Faster, in fact, than the work came in. By his fourth week on the job, Toby was sitting around half the day with nothing to do but read Izzie's copy of *The Worker* or learn the Hebrew alphabet from Bennie's copy of the *Forward*.

During one of these slow stretches, Pete Lomax came by with a job —Comrade Stalin's historic call for a democratic front among freedom-loving people everywhere to fight fascism was to be memorialized in an eight-page party pamphlet. Seeing that Toby had time on his hands, Lomax invited him along the next day to observe, as he had promised to sometime, Communist Party functionaries on the job. Toby looked over doubtfully at his bosses, as if to say he was in no hurry to redeem his pledge to the Red. "Go vit' the *momzer*," Bennie said, patting Lomax on his broad back. "I gotta set his type first, anyvay, or dere vouldn't be no revolution."

They met for coffee at eight in a White Tower. Not owning overalls or knowing how leaders of the proletarian cadres dressed for work, Toby guessed his disintegrating sport jacket would not tag him as excessively bourgeois. Lomax wore a dark-brown suit with patches of sheen and the vestige of a press. His green knitted tie looked as if it had been knotted with one hand. There was little hammer and less sickle in his tool kit—his words of briefing to Toby neither blud-geoned nor slashed, and his eyes, slightly red-rimmed and rheumy at that hour, had none of Saul Orloff's judgmental intensity. A college graduate brought up in the labor movement, he had the disciplined toughness of a man who knew his strength, both physical and intellectual, without the need to spend it on pointless display. He operated instead at a soft, steady drumbeat, advancing his purpose by cumulative effects. It was this calm certainty that won Toby's admiration from the beginning.

The section for which Pete Lomax exercised party oversight, running from Fourteenth Street down to Houston and from river to river at Manhattan's widest point, included thirty neighborhood branches and six industrial ones, the latter all within the union movement. He served also as party liaison with every political, civic, and fraternal organization within his boundaries. On top of that, and as a reward for his diligence downtown, he had recently been appointed interim organizer for the Yorkville section, pending the selection of someone full-time. His work, he told Toby, was one-tenth passion and nine-tenths persistence.

They went first to a meeting at the business office of the Painters Union local in a little office building on Broadway just below Fourteenth. Toby was introduced to the executive council as a graduate student preparing a dissertation on the varieties of social protest. The painters' concern at the moment was that a lot of the union's laid-off rank and file were having trouble collecting jobless benefits due them under the state's three-month-old unemployment insurance program. One of the union councilmen was Lomax's branch organizer in the paint trade and had arranged the invitation so the section organizer could explain how other unions were dealing with the issue.

Lomax spoke slowly, in plain, if not monosyllabic language, making eye contact with each wool-shirted man at the table in clockwise rotation. The problem was twofold, he said—the claim forms were tricky to fill out and business owners were being even trickier in avoiding their legal obligation to pay in their share to the jobless kitty. Viewing the worker benefits as money thrown away or, worse still, as a form of strike insurance, many bosses chiseled every way they could. Some failed to list all their employees when reporting payrolls to the state. Others got cute, changing their firm names, or moving, or going bankrupt needlessly. Least artful were those simply ignoring the law altogether on the premise that the state's enforcement arm was hopelessly puny.

"You have to be your own enforcers," Lomax urged the unionists. First, they ought to form an unemployment committee that familiarized itself with the subject inside out. Then they should advise the membership how to obtain documentary evidence of salary payments, especially since so many painting contractors kept no books or records. Most important, a knowledgeable union official had to accompany every worker when he brought his application in to a state claim reviewer, who often enough proved to be a terrible stickler. "Fortunately, several of the most sympathetic of these examiners are our people," he said, "so if you run into any real son of a bitch over there, let me know and maybe we can do something."

There was no humor and no bombast. And he did not vilify the cheaters as capitalist exploiters of the masses, although he made their meanness clear enough. It was all nuts and bolts. He was there to instruct, not convert them. Toby could detect nothing devious in his approach; hard counsel scarcely qualified as manipulation.

At the end, Lomax solicited their beefs about the state's jobless provisions and promised to pass them on to the C.I.O. people who would be pushing for improvements at the next session of the legislature. Among the worst faults the council scored was the exclusion of payments to unemployed workers who were sick and therefore not available for immediate employment as the eligibility rules required. Such a prohibition had the absurd effect of denying help to those needing it most. On the street, Toby asked what the rationale could have been behind so heartless a provision in a social reform measure.

"Callousness and stupidity," Lomax proposed, "about neck and neck." After a moment he added, "You understand, of course, in Russia they don't have any unemployment insurance whatsoever."

The man's habitual directness had lulled Toby off-guard. "Why not? I thought it was a workers' paradise—"

"Because," Lomax said, plunging a hand into his pants pocket and giving the contents a jingle, "they don't have any unemployment. And if you're sick, the state provides the care—it doesn't punish you."

The unsubtlety of the advertisement came as a surprise. It was as if all the red cards in his hand were trump and he had no need to employ finesse in playing them.

At a tenement on Ninth Street, between Second and First, they trooped up to a fourth-floor apartment, where Lomax's knock was tardily answered by a woman with a face so pinched and worn that Toby could not even guess at her age. Her bulging eyes, like rancid gelatin, met theirs only with palpable pain. Mrs. Miller's situation, Lomax told Toby en route, had been called to his notice by a party member serving as a case worker in the city's Emergency Relief Bureau. But the welfare workers were overloaded, so Lomax himself looked in now and then.

"Emil's took the baby to Bellevue," Mrs. Miller said. "He's gonna give blood, but the poor thing's so anemic they don't hold much hope—"

Defeat had drained her every semblance of childbearing ripeness. Hag's hair tumbled uncombed to her shoulders, and breasts that not long before had nourished hung like shriveled sacks to her waist. The baby had come a month and a half early, she explained to Toby in a thin, grief-rattled voice, and they had told her at the hospital to try to build it up with Viosterol—"only they don't have such expensive stuff at the relief bureau." She had done her best to sustain life for four months, but their relief payments just didn't go far enough. The rent was $32 and the utilities $4.50, which left $54.70 a month for food, clothing, and all the family needs. Her four other children, ranging from six to sixteen, were also seriously malnourished, and the older boy needed an operation but the doctors thought he might not be strong enough to survive it. Her husband had last worked four years earlier as a cab driver. He looked so gaunt and zestless these days, nobody wanted to hire him. "And now they're going to cut the welfare payments," she said, sinking into the one upholstered chair remaining in the living room. "I think maybe I'll jump in the coffin after they put the baby in." She said it without a whimper, as if every tear had long ago been wrung out of her.

Yet she had not surrendered. Frail and tattered as they were, all her grown children attended school—Mrs. Miller saw to that. Her older daughter, Laura, was doing well in art, she said, a glimmer of life awakening her face. There was to be an exhibition at the Astor the following Saturday, and her drawings were among those selected for display. The girl wanted to attend in the worst way, "'but Ma,' she says to me, 'how can I go up there—I got nothin' to wear.'" Her head turned up in appeal. "Maybe you know somebody who's got a daughter? For me, I wouldn't ever ask. . . ."

Lomax made a note to call Adele Orloff and put it in his shirt pocket. "She lost another baby the same way three years ago," he told Toby as they strode north on Second.

"I hate to ask it," Toby said, "but why does she keep having them?"

"I hate to say it," Lomax answered, "but in Russia they'd give her a medal—and all the food and medicine her baby needed."

At eleven, they joined an interracial group planning a rally in Union Square two weeks later in support of the antilynching bill before Congress. Most of the session was devoted to determining who would speak for how long in what order. Lomax was asked if he thought there was a chance of getting Robeson to fly back from Europe to be the star of the occasion. "I'll check," he said, "if you're sure you want a Red star." The representatives of the N.A.A.C.P. and the Urban League, appreciative of his sensitivity, thought not. Neither did they object later to his insistence that a C.P. spokesman be included in the program.

On the way out, somebody told him about an upstanding Negro tenant being evicted from an otherwise all-white house on St. Mark's Place because he refused to pay a rent increase that had not been levied against the other residents. Lomax took down the address and nodded.

"Why did he tell you?" Toby asked.

"I guess he thinks I'll do something about it."

"Like what?"

"It depends. Maybe try to shame the white tenants into signing a petition against the landlord. Some people still have a conscience if you appeal to it right."

"You make it sound like an art form," Toby said as they headed for the Lexington Avenue subway.

"Call it what you want—people here have to be retaught how to care for each other."

Patriotism pushed Toby to a token defensive protest. "I understand they don't have any lynchings in Russia—just firing squads."

"For enemies of the state." Lomax paused at a candy stand and bought a Hershey. "Actually, they have a hundred and eighty different peoples and nationalities living in harmony under a single socialist regime."

"Centralized brotherhood—"

"What's wrong with that? It's pretty amazing if you stop to think about it." He broke the chocolate bar and gave Toby half. "Lunch is on me."

Toby shook his head admiringly. "No rest for the righteous?"

Lomax shrugged. "You've got to keep chipping away at the sons of bitches."

At Hunter College, he stopped by the administrative office to pick up an envelope Nina Orloff had left for him. At her instigation, the graduate seminar in sociology, of which she was a leading light, had been taking an inventory of tenement housing in south Yorkville. She had got her hands on an abstract of the preliminary report and was smuggling it to Lomax to use to the party's best advantage. In his view, that meant being first to bring the Hunter findings to the Yorkville Tenants League, his chosen instrument for expanding the C.P.'s section membership.

While pocketing Nina's envelope, Lomax overheard mention of a joint student-faculty meeting about to begin in protest of the firing of a Jewish instructor in mathematics for no justifiable reason. They hurried to the large lecture room, slipped in the rear door, and hung at the edge of the gathering unnoticed just long enough for Lomax to jot down the particulars on the back of Nina's envelope. In the lobby, he phoned the story in to *The Daily Worker*.

"In Vienna," he said, hanging up, "Jewish women are being made to clean streets with a toothbrush for the amusement of the Nazis. These things can't be allowed to happen here." Nor could the degradation of women as a whole be justified in any humane society. The fact that Hunter had the largest enrollment of any women's university in the world served ironically, he noted on the way out, to dramatize sexual inequality in America. The school system was entirely co-educational in Russia, where 41 percent of all university students were women, more than 35 percent of the work force was female, 47,000 women were doctors, 100,000 were engineers and technicians—

Toby threw up a hand to slow the deluge. The man was a walking encyclopedia of sovietology. But how many of his claims were true? Probably he himself had no idea, so bewitched was he by the rosy glow from the east. If Russia was doing even half as well as he claimed, then why were its people not free? Lomax would say freedom was a relative condition. He would say economic degradation was the worst enslavement. He would say greed was pestilential and the profit system a license to rob. But what made his own motives so selfless? All seekers of dominion, even those in sheep's clothing, had the instincts of oppressors. This one probably just disguised his better than most.

The Hunter report was titled "Yorkville Slum Survey," but Lomax was tactful enough, in disclosing its data to the executive board of the Tenants League, to refer to it as "the tenement study." Covering the housing between Fifty-ninth and Seventy-ninth from Second Avenue to the river, the field survey found that 80 percent had no central heating, half had no private toilets, one third had no running hot water, and that there was a total of 32,000 "dark rooms," windowless cubicles that were potent incubators of disease. Added to the chronic disrepair of the tenements, this grim testimony, which Lomax recited with proprietary vehemence, bespoke a crying need for public funding to house the area's impoverished. He proposed that the league move at once to circulate a massive petition to that effect, based on the Hunter findings, and present it with urgency to City Hall and Albany. "They've sunk hundreds of millions into bridges and tunnels in this town," he said. "Now let them spend for the people."

But the real estate interests, he was told, insisted that East Side land values were too high to sacrifice property there for low-income housing projects. "All they want to do," said the director of a settlement house, "is bring the moneyed crowd in here and drive out the poor. There's no incentive to improve anything."

"Then we have to give them one!" Lomax replied sharply. The force of his thrust gained from its brevity. No one needed a speech.

But Lomax did have one speech to deliver that day. To Toby, it sounded as if it had been conceived with him very much in mind.

By far the strongest industrial branch in Lomax's section operated in the International Fur Workers Union, whose president, not coincidentally, was a C.P. member in good standing. Twenty thousand fur workers had been out on strike for nine weeks, seeking job security—after a week's trial, no one should be fired at the whim of the boss—and equal distribution of the seasonal work so every man would be assured at least eight months of employment a year. Spirit ran so high in the union that instead of letting the strike degenerate into a bleak, embittering campaign of attrition, the leadership had turned it into a rallying time.

There must have been two thousand people, Toby guessed, in the strike hall on Irving Place. In the back of the room, the chessboards and ping-pong tables were thronged. Along the sides, workmen's circles were discussing how to improve health conditions in the fur shops and other subjects of ongoing concern. On the makeshift stage up front, the union choir performed. Periodically, all activity would give way to a documentary movie, a lecture on a pressing social topic, a speech by a dignitary, or a bit of entertainment, all supervised by that convalescent impresario Wally Eichhorn, son of a pre-union furrier renowned for having run a decent shop when decency was in short supply. "Hello, *boychik!*" Wally cried above the din, more verve in his voice than Toby had heard in over a year. "Don't listen to anything the Vulgar Boatman here tells you—or them," he said, giving Lomax a fraternal slug on his padded shoulders. "It's all propaganda."

The hall quieted at once when Wally introduced him. Lomax, without notes, breathed fire he had been stoking up all day. "The bosses say communists don't believe in democracy," he began, just below a shout, "and I say, 'Look who's talking!'" There was an immediate ripple of appreciative laughter. "It's capitalism, my friends, that brings dictatorship to the people—and which of you doesn't know it? Every hour of every day, in every company shop and factory and workroom across the land, the owners enslave us privates in their industrial army with a cold, cruel discipline that tolerates no back-talk. You complain, they take your head off. Some democrats! And they say *we're* the ones who should be suppressed. Well, let me tell you men something. You let William Green and Father Coughlin and Martin Dies and his

Un-American Activities Committee lock up the Communist Party and you can kiss democracy in America goodbye forever—because the unions will be the next ones to go, and then the liberals and the churches and everyone else who gives a damn for the masses of humanity—and we'll wind up right where Nazi Germany is today!"

Stirred by the force and sense of Lomax's language, Toby suddenly saw the C.P. as the lightning rod for the whole Left. Whatever its excesses, however much obeisance it paid to Russia, it was a moving, shaking force indisputably devoted to making America more endurable to the underclasses.

They went to Bellevue Hospital after that and both gave blood for the Millers' baby. When they got up, Lomax asked about the infant's condition. It had died, they were told, at two o'clock.

As if his veins had reopened in sorrow for the nameless, helpless creature and the tormented womb from which it had issued, he felt a seepage of his own vital plasma that no mere sentiment could stanch. The child's epitaph came to him out of the dustbin of his mostly forgotten collegiate readings: "There is no wealth but life." Ruskin. Not a very good communist.

And still Lomax's day was not done. At a bar on Twenty-second Street, he met with a group of clerks from Metropolitan Life, being threatened with firing by their departmental supervisor for talking union. And after that, he gave an informal talk to the weekly meeting of an A.L.P. youth club in the back of a refurbished old grocery at Twelfth and Avenue A. It was after eight by the time they got to Ratner's for soup and a piece of fish.

Fatigue showed at last in the slump of his heavy shoulders as Lomax sat half-leaning against the mirrored wall, oblivious to the clatter of the busy restaurant. Where the man found the strength to drive himself so incessantly, Toby could not fathom; his own energies had waned somewhere around the middle of the afternoon—and he had been only a spectator. What struck him particularly was that none of Lomax's dealings all that day had been a parochial party matter. He was working for the betterment of the needy, regardless of affiliation. Toby wondered why philosophical allegiances did not play a larger role in the allocation of his time. "Philosophers have only interpreted the world," Lomax said. "The point is to change it."

Toby concurred warmly.

"Good—that was Marx—if you'll forgive a little underhandedness."

It was a mild enough deception; the sources of the man's inspiration were hardly secret. "Is it like this every day?" Toby asked him.

"Oh, no—sometimes things get a little hectic."

The food and rest refreshed Lomax to the point of ordering them a piece of strudel to split and probing lightly into Toby's personal and political past. The fusion of the two, he thought after listening with care, was highly significant. Even more revealing was the pattern: At college, in the C.C.C., and on the *Trib*, Toby had wound up in deep trouble for his radicalism, although in each instance he had steadfastly refused to perceive of himself as an extremist.

"Right—because I definitely am not one," he said.

"You know what you sound like to me?" Lomax asked, forking up a chunk of the apple pastry. "A light Negro trying to pass. What's the point? Why don't you admit what you are to yourself—you'll be a lot happier. What's wrong with being what you feel? You're blessed with the compassion to see the failings of the social order and a compulsion to set them right—is there a better thing to do with your life? I've never heard of any."

"Believing is one thing," Toby said. "Doing is another. I don't think I've got the stomach to be much of a revolutionary."

"You never know."

"You mean it just takes conditioning to learn to love violence?"

" 'Love' is a little strong—'tolerate,' maybe."

And did that mean Lomax held out no hope the political system could correct the social disorder—through organs like the A.L.P., for instance?

"The trouble with labor parties is they can't do any more than drag concessions out of the system—they never alter its basic exploitive nature." Roosevelt had proven as much. Nothing essential had changed under the New Deal; concentrated ownership of the means of production and the maldistribution of wealth were unchecked. "A few less people starve now, maybe, but the struggle goes on."

"Until the revolution?"

"A revolution can take many forms, but in a word—yes."

"And when will it come?"

"As long as it takes." Lomax eased forward and massaged the side of his neck. "The truth is, it all depends on people like you." The *Manifesto* prophesied—correctly in the Russian instance—that as the social crisis intensified, a small but enlightened splinter element in the ruling class, recognizing the revolutionary party's claims as just, would break off from its origins, join the cause, and provide it pivotal, triumphal leadership. "And that's why we're here talking."

Toby let out a mordant laugh. "You think *I'm* part of the ruling class—making thirty a week in a grimy loft?"

"Next week you could marry a millionaire's daughter."

"Next week I could mangle my arm in a printing press."

"You'd still have another arm," Lomax said, "and I want its fist." Then he went to phone Adele Orloff about a dress so Laura Miller could see her drawings at the Astor that Saturday.

II

On the evening he attended his first meeting of the Bank Street branch of the Fourteenth-Houston section of the New York City district of the Communist Party of the United States, no intention was farther from Toby's mind than the withdrawal of allegiance to his country.

Of the reasons he gave himself to justify his attendance, the most pressing was the possibility, however slender, that the Communist way of organizing society could in fact provide greater good for a greater number of his countrymen than the prevailing system. It was not a possibility he had been willing even to contemplate seriously before. Only now did it seem truly arguable which of the two opposing systems was the more humane—capitalist democracy or socialist autocracy. That very phraseology revealed his previous bias; the socialists, of course, contended it was they who were the authentic democrats and the capitalists who were the absolutists. All Toby knew for certain was that the American social order had not worked to his advantage. Indeed, it had kicked him around the block a few times like a bundle of misguided rubbish. He was therefore no longer readier to dismiss the possible validity of socialism because of the excesses and shortcomings of the Marxist-Leninist model in operation than he was to ignore the cruelties and failures of American capitalism. He owed it to himself, he thought, to learn what it was the domestic Reds were really peddling.

He owed it as well, he told himself, to Lomax, who had taken the trouble to call him twice and propose the idea. Naturally it was flattering to be valued and wanted. The appeal went beyond that, though. Whoever or whatever Pete Lomax was in the privacy of his soul, that bulky body of his housed the most selfless, saintly man Toby had ever come across.

There were other factors as well that prompted his first tentative step toward organized communism. His work at the print shop offered little intellectual stimulation; he soon began to feel himself mentally as well as physically isolated and feared his brain would atrophy before long. At least as relevant was the comforting knowledge that Adele Orloff served as educational secretary of the C.P.'s Bank Street branch. In the back of his mind lurked the hope that his attendance would restore him to worthiness in Nina Orloff's hard eyes.

Before Toby went, Lomax was shrewd enough to orient him. The meetings would undoubtedly strike him at first as indoctrination. It would be better, Lomax suggested, if he approached them as a seminarian does his studies, steeping himself in the thought, traditions, and program of a lay faith at least as transcendent as any self-proclaimed holy one. The party, Toby would have to understand, was not designed for him alone. Many who found their way to its door had a compelling need to be part of something far larger than themselves and finer than any fallible mortal can manage to become on his own. They wanted structure to their lives, and high purpose. And that socializing content the party gave them mattered more than a surfeit of empty, undirected freedom that left them only confused and lost. "What might strike you as authoritarian could be their salvation," Lomax counseled.

The branch met weekly, alternating between secret sessions for hard-core members only and open ones aimed at attracting fresh recruits. The latter were held in a second-floor storage room above a used-furniture store. Aside from an inoperative wood stove, the only objects in the room were a collection of hard wooden chairs of varying vintage and style—surplus merchandise, Toby surmised—and a pair of standing lamps with torn fringed shades. The place was suffused with soft lighting that gave it the approximate cheer of a séance.

Adele brushed a greeting kiss off his cheek and introduced him to the branch organizer, a lean, middle-aged man named Fletcher, and the educational director, a younger, nice-looking fellow named Solomon. It was not clear whether these were their first or last names or, in either case, simply party pseudonyms. Toby counted fifteen in the room beside himself, five of them women and only two or three, by their look, drawn from the unlettered lower reaches of the labor class. The talk beforehand was animated but hardly boisterous, and what strangeness he had felt on arrival was largely routed by Adele's enveloping sponsorship and the subdued cordiality of the others. The worst that could happen was they would find him unsuitable, or vice versa—in which case the adventure of it alone would more than compensate.

The meeting was a hybrid between a newscast and a sermon—urgent flashes dispassionately delivered but evangelically intended. In his mind, Toby likened the production to crafting a sonnet—its form and limitations were all too familiar, but within them, high virtuosity and universal truth were attainable.

Fletcher's skill was quickly apparent in his fluent blend of words and bearing. The organizer wore a tweed jacket with suede elbow patches and spoke in a somewhat exalted vocabulary that likewise hinted of academic affiliation. The substance that emerged from his small, almost reptilian head sounded at times, though, as if it had been forged at an intensity white-hot but rather too narrow to have permitted much inquiry into first causes. Answers, that is, seemed to matter to him a good deal more than questions.

Fletcher's remarks, which aside from a short discussion period at the end formed the entirety of the program, were an apologia for the recent Moscow trials of Bukharin and twenty other old Bolsheviks sent to their doom for treason. The organizer was incensed that most of the American press viewed this latest exercise in Soviet justice as a frameup and a "show trial" when the evidence abundantly demonstrated that the defendants had long conspired to destroy the government, slay its leaders, and give away the Ukraine and other integral parts of the country to its avowed enemies. No serious student of the testimony, he said, could doubt that these spies, wreckers, and murderers had been part of the counterrevolutionary network masterminded by the archterrorist Trotsky.

It was true enough, Toby conceded, that his disapproving view of the purge trials was shaped exclusively by the skeptical accounts in the papers; these had been only slightly mitigated by the pieces he read in *The Worker*, including long transcripts of the confessions he had been conditioned to suppose were extracted from the accused at gunpoint, or worse. Fletcher was entitled to present his case.

The prevaricating tendencies of the capitalist press, the organizer declared, grew directly out of their bitter hatred for the great achievements of socialism in the Soviet Union, "the guiding light of all toiling humanity." The worst malefactors in the U.S. press—"reactionary sheets like the Hearst chain, the *Herald Tribune*, and the *Chicago Tribune*"—sought by their accounts to lend maximum assistance to the Berlin-Rome-Tokyo alliance, which had been exposed at the Moscow trials as the defendants' primary patron.

However illiberal the *Trib* remained in Toby's thoughts, he was jarred by the charge that it was actively aligned with the forces of darkness. At first he speculated that Fletcher's inclusion of it might have been intended as shock therapy for him—possibly Lomax or Adele had told the organizer of his former connection with the paper. And surely the man was too civilized to blur the distinction between the *Trib*'s honest conservatism and Hearst's witless pugnacity or Colonel McCormick's xenophobia. But then it began to dawn on him, hearing Fletcher's sustained objections, that the differentiation, so important in his own mind while he worked for the *Trib*, was no more than nuance when considered against the broader spectrum of political categories. All that mattered to the Left was that the Right-wing press was monolithically propounding the case that the purge trials proved the moral decay of the Soviet state and socialist system.

"Is it moral decay," Fletcher railed, "for a country to cast up out of its vitals that poison which would destroy it? Isn't it more accurate by far to see this as a sign of youthful vigor and strength of purpose?" Was it a sign of moral decay, he asked, for a country to build a better life for its people, battering down every obstacle in the way? Was it a sign of moral decay when a people eliminated all prejudice among its constituent elements? And freed women from medieval slavery and granted them absolute equality with men? And abolished child labor and substituted compulsory universal education, with students receiving pay instead of paying? And provided for the ill and the aged without cost? And wiped out prostitution and its causes? And . . .

His rebuttal did not sound notably more rabid than the detractors of the Soviet system by the time Fletcher was done with them. Toby was complimentary to the organizer as he walked Adele home after the meeting. She brightened at his appreciation. He was a teacher at the New Lincoln School uptown, she told him—"one of those dollar-a-year types, I've heard. He probably could have had a career of distinction at any college in the country if the party didn't preoccupy him so."

"It hasn't stopped your career," he said.

"Mine's different." She matched him stride for stride down Hudson. "And I don't run the branch—I'm no theoretician—and my work uses up very little of my brain."

She was such a strong, proud, straightforward woman; her indissoluble devotion to the party intrigued him. "Do you accept everything Fletcher said about the trials—uncritically? Don't you have any questions?"

"Like what?"

"I don't know exactly. I mean don't you think it's a little strange, for example, that Stalin let these known traitors run around loose for twenty years? After all, he's got a hyperthyroid secret police and informers coming out of the woodwork."

"Don't tell me you think it's a frameup, too? Toby, they *murdered* Gorki—and others—there's no doubt whatever—"

"I'm not saying it's a frameup—and I don't doubt some people in power were killed. But there weren't all that many and it was a long while back. I'm just wondering a little why the state has kept these loathsome creatures alive all this time."

"I don't know. Maybe the police didn't know where they were—or there wasn't enough evidence yet to convict them for certain."

"Maybe. But they've always known where Trotsky's been. If he's such a monster, why do you think they've kept him alive?"

"As an object lesson, I suppose."

"Even though he's fiendishly plotting the overthrow of the government?"

"Well—they must have their reasons, I guess."

"Isn't it possible the state needs internal enemies to justify its authoritarian measures in controlling the people?"

Their pace slowed as Adele pondered a moment. "Toby," she said earnestly, "I know he was a terribly attractive personality in his younger days, but Trotsky is a traitor to the revolution—there's never been any doubt about it."

"Yes, so I keep hearing. But no one tells me exactly what made him a traitor. The worst thing, I gather, is that he kept saying what he believed out loud. Is that so subversive—daring to criticize and dissent?"

"He tried to wreck policies he didn't like—that the rest of the leadership approved. He was a divisive influence."

"If he was so bad, why didn't they put him on trial? Did he ever commit an overt act against the state before they threw him to the wolves?"

"Yes! He definitely did—in '27, I think it was. He tried to organize a street demonstration against the government, but it turned out a total fiasco, they say—"

"A street demonstration? This desperate, power-mad terrorist tried to overthrow Joseph Stalin and the mighty Soviet apparatus with a public protest? That doesn't sound exactly conspiratorial to me."

Adele stopped defending the Red regime and fell still during the last half block of the walk. At the door to her apartment house she thanked him for his accompaniment and gave him a light touch on the wrist. "I don't know all the answers, Toby, but I know it's easy to poke a hole in anything—I've seen Saul do it for twenty-five years. It's the good things they've done over there that I judge them by and care about—and want to see happen here." She kindled a brief smile. "Try to keep the whole thing in perspective."

Fletcher's bugbear at the next branch meeting two weeks later was the deviousness of Nazi propaganda and the susceptibility of the American media to Herr Goebbels' flimflam. The organizer had just seen the latest edition of *The March of Time*, titled "Inside Nazi Germany," which he said was as blatant a piece of fascist deception as any propagated by the Nazi regime itself. The alleged documentary, Fletcher reported, showed hearty youth working and marching and singing, mammoth steel plants going full blast, babies lovingly cared for and people amply fed, soldiers and brownshirts flawlessly uniformed and trooping in unison—and dictators ranting and pliant masses cheering. "But where is the real story?" Fletcher demanded. "Where are the scenes of strikers being cruelly beaten and jailed and shot because they dared to ask for decent wages?" Where were the faces of the Socialist and Communist members of the Reichstag who were thrown behind barbed wire and left to rot in the mire for five years without hope of pardon? Where was the evidence of anti-semitic and anti-Christian brutality?

The offending newsreel feature was running at the Gramercy Park Cinema. On the walk to her home, Toby proposed to Adele that they go see it one night soon.

"Why?" she asked. "I'll take his word for it and save the money."

"It'll be my treat," he said. "I'm just curious—Luce isn't Hearst, exactly. I'm surprised the *Time* people are that pro-Hitler."

"But Fletcher's got eyes—and a brain—"

"So have I—and so do you."

She considered his argument with a doubtful look. "Toby, I can understand how you feel—really I can. This is all new to you, and you have to work it through. But I have more important things to do than waste my time on garbage. I'm willing to take some things on faith—that's the difference between us at this stage. I think maybe the whole idea of that frightens you a little—it's not surprising—and so you keep looking for perfection, and not finding it gives you the excuse to deny the larger truth of what we already happen to believe in."

"I'm not frightened of anything," said Toby, "except blind faith."

He went to see *The March of Time* himself the next night. Fletcher's account of it was accurate with regard to the visual content, but the branch organizer had omitted mention of the accompanying commentary, which left little doubt in Toby's mind about the producers' sentiments. "Democracy in Germany has been destroyed," lamented the narrator with the Jovian tonsils. "Children as well as adults have been regimented by the Nazis . . . all propaganda must glorify the state . . . every year Germany tries to hide its persecution of the Jews . . . the average German worker earns ten dollars a week. . . ."

On the way out of the theater, he ran into Adele and Nina Orloff. His rush of satisfaction at this apparent concession to his skepticism was short-lived, though. Adele granted him a brief, sheepish smile, but Nina dismissed the film's narration as so much background music. "In the movies," she pronounced, "it's the graphic imagery that stays in your head. Nobody remembers the words."

She had a point, just as Fletcher did, but Toby was not persuaded by it. He needed time and space, frankly, to think the whole proposition through, and so he skipped the next meeting of the branch. Two days later, a note arrived from Adele. "There is such a thing as discovering the self," she wrote, "by denying it through submission. Come next time."

He went for his third meeting just before the Fourth of July. Fletcher's text for the evening was "Let the Spirit of 1776 Unite Us to Defeat the Tories of 1938." Jeffersonian democracy, in his rendering of it, underwent a Caspian Sea change. America's just economic foundation, according to the organizer, dated from the breakup of the great colonial land monopolies and opening of the vast territories of the West by the widespread distribution of free or cheap lands. This agrarian democracy, supplemented by an urban democracy of craftsmen working with their own tools as independent contractors, played out the Founding Fathers' dream of a fair and humane society. This ideal was fatally perverted, however, by the onset of the industrial age, with its exploitation of labor and extreme concentration of wealth. Predatory capitalism had made a mockery of social justice. "If Jefferson were alive today," Fletcher divined, "he would be the first to argue there can be no progress in the course of human events where the selfish private interests of a minority are imposed upon the masses. Government, therefore, must revise the social order in accordance with the will of the majority, democratically expressed—"

"No," Toby heard himself speak up, percussive as a Howitzer in a cavern, "Jefferson wouldn't agree to that." It just came out, with no premeditation.

The organizer glanced over at him without a waver in his intent expression. "We take our questions at the end."

"It—wasn't a question. I was disagreeing with what you said."

Fletcher's head drew back. "That's not how we do things here—shouting out disruptions."

"I didn't shout—I was giving my opinion."

"Your opinion isn't invited in the middle of the chairman's remarks."

He felt the molten glare of everyone in the room. But having started, he would not scuttle back to safety. "I'm sorry—but what you said just sounded wrong to me."

"Probably because you come here with your predispositions still intact." Fletcher recrossed his spidery legs. "That's one of the basic purposes of these meetings—to correct misconceptions with fresh, clear thought. That takes an open mind, Mr. Ronan. Now if you can manage to contain yourself until I'm done, you'll have your chance."

When the time came, Toby was less interested in disputing the organizer's interpretation of Jefferson than challenging him on his adopted ground. "What I'd really like to know," he said, "is how the will of the majority is democratically expressed in the Soviet Union."

Fletcher briefly rearranged his skeletal frame, then tipped his chin sideways, revealing a bladelike profile. "The new Soviet constitution is the most democratic in the world," he stated. "Some ninety-six percent of those eligible actually voted for the deputies to the new parliament in December—more than ninety million people." He turned to Solomon for support.

"Ninety-six point five percent," said the educational director.

Toby was almost amused by the statistical flurry. "But if the party selected every candidate, how is that democracy?"

Solomon's lidless eyes fixed on him. "Of the 1,143 deputies elected to the new parliament," he recited, "288 were not enrolled Communists, according to the Supreme Soviet."

"But they were all still picked to run by the party—and without opposition. How is that democracy—if there's no choice?"

"Soviet voters have the choice," Solomon droned back, "of ratifying the state's candidate or scratching out his or her name to indicate disapproval. In the December elections, 1,334,124 voters elected this option. In no case was the outcome materially affected, however, confirming the people's high regard for their government."

It was like trying to debate a shroud. "One could say also that all it confirms is the government's control of the whole process."

"The Soviet state," Fletcher interjected through wafer lips, "reserves the right to insist on loyalty to the revolution and its aims as a requisite for office, much like the constitutional oaths required in this country. I don't think you'll find anyone in Congress who refuses to pledge loyalty to the system."

A hundred points of protest rushed through his mind, clamoring for expression. But the chair's gifts of adroit rebuttal and deflection defied challenge by anyone unschooled in the inquisitorial arts. He subsided without further argument and went home.

All the following week he considered the merits of the party and its claims on his soul. He could not dwell in limbo forever. There was no denying the skill and dedication of its leadership and a certain plausibility to its positions, taken one by one. But the branch meetings were so tautly controlled and the space containing them so seamlessly hermetic that the very thought of them induced a claustrophobic intake of breath. If their purpose was to condition prospective party members to disciplined acceptance of delivered wisdom, they had succeeded only in persuading him he could not long survive the lack of ventilation. He wrote to Adele, saying he was greatly appreciative of her concern but that he would not be returning to the branch meetings. "I cannot bring myself to affiliate," he explained, "with a party that, however admirable its purposes, assigns itself infallibility and the rest of mankind its scorn."

Even less than a reply from Adele did he expect a phone call from Nina. She sounded gorged with compassion. Her parents had gone off for ten days to an adult camp in the mountains; would he like to come over for dinner the next night? She was involved in something new that she thought might help clear up his confusion.

"You think I'm confused because I don't want to join the party?"

"I think," she said, "that you badly need to be rescued—and I'd like to try to help."

"Rescued from what?"

"From yourself. It's an agonizing process for some people."

"I'm afraid I'm incurable."

"Let me try, anyway."

III

If Nina's problem was that she could not distinguish easily between people and causes, his own was a habit of investing his affections inversely to the overtness with which they were returned. But time had painfully corrected this unrewarding tendency. In view of the volatile course of their friendship, Toby reacted to her new gesture with wariness. He sensed a mortgaged motive, as if the party had put a bounty on his head and Nina had contracted to bring it in on a pike.

She had taken a leave from her job at the hosiery store, where things were slow over the summer, in order to attend a workshop in advanced Marxist theory that the party was sponsoring for fifty handpicked younger members. She paid the twenty-five dollars from her own savings for the six-week session, which featured not only leading American authorities on socialist thought but several Soviet eminences from the Lenin Institute itself. "That's very impressive," Toby said, hearing her expand on the marvel of it all moments after he was inside the door. "There's nothing quite like getting the word straight from the bear's behind."

"Oh, boy," she groaned, "they must have fixed you but good at Bank Street. You need nourishment—mental and physical. I better go check the meatballs."

She was a little late. Her meatballs, on the lavish scale of grapefruits, came out chewy where penetrable. But the spaghetti and sauce were only slightly scorched and the canned peaches were flawless. Her long day of exertion, in class and the kitchen, and the closeness of the July night in the cluttered Orloff apartment left her wreathed in unmistakable musk when they met after coffee for a long, deep reunion kiss unlike any they had shared before she broke off with him. If he had any doubt it was prelude to renewal of their sexual intimacy, which he had tasted with such cruel brevity, it was dispelled by her return from the shower clad only in a slip and bathrobe.

"I think I know what the problem is," she said, redolent now of rose petals, as she dropped down beside him on the loveseat.

"What problem?" He could think only of his raging libido and pending indigestion, neither of which would bear revealing.

"Don't be cute—I know you too well." She gentled the top half of him onto her lap, immeasurably improving his receptivity. "The trouble is you're convinced party membership will somehow diminish you —and the truth is exactly the opposite."

"Oh—is this why I'm here?" he asked, consuming her vertically. "Maybe I should be up taking notes—"

"Shhh—just be still and listen." She stroked his head even as he worked it by degrees into the cushioning warmth of her delta. The party was the only practicable way, she said, of fusing the world and the self. Enlistment and compliance with its directives were acts not of servitude but of profound commitment. As a solitary wayfarer, he was doomed to pass through life like a brief shadow. Bound to the party, his very being would assume a far more substantive meaning. It would integrate him with history's great movement toward social justice while letting him stay whole and good and true to himself.

It was apparent that dialectics acted upon her as a more potent aphrodisiac than his nuzzling of her pelvis. "How can I stay true to myself," he asked, lifting his head from her lap, "with an apparatchik telling me what to think and believe all the time? I already have a brain of my own."

"Which is why the party wants you. But the party isn't a free-for-all—it's a great social movement to save humanity. It needs discipline and cohesion, or else it'll deteriorate into a kaffeeklatsch."

"That's the party's problem. I don't pawn my brain for anybody."

"Hey, no one's asking you to stop thinking, Toby. I mean what do you take me for—Charley McCarthy's sister? I value my brain as much as you do yours." She strummed her fingers down his chest. "What worries me is what'll happen to you if you turn away from the party now."

"How come it hasn't been worrying you for the past eight months?"

"Because I didn't think you were one of us."

"I'm not—I don't think—"

Her hands traveled down to his thighs. "Oh, yes, you are—you're right on the brink. But the whole idea of commitment has you panicky." Her fingers latched on to his inflamed manhood. "Well, part of you, anyway."

He fell asleep after they were done, and she did not rouse him. In the morning, she proposed that he stop up to his hotel room after work for a change of clothes and come back down to Hudson Street. Breaking him was obviously going to take more than one night; it was a matter of education, not seduction. So long as her method continued to involve lobes and loins both, he was open to persuasion.

By the time he returned to the apartment that afternoon, Nina had already done her homework for the next day, but instead of pouncing on him with a full dose of doctrine, she had the good sense to bed him first and drain off his resistance. Then she gave him selected passages to read from her previous day's assignment while she slipped off to fix them a light supper. That became the pattern for the rest of his stay: They would talk seriously throughout the meal, which did not suffer from the inattention, and go out afterward to one of the city's free summer entertainments. But on the way and in between and when they got back, up to the moment of renewing their passion before they slept, she strummed the party lyre and tried to charm him into submission.

Yet no matter how thoroughly giving she was of mind and body, trying to understand him and make him understand in return, that run of intense nights and days together proved endlessly combative. His main problem with her loving assault on him was Marx. The more she made him read, the less he liked it. Most of it was torpid prose. And when he did manage to decipher a passage, it seemed to him either a proposition not worth belaboring or a conclusion warped by the excessive meanness of Marx's age and the bitterness of his life. He soon stopped taking Nina's lectures lying down.

"The socialist man is a happy man," she caroled over dessert their third night, "because his life is enriched by so much more than the possession of material things—by love and thought and real human feeling, and membership in a just social order."

"But why, O Socrates, can only the socialist man be happy?"

"Because private property is the negation of the human personality. It makes man a stranger to his own labor by forcing him to work for hire as a wage slave in order to subsist. Work should be true human expression, free and conscious—not an ordeal."

He shoved a pudding glass aside and dropped his elbows on the table. "You really believe that, don't you?"

"Of course."

"I don't. Most work is repetitive drudgery whether you do it for yourself or some slavedriving son of a bitch. For most people it's not an expression of anything nobler than their need to eat. Also, to stay sane—the only thing more boring than working is not working. And anyway, why can't a proletarian want what a bourgeois wants? Why isn't private property a legitimate reward if you're given a fair shake at acquiring your share?"

Flames shot out of her eyes. "You're not listening!" she hollered instead of answering. "You're so busy being negative that you won't stop and think through anything I'm saying to you." She pushed herself away from the table and began cleaning the dishes with noisy pique. "I don't know sometimes whether you're stubborn or just plain dumb. And you can help me clean these while you're at it!"

But she kept hammering at him, even as he kept greedily accepting her proffered body until deciding it was a sordid bargain on both their parts. His encouragement of their dialogue was as false as her enticement to their lovemaking; each was subordinated to their own separate needs and not accessory to a shared fulfillment.

The inevitable blowup began at a Goldman Band concert in Central Park. A spirited rendering of "Marche Militaire" naturally made her think of Tchaikovsky, who naturally made her think of Russia, communism, and Marx, who made her think of Engels, who—she began telling him at length during the intermission—had long repudiated the bourgeois family structure by living with a woman out of wedlock; what did Toby think of that?

"I think you're playacting that we're like that—and I'm tired of it." She was not interested in him as a human being, he charged—only as clay for the Marxist mold into which she herself was being irrevocably cast.

"That's not true!" she fumed. "I'm doing all this because I care. Why else would I have started with you again?"

"To test your powers—and win a few points with the party."

"That's—horrid of you."

But the accusation registered. By the time the band wound up with a Sousa march that transported Toby back to Pittsfield State Forest and the compulsions of Gordon Sparhawk, she had abandoned her didacticism long enough to detect his reverie and ask about it. He supplied a few generalities, but she pressed him for particulars and soon was caught up in his graphic recall of the camp and his engagement with vest-pocket despotism. "You ought to write about it," she urged. He said he had and, encouraged by her show of interest, steered their homeward course to his hotel, where she waited in the lobby while he ran up to his room.

He had written it on the well-seasoned typewriter he bought for sending out his job-application letters after the *Trib* fired him. The story, titled "Upon the Tenderest Heart Falls the Deepest Shadow," was about David Schumacher's misadventures and tragic end under the captain's modified reign of terror. She read it the moment they were back in the apartment, with an eagerness that pleased him and a speed that did not. How could she extract the fine texture of his language and nuances of character while flipping the pages that fast? At the end, she looked up, nodded, and said she would have to reread it. This time she went more slowly—for that he was grateful—but he feared her whirring mind was gearing up for an assaulting exegesis. She limited her demolition to a single sentence: "It's awfully well-written—really it is—but I'm not sure I see the point."

"The point is up to you to decide—it's not an essay."

"I'm not illiterate, Toby. It's just that I'm not exactly sure what it is you're driving at."

He understood her fondness for Odets. "I'm not driving at any one particular thing. I'm writing about being awkward and lonely and powerless in an alien place—and the courage it takes to survive—"

"But the boy doesn't survive—that's what confuses me. Are you saying it was the fault of the captain—and what he stands for?"

"I'm not saying it's anybody's fault—most things that go wrong in life aren't that simple." He wanted her to see the conceptual gulf that separated them. "That's what Marx couldn't accept—not everything that happens is cause and effect. You can't turn history into a formula—or all human behavior into categories—"

"You pompous ass!" she burst out, caught up short by his cross-reference and infuriated, as if he were raiding her territory to gain an illicit advantage. "What do you know about Marx—except to carp? What do you know about anything? All you can do is ask questions! No one ever changed a damned thing that way—"

"I don't agree—"

"I don't care!" She tossed his story back at him, but the motion was too quick for him to grasp the pages, and they fluttered to the floor in jumbled sequence. "You don't agree with anything!" she railed. "I've been blabbing my stupid head off for a week trying to put some courage in your convictions, and it turns out all you've got on the inside is a whole lot of reservations. What a damned waste of time and effort!"

"I'm sorry I'm not a fanatic—isn't that what you want?"

"Who are you calling a fanatic?"

"I—didn't call anybody anything—"

"Why not? Why don't you just come right out with it and say what you think already? You're such a damned repressed—wishy-washy—"

"Because I don't have an 'it' to come out with—because I'd much rather doubt everything than put my faith in something that's a mirage—that's a bunch of lies and half-truths—that's just another stinking pile of orthodox shit!"

She scooped up a pile of her father's socialist magazines from the chair next to her. "Oh, you think all this is a lot of shit? Anything you're too thick to understand is shit, right? Anything you haven't the guts to stand up for—"

"I wasn't talking about any one thing—"

"Oh, who the hell are you kidding?" she raged and sent the magazines flying at him. The flapping pages flew around his face and shoulders but inflicted no damage. "It's your stuff that's shit, if you want to know the truth," she went on in a frenzy, kicking blindly at the pages of his story and then marching off to her bedroom. "And you can keep your goddamned dirty hands off me from now on!"

He would not let their affections die a final time by slipping off forsaken into the night. In the morning, she was less than contrite but no longer explosive. It was Sunday, their last day together before her parents came home. They decided to take the Day-liner up the Hudson to West Point. By mutual assent there were no homiletics; it was too late for that. They clung to the boat rail, drinking in the spume of the river, the faceted grain of the hulking Palisades, the glory of summer at its bluest and brightest—and wondering what it was that had kept them from loving each other.

Opposite Piermont, rising drably and obliquely from the western shore, he pointed out to her where he had grown up. But their old house was hidden by foliage and, at any rate, her curiosity about his boyhood in that backwater was perfunctory at best—a sure signal that in withstanding her siege, he had lost whatever fascination he might have held for her. Their pauses lengthened. Only on the way back, when he asked her why it was that Jews were so active on the political Left, did she tune back on.

"What brings that up?" she asked.

"I don't know—these whole nine days, I guess—and you—your family—Marx—the party—" He supposed the Jewish passion for social justice to be grounded in their persecuted past, but other historical peoples had the sense to lapse into passivity when their conquerors and tormentors eased their grip; Jews remained insurgents.

"We're history's nag," she said, turning her face to catch the breeze that lightly infiltrated her curly dark nimbus. "We bear witness to man's inhumanity—that's what we were chosen for, didn't you know? Jesus was nothing new. And we haven't stopped since he came—and left." She filtered a breath out of the suddenly rising wind. "It doesn't exactly win you a lot of friends, though." She thought a bit more, then smiled and said maybe that was why so many of the great violinists were Jews—no other instrument issued strains of such poignant lamentation. She moved a few yards down the railing; he did not follow.

Thus, in spite of all Nina Orloff's efforts, and her mother's, and father's, and the party's, Toby Ronan did not join the Communist camp. He had heard the party's tempting song, marched in alliance with it, flirted with it, slept with it gladly, but in the end, he could neither carry its tune nor dance to its cadence.

The party did not let him off scot-free.

The partners at the print shop said they could not afford to keep him on with business the way it was. When Toby asked how that could be if they had just bought a new Ludlow at his urging, Bennie said Izzie had made the deal without his knowledge and the purchase had caused fresh bickering between them. Doubtful of that story as well, Toby accompanied Isidore Sonnschein on his walk home for lunch and got fed a chopped-liver sandwich and the truth.

Lomax had brought them Toby, and now Lomax said it was time to let him go—there was someone else needier to take his place. Since Lomax had the power to cut off half their business with a word, there was no debating his edict. "A shame," Izzie said, "to happen to such a nice boy as you."

So far, it had been a banner year. The Right had garroted him for being a radical agitator—and the Left for refusing to become one.

Nihilism took on more allure for him by the day. By night, he fed on self-pity, and then could not keep it down.

IV

He had never seriously considered fulfillment in the form of money —cash, greenbacks, moola, and all it could buy—until Dan Jonas, late of the *Trib*, made a timely call to him and raised the immediate prospect.

There was an opening at the public-relations firm where Dan had been working for several months, having quit the shipping-news beat to which the paper had relegated him, and he thought of Toby for it at once. The pay was very good; he had started at sixty a week and was already up to seventy-five—"plus an expense account. And the work's really very challenging."

No doubt Dan was penitent for his complicity in Toby's sacking at the paper and sought to make amends. But a ticket to a career in press-agentry sounded more like adding insult to injury. Toby's steepening disillusionment had not yet turned into terminal cynicism. Something in him still held that money less than honorably come by cheapened his worth, however much the world sneered at such pious accounting. And short of verifiable banditry, was there a more ignominious profession than the tinseled con game of confecting celebrity? "I don't think it's for me, Dan," he said, "but thanks for keeping me in mind."

"Come on, Toby, I know exactly what you're thinking, but it's not like that at all," Dan persisted. "You have to be very resourceful—at least as much as a reporter—and the stakes are higher. It's not a question of selling out, either. It's more a matter of—well, a mature outlook, you could call it." Besides, it was a kick to match wits with the press all the time. That very day's *Mirror*, for instance, carried an item Dan had planted in the café-society column about one of his firm's client restaurants. Its chef was quoted as advising that, when ordering a ham from the butcher, you should specify the left one because pigs used only their right hind leg to scratch themselves. "Isn't that a pip?" Dan snorted.

"I suppose it's terribly naïve to ask," said Toby, "but does that happen to be true?"

An awkward pause revealed their divergent standards. "Sure—I guess. The guy's a famous chef—he'd never make up a thing like that. Anyway, what the hell difference does it make? Any housewife who cares that much about the tenderness of a ham deserves to have her ass tweaked a little." Not that you could play fast and loose with the truth, he added, and get away with it for long. In fact, the guy Toby would replace had called the papers about another client, the Park Central Hotel, and told them that one of its notable guests, an Indian rajah, had lost his pet python on the premises for a couple of hours. The idea, of course, had been to suggest that the hotel was grand enough to cater to royalty. The rajah was real, but the snake was not; on balance, in management's view, all the story did was imply that the hotel was infested with vermin. The firm lost the account, and swift retribution took the brainstormer.

"I'm glad there's still some honor among thieves," Toby said, beginning to think perhaps he ought not to be so negative about gift horses just because his last one proved a plug. If Lomax, presumably a paragon of the proselytizing trade, had lied to him about no strings

being attached to the job at the print shop, then maybe—by reversing
the coin—a certain bluff virtue thrived amid the ulterior motives of
the ballyhoo business. And who else was beating down his door with a
job offer?

"It's not thievery at all," Dan said. "In fact, I'd say it's at least as
honest as the newspaper racket and not half as grubby. Also, genuinely creative—which is one reason my boss is interested in you. I told
him you quit the paper to write a novel. And he likes the idea of Harvard—he thinks it would help the firm land some of the civic and
charitable organizations we're after as clients. Why don't you at least
come by and see the guy—he's a straight shooter."

From the smart look to the reception area—shiny dark-green leather
chairs, a gleaming black linoleum floor with an octagon inlaid in
white, heavy mahogany tables holding brass lamp bases with shades in
tortoise-shell paper, and over the mantel, a big electric clock in white
plaster topped by a carved black eagle—Arvin St. Cyr & Associates
was prospering nicely at 180 Madison Avenue, a block below the Empire State Building. As reformed carny touts went, the proprietor bore
himself with nice understatement. Toby watched him waft into work
just before their eleven o'clock appointment in a polo coat and
matching camel's-hair cap. Beneath, he sported expensive twills, a pais-
ley tie, and the smallest pair of brown wingtips ever seen on an otherwise fully grown man. For flair there were rococo sideburns and a
British accent, somewhat more Blighty than Blenheim, that the former
Joe O'Malley had picked up during his days as a Chicago vaudeville
publicist. Moving to New York, he adopted the more elegant mon-
icker, went to work with the Ziegfeld office, hung on there through
the worst of the depression, and opened his own shop in '35. "Illusion
is not delusion," he told Toby by way of unfurling the agency creed.
"We sell the shine, not the shoes—one's no good without the other."

Theirs was a fast-moving, fast-growing outfit, Arvin St. Cyr explained, and no place for mooning aesthetes. What Toby did with his
writing talent on his own was his business; in the office, it had to be at
the full disposal of the clients, along with the rest of him. Only self-
starters and go-getters were wanted. There was no training course and
no one to hold his hand; either he had a flair for the thing or he didn't
—time would tell them both soon enough. The job was his if Toby
wanted it.

"Absolutely," Toby said, accentuating the positive approach, "assuming that the—"

"Oh, yes. Well, let's say seventy to start with—Harvard's worth a
bit of a premium." There weren't any fixed hours. He might have to
be up till three accommodating a client and then be at another one's

desk at nine, fresh as a daisy. "Speaking of which," the proprietor added, studying Toby's tiring gray suit, "I think you'd better put half your first month's salary into a little snappier wardrobe. We have to give the clients a bit of a show for their money."

"Yes, sir."

"Nothing flashy now, though."

"No, sir."

"And tell me, Ronan, what's the first thing you do after getting home from the office."

"Excuse me, sir?"

"I say, once you've got back to your place—"

"I—don't think I—"

"Take your clothes off, man, and hang them in the closet. Don't lay around in your good things or you'll look like a tramp next day."

"Yes, sir."

He would have an expense account, too, amounting to a third of his salary—it was mandatory. "Use it any way you'd like—take a client to lunch or a contact to theater or a useful friend to a Turkish bath, even, but if you don't spend it, you're not doing the job right."

"Yes, sir."

Beyond the *moderne* reception area and the boss's lair, done up in red morocco and rosewood, the office was cramped and strictly functional. Six associates shared three tight cubicles, offering just enough space for a desk, phone, and typewriter apiece; most of the work, after all, was on the outside.

Toby's first assignment was to write a eulogy that an actor client wished to run in *Variety*, mourning the death of his beloved manager-agent while advancing his own celebrity. "A little *schmaltz*," St. Cyr ordered after Toby had spoken on the phone with the bereaved client.

An hour later, Toby presented an encomium so extravagant it could have been surpassed only by Mussolini addressing his mirror. "More feeling," he was commanded. Toby invaded the higher reaches of hyperbole, bordering on the ludicrous. "Better," St. Cyr said, taking out his pen and attacking the composition himself, "but not perfect." Their joint creation began:

> God has lifted his option on Tyrone Constable.
> The Supreme Manager, in that Great Studio in the Sky, has summoned one of His classiest representatives to a heavenly reward. There, mingling with an all-star cast, he will continue to offer the same tender counsel and loving generosity he provided his earthly clientele.
> No finer man ever lived, no more loyal friend, nor a father as devoted nor a better husband. In the script of his life, now bound

together with silken cords, not a page is blemished by a black mark. At the Pearly Gates, no angel is more suited to tend the box-office take. . . .

"Better check," St. Cyr warned, "and see if the guy ever had any kids."

This lustrous gem earned Toby authorship of a ten-page press release heralding the gala New York debut of the House of Orsini, dispensers of "Perfumes from Paradise." The matchless exquisitry of the establishment had to be rendered in prose of similar adoration. "The Grand Salon is furnished," he wrote, "with fifteen *empire* sofas upholstered in regal purple and rarest orchid felt, fringed in black, with low, lacquered tables of sculpted onyx, on carpeting of scarlet plush." The walls were of pearly moiré; the light fixtures, side brackets from the great palaces of Tuscany; the recessed display cases, of travertine marble and antiqued mirror, and "throughout the dream-like chamber a veritable grove of orange trees springs up from giant filigreed urns." The adjacent "Heritage Room" authenticated the pedigree of the product. It featured, in Toby's words, "a full-length portrait of Count Orsini della Robbia, the legendary hero-lover and statesman-prince, in battle regalia, and a thousand-square-foot rug in peacock blue, gold, and cerise bearing the Orsini coat of arms with its internationally renowned insignia, a sword crossed with a long-stemmed rose." Framed on the walls were prize certificates from a century of fairs and expositions and the Count's original appointment as Royal Perfumer to King Gretz of Herzegovina. Throughout the premier month, the release concluded, "the timeless music of romantic love would be performed in the salon on an all-ivory piano, an Orsini heirloom."

"Is it a store or a seraglio?" Dan asked, awed by the lush prose.

"Illusion is not delusion," Toby instructed. "The sofas are on loan. The side brackets come from Whippany, not Tuscany. The orange trees are cellulose. The travertine is plaster. The rug is only four hundred square feet. The piano is painted to look ivory. And there's no mention anywhere in the New York Public Library of anyone named Orsini della Robbia, in fact or fiction. But the spread sure beats Woolworth's, and your car could run from here to Wyoming on one whiff of that perfume."

Success begat success. The Orsini opening, played lavishly in the papers, won Toby the glamorous task of engineering a quick promotion campaign for Sherry Rutledge's new movie, *Belles at Dawn*, being released by the studio ahead of schedule. Toby recommended renting the biggest billboard in town, which research disclosed was

115 feet long and forty-five feet high and located at Fourth Avenue and Astor Place, across the street from Wanamaker's. Miss Rutledge's colossal contours could entice Gotham for nine hundred a month, including the cost of the paint and the painters.

"Anyone can buy space," St. Cyr said. "Our job is to get it free."

Toby thought some more and came up with the idea of offering Miss Rutledge's free endorsement of appropriate nationally advertised products in exchange for prominent mention of her new movie in the ad copy.

"Top drawer," said the boss. "Send out a night letter to every ad agency in town but tell them the lady's got only one free day to pose on her way to Europe—that'll goose their interest. And book a suite at the St. Regis." Toby was to exercise rigorous discretion in deciding which products the star would shill for. "And remember—no laxatives!"

Thirty-seven photographers trooped by her hotel suite with a million watts of light before the ethereal actress escaped only slightly singed. The ultimate measure of the scheme's success was the next number of the *Woman's Home Companion*, which carried eight separate ads in which the star and her film were cited; products endorsed were a candy bar, a facial soap, a line of golf clubs, a make of wardrobe trunk, hosiery, bedroom slippers, a brand of bedding—and a depilatory.

"For crissakes!" St. Cyr roared, dropping all airs on seeing the magazine. "Unwanted hair is like unwanted shit—glamour queens don't have either! No laxatives and no depilatories from now on, you got it?"

The fanfare notwithstanding, *Belles at Dawn* laid an egg.

Toby walked the crooked line between harmless showmanship and active counterfeiting when assigned to generate hoopla for a new line of men's sportswear under the brand name Sheik. Fashion writers and editors were lured to an all-afternoon bash at a ballroom in the Drake, gussied up in a mock-Arabian motif. After a luncheon of *couscous* and the fashion show, the program offered a special screening of Valentino as *The Sheik* and the personal appearance of a purported real-life counterpart, His Excellency Sheik Fahzi Wahba, Envoy Extraordinary and Minister Plenipotentiary of His Majesty King Ibn Mufta of the Arab Protectorate of Abu Dahbi.

Sheik Fahzi, a fake from start to finish, was St. Cyr's idea, but Toby was charged with perpetrating it to the press. "You be his interpreter," the boss instructed. "They'll get the idea."

Toby tried at first to bore the writers out of the personal angle as they clustered around the small, bearded actor in dark-rimmed glasses who had been hired to play His Serene Fraudulence. With pedantic precision, he ran through every item in the sheik's elaborate costume, from his *kaffiyah* to his *zubool*, taking pains to give the correct English spelling of each; that much was authentic. But the press wanted human-interest quotes. By prearrangement, however, the sheik was restricted to a single line of his own—"I am very happy for this visit in America"; the rest of his answers, in pidgin Arabic, were funneled through Toby. Why had the sheik come here? "He was sent as a delegate of Islam to the opening of a mosque in Yokohama, and finding himself relatively so near the U.S., thought he would drop by." What did the sheik think of America? "He likes it because there are so many cars and so few flies." How was the sheik occupying himself in New York? "Lunches with the oil companies and dinners with transplanted Arabs—he says there are fifty thousand here, all related." Since his religion denied him alcohol, what was the sheik's favorite liquid refreshment? "Piña colada." Did the sheik own a palace? "A small one— he is not a major sheik. And he won't answer any questions about his harem. In fact, the sheik respectfully asks that all his answers be regarded as off the record"—Toby cranked up a giveaway grin—"or Allah will blow you away with the breath of a thousand camels."

For carrying off this masquerade in raffish style, Toby was rewarded with a ten-dollar raise. They were not the wages of sin, precisely, but he could not separate the compensation from the toil. Practicing these meretricious arts bothered him less somehow than being acclaimed for it. If he was going to get dirty again, it ought not to be from gilding trinkets; gravediggers, for all their degraded lot, did not profane themselves.

He was in this muddled mood when Dan Jonas came back to the office from lunch with regards for him from Eden Chafee. She had been at a nearby table at his restaurant. "Looks terrific, too," he reported. She had been working as a researcher on *Time* since coming back to town in the spring. According to his lunch partner—"he knows the Luce shops inside out," Dan confided—she was also sleeping with half the office. "She said to be sure to remember her to you," he added with a leer.

This stabbing news threw his already swirling spirits into high turbulence. She had gone out of his life without a trace, never even sending regrets. In fairness, he had told himself, there was nothing real between them. They had been office friends, no more, whatever fantasies he had invested in their acquaintance. And she had gone off to recover from her own emotional wounds; his were hardly her doing—or concern. Her reappearance now, just when he finally had a little spending money that might allow him to contend for her attentions, was like a sudden starburst in his overcast firmament. That she came sullied by scandalmongers he chose to read as evidence of a rocky rebound from her breakup with Richard. He ought to call her.

All that night he debated the step. Every conversation they had ever had ran through his head. They were tense, compact, combative, overcharged with an energy that had to have a purpose. Some unknowable force meant their lifelines to cross again—and then what, mingle or keep moving? He could not bear the latter. What point would there be in his investing in her anew? To risk a fresh rebuff for what —hope against hope that, with the passage of time, she had come to recognize his true qualities? To satisfy his deathless longing to seize her up and hold her and subdue her? It seemed an insane gamble. If she understood him now and reciprocated even a part of his passion, she would have let him know in her reckless fashion; she was not given to inhibition.

But she had told Dan to say hello, had sent him a message at the first opportunity—there was no need for her to have done that if she cared nothing for him. There was a vast range, though, between a little residual feeling and an incurable yearning of the intensity he sensed retaking possession of his own being. He had to find out, at whatever cost, how much he mattered to her. One unrequited love was every man's lot; was a second beyond his endurance? This was the girl who could change the world for him, reverse his fortunes, embolden his life and vitalize it. He could forgive her rejection but not himself the failure to try.

He telephoned in the morning from a booth near his office. A hundred wisecracks kept not quite forming in his brain. He must not seem too ardent, or too grieved, or too anything but steadfast and strong and gaily attractive and—

"Hello—Miss Chafee speaking."

"Oh, hi, Miss Chafee. I am an itinerant blacksmith doing some research on *Time* researchers and thought perhaps you could—"

"Toby! For heaven's sake! I was going to call you—can you believe that? I only just got in—the office, I mean. I didn't know where you were or anything until yesterday—"

Her voice sounded rushed, but it had that same disquieting vibrancy that had so attracted him from the first moment he heard it. "Sure," he said, "I know."

"I wanted to tell you how pleased my father has been with the Bloomgarden boy you sent him. His plant manager says he's absolutely the best worker in the whole place."

"Yes. Well, it's nice to be of help to two appreciative parties."

"I'll remember that. And you—is everything okay?"

"Fine—excellent."

"I'm glad. I guess it can't be easy for you—doing that. You're in it for the money, I suppose?"

"It's not at all bad, really. Some of it's quite challenging."

"I'll bet."

"No, really—"

"Whatever you say."

"I guess you think it's just a lot of flimflam—"

"What I think doesn't matter. You're the one who's got to do it. I just hope it's worth giving up journalism for."

"I didn't give it up—it gave me up—in case you hadn't heard."

"I heard. In fact, I joined *Time*'s guild unit on account of you."

"Well-well," he said, a pleased tremble taking hold of him, "will miracles never cease?" The line fell flat. "Anyway, I'll probably go back into journalism someday. This is temporary."

"Are you serious, Toby?" A freezing incredulity.

"Sure—why not?"

"You can't go back—don't you know that? Once you've been a damned press agent, no decent newspaper in the country will touch you. You've crossed your Rubicon." Her disapproval was thunderous.

"You sound angry."

"Because it's pathetic—someone with your talent throwing it away as a publicity hack! How could you *do* that?"

He felt a suddenly familiar rush of fury at the merciless tone. "How could you have gone away and never said goodbye?"

The thunder ceased. "You're—evading the issue."

"I knew we had something in common," he said. "Anyway, you never told me I was talented before—"

"I thought you had a swelled head."

"Have lunch with me—"

"I can't—I only get a short break."

"But Dan saw you—"

"That was with one of the editors—a command performance."

"I see. Do you give a lot of those?"

"As few as I can get away with."

"How about dinner, then?"

There was a pause of palpable discomfort. "Dinners are hard, too."

"I see. You must be terribly popular—"

"It's—more complicated than that."

Her almost insulting shortness shredded his composure. "Thanks," he said, "it's been wonderful talking to you again—unbelievably thrilling."

In the background, somebody said something to her. "I've got to run now. Can you meet at eight tomorrow morning and walk around the reservior with me? I do it every day to stay trim. Eighty-sixth and Fifth, the park side—okay?"

She was already pacing the corner when the bus let him off. The sight of her, sustained by unflagging memory for nearly a year, hurried him forward. His arms climbed above his waist in an involuntary disclosure of longing. How he craved to fold her into him and press her tight and squeeze the acid from every mean cell. But she remained forbidding and eluding; only their hands meshed, and briefly, before she drew back again.

There was a change in her. Her hair, once always so carefully waved and set, was parted to one side now and drawn straight across by a pair of tortoise-shell combs holding it in place above the ear. Her coat was plain navy wool, and beneath she wore a subdued tartan skirt and simple white blouse. The elegance was gone from her look. Only the undiminished blue blaze to her eyes announced a latent swagger.

She steered him into the park and, cued by his civilities, reported what she chose. Her work was uninspiring, but it offered at least the possibility of promotion to a writing job—"if I play my cards right." Was this a dismaying hint that her fastest route upward was traveling on her back? "The researchers actually keep the place honest," she said by way of rationalizing her work. "If the magazine fouls up the little things, the credibility of the whole shebang is undermined. Only how would you like to spend half your life on the phone asking some geezer if he's really and truly altogether bald?"

She set a cracking good pace around the basin, its drab waters choppy and uninviting in the October morning. Walden in the park. Nature denatured. A redemptive bath for Sodom's sinning multitudes; it worked by means of contemplation instead of immersion. Through its fence, she waved to a worker paddling a rowboat near the north gatehouse. He responded by lifting a long pole with a landing net on the end. The lone boatman, there to fish out debris, knew all the regular reservoir-walkers, she said. George M. Cohan, for example, came every day. And on Saturday mornings, District Attorney Tom Dewey.

"Dewey? Isn't he afraid some mug'll toss him in?"

"I might do it myself," she said. "He's a fascist if you ask me."

"Gee, I rather admire the man."

"That's how much you know. How do you think he put away Luciano?"

"By working hard at it?"

"Ha!" He had held well over a hundred witnesses incommunicado, she said, so the defense couldn't get to them before the trial. And he browbeat reluctant ones to testify for the state by threatening to prosecute them for income-tax evasion. And he routinely got the courts to set excessive bail. "I happen to think those methods stink."

"Luciano isn't Robin Hood. These people are animals."

"That doesn't excuse running roughshod over the Bill of Rights. You let a fanatic like Dewey loose and soon you've got hordes of storm troopers marching."

He fought to keep a smile from creeping onto his lips. Probably she had fallen in among a den of closet libertarians at the magazine and was spouting the current line. The sight of a heel-and-toe walker twitching by them in the opposite direction at a furious pace forced his grin into the open. "Looks as if his arms are going to fly off any second," he said.

"That's Arnold—he makes it around in fifteen minutes."

Her supreme authoritativeness began to grate on him. "You certainly know a lot about everything, don't you?"

"It's my job—and what I don't know, I can find out fast."

"What a marvelous gift."

"I'm perfectly serious." She glanced out over the reservoir. "Now how much water's in there, would you think?"

"I couldn't begin to guess."

"Well, just suppose you had to find out. How would you go about it?"

"I don't know. I suppose I'd have to measure the dimensions of the thing and then make all kinds of modifications because it's irregular—"

"It holds a billion gallons."

"How'd you figure that out?"

"I didn't. I called the Water Department. Aren't I smart? Sometimes you're allowed shortcuts if the long way around isn't likely to work."

He nodded appreciatively. "Maybe that's what Dewey figured, too."

"Good Christ!" she blew up. "The two aren't even vaguely connected. No one's entitled to stomp all over other people's rights."

Her imperious instruction and studied remoteness were worse than outright rejection would have been. "How about their emotions?" he asked.

She slowed their pace. "What about them?"

He clamped his hands to the sides of her shoulders to freeze her attention. "I mean why am I relegated to your morning walk? If you want to see me, pick a civilized time when we can have a little leisure. If not, just say so. But you don't have the right to treat me like your dog."

His reproach muffled her entirely for the last part of their circuit.

"Okay," she said when they re-emerged on the avenue, "but I need a little time." Then she lifted her faintly flushed face to his, kissed him softly on the mouth, and slipped off to catch an approaching bus down Fifth.

It was a day of dubious auguries and angry embers. At his hotel after work, he was greeted by a letter from Nina Orloff. Her mother had been expelled from the party for deviationist thought and divisive conduct, she wrote and accused him of Rasputin-like sorcery in fomenting Adele's disaffection. The process, Nina was certain from firsthand observation, dated from the moment Toby showed up at the Bank Street branch. "You're the most pathetic person I've ever known —too weak to give yourself to a truly moral world order so you're reduced to slandering and smearing it for the rest of us," she ended. "I'm ashamed to have known you."

Her hateful words were no doubt prompted by hysteria. He began to draft a reply. Why, he asked, did she blame him instead of the party, which was incapable of tolerating a particle of independent thought among its recruits? He got as far as contending that communism was at least as dehumanizing as capitalism—worse, probably, because it turned family members on one another and knew no love but the party—and then stopped writing. Nina's indictment was absurd on its face. There had to be more to Adele's expulsion, especially in view of Saul's party rank. Toby smelled a plot and knew where to go to unravel it.

"You want it straight, *boychikel,* or sugarcoated?" Wally asked. His closeness to his sister, and Kenny Lomax's to his brother, had allowed the roommates to piece the puzzle together.

"The works—I guess," Toby chose, falling onto Wally's daybed.

Adele, a husky and passionate woman too little satisfied by her chronically preoccupied husband, slept from time to time with Fletcher, the Bank Street branch organizer. Lomax had been apprised of the relationship by Solomon, the branch educational director and a mainstay in the section organizer's network of loyal informants. Fletcher's wife, too, had found out and threatened to tell Saul Orloff, who would surely have had Fletcher purged, if not killed. But Fletcher was a major donor to the party treasury and could hardly be turned out for mere adultery as long as he remained doctrinally pure. Saul was still more valuable to the party; in line to become vice chairman of the state committee, he could not afford to have his name linked openly with scandal. Thus, Adele, who had proven herself indiscreet, was judged expendable and a charge of deviationism plausibly contrived. She herself knew the real reason for the purge but could not share it, of course, with her family. And Lomax, naturally, wanted to spare Nina news of her mother's infidelity, especially since Nina was sure to have insisted that Fletcher be purged instead.

But how, Toby wondered, could Nina have possibly exerted such suasion on the powerful section organizer?

"By telling him," Wally said, "she wouldn't sleep with him anymore."

Toby's face misted with disbelief.

Wally was unsympathetic. "What did you think—the comrades spend all night kibitzing about historial materialism?"

TWENTY

NOVEMBER ran its chilling fingers over the sentient surfaces of the city, and still no word came from her. Life had never seemed so barren of purpose to him, his heart heavier nor hope as fugitive. Possibly it was the wistful season, or the state of the world, or the triviality of his work—or the sum of them all. Mostly, he knew, it was Eden. Half his waking hours and all his dreams were suffused with her alternately encroaching and receding image. On a whim, he mailed her his story about David and the camp and invited her verdict.

She woke him on the phone in the middle of the night and, sniffing back tears he had never seen her shed, blurted her pleasure with his offering. She had read it through three times just to be certain, and was still deeply touched, and had to tell him that instant. "Only why did you have to make him die?"

He was instantly, gloriously awake. "Because he really did."

"But that's terrible—just awful. I'm so sorry for him." She gave a final sniff. "You've got to send it around to the magazines, Toby—it's too good not to. Promise?"

"Only if you'll spend Saturday with me." She could not deny him the reward.

"I can't—I'm working this Saturday."

"Sunday, then—make it Sunday."

"This Sunday's no good—I've got something I—"

Sweet reason rebelled; manners no longer mattered. "I don't care!" he cried. "Get rid of it! Walk with me, Eden—talk with me—spend the afternoon with me! Spare me one goddamned afternoon out of your precious life, can't you do that for once—for crissakes—"

For an instant, he was sure she was gone, contemptuous of his impotent fury. "All right," she said finally, "since you have such a fetching way of putting it. But promise me you'll send the story around—everywhere."

"Maybe I'm not a glutton for rejection—appearances to the contrary."

"You've already got one acceptance," she said. "Sleep tight."

It was a blowy afternoon that ended with them taking hot chocolate at the boathouse by the lake. The rowboats were long in storage and the place all but deserted that time of day, so they appropriated a whole corner of the enclosed porch and talked freely. The lake, without its usual flotilla of colliding oarsmen, barely stirred in grateful serenity as they gazed out over it in the pauses between revelations.

He told her about everything from his first boyhood brush with the muse—the essay memorializing the dead cat—to his hugely ambivalent affair with the C.P., winding up with a confession of ardent disbelief in anything and anybody beyond himself. This latter confidence, he neglected to add, was of a fragility threatening momentary dissolution.

She was less revealing at first but let out enough by degrees for him to begin to understand. After Richard, she had had to get away and re-examine everything about her life and thoughts and feelings. In Florida for the winter and on a Caribbean cruise with Aunt Winnie, she reassembled the pieces slowly, discarding half the facile assumptions of her past. "You started me on it," she conceded, "but I wasn't much for listening then." She read, without the duress college imposed, and discovered she had known practically nothing. With spring, her spirits revived, only accompanied now by an extreme tentativeness as she returned to the city, uneager for a consuming job or emotional involvement until she was stronger and surer of her values. "And you, baby," she smiled, spreading a hand lightly over his, "were no one to dabble with."

"You didn't seem to mind when there was a Richard."

"I know—I was very naughty. And you were charmingly vulnerable."

At the magazine, she could not repulse the advances of an attractive older man, married, unhappy, and too Catholic to contemplate escape. They both had wanted the relationship to stay casual, but his interest in her was not to be contained. Though her feelings were less than entirely reciprocal, she ordered her after-hours life at his convenience. "I'm still seeing him," she said, leaving the intensity and likely duration of her fondness in doubt.

" 'Seeing him'? Is that your euphemism of the week?"

"Why—isn't that plain enough English?"

"It's mid-Victorian."

"What am I supposed to say?"

"If you're sleeping with him, say you're sleeping with him."

She hurried a cigarette into place. Over the year, she had cut down on her smoking but learned now to inhale. "Some things needn't be said."

"You mean you're sparing me?"

"I didn't think I was sparing either of us." She let him give her a light. "Of course I'm sleeping with him—adults do, you know."

"No—not a self-respecting woman—in your circumstances—"

She punished her cigarette, practically biting off the end while drawing in its smoke. "What the hell are you talking about?"

He studied the last patches of light coming off the wind-skimmed lake. "You're something, you know?" he said. "You've got the nerve to tell me *I'm* pathetic for going into public relations to make a buck, but it's perfectly okay for you to become the mistress to a bigshot in your office—"

"I'm nobody's goddamned mistress!" she stormed back at him. "It's my apartment—it's my life—it's my decision how long it lasts—"

"But you arrange your life around him—and his needs. You just said as much a minute ago. Why don't you face it?"

The smoking simmered her down. "Okay, I'm feeling trapped," she admitted, facing him obliquely, "and debased—but that's more my fault than his." She was trying hard to figure a way out without hurting him—or herself, professionally, if that were possible. She had already hurt herself, he said, without cushioning the blow; stories alleging her promiscuity were current around town. "Shit," she said, "sometimes I hate this lousy city."

He fought through the haze to find her narrowed, hurt eyes. "It's not the city that's doing it to you."

Beneath ragged streaks in the kneeling sky, they forged a treaty. He would abandon the publicity dodge, and she would disentangle herself from her bedmate—both at their earliest convenience. After that, the protocols remained to be written.

His first clue that she might really be interested in him came the following week when she called with news that *Life* was looking for a caption-writer, a highly demanding job that could lead him almost anywhere within the Lucean stable. "If you're interested, I think you'd qualify."

"I thought publicity hacks had invalidated press credentials?"

"Well," she said, "I think maybe I can take care of that."

"Through your friend?"

She paused. "What do you care how? I think you ought to take a shot at it, Toby—I don't know if a lot of things will be coming along."

"You mean I need special pleading to get back my legitimacy?"

She sighed. "Why are you making this hard on both of us? If you really want out of where you are, stop being fussy about your sponsorship."

"I don't want your friend's help—okay?"

"It's not okay—it's dumb. Look, just forget about him—and me. If you want the interview, I can arrange it. You don't have to know who says what in your behalf."

"No thanks—unless you swear to me he'll have nothing to do with it."

"Christ, you're a pain." She thought for a minute. "All right, I'll take care of it myself, but listen, just don't tell them what you're doing now—pretend you're writing fiction fulltime. The *Trib* thing we'll blame on reactionary politics. Got it?"

"No. I've got nothing to apologize for."

"Will you please be practical for once in your dumb life?"

"You're the only dumb part of it," he said and hung up.

But she arranged the interview for him and he went, holding back nothing of his past or present. They did not offer him the job. Eden, infuriated with everyone concerned, struck hardest at him. "Why are you still such a pigheaded ass?" she yelled into the phone.

"Why are you still spreading your legs out of martyred compassion?"

"Oh," she groaned, "what a nasty bastard you turned out to be!"

And yet, with each punishing exchange, they grew closer. However fiercely they flew apart, a forgiving tenderness was beginning to work centripetally on them. They would talk on the phone a couple of times a week, and on weekends, when her friend was with his family, go somewhere free or inexpensive and have a meal out afterward. But she did not ask him up to her place, and he did not ask her why. Nor did he invite her to his room; it was a courting almost entirely uncarnal. There were brief embraces now and then behind a tree in the park or on the few cab rides they took, but mostly, an aching abstinence. It was as if they both had to be terribly sure, and while the process of exploration unfolded, they held each other close yet in abeyance.

One Saturday they went for lunch to Sweet's, near the Fulton Fish Market, and afterward drifted out along the nearby docks. On a pier behind the market, they saw a group of derelicts hovered around a fire made from splintered packing crates, cooking fish in the ashes and eating the scorched chunks off a stick. Inside the market, Eden asked about the men and was told they were always out there on the pier, in all seasons, feeding off the stale or undesirable cuts given them out of pity. Whereupon she bought five pounds of halibut steak and, unaccompanied by Toby, presented the prime slabs to the woebegone drifters.

"Very nice," he said when she rejoined him. "You've made their day."

"Is there something wrong with that?"

"I didn't say there was."

"It's your tone—and that lousy look. I hope you're not going to turn out like the liberal phonies at the magazine. They're some bunch." When she asked the Leftist office contingent to a fund-raiser for the Loyalists she had been wheedled into co-sponsoring, half of them said it was a futile gesture, just like her pledge of a week's salary to the cause. "I don't happen to believe that. If you have compassion, you do what you can for people—you don't try to calculate the results ahead of time."

"Maybe only rich people can be truly charitable."

"Helping the Loyalists isn't charity—it's a vote against tyranny. Anyway, I'm against charity—it only depresses the recipients."

"And those guys on the pier just now—what was that?"

"Impulse," she said. "They looked like such sick dogs."

"And you thought some nice, fresh halibut would cure them—"

"I didn't think anything—I just wanted to do it."

"Is that how you do everything—on impulse?"

"Not the way I used to. Can't you see—I've become more calculating—out of self-preservation."

"I see. Is that what happened with your friend on the magazine—you calculated yourself right into his arms—out of self-preservation."

"Don't be nasty."

"I'm just trying to understand you."

"Sure-sure." Her eyes flashed at him and then relented. "If you want to know the truth, I thought I'd be able to control the situation better."

"You mean more like you do ours?"

"I don't see them as comparable in any way."

"Naturally—you're going to bed with only one of us."

"Oh, Lord. Is that all that matters to you in a relationship?"

"Some people consider it one of the revealing signs of affection."

"There are others—plenty of them—and you know it."

"I don't know anything you don't tell me—I'm not a mind reader."

She brought her face close to his on that seedy street corner and traced a finger around his mouth. "I'm doing the best I can, Toby," she said. "If it's not good enough for you, then we don't have to see each other anymore."

It rained the Sunday after, so they went to see Katharine Hepburn in *Holiday*, the film version of a Philip Barry play about an heiress who hated her wealth. Eden took exception to the premise. "The worst it does," she said, "is inflict a little guilt—until you consider the alternatives."

"You won't donate your entire inheritance to the needy?"

"I've told you—I'm against charity. I'd rather pay higher taxes so government can handle it all impersonally."

"But not enough to cost you any of your deserved comforts—"

"Who said they were deserved? I've never thought that. It's just that the unfairness hasn't bothered me at all until recently."

"But you still won't give up your advantages willingly, of course."

"You mean voluntarily—if no one else did?"

"I mean without someone pointing a gun at your head."

"Why should I? My father didn't steal his money to get it."

"That's not what Marx says. Every worker in his factory gives him surplus value—which is how come you own an alligator bag."

"Oh, that I'd give up. In fact, I've turned practically ascetic—haven't you noticed?"

"If you don't count an apartment at Madison and Seventy-first."

"Well, I have to live somewhere. And it's not all that big."

"Some swell sacrificer."

She grew pensive. "I read Aristotle in Florida. There was a copy in the Palm Beach library—no one had taken it out since 1923. He says all politics is just a struggle between the rich and the poor. I never thought of it that way before."

Her social consciousness was still nearly a desert island; mocking it would have been cruelty. "Look, it's not just politics—all history is a class struggle. Politics is just a question of how you approach it. The Left wants to negotiate between the classes. The Right thinks privilege is a state of nature."

"Not my father. He says privilege has its obligations."

"Of his choosing."

"But if he's humane, what's wrong with that?"

"No despot is humane except when it suits him."

"He's no despot—I've told you that."

"He doesn't let his employees vote on company policy, does he? He does what he wants and imposes the decisions on them, whether they like it or not."

"Because it's his business—and money—and brains—and drive—"

"And their sweat and toil that makes it happen."

"They're not equivalents at all."

"So sayeth the despot's daughter."

As if to dispel his convictions about the Chafees' severity, she asked him to the family dinner in Chappaqua over Thanksgiving, never the happiest time of year for him.

The invitation surprised and pleased him. But he was at pains not to read too much into it. That was wise, as it turned out, because only Aunt Winnie among Eden's relatives was on hand; even her sister, Alicia, and her husband, alternating years between the Chafees and the Pelhams, were not there. Despite the smallness of the gathering, he was uneasy and subdued during the meal. He felt himself not so much an outsider as an imposter, with little to recommend him as a suitor for Eden in her parents' eyes.

She sensed his discomfort and mentioned it afterward as they walked the grounds side by side but not hand in hand. "You're too tense," she said. "Don't worry what they think—you're my friend. You don't have to impress anybody around here."

"Including you?"

"I'm already impressed."

"By my many dazzling accomplishments and vast wealth?"

She smiled but declined to elaborate on her reasons; his being there would have to suffice as testimony. With Jefferson yapping happily at their heels, they headed out of the driveway on bikes for a ride down into the village. They had not gone very far when a car came along traveling much too fast for its narrow passage and sent the pair of them hurtling off the road to avoid being run down. They landed roughly on the roadside, momentarily dazed but otherwise unhurt, as the car braked to a shrill halt a few hundred yards past them.

Toby drew himself up on his knees, checked to make sure Eden had no breaks or bruises, then noticed that the car was still there, neither returning toward them to assess their condition nor driving on in criminal disregard. But once the driver saw Toby stirring, he must have supposed he would do himself no good by lingering on the scene and began wheeling the car back into position. Without explanation, Toby sprang to his feet and started pounding down the road in pursuit of the vehicle before it could work up speed. The sight of him churning in hopeless chase spurred the driver and in another instant the car had roared off around the next bend.

He was still panting when he reclaimed his bike, its front wheel twisted out of shape from the impact of the forced landing. Eden, watching him silently as his gasps subsided, finally burst into laughter. "Hey, it's not funny," he said. "The son of a bitch could've killed us. He didn't miss by much."

"I know," she said, trying to stifle her mirth, "but if you could have seen yourself running after him—it was a picture of utter futility. What on earth possessed you?"

"I—was goddamned angry."

"But the man was in a car. What did you expect him to do, with you tearing after him like that—wait to shake your hand?"

"I—wasn't thinking—I guess."

"Maybe you wanted to catch a glimpse of his license plate—that's what I thought you were doing."

"Yes, I guess so. I don't know—maybe I was in shock."

"And what would you have done if you'd caught him somehow and he turned out to weigh three hundred pounds and be built like Joe Louis?"

"I don't know. I would have worried about that then."

She wrapped both arms around his middle and gave him a happy hug. "How come, baby, you didn't act the same way in Brooklyn that night—at the strike—when I yelled at you?"

He felt the gladdening press of her against him and understood less than ever what it took for him to awaken her deepest affection. "I don't know—I guess I wasn't as angry then—and there were more of them. The odds were better here."

"What—of your running on foot to catch up with a car? That's crazy!" She rested the side of her head against his cheek. He felt her warm breath on his neck. "Shall I tell you why you did it, baby?"

"My head hit a rock landing and I had a delusion I was Superman."

"That's one theory. But I have another."

He tried to locate her lips, but her face kept avoiding his. "I thought I died and was an angel expecting my wings to sprout any second?"

"How about you chased him because there was no possibility of your catching him?"

"That's—really crazy."

"Is it?"

He reached around for her face and drew it up toward his with more roughness than he had intended or she cared for. "That's not a very nice innuendo. In fact, I'd say it's damned uncomplimentary."

"What is—that you're a man addicted to hopeless pursuits?"

"If that's what you mean."

"I'm not sure—but I think so. There's a substantial body of evidence. Part of it's terribly endearing, you know—"

"But mostly it's just ludicrous."

"I didn't say that."

He searched her face. "Look, are you included—because you can just come out and say so and not go into—"

"What—among your hopeless pursuits?"

"Yes."

"I wasn't thinking of you and me—just you. It's time you figured what you want out of life."

"I don't have that luxury."

"You're wrong," she said. "In fact, it's the only one you've got."

They went up to the Cloisters the next weekend to see the new building that housed the Metropolitan's collection of medieval art. The hushed surroundings and sacred relics moved her to primal thoughts. "Don't you really believe in anything?" she asked. "I'm not sure I do anymore." She still went to church Sunday mornings with Aunt Winnie, more out of habit than piety, she insisted.

"What did you have in mind," he answered, "other than the efficacy of prayer?"

"Faith—history—science—asparagus—anything you'd like. Just tell me life has meaning—and mankind is evolving into even-higher forms of civilization."

He shook his head. "There's going to be another war," he said, "more horrible than the last." From end to end, Europe was in turmoil. The Munich Pact, just a few months old, had only emboldened the Nazis. In a state-ordained atrocity, they broke into thousands of Jewish homes and shops and synagogues, pillaging, maiming, murdering through the night. The extinction of the Jews was now national policy. Czechoslovakia, yielded up as a sphere of influence on the altar of appeasement, was to be the jackal's next meal. And its ravenous eyes were already cast on Poland and the Ukrainian breadbasket beyond. The Soviet Union responded only with its own ongoing orgy of political terrorism, although the bloodletting was more selective. In Spain, the *guardia civil* was lining up peasants in the streets and stabbing them to death; Iberian liberty had entered its terminal agony.

"What are we supposed to do about it?"

"Why ask me? You're the one who goes to church. Last time I went, your holy rector at St. Bart's was cursing Europe as the pit of barbarism and thanking God He had made America so righteous. For all I know, he's got something there. Let the rest of the world blow each other's brains out, and we'll inherit the earth."

"You don't really believe that."

"I told you—I don't believe in much of anything—"

"Sometimes I think your problem is you believe in too much—except yourself." She took his hand as they hiked down from the monastery toward the subway and swung their linked arms in a slow, exaggerated pendulum stroke. "What's your grand ambition in life—and don't tell me you don't have one. I mean you must want to do something terrific you'll always be remembered for. What is it—write a masterpiece? Five masterpieces? Stamp out starvation? Sail around the world in a washtub?"

"Those aren't mutually exclusive."

"I'm serious, Toby—I want to know."

Did she? What did she really want to hear from him? What would it take to purchase her love and respect? Was there any price he could pay? Why was his love, his devotion, his very being not enough? He had nothing else, really, and she had to know that by now. What kind of trick was it, then, she was up to? What sort of answer could he give to satisfy her who had everything or could summon it on command?

"I'd just like to be happy," he said.

"That's begging the question. What would *make* you happy?"

"Not having a grand ambition to consume me."

"Oh," she said, "you're just being contrary to spite me. I mean wouldn't you give up even a part of your life in return for performing something shining and wonderful—to know you'd been somebody really special?"

He squeezed her hand harder. "I know it's madness, but I have this notion that I already am somebody special."

"Oh, sure—nobody's nobody. But I'm talking about being extraordinarily remarkable—an historical personage."

"I thought you were against my chasing rainbows?"

"I'm not against dreams, though."

"My dream is to live a long, happy life and share it with somebody I love ecstatically. The end."

"And not care if the world recognizes your specialness?"

"Suppose I try and it never does—then what? Why die of bitterness?"

"Maybe you should just become a milkman."

"Why not? Every life's heroic—and every death inglorious."

She considered the sentiment carefully. "What an extraordinarily prosaic thought."

"It's my epitaph. Maybe that's what they'll remember me for."

"I wouldn't count on it."

"Oh, no," he said, freeing his fingers from hers and plunging both hands into his pants pockets, "I'm not counting on anything. See, I've figured it out—that's the secret to it all. The more you need the world's reward, the surer it is to deny it to you. And the more good you try to do, the sorrier mess you make of it."

She wrestled one of his arms loose and latched on to it. "You're still fooling with me, aren't you? Why are you so afraid to be serious?"

"Because what the hell difference does it make?"

"It makes a difference to me. I need to know what's going on inside you."

"So you can laugh at it—or tear it apart?"

Pain filmed her eyes before she closed them and tugged him to a halt. "Toby," she cried, "I care about you! What do I have to do to convince you—write it in chalk on the side of the Empire State Building?"

"You can stop fucking your friend on the magazine."

She balled her fingers into fists and began to grind them slowly against his chest. He could not tell whether it was a gesture of expiation or attack. "All right," she said softly, "all right." Her face tilted up at his. "And what about your part of the bargain?"

"I'll get to it," he said.

He looked actively now for other work, concentrating on the publishing houses and copy departments of advertising agencies, where his public-relations job would not taint him severely. Eden rated advertising only one rung higher from purgatory than press agentry but granted that it more nearly qualified as a legitimate craft. Her reservations meant little, though, for he could find no openings, even in a mail room. And by Christmas week, his short story had been rejected by five magazines. What joy he managed to generate that season, due solely to Eden's ambiguous presence in his life, was all but canceled by his dour prospects professionally.

His negative attitude toward his work and growing self-disapproval for ever having fallen into it manifested themselves in self-destructive performances on the job, and two days before Christmas, with a display of regret and a week's severance, Arvin St. Cyr let him go. It was the third workplace from which he had been dismissed that dismal year.

But the year was not over. On its next to last business day, Garrett Chafee invited Toby to his family company's decorous offices in the Chrysler Building. A welcome warmth radiated from that benign capitalist countenance, with its high, wise forehead, emphatic jaw, and the irrepressibly taunting eyes he had passed on to his younger daughter. Beside him, outfitted in smart glen plaid, was his son-in-law, the courtly Remington Pelham, Dartmouth '27 and strapping scion of Maryland Eastern Shore gentility. A few moments of proper pleasantries preceded their business proposition to him.

The Chafees' paper-bag plant in North White Plains was running into problems. Unit costs were out of line; too much fat had somehow developed in the production process, seriously threatening profits. "And all of a sudden, a lot of defective bags are showing up in our customers' hands," Rem Pelham put in. "That has to stop fast, or our name's mud." The plant manager had held his job to the Chafees' satisfaction for a dozen years and apparently not introduced any changes that could explain the production slippage. What they wanted, therefore, was an alert man with fresh eyes to go in as the assistant plant manager, a post being vacated momentarily by a retirement, to locate the trouble, and report back as soon as possible to the executive office. From there, depending on the newcomer's acumen, the sky was the limit. "Rem's got some big plans for us," Mr. Chafee said with an indulgent wink, "and we're going to need people with brains and initiative."

Toby laughed—whether more from the attraction or the absurdity of the idea, he was too stunned to judge. "Me?" he asked. "You want *me* to find out what's wrong with your plant?"

"True, you would have to put aside at least a few of your anticapitalist biases," Chafee said, "but something tells me your native good sense would attend to that."

"Thank you, sir, but I wasn't thinking of ideology. I was wondering why on earth you think I'm qualified."

Chafee toyed with the telephone dial under his right hand for a moment. "Toby, let me give you a short lesson in worldly success— even if it turns out to be my only one. Never, ever, talk yourself down. If somebody else thinks you've got something on the ball, don't disabuse him of the notion—life doesn't offer anyone enough breaks for imprudent modesty." He picked up a pencil and fluttered the eraser end at Toby. "Now I'll answer your ill-advised question. You're young. You're energetic. You're well-educated. You've worked with your hands, know something about machines, and aren't afraid to get a little dirty. You were also close with laboring people in the C.C.C. And if the fellow you sent us is anything to go by, you're a helluva good judge of a man's work aptitude."

Toby shook his head with a wan smile. "That's very flattering, sir, but with all due respect, I think somebody's been selling you a bill of goods."

Chafee drew back sternly. "Let's be clear about that somebody from the start. Whatever course your friendship takes with Eden will in no way affect your standing with Rem and me, I give you my word. This is strictly a business proposal. Capitalism doesn't run on sentiment—not for long, anyway—as I'm sure you don't need reminding." The pay was a hundred a week to start; he suggested Toby take overnight to decide.

That evening Eden finally asked him to her apartment. He went torn between the suspicion he had become her favorite charity and gratitude that she thought enough of him to have interceded with her family to bring him in out of the cold. Either way, he was thoroughly embarrassed. She saw it at once and approached the subject in a low key.

She fixed them some scrambled eggs and coffee and then sat him down in her snug living room. "It's a good company and honorable work," she said, "and you could bring decency and compassion to its management as it grows." Then there was the matter of money, unless he was allergic to it; if he helped build the business, comfort and security could be his for life. As to his writing, he could do that after hours and on the weekend, and if fortune smiled on his talent, he could always quit and write fulltime; no one was asking him to marry Chafee Industries.

"And what happens to us," he asked, "if I'm stuck away somewhere in the middle of Westchester and you're down here?"

She tossed her head back and to the side and began anxiously smoothing her hair. "They say absence makes the heart grow fonder."

His throat thickened. A hideous welling within announced he was about to be bought off with kindness, not for the first time. "They also say out of sight, out of mind."

"You think you're being farmed out—isn't that the baseball term?"

"Something like that."

"And it bothers you?"

"Immensely."

"That's good," she said, "because I happen to have a home stuck away somewhere in the middle of Westchester—and there's a not half-bad newspaper in White Plains that wants me to be its assistant women's page editor." She was in his arms then and splashing big happy tears down his face and crying, "Oh, do it, Toby—do it!"

He fought for breath against his ecstasy. "But what about your—"

"He's not my friend anymore. He took it hard—which is one reason I've left the place." She kissed him so he would not ask for others.

They spent the night on her living-room sofa, limbs locked but love unconsummated. Their prospective joint pursuit of happiness was bliss enough just then.

Toby stayed over New Year's with his father in South Nyack. The senior Ronan was overjoyed at the thought of having another industrial manager in the family, especially one who could claim an inside track with the ownership. "And when you've been there a couple of years, start talking pension to them," he counseled his son, "or you may wind up high and dry."

II

Skeezix's squat, muscular form was posted by the door in wait for him. They clasped each other for a moment like long-lost comrades-in-arms, noting the small ravages adversity had worked but glad enough they were both intact and upright.

Skeezix drew back first, remembering that rank still separated them, and led Toby through the clattering aisles of incongruously green machinery to the manager's office at the rear. "The noise'll give you a fuckin' headache the first couple o' weeks," Skeezix said. "After that, you're either deaf or don't notice no more—" He caught himself with a smile. "*Any* more."

Merlo Ratterman, seemingly unaware his new deputy had been dispatched from New York to inform on him, was a mutton of beaming affability. Silver-haired in his mid-fifties, with an unsightly spill of gut over his low trouser tops, he evinced no little pride in his realm. Since he became manager, the plant had missed only one order deadline—due to a power outage beyond their control. The place, Toby should note, was whistle-clean, and in the twenty years since he had first come to work in it as a master mechanic, they had never had a real fire. Safety was the watchword; smoking was strictly prohibited on the premises. And labor unrest was unknown. "It's a nice, friendly shop," the manager said. "I want you to call me Merlo—everyone does."

In an hour's tour of the two-story brick building, Merlo fed him the essentials of the operation. It was blessedly uncomplicated. Everything began with the giant rolls of brown kraft paper, the plant's life supply, that came in on the railroad siding at the back of the building and were hoisted by freight elevator to the second-floor storage area. Each roll, about four feet in diameter and a yard wide, weighed three quarters of a ton and yielded 25,000 "sacks," as they called the sixth-of-a-bushel grocery bag that was the plant's staple. "You don't want to leave your little toe too close to one of them babies when it's being rolled into place," Merlo advised.

The first-floor production area was divided into sections A through D, each containing six bag-making units—four for sacks, one for medium-sized delicatessen bags, and one for small lunch bags—and presided over by a supervisor. Each supervisor was responsible for the flow of production in his section. Any deviation of more than 5 percent from the average output told Merlo that a section was having trouble. "That's why every morning we go over the numbers from the day before with a fine-tooth comb," he said, exuding competence. It did not seem to bother him, or perhaps even to have occurred to him, that by a comparative standard the sections might have been performing consistently with one another but, in absolute terms, slipping below an acceptable operating level.

The bag-making machines themselves were minor miracles of modern technology. Each unit, about thirty-five feet long from the giant roll of kraft paper mounted at the front end to the metal-roller conveyor hauling off the finished product, had hundreds of ceaselessly moving parts—drums and wheels and gears, feeders and cutters and folders, appendages that printed and pasted and counted, all of them whirring and clacking and howling in choral dissonance. Instead of a menacingly lustrous gun-metal finish, they were coated with paper dust that gave them something of the look of a fuzzy caterpillar—only these were still more voracious creatures, ready to gobble up anything that neared their iron jaws. "We lose about a finger a year," Merlo conceded; it was impossible to avoid. During his entire tenure, just one man had had his hand severed, adjusting a blade, and another had had his arm crushed realigning a score finger. The new units now required two hands and a foot to operate, greatly reducing the chance of an accident. "But you still want to watch where you lean around here," the manager cautioned.

Just then another source of peril loomed behind them. A tow-motor truck bearing two full pallets of bundled bags on its hydraulic lift honked once and rolled by at a stately ten miles an hour, nearly sideswiping them on its way to the shipping area. "That's Cowboy Clyde," Merlo said without irritation. When things were slow on the loading platform, the Cowboy would get his vehicle into high gear and then jam the brakes to skid into a spin. "He puts on a helluva show." Toby inquired judiciously why such daredeviltry was condoned. "Because he knows what he's doing," replied the manager, with a trace of testiness, "and he works twice as hard as any other mover."

In addition to Cowboy Clyde, there were five inside towmen in the plant complement, eight truck drivers to deliver finished orders, four mechanics in the maintenance shop, and on the line itself, grinding out hundreds of thousands of bags a day, a regiment of two hundred machine-tenders, balers, porters, cutters, printers, pastemakers, checkers, and inspectors. The white-collar contingent included six clerks, a secretary, a bookkeeper, and two watchmen beside the manager, his assistant, and the four supervisors—a grand total of 234 employees. "And I know everyone of 'em by name, address, and favorite excuse when they call in sick," said Merlo.

He took Toby to lunch at a bar and grill owned by his wife's family on Getty Square in Yonkers. Mrs. Ratterman, a diminutive pouter pigeon with a salt-and-pepper bun affixed to the rear of her small, fierce head, stood watch over the downtown refectory with a meat cleaver beside the cash register. Merlo, though otherwise employed, plainly functioned as the major domo, greeting customers, monitoring receipts, and popping in and out of the kitchen from his booth strategically placed on the rear wall. Between his salary at the plant and his wife's share of the restaurant take, he told Toby, the Rattermans had managed to buy a fine home in the second-best section of Yonkers, two cars, a vacation cottage in the Adirondacks, and a small motorboat, all while sending their two sons to college and a daughter through nursing school. "Don't let this fool you," he said, indicating his excessive belly. "I got no moss on me."

It was half past two, Toby noted, when they got back to the plant.

For the first week, with Skeezix as his most reliable guide, he watched and learned. His staunch junior confidant from the C's had moved up the plant ladder from baler to operator to checker to inspector, just one rank below supervisor, with uncommon speed. Most of the work required only low-level skills—"and it's boring as shit," he said, "but the pay's okay and the hours are steady." The workday ran from seven to five, with a half-hour for lunch and two fifteen-minute cigarette breaks on the loading platform: a forty-five-hour week, with occasional Saturday overtime at the standard rate. The work force was nice enough—"except for that crazy bastard," Skeezix said as Cowboy Clyde chugged by them at battle speed. "He oughta be out on his ear."

"Merlo says he's an ace workman."

"Horseshit! The Cowboy is Merlo's wife's nephew, so everyone's afraid to say boo to him. The dumb fuck tips his loaded truck over once a week and all Unc does is make him clean up the spill." In June, the speed demon had almost set himself on fire filling his gas tank on the loading platform with a cigarette in his mouth. "But don't cross him or he'll go running to Merlo."

Aside from steering clear of the Cowboy, the whole trick of succeeding as a plant overseer was learning how to "read" the bags as they came out of the machines, spot any imperfections, and cure the causes as fast as possible. The printing register could be off or the seams jagged or—Skeezix grabbed a bag from the conveyor they were passing—"they could have a puffy bottom like this one, which means it won't hold shit. Probably the paper isn't breaking on a score because the bottom former or the tucker blade's not set right." And he went to tell the section supervisor.

If Toby was to understand the mechanical operation thoroughly, he decided he had better get down to nuts and bolts. On Saturday, after moving into a small apartment in New Rochelle not far from where Skeezix lived with an aunt and uncle, he invested in a '34 Chevy and drove over to the plant, which was not operating that day. As a favor to him, one of the maintenance mechanics, a normally taciturn fellow named Emery Poole, came in on his own time and gave Toby an anatomy lesson in bag-making, stripping one of the big machines down to its elements. It made the linotype look like a toy.

"Goin' good," Poole explained with proprietary pride, "this gadget'll turn out five hundred bags a minute." But that required, first of all, the paper roll to be threaded with neither too much nor too little tension and to have just the right moisture content—7 percent was ideal. Every machine tender was equipped with a moisture gauge he was supposed to stick into each roll before hooking it up. If it was too wet, the paper would feed through sluggishly, reducing output to maybe 350 or even 300 bags a minute, or the slitters might not cut well, causing malformed bags. If the roll was too dry, the brittle paper would crack under tension, causing downtime for rethreading. A paper-steamer was supposed to be attached to the machinery just before a dry roll was fed into the printer, making it flexible enough for a smooth run. But often the operators were too lazy to go through the labor of setting up the steamer, assuming they had bothered to use the moisture-gauge in the first place. Similar neglect infected the guts of the machinery, where the intricately arranged metal fingers that formed the bags on the constantly revolving drums were always loosening and slipping out of alignment; if they were not closely superintended, along with the sharpness of the cutter and tucker blades, the wastage could be formidable. "Even the paste needs steady checking," Poole concluded, like a surgeon addressing an operating theater on stitchery—"if there's not enough borax in the mix, your seams are never gonna hold."

Armed with a modicum of technical knowledge and intense motivation, Toby came to the plant early every morning and left late as he tried to familiarize himself rapidly with its faltering rhythms, patterns, and personnel. He wore a white collar to work but no tie, except on Wednesdays, when Merlo staked him to lunch at his place in Yonkers. This informality, aimed at infiltrating the rigid caste lines of the workplace that first-naming did not alter, earned him only suspicion in the blue-collar camp and disdain from the supervisors and office staff.

Direct contact with the workers was difficult. The chain of command called for the assistant manager to deal largely with the supervisors; to approach the men on the floor with any frequency would have been to usurp the supervisory prerogative. There was the added practical problem of the noise level; it was so high that no conversation could be sustained much below a shout—and given Toby's somewhat delicate mission, such broadcasting of it would hardly have been wise. Now and then he tried drifting out onto the loading platform during the cigarette breaks in order to mingle with the men and perhaps intuit their attitudes toward their work and overseers. But since he neither smoked nor affected casualness better, say, than the Lone Ranger dropping in at the Lucky Nugget Saloon, his transparency left him a pariah. It was the same when he tried to brown-bag lunch with them; despite Skeezix's efforts to persuade the rank and file that Toby was a regular guy, no one who had graduated Harvard could escape being branded either a rich man's son or a pansified genius—and surely no pal of the working stiff.

He overcame these sizable handicaps by heroic eyeballing from near and far and fondly plying Skeezix Bloomgarden on the two nights a week they had beers together—surely defensible exploitation, Toby told himself. By the end of his third week there, it was obvious that what ailed the plant was lax surveillance all along the line.

Merlo Ratterman, in addition to making three-hour lunchtimes a habit, attended his office only fitfully the rest of the workday. It was his way, he said, of breaking Toby in. As a restaurateur, he made an expansive host; as a plant manager, he was a truant. With him away so much, the supervisors passed a good deal of their time smoking in the can, cracking wise, and collusively camouflaging their delinquency by comparing daily production reports before handing them in and making what adjustments prudence dictated. With the supervisors indifferent, the inspectors did a minimum of inspecting—those too zealous at their task, Skeezix confided, were told to join the Boy Scouts.

The net effect of this contagious sluggishness was readily detectable throughout the plant floor. Workers often operated in slow motion. Machine tenders regularly took twenty minutes or more to hook up a new roll of paper to the bag-makers—a function that could be ably performed in half that time. Such a loss, multiplied by the eight or nine rolls each machine was rated to consume per workday, constituted gross managerial negligence. The casual and irregular maintenance inspections, moreover, led to repeated breakdowns of the production machinery. Toby logged the downtime of some units at 20 percent; a phone call to the manufacturer of the machines revealed that this level of dysfunction was twice the acceptable level for the bag industry as a whole. And the proportion of defective output, whether spotted in time by the plant's checkers and inspectors or, to the company's far greater detriment, shipped out to customers, was a scandal.

Each time Toby drove up the Saw Mill to visit Eden in Chappaqua, her father would serve him a drink and press him smoothly on how his mission was going. The setting *chez* Chafee was so seductively gracious—an expansively comfortable living room, a crackling fireplace, intelligent and engaging people, an adoring Irish setter nestled beside his feet, and the promised tender of wealth for his complicity—that he was hard put not to issue piecemeal bulletins on his findings. "If you don't mind, though, sir," he said instead, "I'd like to be sure before I go popping off."

His hope was to persuade Merlo Ratterman to mend his ways so he would not have to be squealed on. Toward that end, Toby presented the plant manager with a respectfully hortatory five-page memorandum. It proposed, among other innovations, twice-a-day maintenance adjustments of all the machines, a daily change of all cutter and tucker blades, dismissal from employment for failure to test any roll of paper with the moisture-gauge before putting it in place, and, above all, recording the precise output and downtime of every unit so that the personnel responsible for substandard performances could be identified and reformed, or fired.

Toby's act of presumed kindness—in contravention of his orders to report directly to the Chafees with his analysis of the plant's ills—was met at first with silence and then hostility. Merlo volunteered nothing at all to him about the memo but pointedly failed to invite him to lunch in Yonkers that week. When Toby finally asked him his reaction, Merlo said only that the memo reflected primitive understanding of plant procedures and operating costs and it would have been smarter for him to have gathered six months' or a year's experience before venturing to prescribe how the place should be run. Nor were any of Toby's proposals subtly instituted. Indeed, rumor reached him via Skeezix, who heard it from one of the supervisors, that his days at the plant were numbered—that he had been provisionally hired and Merlo would shortly inform the New York office that his new assistant manager had flunked the test.

The rumor was not entirely implausible, to Toby's mind. For the ownership to have set their plant manager and his assistant to coldly assessing each other might well have been standard internecine practice in the business world: out of deadly scrutiny, profits. But if he could not take the Chafees at their word—if they could not weigh his competence without stooping to subterfuge—it was better to find out soon. He decided to give Merlo two weeks more to change his tune.

The first week, Cowboy Clyde came within a fraction of an inch of killing himself. Pretending the loading dock was the Indianapolis Raceway, the tow-motor operator tried to make a sharp turn with his ungainly vehicle, hit an ice patch, and went skidding off the platform onto the railroad siding below. The Cowboy, pinned to the track under the weight of his truck, sustained a fractured skull, three broken vertebrae, and four cracked ribs, one within a hairline of puncturing his aorta. The incident, in Toby's view, symptomized Merlo's indulgence not merely of one witless relative but of a whole plantful of slackers.

The following week, quite by chance, Toby discovered that the problem was pathological in nature.

Just before noon one morning, a claims examiner from the state's Division of Unemployment Insurance called Merlo about a discharged worker named Sauer who had filed for benefits. Since Merlo was on his usual protracted lunch hour, Toby took the call. According to the examiner, the state's records showed the company had failed to pay in its proper share to the unemployment pool for the last few weeks Sauer was on the job. Could the company please check its payroll files to determine whether its payments to the state were in arrears or Sauer was making a false claim? Toby said he would pass the inquiry along to the manager, but when his caller advised that this was the third time he had been in touch, Toby said he would try to expedite the matter himself.

He went directly to the bookkeeper's office, but she had just left for lunch. The payroll ledger, though, had been left on her desk. Thinking to dispose of the chore in a moment or two, he began to flip back through the ledger to find out when Sauer had been removed from the payroll. What he found, to his puzzlement, was that at $36.75 a week, the discharged employee was still listed as receiving his pay.

Sniffing embezzlement, Toby checked with Skeezix. Sauer had indeed been fired two months earlier for smoking on the premises. Either the bookkeeper alone or, more likely, she and the plant manager —he who knew everyone on the plant payroll by heart and otherwise would surely have picked up the scheme at a glance—were pocketing the money. And if it was being done with Sauer's name, perhaps the ruse was being worked with other phantom employees. True, the company's regular auditing procedures would have noted the payments, but the accountants would not have known that they were fraudulent without taking a census of the plant; instead, the money would simply have shown up as part of excessive operating costs.

Next noontime, he went back to the bookkeeper's office, but this time the payroll ledger was locked up. Toby rummaged through Merlo's set of plant keys hanging in a cabinet over his desk and, finding none marked for the bookkeeper's closet, tried all the unlabeled ones in her lock. The next to last one worked. In fear of her imminent return, he scribbled down every name on the current payroll that he did not recognize. There were about forty in all, most of them delivery drivers or balers or others marginal to the problem he had been sent to cure. Just as he was taking down the last few names, the bookkeeper walked in on him. "The state unemployment people called," he blurted. "I thought I'd try to—"

"You have no right to—" the bookkeeper began and, suspecting the worst, cut herself off at once to await Merlo Ratterman's return.

In the interim, Toby ran over his list with Skeezix, a veteran at keeping track of personnel rosters. Beside Sauer's, there were five names of workers who had been let go over the previous six months. The plant was not only being run into the ground; it was also being systematically robbed.

Professing illness, he took the rest of the afternoon off and went home to write up his findings in detail. In addition to charging Merlo with malfeasance, misfeasance, and nonfeasance, Toby listed his proposals for imposing strict accountability on every man and machine in the plant. As a fillip, he suggested an extension be built onto the plant's first floor, saving all the time and effort required to haul the incoming paper rolls up to the second-floor storage area. The latter, he thought, might be converted to offices and a modest lunch room, with vending machines and ashtrays.

He delivered the report to Garrett Chafee that same evening and then took Eden to the movie in Mt. Kisco. When they got back, his liege was both aroused and relieved. "You're a God-send," he said, coiling a long arm around Toby's shoulder. "Don't you go in tomorrow—Rem and I will come up from the city, along with a couple of our security people. Meanwhile, see if you can scout us up a new bookkeeper on the double."

By the next nightfall, the plant had a new manager as well. Chafee promised he would not be posted to the assignment longer than a year; by then, if everything was going well, he would probably be asked in to the New York office. For the moment, his pay was put up to $125 a week, and Eden insisted he get his flaking black Chevy repainted if he expected her to ride in it anymore.

The reversal in his fortunes had been so swift that he did not entirely trust it. A week passed before he was willing to celebrate. They went for dinner at the restaurant in the castle on the hill in Tarrytown and had an expensive bottle of wine with it. Barcelona had just fallen, but politics was a world away just then; he could not grieve for liberty's latest casualty. Across the table sat a young woman of rare spirit, quick wit, knowing taste, and radiant looks who—there was growing reason to hope—cared for him deeply. He gorged on his luck and savored a happiness he had not known. In the Chafees' driveway, at the end of the ride home, he told Eden, tenderly if somewhat somberly, that his love for her went beyond any artful phrasing of it.

"Thank God," she said, still a little giddy from the wine. "Was that so very hard to say?"

"Excruciating."

"Why—because you aren't sure I feel the same?"

"Partly that—"

"And partly your insufferable reserve." She swiveled toward him. "What am I doing stuck away in the middle of Westchester—if not to be near you? Or were you afraid you weren't good enough for the flawless pearl of the Chafee dynasty—the rarest blossom in Christendom—"

"Would that have been so odd—to think you were set on someone with a long pedigree—after what happened before—"

"With Richard?"

"Yes."

"Oh, fuck Richard!" she spat. "Which I never did, by the way—not even a tiny bit." She touched his nose with hers and cupped his head between her hands. "May I say to you, Mr. Alonso Tobias Ronan, Junior—oh, when do I get to meet your dad, by the way?"

"Any day."

"A deal," she said and started over. "Toby Ronan," she said, giving the end of his nose a small lick, "I adore you as I have no other man. You are impossibly complicated—and hopelessly undevious. You are incredibly brave—and terribly vulnerable. And I know I love you madly because I don't need anyone else in the world now to make me ecstatically happy—or shatteringly sad." Their mouths and arms meshed for so long and so rapturously that Jefferson, nostrils aquiver, began barking away out of neglect inside the house.

Toby went to New York the next morning and bought a 1.12-karat, emerald-cut diamond ring at Black, Starr & Gorham. The purchase left him with $116.47 and a five-year-old coupe as his only liquid assets in the world. But you could hardly give a girl like Eden Chafee a trinket from a Crackerjack box. "My God!" she gasped on receiving the jewel. "It must have taken every cent you had."

"Not quite."

She wept and hugged him with unutterable gratitude. "You'll never get ahead in the world," she snuffled joyously, "if you're going to be this extravagant."

"It's not extravagant—it's a solid investment."

She wiped away the tears. "What a romantic!"

At their festive engagement dinner in New York that weekend, attended by Garrett and Rae Chafee, Rem and Alicia Pelham, and a mildly stunned Aunt Winnie, the talk was all of Toby's painless conversion to capitalism and the charms of a June wedding.

III

It was Eden who thought of hiring his father as the assistant plant manager, but it was her brother-in-law who actually proposed the idea to Toby. "Why not?" Rem asked. "He's highly experienced. He'd be exceedingly loyal and lend a lot of encouragement to the manager. And a little bird told me he's still pretty spry—fifty-nine's not Methuselah."

Toby had his doubts. It was bad enough to have attained his exalted new rank courtesy of the boss's daughter; to appoint his own father as first deputy was rampant nepotism, a vice particularly to be avoided in view of his predecessor's record. He was determined to use his fresh authority justly and impartially. On the other hand, it was perfectly true that his father had put in many years running a similar and, indeed, considerably larger factory; whether it was making paper bags or tin cans, the operating principles had to be about the same. And who could be more supportive yet constructively critical of him? What a fine thing, moreover, to rescue him from the indignity of serving as a bank guard his final active years. Or was there perhaps worse indignity in playing second fiddle to a son?

"Not in the least," his father said. "I'd be highly honored—if you don't mind working with a retread."

As plant manager, Toby wore a tie in every day now. He would usually undo his top shirt button and tug the tie knot down an inch or two, but the tie itself never came off. It was not so much a symbol of his dominion as a declaration that the whole place had to shape up, the manager included.

The reform program initiated by the Ronan regime, *fils et père*, had somewhat more stick than carrot to it. The pace of production was speeded throughout the plant. Several of the most notorious foot-draggers were let go, and new maintenance men were taken on in their place. Twice-a-day inspection of the machinery became routine; downtime and wastage quickly dropped. Every unit and its work crew were monitored, and their daily output closely charted. Workers caught sneaking a smoke, violating the safety rules, failing to use their moisture-gauge on the paper rolls, or otherwise blatantly malingering received demerit points from their supervisors. "Three of them," Toby said in explaining the new work rules to a plant meeting, "and you're out of the old ball game."

But there were to be improvements in working conditions as well, the manager announced. Part of the second floor would be converted to a lunchroom, where the men were also welcome to smoke during their morning and afternoon breaks. All the old machines were to be modified to incorporate the safety features of the new models. Ear plugs would be provided free of charge to all workers who wanted them against the constant mechanized timpani. Members of the floor section that posted the highest output for the week would receive a 3 percent cash bonus in their pay envelopes. And employees with three or more years of service at the plant would henceforth be entitled to a second week of paid vacation annually.

Improved results did not come trouble-free. There was some grumbling at first about sweat-shop methods, although it was plain to many in the place that beneath its cosmetic cleanliness, anarchy had threatened under Merlo Ratterman's licentious rule. Five more laggards had to be fired after repeated warnings, the final one from Toby himself, who later administered the *coup de grâce* in person instead of delegating the task to the assistant manager, as had been Merlo's practice. Nothing demonstrated the new manager's resolve better than his dismissal of one of the supervisors, a prime line officer in the plant command. Not only had the fellow been a ringleader of the collusive slowdown in Merlo's day and barely reformed since but he was indiscreet enough to disparage. "Ronan's old man" within Skeezix's hearing. Toby's sidekick called the man on it, the supervisor accused Skeezix of being the manager's toady, and the two came to murderous blows on the loading platform. When Toby learned of the fracas and its cause, he replaced the offending overseer with Emery Poole from the maintenance department. "The next supervisor's slot that opens," he quietly told Skeezix afterwards, "is all yours."

"Yassuh, Mr. Ronan—suh," Skeezix said and shuffled obsequiously out of the manager's office.

For the most part, though, Toby's reformation of the plant proceeded without friction and, by spring, had yielded substantial economies. As a validation of his competence, the upturn left him heady, bordering on euphoric. After all, he had never really run anything before in his life. To his surprise, wielding power was a decidedly pleasurable sensation. He took pains not to be arbitrary or brazen about it, but it was satisfying to note a certain deferential movement that greeted the merest hint of command in his voice or the purposeful approach of his step. Even the upbraiding or termination of unworthy underlings proved less painful to him than he would have guessed; as long as some men had to sit in judgment of others, authority was best vested in sensitive and merciful taskmasters.

Although the product was humble enough and the labor that went into it by no stretch ennobling, Toby conceived of his role as very constructive socially. The plant was perhaps not contributing decisively to the redistribution of American wealth, but by providing humane incentives for efficiency, better conditions in the workplace, and at least some improvement in the workers' standard of living, it served as a promising refutation to doctrinaire Marxism. Someday, conceivably, he would prevail upon the ownership to grant worker participation in profits—to each, according to his merit.

Among the nicer benefits of his new arrangement was the chance to become acquainted with his father as he had never been in boyhood. They were equals now and both glad of companionship enriched by a shared frame of reference. The elder Ronan supplemented those memories with tales of his own young manhood, his first job in the Haverstraw brickyards, how he went canoeing on the Hudson with Toby's mother in their courting days and once turned over in Tomkins Cove with much desperate thrashing—a living scrapbook that left his son feeling less rootless and more appreciative of values and yearnings that had shaped him. Neither sloth nor greed was part of the family makeup, any more than demonstrative love had been. "So much was understood between your mother and me," his father allowed, "but one of my sorest regrets since she died was all the things that never got said and should have been. Don't you make the same mistake."

Accordingly, Toby's communication with Eden ripened with the season. Qualms and crotchets were exchanged so they would not enter matrimony as strangers, full of unpleasant surprises and unreal expectations. Their sexuality, too, grew more intimate, though not consummate; their bodies burned for fulfillment, but by mutual, unspoken pledge, it was to be withheld as their ultimate wedding gift to each other. Meanwhile, plans for the great event advanced. The ceremony, on the Chafees' flawless lawn, was to be limited to a hundred guests— fewer would have been unforgivable in view of Rae Chafee's social position; more, intolerable to the loving couple. In mid-April, Eden's parents disclosed their wedding present—a modestly scaled Victorian in mint condition that the Chafees had found for them in Irvington, with a positively poetic prospect of the Hudson—or, if it did not suit them, any house they chose of comparable cost. And to guard the newlyweds' hearth, Jefferson the setter. Toby's cup runneth over.

The request, then, soon after by a seven-man committee of employees for a meeting of the work force to discuss unionizing the plant came as a particularly ill-timed shock.

Toby's first reaction was annoyance with Skeezix for not having tipped him off about what was brewing. When Skeezix turned out to be a member of the organizing committee, Toby saw betrayal. Nor was the feeling directed against Skeezix alone. The very notion of a union smacked of ingratitude for the improvements he had brought and implied distrust of his intention to extend progressive policies. "You're a victim of your own kindness," Toby's father reasoned with him. "Give an inch and they want a mile."

Deeper reflection left Toby freshly appreciative of life's rich irony. It had cast him now as the autocrat of plant operations, not merely a neutral monitor and certainly not an order-taker as had been his fate till then. If his past allegiances had been with the union struggle, his current posture left him indifferent at best to its justification, particularly at his expense. His concern, he told himself, was entirely practical, his objections non-partisan. It was not a question of his sway being diminished if the plant went union but the consequences of the fact. Authority, once diffused and shared, lost all its dread. Disobedience and discord were sure to follow, and with them, poorer performance on the production line—and the fouling of his dreams.

Satisfied that the stirrings of unionism did not reflect disapproval of his managerial performance—perhaps the opposite, even—Toby resolved to meet the issue by reason and resilience; suppression, he knew firsthand, only fed the flames of insurgency. The organizing committee was permitted to hold an informational meeting in the lunchroom after work on the proviso he could address it at the end. The place was packed when he got there; this was plainly no splinter movement. Their ranks parted readily before him, but instinct advised him at once that his relationship to them now and forever more was as an adversary.

"I've been a union man myself," he told them, "and paid the price proudly. There's strength in numbers when there's justice in the workingman's demands and management is a stone wall. But I'm not stone, and if you want my opinion, you'll get farther with this company by talk than by muscle." Let them put forward their requests by peaceable discussion. And if they wanted to band together formally, they did not need to affiliate with any outside organization; company unions were known to work well where ownership was enlightened.

Their requests, replied the chairman of the organizing committee, a machine tender with the company seven years, could be stated briefly: better pay, shorter hours, job security. Details would be forthcoming.

When Toby advised Garrett Chafee and Rem Pelham of the unwelcome development, they were flatly opposed to a union from the first. "It's one of the prime reasons we located out of the city," his prospective father-in-law explained. The company paid better than the going rate for industry as a whole, and working conditions, at Toby's behest, had been improved. A union would simply renew the squeeze on company profits by cutting productivity that Toby had worked so hard to raise. "We'll be fair," Rem said, "but we won't go soft. Your job is to nip this thing in the bud."

"And how do I do that?"

"You fire the agitators, that's how—all of them, right away."

"I think that's just inviting disaster." Toby appealed to Chafee for restraint. "I'd rather try to ride the thing out."

"You're playing with fire," said Rem. "You don't put out fires by giving them a chance to work up a head."

"Or by pouring on oil," Toby argued.

Chafee chose the waiting game. The plant organizing committee, however, would not oblige. During lunch hours and cigarette breaks, its members circulated everywhere, agitating for collective action. Toby took no restraining measures; instead, he sought Skeezix's counsel to figure out what had sparked the uprising despite management's relative benevolence. Skeezix shrugged but made a guess: "These guys got nothin' much goin' for 'em—except each other." The largely low-skilled work engendered no pride, and opportunities for real advancement were few. Life at the plant, its tolerable bosses notwithstanding, was a deadend. Better pay, job security, and more time away from the ear-splitting grind were the only meaningful compensations—and no company ceded them willingly.

At the next organizing meeting, a representative of the Paper Workers Union was on hand; the plant manager was not. Toby's father counted as the session convened; more than half of the blue-collar force trooped upstairs to attend. "I don't like the looks of it nohow," he told his son.

Nor did the New York office. Rem Pelham renewed his call for draconian countermeasures. "Lop off a few heads, and you'll see how fast the thing fizzles." Garrett Chafee, lamenting that outside union affiliation would assure minimum output at maximum pay, prepared to side with his son-in-law.

Toby held out for compromise. "If you'll give up something, I think maybe I can get good value back."

Convinced time was running out, Chafee granted him a few days' reprieve to put together the package. Toby was back in twenty-four hours with his proposal. Management would recognize a company union and issue it a contract that provided for a forty-two-hour week instead of forty-five, with time and a half now for overtime; a three-step incentive pay scale, with grade C workers receiving the base pay, grade B workers earning 5 percent above base, and grade A workers 10 percent above; a second week of paid vacation after two years on the payroll instead of three; severance pay of one week for each three years of employment, and a formal grievance committee to consider firings and the fairness of other management actions and policies—though the employee panel would be powerless beyond expressing its views. The offer would be left on the table for exactly one week, at the end of which the entire plant would vote on it. Approval would effectively repulse affiliation with the greater American labor movement; rejection, Toby agreed, would be followed by unkinder forms of discouragement.

Rem was calm but adamant. "I think you're giving away the store."

Garrett Chafee thought Toby was being generous to a fault—"but I suppose it's the lesser evil. Try it—only I'm holding you to Rem's alternative if this doesn't go."

He felt as if he had been practicing for years on a high wire between self-interest and conscience, and his debut under the big top was finally at hand. Eden, by now, understood the nature and difficulty of his act and, while doubting it would succeed in the long run, applauded his effort. "And thank God for Daddy," she said. "I told you he's always been marvelous with the help—or whatever you call them."

It remained questionable in the extreme whether the help shared her view. Secure that he had extracted the fairest possible offer from the owner, Toby pitched it hard at the plant. He had the terms mimeographed and distributed to everyone on the payroll. He went to the lunchroom every day that week to answer questions about the proposed contract. And he barred the Paper Workers Union organizer from the premises, although C.I.O. operatives distributed leaflets at the plant gate, inveighing sharply against the company union plan.

"Everyone thinks you done a good thing," Skeezix told him while the issue hung in doubt, "and we already come out ahead in this." But what would happen when someone succeeded Toby? A less compassionate plant manager might already have fired half the work force if threatened with unionization. Worker rights ought not to depend on management's indulgence—and house unions were almost always puppets of the company. And for good measure, the C.I.O. was attacking the graduated-pay incentives under the proposed company contract as a blatant sweat-shop technique.

Toby did his best to blunt all such arguments, but when the plant was formally polled at the end of the week, barely 40 percent of the workers favored the company union.

Over the weekend, Eden steeled him for the coming ordeal. "You gave Father your word," she said. "There comes a time when you have to decide who and what you are."

On Monday, without pretense that the reason was other than punitive, he fired two members of the organizing committee—though neither the chairman nor of course Skeezix—and one outspoken supporter among the rank and file.

"I never figured you," said Skeezix, eyes pain-glazed, "for a fuckin' fascist."

The effect of the firings was what Toby had expected—explosive resentment. A work slowdown spread throughout the plant, and none of the men spoke to the manager, his assistant, or the supervisors. Into this combustible environment, wearing a dark suit and tie that looked incongruously formal beneath his laurel wreath of bushy gray hair, strode Saul Orloff, of counsel to the International Paper Workers Union.

Toby's worried eyes widened. "Gee," he said, "small world."

"Getting smaller all the time," said Saul, with a chilling handshake. His involvement was no coincidence. He had retained a vivid memory, he said, of the Chafees from Nina's account of their conspicuous plunder, and when the union requested legal help from the International Defense Fund in organizing the paper-bag plant, Saul volunteered. "I only just found out, though, that you went over to the aristocracy. Well, I guess congratulations are in order—another Harvard man makes good."

The sight and sound of this professional avenger, appearing so unexpectedly amid the turbulence around and within him, flooded Toby with distaste, then venom, then guilt. "Thanks," he said. "Now why don't you just get on with whatever it is that brought you here?"

Saul sat, uninvited, and turned those long, tapered, implacably judgmental eyes on him for an eternal moment. "Toby, Toby, Toby," he finally said just above a whisper, with an accompanying series of tiny headshakes. "How can you live with yourself?"

To flee that scalding look and damning question, Toby retreated behind the desk and folded his arms across his chest. "Look, I've done whatever I could. We offered a contract with much better terms than—"

"You didn't *offer* anything—you were forced to respond to the collective courage of your workers. And now you're trying to bribe them into not organizing."

"It's not a bribe—it's a damned good contract—"

"Rammed at them on a take-it-or-leave-it basis and followed by immediate reprisals because they want the right to real collective bargaining." Active revulsion disfigured Saul's mouth. "Give your new in-laws a message from me—okay? Tell 'em it doesn't matter what else they own, they can't possess the working class—and someday, not too far off now, the working class is going to possess them."

"They don't think like that, if you want to know—and neither do I. No one's supposed to possess anyone. People are supposed to be free."

"Right—just like you were—to do whatever you wanted with your life. And what do you become? A parasite to capitalists who extorted their fortune from the labor of helpless wage slaves. I hope you'll be able to sleep at night between all those nice silk sheets." His punishing eyes suddenly turned wicked. "They say pampered pussy infects you with terrible social diseases—like swollen spite glands and shriveling of the heart—"

"Fuck yourself!" Toby yelled, arms dropping in dumb fury.

"I'm not your problem." Saul reached into a zippered briefcase and handed him a formal petition in behalf of the plant's workers, under procedures set forth in the National Labor Relations Act, requesting a shop-wide election under federal supervision on affiliating with the paper workers union and designating it as official bargaining agent. "You've also got forty-eight hours to reinstate the three guys you fired or all hell's going to break loose. Ask your bosses how their customers would feel about a picket line in front of their stores all over the East." Saul stood and cast a last sad look across the desk. "Tell me just one thing—how in the name of simple decency could you throw those guys out the door for having had the guts to do just what you did at the *Trib?* Didn't that whole business at the paper mean anything at all to you, Toby?"

"Sure. It meant I'd better stop trying so hard to save everyone else and start worrying about my own ass a little. That's what Nina said preoccupied me all along, anyway—speaking of shriveled hearts—"

"You're wrong again. She's marrying Mel Kantor a week from Sunday."

The news surprised him. Perhaps Melvin had curbed Nina's consuming partisanship. "Give them my best," he said. "I hope she raises a whole brood of little deviationists."

The morning after Saul's two-day deadline had elapsed for rehiring the fired pro-union workers, Toby got to the plant early and sniffed trouble the moment he opened the door. His father was already there, assessing the damage. Three of the big bag-making machines had been wrecked—rammed repeatedly with the giant rolls of kraft paper, as if

Gulliver had gone on a mad bowling spree. Repairs would run into the thousands.

The onset of violence jarred Garrett Chafee. No longer trusting his own conciliatory inclinations or Toby's, he deferred wholly to his son-in-law from that point on. "Find out who did it—any way you have to," Rem ordered, "and press charges. We want those bastards behind bars, and quick." Meanwhile, the plant was to go under Pinkerton guard night and day.

He decided to put unmerciful heat on Skeezix. It was a contemptible thing to do, but all the alternatives that occurred to him would have been worse. "I need the names of everyone who did it," Toby told him, "or I'm going to have to fire people right and left, hit or miss."

Skeezix sat with his head lowered. "You know damned well I'm no fuckin' squealer," he said, "even if I did know—which I don't."

Toby nodded. Then he said quietly, "Look, you asked me for my help once in getting a job, and you got it, gladly. Now I need yours."

Skeezix's head shot up. "Hey, I helped you plenty o' times."

Toby nodded again and sighed. "Look, this whole thing is getting very ugly. I've been trying to do my level best to keep it from blowing up, and then your people did a dumb thing like this—"

"The dumb thing was firing our three guys."

"I had to, Skeezix—"

"Nobody has to do nothin'—it's a free country."

"Look," Toby began again, growing desperate, "if I have to fire more men, it's going to be on your conscience."

Skeezix hunched his stocky shoulders. "At least I still got one."

He gave Skeezix overnight to change his mind, and when that did no good, Toby fired three more workers, including the chairman of the organizing committee. During lunch, Skeezix was elected to replace him.

By the next morning, the doughty new leader had help. Saul Orloff reappeared at the manager's door, this time accompanied by the law— in a form achingly familiar to Toby. "Francesca Platt, from the National Labor Relations Board staff," Saul introduced her. "I believe you've met."

Her name was different and her hair shorter, but there was no mistaking that proud, heart-shaped face with its high cheekbones and dark almond eyes swimming shrewdly about behind her glinting glasses. "Hello, Toby," she said, smiling slightly and extending a firm hand for him to take.

Her touch, certifying a reality wilder than any moment he had ever dreamed, turned him to lead. "Hello, Cheska," he said. No saving pleasantry entered his arrested brain. He stood there gaping at her, flanked by Skeezix and Saul Orloff in an uncanny triptych—bearing witness, among the three of them, to the whole muddled journey his young adult life had taken. A dull, persistent pain he could not localize assaulted him.

"Perhaps if you'd excuse us for just a couple of minutes," Cheska said to Skeezix and Saul, "Mr. Ronan and I might settle all this."

Her husband had transferred from the Berkeley law faculty to Columbia, she explained when they were alone, and the N.L.R.B. had taken her on in its New York field office. "That's excellent," he said, still standing awkwardly over her as she sat beside his desk. "I'm glad you've put your brains to work for a good cause."

"Thanks," she said. "I only wish I could return the compliment."

He perched on the edge of the desk, one foot toeing the floor for balance. "It's not really the way things may look. Orloff's a fanatic—"

"That's funny—he thinks the world of you—or did, until all this happened." She looked up at him kindly, as if trying to bridge the years and vicissitudes that had altered them both. "Well, I guess you've finally figured out who you are. I used to think you were too civilized to survive in the real world—and you turned out to be more corrupt than any of us."

He could not bear indictment by this first, sweetest, harshest love of his life. "What the hell makes me corrupt—firing people who sabotaged the plant?" His arms flung out. "That's inexcusable lawlessness—"

"I understood you fired people before anyone damaged anything."

"That's no excuse for destroying property."

"People matter more than property," she said, "or hadn't you heard?" Her eyes narrowed. "And you discarded them—like waste paper. That's corruption, Toby. And the new bunch you threw out yesterday—who said they were the ones who did the dirty work? And when you fired them, you also broke the law. You can't toss out pro-union workers once they've filed with the government to hold a shop election." She took out a long envelope from her purse. "This is an injunction issued in federal court yesterday afternoon, ordering you to stop it." She rose and handed it to him. "And if you don't obey it, I'm going to make it my personal business to put you in jail." She fell still a moment, then blinked hurriedly, dissipating their shared memory. "Last time you went, if I'm not mistaken, we were on the same side."

"Cheska, I'm not against—"

"Oh, Toby," she said, eyes shut hard against the revealing emotion the interview had provoked in her, "how could you have given in to them so easily? You were so good—and sensitive—and principled—"

With all his draining strength, he fought back the impulse to fall at her feet and beg for understanding. He reached a hand out and brushed it the width of her pained warm forehead. "There isn't any 'them' to give in to," he said. "There's only us, Cheska—and I'm doing the best I can."

"Sure." She turned sideways to him. "I hope that'll get you by." At the door she stopped and added over her shoulder, "I never expected to run in to you again—and now I wish to God I hadn't."

IV

On learning of the federal injunction, Rem Pelham grew still more defiant toward the union effort. "You call a meeting of those lugs," he commanded Toby, "and tell 'em if they don't drop this whole thing fast, there's damned well going to be a lockout one of these mornings."

"I don't think it'll do much good, Rem—we're past that now."

"Toby, I'm beginning to think you don't have the balls for this thing. You tell 'em—and sound like you mean it—because it may come to that."

"I'm beginning to think," he told Eden that night, "that your dear brother-in-law is a prize prick."

"He's just trying to keep your morale up," she said. "He knows how hard all this is on you. They never told you the job would be a picnic."

He called a plant meeting the next day and did his best to sound convincing. They would have to choose, he told them, between the union and the plant—management was through coddling them.

When he came in the following morning, the entire duct system connecting the paste-making vat to the bag machines was gummed up; somebody had added extra borax to the mix and turned the pumps off overnight. By the time the mess was cleaned up, the plant had lost a whole day's production.

Rem retaliated by ordering the Pinkertons to carry shotguns and patrol inside the plant as well as outside. Toby protested that the step was unnecessarily provocative. "In your opinion," said Rem, "and you've been wrong from the start."

Toby took his objection to Garrett Chafee. "We've tried your way," Chafee told him sadly, "and it didn't work."

"The game's not worth the candle," he said to Eden. "The union isn't all that monstrous—or worth shooting people over."

"It's the principle of the thing," she replied. "Daddy and Rem just don't want to be bullied into it—and I think they're being very courageous." She kissed him hard. "And you, poor baby—you're the one on the firing line, aren't you? Just do your best—they understand."

On the second day the Pinkertons were patrolling the premises, shotguns at the ready, a terrible noise came from the loading platform just after lunch. Someone had aimed one of the tow-motors toward the edge, turned on its switch, and run for it; the small, heavy truck went crashing over the side onto the railroad track—a flaming wreck. One of the guards spotted someone fussing suspiciously with a second tow-motor at the opposite end of the platform and yelled for him to stop. When the fellow darted off instead, the Pinkerton pursued, kneeled, and fired. The shotgun pellets turned the left eye of a young baler into bloody pulp. He screamed his innocence all the way to the hospital.

The shattering report of the gun left Toby shaken and somber. He had tried to interpose himself between an immovable management and an irresistible work force. In satisfying the ownership by better cultivating the plant labor, he had also awakened the workers' aspirations, but without a vested interest in the enterprise, their loyalty was reserved for themselves. Indignity was met with vandalism that undercut their moral ground and left Toby nowhere to stand, in the end, but as a collaborator with martial law. The shooting told his whole trembling body in an instant that the position was untenable.

While the police were on the way to the plant, emotions within it boiled toward a flash point. Workmen converged on all sides of the six armed guards, one with his gun still smoking, and looked ready to wrench away the weapons and turn them on their owners. There was no time to negotiate. Toby pushed determinedly through the bristling blue-collar ranks and confronted the chief guard with an outstretched hand. "You people are done here," he said. "We'll hold your weapons till the cops are done."

"The guns go with us," came the panicky reply.

"If you value your lives," Toby said, "you'll hand them over."

Fearful of a lynching bee, the uniformed men hesitated. Toby, with numbers on his side, stood his ground. One by one, the shotguns were surrendered. He handed the first two to his father, the next three to Skeezix, and kept the fired one himself. His father ushered the trigger-happy guard to the manager's office, and the other five filed out the front door of the plant through a gauntlet of curses.

"All right," Toby said, scanning the heated workers who pressed in on him, pleased by his retaliatory action but still brimming with larger resentments, "we're closing up for the rest of the day. Go home—cool off—and think hard about what just happened and why. Violence only feeds violence. Don't come back tomorrow unless you're prepared to wage your fight legally."

For a long, electric moment, no one moved. It was not impossible, he thought, every vein in him throbbing, that in the next instant they would tear the place to pieces. In that wavering breach, Skeexiz, like a revolving gun turret, turned to the rank and file and snapped out in a sharp, stinging voice, "You heard the man—hit the trail!"

The withdrawal was glum but orderly.

On his way into the city, Toby stopped off at the *Reporter-Dispatch* office in White Plains to tell Eden what had happened. Finding she was out to a benefit luncheon, he sat at her typewriter, wrote up a one-take account of the shooting incident, and handed it in to the city desk. Supplemented by the police report and confirmation from the hospital that the workman had lost an eye, the item made the front page of the final edition.

In his New York office, Garrett Chafee was genuinely, if briefly, disturbed by the news Toby brought him. After a brooding look out over the city spread below his comfortably appointed redoubt, he turned back and said, "I know it's awful that a thing like this had to happen, but maybe that's what it takes to bring these people to their senses."

Toby measured his words. "I don't believe a thing like this did have to happen. And with all due respect, sir, 'these people' have helped make you a comfortable man. All they're after is a little more of the pie and an acknowledgment of their dignity—and I think they're entitled to them."

Chafee tilted back and fiddled with his phone dial. "Toby, I don't have any problem with the workers of the world wanting to lose their chains. It's when they start clobbering me with them that I get my back up."

"I believe we're the ones who started swinging first."

"In self-defense."

"I don't accept that. And I can't accept Rem's philosophy of labor relations. If you want to stick with Rem as the plant policy-setter in view of what's happened, then I guess you need a new manager up there."

Chafee's distress was immediate. "That's a helluva position to put me in, Toby. I need both of you—and he's got seniority." He climbed to his feet and rested a cautioning hand on Toby's shoulder. "Why don't you wait and see how you feel in the morning before deciding for certain?"

"There's nothing for me to decide. I'm no good at implementing policies I think are tyrannical."

He was there waiting for her when Eden drove home to Chappaqua at the end of the day. She was still steaming with defeat after her effort to keep the story about the plant shooting off the front page. "And you," she said, "how could you *do* that—dropping the thing right in their laps?"

"I didn't want it blown out of proportion."

She flung the paper at him. "Well, I hope you're satisfied then."

He read over the printed version. "It's accurate, anyway."

"It's terrible publicity, don't you understand?"

He watched her circling and smoking. "How can you talk about publicity when someone got his eye shot out down there?"

"Oh, I get it—Toby needs instant expiation so he goes running to the paper with the story." Her hot, blue glare sizzled him. "Don't you have any sense of loyalty to this family?"

"Not when it condones brutality."

"They're the brutes! They started destroying things—"

"Out of fear and anger they were all going to lose their jobs. You don't treat people like that—unless you're full of fear and anger yourself—which is what I think Rem's trouble is."

"Rem! Rem's ten times the businessman you'll ever be."

He picked the newpaper up from the floor and put it on the hall table. "That's what I decided, too," he said, "so he's the only one of us working for Chafee Industries at the moment."

"Oh, great!" Her rage billowed. "You mean you're walking out when the going gets rough—is that it? That's very goddamned heroic!"

"I'm doing what I have to do."

"What you're doing is tossing away your whole stupid future!"

"I don't buy that."

"No—you wouldn't. Everything's been handed to you on a silver platter—and you can't wait to dump it over. What total idiocy!"

All their carefully accumulated civility went whipping away in anger. "I can't live with myself if I have to spend all day jabbing people in the ass with a bayonet. It's too high a price to purchase my comfort."

"I see. And what about living with me—and my comfort? What the hell am I supposed to do—turn my back on my own family?" Her arms sprang sideways and her palms turned up. "You want me to walk away from all this—just because you have a distorted, infantile value system?"

"Your family's not going to excommunicate you because of me."

"Good Christ in heaven! Three weeks to the wedding Lochinvar decides to hurl shit all over the bride's family—and thinks they won't mind it a bit." She gave her head a flutter. "I sure do pick 'em."

"I'm sorry that's how you feel."

"What did you expect? I think you've lost your senses."

"No—just the opposite."

She threw herself into a plump white sofa. "Then how can you be so goddamned selfish—to drive a wedge like this between me and my family? If you really loved me, you'd never have dreamed of such a thing."

"I didn't think I was marrying your family," he said.

"I *love* my family!" she shouted. "And I want them to love my husband—can't you understand that? I don't want them to think I married a nincompoop—not to mention a thankless freeloader."

"I never asked your family for a damned thing!"

"But you didn't mind accepting its generosity—only you wouldn't think of repaying it by swallowing some of your big fat pride for a little while."

"You don't want a husband at all—you want a consort—somebody to genuflect at the Chafee family shrine—a loyal retainer who'll perform stud duty and never ask embarrassing questions—"

"I think you're an ungrateful, nasty bastard!"

He turned from her. "I think maybe we've both said enough for now." The emotional drain of the whole afternoon nearly overtook him as he headed out the front door. "I'll talk to you."

"No!" she yelled after him. "We don't have anything more to say." She stood framed in the doorway, quaking with fury and confusion. "And you can take this fucking thing back to the pawnshop you got it from!" The ring went skipping off the porch steps into the driveway gravel.

He crawled around for ten minutes before finding it in the fading light. Then he drove to New Rochelle and went out drinking with Skeezix until they both were exceedingly plastered.

V

What amazed Skeezix most was not the bizarre shapes of the buildings or the dramatic lighting inside them or the profusion of bright colors everywhere or the massiveness and modernity of the whole lavish contraption but the appalling fact that it would all be pulled to the ground the moment the event was over. "It don't make any sense," he said, wide-eyed now, though still a little hung-over.

"It's a carnival," Toby instructed him. "They don't have to make sense as long as the hustlers find work and the customers stay happy."

Having opened on May Day, the World's Fair was not nearly as crowded in its third week of operation as it would be when the summer tourists came thronging in. It was the perfect time and place for the pair of them to escape from reality for a day.

They were drawn almost at once to the two enormous white shapes that had already become the linked symbols of the streamlined extravaganza. The trylon, Toby read to him from the official fair guide as Skeezix snapped away at the sleek, three-sided spire with his uncle's camera, was seven hundred feet high; the perisphere beside it, the largest globe ever constructed by man, measured two hundred feet in diameter. Skeezix thought the trylon the greater engineering feat. "I wonder how they got a thing so fuckin' skinny up in the air that high."

"Maybe they put Link in charge of the crew," Toby suggested.

"Link who?"

"Link, Link—the colored kid at the camp. Remember the fire tower?"

"Oh, yeah—Link. I wasn't thinkin'."

"It says in here the trylon stands for aspiration."

"Oh, yeah? And what's the globe for—constipation?"

They saw Democracity, the giant model of a future metropolis, from the revolving balcony inside the perisphere. And then the huge diorama travelogue of America from the moving chairs in the General Motors Building. And an eight-foot robot counting on its fingers at the Westinghouse exhibit. And the world's largest locomotive, churning in place at seventy miles an hour. And a drop of water magnified two thousand times, and electric eels lighting lamps and ringing bells, and a hundred other marvels you would never see elsewhere in a lifetime. By the time they headed toward the foreign pavilions down Constitution Mall, the broad avenue enlivened by trees and fountains and floral beds that formed the fair's main promenade, Skeezix had run out of film and energy. He elected to take a rest while Toby toured the Soviet Union's display.

The two-story structure formed a marble-clad semicircle, broken into two wings, one bearing on its facade a mammoth bas-relief portrait of Lenin, the other of Stalin. At the head of the stairway leading into the exhibition hall, in a white shirt and slacks with a tennis sweater over her shoulders, its sleeves looped around her neck like a big bow tie, stood Eden Chafee, waving a blue and orange World's Fair pennant at him. "Hello, comrade," she said as Toby took the steps two at a time. "What took ya?"

The laughter spilled out of him, and with it the bitterness of the previous night. "What the hell are you doing here?"

"Waiting for you," she said.

"How'd you know I was here?"

"I called the plant—your father said you were playing hookey with Skeezix. Then I called his aunt, and she said you guys were headed here."

His joy and amazement collided. "But how did you expect to find us—there's three hundred buildings."

"I figured you'd be in sort of an anticapitalist mood just about now, so if I hung around here, sooner or later you'd show up. It's only been a four-hour wait—buy me a hot dog inside, I'm starving."

They stiffly ate chicken blinis and tea while serenaded by the heroic singers of the Red Army. Neither offered a word of reconciliation. Nor in their tacit truce was physical contact permitted; together but apart, they toured the exhibitions: carpets from the Caucasus, wood carvings from Tashkent, lacquer work from Baku, a reproduction of a station in Moscow's ornate new subway system, the first plane to fly from Russia to America by the Arctic route, a twenty-foot-high model of the Palace of the Soviets made entirely—for some unfathomable reason—of semi-precious stones. . . .

"What do you think, comrade?" she asked as they headed down a broad flight of stairs into the courtyard between the wings of the pavilion.

"Not enough tractors."

She smiled and led him toward the base of the immense pylon that soared up out of the center of the courtyard in conscious imitation of the trylon, though it was not half so tall. Faced in red porphyry framed with paler marble, it was surmounted by a giant, polished-metal statue of the quintessential workingman of the world, muscular, dutiful, and mute. "I'll bet he's from the People's Paper-Bag Factory," she said with an upward glance, "and they bronzed him when he asked for higher pay."

"It's stainless steel, actually—"

"So they couldn't afford bronze," she said airily and then, all restraint shredding, buried her face against his chest. "Oh, Toby—I was wrong—so, so wrong—"

He wrapped his arms around her and lowered his cheek against her hair.

"I said if you loved me enough, you wouldn't have done a thing like that—quitting, and humiliating me, and cutting me off from everyone—"

He felt her warmth hard against him and the pounding of both their hearts. "It sounds vaguely familiar—"

"But if I loved you enough, I should have understood—what makes you you—and not spat on your dumb—beautiful—principles."

People passing glanced at them and then away. "You could say that."

"Then why didn't you, damn it! Why did you just stand there and let me abuse you—like the spoiled little bitch I can be?"

He locked her tighter to him. "Because—if you didn't know that, I didn't want you. It's something you had to feel—not be argued into believing."

"I feel, Toby—oh, Christ, I feel." Slowly and gently then, she pulled away from him, made a pass at blotting her drenched face with a sleeve, and reached into her pants pocket for a small, square blue-felt box. "This came in a week ago," she said, conveying it to him with both hands and brimming eyes. "I didn't want it to go to waste."

He opened it. The gold band gleamed and winked in the early-afternoon sun. He pincered it between his fingers and read the inscription, engraved in tiny italic capitals: "MY LIFE, I LOVE YOU. EDEN 6-20-39."

"It's Byron, I think. I read so much in Florida I can't remember—"

"It's—just—I—"

She put a finger to his lips. "And they're going to make your father plant manager—for the time being, at least—till they see if he can handle it. Rem said to Daddy, 'Let's hope he's not a block off the old chip.'" Her eyes danced.

"That's—I—"

Her finger pressed against his mouth. "I think he ought to come live with us, Toby—I mean if he wants to. There's plenty of room, really —and he must be awfully lonesome."

"I—"

"Besides, we'll probably need his help with the upkeep. I told Daddy we couldn't accept anything—the house is more than generous of them. And since you're going to be gainfully unemployed for a while—"

"Oh?"

"Yes—Columbia, I think. Two years and one dissertation. That's what you're best at—truth, beauty, and all those forsaken precepts. Lord knows there's enough other people out there tearing them apart."

They kissed without shame. When they looked up, it was into Skeezix Bloomgarden's awed, approving face. "Somethin' tells me," he said, "three's a crowd."

EPILOGUE

AS MY MOTHER'S DEATH had foreshadowed the solitary ordeal I would pass through in that decisive decade of my life, so at the end of it was I instructed by the dying of another strong, sweet soul.

Wally Eichhorn's second stroke was fatal. I saw his death notice in the paper—there was no obituary. By New York newspaper standards, he was nobody special. So much else had died that final autumn of the 'Thirties that my mood was one of almost generalized bereavement as I abandoned an afternoon seminar in linguistics and took the subway down to Wally's memorial service at Riverside Chapel.

The large turnout made me happy. Being Wally, he had forbidden a dirge. Instead, a small chorus sang three familiar songs of his choice, each followed by a short eulogy explaining its connection to his life.

First came a plaintive rendering of "The Whiffenpoof Song," to mark the anomalous fact he had graduated from Yale. "He was no poor little lamb who had lost his way," his sister Adele said in firm-voiced tribute, "but he did believe all of us are doomed from here to eternity, so we'd better make the most of what we're given." What I remembered was his telling me once that the nicest part of being a Jew was not having to worry about a hereafter; you could be a *mench* or a miserable bastard your whole life—and both would get you to the same place.

Then they sang "Manhattan," the Rodgers & Hart anthem to the city. "The pushcarts were not sweet and they did not glide gently by where he grew up," said his dear friend, Kenny Lomax, "but for all his cynicism, he was a hopeless romantic about this place. He used to say people are just more alive here than anywhere else—and he'd been a lot of places." Me he told that every place outside New York was the sticks, and the sticks were all right but being boffo there was like having sex with your sister.

Finally, the chorus performed "God Bless America" at a very slow and stately tempo, and a little old man from the fur union got up and said he had known Wally from the days his father had first brought him as a boy to visit the Eichhorn workshop and he had done a little jig up on one of the tables. Wally always loved America, the old-timer said, but he hated patriotism. He had never understood why anyone should be more loyal to his country than to, say, his city or family or faith or party or himself. And he thought all sorts of terrible things were done in the name of patriotism, like making war and oppressing people with the courage to cry out that justice needed to be done throughout the land before any country could be truly proud of itself. What Wally had loved most about America was not its wealth or strength or vitality or undying hope but a shared humanity that no government could ever impose. "It was the only thing he really believed in—that beyond all our strife and struggles, we care for one another very much."

He had told me of another national distinction. Americans, he said, were the only people on earth both certain their blessings were divinely granted and decent enough to feel guilty about the honor.

On the way out of the funeral home, I ran into Melvin Kantor. He and Nina had come down to the city from Syracuse, where he was now an assistant professor at the university. For metaphysical reasons I did not pursue, he declined to accompany Nina and the Orloffs to the cemetery. Instead, he joined me for a cup of coffee and some counsel on careers in academia.

"I suppose the Pact has only deepened your conviction about the inherent evil of communism," he said when we got around briefly to politics.

What I had supposed was that the infernal Nazi-Soviet treaty, sealed that August and followed at once by their joint dismemberment of Poland and the outbreak of world war, had finally opened the eyes of fanatic party-liners like Nina. "All it confirmed for me," I said, "is that socialist warlords aren't the moral superior of any others."

"Which means you can't distinguish between Stalin and Hitler."

"*Won't* distinguish—treachery is treachery."

"You don't understand *realpolitik*. Precisely because a system is morally superior, even its most expedient policies are justifiable in the long run. Stalin has to keep Russia alive."

I understood what expedient policy the formerly skeptical Melvin Kantor had adopted to win the former Miss Nina Orloff—abject surrender. "So the ends justify the means?"

"Certainly."

"No," I said, weary by then with all peddlers of venal sophistry, "there's only one end in life, and that's death—the means are all that really matter."

He gave a supercilious snort. "Where'd you dig that one up?"

"A little here," I answered, "and a little there."

When I reached home that night after a fuller day than I had bargained for, my wife kissed me warmly, my father looked up from his newspaper with a fond smile, and my faithful dog swished its auburn tail. In the mail was yet another rejection slip for my story about David Schumacher. "Why don't you put it aside?" Eden said. "You and I know it's good—that's enough for now. Someday you'll get back to it all again."

So I have.